What ʿĪsā Ibn Hishām Told Us

Volume One

Letter from the General Editor

The Library of Arabic Literature series offers Arabic editions and English translations of key works of classical and pre-modern Arabic literature. Books in the series are edited and translated by distinguished scholars of Arabic and Islamic studies and are published in parallel-text format with Arabic and English on facing pages. These titles are also made available as English-only paperbacks. The Library of Arabic Literature includes texts from the pre-Islamic era to the cusp of the modern period, and encompasses a wide range of genres, including poetry, poetics, fiction, religion, philosophy, law, science, history, and historiography.

Supported by a grant from the New York University Abu Dhabi Institute, and established in partnership with NYU Press, the Library of Arabic Literature produces authoritative Arabic editions and modern, lucid English translations, with the goal of introducing the Arabic literary heritage to a general audience of readers, as well as to scholars and students.

Philip F. Kennedy
General Editor, Library of Arabic Literature

حديث عيسى بن هشام

أو

فترة من الزمن

المجلّد الأوّل

محمد إبراهيم المويلحي

What ʿĪsā Ibn Hishām Told Us

or

A Period of Time

Volume One

Muḥammad al-Muwayliḥī

Edited and translated by
Roger Allen

Volume editor
Philip Kennedy

NEW YORK UNIVERSITY PRESS
New York and London

NEW YORK UNIVERSITY PRESS
New York and London

Library of Congress Cataloging-in-Publication Data

Muwaylihi, Muhammad.
What ʿIsa ibn Hisham told us, or, A period of time / Muhammad al-Muwaylihi ; edited and translated by Roger Allen.
volumes cm -- (Library of Arabic literature)
In English and Arabic.
ISBN 978-1-4798-1388-9 (cl : alk. paper) -- ISBN 978-1-4798-9511-3 (e-book) -- ISBN 978-1-4798-0441-2 (e-book)
I. Allen, Roger, 1942- editor, translator. II. Muwaylihi, Muhammad. Hadith ʿIsa ibn Hisham. III. Muwaylihi, Muhammad. Hadith ʿIsa ibn Hisham. English. IV. Title. V. Title: Period of time.
PJ7850.U9H313 2015
892.7'35--dc23
2014044218

New York University Press books are printed on acid-free paper, and their binding materials are chosen for strength and durability.

Series design by Titus Nemeth.

Typeset in Tasmeem, using DecoType Naskh and Emiri.

Typesetting and digitization by Stuart Brown.

Manufactured in the United States of America
c10 9 8 7 6 5 4 3 2 1

Table of Contents

Introduction

The Author: Muḥammad al-Muwayliḥī

Muḥammad al-Muwayliḥī was born on the 30th of March, 1858, into an illustrious family that traced its origins to the town of Muwayliḥ on the coast of the Ḥijāz in the Arabian Peninsula. His father, Ibrāhīm al-Muwayliḥī (1843–1906)—only fifteen years older than his son, had inherited the family silk business along with his brother ʿAbd al-Salām, and both brothers were closely involved in the political life of Egypt during the reign of the Khedive Ismāʿīl (r. 1863–79).

For a brief period at the age of ten, Muḥammad attended the famous school at Khurunfish in Cairo which was run by the Jesuit order and catered for the sons of the aristocracy, but from the time he was fifteen he was taught privately. As a young man he made the acquaintance of many of his father's friends, among whom Jamāl al-dīn al-Afghānī and Muḥammad ʿAbduh.[1] Muḥammad later attended ʿAbduh's lectures at al-Azhar, the same institution that he was to criticize with such vehemence in the newspaper articles that were later to be published in edited form as *Ḥadīth ʿĪsā ibn Hishām* (*What ʿĪsā ibn Hishām Told Us*). He also had occasion to meet other important figures in Egyptian cultural life of the times, including Shaykh Ḥusayn al-Marṣafī and Maḥmūd Pāshā Sāmī al-Bārūdī, the famous statesman and poet, both of whom took an interest in his education.[2]

In 1872, Ibrāhīm's fortunes suffered a severe setback. He had been attracted to the newly founded Stock Exchange, and in the course of speculation lost the 80,000 pounds which had been bequeathed to him by his father.[3] Leaving ʿAbd al-Salām to manage the business as best he could, Ibrāhīm retired to his house for three months. We learn from various sources that when the Khedive Ismāʿīl heard about this, he summoned both brothers to the palace, gave each the title of Bey and 3,000 pounds, and ordered his entourage and harem to dress themselves exclusively in al-Muwayliḥī silks.[4]

Following the financial crisis of 1879, the Khedive Ismāʿīl was forced to abdicate and went into exile in Naples. He invited Ibrāhīm al-Muwayliḥī to join him as his private secretary and tutor to Prince Aḥmad Fuʾād (later King Fuʾād the First).[5] Putting Muḥammad in the care of his uncle, ʿAbd al-Salām, Ibrāhīm left Egypt for Italy. Through his uncle, Muḥammad met Ibrāhīm al-Laqqānī, a barrister and writer who was also a friend of Ibrāhīm al-Muwayliḥī. Al-Laqqānī introduced Muḥammad to some of his own friends, amongst whom were ʿAbdallāh Nadīm and Ḥasan Mūsā al-ʿAqqād. These three men were the protagonists of the "Egypt for the Egyptians" movement, and Muḥammad wrote regularly to his father in Italy describing the discussions he heard and the general political situation in Egypt.[6] On April 5, 1882, Muḥammad became a clerk in the Ministry of Justice, but he did not remain in the post for long. In June, ʿAbd al-Salām al-Muwayliḥī left for Syria to convalesce from an illness, and Muḥammad was left on his own during the turmoil which led up to the revolt of Aḥmad ʿUrābī, the riots in Alexandria, and the subsequent British landing and occupation. Ibrāhīm had sent his son a leaflet he had written in support of the Nationalists, entitled *Al-Jannah taḥta ẓilāl al-suyūf* (*Paradise Under the Shadow of Swords*), and Muḥammad was arrested distributing copies of this document. Put on trial before a military court on the orders of ʿUthmān Pāshā, the Minister of the Interior, he was condemned to death. However, Buṭrus Ghālī Pāshā, a friend of the Muwayliḥīs who was Permanent Under-Secretary to the Minister of Justice (*Wakīl al-ḥaqqāniyyah*), interceded on Muḥammad's behalf with the Khedive Tawfīq, claiming that Muḥammad had been encouraged by his father, that his uncle—who was his official guardian—was convalescing in Syria, and that he was not old enough to be considered politically troublesome. The sentence was commuted to exile.

Muḥammad now joined his father in Italy, where he learned Italian and some Latin, and continued his studies of French with a lawyer friend of his father. He also helped his father to produce the newspaper *Al-Ittiḥād*. But the Ottoman Sultan wrote in 1880 expressing his displeasure at the views published by the newspaper, so the Khedive Ismāʿīl was compelled to order Ibrāhīm to stop printing. In 1884, Ismāʿīl sent Ibrāhīm to Paris from Italy, and Muḥammad accompanied his father. In the French capital both Ibrāhīm and Muḥammad al-Muwayliḥī helped Jamāl al-dīn al-Afghānī and Muḥammad ʿAbduh with the publication of *Al-ʿUrwah al-Wuthqā*. This newspaper was to have a tremendous influence in the Arab Middle East, not only because of its outspoken attacks on the British presence in Egypt and the evils of excessive Westernization, but also because of its advocacy of the idea of Pan-Islam based on the Ottoman Caliphate. The Muwayliḥīs were later to support all of these points of view with vigor in their own newspaper following their return to Egypt.

The fourth issue of *Al-Ittihād* was circulated in Europe, Turkey and Egypt, and its criticism of the Ottoman Sultan caused a considerable stir. The Ottoman court contacted its ambassador in Paris, and, despite protests in *Le Figaro*, Ibrāhīm was expelled from the country and traveled to Brussels.[7] Al-Afghānī wrote from London at that time, and suggested Ibrāhīm and Muḥammad come to England. Father and son accepted the invitation. Once there, they assisted al-Afghānī in the publication of further issues of *Al-ʿUrwah al-Wuthqā*. Ibrāhīm himself produced further issues of *Al-Ittiḥād* and *Al-Anbāʾ* as well as a new newspaper called *ʿAyn Zubaydah*. During their stay in London, the Muwayliḥīs were introduced to Lord Randolph Churchill and Lord Salisbury, but any further entrées into British political society were cut short by another turn of events.

Ibrāhīm had been changing his tack somewhat by supporting the Ottoman government in his newspapers through fierce attacks on the policies of Gladstone's government, and this seems to have pleased the Sultan. Hagopian Pāshā, the "Nāẓir al-Khaṣṣah al-Sulṭāniyyah" (Supervisor of the Sultan's Entourage) was sent to London in January 1885. We learn that he, together with Qastākī Pāshā, the Ottoman ambassador in London, tried to persuade Ibrāhīm to go to Istanbul where, they asserted, he would discover that the Sultan had forgiven him for the unfavorable comments he had made in his newspapers in the past. But, with the memory of his recent expulsion from France still fresh in his mind, Ibrāhīm was (not unnaturally) dubious about the Sultan's intentions, and sent Muḥammad to Istanbul to find out the real terms of the invitation. When Muḥammad confirmed that the Sultan's offer was sincere, Ibrāhīm came to Istanbul and was appointed a member of the Education Council. Ibrāhīm soon made the acquaintance of Munīf Pāshā, the Minister of Education, who allowed Muḥammad to use the Fātiḥ Library with its large collection of manuscripts. Among the works which Muḥammad al-Muwayliḥī transcribed were *Risālat al-ghufrān* (*The Epistle of Forgiveness*) by the famous poet, Abū l-ʿAlāʾ al-Maʿarrī, several treatises by al-Jāḥiẓ (including one on magnanimity, *al-Nubl*, and another on envy, *al-Ḥasad*), and the *Dīwān* of Ibn al-Rūmī. Another friend of Ibrāhīm whom Muḥammad met at this time was al-Shinqīṭī who is one of the dedicatees of *Ḥadīth ʿĪsā ibn Hishām*.[8] In addition to all this, Muḥammad found time to write some articles for the newspaper, *Al-Munabbih*, at the invitation of ʿAbdallāh al-Mughīrah.

In 1887, Muḥammad left his father in Istanbul and returned to Cairo where he helped ʿĀrif Bey al-Mardīnī (the private secretary of Mukhtār Pāshā, the Ottoman Commissioner in Cairo) to edit *Al-Qāhirah al-Jadīdah*, a daily newspaper which had first appeared in 1885 but ceased publication when al-Mardīnī was invited back to Istanbul by the Sultan a few months after Muḥammad's return to Egypt.[9] Muḥammad continued to write articles for other newspapers in Egypt; *Al-Muqaṭṭam,* for example, he wrote under a variety of pseudonyms such as "an Egyptian who knows his country" and "*al-Badīʿ*." At the head of these articles he was described as "a distinguished man of letters in Egypt whose eloquence will fascinate all those who are fond of literature." In them he broached a variety of topics including the Nationalist Party, slavery, and the Legislative Council and its schemes.[10] On his return from Istanbul, Muḥammad had renewed his acquaintance with Ibrāhīm al-Laqqānī and Buṭrus Ghālī. These two men were among the circle of friends who would meet regularly at the house of Princess Nāzlī Fāḍil, the niece of the ex-Khedive Ismāʿīl and wife of Salīm Abū Ḥajib, the Mufti of Tunis. This circle served as the meeting place for a remarkable collection of figures from Egyptian political and intellectual life, and of some non-Egyptian ones as well; we are told that Lord Cromer attended occasionally.[11] In addition to those already mentioned, the members included Muḥammad ʿAbduh, Saʿd and Aḥmad Fatḥī Zaghlūl, Qāsim Amīn, Muṣṭafā Fahmī, ʿAlī Yūsuf, and Ḥāfiẓ Ibrāhīm, a list which includes some of the leading spirits in the movement to reform Egyptian society. There seems little room for doubt that much of the discussion which must have taken place at the meetings of this circle is directly reflected in the series of articles that al-Muwayliḥī was to publish under the title *Fatrah min al-Zaman.* Another interesting figure with whom Muḥammad al-Muwayliḥī was acquainted at this time was the Englishman, Wilfrid Scawen Blunt, who had been very closely involved in the defense of ʿUrābī after the collapse of the 1882 revolt. Blunt mentions the "Moelhis" many times in his *Diaries,* and from this source we can obtain some interesting pieces of information about Muḥammad's activities during this period. Blunt tells us for instance that Muḥammad was a close friend of Mukhtār Pāshā: "To these Arabist visitors from Cairo were gradually added other sources of native information, the most important of whom were my old friends Aarif Bey and Mohammed el Moelhi, nephew [sic] of my old friend Ibrahim el Moelhi, both of whom were now much in the confidence of the Ottoman High Commissioner in Cairo, Mukhtar Pasha Ghazi."[12] Blunt also tells us that ʿAbd al-Salām, Ibrāhīm, and Muḥammad al-Muwayliḥī were all involved in the intrigue of 1893, as a result of which Muṣṭafā Fahmī was dismissed as Prime Minister by the Khedive ʿAbbās the Second and replaced for a period of days by Fakhrī Pāshā.[13] Ibrāhīm may have been informed about these events through correspondence with his son, but in any case, Muḥammad was a frequent visitor to Istanbul during this period; in 1892, he was there to be decorated as a Bey (second class), and again in 1893 when Blunt went to Istanbul in an unsuccessful attempt to gain an interview with the Sultan. In this same year, Muḥammad delivered a lecture to the Language Academy (*al-Majmaʿ al-ʿIlmī*) on the acquisition of the talent for creative writing by learning poetry.[14]

In 1895 Ibrāhīm al-Muwayliḥī decided to leave Istanbul. He had made many friends in the Ottoman capital, including al-Shinqīṭī, Munīf Pāshā, and Ibrāhīm Bey Adham, for whose newspaper, *Al-Ḥaqāʾiq*, he had written several articles describing state occasions. He had, however, grown tired of the court intrigues and decided to return to Egypt. He was unable to keep this fact a secret from the Sultan's spies, and Sultan ʿAbd al-Ḥamīd sent someone to find out why he wished to leave. Ibrāhīm sent back the reply that he wished to return to his own country and see his son and friends again. The Sultan seems to have been satisfied and did not prevent him from leaving. In 1896, Ibrāhīm collected the articles which he had written about life in Istanbul and published them at the Egyptian *Al-Muqaṭṭam* press under the title *Mā Hunālik*. When copies of the book reached Istanbul and were brought to the Sultan's attention, however, he dispatched a letter to Egypt with the order that they should all be collected and sent to him in Istanbul. Ibrāhīm had no wish to incur the Sultan's hatred and set about collecting as many copies of the book as he could, which he duly sent to Istanbul.[15]

In December 1895 Muḥammad had been appointed Muʿāwin of the province of Qalyūbiyyah and later Ma'mūr of the district of Burullus, but he resigned the latter post after a short while and in 1898 joined his father in producing his new newspaper.[16] The first issue of *Miṣbāh al-sharq* appeared on April 14, 1898, and the paper soon established a high reputation for itself. This was due in no small part to the fact that the majority of the content was written by the Muwayliḥīs and indeed was frequently unsigned, a fact which was later to give some of Muḥammad's enemies the opportunity to dispute the authorship of the articles that eventually became the book *Ḥadīth ʿĪsā ibn Hishām*. The paper contained news from Istanbul and items of local interest as well as extracts from Arabic literature, including essays of al-Jāḥiẓ and poems from the *Dīwān* of Ibn al-Rūmī which Muḥammad had transcribed in Istanbul. The leading articles dealt with such topics as the Pan-Islamist movement, the British occupation of Egypt, the war in the Sudan, the religious reform movement, and the comparison of Oriental and Western customs. Muḥammad also caused a considerable furor in the literary world of Cairo by publishing a series of articles in which he subjected the *Dīwān* of the famous Egyptian poet, Aḥmad Shawqī (1868–1932), together with its introduction, to some exacting but constructive criticism.[17] Such material as this was rarely found in newspapers of the time, and many writers have acknowledged the effect which its contents and style had on them; Muḥammad Kurd ʿAlī says that "*Miṣbāḥ al-sharq* was the best weekly," while Salāmah Mūsā tells in his autobiography how he acquired "a taste for artistic beauty" by reading the articles it contained.[18]

In November 1898, Muḥammad began to publish under the title *Fatrah min al-Zaman* the lengthy series of articles that form the text of these volumes; later, after much editing, these articles became the book *Ḥadīth ʿĪsā ibn Hishām* (their precise history is discussed in the section "A History of the Text" below). They appeared each week on the front page of the newspaper. At first they were unsigned, but, when Ibrāhīm began to publish his own story in a series of articles entitled "Mirʾāt al-ʿĀlam," Muḥammad signed his name with the letter *mīm* and Ibrahim used an *alif*. Muḥammad continued to publish these articles until June 1900, when he went to London to cover the state visit of the Khedive to the homeland of Queen Victoria (in whose honor Ibrāhīm composed an ode which was printed in the newspaper). Muḥammad sent back an article describing this visit,[19] and then went to Paris to visit the Great Exhibition (*Exposition universelle*), which he described for the readers of *Miṣbāḥ al-sharq* in a series of episodes entitled "Paris."[20] In describing his visit to the French capital, al-Muwayliḥī was following the precedents set by such figures as al-Ṭahṭāwī, al-Shidyāq, and ʿAlī Mubārak. Unlike these writers, however, he confined most of his descriptions to the Paris Exhibition of 1900.

Although *Miṣbāh al-sharq* was officially owned and edited by Ibrāhīm al-Muwayliḥī, Muḥammad gradually took over the management of the newspaper, and Ibrāhīm became a political adviser of the Khedive. In 1902, Muḥammad found himself at the center of a social scandal. While sitting in a café, he appears to have insulted a young nobleman, Muḥammad Bey Nashʾat (whom ʿAbd al-ʿAzīz al-Bishrī—a friend and young protegé of Muḥammad al-Muwayliḥī—describes as "a frivolous fool"). Apparently the whole thing was intended to be a joke, but it seems to have been misinterpreted because the irate young man slapped al-Muwayliḥī on the face.[21] ʿAlī Yūsuf, the editor of the newspaper *Al-Muʾayyad*, then published a series of reports of the incident which considerably dramatized the whole affair and cast a slur on Muḥammad. Muḥammad wrote a rather stupid and vitriolic reply in *Miṣbāḥ al-sharq* called "Al-Jarīdah al-ʿĀmmiyyah" ("The Plebeian Newspaper") in which he declared that *Al-Muʾayyad* represented the gutter press and was read only by the lower classes of society.[22] ʿAlī Yūsuf countered his attack with a regular column in his newspaper called "ʿĀm al-kaff" ("The Year of the Slap"). Al-Bishrī points out that many people in Cairo had suffered from the barbed pens of the Muwayliḥīs and thus there was no shortage of material with which ʿAlī Yūsuf could fill his column. Indeed, the poet Ismāʿīl Ṣabrī (1854–1923) was among those who composed poems for this purpose.[23] ʿAlī Yūsuf kept the column going for twelve consecutive daily issues of the newspaper and continued to taunt Muḥammad for not replying to his critics.[24] Eventually however, the common friends of both men including, no doubt, many members of the Nāzlī circle which both men attended, appear to have arranged a cease-fire, and no more was heard of the subject—for a while at least.

According to his closest friends, Muḥammad was deeply affected by this campaign against him; based on descriptions of his retiring nature and hatred of crowded places, this seems very likely. To some degree, his generally unsociable temperament can be attributed to the chronic stammer from which he suffered; apparently it was so bad that he would often be unable to finish a sentence at all and would have to resort to an embarassed silence. This fact may not only explain why he preferred to be educated at home as a boy, but also may provide a clue to the drastic effect which this incident in the café had on him. It is certainly true that the gradual decline of *Miṣbāḥ al-sharq* and *Abū Zayd* (a satirical magazine started by his father) can be traced to this period. The articles on topical subjects written by the editor, which had been a hallmark of the earlier issues and had accounted for much of the paper's popularity, became less frequent and were replaced by long extracts from French newspapers, some of which extended over several issues. Advertisements and announcements were allowed to take an ever-increasing amount of space in a paper which had only four pages to fill. It may have been at this time that Muḥammad decided (or perhaps it was suggested to him) to collect the episodes of *Fatrah min al-Zaman* into book form, so he closed down the newspapers to allow himself more time to concentrate on his revision of the text. Whatever the cause of closure may have been, *Miṣbāḥ al-sharq* ceased publication on August 15, 1903.[25]

The Muwayliḥīs continued to write for other newspapers. Ibrāhīm sent articles to *Al-Mu'ayyad* and *Al-Muqaṭṭam*, and in 1905 even founded a new newspaper called *Al-Mishkāt* in the name of his son Khalīl and Ḥamdī Bey Yakan.[26] Meanwhile, Muḥammad saw revenge taken on ʿAlī Yūsuf. In 1904 the latter was involved in a scandal when he proposed to Ṣafiyyah al-Sādāt, a woman of high birth, and was refused by her father, although the woman herself had consented to marry him and seemed to want to do so. The woman's father based his refusal on the fact that ʿAlī Yūsuf was an Upper Egyptian (Ṣaʿīdī) and was not worthy of his daughter because he was not a *sharīf*. The case was taken to court, and ʿAlī Yūsuf lost both the initial case and the subsequent appeal.[27] During all this, the daily newspaper *Al-Ẓāhir* printed a column with the title "ʿĀm al-Kufʾ" ("The Year of Equality")—an obvious echo of the series of articles against Muḥammad mentioned above, except that this series continued for thirty-four consecutive issues.[28] In poems that appeared in the column, ʿAlī Yūsuf's suitability for such a marriage was questioned, his claims to be a *sharīf* were ridiculed, and he was made out to be a person totally unsuitable to take over the supervision of the Ṣūfī *waqf* properties, a post for which his name had been put forward.

Ibrāhīm al-Muwayliḥī fell ill in December 1905 and died on January 29, 1906. It was also in that year that ʿAbbās the Second decorated Muḥammad with the order of Bey second class (Mutamayyiz), but Muḥammad now appears to have preferred to remain at home as he had done as a boy, reading and holding discussions with his friends. Among the people who used to frequent his house during this period were ʿAbd al-ʿAzīz al-Bishrī and ʿAbbās Maḥmūd al-ʿAqqād, both of whom have left descriptions of the friends who used to come to these discussions—Ḥāfiẓ Ibrāhīm, ʿAbd al-Salām al-Muwayliḥī, Muḥammad Tawfīq al-Bakrī, Muḥammad Bey Rashād, and ʿAlī Yūsuf (with whom Muḥammad appears finally to have been reconciled).[29] Muḥammad left his house rarely and wrote very little. The series of articles *Fatrah min al-Zaman* appeared in book form as *Ḥadīth ʿIsā ibn Hishām* in 1907. On February 9, 1908, an article entitled "Kalimah Mafrūḍah" ("An Obligatory Word") appeared under his name in *Al-Muʾayyad*. The occasion of this article's appearance is described by Sir Ronald Storrs:

> The Italians of Alexandria have chosen this juncture for proposing that the Municipality should erect a large statue to Dante, which plan, seeing that Dante placed Muhammad and Ali in hell with the other Schismatics, cleft from chin to tank with their insides hanging out, is meeting with frantic opposition from united Islam.[30]

Muḥammad's article was an important contribution to this united Islamic front. He began by quoting in Arabic for the readers of the newspaper exactly what Dante does say about Muḥammad in the *Divine Comedy*, and from there went on to demand that all Muslims should rally to the cause of their religion instead of sitting back lethargically and watching while it suffered such a gross insult. It is almost certainly significant that a few pages later Storrs records the disgust of Princess Nāzlī herself with what Dante had written. In the following year, Muḥammad allowed himself to be drawn even further out of his seclusion and retirement when he accepted an invitation to attend the opening of the Ḥijāz railway, traveled to Medina and is said to have been one of the anonymous contributors to the series of articles on the railway which appeared in *Al-Mu'ayyad* at the time.[31]

On May 15, 1910, he was appointed Director of the Waqf Administration. Al-ʿAqqād records that al-Muwayliḥī found the work very tedious, and so it is hardly surprising that he resigned from the position four years later, and retired to his home again. He apparently felt that his talents were being wasted and that a man of his standing should not have to work in such a fashion.[32]

From now on, he seems to have lived a modest life which at times descended to poverty, but the pride which had prompted him to leave his post in the Waqf Administration apparently helped him to live through such trials with dignity.[33] He ventured into print only once more before his death in 1930. On December 30, 1921, an article of his appeared in the newspaper *Al-Ahrām* under the title "Ṣawt min al-ʿUzlah" ("Voice from Retirement") in which he began by giving his reasons for retiring from a life of journalism and then proceeded to express his feelings about the second expulsion of Saʿd Zaghlūl from Egypt. He pointed out that the situation was one which could bring Egyptians together as one nation and that Jamāl al-dīn al-Afghānī would rejoice at the thought. Apart from this article, Muḥammad divided his time during the remaining years of his life between his home and Alexandria with occasional visits to sporting events such as horse racing. In 1925, "the owner of a well-known newspaper" (unfortunately anonymous) is said to have asked him to write two articles expressing a certain point of view on a subject for the sum of eighty pounds, but Muḥammad's alleged reply sounds typical enough: "Al-Muwayliḥī's pen is not for sale."[34]

In 1927, *Ḥadīth ʿĪsā ibn Hishām* was published as a textbook by the Ministry of Education for use in secondary schools. Muḥammad undertook an extensive revision of the work before its publication (see more details in the following section). In this process, he excluded many of the book's most controversial pages and included the episodes from Paris mentioned above as "Al-Riḥlah al-thāniyah" ("The Second Journey"). He also began to work on the production in book form of a set of essays on various philosophical topics, most of which had also appeared on the pages of *Miṣbāḥ al-sharq*. A few weeks after finishing work on these essays, on February 28, 1930, he died in Ḥulwān, and it was left to his brother Khalīl and his friend Salīm Abū Ḥājib, Princess Nāzlī's husband, to prepare the book for publication. It appeared as *ʿIlāj al-nafs* (*Cure for the Soul*)—also a school text—in 1932.[35]

A History of the Text

Ḥadīth ʿĪsā ibn Hishām, Muḥammad al-Muwayliḥī's famous turn-of-the-century narrative, was an instant success when it appeared as a series of articles under the title *Fatrah min al-Zaman* between 1898 and 1902 in the family's Cairo newspaper, *Miṣbāḥ al-sharq*. It became even more successful when it appeared as a book in 1907, now under the title *Ḥadīth ʿĪsā ibn Hishām*. Multiple editions of the work have been published in the century or so since that first edition—the most recent of which is edited by me—appeared as part of a collection of the author's complete works in 2002.[36] While all these editions of the work may be considered as versions of the text, they are by no means all the same. Behind that fact lies a tale that I would like to relate in this section of the Introduction.[37]

As noted in the previous section, the Muwayliḥīs—father Ibrāhīm and son Muḥammad—had been vigorous participants in Egyptian political and cultural life beginning in the reign of the Khedive Ismāʿīl (r. 1863–79). The father had held prominent positions, and his son often joined his father in such activities. Both men were acquainted, for example, with the renowned Islamic activist, Jamāl al-dīn al-Afghānī, and his colleague, Muḥammad ʿAbduh, who was to become a major figure in the Islamic reform movement in Egypt.[38] As a direct result of the Muwayliḥīs' involvement in such controversial debates, activities, and intrigues, Ibrāhīm al-Muwayliḥī clearly felt it wise to accept the Khedive Ismāʿīl's invitation to travel with him when he was exiled in 1879, and Muḥammad was also compelled to leave the country when he was arrested for distributing leaflets written by his father during the 1882 ʿUrābī Revolt, a direct consequence of which had been the British occupation of Egypt. Thereafter father and son traveled widely, to Italy, to Paris, to London, and finally to Istanbul when, as noted earlier, Ibrāhīm received an "invitation" from the Sultan ʿAbd al-Ḥamīd to come to the Ottoman capital—an invitation, one suspects, it would have been unwise to turn down. Both Egyptians spent a number of years in Istanbul, and Ibrāhīm wrote a famous account of his time there (*Mā Hunālik*) which was published in Cairo following his return in 1896 and immediately banned. Now that father and son had returned to their homeland, their broad acquaintance with the intricacies of Egyptian political and intellectual life, their wide experience of European culture, their exposure to life in the Ottoman capital, and, in the case of Muḥammad al-Muwayliḥī, long hours spent reading texts and manuscripts in Istanbul's Fātiḥ Library, were all qualities that made them ideal candidates for the foundation of a new weekly newspaper, one that would join an already crowded field that included, besides *Al-Muqaṭṭam*, the long-established *Al-Ahrām* (founded in Alexandria in 1875 by the Syrian Taqlā brothers) and the more populist *Al-Mu'ayyad* (founded in 1889 and edited by ʿAlī Yūsuf).

The al-Muwayliḥī newspaper, *Miṣbāḥ al-sharq*, soon established a wide reputation, not only for its trenchant commentary on current events and political developments, but also for its elevated style.[39] As if to emphasize the erudition of the composers of the articles (which were not initially signed), readers may have been somewhat surprised when issue number 21 of the 8th of September 1898 contained an article—published as section 0.1.1 in this edition—that begins with a line of poetry and then introduces the name of ʿĪsā ibn Hishām as the narrator of a sarcastic piece in the form of a fictional conversation between three well-known Egyptian political figures and holders of Egyptian ministerial office, Fakhrī Pāshā, Buṭrus Pāshā, and Maẓlūm Pāshā, about the latest developments in the Sudanese War. Quite apart from the obviously critical posture that the article adopts, of interest here is the process of fictionalizing the commentary and also the invocation of an illustrious name from the heritage of Arabic premodern narrative, ʿĪsā ibn Hishām, the narrator of and often participant in the famous collection of *maqāmāt* composed centuries earlier by Badīʿ al-Zamān al-Hamadhānī (358–98/969–1007). Given that the contents of newspapers usually brought (and indeed bring) almost instantaneous reactions from their readerships, we have to assume that the initial foray into this type of composition was well received, in that it was followed in quick succession by three others, all of them relating to the Sudanese War and the involvement (or rather non-involvement) of the Egyptian government and its ministers in what was projected as a joint enterprise (the so-called Anglo-Egyptian Sudan). The significance of these four initial articles introduced by ʿĪsā ibn Hishām is firstly that they are directly concerned with one particular aspect of Egyptian political life in the final years of the nineteenth century—the Sudanese war—which is completely missing from the published book text of *Ḥadīth ʿĪsā ibn Hishām* to appear later (1907). In addition, the final article of the four appears just one week before the first "episode" of *Fatrah min al-Zaman*, the series that, in heavily edited and rewritten form, was later to become the text of *Ḥadīth ʿĪsā ibn Hishām*. One is left to wonder whether this initial set of four articles (*Miṣbāḥ al-sharq* 21, 23, 24, and 30) was a kind of "dry run" for what was to become a much longer project—

even though it is almost certain that, at this initial stage, Muḥammad al-Muwayliḥī himself could have had no idea of the runaway success that was to greet his work nor the length of time that weekly publication of episodes would involve.

The first episode of the series of articles entitled *Fatrah min al-Zaman* appeared in issue 31 of *Miṣbāḥ al-sharq* (November 17, 1898). The new title and the fact that ʿĪsā ibn Hishām, the narrator who is wandering in a graveyard, encounters a Pāshā from the era of Muḥammad ʿAlī, clearly implies that something new and different is intended, although the existence of the four previous articles also implies a clear and continuing linkage to current events. Another feature that marks this episode as being something different is the author's virtuoso use of the traditional style known as *sajʿ*, literally the cooing of a dove, but used to represent the ancient style of cadenced and rhyming prose that is first encountered in the pre-Islamic era in the utterances of preachers and soothsayers, then found as the primary stylistic feature of the Qur'anic revelations, and later adopted by Badīʿ al-Zamān al-Hamadhānī in his innovative narrative genre, the *maqāmah*. Over the course of the series—spread out over four years in total—almost every original episode begins with an extended passage of *sajʿ*, more often than not setting the scene and establishing the context.

The initial four episodes of *Fatrah min al-Zaman* were published in a flurry, one week after another, suggesting that their author had a basic "plot" in mind for at least the initial encounter of his Egyptian narrator and the resurrected Pāshā with the complexities of Egyptian law—a French-based system being applied to Egyptians during a British occupation. At the same time however, he clearly needed to assess the reaction of the continually growing readership of the newspaper to this new experiment, one that combined astute observation of late nineteenth-century occupied Cairo with a style redolent of the most famous of pre-modern Arabic narratives.[40] Bearing in mind the reaction to both the original episodes and the subsequent book, one has to assume that the response was extremely positive. The episodes therefore continued after a five-week gap. The trials and tribulations of the Pāshā following his arrest for assault—his court case and eventual acquittal, and his quest for the misappropriated endowment that he had bequeathed to future generations—were recounted in a series of articles that take us to March 1899. What is significant in view of our current concern with the textual history of the narrative is that the publication sequence is interrupted with an episode in *Miṣbāḥ al-sharq* 40 (January 19, 1899) which is entitled "The Sudanese Government Monopoly" and involves yet another conversation between a newspaper reporter and a minister in the Egyptian government about events in the Sudan; in other words, we see a return to the topic dealt with in the four episodes preceding the opening episode of *Fatrah min al-Zaman*. Here is how this intrusion is justified by the author:

> ʿĪsā ibn Hishām told us: I heard a story about a minister concerned with that topic which is on everyone's mind at the moment. This happened when a newspaper reporter came to see him to try to get the benefit of his enlightened views and learn some accurate information about the new government in the Sudan. Because it seems to me so remarkable, I have decided to relay it to our readers immediately before we go back to the story of the Pāshā and his trial.

The insertion of this article into the sequence of episodes involving ʿĪsā ibn Hishām's narration of the Pāshā's encounter with the Egyptian legal system is certainly a symptom of the vagaries of serialized publication—as the careers of earlier generations of novelists in Europe can readily illustrate. But the insertion also shows that the situation in the Sudan was a preoccupation of the Egyptian press at the time when Muḥammad al-Muwayliḥī began to publish his narrative, and that it is clearly reflected in the original sequence of articles.

This concern with the Sudan is also responsible for another break in the publication sequence, but this time for a different reason. In ʿĪsā ibn Hishām's *Fatrah min al-Zaman* narrative, the Pāshā is both emotionally and physically exhausted after his experiences with the law. A period of rest and contemplation is recommended, and it coincides with an actual occurrence of the plague in Egypt. Several episodes are thus concerned with medicine, the plague, and a resort to literature as a source of relaxation and contemplation. This brings the publication sequence of episodes to June 1899, at which point Muḥammad al-Muwayliḥī pauses. The gap is filled by his father, Ibrāhīm, who publishes three episodes of a narrative of his own, *Mir'āt al-ʿĀlam* (*Mirror of the World*), where there is also an intense focus on the poor conditions under which the Egyptian army is laboring in the Sudan and, as experienced by Ibrāhīm directly, on the perils of speculation on the Stock Exchange.[41]

When Muḥammad al-Muwayliḥī resumes his narrative (*Miṣbāḥ al-sharq* 63, July 13, 1899), it is with a visit to a wedding hall, as part of which there is a section devoted to a lengthy history of singing. At the conclusion of an episode, the protagonists encounter a number of different social groups who have gathered at the wedding celebration—al-Azhar shaykhs, merchants, royal princes, and civil servants. Each of these categories subsequently becomes the topic of a later episode in *Fatrah min al-Zaman*. These shifts in narrative focus, each one involving a gap of varying duration in the publication of the articles, give us a hint as to how al-Muwayliḥī's responded to reader interest in the way he composed and sequenced episodes, again a replication of the circumstances under which novelists like Charles Dickens frequently functioned in composing and publishing novels. It is in the episodes that follow the description of these "meetings" (*majālis*) that al-Muwayliḥī comes up with his most inspired creation, the provincial *ʿumdah* (village headman) who comes to the rapidly Westernizing capital city from the countryside in search of fun and is mercilessly exploited by a duly Westernized fop (*Khalīʿ*, which I have translated as "Playboy") and his accomplice, a Merchant. The juxtaposition and confrontation of traditional mores and Western fashions is explored through a number of different venues and situations: restaurants and food, bars, tourism, money borrowing, and the theater. After a visit to the Pyramids, ʿĪsā ibn Hishām, the Pāshā, and their "Friend" (*ṣadīq*) leave the other group to their own devices and return home (*Miṣbāḥ al-sharq* 107, June 8, 1900). Given that Muḥammad al-Muwayliḥī was leaving almost immediately for Paris and the *Exposition universelle*, it is not surprising that, in what was at the time a final episode in the series, the Pāshā expresses to ʿĪsā his desire to see Western civilization firsthand. Plans are made to travel to France.

As already noted, Ibrāhīm al-Muwayliḥī made use of his son's journey to France to publish further episodes of his own narrative. Not only that, but *Miṣbāḥ al-sharq* 107 also contains the following announcement:

> ʿĪsā ibn Hishām: Muḥammad al-Muwayliḥī is traveling to the Paris Exposition this coming Sunday. Once he has gathered his impressions of the entire scenario and its details, *Miṣbāḥ al-sharq* will be publishing his description of its marvels and curiosities.

Muḥammad al-Muwayliḥī traveled first to London in order to write about the Khedive's visit to England,[42] but he then traveled to Paris. The first Parisian episode of *Fatrah min al-Zaman* was published in *Miṣbāḥ al-sharq* 116, August 17, 1900, with the following preface:

> This is the first episode of *Ḥadīth ʿĪsā ibn Hishām* concerning the visit to the Paris Exhibition. It has been sent to us by Muḥammad al-Muwayliḥī following his previous report on the visit of the Khedive of Egypt to Her Majesty the Queen of England.

Among the things to note from this introduction is that the series of episodes, originally (and still) called *Fatrah min al-Zaman*, has now acquired another title, *Ḥadīth ʿĪsā ibn Hishām*, which had been used on a few occasions in announcements before, but seems to have become the preferred title—indeed the one under which the eventual book was to be published in 1907. This trend is further emphasized by the fact that Ibrāhīm al-Muwayliḥī's narrative is assigned the subtitle *Ḥadīth Mūsā ibn ʿIṣām*, invoking the name of his own narrator and at the same time echoing in the clearest possible way the emerging title of his son's work.

Eight episodes describing (and, more often than not, harshly criticizing) the *Exposition universelle* in Paris were published between August and December 1900.[43] The last of them finishes with the usual statement, "To be continued," followed by the letter "M." Muḥammad al-Muwayliḥī had used this formula at the end of his articles ever since his father had begun publishing them. And yet the articles didn't continue. Or, at least, nothing followed until February 1902 (in other words, long after his return to Cairo) when, without any further explanation, three further episodes of *Fatrah min al-Zaman* were added. The first simply opens with the following statement:

> ʿIsa ibn Hisham said: Our coverage of the visit we paid to the mother of all European capitals and our stay in the hub of civilization finished with a description of the Great Exhibition: the different people we met there, the strange happenings day and night, the variety of exotic items, the precious and creative objects of every conceivable kind of craft that were on display, the nightclubs and music halls scattered across the grounds, the splendid views it afforded visitors, and the undesirable subtext out of sight. The Pasha, our Friend, and I had emerged from it with a mixture of feelings: praise, criticism, and outright condemnation. We were still in the company of the sage Frenchman, his temples whitened by his willingness to share with us his culture and learning.[44]

These three articles, which form an uninterrupted continuum and only the first of which contains an example of their author's virtuoso use of *sajʿ*, offer a detailed description of the French system of government—its presidency, election processes, senate, and chamber of deputies. The third of these episodes ends again with the usual "To be continued," and yet nothing followed. And this time it was indeed the end of the *Fatrah min al-Zaman* series the author had initiated four years earlier.

For whatever combination of reasons, al-Muwayliḥī was to take his time in converting his series of newspaper articles into book form. It seems clear that he had already been receiving encouragement to do so from the enthusiastic response of readers of the newspaper, not to mention many of his literary colleagues, including the renowned nationalist poet, Ḥāfiẓ Ibrāhīm (1871–1932). Indeed the latter's own contribution to the neoclassical revival of the *maqāmah* narrative *Layālī Saṭīḥ*, first published in 1906, contains an extract from al-Muwayliḥī's as yet unpublished book (and incidentally concentrates heavily on the situation in the Sudan, not surprising in view of the fact that the poet served as an Egyptian army officer there).[45]

The first edition of *Ḥadīth ʿĪsā ibn Hishām* was published in 1907, *Fatrah min al-Zaman* becoming its subtitle. In the introduction to this (and only this) edition, al-Muwayliḥī explains his method and rationale:

> After reviewing the articles carefully—a process that has demanded revisions and corrections, as well as alterations, substitutions, omissions and additions, I have now converted the story into book form. After all, the contents of newspapers are by definition ephemeral, mere thoughts of the day. They cannot claim a place in a book that will move with the times and be read over and over again.[46]

A comparison of the text of the 1907 edition of *Ḥadīth ʿĪsā ibn Hishām* with articles in the series *Fatrah min al-Zaman* does indeed corroborate the author's description of the conversion process. The wording of individual phrases is changed, and clarifying detail is often added; the major emphasis is on expansion and clarification rather than contraction. For the second edition of 1912, the author adds a glossary at the end of the text. However, what is most striking about the first edition of the book is that it does not include any of the material in which the Sudan situation is the primary topic; secondly, the original sequence of episodes is altered, requiring a good deal of rewriting and reorganization. In the original articles the visit to the wedding hall comes much earlier in the sequence and is followed by visits to the series of assemblies (*majālis*), whereas in the book version the assemblies come first in the ordering of episodes. Furthermore, completely new material is included about the plague, derived from a factual article, "Al-Akhlāq fī l-Wabāʾ" ("Ethics During the Epidemic") that was published in *Miṣbāḥ al-sharq* 221, September 13, 1902. The first edition (and the two subsequent ones, 1912 and 1923) all finish with the expressed desire to add "the second journey" (*al-riḥlah al-thāniyah*)—the episodes describing the visit to Paris—to the first (*al-riḥlah al-ūlā*) at some point in the future. Meanwhile the first three editions of *Ḥadīth ʿĪsā ibn Hishām* were and are only concerned with the Egyptian context. A further addition to the third edition (1923) was that of titles to the newly established "chapters" created either from the contents of the original articles or, more often, by consolidation of articles into larger units.[47]

At some point in the 1920s, *Ḥadīth ʿĪsā ibn Hishām* was adopted as a text for secondary school, and al-Muwayliḥī was invited to prepare a new fourth edition, which was published in 1927. I have not thus far found any specific evidence as to instructions that the author may have received regarding expectations for such a school text, but it is clear that the revision process he undertook before publication of this fourth edition radically altered the critical tone of the work—one that had already been somewhat muted by the process of converting the newspaper articles into a book. His now twenty-year-old wish to include the Paris episodes (*al-riḥlah al-thāniyah*) to the book was also finally fulfilled. Thus the second part of post-4th edition versions of *Ḥadīth ʿĪsā ibn Hishām* was added to the list of several previously published contributions by Arab visitors to the analysis of European civilization—in the case of Egypt a trend initiated in the nineteenth century by Rifāʿah Rāfiʿ al-Ṭahṭāwī (1801–71) with his *Takhlīṣ al-Ibrīz fī Talkhīṣ Bārīz* (*The Purification of Gold Concerning the Summary of Paris*), originally published in 1834. However, along with this addition to the text, some extremely significant omissions were made. Two complete "assemblies," one devoted to the shaykhs of al-Azhar discussing the heretical sciences of philosophy and geography and the other to the princes of the royal family who were squabbling with each other over expensive racing stallions, were completely omitted, along with a number of uncomplimentary anecdotes about Muḥammad ʿAlī, founder of the dynasty to which the current Egyptian ruler—now called "king"—belonged. One can only surmise about the decision-making process involved in these omissions, and whether they were made on the author's own initiative or as the result of a "recommendation" from some official channel, possibly because it was now almost thirty years after the time when the original articles had been composed. Indeed the none too subtle criticism in these episodes may have been reckoned inappropriate for the Egyptian teenage minds who would be studying *Ḥadīth ʿĪsā ibn Hishām* for the secondary-school examinations known as the *thānawiyyah ʿāmmah*.[48]

Whatever the case may be, the book version of Muḥammad al-Muwayliḥī's narrative *Ḥadīth ʿĪsā ibn Hishām*, originally published in 1907 and the one that has become the best known through a number of subsequent editions and reprints, already differs considerably from the original newspaper articles, and its fourth edition of 1927 takes the process of change still further. When I was asked by Professors Gaber Asfour and Sabry Hafez in the 1990s to prepare a new edition of the author's complete works (and those of his father) for a new series, *Ruwwād al-Fann al-Qaṣaṣī* (*Pioneers of the Narrative Art*) to be published by al-Majlis al-Aʿlā li-l-Thaqāfah (Supreme Council for Culture) in Cairo, I was already aware of the differences between the various editions of this work which had long since come to be regarded as a foundational contribution to the development of modern Arabic narrative—looking both forward and backward in time, a genuine "bridge-work." It was on that basis that I prepared the text for publication, using the resources that I had myself collected—in handwritten form—as part of my Oxford doctoral research in 1966. That work was published in two volumes in 2002. However, with advancements in computer technology and research methods, I have now been able to access the complete archive of the al-Muwayliḥī newspaper, *Miṣbāḥ al-sharq*, and have discovered that even what I thought was a "complete" edition of the text is in fact not entirely complete.

It is in that context that the invitation from the Library of Arabic Literature (LAL) to prepare a parallel-text version of what I have titled *What ʿĪsā ibn Hishām Told Us* is so welcome, in that it gives me the opportunity to produce for the first time in book form an Arabic and English version of the sequence of all the episodes of the original series of articles al-Muwayliḥī wrote and published that are introduced by a narrator named ʿĪsā ibn Hishām, whether or not they are part of the series called *Fatrah min al-Zaman*. That decision on my part, of course, raises some significant questions. Al-Muwayliḥī's description of his own revision process in converting the original articles into book form clearly indicates an aspiration on his part to turn something that was published in a context that he describes as "ephemeral" into a more permanent form. However the notion of ephemerality that he associates with newspaper publication and invokes to explain his rationale for revision is only part of the story. If we examine the sequence of the original articles closely and follow his lead in omitting entirely the "dry run" set of four articles devoted to the Sudan (and the somewhat curious return to the topic inserted in the initial sequence of *Fatrah min al-Zaman*), then the series seems to fall into four subseries: the Pāshā's initial encounter with the Egyptian legal system in which both he and ʿĪsā ibn Hishām are centrally involved in the action; the period spent away so as to avoid the plague and allow the Pāshā to recover, in which there is considerably less action; the series of "assemblies"; and finally the episodes involving the ʿUmdah and his two colleagues—in both these last two sequences ʿĪsā and the Pāshā fade almost completely into the background once the context has been established. Thus, if one is to apply some notions of Western narratological analysis to the resulting book text, one can say that al-Muwayliḥī's careful reworking of the newspaper articles does provide for a more convincing sequence of "events," but does little or nothing to affect the varying roles of two of the principal "characters."

Several Egyptian critics have tried to make of *Ḥadīth ʿĪsā ibn Hishām* an incipient novel, but I would suggest that an investigation of the work's origins ties it as closely, if not more so, to the more episodic model of the classical *maqāmah* genre that is deliberately being invoked by the use of ʿĪsā ibn Hishām as a participant narrator, duly derived from al-Hamadhānī's tenth-century model. To the episodic nature of the individual articles can be added yet another feature of al-Hamadhānī's creations, namely their resort to "prosimetrum," the regular inclusion of lines of poetry within a cursive prose narrative. One might even go on to suggest that, if al-Muwayliḥī's attempt at producing a more logically sequenced narrative out of the original article series *Fatrah min al-Zaman* was a reflection of his acquaintance with and understanding of fictional models of that era, then the episodic and even fragmented nature of the story in its article format is a much closer reflection of his "classical" model in al-Hamadhānī's *maqāmāt* and may indeed emerge therefrom as almost postmodern.

This edition, the first ever in book form to include all the original articles narrated by a nineteenth-century Egyptian called ʿĪsā ibn Hishām and published in *Miṣbāḥ al-sharq* at the turn of the nineteenth century, will thus re-establish their author's text firmly within the political and cultural context within which they were conceived and on which they regularly commented. The availability of different versions of this famous narrative—the original articles of *Fatrah min al-Zaman*, the collected works of Muḥammad al-Muwayliḥī, and the various editions of *Ḥadīth ʿĪsā ibn Hishām*—will make it possible to examine in detail the role that this "bridge-work" played in linking the pre-modern heritage of Arabic narrative to his lively portrait of a tumultuous and changing present in nineteenth-century Egypt and the ways in which the story has been transformed during a timeframe that now exceeds a century.

Note on the Text and Translation

In view of the complex textual history, it should again be made clear that the text and translation presented here are *not* based on any published book version of Muḥammad al-Muwayliḥī's *Ḥadīth ʿĪsā ibn Hishām*. Rather they offer for the first time the original texts and translation of the series of articles, entitled *Fatrah min al-Zaman*, which were originally published over a four-year period (1898–1902) in the al-Muwayliḥī newspaper, *Miṣbāḥ al-sharq*, and later converted by the author—after significant editing, into the book, *Ḥadīth ʿĪsā ibn Hishām*, first published in 1907. In that connection, it should be noted that the Arabic text presented here is an exact replica of the original newspaper articles, including the printing conventions that the editors chose to follow.

It might seem more appropriate to select *A Period of Time* as a title for this edition, that being a literal translation of the original Arabic title for the series of articles. However, since I had already used that title for my published study and translation of the third edition of *Ḥadīth ʿĪsā ibn Hishām* (1923—originally my doctoral thesis at Oxford submitted in 1968, published originally in microfiche form in 1974 and later in a second edition in 1992), I have decided to use another title, *What ʿĪsā ibn Hishām Told Us*, my aim being to reflect the fact that the contents of this version of al-Muwayliḥī's text and its translation into English involve *all* the articles that he published in *Miṣbāḥ al-sharq* that are introduced by a narrator named ʿĪsā ibn Hishām, both those that made their way, albeit in altered form, into the book *Ḥadīth ʿĪsā ibn Hishām* and those that, for a variety of reasons, were not included.

In the sections above we have already noted that Muḥammad al-Muwayliḥī, through his mostly private education, his travels, his interests, and his research in libraries, was extremely erudite, as indeed was his father, Ibrāhīm al-Muwayliḥī. That much is abundantly clear from the elevated style that characterizes the articles published in their newspaper *Miṣbāḥ al-sharq*, and thus in the works in which those articles were assembled in book form. Whereas some of their contemporaries—such as Jūrjī Zaydān (1861–1914) and Muṣṭafā Luṭfī al-Manfalūṭī (1876–1924)—may have striven to develop a less elaborate and more accessible style with which to attract a broader readership to their works and especially the newspaper and journals in which they published, such, it would appear, was not a goal of the Muwayliḥīs in their choice of style.

In the particular case of Muḥammad al-Muwayliḥī and the text that makes up this edition, we are dealing with a conscious revival of a pre-modern narrative genre (including its narrator by name) and its characteristic stylistic features. Like al-Hamadhānī many centuries earlier, al-Muwayliḥī has a narrator and a main character (the Pāshā) travel to various places where they react to and comment on what they encounter, in this case the Egyptian legal system, the onset of the plague, the wide variety of meeting venues in Cairo, the clash of indigenous and imported values exemplified by the tastes of the ʿUmdah and the "Playboy," and, at a later stage, the various pavilions of the Paris Exhibition of 1900. Also like his illustrious forebear, al-Muwayliḥī indulges in a variety of pastiches of other forms of discourse: among many possibilities, we might mention the overblown rhetoric of the groomsman's speech at the Wedding (20.10), and the absurdly complex and obscure reasoning of the newspaper article allegedly written by the al-Azhar shaykh (22.14–22.18). But from the point of view of this text and its translation into English, the most prominent feature of the *maqāmah* genre was its revival of the ancient style known as *sajʿ* and the resort at the same time to the use of "prosimetrum," the inclusion of lines of poetry and sometimes complete poems in what is otherwise considered to be a work of "prose." A comprehensive history of the stylistic phenomenon of *sajʿ* within the literary heritage of the Arabs has yet to be written, but the style is certainly to be found during the pre-Islamic era and is the primary characteristic of the Qurʾanic text; indeed in his important study *Introduction to Arabic Poetics*, the Syro-Lebanese poet and critic Adūnīs (b. 1930) suggests that in the Arabic literary tradition, *sajʿ* may not be the first manifestation of poetry per se, but is certainly the first manifestation of the poetic. Here is not the place to explore these issues in detail, but merely to point out that the linkage of *sajʿ* and poetry in Arabic, and in the writings of al-Muwayliḥī with which we are concerned here, can be traced back to the very origins of its literary history.

The articles narrated by ʿĪsā ibn Hishām which al-Muwayliḥī published in *Miṣbāḥ al-sharq* are characterized by a very elevated style of prose writing, and they also replicate the drama genre to a degree by including lengthy examples of dialogue, still composed of course, in the same elevated style. However, the initial paragraphs of each original article also involve the kind of virtuoso displays of style that are an intrinsic feature of *sajʿ*. As any learner of Arabic soon discovers, the language is one in which morphological patterns are not only widely prevalent but form the very basis of its lexicography (one might even suggest that the entire process is not a little "algebraic," algebra being itself a subdivision of mathematics and indeed the term itself being of Arabic origin, *al-jabr* [contraction]). The *saj*ʿ style exploits this feature to the maximum: not only is there regularly a sequence of phrases with a rhyming syllable at the end (thus replicating the prosodic system of Arabic poetry), but it would also appear that the rhythmic cadence of each phrase also needs to parallel the others in each rhyming sequence (which, when done by a virtuoso composer of *maqāmāt* such as al-Ḥarīrī [1054–1122], might extend for eight consecutive phrases). An almost axiomatic consequence of these "expectations" of the *saj*ʿ style (one that admittedly has been scantly analyzed by scholars, perhaps because of the presence of the phenomenon in the Qur'an and the notion of that text's "inimitability") is that the same incidents and images are depicted numerous times with different phraseology, allowing the composer not only to display his linguistic virtuosity but also to exploit Arabic's myriad possibilities in the realms of morphology and synonyms.[49] When we add to this al-Muwayliḥī's acknowledged erudition and wide exposure to both Arabic and European cultural and literary traditions, the challenges that confront the would-be translator of this text seem clear.

Turning now to the translation process itself, I have to acknowledge that, even when faced with the challenges a text such as that of al-Muwayliḥī presents to both the translator and the anticipated reader of the resulting translation, I still find myself resorting to the logic presented by the renowned German theologian, philosopher, and commentator on translation, Friedrich Scheiermacher (1768–1834) when he states:

> Either the translator leaves the author in peace as much as possible and moves the reader towards him, or he leaves the reader in peace and moves the author towards him.[50]

While there are, of course, a number of theoretical and practical issues that any translator has to resolve in the process of "transferring" a text from one culture and reading public to another, I have as a basic principle always much preferred the former of these two possibilities, that of "foreignizing the reader" rather than "domesticating the text." With that in mind, I should therefore state clearly that, when I have been confronted, for example, at the beginning of each article in this text with a series of phrases in Arabic *saj*ʿ which portray with multiple variations the same image or create a scenario—that being the most usual function of the introductory paragraphs in each article, I have resorted to a process of repetition and a copious use of synonyms which is perhaps not characteristic of English-language discourse, but a clear replication (translation) of the original Arabic text. Meanwhile, the often lengthy passages of cursive Arabic prose have been rendered into what I hope will be regarded as an appropriate level of English discourse. It is only in the marginally more spontaneous sections of dialogue (especially those involving the ʿUmdah and his two companions) that I have made any attempt at a more "conversational" style, but even there the constraints of al-Muwayliḥī's choice of Arabic language register do not encourage any efforts at producing a series of more spontaneous exchanges.

To conclude, al-Muwayliḥī's long-acknowledged masterpiece—whether in its original newspaper article form as in this edition or in one of the many and varied book editions of the work—is not only a wonderfully trenchant survey of turn-of-the-century Egypt under British occupation as it was involved in a complex process of cultural assimilation and transition, but also a conscious attempt to link developments in Arabic language and its literary forms during the nineteenth century (a movement generally known as the *nahḍah* [revival]) to the Arabic heritage of the pre-modern centuries. For that reason I have already characterized here it as being a genuine "bridge-work," one that adopts a kind of Janus-like posture, looking in two directions simultaneously. It can be argued, and indeed several Egyptian scholars have argued, that the editorial process al-Muwayliḥī undertook before the publication of *Ḥadīth ʿĪsā ibn Hishām* in 1907 may have been an attempt to turn the text into a kind of "proto-novel." However, as I have also endeavored to show previously (especially in *A Period of Time*, 1992, Section III), the revised text is less than successful in meeting even the minimal goals of such a designation. While one may be able to offer different views within that critical generic context, there can be little doubt that the original newspaper articles, published here for the first time in their original format and sequence, are the clearest possible reflection of the political, social, and cultural concerns that were the central focus of both al-Muwayliḥīs in their newspaper. That is, it seems to me, their enduring value, added to which is the fact that the vast majority of the text that was eventually to be published as *Ḥadīth ʿĪsā ibn Hishām*—with either its "first journey" only (1907, 1912, and 1923) or both journeys (1927 and thereafter)—is present in the current text, albeit in a different sequence.

Given the multiple cultural and cross-cultural references in the text, I have provided both a Glossary of Names and Places and a series of detailed endnotes. The latter includes references to the equivalent chapters of the book version of

Ḥadīth ʿĪsā ibn Hishām, as well as citations of as many of the sources of the copious amount of poetry in the text as I have been able to find. In that context, I have to express particular gratitude to Professors Geert Jan van Gelder, James Montgomery, Maurice Pomerantz, Bilal Orfali, and Philip Kennedy, all of whom have allowed me to tap their knowledge of the Arabic poetic tradition in quest of the identities of the many unidentified poets whose lines are cited in this text. I would also like to thank my colleague, Professor Joseph E. Lowry, for his assistance with the identification of the legal sources that are cited in the text.

In conclusion, I would like to avail myself of this opportunity to express particular thanks to Professor Philip Kennedy, the General Editor of the Library of Arabic Literary series (and also editor of the project that consists of these two volumes) and the other members of the project's Editorial Board.

Roger Allen

Notes to the Introduction

1 Ibrāhīm's dealings with al-Afghānī are fully covered in Keddie, *Sayyid Jamāl ad-Dīn "al-Afghānī,"* 235ff. and 246ff.

2 Al-Bishrī, *Al-Mukhtār*, 1:246.

3 The al-Muwayliḥī newspaper *Miṣbāḥ al-sharq* is full of articles concerning the perils involved in speculation on the Stock Exchange and the wiles of brokers in tricking the unwary. The topic of speculation is also a major theme of Ibrāhīm al-Muwayliḥī's *Mir'āt al-ʿĀlam* discussed below.

4 It should be pointed out that the most detailed source of information on the lives of Ibrāhīm and Muḥammad al-Muwayliḥī is Ibrāhīm al-Muwayliḥī the younger, and that, although the family anecdotes do throw considerable light on various aspects of the lives of the two men—and particularly the atmosphere of political intrigue which is further illuminated by al-ʿAqqād in "Mā warā' al-tarājim"—many of these stories may have been embellished to some degree in order to amplify the influence which Ibrāhīm al-Muwayliḥī is alleged to have had.

5 Ibrāhīm al-Muwayliḥī the younger quotes a letter written by Ibrāhīm to Muḥammad on March 15, 1880 asking for junior grammar books to be sent to Italy. See *al-Risālah* 6 (1938): 617ff.

6 *Encyclopaedia of Islam*, 2nd ed., s.v. "Arabi Pasha"; Landau, *Parliaments and Parties in Egypt*, 94ff.

7 *Le Figaro* (Paris) 331, November 26, 1884.

8 "Ihdā' al-Kitāb," in all editions of *Ḥadīth ʿĪsā ibn Hishām*. Al-Shinqīṭī died in Cairo in 1904.

9 Tarrāzī, *Ta'rīkh al-ṣiḥāfah al-ʿarabiyyah*, 4:165. ʿĀrif Bey later rose in the Ottoman administration and became governor of Sūriyā (Damascus).

10 These articles appeared irregularly in *Al-Muqaṭṭam* between December 8, 1887 and November 19, 1894.

11 Muḥammad Farīd comments in his unpublished memoirs that the Princess had a penchant for British officers. The setting for these meetings is well described by Sir Ronald Storrs in his *Orientations*, 87ff. The circle is discussed in greater detail in my "Writings of Members of the Nazli Circle."

12 Blunt, *My Diaries*, 1:14.

13 Ibid., 1:106. See also Lord Cromer, *Abbas II*, 7ff.

14 Published in *al-Muqaṭṭam*, August 18, 1893.

15 The Arabic text of this work was (re-)published in Ibrāhīm al-Muwayliḥī, *Al-Mu'allafāt al-kāmilah* in 2007. My English translation of this work is published as *Spies, Scandals, and Sultans.*

16 The former of these two appointments was announced in *Le proche Egyptien*, December 3, 1895.

17 The articles are reprinted in al-Manfalūṭī, *Mukhtārāt al-Manfalūṭī*, 139ff. I discuss both the articles and the accompanying furor in "Poetry and Poetic Criticism at the Turn of the Century."

18 Kurd 'Alī, *Memoirs*, 89; Mūsā, *The Education of Salāma Mūsā*, 38.

19 *Miṣbāḥ al-sharq* 112, July 12, 1900.

20 *Miṣbāḥ al-sharq* beginning August 17, 1900.

21 Al-Muwayliḥī's version of the incident is given in "Ḥādithat Darāktūs," *Miṣbāḥ al-sharq* 229, November 8, 1902.

22 *Miṣbāḥ al-sharq* 230, November 15, 1902.

23 Ismā'īl Ṣabrī, *Dīwān*, 94ff.

24 *Al-Mu'ayyad*, November 9–30, 1902.

25 The last issue of the newspaper to appear (August 15, 1903) contains the following announcement: "Apology: the editor of this newspaper has fallen ill and must have a change of air and some relaxation for a while. He asks the esteemed readers of the newspaper to accept his apologies for being away from work for a period of thirty days so that he may recover, God willing." No formal announcement of permanent closure was made, and there was no comment on the subject from the rest of the press.

26 Tarrāzī, *Ta'rīkh al-ṣiḥāfah*, 4:185.

27 For further details of the case, see *Al-Kātib* 28 (July 1963, 74). For one of the poems on this subject, see Ḥāfiẓ Ibrāhīm, *Dīwān*, 1:256.

28 *Al-Ẓāhir*, August 2–October 3, 1904.

29 Al-Bishrī, *Al-Mukhtār*, 1:244ff.; al-'Aqqād, *Rijāl 'araftuhum*, 79ff.

30 Storrs, *Orientations*, 74.

31 Al-Bishrī, *Al-Mukhtār*, 1:249.

32 Al-'Aqqād, *Rijāl 'araftuhum*, 82–4.

33 One of the articles by Zakī Mubārak published in *al-Risālah* (10:995ff.) contains a section called "The Captive of Poverty and Hardship."

34 Mubārak, *al-Risālah*, 10:1049.

35 Al-Muwayliḥī, *'Ilāj al-nafs*.

36 Al-Muwayliḥī, *Al-Mu'allafāt al-kāmilah*.

37 This history of the text should be regarded as a much-updated version of the section in my earlier study and translation of the text: Allen, *A Period of Time*, 32–48.

38 For fuller details on the two men's involvement in Egyptian and Ottoman politics, see Allen, *A Period of Time*, 1–14.

39 I must take the opportunity here to express my gratitude to my colleague and friend, Professor Gaber Asfour. While he was serving as Secretary-General to the Supreme Council for Culture in Cairo, I arranged for him to meet (now Dr.) Marie-Claire Boulahbel, at the time a French doctoral student writing a dissertation under my supervision on the works of Ibrāhīm al-Muwayliḥī at INALCO in Paris. He provided her with a CD-ROM of the complete run of issues of *Miṣbāḥ al-sharq* in the Dār al-Kutub newspaper archive that she subsequently catalogued and of which I now possess a copy. I need to express my gratitude to her as well for making access to the materials that much easier. All my subsequent research on the works of the Muwayliḥīs has been based on the ability to consult the original articles in the newspaper.

40 While Aḥmad Fāris al-Shidyāq includes examples of the *maqāmah* genre in his famous work, *Al-Sāq ʿalā al-sāq fī-mā huwa al-Fāryāq*, al-Muwayliḥī uses the *sajʿ* style as an opening feature to all his articles. For a virtuoso translation of al-Shidyāq's work, see Humphrey Davies's recent translation of al-Shidyāq, *Leg Over Leg*.

41 The complete text has been published in Ibrāhīm al-Muwayliḥī, *Al-Muʾallafāt al-Kāmilah*, 161–202. My English translation of the text has appeared in the journal *Middle Eastern Literatures*, 15, no. 3 (December 2012): 318–36; 16, no. 3 (December 2013): 1–17. It would seem that the father was willing to subordinate the publication of his own story to that of his son, in that, after publishing an initial three episodes in June–July 1899, he was willing to wait an entire year before publishing the remainder (while his son was traveling to Paris to report on the *Exposition universelle*).

42 Al-Muwayliḥī was clearly not enamored of English weather: "To Almighty God is the complaint about London weather! The sun has vanished and the moon is nowhere to be seen. Do you have any information to share with me about the sun or news of the moon? It has been such a long time, and I can only hope that God will compensate me for London weather with better in Paris. Farewell." *Miṣbāḥ al-sharq* 112, July 13, 1900.

43 *Miṣbāḥ al-sharq* 116, 117, 118, 121, 123, 126, 130, and 133.

44 *Miṣbāḥ al-sharq* 192, February 14, 1902.

45 Ḥāfiẓ Ibrāhīm, *Layālī Saṭīḥ*, 29.

46 Cairo: Maṭbaʿat al-Maʿārif, 1907.

47 Where original articles are combined to make a single chapter in the book version, the beginning of the second original article can easily be identified by its opening with a characteristic passage of *sajʿ*.

48 While conducting research for my Oxford doctoral thesis in Cairo in 1966, I had occasion to ask many Egyptians for their opinions of *Ḥadīth ʿĪsā ibn Hishām*. Their reactions were very similar to my own regarding the work of Geoffrey Chaucer, namely that, while it was and is recognized to be a great work, the very fact that it had been a "set text" for important examinations (and thus involved dealing with considerable linguistic complexities at a certain age), had radically affected their views of it.

49 An exception to this situation is Stewart, "Sajʿ in the Qur'an: Prosody and Structure."

50 Quoted in L. Venuti, *Translation Studies Reader*, 2004, 49.

حـديث عيسى بن هشــام

المجلّد الأوّلـــ

What ʿĪsā Ibn Hishām Told Us

Volume One

مصباح الشرق ٢١، ٨ سبتمبر ١٨٩٨

ثلاثةٌ تشرق الدنيا ببهجتهم ١،١،٠

شمس الضحى وأبو إسحاق والقمر

حدثنا عيسى بن هشام أنه رأى في المنام، ثلاثة من الحكام، يتحدثون على الطعام، فنقلنا لك رؤياه على ما تراه ،

بطرس (متطرفا متخففاً متألقا متأنقا) أين الخطباء السابقون، والبلغاء الأولون، والشعراء المادحون، والفصحاء الواصفون، وأين ابن الوليد وأبو تمام، والفردوسي والخيام، وأوربيدس وهوميروس، وهوراس وفيرجيليوس، يصفون لنا نصيبا من هذا الانتصار، وحظنا من هذا الافتخار، ويدونون لنا حسن الذكر في سجل الزمان. ويبيضون صفحات تاريخنا بفتح السودان. وما أشبه حال السردار في هذا المضمار، معنا معشر النظار بحال يوليوس سيزار. لما أرسل خبر انتصاره السريع من آسيا، إلى مثل مجلسنا المثلث في روميا، في ثلاث كلمات بينات موجزات: * وصلت * رأيت * انتصرت. ٢،١،٠

مظلوم (منذهلاً منبهتاً مندهشاً منبهراً) سألتك يا صاحبي بالله - ما هذا اللاتيني الذي تنطق به وما معناه.

بطرس ليس هو بلاتيني ولكنه عربي فصيح، يقتضيه الوصف والمديح في الكلام عن الفتوح والغزوات، والوقائع والغارات، ولكن الأجدر والأحرى، أن أعبر لك عنه بعبارة أخرى.

عـاد لِمصْرِكَ خَرْطُومُهـا.

٨٦١ ٣٨٠ ٧٥

سنة ١٣١٦

فقد وافانا السعد ، وأسعدنا الجد، فجعل فتح السودان في مدة حكمنا الميمون المنظوم، وذهب الظالم يا مظلوم، فسبحان المنعم الذي ادخر لنا هذه المواهب وتفضل علينا بحسن المواقب.

Miṣbāḥ al-sharq 21, September 8, 1898[1]

Three things shine in glorious splendor on this earth: 0.1.1

The noonday sun, Abū Isḥāq, and the moon.[2]

ʿĪsā ibn Hishām told us that in his dreams he saw three rulers conversing over their meal. As you will see, this is what he dreamed:

Buṭrus (*making a show of his refinement, full of good cheer, and feigning elegance*) Where, O where, I ask, are those orators of olden times, men of eloquence, poets who could sing paeans of praise, littérateurs who would record people's names for all time? Where are Ibn al-Walīd and Abū Tammām, Firdawsī and al-Khayyām, Euripides and Homer, Horace and Virgil? Who will record the part we have played in this great victory and our share of the glory? Who will note down the marvelous record in the archives of time and make the white pages of our history glow with stories of the conquest of Sudan, the lands of the blacks? At this moment, the Sirdar[3] and we ministers resemble Julius Caesar himself when he sent back from Asia the news of his rapid victory to a Roman senate which must have been much like our own tripartite meeting here. Caesar used just three crisp words: "*Veni, vidi, vici.*"[4] 0.1.2

Maẓlūm (*astonished and baffled*) Tell me for heaven's sake, my friend, why on earth are you speaking in Latin? What does it mean?

Buṭrus It's not Latin! It's pure Arabic. Whenever victories, campaigns, and battles are to be recorded, such are the demands of description and panegyric. But I can describe it for you in another way which might be more appropriate:

"To your Egypt has her Khartoum been returned."
The year 1316.[5]

Our fortune has been fulfilled, and destiny has come to our aid. The conquest of the Sudan has occurred during our blessed and orderly period in office. Now the tyrant has gone, Maẓlūm. So all praise be to God who has reserved these gifts for us and afforded us such a wonderful conclusion to events!

٣،١،٠ مظلوم (واجماً وجوم شحيح ضاع في الترب خاتمه) قد فهمت أنك تتكلم عن السودان، ولكن ما معنى هذا الابتهاج والاستحسان، الذي جعلك تسجع بسجع الكهان، وأية فائدة تسود علينا معشر نظار مصر، من هذا الفتح ومن هذا النصر.

بطرس (تائها معجبا) فائدتنا منه أننا نصبح نظاراً على أربعة وعشرين مليوناً من النفوس وينوّه باسمنا في أقطار شاسعة ومملكة واسعة، أرضها بكر، وترابها تبر.

مظلوم (محتقرًا مزدريا) لا أرى في كل هذا من فائدة، إلا إذا زاد مرتبنا على نسبة البلاد الزائدة.

بطرس (متضجرا متأففا) عفا الله عنك ماذا تريد من زيادة المرتب وهم يعترضون علينا وينتقدون، ويلومون ويندون، لقلة ما نعمله، وجسامة ما نتناوله، ولكن إن كان ولا بد من فائدة جوهرية، فأمامنا هناك سهام الشركات الانجليزية.

مظلوم (يفتر عن لؤلؤ رطب وعن برد) ومن لنا بالعلم بهذه الشركات وسهامها.

بطرس ألم تعلم أنّ هذه الشركات لا يمكن لها أن تستعمر أرض السودان إلا بعد أن يؤذن لها من حكومة مصر وتعقد الشروط عندك في المالية مادامت راية مصر خافقة في أفق السودان.

٤،١،٠ فخري (مهموماً مغموماً) أرجوك أن لا تذكر أمامي لفظ الراية فإني أقشعر من ذكرها ويكفيكما ما أنتما فيه من الأماني والآمال وما أنا فيه من الهموم والأحزان فقد قدّر الله عليّ أن أتولى الوزارة مرتين مرة أصيلا يوماً واحداً ومرة وكيلا أياماً. فأما الأصيل فقد كتب على مصر في ذلك اليوم أن لا تعمل عملا ولا تغير وزارة إلا بمشاورة المحتلين، وسجل عليها ذلك في الكتاب الأزرق، وأما الوكيل فقد كان ما كان من رفع الراية الانكليزية على السودان.

بطرس (مهوّنا مسلياً) خفض عليك وهوّن فإن كان بعض من لا يعلمون عويصات الأمور من السياسة يرون في نظارتيك ما تراه فإن الواقفين على الحقائق يعترفون لك باليد البيضاء على كل ناظر من النظار إذ كنت السبب في دوام هذه النظارة وعدم التعرض لها بشيء ما دام المحتلون راضين عنها وما أسهل رضاء المحتلين

Maẓlūm (*who still seems baffled, like a miser who has just lost a ring on the ground*) I can understand that you're talking about the Sudan. But why this jubilant celebration that's making you rhapsodize like a soothsayer? What benefit will we Egyptian ministers get from this victorious conquest? 0.1.3

Buṭrus (*arrogantly*) We've now become ministers who are in charge of twenty-four million people. That's the benefit we get from it all. Our names are to be proclaimed over huge areas, and we will have wide dominion in a place where the earth is virgin and the soil is pure gold.

Maẓlūm (*disdainfully and in utter contempt*) The only advantage that I can see would involve us getting a salary raise equivalent to the territorial expansion.

Buṭrus (*exasperated*) God forgive you! How can you talk about a salary increase when people are already criticizing and excoriating us for the little work we do and the piles of money we get for it? Even so, if there's to be substantial benefit gained from it all, then it will be in shares in English companies which are now at our disposal.

Maẓlūm (*revealing a set of pearly white teeth*) Whom do we know who is *au fait* with companies and shares?

Buṭrus Don't you realize that those companies will only be able to colonize the country if the Egyptian government gives them permission? As long as the Egyptian flag is flying over the Sudan, you can impose restrictions through the Finance Ministry.

Fakhrī (*distressed*) Please don't mention "flags" in my presence; the very word makes me shudder in horror. As it is, your hopes and expectations and my own anxieties are quite enough. God has willed that I should twice hold ministerial office: once as a real minister for a single day, and once as a deputy minister for several days. When I was a real minister, fate decreed that Egypt was not able to make a single move or change any ministry without consulting the occupying power, and this was recorded in the Blue Book.[6] When I was a deputy minister, the English flag was raised over the Sudan, as everyone knows full well. 0.1.4

Buṭrus (*trying to console him and make light of the situation*) Calm down, my friend! Some people who have no idea of the difficulties involved may look on your two ministries as you do, but those of us who know the real situation can acknowledge the great expertise that you possess. It's because of you that

على النظار فهم خالدون ما خلد الاحتلال، وأما الراية الانكليزية فإنها رفعت في أثناء الصلاة على روح غوردون إحياء لذكره لا إلحاقا للسودان بالانكليز فليس عليك في الحالتين من غضاضة ولا في وزارتيك لدينا من مضاضة.

مظلوم (متطلعا مشرئبا) ومن أين جاءكما الخبر برفع الراية الانكليزية على الخرطوم وما أتانا به نبأ رسمي.

بطرس جاء الخبر في عرض تلغراف السردار الذي أرسله إلى قائد جيش الاحتلال فتلقفته الجرائد وأخذت في التشنيع عليه والتوسيع فيه كعادتها فحصل لنا العلم به.

فخري ألا تنظران أيها الناظران إلى حزم الانكليز وحكمتهم فقد عضوا بالنواجذ في جميع أعمالهم على قول من قال «استعينوا على قضاء حوائجكم بالكتمان» فهم يعملون أعمالهم بينهم في الحكومة المصرية في أخفى من دبيب النمل فلا يصل إلينا علمها إلا في نعاق الجرائد والناس يظلموننا بأننا داخلون في سرهم ونجواهم.

مظلوم وما لنا ولهذا العلم وماهيته إذا خلص الناظر منا بماهيته.

فخري (متأسفاً متحسراً) ويل للشجي من الخلي لو كنت مثلي ممّن لاك بين فكيه حلاوة الأمر والنهي في نظاراتنا قبل الاحتلال لعلمت أن حرماننا من أخبار الحكومة ونحن الحكام يذهب باحترامنا عند البسطاء المغفلين.

مظلوم (مستغرباً متعجباً) ما هذه الحلاوة التي كنت تذوقها.

فخري هي أن يفد على بابك الوافدون ويقصد رحابك القاصدون. ٥،١،٠

مظلوم (جزعاً فزعاً) لا. لا. دعني وحقك من هذه الحلاوة فهي في الحقيقة مرارة وخسارة.

فخري إنّ ما تفزع منه من كثرة الوفود على بابك، وازدحام القصاد حول رحابك، لا يذكر في جانب خضوع الرقاب إليك، وتراميهم على قدميك، وتطاول الأعناق للرجاء فيك، وامتداد الآذان لسماع كلمة من فيك، ثم اعلم أني لا أطمع في سهام الشركات، ولا في زيادة المرتبات، بل أكتفي بمثل بيت العباسية الذي يحكي بين

this ministry has carried on for so long without incident, that is as long as the occupying powers has been happy with it. But then, it's so easy for our ministers to keep the occupying forces happy; they'll stay on forever, as long as the occupation lasts. Actually the English flag was only raised during the memorial service for Gordon and not on the occasion of the annexation of the Sudan to England. There's nothing for you to be ashamed of on either count; your twin ministries did not cause us any grief.

MAẒLŪM (*leaning forward attentively*) Where did you both get the news about the English flag being raised over Khartoum? We haven't received any official word.

BUṬRUS From the telegram which the Sirdar sent to the General commanding the occupation army. Then the papers picked it up. As usual, they started denouncing it at length, and so we got to hear about it.

FAKHRĪ My dear Ministers, can't you both see how determined and prudent the English are? In everything they do, they abide by the dictum: "To get what you want, make full use of secrecy." Just like ants crawling noiselessly around, the English run the Egyptian government among themselves in such secrecy that the only way we get to hear about things is when newspapers get information and start croaking. Then people start maligning us by suggesting that we're involved in the secret sessions too.

MAẒLŪM Why do we need to know such things as long as the minister among us gets paid his salary?

FAKHRĪ (*with a sigh*) How can you possibly know as much about it as I do?! If you'd tasted, as I have, the sweet savor of absolute authority that we had in our ministries before the occupation, you'd realize that being starved of government news, when we are supposed to be in charge, detracts from the respect which simple ignorant people feel for us.

MAẒLŪM (*baffled*) What was that sweet savor you used to taste?

FAKHRĪ Delegations would crowd your door, and people with petitions would head for your ministry. 0.1.5

MAẒLŪM (*horrified*) Stop, stop! Spare me such sweet delights! In actual fact it's all bitterness and loss.

FAKHRĪ The horror that you envisage from all those delegations and people with petitions that seem to aggravate you so much are nothing when compared with the pleasure to be gleaned from the way people bow and throw themselves at your feet. They crane their necks to make their pleas and

قصور الجيران، بيتا من بيوت أم درمان، ولا أتطلع أن يضاء بالكهرباء ولا أن يكون على مائدتي الهليون والهندبا، وإنما لذتي الدنيوية، في تلك اللذة المعنوية.

مظلوم يظهر لي من تزهدك وتقشفك وتولعك بهذه اللذة المعنوية أنها لذة تفوق اللذات فما هي الطريقة التي توصلنا إليها وتقدرنا عليها.

فخري أما الأمر والنهي فقد مضى لسبيله ولم يبق إلا أن نعلم علم الحكومة قبل الناس وغاية ما في الوسع اليوم أن نسأل الله إلهام المحتلين بأن يوقفونا على أخبار حكومتنا قبل أن تقف الجرائد عليها.

الجميع آمين.

بطرس (وهو خارج يناجي نفسه هازا كتفيه) إنّ أمر الراية لخطب كبير، والخلاص من مسؤوليته عسير، ولكن كم سمعنا وكم رأينا، وكم خلصنا وكم نجونا، وإذا كان بطرس بولس مأمور خزينة الخرطوم عند قتل غوردون ومن معه كان المفرد الوحيد الذي خلص من فتك الدراويش فلا يصعب على بطرس غالي أن يتخلص من مثل هذه الملاعب التي يسمونها في السياسة بالمصاعب.

strain their ears to hear a single word from your mouth. I don't want either shares in companies or a salary raise. I'm quite content with my small house in al-ʿAbbāsiyyah which is like a primitive place in Omdurman when compared with the huge mansions all around it. I've no desire to have it lit by electricity, or to have asparagus and chicory on my table. My own worldly pleasures now reside in more spiritual realms.

MAẒLŪM Your withdrawal from worldly affairs like some ascetic and your obsession with spiritual pleasures gives me the impression that they surpass all other pleasures. So, tell me, how can we find it and make use of what they have to offer?

FAKHRĪ The days of absolute authority are over. All that remains is for us to hear about what is going on in the government before anyone else. All we can do is to ask God to inspire the occupying power to let us know about our government's affairs before the newspapers get hold of it.

EVERYONE Amen to that!

BUṬRUS (*as he takes his leave, he is talking to himself and shrugging his shoulders*) This flag business is very serious. It's a difficult problem to shrug off. But then, we've heard and seen a good deal. How often have we managed to save ourselves and others?!

(Since Buṭrus Paulus was in charge of the Khartoum treasury when Gordon and his men were killed and was the only one to escape the Darwīsh slaughter, it should not be too difficult for Buṭrus Ghālī to rid himself of silly games like these which people in politics call "difficulties.")

مصباح الشرق ٢٣، ٢٢ سبتمبر ١٨٩٨

١،٢،٠ للحرب قوم أضلّ الله سعيهم
إذا دعتهم إلى حوماتها وثبوا
ولست منهم ولا أهوى فعالهم
لا القتل يعجبني منها ولا السلب

٢،٢،٠ حدثنا عيسى بن هشام، قال: بلغني أنّ بعض ذوي الأقلام، رأى أحد نظارنا العظام يدور في ساحة حمام من حمامات المياه المعدنية في البلدان الأجنبية فاستدل من تبختره في مشيته، أنه ناظر حربية في بلدته للخبر المشهور، والقول المأثور، عن مشية التبختر، أنها مشية مكروهة في كل مكان، إلا في ساحة الحرب والطعان، فقصده قصد سائل أخبار، لا سائل درهم أو دينار، قائلا في نفسه الآن أستقي الخبر من عينه، وأستخرج الأمر من معدنه ، وما لإخواني من مكاتبي الصحف والجرائد، يهيمون في الفيافي والفدافد . وما لهم والمسير في نار الهجير، يهجرون الأقارب والآل ويسبحون في بحور من الآل، ليس لهم من شراب، إلا من السراب، ولا طعام يصاب، إلا من الصاب، ولا رقاد إلا فوق شوك القتاد، ولا ظل إلا ظل البنود، تخفق بين الجنود، يدورون مع الجيش في المغاور والغابات، دوران الآذريون من النبات، والحرباء من الحيوانات حول قرص الغزالة في الأفق إلى أن تغيب في الشفق، حتى إذا التحم القتال واحتدم النزال، وتصارعت الأبطال وتقارعت الرجال، وأقبلت الآجال تفترس الآمال، وتقطع الأعمال، وهم يتطلعون طلع الأخبار، كما يتطلع المسهد إلى ضوء النهار. انكشفت الملحمة عن القتيل منهم والجريح، والذبيح والطريح، ولكن نعم ما أحسن عليّ به الحظ وجاد وأسعفني به اليمن والإسعاد. وأبلغني المراد على غير ميعاد، فأنقذني مما أصاب أصحابي من الحمام. وجعلني أصيب غرضهم وأنا في نعيم هذا الحمام، وهكذا الدنيا يسعد فيها المقيم المكسال، ويشقى من يشد الأزمة والرحال.

ثم تقدم إلى الناظر بعد أن سلم فقال:

Miṣbāḥ al-sharq 23, September 22, 1898

War engenders its own folk whom God leads astray;
When it summons them to its turmoil, they leap.
I am not of such people; I abhor what they wreak;
Neither conflict nor plunder give me pleasure.[7]

0.2.1

ʿIsā ibn Hishām told us: I heard that a newspaper correspondent spotted one of our senior ministers walking around the courtyard in a spa abroad. From his prancing gait he gleaned that it was the Minister of War. As the common expression has it: such a gait is detested everywhere except in the sphere of conflict. So this reporter went up to beg him for something: not for money, but rather for information. He told himself that he would now be getting the news from the very source. At the same time he kept thinking about his fellow reporters who would be roaming around in the deserts of the Sudan, wandering in the steaming heat of the midday sun, far away from their families and relatives, as they sweated in seas of humid air—their only water a mirage; their only food bitter-tasting colocynth. They would be sleeping on prickly thorns, and their only shade would come from flags fluttering over the army. They would be doing the rounds of caves and forests, just like anemones in plant-life and chameleons among animals as they encountered the sun's disk hovering over the horizon until evening sunset. Then conflict would erupt, fighting would flare up, heroes would battle each other, and men would confront their foes. Fates would rush in to snatch away hopes and put an end to all activity. The reporters meanwhile would be eager for news, like insomniacs craving the light of day. The entire saga would then proceed to recount its tales of dead and wounded, those slain and maimed. But fate has indeed been kind to me, he told himself, and my lucky stars have come to my aid. I have achieved my goal and escaped the hardships and risks that my colleagues are facing; and all that in this luxurious European spa. But then, that's the way of the world: the layabout who stays home gets all the luck, while those who ride their mounts into danger have to suffer.

0.2.2

The reporter then went up to the Minister and said:

الكاتب (متحمساً) قد دلتني مخايلك وشهدت لي شمائلك أنك مصري من رجال الحرب فهل لك أن تسمح لي بمحادثتك، وتجيبني إلى محاورتك لأنشرعنك في الجرائد من أمر السودان ما يرفع ذكرك ويعلي قدرك. ٣،٢،٠

ناظر الحربية (شامخاً باذخاً) أنا ناظر الحربية المصرية.

الكاتب (مستبشراً مستخبراً) لا شك أنّ عهد سيدي الناظر ببلاده غير بعيد وأنه لم يحضر إلى هذه البلاد لترويح النفس إلا بعد أن قاسى أعظم المشاق وعانى أكبر المصاعب في فتح البلاد السودانية.

الناظر (متحيراً متوجساً) نعم حضرت إلى هنا ولكن قبل الفتح بشهرين.

الكاتب (متعجباً) وكيف يصح ذلك وكيف يجوز لناظر الحربية أن يترك الحرب وتدبيرها وهي مشتعلة في بلاده وينسحب عنها نازحاً متروحاً.

الناظر (محتجاً) لا عتب على ناظر الحربية في ذلك فإنه يباشر جميع أعماله وهو بعيد عن بلاده كما أنّ قائد الجيش الذي يدير حركته يكون وراء الجيش.

الكاتب نعم إنّ مركز القائد وراء الجيش لا يمنعه من إدارة الجيش ومعرفة حركاته فهل تصلك الأخبار في أوقاتها كما تصله في أوقاتها.

الناظر (مفتخراً) اعلم أن لي وكيلين على الحربية ناظر المالية ووكيل الحربية وهما لا يغفلان عن إرسال الأخبار إليّ في أوقاتها من سان ستيفانو.

الكاتب (مستفهماً) سان ستيفانو! وهل في البلاد السودانية ما يطلق عليه هذا الاسم.

الناظر (مستدلاً متمثلا) ليس هو من البلاد السودانية وإنما هو محل حمامات في الإسكندرية وأنت تعلم أن تلغراف الشيفرة لا يبعد عليه مكان، ولا يمضي عليه زمان، وإذا كان لاعب الشطرنج يلعب مع آخر من بلدة وهو في بلدة أخرى وميدان الحرب هو أصل الجد المأخوذ عنه هذا اللعب فهل يعتريك شك من وصول الأخبار إليّ بهذه الطريقة.

الكاتب إذن أخبرني ما هي أخبار اليوم.

0.2.3 REPORTER Your demeanor leads me to believe that you're an Egyptian and a war veteran. Will you allow me to interview you so that I can publish some news about events in the Sudan in the newspapers? That will bring your name to people's attention and enhance your prestige.

MINISTER OF WAR (*arrogant and contemptuous*) I'm the Egyptian Minister of War.

REPORTER (*encouraged*) I'm sure you've only recently left Egypt, Sir. You must only have come here for a rest after enduring severe hardships and difficulties during the Sudanese campaign.

MINISTER (*flustered*) Yes, I was there. But that was two months before the conquest.

REPORTER (*astonished*) How can that be? Can the Minister of War simply stop supervising the campaign when it's at its height and slip away for a holiday abroad?

MINISTER There's nothing wrong with the Minister doing that. He can supervise everything from abroad. After all, an army general directs operations from the rear.

REPORTER That's quite true, but it doesn't stop him from directing operations and knowing what's going on. Do you get news as quickly as he does then?

MINISTER (*boastfully*) You should realize that I have two deputies in the Ministry of War: the Minister of Finance and the Permanent Undersecretary of War. They both make a point of keeping me informed from San Stefano as soon as anything happens.

REPORTER (*seeking information*) San Stefano? Is there a place of that name in the Sudan?

MINISTER (*explaining*) It's not in the Sudan; it's a spa in Alexandria. You know full well that time and distance mean absolutely nothing now that telegrams are available. One chess player can play with another in a different country. In fact war is itself the very foundation on which that particular game is based, so how can you have any doubts that I can get the news in the same way?

REPORTER So tell me then, what's today's news?

الناظر اليوم هواؤه عليل، ونسيمه بليل، وسماؤه صافية، وشمسه زاهية.

الكاتب (باسماً) لكم الله معشر الشرقيين ما أقدركم على التقليد وما أسرعكم في محاكاة الغربيين فقد كنا نعتقد أنّ أمراءنا ووزراءنا انفردوا وحدهم بفن المراوغة والمحاولة للتخلص من مكاتبي الجرائد حين يتفننون في استكشاف الأخبار من مكامنها من صدورهم، فهل لك أيها الناظر أن أتنازل لك عن مهارتي في فن التحايل وأن تنزل لي عن دهائك في فن المحاولة والمراوغة فلا يضيع الوقت بيننا فإذا رضيت فأخبرني عن رأيك في التعايشي. ٤،٢،٠

الناظر (متكهناً) إذا ذهب التعايشي إلى كردفان، فإنه فان، وإن خلص إلى دارفور، فهو معفور، وإن عاد إلى أم درمان، فلا أمان، وإن رجع إلى الخرطوم وسم على الخرطوم .

الكاتب لم تزدني يا سيدي شيئا في أمر التعايشي عما كنت أعلمه ولا ألح عليك في كشف الخفي من أمره فإنّ لك الحق في كتمانه وربما كانت الإباحة به مما تحول دون القبض عليه فأنا أترك لك ذلك وأطلب منك أن تخبرني عن النبأ العظيم والحادث الكبير في توجه السردار إلى فشودة.

الناظر (مستهيناً) أمر السردار فيها بسيط فإنه يريد الرجوع إلى مصر ليتمتع بذلك الانتصار، ويستريح برهة من عناء تلك الأسفار.

الكاتب (متأسفاً) أراك لا تزال على محاولتك لي.

الناظر (معتذراً) أقسم لك بكل يمين أن مثلي لا يمين، بعد الاتفاق على نبذ المحاولة والاختلاق.

الكاتب (مستنكرا) كيف تقول أنّ الأمر بسيط وهو نبأ عظيم وحادث كبير يهتم له وزراء السياسة عموما ويهم نظار مصر خصوصا وكيف تقول أنّ السردار يرجع من فشودة إلى مصر وهو إنما يتقدم إليها بعد فتح أم درمان ليتمم فتح السودان فإنها قريبة من منابع النيل.

MINISTER The weather's fine; there's a cool breeze and clear sky, and the sun is shining brightly.

0.2.4 REPORTER (*with a smile*) Easterners are certainly quick to imitate Westerners, aren't they? Talking about the weather! We used to think amirs and ministers were in a class of their own when it came to prevarication and ruses to get rid of newspaper reporters who were trying to get some information out of them. May I suggest, Minister, that I stop using tricks to get information from you and you in turn stop hedging; that way we won't waste any more time. If you're agreeable, would you mind telling me what you think about al-Taʿāyishī?

MINISTER (*offering a prediction*) If he goes to Kordofān, he's a dead man; if he escapes to Darfūr, he'll be obliterated for sure; if he comes back to Omdurman, he won't find for protection any remand; and, if he goes back to Khartoum, then for that city it's doom.[8]

REPORTER So far you've not told me anything I didn't know already. But I'm not going to press you to reveal any secrets; you have a right to keep them to yourself. Disclosing such information might prevent his being captured. I'll leave that point and ask you about the most significant news of all; the fact that the Sirdar is heading for Fashōda.

MINISTER (*derisively*) The Sirdar's actions can be easily explained. He wants to get back to Egypt to enjoy his triumph and is just resting for a while.

REPORTER (*sighing regretfully*) I see you're still dodging the question.

MINISTER (*making excuses*) I assure you, someone such as myself doesn't tell lies after agreeing to talk frankly.

REPORTER (*exasperated*) Then how can you say that things are so simple? It's a matter of great importance, one that is preoccupying all the ministers of the European powers and especially those of Egypt! How can you say that the Sirdar is coming back to Egypt from Fashōda? He only went there after entering Omdurman in order to complete the conquest of the Sudan. It's quite near the source of the Nile.

الناظر (هازئا ضاحكا) أراك تخطئ فيما تقول والخطأ بيّن في عبارتك فإنّ فشودة ما دامت واقعة على منابع النيل فلا بد أن تكون واقعة عند الشلال حيث يبنى الخزان هناك.

المكاتب (مندهشا ساخطا) لم أخطئ أيها الناظر ولكني أراك قد خرجت من طريق المحاول إلى طريق المتجاهل فإنّ فشودة واقعة بعد أم درمان على النيل الأبيض على مسافة تزيد عن الأربعمائة كيلو، فأصدقني عما تعلمه من أمرها وأمر مرشان (ومرشان كلمة فرنسوية معناها بائع). ٥،٢،٠

الناظر (متخلصا) الآن ظهر لنا معنى تعريج السردار على فشودة لأجل هذا المرشان ديسكلاف (بائع الرقيق) فإنّ انكلترا هي الدولة الوحيدة التي اشتهرت بالدخول في كل الأقطار لمنع الرقيق.

المكاتب (متضجرا) لقد أعياني الأمر معك أيها الناظر فمرشان رجل فرنسوي حضر مع حملة فرنسوية ليستولي على بعض الجهات القريبة من منابع النيل لتمنع انكلترا من الاستيلاء على السودان كله.

الناظر (متذكرا مستدلا) نعم ذاك رجل خاب في مسعاه إذ تعطل في طريق الحبشة فرجع ولم يحتل أرضاً في السودان.

المكاتب (محتدا منفعلا) واحسرتاه أنا أتكلم عن مرشان وهو يتكلم عن بونشان.

الناظر (مختصرا) لا تحتد أيها المكاتب ولا تشتد فأنا أقول لك عن جلية الأمر وفصل الخطاب في كلمتين، إن كنت تتكلم عن مرشان، فالسردار يقصده لمنع الرقيق في السودان. وإن كنت تتكلم عن بونشان (وهي كلمة فرنسوية أيضا معناها المزرعة الجيدة) فقد توجه السردار إلى فشودة لاختيار الأراضي الصالحة للزراعة والاستيطان.

المكاتب (ممزقا ثيابه خارجا من أهابه) اعلم يا حضرة الناظر أنّ مرشان وبونشان من أسماء الأعلام لا أسماء المعاني كما تسمون مظلوما وغاليا وعبائيا وليس ثمت ظلم ولا غلاء ولا حمال ضخام وكما تقولون ناظر حربية وليس له نظر في حرب ٦،٢،٠

Minister (*laughing scornfully*) You're obviously wrong. If Fashōda is really at the source of the Nile, then it must be at the cataract where the dam is being built.[9]

Reporter (*amazed and increasingly angry*) I'm not mistaken, my dear Minister. I see you've changed your tactics now; instead of hedging, you're feigning ignorance. Fashōda is more than four hundred kilometers above Omdurman on the White Nile. Tell me, what do you know about it and Marchand?[10] 0.2.5

Minister (*relieved*) Now I see why the Sirdar is moving towards this Fashōda place—it's because of this *marchand d'esclaves*![11]

Reporter (*angrily*) My dear Minister, I'm fed up with talking to you. Marchand is a Frenchman who's come with a French force to take control of some areas close to the source of the Nile. The aim is to try to prevent England from controlling the whole of the Sudan.

Minister (*using his memory*) Yes, he failed. He was delayed in Ethiopia and gave up; he never occupied any part of the Sudan.

Reporter (*furious*) Good grief! Here I am talking about Marchand, and he's talking about Bonchamps!

Minister Don't lose your temper, my dear sir! I'll tell you the complete truth in a couple of words. If you were talking about Marchand, then the Sirdar is going there to put an end to slavery in the Sudan. If it's Bonchamps you were referring to, then he is heading for Fashōda to choose some lands which can be used for cultivation and settlement.[12]

Reporter (*tearing at his clothes and losing all patience*) My dear Minister, Marchand and Bonchamps are proper names belonging to famous people; they're not being used as nouns with semantic connotations. When people are called Mazlūm, Ghālī, and 'Abbā'ī, it doesn't mean there's any reference to tyranny, overcharging, or heavy loads.[13] 0.2.6

Here we are with a Minister of War who knows nothing about fighting and is not even supervising the campaign. What bad luck! I'm wasting my time. I came to get information and I end up giving it instead! The nightmare of this confrontation makes me envy my colleagues who are facing death on the

ولا علم بقتال فما أسوأ بختي، وأضيع وقتي، جئت متعلما فأصبحت معلما وصرت بعد أهوال هذا الجدال أحسد إخواني أمام الموت في ساحة القتال، فقد نالوا المآرب بعد المصاعب. ونلت المصاعب قبل المآرب وخرجت خالي الوفاض من نيل الأغراض، وهكذا تكون عاقبة من اعتمد على التقاعد ولم يشمر في أموره عن الساعد.

Sudan battlefront. At least they will have got what they want after some hardships, whereas all I've got are still more problems after thinking I had found what I was seeking! That's what happens when you stay aloof without getting involved in the task at hand.

ثلاثة في واحد، وواحد في ثلاثة

مصباح الشرق ٢٤، ٢٩ سبتمبر ١٨٩٨

حدثنا عيسى بن هشام قال: بلغني عن نائب القائمقام أنه زاره خليط من خلطائه، وصفيّ من أصفيائه، فلمّا دخل عليه متطلعاً طلع أخباره، وجده مطرقا لتزاحم أفكاره، مقطب الوجه عابساً، ظاهر القنوط يائساً، يتلألأ العرق على جبينه فيمسحه بشماله ويمينه، ثمّ يزمجر في نفسه، ويهمهم، ويجمجم ويدمدم، فأخذ الزائر في سؤاله عن أمره وحاله. ١،٣،٠

الزائر ما لي أرى النائب غريقاً في بحر الأفكار، مستسلما للأحزان والأكدار، وليس من جديد يقضي بهذا الهم الشديد. ٢،٣،٠

النائب (مشتغلا بحاله، غير ملتفت إلى زائره وسؤاله) ....

الزائر لعل النائب يقدح فكره في كشف ما يكون من نتيجة المخابرات بين الدولتين في مسألة فشودة.

النائب (متهاونا مستصغرا) ذاك أمر يهم الجرائد.

الزائر لعلك تفكر فيما يؤول إليه الأمر في مسألة رفع الراية الانكليزية.

النائب هذا يشغل الأستانة ولوندرة.

الزائر أظنك تشتغل بمخابرة الجناب العالي للاحتفال بقدوم الإمبراطور.

النائب هذا لفابريسيوس.

الزائر كأني بناظر الأشغال يدبر طرق الوقاية من فيضان النيل في هذا العام.

النائب هذا لمشايخ البلاد.

الزائر عساك تجتهد في استنباط عذر لبيع سكة حديد السودان.

النائب وهذا ممّا يعنى به سوراس، وليس بي ممّا ذكرت من هذه الأمور العمومية شيء، وإنما هو أمر خاص بي.

Three in One and One in Three

Miṣbāḥ al-sharq 24, September 29, 1898

ʿIsā ibn Hishām told us: I heard that the deputy *qāʾim maqām* had a visit from one of his coterie. When the latter came in to ask for the latest news, he found his friend with his head lowered, deep in thought. He was frowning and scowling and looked disheartened. Sweat was glistening on his forehead, and he was wiping it off with his left and right hand in turn. He began to mutter and grumble to himself. His visitor asked him what was the matter: 0.3.1

VISITOR How is it I see you looking so pensive and worried? Surely nothing's happened to make you so anxious? 0.3.2

(*The deputy pays no attention but remains deep in his own thoughts.*)

VISITOR Maybe you're racking your brains to work out what will be the result of the negotiation between the two powers on the Fashōda question?

DEPUTY (*scornfully*) The papers are fussing about that.

VISITOR Then perhaps you're thinking about what will happen over the question of the raising of the British flag?

DEPUTY That's for people in Istanbul and London.

VISITOR Then you must be busy contacting the Khedive over the arrangements for the Emperor's arrival?

DEPUTY That's a job for one of his aides.

VISITOR Could it be then that, along with the Minister of Works, you're involved in organizing the precautionary measures to be taken against the Nile flood this year?

DEPUTY That's for local authorities to worry about.

VISITOR Then maybe you're trying to come up with an excuse for selling off the Sudanese Railway.

DEPUTY Suarez is working on that. I'm not concerned with any of those public interest items you've just mentioned. It's a purely private matter.

الزائر يجوز أن يكون الخواجة رولوسمح أن يبيعك بيت باب اللوق بمبلغ الثلاثة آلاف جنيه الذي قدرته له عندما طلب فيه اثني عشر ألف جنيه.

النائب لا هذا ولا ذاك وإنما الذي أوجب همي وحزني هو انقضاء زمن الحكم المثلث أولا وانتهاء أمد النيابة عن القائمقام ثانيا ولم يبق إلا البحث عن طريقة تخلد لي ذكرى هذا الحكم فأتلذذ به في خلواتي، ويلبس به أعقابي ثوب فخري بعد مماتي.

الزائر نعم الفكر لتخليد الذكر.

(وهنا يعود النائب إلى قدح القريحة كما كان، وبعد هنيهة ينتفض جذلان فرحا مبتهجا منشرحا ويصيح قائلا «وجدتها» كما قالها أرخميدس من قبله). ٣،٣،٠

الزائر (متشوقا متطلعا) ما هذه الخبيئة التي وجدتها، والرغيبة التي نلتها، فأراك قد لمعت أسرتك، وأشرقت غرتك.

النائب ثلاثة في واحد وواحد في ثلاثة.

الزائر لم لا تخبرني في أول الأمر أنك تبحث في مسألة من الهندسة أو الجبر.

النائب نعم ثلاثة في واحد وواحد في ثلاثة.

الزائر فهمت، ولكن ما هي هذه المسألة التي تحار فيها الألباب، وتخلط بين تخليد الذكر ومسائل الحساب.

النائب ستفهم الآن مرامي بهذا الدكريتو الذي تراه أمامي.

الزائر لم تزدني في الأمر إلا تعمية وإبهاما.

النائب هاك ما يكشف لك العمى (يتناول القلم ويسطر به على قرطاس ثم يدفعه إليه فإذا هو الأمر العالي بتعيين رئيس قوميسيون السكة الحديد وقد أمضاه على هذه الصورة):

بأمر الحضرة الخديوية عن رئيس مجلس النظار

فخري فخري

ناظر الأشغال العمومية

فخري

VISITOR Could it be that Mr. Rollo has authorized the sale of his house in Bāb al-Lūq to you for the three thousand pounds that you've offered, when he'd been asking for twelve thousand?

DEPUTY It's not that either. Two things are bothering me: the term of tripartite rule has come to an end; and secondly my own term as deputy *qā'im maqām* is over. All I can do is to try to find some way of keeping alive the memory of my period in government, something that'll give me pleasure in retirement, something my children can wear as a badge of pride. Then after my death, my descendants can assume the Fakhrī mantle.[14]

VISITOR What a marvelous idea.

0.3.3 (*The deputy continues to rack his brains. After a while, he leaps to his feet in joy. "I've found it," he yells, just like Archimedes before him.*)

VISITOR What secret treasure have you uncovered? What cherished dream have you now realized? Why such a radiant smile on your face?!

DEPUTY Three in one and one in three.

VISITOR Why didn't you tell me at the start that it was an engineering or algebra problem you were trying to solve?

DEPUTY That's it: three in one and one in three.

VISITOR I understand. But tell me, what is this problem which has been bothering you—one that manages to combine arithmetic with keeping memories alive?

DEPUTY Now you'll understand the import of the decree that you see in front of me.

VISITOR You're just making me even more confused and baffled.

DEPUTY This will solve the riddle.

(*The deputy takes out a pen, writes something on a piece of paper, then hands it to his visitor. It concerns the important matter involving the appointment of the chairman of the Railways Commission. Here's how he has written it out:*)

By order of His Excellency the Khedive from the Prime Minister:

FAKHRĪ FAKHRĪ

Minister of Public Works

FAKHRĪ.[15]

الزائر أما خطر لك أنّ الناس في مستقبل الدهر يظنون أنه كان في الحكومة المصرية ثلاثة من الحكام بهذا الاسم في آن واحد. ٤،٣،٠

النائب وهل تظن أن الدهر يسمح في آن واحد بثلاثة من مثلي، أما سمعت قول الشاعر:

هيهات أن يأتي الزمان بمثله
إنّ الزمـان بمثله لبخيـل

الزائر سبحان من هداك وأرشدك إلى هذا الاختراع فهو أشبه بالمرآة الثلاثية يرى الناظر فيها نفسه ثلاثة في وقت واحد.

Visitor Hasn't it occurred to you that in future people may think there were three people with the same name in the Egyptian government at the same time? 0.3.4

Deputy Do you imagine that the fates would allow there to be three people like me at any one time? Haven't you heard the words of the poet:

Small chance that time will ever produce his peer;
with people of his ilk it is miserly indeed![16]

Visitor Thank God you have been able to devise this plan. It's like a three-way mirror in which the Minister can see himself three times at once!

النظار والمساواة

مصباح الشرق ٣٠، ١٠ نوفمبر ١٨٩٨

١،٤،٠ حدثنا عيسى بن هشام، قال رغبت في سماع الكلام، من أفواه العوام، عما في الحال العام، من خلل ونظام، وحرب وسلام واختلاف ووئام، فعمدت إلى سوق لا تستقر فيها الأقدام، من شدة الزحام، فوجدت معرض أيمان، لا معرض إيمان، كل يحلف ويخث ويبرم وينكث لترويج سلعته وبيع بضاعته، فلم أحظ من غرضي بطائل ولم أرجع من مقصدي بنائل، فعدلت عما نويت، ورجعت من حيث أتيت، فصادفت في طريقي مركبة الكهرباء تسير سير الفضاء في نزوله من السماء، فركبت فيها فوجدت صنوفا من الناس مختلفي الأشكال والأجناس، والوجوه واللباس، وهم بين واقف وقاعد، ونازل وصاعد، وامرأة وطفل، وزوجة وبعل، وأهيف وهيفاء، ودميم وشوهاء، ومخمور ونشوان، ومخدر وسكران، وكلهم في همس وصياح، ونزاع وارتياح، وخلاف في دفع الأجرة، واتفاق في رد التذكرة، مع مطالعة جرائد، ومغازلة خرائد.

٢،٤،٠ وبجانبي رجل يملأ العين فخامة، والمكان ضخامة، هذبت السذاجة طبعه ومزاجه، وهو لاهٍ باستماع ما يقال، في مكاشفات الأحوال، فيستر وجهه بمنديل، كلما أضحكته تلك الأقاويل، ومما أعجب به وأخذ بلبه اشتداد الخصام بين راكبين متزاحمين، حتى سب أحدهما الآخر وشتمه، ولكمه ولطمه، وكاد يفضي الأمر إلى مناداة الشرطة من النقطة، لولا أنّ السائق أفهم المشتوم السر المكتوم، وهو أنّ الشاتم ممن يجب له الاحترام والاعتبار، لأنه خادم لأحد النظار، فأخذ المشتوم يعتذر ويتودد والشاتم يتكبر ويتمردز

٣،٤،٠ وبينا نحن نسير، إذ أوقف المركبة الصفير، وإذا برجلين يتساران وهما سائران،

Ministers and Equality

Miṣbāḥ al-sharq 30, November 10, 1898

ʿIsā ibn Hishām told us: I was keen to hear from people about various aspects of the current situation: the mixture of organization and chaos, of war and peace, and agreement and discord. So I made for a market. It was so crowded there that you could barely put your foot on the ground. What I found in fact was a showroom of oaths rather than of faith; everyone was breaking their word and infringing regulations so that they could get rid of their merchandise and sell their wares. When I failed to get what I wanted, I changed my plans and retraced my steps. 0.4.1

On the way I came across a tram moving along like fate itself descending from heaven. I got on and found myself among a whole variety of people. Some were standing, others sitting, and people kept getting on and off. There were women and babies, wives with their husbands, good-looking men and women and ugly ones too, and some drunken fools as well. They were all yelling and screaming, arguing, or whispering to each other, bickering with the conductor over the fare and then agreeing when the ticket was handed to them. Others were reading newspapers or else making eyes at pretty girls.

Next to me sat an imposing man who was so bulky that he filled up the entire space. He seemed to value the simple life and was keeping himself amused by listening to people talking about themselves and then covering his face with his handkerchief every time such talk made him laugh. He was particularly happy when two passengers who were squeezed together started arguing. Eventually one of them swore and cursed at the other and then proceeded to cuff him. The police would have been called then and there if the driver had not told the injured party that the person who had cursed and cuffed him had to be shown great respect since he was a minister's servant. The man at whom the curses had been aimed immediately apologized profusely and tried to make amends while the curser gave him an arrogant stare. 0.4.2

As we proceeded on our way, the tram ground to a halt with a whistle. There were two men alongside each other, one riding a bicycle and the other 0.4.3

أحدهما راكب دراجة، والثاني قد نفخ المشي أوداجه، فما وصلا إلى المركبة حتى قام لهما مكاتبي احتراما، يستقبل منهما تحية وسلاما، فامتطى الماشي كرسي الترامواي امتطاء صهوة الجواد، فعل الفارس في ميدان الجلاد والطراد، وبقي صاحب الدرّاجة يساير المركبة بجانبنا فصرت بينهم، ولم أدر من هم، حتى ظهر لي من تهاديهم تحية الإمارة أنهم من ذوي النظارة، وعلمت من حديثهم أنّ الراكب الأول بجانبي وكيل الحقانية والماشي ناظر الحربية والدارج ناظر المالية، وإليك ما سمعته من محادثتهم، والتقطته من محاورتهم تارة بعربيتهم وأخرى بفرنساويتهم.

٤،٤،٠ وكيل الحقانية (لناظر الحربية وناظر المالية) كيف تمشيان وتدرجان على هذه الحال وأين خيلكما ومركبتكما.

ناظر الحربية (متهللا فرحا) وقع الحجز عليهما من نظارة المالية.

وكيل الحقانية (وهو لا يكاد يسيغ ريقه من الدهشة) وكيف يقع الحجز على مركبة ناظر المالية وهو الحفيظ على خزائن الأرض وعلى مركبة ناظر الحربية وبخيله ورجله فتح السودان.

ناظر الحربية إننا قد أغفلنا أعطاء العوائد عليهما فأراد المحتلون أن يظهروا للملأ عدلهم بإطلاق المساواة بيننا وبين كافة الناس فبادروا بالحجز عليها وبادرنا إلى المسابقة في غرضهم فأعلنا ذلك بمشينا في الشوارع والأزقة وركوب الترامواي إخلاصا في الموافقة على ما يريدون، وتزلفا إليهم بفعل ما يشتهون.

وكيل الحقانية لقد حق لنا السرور والفرح بهذا فقد أعاد لنا المحتلون ما نسمع به من المساواة في صدر الإسلام من نزول الأمراء إلى درجة الرعية وما يفرق ركوبك الترامواي من ركوب مروان الحمار عند دخوله الشام، في خلافة أبي سفيان بن هشام، حين اعترض على موكبه ومخالفة المساواة به.

ناظر الحربية قل لي بالله في أي كتاب وجدت هذه الحكاية.

quite out of breath from keeping up with him. They had barely reached the tram before the man next to me stood up respectfully and accepted their greetings. The man who had been walking took a seat, looking as though he were mounting a splendid steed like some horseman on the battlefield. The man who was riding the bicycle stayed on his machine and pedaled alongside the tram. I was sitting between them. I had no idea who they might be until they greeted each other with an air of authority, from which I gathered that they were ministers. From their conversation, it emerged that the passenger sitting beside me was the Permanent Undersecretary of Justice, the person who had been walking was the Minister of War, and the man on the bicycle was the Minister of Finance. I will now give you a version of the conversation I heard; they were speaking sometimes in Arabic and at others in French:

0.4.4 PERMANENT UNDERSECRETARY (*to the Ministers of War and Finance*) Why are you both walking and riding like this? What's happened to your horses and carriages?

MINISTER OF WAR (*chuckling*) They've been sequestered by the Ministry of Finance!

UNDERSECRETARY (*almost skipping a heartbeat from shock*) How can they sequester the Minister of Finance's carriage? He's the guardian of the country's treasury after all. They can't do that to the Minister of War. After all it was his horse and foot which helped conquer the Sudan.

MINISTER OF WAR We've overlooked sharing the revenues accrued from both of them, so the occupying powers were eager to show how just they were by applying the principle of equality and by treating us in exactly the same way as they do ordinary people. They confiscated the carriages on the spot, and we've rushed to oblige them by walking in the streets and riding on trams. By so doing, we can show how compliant we are to their wishes and thus ingratiate ourselves to them.

UNDERSECRETARY We should be delighted by the present situation. The occupying powers have restored the principle of equality from the very first days of Islam that we've all been hearing about. In those days of old, amirs used to descend to the same level as the people. The way you're riding on a tram is no different from the way Marwān came into Damascus riding a donkey during the caliphate of Abū Sufyān ibn Hishām; he had objected to his procession and the way it contravened a sense of equality.[17]

MINISTER OF WAR In which book did you find that story?

وكيل الحقانية لم أنقلها عن كتاب حيث لا وقت عندي لقراءة الكتب وإنما سمعتها موثوقًا بها من منقولات الناظر من شيخه الحداد.

ناظر المالية (متلفتا فوق دراجته يمينا وشمالا) ذكرتم شيئا وغابت عنكم أشياء فإنه لم يدخل في حسابكم تلك الفائدة التي تفوق فائدة الطاعة في أمر المساواة وهي صعود قيمة الأسهم في شركة الترامواي إذا ركبنا فيه فإنّ الناس يتزاحمون للركوب فيه صغيرهم وكبيرهم لمشاهدتنا ومماثلتنا والركوب بجانبنا فتصعد أسعار السهام فيربح كل من أناله الحظ نصيبا منها.

ناظر الحربية نعم الفكر ونعمت الفائدة لو أنّ شركة الترامواي تعجل باستحضار ما وعدت به من مركبات الدرجة الأولى لنأمن فيها من مخالطة العامة وسماعها ما عساه يجري بيننا في ركوبنا من مداولاتنا في أعمال الحكومة السرية. ٥،٤،٠

وكيل الحقانية والمركبات من الدرجة الأولى لا بد من الزحام فيها أيضا.

ناظر الحربية إنّ الذين يركبون في الدرجة الأولى هم من الطبقة العالية ولا بأس أن يقفوا معنا على بعض هذه الأسرار، إنما الخوف من العامة الذين لا يقرؤون الجرائد.

ناظر المالية أرى أنكم كلما وقفتم على فائدة أغفلتم أخرى ألم تعلموا أنّ ركوبنا في الدرجة الأولى يزيد عن أجرة الدرجة الثانية وحسن الاقتصاد يحرم هذا الإسراف.

ناظر الحربية لا تظن أننا نسينا هذا الاستدراك وعندنا مثال في دوائه وهو أنّ سعادة فخري باشا ناظر الأشغال العمومية والمعارف العمومية كان إذا ركب سكة حديد الرمل في الإسكندرية قطع نصف تذكرة فإذا سأله مفتش القطار في ذلك أفحمه بقوله إني ناظر ولي الحق في الركوب بالنصف والمعافاة من النصف الآخر ولا شك أنّ شركة الترامواي تكون أخضع في هذا الباب من شركة سكة الرمل.

UNDERSECRETARY I didn't get it from a book; I don't have any time to read such things. I heard it from the Minister, and he in turn heard it from his teacher, Shaykh Ḥaddād.

MINISTER OF FINANCE (*looking right and left over his bicycle*)

"For all the things you've mentioned,
there are several you've overlooked."[18]

There is something else which goes far beyond the benefits we get from merely complying with this idea of equality. If we ride on trams, the price of shares in the tramway company is bound to go up. People will start crowding each other out so that they can all ride on trams and have an opportunity to see us and copy everything we do. The price of shares will rise; people who are lucky enough to own shares in them will make a large profit.

0.4.5

MINISTER OF WAR If the tramway company did what it has promised to do and introduced first-class carriages, that would be fine. Then we wouldn't have to mix with common people and run the risk of their hearing our conversations about secret government matters while we're riding with them.

UNDERSECRETARY The first-class compartments would be bound to get overcrowded as well.

MINISTER OF WAR People who ride in first-class carriages are from the upper class. It doesn't matter if they hear some of the secret business we're discussing. The people to worry about are the common folk who don't read newspapers.

MINISTER OF FINANCE Every time you come up with a way of making a profit, you miss another one. Don't you realize that it costs more to ride in first class than it does in second? Sound economics won't allow such extravagance.

MINISTER OF WAR Don't you think we should forget this whole idea? After all, we already have an example of a way to remedy it. When His Excellency Fakhrī Pāshā, the Minister of Public Works and Public Education, used to travel by rail from Ramla to Alexandria, he would cut his ticket in half. If the inspector asked him, he completely nonplussed him by replying that he was a minister. As such, he was entitled to travel at half fare and to be exempted from the return half. I'm sure the tramway company here will be more amenable on this point than the Ramla Railway Company.

قال الراوي ولما دنا وقت الافتراق نزلت ونزلوا وانصرفت وانصرفوا وتركتهم في آمالهم ٦،٤،٠
من الربح والتزلف والاقتصاد. وتركوني بما سمعته من محاورتهم فائزا بالغرض والمراد،
من امتياز الشاتم على المشتوم، ومساواة الحاكم بالمحكوم.

Our narrator told us: When the time came for us to part company, I got off and so did they. We all went our own ways. I left them to their dreams of profit, economy, and flattery. They meanwhile left me with their conversation, achieving thereby the cherished goal of distinction between the curser and the cursed and of equality between ruler and ruled. 0.4.6

مصباح الشرق ٣١، ١٧ نوفمبر ١٨٩٨

١،١ حدثنا عيسى بن هشام، قال رأيت في المنام، كأني أمشي في صحراء الإمام بين القبور والرجام، في ليلة قمراء، يستر بياضها نجوم الخضراء، فيكاد في سنا نورها ينظم الدر ثاقبة، ويرقب الذر راقبه، وكنت أحدث نفسي بين تلك القبور، وفوق هاتيك الجنادل والصخور، بغرور الإنسان وشممه، وافتخار بمساعيه وهممه، وإغراقه في دعاويه، وتغاليه في تعاليه، واستعظامه لنفسه، ونسيانه لرمسه، فقد شمخ الإنسان بأنفه حتى رام أن يثقب به الفلك، استكبارا لما جمع وما ملك، فأرغمه الموت حتى سد بذلك الأنف شقا في لحده، بعد أن وارى بين صفائحه صحائف عزه ومجداه.

٢،١ وما زلت أسير وأتفكر وأجول وأتدبر حتى تذكرت في خطاي فوق رمال الصحراء، قول الشاعر الحكيم أبي العلاء :

خفف الوطء ما أظن أديم ال
أرضِ إلا من هذه الأجساد
وقبيح بنا وإن قدم العه
دُ هوان الآباء والأجداد
سر إن اسطعت في الهواء رويدا
لا اختيالا على رفات العباد

٣،١ فخففت الوطء وعلمت أن تلك الثغور التي طالما حوّل العاشق قبلته لقلبها، وباع عذوبة الكوثر بعذوبتها، قد اختلطت بالحصباء، وامتزجت بغبار الغبراء .

وأن تلك الخدود التي كان يغار منها الورد فيبكي بدموع الندى، ويشتمل الفؤاد منها بنار الجوى ويقف الحال منها موقف الخليل من النيران، أو ابن ماء السماء في شقائق النعمان، ويتموج فيها ماء الشباب، قد طوى الدهر حسنها طي الثياب، وصارت بحكم القضاء أديما لوجه القضاء.

وإنّ تلك العيون التي صادت بأهدابها الملوك الصيد، رعاة الأمم ورعايا الغيد،

ʿĪsā ibn Hishām told us: In a dream, I saw myself walking among the tombs and gravestones in the Imam Shāfiʿī cemetery. It was a brilliant moonlit night, bright enough to blot out the stars in the sky; in fact, so gleaming was the light, one could have threaded a pearl and watched a speck of dust. As I stood there amid the graves atop the tombstones, I contemplated man's arrogance and conceit, his sense of his own glory, his pride, his total obsession with his own pretensions, his excessive desires, his sense of self-aggrandizement, and the way he chooses to forget about the grave. In his deluded arrogance he hoists his nose into the air and endeavors to pierce the very heavens with it. Then he can boast about the things he has collected and use what he owns to claim some kind of superiority. But then Death always coerces him. Once it has enshrouded his artificial splendor and glory beneath its slabs of stone, it uses that very same nose to block up a crack in his tomb. 1.1

Deep in thought I continued my walk. I recalled the words of the sage poet, Abū l-ʿAlāʾ al-Maʿarrī: 1.2

Tread lightly, for methinks the surface of the earth
is made only from these bodies.
It would be wrong of us to treat our forefathers
and ancestors lightly even if they lived long ago.
Walk slowly abroad, if you are able,
and do not strut over the remains of God's people.[19]

So I repented and trod lightly. Among these numerous corpses and remains of the dead there would be mouths. For a single kiss from them, lovers in the past would often have changed course and bartered the very sweetness of Kawthar for their sweet taste. But now they are blended with the dust of the earth, and their teeth mingle with pebbles and small stones. 1.3

I also remembered those cheeks the rose so envied that it wept dewy tears, which would arouse people's hearts to a fiery passion. The beauty spot on their surface looked exactly like the faithful companion Abraham in the fire, or the black-skinned Nuʿmān of al-Ḥīrah in the midst of red anemones. Through them flowed the glow of modesty and youth's gushing spring, but now fate has folded away their beauty just as one shuts a book; by destiny's decree they have become a mere layer on the earth's surface. The lashes of those eyes ensnared

وسحرت ببابل هاروت وماروت، وأوقفت موقف الاستكانة رب الجلال والجبروت، يلتمس والتاج في يمينه وعرق الحياء فوق جبينه، من خلال لحظاتها قبولا، كسائل يمد الالتماس الإحسان كشكولا، صارت ترابا تحت الرمس كأن لم تفتن بالأمس.

وإنّ ذلك الشعر، الذي تعلق به سواد القلب والبصر أسقطته من منابته يد الزمن، فنسج الأجل منه ثوب الكفن.

وإنّ تلك النهود التي كانت زينة للصدر، أصبحت مخلاة تحمل الزاد لدود القبر. ٤،١

كم صائن عن قبلة خده
سلطت الأرض على خده
وحامل ثقل الثرى جيده
وكان يشكو الضعف من عقده

وإنّ تلك العظام، من بقايا الملوك العظام، الذين كانوا يستصغرون الأرض دارا، ويحاولون عند النجوم جوارا. وإنّ تلك الضلوع التي انحنت على الحلم والعلم، والثنايا التي طالما خرج من بينها أمر الحرب والسلم، وأنّ تلك الأنامل التي كانت تبري القلم للكتّاب وتبري بالسيوف الرقاب، وأنّ تلك الجماجم والرؤوس، التي استعبدت الملايين من النفوس، اختلط الرئيس فيها بالمرؤوس، فلا تبيين ولا تمييز بين الذليل منها والعزيز

هو الموت مثرٍ عنده مثل مقتر
وقاصد نهج مثل آخر ناكب
ودرع فتاة عنده درع غادة
وأبيات كسرى من بيوت العناكب
فرجل في غبراء والخطب فارس
وما زال في الأهلين أشرف راكب
وما النعش إلا كالسفينة راميا
بغرقاه في موج الردى المتراكب

mighty kings, so that the rulers of people became the subjects of girls. They bewitched Hārūt and Mārūt in Babel and humiliated the majestic tyrant as he sought some glimmer of approval in their glances. There he stood, crown in hand. Beads of perspiration on his forehead were evidence of his shyness; he was like a beggar seeking alms. These same eyes have now become soil within the tombs; it is as though they had never infatuated anyone. That luxuriant black flourish of hair whose glitter dazzled both heart and eyes to the core has been plucked from its roots by Time's hand, and from it fate has woven a funeral shroud.

1.4 Those breasts, that once seemed like boxes of silver decorated with pearls or balls of snow with a pomegranate flower at center, now look like leather bags with food for worms in the grave.

How many a maid who withheld her cheek from a kiss
has had her cheek mastered by the earth!
How many a girl whose neck now carries the weight of the earth
used to complain of the unbearable weight of a necklace.[20]

Those decaying bones, remains of mighty kings who considered the earth too paltry a domain and tried to attain regions bordering the very stars; those chests which contained courageous and prudent hearts; those lips which often uttered orders of war and peace; those fingertips which used to sharpen quills for writing and trim necks with the sword; those faces and heads which enslaved bodies and souls and which were described as full moons at one moment and as suns at another; among the dead, such rulers are peers of the ruled, nor is there difference or distinction between the lowly and mighty.

He is Death for whom rich and poor are both the same;
a man who knows his way is like another who has gone astray.
In his judgment, the warrior's shield and maiden's shift are both alike;
an emperor's dwellings are mere spider's webs.
Such folk are trodden in the dust, while misfortune rides rampant;
among people fate is still the best rider.
The bier is like a ship casting its contents to drown in the sea of death,
piling up and up.[21]

٥،١ وبينما أنا في المواعظ والعبر، والخواطر والفكر، أتأمل في عجائب الحدثان، وأتعجب من تقلب الأزمان، مستغرقا في تصور بدائع المقدور، منهيا بالفكر إلى أسرار البعث والنشور، إذا برجة من خلفي كادت تقضي بحتفي، فالتفت لفتة المذعور فإذا هو قبر قد انشق من بين تلك القبور، وخرج منه رجل طويل القامة، عظيم الهامة، عليه سيما المهابة والجلالة، والنجابة والنبالة، فصعقت صعقة موسى يوم دك الجبل، وكاد يذهب بنفسي الوجل والخبل، ولما أفقت من غشيتي، وانتبهت من دهشتي رأيت الرجل قد داناني، وناداني، نداء القائد العسكري بصوت جهوري، فدار بيننا الحديث وجرى على ما ترى:

٦،١ **الشيخ** أُدن أيها الرجل مني.

قال عيسى بن هشام فارتعدت فرائصي ولم أر بدا من الدنو منه فدنوت ولبيت.

الشيخ ما اسمك وما صنعتك ولم جئت هنا.

عيسى بن هشام يقول في نفسه: هذا الشيخ قريب العهد بسؤال الملكين فهو يسأل على منواله فاللّهم أنقذني من هذا الضيق، وأوسع لي في الطريق لأخلص من مناقشة الحساب، وأكفني شر العذاب ثم يلتفت إليه ويقول:

عيسى بن هشام اسمي عيسى بن هشام وصناعتي كاتب وجئت لأعتبر بزيارة المقابر، فهي أوعظ من خطب المنابر.

الشيخ وأين دواتك يا معلم عيسى ودفترك.

عيسى بن هشام أنا لست من كتّاب الحساب ولكني كاتب منشئ.

الشيخ لا بأس فاذهب ياكاتب منشئ فاطلب ثيابي وليأتوني بحصاني (دحمان) وبالجنيب معه.

عيسى بن هشام وأين يا سيدي بيتكم فأنا لا أعرفه.

الشيخ (مشمئزا) قل لي من أي الأقطار أنت فإنه يظهر لي أنك لست من أهل مصر إذ ليس في مصر من أحد يجهل بيت أحمد باشا المنيكلي ناظر الجهادية المصرية.

As part of such sobering notions, I was considering the remarkable things that happen and marveling at the way in which times change. Deep in thought about the extraordinary things which fate brings about, I was trying to probe the secrets of the resurrection. Suddenly, there was a violent tremor behind me which almost brought my life to an end. In terror I looked behind me. I discovered that one of the graves had opened, and a man had appeared. He was tall and imposing, carried himself with dignity and a majestic aura, and displayed all the signs of nobility and high birth. I felt as stunned and terrified as Moses on the day when the mountain was destroyed.[22] Once I had recovered from the shock, I noticed that he was walking toward me. He shouted to me like an army commander issuing orders. The conversation went as follows: 1.5

GHOST Come closer. 1.6

ʿĪsā ibn Hishām said: My whole body shook, but I could see no way out, so I obeyed his instructions and moved closer.

GHOST What's your name and profession? What are you doing out here?

This man must have been interrogated recently by the two Questioning Angels, I told myself; that is why he is using their procedure. I asked God to rescue me from these dire straits and come to my aid so that I could escape the arguments of the Day of Reckoning and be protected from this terrible punishment. Then I turned in his direction and answered:

ʿĪSĀ IBN HISHĀM My name is ʿĪsā ibn Hishām, my profession is the art of writing, and I came here to find some inspiration by visiting the tombs. I find it more effective than listening to sermons from pulpits.

GHOST Well then, secretary ʿĪsā, where's your inkwell and notebook?

ʿĪSĀ IBN HISHĀM I'm not a secretary in the Treasury or Secretariat, I'm an author.

GHOST Never mind! Go then, my good author, and look for my clothes and bring me my horse, Daḥmān!

ʿĪSĀ IBN HISHĀM But where's your house, Sir? I don't know it.

GHOST (*in disgust*) Tell me, for heaven's sake, which country are you from? You can't be an Egyptian. There's no one in the whole country who doesn't know where my house is. I'm Aḥmad Pāshā al-Manīkalī, the Egyptian Minister of War!

عيسى بن هشام اعلم يا مولاي أنني رجل مصري وطني عريق في المصرية والوطنية ولم أجهل بيتك إلا لأنّ البيوت في مصر لا تعرف بأسماء أصحابها بل بأسماء شوارعها وحاراتها ونمرها فإذا تفضلتم وأوضحتم لي شارع بيتكم، واسم حارتكم ونمرة البيت ذهبت إليه كما أشرتم.

المنيكلي (مغضبا) ما أنت يا كاتب منشئ إلا مجنونا فإني لم أسمع في حياتي بنمر للبيوت فهي ليست إفادات أحكام أو عساكر نظام فناولني عباءتك أستتر بها وأعطني أيضا طربوشك ونعلك وصاحبني حتى أصل إلى بيتي.

عيسى بن هشام إذا كانت المصيبة في العباءة والطربوش والحذاء كان الأمر هينا. ولقد كان المعهود ان سلب المارة لا يقع إلا من قطاع الطريق أما أنا فماذا أقول إذا كان من سلبني شبحا من سكان القبور. ٧،١

المنيكلي يأخذ العباءة فيستنكف منها ثم يلبسها بعد تردد ويقول:

المنيكلي للضرورة أحكام ولكننا قد لبسنا أدنى من هذه العباءة في مسايرتنا لأفندينا المرحوم إبراهيم باشا على طريقة التخفي والتبديل في الليالي التي كان يصرفها في البلد ليستطلع بنفسه أحوال الرعية.

قال عيسى بن هشام ولما أخذنا في السير وقف بغتة وقال:

المنيكلي كيف العمل؟

عيسى بن هشام ماذا؟

المنيكلي أنا نسيت أنا في الليل وأنا بهذه العباءة لا يعرفني أحد فكيف ندخل من أبواب مصر وليس معنا كلمة «سر الليل».

عيسى بن هشام كما أنك يا سيدي لم تسمع بنمر البيوت في حياتك فإني لم أسمع بسر الليل في حياتي. ما هو؟

المنيكلي (مستهزئا ضاحكا) ألم أقل أنك غريب غير مصري، اعلم أنّ «سر الليل» كلمة تصدر من القلعة إلى جميع القره قولات والأبواب والضبطية فلا يصرحون لأحد يمشي بالليل إلا إذا كان حافظا لهذه الكلمة يلقيها في أذن البواب فيفتح له

'Īsā ibn Hishām Believe me, Pāshā, I'm from pure Egyptian stock. The only reason why I don't know where you live is that houses in Egypt are no longer known by the names of their owners, but by the names of their street, lane, and number. If you would be so kind as to tell me the street, lane, and number of your house, I'll go there and bring you the things you've requested.

Al-Manīkalī (*annoyed*) It's clear to me, my good author, that you're out of your mind! Since when have houses had numbers to be known by? What are they? Some kind of government legislation or army regulations? Anyway give me your overcoat to wrap myself in and your tarboosh and sandals too. Then accompany me till I reach my house.

1.7 'Īsā ibn Hishām said: Since it was only my overcoat, tarboosh, and sandals that were involved, it was fairly easy. Usually it is highwaymen who rob passersby, but now here was this ghost, a grave-dweller at that, doing it to me as well.

Al-Manīkalī took the coat and put it on with a reluctant disdain:

Al-Manīkalī Well, "Necessity has its own Rules!"[23] But then, I have disguised myself in even shabbier clothes than this while accompanying our late revered master, Ibrāhīm Pāshā, on the nights he used to spend in the city so that he could see for himself how people were faring.

Īsā ibn Hishām said: We started walking, but then he stopped abruptly.

Al-Manīkalī But what's to be done?

'Īsā ibn Hishām What do you mean?

Al-Manīkalī I've forgotten that it's nighttime. There's no one on duty who'll be able to recognize me in this overcoat. How can we get the gates opened when we don't have the password?

'Īsā ibn Hishām You've just told me, Sir, that you don't know anything about houses having numbers. Well, I don't know anything about a "password." What is it?

Al-Manīkalī (*laughing contemptuously*) Didn't I say you had to be a foreigner? Don't you know that the "password" is a word issued each night from the Citadel to the officer of the watch and all the guardhouses and gates? No one is allowed to travel at night unless he has memorized this word and can repeat it to the gatekeeper, whereupon the gate is opened for him. It is given

وهذه الكلمة تعطيها الحكومة سرا لمن يطلبها منها لقضاء أشغاله بالليل وهي تتغير في كل ليلة، فليلة تكون «عدس» وليلة تكون «خضار» وليلة تكون «حمام» وليلة تكون «فراخ» وهلم جر.

عيسى بن هشام يظهر لي من كلامك أنك لست من أبناء مصر فإن هذه الألفاظ تطلق فيها على المأكولات لا على التصريح للناس بالسير في ليلهم، ومع ذلك فقد دنا الفجر ولا لزوم لكل هذا.

٨،١ قال عيسى بن هشام: فمشينا في طريقنا وأخذ يقص عليّ حوادث الحروب والوقائع التي شاهدها بعينه وسمعها بأذنه ويذكر مآثر محمد علي وشجاعة إبراهيم وما زلنا على تلك الحال حتى وصلنا في ضوء النهار إلى قرب القلعة فوقف وقوف الخاشع يقرأ الفاتحة لمحمد علي ويخاطب القلعة بقوله:

المنيكلي «يا مصدر النعيم، ومصرع الجبابرة من عتاة المماليك، ويا بيت الملك، وحصن المملكة، ومنبع العز، ومهبط القوة، ومرتفع المجد وموئل المستغيث وحمى المحتمي، وكنز الرغائب ومنتهى المطالب، ومثوى الشهم، ومقر الهمام. أيها الحصن كم فككت عانيا وقيدت بالإحسان عافيا وكم أرغمت أنوفا وسللت سيوفا، وجمعت بين البأس والندى والحياة والردى».

٩،١ قال عيسى بن هشام: ثم التفت إليّ وقال:

المنيكلي علينا أن نختار أقرب الطرق لنذهب إلى بيتي فألبس ثيابي وأتقلد حسامي وأركب جوادي ثم أعود إلى القلعة لألثم أذيال ولي النعم الدواري الأع.

فأخذني العجب لهذا الكلام وأحببت أن أوافقه إلى التمام.

out in secret to the people who ask the government for it so that they can carry on their business at night. It's changed every night. So, one night, it will be "Lentils," the next night "Greens," the next night "Pigeons," the next night "Fowl," and so on.

'Īsā ibn Hishām It's clear to me that you're the one who's not Egyptian. The only use we have for such words is as food. We've never heard of their being used to convey permission to travel at night. In any case, it's almost dawn, so we'll have no further need of such words or any others.

'Īsā ibn Hishām said: So we went on our way. The Pāshā began to tell me more about himself. He told me tales of wars and battles which he had either witnessed himself or heard about and then went on to recall any number of exploits of Muḥammad 'Alī and the great courage of Ibrāhīm. We continued in this fashion till we reached the Citadel Square, by which time it was daylight. The Pāshā halted in humble respect, recited the Fātiḥah to Muḥammad 'Alī's tomb and then addressed the Citadel: 1.8

Hail to thee, source of bounties, treadmill of the violent Mamluk tyrants, haven of sovereignty, fortress of royal sway, source of might, birthplace of power, and height of glory. You are the refuge of the pleader for help, protection for him who seeks it, treasure-house of people's desires, goal of their aspirations.

O Cairo Citadel, how many people who came to you in search of kindness you have obligated with your charity! How many pompous men have you coerced, and how many swords have you drawn. You combined power and generosity, and could decide as alternatives between life and death.

'Īsā ibn Hishām said: Then the Pāshā turned towards me. "Hurry to my house with me," he said. "I can put on my proper clothes, buckle my sword, and mount my horse. Then I'll return to the Citadel and pay my respects to his exalted highness, the dispenser of bounty." 1.9

All this astonished me, and I decided to follow his story to its conclusion.

قال عيسى بن هشام: ولما زايلنا ساحة القلعة انحدرنا في الطريق وبينا نحن نسير إذ تعرض لنا مكارٍي يسوق حماره وقد راضه الخبيث على سد الطريق فكلما سرنا وجدنا الحمار أمامنا والمكاري ينبح بصوت قد بح حتى أمسك بذيل صاحبي يقول له: ١،٢

المكاري (للباشا) اركب يا بك فقد عطلتني من الصبح وأنا أسير وراءك. ٢،٢

الباشا (للمكاري) كيف تدعوني أيها الشقي إلى ركوب الحمار وما رغبت فيه وما دعوتك وكيف استبدل ركوب الضمر السوابق، بالحمار الناهق.

المكاري كيف تنكر إشارة يدك وأنت تتكلم مع صاحبك عن طريق الأمام وقد دعيت مرارا من السائرين فلم أقبل منهم لارتباطي بتلك الإشارة فاركب أو أعطني أجرة العطل.

الباشا (وهو يدفع المكاري بيده) اذهب عنا أيها السفيه، فلو كان معي سلاحي لقتلتك.

المكاري (متسافها مفحشا في القول) كيف تجسر على التفوه بهذا الكلام فإما أن تعطيني أجرتي وإما أن تذهب معي إلى القسم وسترى ما يعاقبونك به على تهديدك لي بالقتل.

الباشا (لعيسى بن هشام) إني لأعجب من صبرك منذ اليوم على هذا الفلاح السفيه الذي يزفنا بسفاهته وقباحته فهلم فاقتله بالنيابة عني وأرحه من عيشته وأرحنا منه.

عيسى بن هشام كيف أقتله وأين القانون وهؤلاء الحاكمون.

الباشا ما لي أراك قد شق الخوف قلبك وقطع أنفاسك أيعتريك خوف وأنت معي؟ إنّ هذا لعجيب.

المكاري العفو! العفو! من هو أنت ومن هو غيرك ونحن في زمن الحرية لا فرق بين المكاري وبين الباشا.

Leaving the Citadel Square, we walked downhill. As we proceeded, we found our path blocked by a donkeyman pulling his donkey behind him. The rogue had the animal trained to stand in the way of passersby and block the road. So, every time we tried to move on, we found the donkey in front of us and the Donkeyman shouting at us in a hoarse voice. Eventually he grabbed the edge of my companion's coat: 2.1

DONKEYMAN Get on my donkey, Sir—you've kept me from my business. I've been walking behind you. 2.2

PĀSHĀ (*to the Donkeyman*) You miserable wretch, do you really expect me to ride your donkey? I've never had the slightest desire to ride it, nor have I hailed you at any time while I've been walking. How could someone such as myself possibly mount a braying donkey rather than a rearing thoroughbred?

DONKEYMAN How can you deny summoning me with the gesture you made with your hand while you were talking to your companion on the way from the cemetery? I've been hailed by travelers several times since then, but I didn't respond or pay any attention to their calls because I was obligated to you by that gesture of yours. Either get on my donkey or else pay me the charge for hiring me.

PĀSHĀ (*pushing the Donkeyman with his hand*) You insolent devil! Go away! If I had my weapon with me, I'd kill you.

DONKEYMAN (*defiantly*) How dare you talk to me like that! Either you give me my charge, or else come with me to the police station. You'll find out there how they'll deal with you for threatening to kill me!

PĀSHĀ (*to ʿĪsā*) I'm surprised you're being so patient with this bumptious yokel who is being so persistently rude and cheeky to me. Get on and kill him for me; that way we'll relieve him of his life and ourselves of him!

ʿĪSĀ How can I possibly do that? What about the law and the authorities?

PĀSHĀ Heavens above, am I really to believe that fear has cleft your heart in two and cut short your breath? Are you really afraid in my company? That's incredible!

DONKEYMAN (*scoffing*) Oh, begging your pardon, Sir, begging your pardon! Who do you think you are, or who is anyone else for that matter? We're living in an age of freedom now when there is no difference between a donkeyman and a Pāshā.

٣،٢ عيسى بن هشام أنا لا أضرب أحدا وأنت لا تقتل وأنت معي أحدا واعلم أنه لا تصدر منا مخالفة أو جنحة أو جناية إلا والعقاب من ورائها وإني أقول لك ما قاله الخضر لموسى عليه السلام ﴿إِنَّكَ لَن تَسْتَطِيعَ مَعِيَ صَبْرًا * وَكَيْفَ تَصْبِرُ عَلَىٰ مَا لَمْ تُحِطْ بِهِ خُبْرًا﴾ والطريقة الوحيدة للخلاص من هذا السفيه أن أعطيه شيئا من الدراهم واسأل الله أن يوصلنا إلى بيتك بالسلامة.

الباشا لا تعط هذا الكلب السفيه درهما بل اضربه فإن لم تفعل فأنا أتنازل إلى ضربه وتأديبه فإنّ الفلاح لا يصلح جلده إلا الجلد.

(ثم يمسك الباشا برقبة المكاري ويضربه بيده).

المكاري (صارخا مستغيثا) يا بوليس! يا بوليس!

عيسى بن هشام (وهو يجتهد في إنقاذ المكاري) اللّٰهم خلصني من شر هذا اليوم فإنّ شره مستطير، اتق الله أيها الأمير في عباد الله.

٤،٢ قال عيسى بن هشام: فما أتممت هذا الكلام حتى اشتد الغضب بصاحبي فرأيت حماليقه قد انقلبت وشفته تقلصت وجبهته ضاقت ومنخره اتسع فخفت أن يبطش بي ويلحقني بالمكاري فتداركت نفسي وقلت له:

مثلك لا يضرب بيده فأنت أرفع قدرا من أن تمس بيدك الشريفة هذه الجيفة.

فسكنت حدته وامتنع عن الضرب فعمدت إلى المكاري فوضعت في يده دريهمات على غير علم من صاحبي وطلبت منه أن ينصرف عنا فما ازداد اللئيم بذلك إلا صياحا وعويلا ونداء للبوليس واستنجادا به.

الباشا (لعيسى بن هشام) ألم أقل لك أنّ الفلاح لا يصلحه إلا الضرب؟ ألم تر أنّ غاية ما ينتهي إليه في رفع الألم عنه أن يستغيث بالمشايخ والأولياء؟ ولكن قل لي بالله هل بولس هذا الذي يناديه وليّ جديد.

عيسى بن هشام نعم إنّ هذا البوليس هو وليّ الأمر احتلت فيه القوة الحاكمة.

ʿĪsā I'm not going to hit anyone, and, as long as you're with me, you're not going to kill anyone either. You must realize that if we commit an infraction, misdemeanor, or felony, we will be punished for it. So don't be surprised that I am so patient and long-suffering. I will say to you exactly what al-Khiḍr told Moses (peace be upon him): «You will not be patient with me, so how can you endure things of which you have no experience?»[24] The way to get rid of this insolent fool is for me to give him some dirhams. Then he will bother someone else. I just pray that we reach home safely. 2.3

Pāshā You'll not give this barking cur a single dirham. Beat him! If you won't do it, then I'll have to stoop so low as to beat him myself and teach him a lesson. The only way to improve a peasant's skin is by flogging.

With that the Pāshā grabbed the Donkeyman by the neck and started hitting him.

Donkeyman (*yelling for help*) Police! Police!

ʿĪsā (*doing his best to rescue the Donkeyman from the Pāshā's clutches*) O God, save me from this ill-starred day full of disaster!

I spoke to the Pāshā: Show the fear of God, Amir, in your treatment of His servants!

I had barely finished saying this to him when I saw his temper get the better of him. His whole expression changed, his eyes began to roll, his lips tightened, his nostrils expanded, and his forehead contracted into a frown. I was afraid that his crazy temper would lead him to do me an injury as well as the Donkeyman. I tried a more rational approach. I told him that a personage of his eminence should not demean himself by behaving in such a manner; he was far too exalted a figure to foul his noble hands by touching a corpse like this one. Using such a stratagem I managed to calm him down. I went over to the Donkeyman and put some dirhams into his palm without the Pāshā knowing. I asked him to go away and leave us alone, but that only made the wretch shout all the louder for the police to help him. 2.4

Pāshā (*to ʿĪsā*) Didn't I tell you that peasants can only be reformed by beating? Don't you realize that the only thing he can do to get rid of the pain he's going through is to yell for help to Shaykhs and Saints! But tell me, is this "Police" he keeps shouting for and asking to help him some new kind of saintly figure?

ʿĪsā Well, yes. The "police" is the agency responsible for public order and vested with the government's executive powers.

الباشا أنا لا أعرف هذا البوليس فبين لي حقيقته.

عيسى بن هشام هو القواس الذي تعرفه.

الباشا وأين هذا القواس الذي لا يسمع هذا النداء فإني أرغب في حضوره ليتلقى أمري في هذا الشقي.

المكاري يا بوليس! يا بوليس!

الباشا (لعيسى بن هشام) هلم إلى مساعدته في نداء هذا القواس.

عيسى بن هشام (في نفسه) كيف أنادي البوليس وأنا أحمد الله على سكوته وسكونه وهو بمقربة منا لا يكترث بنداء المستغيث. ثم يلتفت إلى الباشا فيقول له: لا يفيد النداء فإنه مشتغل ببائع الفاكهة كما ترى. (ويشير إليه)

٥،٢ فيلمح المكاري البوليس أمامه فيسرع إليه ويتبعه من تجمع من النظارة فيجدونه واقفا وفي يده منديل أحمر قد امتلأ مما جمعه في صباحه من باعة الأسواق في حفظه للنظام وهو يأمر صاحب الدكان بإدخال ما وضعه خارجها من عيدان القصب وفي يده عود منها يهدده به ويهزه في وجهه هزة الرمح ثم يضاحك طفلا على كتف امرأة ولما حضرنا إليه أقبل نحونا والمنديل في يد وعود القصب في اليد الأخرى.

البوليس (للجمع) ما هذا الصياح على الصباح وما هذا العناء وهذا النداء كأن كل واحد من أهل هذا البلد يريد أن يكون له واحد من البوليس في خدمته.

المكاري أغثني يا سعادة الجاويش فإنّ هذا الرجل ضربني ولم يعطني أجرتي وأنت تعرفني في هذا الموقف وتعرف أنني لست ممن يتشاجر ويتخاصم.

الباشا خذ أيها القواس هذا السفيه وضعه في السجن حتى يأتيك أمري فيه.

البوليس (للمكاري) من أين ركب معك هذا الرجل يا مرسي.

Pāshā I don't understand. Explain to me what this "police" you're talking about really is.

'Īsā It's what you used to call "Kavvas."[25]

Pāshā So where is this kavvas who cannot hear all this yelling and screaming?! I want him to appear so that he can receive my orders regarding this wretch.

Donkeyman Police! Police!

Pāshā (*to 'Īsā ibn Hishām*) Come on, let's help him yell for the kavvas!

'Īsā ibn Hishām said: I asked myself how I could possibly yell for the police when I was really thanking God because I'd managed to quiet him down. All the while, the Policeman was standing close by, not paying the slightest attention to the shouts for help.

I turned to the Pāshā and told him that there was no point in yelling and screaming; as he could see, the Policeman was preoccupied with the fruit seller.

2.5

When the Donkeyman spotted the Policeman directly in front of him, he dashed over to speak to him. All the spectators who had gathered round us followed. They found the Policeman standing there holding a red napkin full of various oddments which he had collected from the market traders during the course of his supervision of the "regulations." He was busy talking to the owner of the shop, instructing him to put inside the shop the stalks of sugarcane which he had on display outside. In one hand, he was holding a stalk of cane and threatening the owner with it, shaking it in his face like a spear. At the same time, he was looking in another direction, and giggling and babbling at a baby on a woman's shoulder.

He carried on like this till we all came towards him, then turned round with the napkin in one hand and the sugarcane in the other:

Policeman (*to everyone*) What's all this row about in the early morning? Why so much yelling and commotion? Anyone would think that every single person had to have his own private policeman at his service.

Donkeyman Please help me, Sergeant Sir. This man here assaulted me and has refused to give me my charge. You know me on this beat and realize that I'm not one to argue or pick a quarrel for nothing.

Pāshā Guard, take this insolent wretch and lock him up in prison till someone brings you my orders concerning him.

Policeman (*to the Donkeyman*) Tell me, Mursī, from where did this man ride with you?

المكاري ركب معي من الإمام.

الباشا (للبوليس) ما هذا الإبطاء في تنفيذ أمري، أسرع به إلى السجن.

البوليس (ضاحكا مستهزئا) أظنك أيها الرجل من مجاذيب الحضرة في الأمام فهلم معي إلى القسم فإن هيئتك تدلني على إفلاسك وعجزك عن الدفع.

٦،٢ قال عيسى بن هشام: فجذب البوليس صاحبي من ذراعه فكاد يغمى عليه من الدهشة فلم يدر ما يصنع وسلم البوليس ما في يديه من المنديل والعود إلى الرجل الذي أودع المكاري حماره عنده وسار صاحبي في قبضة البوليس والمكاري خلفهما والجمع على أثرهم إلى القسم. ولما صعدوا إلى السلم أخذ المكاري يصرخ ويصيح فقابله أحد عساكر المراسلة فضربه ليسكت لأنّ المعاون غريق في النوم فدخلنا في حجرة الصول لضبط الواقعة فوجدناه يأكل والقلم على أذنه وقد نزع طربوشه وخلع نعله وحل أزراره وبجانبه اثنان من أقربائه الفلاحين يتلذذ بما يبهرهما من سلطته على الكبير والصغير في عاصمة القطر وتخت الحكومة وما في قدرته من حبس أي شخص كان والشهادة عليه بما يهواه

فطردنا جميعا من أمامه حتى ينتهي من طعامه فخرجنا ننتظر وقد أراد صاحبي من شدة ما ألمّ به من الدهشة أن يستند على الحائط فخانته يده فوقع فوق عسكري كان يكنس بغير كسوته العسكرية فأخذ العسكري في الشتم والسب ودخل على الصول هاجما فقال إنّ المتهم الذي يشتكي منه المكاري تعدى عليّ في أثناء تأدية وظيفتي فرفسني برجله فأمر الصول بإحضاره ونادى على كاتبه العسكري فطلب منه أن يحرر محضرين محضر مخالفة ومحضر جنحة فأملى عليه الصول اصطلاحات لهم في الكلام لا أفهمها.

DONKEYMAN From the Imam district.

PĀSHĀ Why are you being so slow about carrying out my instructions? Take him to prison at once!

POLICEMAN (*with a scoff*) My dear fellow, it seems to me you must be from the lunatic asylum in the Imām district. Come to the station with me. Your scruffy clothing makes it quite clear that you're penniless and cannot pay the charge.

2.6 ʿĪsā ibn Hishām said: The Policeman dragged my companion along by the arm. The Pāshā almost collapsed in astonishment; he had no clue about what he was doing. The Policeman handed the fruit and other things he was holding to the man whom the Donkeyman had asked to take care of his donkey. My companion was dragged along to the police station on the Policeman's arm. The Donkeyman followed behind them and the crowd came along at their heels.

They all reached the station and climbed the steps. At this point, the Donkeyman started yelling and screaming again. One of the policemen on duty came up and hit him; he had to quiet him down because the Precinct Adjutant was sound asleep. He went into the Sergeant-Major's room to enter the charge, but found him there with his pen in his ear, eating; he had taken off his tarboosh, removed his shoes, and undone the buttons on his uniform. At his side were two peasants whom I presumed to be relatives of his; they were seeing for themselves the enjoyable way he could exercise his influence in the country's capital city and seat of government, the extensive authority which he had over people whether important or of little significance, and the power he had to imprison anyone, whoever he might be, and to use whatever testimony took his fancy as evidence against accused people.

At this point we were all ejected from the room until he had finished eating, so we went outside in the hall to wait. The Pāshā was so distressed that he needed somewhere to lean against. He propped himself up against the wall, but unfortunately his hand gave way and he fell right on top of a policeman out of uniform who was sweeping the floor. This policeman started cursing and swearing, then rushed into the Sergeant-Major's office and told him that the accused person against whom the Donkeyman was bringing a charge had assaulted him "during the course of the execution of his duties" and had kicked him. The Sergeant-Major ordered the Pāshā to be brought in, called for his police clerk, and told him to take a statement for an infraction charge and

وبعد أن شهد البوليس الأول في محضره المخالفة بما ينفع المكاري وشهد الصول نفسه في محضر الجنحة بأنه شاهد المتهم يتعدى على أحد عساكر القسم في تأدية وظيفته ختم الصول المحضرين وأمر أن يأخذوا المتهم إلى خشبة المقاس وتحرير ورقة التشبيه فجاء العسكري المدعي نفسه الذي كان يكنس لأخذ صاحبي فأفاق من دهشته تحت خشبة المقاس وعنف العسكري وإيذائه والتفت إليّ يقول:

٧،٢ الباشا أنا لا أتصور فيما أنا فيه من هذه الحالة إلا أن يكون اليوم يوم الحشر أو أكون حالما في المنام أو أنّ الداوري الأفخم غضب عليّ فأمر بإهانتي على هذه الصورة العجيبة.

عيسى بن هشام لا بد من التسليم والصبر على أي حالة حتى نخلص من هذه الورطة.

العسكري (لعيسى بن هشام بعد أن وضع الخشبة على رأس المتهم) انظر يا شيخ في المقاس فاقرأ لي الرقم.

٨،٢ قال عيسى بن هشام: وبعد أن قلت له عنه توجه بصاحبي إلى الكاتب لتحرير ورقة التشبيه فسأله هل له ضامن فتعرضت لضمانته فلم يقبلوا مني إلا بتصديق شيخ الحارة فحرت في أمري ومن أين أجده فغمزني بعض العساكر وقال لي اخرج فإنك تجد شيخ حارة بالباب فاعطه عشرة قروش للتصديق على الضمانة فخرجت فوجدت العساكر يضربون أصحاب القضايا لإسكاتهم عن الصياح والضوضاء حتى لا ينزعج المعاون من منامه. وقد لحقني العسكري الذي نبهني فدلني على شيخ الحارة وطلب لي منه التصديق على الضمانة وتوسط في مناولته الدراهم. وعند دخولي مع شيخ الحارة في

another for a misdemeanor. He dictated some technical jargon to him, but I didn't understand a single word of it.

The Policeman whom we had accompanied to the station gave his evidence on the infraction which helped the Donkeyman substantiate his charge, and then the Sergeant-Major himself testified on the misdemeanor charge that he had seen the accused assault one of the station personnel during the course of his duties. The two charges were thus completed. The Sergeant-Major then gave orders for the accused to be taken to the measuring-beam and his identification dossier to be drawn up. The Policeman who had brought the charge against the Pāshā came up, took my companion by the right arm and carried out the order himself, subjecting the Pāshā to all manner of pain in the process of measuring him. While all this was going on, the Pāshā looked like someone who has just fainted from sheer bafflement and distress. But eventually, when he had roused himself a little from his stupefaction, he turned to me and said:

Pāshā I can only imagine from the situation I'm in that today is Judgment Day itself, that I'm dreaming, or else that His Mighty Excellency is so furious with me that he has given orders that I be humiliated in this dire fashion. 2.7

ʿĪsā The only thing you can do is to resign yourself and be patient till we can escape safely from this misfortune.

Policeman (*to ʿĪsā ibn Hishām, after he has placed the measuring beam on the accused's head*) Look at the scale, Sir, and read off the number.

ʿĪsā ibn Hishām said: Once I had done that, he took my friend to the office secretary to put together the Pāshā's identification dossier. The secretary asked him whether he had anyone to stand bail for him. I put myself forward as surety for him, but they wouldn't accept my offer without verification from the Shaykh of the Quarter. I was at a loss as to what to do; where could I find the Shaykh of the Quarter at a moment's notice? One of the policemen whispered in my ear that I should go outside; I would find the Shaykh of the Quarter at the door. I should give him ten piasters, he said, for verifying the bail. The policeman caught up with me, pointed out the Shaykh of the Quarter, and even acted as go-between in handing over the fee for the verification. When I returned to the secretary's office with the Shaykh of the Quarter, it was to discover that the policeman, who had been inflicting the most pain on God's people and had seemed the most eager to ensure that the Adjutant was allowed to sleep in peace now, was rushing to the door of the Adjutant's room, shoving 2.8

حجرة الكاتب وجدت أشد العساكر حرصا على راحة المعاون ونومه وأقساهم ضربا للناس قد هجم على باب حجرة المعاون يدفعه بكل قواه حتى فتحه وأخذ يهز السرير بعنف فاستيقظ المعاون فزعا فعلم أنّ المفتش قد دخل من باب القسم فأسرع إلى ملابسه فلبسها في لحظة وهرول إلى استقباله فلما قدم عليه المفتش وقف المعاون وقفة النظام بعلامة التعظيم ولكن من سوء حظه أنه ذهل عند لبس الطربوش فلم يجعل زره جهة اليمين بل كان فوق الجبهة وأنّ الشعر كان قد تجدد في ذقنه لأنه لم يتمكن من حلقه في يومه، وبعد أن نظر إليه المفتش شزرًا دخل في الحجرة وأخذ يشتغل في كتابة تقرير لمحاكمة المعاون على مخالفته في زيه للأوامر المستديمة.

٩.٢ ولما رأى صاحبي سكون الصياح دفعة واحدة في القسم واستيلاء الخوف واضطراب أعضاء العساكر وحركات المعاون في قيامه وجريه سألني عن شأن ذلك الداخل الذي قلب القسم من حالته الأولى إلى هذه الحالة فقلت له إنه المفتش قد حضر للتفتيش والتنقيب على أعمال القسم والنظر في شكوى الشاكين وتطبيق أعمال العمال على النظام والقانون. فطلب مني أن ندخل عليه لنعرض عليه ما أصابنا فدخلنا فوقفنا أمامه وهو يكتب في تقريره فسألنا عن أمرنا فبدأنا بالقصة فأمر أحد العساكر بإخراجنا، وبعد أن أتم تقريره وضعه في جيبه ونزل مهرولا ولم يلتفت في القسم إلى غير زي المعاون فرجع الصياح والضرب والضجيج كما كان عليه قبل دخول المفتش، وصاح أحد المضروبين بأنه لا بد أن يشتكي القسم إلى النيابة فدخل أحد العساكر ليخبر المعاون بذلك - وقد وضعت أذني على الباب - فوجده يهمس بقوله:

ما هذه الخدمة وما هذا الذل لعن الله الاحتياج، ومع ذلك فالحمد لله الذي جعل المفتش من الإنكليز فهو خير من أولاد العرب فإنه لعجزه في اللغة وجهله بالأعمال

it with all his might, and going in. He shook the bed vigorously. The Adjutant woke up with a start to be informed that the Inspector had been seen entering the station gate. He rushed over to his uniform, put it on in a trice and rushed out to meet the Inspector. He stood there at attention, but unfortunately for him he had put his tarboosh on carelessly with the tassel over his forehead instead of putting it on the right side. In addition to that, there was a fresh growth of hair on his cheeks because he had not yet found time to shave. The Inspector glared at him, went into the room in a rage, and began to write out a report charging the Adjutant with contravening "standing regulations regarding dress and turnout."

2.9 When the Pāshā noticed that the beating and yelling had stopped all of a sudden and witnessed the alarm and confusion among the policemen, let alone the actions of the Adjutant, he asked me what was the significance of this man whose entry had caused such a flurry of activity. I told him that the Inspector came to the station to inspect and supervise "conditions," to look into people's complaints, and to make sure that the actions of officials conformed with the demands for law and order. The Pāshā then asked that we go inside and bring to his attention the insult we'd endured.

We went in and stood in front of him. We found him writing his report. He turned towards me and asked us our business. But no sooner had we begun to tell him our story than he ordered one of the policemen to remove us from his presence. When he had finished writing the report, we saw him put it into his pocket. With that, he rushed away without bothering to inspect or supervise anything, apart, that is, from the Adjutant's turnout.

When he had left, the beating, yelling, and general din resumed in every part of the station with an even greater intensity than before his arrival. One of the people who had been severely beaten and was in intense pain yelled out that he fully intended to make a complaint against the station officers at the Parquet Office. One of the policemen went in to tell the Adjutant what the man had said. Placing my ear to the door, I could hear the Adjutant talking to himself:

"What's the point of this job," he was saying, "and all the humiliation I have to suffer? God's curse on the need to earn a living! Even so, thank the Lord this Inspector is English and not a native Arab. He's much better than they would be. He doesn't understand Arabic and knows absolutely nothing about the job. All he's worried about is inspecting my tarboosh and beard. If he were an Arab,

اقتصر في التفتيش على طربوشي ولحيتي ولوكان من أبناء العرب لاطلع على اختلال القضايا وما يرتكبه عمال القسم من مخالفة الأصول.

١٠،٢ ولما أصغى المعاون إلى العسكري في تبليغه ما قاله ذلك الرجل من الشكاية إلى النيابة ازداد كدره فأمر بحبس المتهمين جميعا من أرباب القضايا أربعا وعشرين ساعة وفيهم صاحبي. فذهبت إلى المعاون أطلب أن يطلق سراحه بعد ضمانتي له فقال بوجه عبوس:

الأولى بقاؤه في القسم للصباح حتى يكشف على السوابق ويرسل إلى النيابة.

فدخل الحبس.

he'd have managed to find out what a chaotic state the court cases are in and the way the station officers break all the rules."

2.10 He then turned to the policeman and listened as he told him what the man who was determined to complain to the Parquet Office had said. At this, he became even more worried and annoyed. He issued orders that all the suspects were to be imprisoned for twenty-four hours, including my friend, the Pāshā. I went to see the Adjutant and requested that he release the Pāshā after I had stood bail for him. He refused and told me with a frown that the best thing was for the Pāshā to remain at the station till the next day so that his previous convictions could be investigated. Then he would be sent over to the Parquet Office.

With that, the Pāshā went to prison.

مصباح الشرق ٣٤، ٨ ديسمبر ١٨٩٨

قال عيسى بن هشام: وتركت صاحبي في حبسه وبت ليلتي في هم وأرق واضطراب وقلق لما أصاب الرجل من ضربات الدهر المتتاليات وهو غريق في دهشته وحيرته لا يدرك مضي الزمن ولا يدري ما الحال ولا يعرف ما الانقلاب ولا يعلم ما التغيير الذي أحدثه الدهر من بعد عهده وانقضاء نحبه وزوال دولته واندراج تلك الأيام في ثوب البلى. وكنت هممت أن أكاشفه بجلية الحال وكنه الأمر عند الوهلة الأولى من مصاحبتي له لولا ما دهمنا به القضاء المحتوم والخطب المقدور فأوقعنا فيما ألم بنا وفكرت بعد ذلك فكان من حسن التدبير وسداد الرأي أن أتركه جاهلا بالأمر حتى ينتهي من خطبه ويكون جهله بتغيير الحال قائما بعذره في التخلص من ورطته، ثم عقدت الطوية على أن لا أفارق صحبته حتى أريه ما لم ير وأسمعه ما لم يسمع وأشرح له ما غمض وانبهم عليه من تاريخ العصر الحاضر لأطلع على ما يكون من رأيه فيه ومقابلته بالعصر الغابر وأي العهدين أجل قدرا وأعظم نفعا وما الفضل بينهما وما يمتاز به كل منهما، فبكرت إلى القسم في اليوم الثاني من حادثتنا وأنا أحمل معي ما يليق به من ثياب ليرتديها في خروجه من حبسه فوجدت العسكري يستعد به ليتوجه معه إلى قلم السوابق في دار المحافظة، فلما بصر بي الباشا ناداني بقوله: ١.٣

الباشا ما هذه الخطوب والحوادث وما تلك الملمات والكوارث قد كنت أظن أنّ ما وقع لي في أمسي كان لسخط أفندينا الداوري الأفخم ولي نعمتنا وغضبه على عبده بمكيدة كادها لي أعدائي أو فرية افتراها حسادي فلذلك صبرت لحكم الضرورة وامتثلت على تلك الصورة حتى أتمكن من التشرف بالإعتاب والمثول بين يدي مالك الرقاب فأزيل الشبهة وأنفي الريب وأبرأ له مما رماني به الساعي والواشي وأجلي له ٢.٣

3.1 ʿĪsā ibn Hishām said: I left my companion in prison and went home. I lay awake all night, feeling restless and unable to sleep because I was so worried at the way fate had struck the Pāshā down with such a succession of blows. There he was, utterly baffled and bewildered, unaware that time had passed. He was completely unfamiliar with the present state of affairs, and had no idea that, with the passage of time since his own era and the decline of the dynasty of his time into the folds of decay, things had changed. I had intended to tell him about all this when I first met him by explaining the circumstances involved, but then fate had struck us a blow by landing us in the chain of events which had befallen us. Afterwards, I had thought for a while and decided that the best plan would be to let him remain ignorant about the way things were until his misfortunes were at an end. The fact that he had been unaware that conditions had changed would serve as a pretext in clearing him of the charge against him.

I decided not to leave his company until I had managed to show him the things he had not seen, tell him about the things he had not heard, and explain those aspects of modern history which he did not know or might find perplexing. In that way, I would discover what his opinion was of the present in comparison with the past, and learn which of the two was of greater worth and brought more benefits, and in what ways one was superior to the other.

Early the next day I went to the station, taking with me some suitable clothing for my companion to wear when he came out of prison. I found the policeman ready to take the Pāshā to the Register of Convictions in the Government Building. As soon as he spotted me, he started yelling at me:

3.2 PĀSHĀ What's the meaning of all these misfortunes and calamities? I imagined that the sufferings I endured yesterday were the result of His Mighty Excellency's anger at his obedient servant, that my enemies had managed to devise some kind of plot against me, or else that people who envy me had trumped up some false story. So I endured the things which necessity decreed I had to suffer and submitted myself to these indignities till such time as I would be able to present myself at the doorstep of the palace and appear before the master of all slaves. Then I would dispel all suspicions, banish any doubts, and show him that I was innocent of whatever charges slanderers and calumniators had trumped up against me. I would make clear to him how genuine was my devotion and loyalty to him. As a result he would be doubly

حقيقة إخلاصي وعبوديتي فيضاعف عليّ رضاه لحسن الطاعة في احتمال هذا الهوان.

طال مني تحمل خلت أني
قابض من أذاته فوق جمر

ثم أعمد بعد ذلك إلى إفشاء العقاب عقاب القتل والصلب في هؤلاء الأوباش السفهاء، والأشقياء الأغبياء جزاء ما اجترؤوا عليه في معاملاتي واقترفوه من جهل منزلتي ولكني سمعت في الحبس- ويا سوء ما سمعت وعلمت ويا شر ما علمت - أنّ الدول دالت والأحوال حالت وأنكم أصبحتم في زمان صحّ فيه قول ذلك المكاري إنه هو والباشا في المنزلة سواء وتلك التي

تصم السميع وتعمي البصير
ويسأل من مثلها العافيه

فاللهم عفوك وصفحك هل قامت القيامة وجاء يوم الحشر وانتصب الميزان وانحلت الرئاسات وانطوت المراتب واستوى العزيز بالذليل والكبير بالصغير والعظيم بالحقير والعبد بالمولى ولم يبق لقرشي على حبشي فضل ولا لأمير منا على مصري أمر، ذلك ما لا يكون ولا تحتمله الظنون، واعلم أيها الرجل أنّ ذنب أولئك السفهاء فيما جنوه عليّ لا يعدّ في جانب ذنبك إلا كالخردلة من الصخر والقطرة من البحر لكتمانك عليّ الأمر حتى دخلت بي بلدا هذا حالها وذاك شأنها وأعوذ بالله منك ومن شياطين الجن. ٣٠٣

عيسى بن هشام ﴿لَا تُؤَاخِذْنِي بِمَا نَسِيتُ وَلَا تُرْهِقْنِي مِنْ أَمْرِي عُسْرًا﴾. لقد نزل بي الذهول والتبلد والخوف والتحير عند قيامك من القبر ما منعني من تبصرتك بالواقع وتنبيهك إلى تغيير الحال وما كدت أتيقظ إلى تعريفك بها حتى دهينا بذلك المكاري ودهمنا بتلك الحادثة ولا ذنب لي فيما أتيت والعذر مقبول لديك،

pleased with me because of the dignified way in which I had submitted to this humiliation.

Long was my endurance.
I imagined I was grasping miseries hotter than coals.[26]

Thereafter I would make it my business to inform everyone of the penalty of death and crucifixion that I proposed to wreak on those insolent wretches and ignorant scoundrels in recompense for the way they treated me and ignored my status in society. But I heard in prison—what a dreadful thing to hear!—that dynasties have succeeded one another, conditions have changed, and that you really are living in a different time from the days of old, and in a state of anarchy in which the Donkeyman's assertion that both he and a Pāshā are of equal standing is true. This is something that:

Deafens the hearer, blinds the person who sees;
we ask deliverance from the like of it.[27]

3.3

Oh God, by Your pardon and forgiveness, has the last day come, is this the Day of Gathering? Have classes disappeared and dynasties disintegrated? Is the mighty man on a par with the lowly, the powerful dignitary the equal of the small, the great man the equal of the despised, the servant the equal of the master? Has the Qurayshī no longer any superiority over the Abyssinian,[28] and is a Turkish amir not of higher status than a mere Egyptian? This cannot be true! It is quite beyond the powers of comprehension.

And as for you, my good fellow, I want you to know that, compared with your outrageous conduct, I consider the crime those insolent wretches have committed against me to be nothing more than a grain of mustard seed as compared with a rock, a mere drop in the ocean. You have kept me in the dark and even introduced me to a country where this is the state of affairs. So God protect me from the likes of you and all the devil's demons.

ʿĪsā «Don't blame me for my forgetfulness, nor burden me with any difficulty in my affairs.»[29] When you emerged from the grave, I was so scared and bewildered that I behaved stupidly. I wasn't able to tell you about present conditions and the way in which things have changed since your own lifetime. I hardly had an opportunity to tell you about it before the Donkeyman started bothering us, and we were beset by these misfortunes. I've done nothing wrong, and you should accept my excuse. Endure whatever you may

فاصبر على ما تلاقيه واحتمل ما أنت فيه، وتقبل القضاء بوجه الرضاء، ولا تأس على ما فات ليكفّر الله عنك السيئات.

العسكري (للباشا) هلم إلى السوابق.

الباشا أترى قد زال عني بؤسي وانقشع نحسي ورجع إليّ عزي فجاؤوني بموكبي وخيلي.

عيسى بن هشام (للباشا) ليس المقصود بالسوابق تلك الجياد الصافنات والعتاق الصهلات وإنما هو ديوان تقيد فيه سحنة المتهمين وسيماهم ويكشف عما جنته أيديهم في ماضيهم.

العسكري للباشا (هو يسحبه) دع عنك كثرة الكلام وامش معي ساكتا ساكنا.

الباشا (وهو يمتنع) ما الحيلة في القضاء والعمل في المقدور وكيف الخلاص وأين النجاة ومن لي بالموت يدفعني في صدري فيردني إلى قبري.

عيسى بن هشام (وهو يتضرع) أقسمت عليك بدفين القلعة ووقع سيوفك في المعمعة ألا ما قبلت نصيحتي وعملت بمشورتي فلا تعاند ولا تعارض فإنّ الامتناع لا يفيد ولا يزيد في ملمتنا إلا شدة وفي مصيبتنا إلا حدة والعقل يرشدنا أن نسلم للأقدار حيث لا عمل وأن نلبس لكل حالة لبوسها إمّا نعيمها وإمّا بؤسها.

٤٫٣ قال عيسى بن هشام: فسمع الباشا لقولي ورضي بحكم القضاء على المضض، وسرنا مع العسكري فوصلنا إلى قسم السوابق وتحقيق الشخصية فرأى الباشا هناك من أعمال التشبيه ما تخلع له القلوب وتشيب منه النواصي فعرّوه من ثيابه وفحصوا بدنه عضوا عضوا ووجهه وحدقوا في عينيه وصنعوا ما صنعوا وهو يحرق الأرم ويتنفس الصعداء حتى انتهوا من عملهم وسألوا عن ضمانته فلم يجدوا له ضمانة لأنّ المعاون قاتله الله رد شيخ الحارة عن التصديق على ضمانتي ليجوز له الحبس فأرسلونا مع العسكري إلى النيابة فدخلنا على عضو النيابة فوجدنا أمامه قضايا جمة وأصحابها

encounter and put up with the situation in which you find yourself. Accept fate with a good face and don't grieve over the past in order to atone for your present misdeeds.

POLICEMAN (*to the Pāshā*) Come on, we're going to the Register of Convictions.

PĀSHĀ The Lord be praised! I do believe my suffering is over and my misfortunes have been driven away. I have regained my former status, and they have brought me my retinue and horse![30]

ʿĪSĀ That word doesn't mean rearing steeds and neighing thoroughbreds. It's a department where they record the features and characteristics of the accused and find out if he has committed any previous offences.

POLICEMAN (*to the Pāshā, as he drags him along*) Stop all this chatter. Come with me quietly and in an orderly fashion.

PĀSHĀ (*holding back*) What can one do in the face of predestined fate? How can I escape? Who will dispatch me to death a second time and return me to my grave?

ʿĪSĀ (*pleading*) I beg you, in the name of the one who is buried in the Citadel and by the clash of your swords in battle, please take my advice and behave as I suggest. Don't resist or object. Reluctance will serve no purpose and only make our misfortunes worse. When we have no choice in the matter, the sensible thing to do is to resign ourselves to fate and to wear the appropriate garments for every situation, whether cheerful or miserable.

3.4 ʿĪsā ibn Hishām said: The Pāshā heard what I had to say and reluctantly accepted the decree of fate. We duly accompanied the Policeman until we reached the Register of Convictions and Substantiation of Identity. There the Pāshā endured enough identity procedures to give anyone heart failure and turn his hair white. They stripped him of his clothes, examined him limb by limb, measured his face and body, stared into his eyes, and did all kinds of things to him. He just kept sighing deeply until they had finished with him. They asked about bail and discovered that he had none because the Adjutant—God curse him!—had refused to accept the verification of his bail which the Shaykh of the Quarter had provided, so that he could legally keep him in prison for the night.

مزدحمون ينتظرون دورهم فانفردنا ناحية ننتظر دورنا والتفت صاحبي إليّ يسألني:

الباشا أين نحن الآن ومن هذا الغلام وما هذا الزحام.

عيسى بن هشام نحن أمام النيابة وهذا عضو النيابة وهؤلاء أرباب الدعاوى.

الباشا وما هي النيابة.

عيسى بن هشام النيابة في هذا النظام الجديد هي سلطة قضائية مكلفة بإقامة الدعاوى القضائية على المجرمين نيابة عن الهيئة الاجتماعية. والغرض من إنشائها أن لا تبق جريمة بلا عقوبة ووظيفتها أن تدافع عن الحق فتظهر ذنب المذنب وبراءة البريء.

الباشا ما هي الهيئة الاجتماعية

عيسى بن هشام هي مجموع الأمّة.

الباشا ومن هو هذا العظيم من الأمّة الذي اتفقت عليه لينوب عنها.

عيسى بن هشام ليس هذا الذي تراه بعظيم من عظماء الأمة وإنما هو أحد أبناء الفلاحين أرسله أبوه إلى المدارس فاكتسب الشهادة فاستحق النيابة عن الأمّة فتولى دمائها وأعراضها وأموالها.

الباشا نعمت المنزلة عند الله منزلة الشهادة، وللشهيد في الجنة أعلى الدرجات ولكن كيف تتصور عقولكم - وأظنهم فقدتموها- أن تجتمع الشهادة في سبيل الله والحياة في الدنيا لإنسان. ولكن الذي يفوق ذلك عجبا ويزيد العقل خبالا أن يحكم الناس فلاّح وينوب عن الأمّة حراث، ولقد خرجت من شدة إلى شدة ومن ويل إلى ويلٍ فسلمت وصبرت ولكن لا صبر لي على هذه الخارقة فما أعظم الفاجعة وأشد النازلة، فِنَيَ مني الصبر ومن لي بفناء القبر.

عيسى بن هشام اعلم أنّ هذه الشهادة ليست شهادة الجهاد بل هي ورقة يأخذها التلميذ في نهاية دروسه ليثبت بها أنه تلقى العلوم وبرع فيها وقيمتها لمن يرغبها ألف وخمسمائة فرنك. ٥،٣

With that, they sent us over to the Parquet with the Policeman. When we entered, we found the Parquet Attorney with a load of cases on his hands and hordes of litigants waiting their turn. So we went over to one side to wait our turn as well. My companion turned to me.

PĀSHĀ Where are we now? Who's this young fellow? What's this mob of people?

ʿĪSĀ We're in the Parquet office. This man's a member of the Parquet, and all these people are litigants.

PĀSHĀ What is this "Parquet?"

ʿĪSĀ In this new legal system, it's the judicial authority responsible for bringing criminal charges against offenders, acting on behalf of society. It was introduced so that no crime should go unpunished. Its duties are to uphold the truth and prove the guilt of the guilty and the innocence of the innocent.

PĀSHĀ What is this "society" on whose behalf it acts as deputy?

ʿĪSĀ The people as a whole.

PĀSHĀ Who is this mighty person whom the people agree to act as their deputy?

ʿĪSĀ The man you see in front of you is not a man of enormous importance. He's just a peasant's son whose father has sent him to schools where he's obtained the certificate. He's thus entitled to act as an attorney of the Parquet. His authority to deal with people covers matters of homicide, property, and finance.

PĀSHĀ In God's eyes the martyr has an exalted status; in heaven, he occupies the very highest position.[31] But you seem to have lost your mind! How can you suppose that martyrdom in the way of God and life here on earth can both apply to one man at the same time? What is even stranger and more confusing is that a peasant can have authority over people, and a farmer is the community's deputy! I've gone from one misfortune to another but still remained calm and patient. But I can't do so any longer in the face of this incredible state of affairs. What an utter disaster! What a terrible catastrophe! I've no patience left. Will someone help me return to the oblivion of the grave?

3.5

ʿĪSĀ You must realize that this "certificate" does not mean the same thing as martyrdom in holy war. It's a piece of paper received by students at the end of their studies to confirm that they have studied and achieved excellence in the various branches of learning. Sometimes people who want to get one have to pay one thousand five hundred francs.

الباشا مه مه، كأنك تريد الإجازة التي يجيزها علماء الأزهر لمن حضر عليهم العلوم من الطلبة وفاق فيها. ولكننا ما سمعنا في دهرنا بهذه الأثمان وما عهدنا أنّ الأزهر الشريف يتعامل بالفرنكات.

عيسى بن هشام ما هذه العلوم بعلوم الأزهر ولكنها علوم افرنكية يتلقونها في بلاد الإفرنج والفرنك عملة تلك البلاد وتلك القيمة يقال لها رسم الشهادة وهي لا تذكر بالنسبة إلى فوائدها فإنّ القاعدة في هذا النظام «إنّ الشهادة بلا علم خير من العلم بلا شهادة» وصاحبها إذا قدمها للحكومة يكون له الحق في الاستيلاء على مرتب وظيفة شهري يزيد على الدوام ويرقى.

الباشا الآن كدت أفهم. أظنها مثل أوراق الالتزام وسراكي الروزنامجة في حكمنا.

٦.٣ قال عيسى بن هشام: وبينما نحن في هذا الحديث إذا بشابين رشيقين رقيقين أقبلا يخطران في مشيتهما ويعبق الطيب من أردانهما، ويترنمان بالحديث بينهما، ولا يلتفتان إلى من حولهما، أحدهما يلاعب الجو بعصاه، والثاني تلعب بالنظارة يداه. فشخصت الأنظار، ووقفت الأبصار، والحاجب يدفع الناس من طريقهما حتى وصلا إلى الباب فأمر النائب بطرد من كان واقفاً بين يديه من أرباب القضايا والدعاوى واستمرّ الحاجب يسحبهم ويجرّهم وينهرهم ويسبهم والنائب يطوي المحاضر ويسد المحابر ويستعجل في فض الزحام وإخلاء المكان استعداداً لاستقبال الشابين. وسألني الباشا قائلا:

الباشا يظهر أنّ هذين الشابين من أكبر أولاد الأمراء أو أعظم مفتشي الحكومة لشدة الاحتفاء باستقبالهما كما رأيناه في القسم.

عيسى بن هشام ما أظنهما إلّا زائرين من قرناء النائب في المدرسة كما يظهر لي من شمائلهما.

وأردت استطلاع خبرهما واستكشاف أمرهما فانتهزت فرصة الزحام واختفيت

PĀSHĀ Oh, I see! You mean the certificate awarded by scholars at al-Azhar to the students who have studied with them and achieved distinction. But I never heard of such expenses in my time, nor have I heard of the noble al-Azhar dealing in francs.

ʿĪSĀ The subjects they study are not the traditional al-Azhar ones, but Western ones which they learn in Europe. The franc is the French unit of currency, and they call that amount the fee for the certificate. It is a trifling sum when you bear in mind the many advantages it brings. In this system, the basic principle is that "a certificate without any learning is better than learning without any certificate." Anyone with a certificate can present it to the government department and have the right to receive a salary and continuing increments.

PĀSHĀ I almost follow you now. I think this certificate corresponds to the tax-farm lists and ledgers of treasury officials in the time of our government.

3.6 ʿĪsā ibn Hishām said: While we were chatting, two young men suddenly appeared. They looked very suave and elegant as they strutted their way through the crowd. Their sleeves exuded perfume into the air. Conversing volubly with each other, they managed to ignore everyone around them. One of them kept cleaving the air with his cane, while the other fiddled with his spectacles. Everyone stared at them agog. The Policeman walked ahead of them, pushing people out of their way. Eventually they reached the door of the Attorney's office. He told the litigants in the various cases to leave, whereupon the usher proceeded to force them all out, cursing and swearing as he did so. Meanwhile the Attorney himself set about finishing up the minutes and removing the inkwells. Having cleared the entire place, he made ready to welcome the two young men. The Pāshā asked me:

PĀSHĀ (*to ʿĪsā*) It looks to me as if these two young men must be the sons of very important princes, or else they are inspectors of the Parquet like the police station Inspector whom we saw earlier.

ʿĪSĀ No, I think they're just friends of the Attorney from his college days paying him a visit. That's clear enough from their general appearance.

I wanted to find out more about the two of them. So, while everyone else was milling around, I took the opportunity to sneak up close to the door

في عقب الدار وراء الستار بحيث أسمع وأرى وهذا ما دار بينهما وجرى.

الزائر الأول (بعد السلام والجلوس) لماذا تركتنا أمس من قبل أن ينتهي اللعب. ٧،٣

النائب لأنه كان قد مضى من الليل أكثره وعندي من القضايا ما يضطرني إلى التبكير.

الزائر الثاني وهل القضايا تعوقك عن البقاء مع إخوانك. وقد يمكن لك أن تعتذر بهذا العذر لغير الواقفين على أعمال النيابة أمّا أنا فقد رأيت فلاناً صاحبي لا تحمل قضايا اليوم كله أكثر من ساعة واحدة فإنه يمر عليها بلحظة منه ويستغني عن مطالعتها ويكتفي بتوقد ذهنه ونباهة قريحته وما دام الشقاق والنزاع انتهى من بين النيابة والبوليس فالأولى الاكتفاء بمحاضر البوليس أو ردّها لاستيفائها ولا محل لتجديد التحقيق وتضييع الوقت في إعادة السؤال دفعاً لما عساه يتولد مرة أخرى من الخلاف والشقاق.

النائب هذا ما أفعله ولكن لا بد من التمسك بالظواهر والأصول.

الزائر الأول أفما عندك الكاتب يقوم عنك بهذا ويكفيه.

النائب نعم صدقت. وأنا أقول لك أنّ السبب الحقيقي في مفارقتكم وطرح اللعب هو أنني خسرت ما كان معي من مرتب الشهر ولم يبق منه إلّا النزر اليسير ونحن لا نزال في أوائله.

الزائر الأول هذه هي عادتك في ادعاء الخسارة دائماً مهما ربحت وكسبت وما سمعت منك في عمري إلا أنك خسران. أفلم تربح مني في اليد الأخيرة التي كانت بيننا أكثر من خمسة جنيهات.

النائب وحياة شرفي وذمتي ومستقبلي إني قمت من عندكم أمس بالخسارة.

الزائر الثاني ما علينا. هل أنت لا تزال على وعدك معنا في التوجه عند صاحبنا فلان للتفرج على الرقص البلدي من فلانة المشهورة.

النائب لا يمكنني ذلك، أوّلاً لأنّ هذا الرقص الذي يجب أولاد البلد

behind the curtain from where I could both see and hear. This is the conversation I heard:

3.7 FIRST VISITOR (*after greeting the Attorney and sitting down*) Why did you leave us yesterday before the game was over?

ATTORNEY It was long past midnight, and I had so many cases to deal with that I had to get up early.

SECOND VISITOR Whoever heard of cases keeping anyone away from his friends' company? That excuse is only handy when you're talking to people who aren't familiar with the Parquet's business! I personally am acquainted with a colleague who only spends an hour a day on cases! He's satisfied just to look them over for a moment. He doesn't bother to peruse them, but relies instead on a combination of his sheer mental acumen, his alert intellect, and his wide experience in order to discover the relevant facts. Not only that, but now that there's no longer any disagreement or bad feeling between the Parquet and the police, the best idea is to make do with police evidence or else send it back it to them for completion. There's no point in reopening inquiries and wasting time on something which may lead to more bad feelings and arguments all over again.

ATTORNEY That's exactly what I do, but one has to adhere to outward appearances as far as possible.

FIRST VISITOR Haven't you got a secretary who can take over and save you all the bother?

ATTORNEY You're right. The secretary can do it perfectly well. The real reason why I stopped playing and left yesterday was that I'd already lost the month's salary I had with me, and it's still only the beginning of the month.

FIRST VISITOR You're always claiming to have lost, however much you've won. In my entire life the only thing I've ever heard you say is that you've lost. Didn't you win five pounds off me on the last hand we played?

ATTORNEY I swear to you on my honor, conscience, and future career, that I'd lost money when I left yesterday.

SECOND VISITOR Never mind! Tell me, are you still going to keep your appointment with us to go to our friend's house to see that famous belly dancer?

ATTORNEY I can't make it. In the first place, I don't like that type of dancing. Only locals and peasants enjoy that sort of thing. Secondly, I've invited

والفلاحين لا يجبني، وثانياً لأني دعوت مادموازيل ...... المشخصة في الأوبرا مع فلان وفلان المشخصين للغذاء عند سانتي وسنذهب بعد ذلك إلى خان الخليلي وقصبة رضوان وبعض المحلات القديمة البلدية للتفرج عليها.

الزائر الأول أنت تدّعي الآن أنه لم يبق معك من مرتبك إلا النزر اليسير فكيف لك بهذه النفقات. ٨،٣

النائب فإنني إن أذكر لكما أنّ معنا فلاناً الأفوكاتو وصاحبه فلاناً العمدة.

الزائر الثاني وكيف يميل هذان إلى مجلس افرنكي ويستريحان إليه وهما لا يعرفان شيئاً من اللغة والاصطلاحات الأوربية.

النائب ألم تعلم يا أخي أنّ أمنية الأفوكاتو أن يكون مصاحباً لأهل القضاء وأمنية الفلاح أن يكون في وسط مجلس افرنكي وإن لم يفهما منه شيئاً وكلفهما ما كلفهما.

الزائر الثاني من أين اشتريت هذا الكرافات (رباط الرقبة).

النائب هذا جاءني به يا مونشير (عزيزي) مع ملابسي من عند الخياط في باريس.

الزائر الأول هل بلغك استعفاء فلان.

الزائر الثاني هل رأيت الدراجات الكهربائية.

النائب قد وقفت لكما على سبب انتحار ابن سوارس.

الزائر الغرام

النائب لا

الزائر المال

النائب لا

الزائر المرض

النائب لا. وإنما هو آخر موده في باريس.

Mademoiselle X, the opera star, and two of her colleagues to dine with me at "Santé" in the Ezbekiyyah Quarter. Afterwards, we're going to have some fun and visit Khān al-Khalīlī, Qaṣbat Ruḍwān, the Tombs of the Caliphs, and other ancient sites in the city.

3.8 FIRST VISITOR You were just claiming you didn't have any of your month's salary left. How are you going to afford such expenses?

ATTORNEY I forgot to mention that a lawyer and his friend, the *ʿumdah*,[32] are coming with us.

SECOND VISITOR How can two such people make any pretense of liking French soirées or getting the slightest enjoyment out of them? They don't know a word of the language or any European phrases.

ATTORNEY My dear friend, don't you realize that lawyers want to keep the company of the judiciary, and peasants want to brush shoulders with us? But both alike dearly want to attend French soirées, even though the cost is so high and they get no benefit or enjoyment whatsoever.

SECOND VISITOR (*tersely*) Where did you get that cravat?

ATTORNEY I didn't buy it, *monsieur*. It came with my clothes from my tailor in Paris.

FIRST VISITOR Did you hear that X has resigned?

SECOND VISITOR Have you seen those electric carriages?

ATTORNEY I've found out for you why Suarez's son committed suicide.

FIRST VISITOR I know—love!

ATTORNEY No.

VISITOR Money?

ATTORNEY No.

VISITOR Was he ill?

ATTORNEY No, the poor chap was copying the latest rage in Paris!

الزائر الأول وأنا قد وقفت لكما على سبب انفصال عثمان بك غالب من وظيفته.

النائب سيرته

الزائر لا

النائب وطنيته

الزائر لا

النائب فرنسويته

الزائر لا. وإنما هي انكليزيته.

٩،٣ قال عيسى بن هشام: فسئمت من هذا الكلام الفارغ والحديث المقتضب وانتهزت دخول الحاجب فخرجت من مكمني في غضون ذلك فوجدت أحد سماسرة المحامين قد التصق بالباشا يحاوره فأنصت من بعيد فمّا سمعته قوله:

السمسار اعلم أنّ المحامي في يده القضاء يبرئ ويعاقب من يشاء وما النيابات وما المحاكم وما القضاة إلا طوع إشارته ورهن كلمته فلا حكم إلا بأمره ولا قضاء إلا برأيه وأنت رجل غريب حقيق بالرحمة والشفقة وتدعوني الإنسانية والمروءة أن لا أدعك طعمة في أيدي المحامين الذين يسلبون الناس المال بطرق النصب والاحتيال وكاذب الوعود والآمال، وصاحبي فلان المحامي رجل صادق أمين وأصولي شهير صاحب مقام سام بين الأمراء والحكام فهو صديق الناظر وجليس المستشار ونديم القاضي وخدين النائب ووكيل البرنس ولو شاهدته يا سيدي في اجتماعه معهم في السهر والسمر والحظ والأنس يشاربهم ويؤاكلهم ويمازحهم ويقامرهم لأيقنت أنّ كل طلب له يجاب وليس لأمره من راد، والمجرم بريء والبريء جان على حسب المراد، فقل لي عن مقدار ما تستطيع دفعه في المقدم.

First Visitor And I've found out for you why ʿUthmān Bey Ghālib was fired from his post.

Attorney Was it his conduct?

Visitor No.

Attorney His job?

Visitor No.

Attorney His French?

Visitor No, his English!

ʿĪsā ibn Hishām said:[33] I found this terse and vacuous conversation boring, so I took advantage of the guard's entry to leave my hiding place and return to my companion, the Pāshā. I found a lawyer's agent beside him. He had come over and was talking to him. So I stood at a distance. Here is some of what I heard him say: 3.9

Agent You should realize that the lawyer can direct the judiciary exactly as he wishes, punishing and acquitting anyone according to whim. The members of the Parquet, the courts, and judges merely follow his instructions. No decision can be made unless he says so and no verdict can be reached without his instructions. You're a stranger here, someone who deserves sympathy and forbearance. Mere human decency forbids me to let you fall into the clutches of some low-class lawyers who regularly use deceitful and crafty methods and make false promises that raise all kinds of hopes, and all that merely to rob people of their money. My colleague on the other hand is honest and reliable, a well-known man of principle who is highly regarded by princes and government officials alike. He's the inspector's friend, the counselor's companion, the judge's intimate companion, the attorney's confidant, and the prince's agent. If only you could see him just once, my dear Sir, when he meets them for a late-night chat. You would immediately notice the informal atmosphere they share as they enjoy themselves in each other's company and watch him as he eats and drinks with them, chats and jokes, debates and gambles. You would then be convinced that every request he makes is granted and no one would refuse to do what he orders. As a result, the guilty man can be innocent in accordance with his wishes, and the innocent man guilty. So tell me, how much can you afford to pay in advance?

الباشا أنا لا أعرف المقدم ولا المؤخر ولم يخبرني صاحبي عن هذا الحاكم المطلق فإذا استفهمت عنه . . . .

السمسار (مقاطعاً) لا لزوم للاستفهام من أحد فها هو حضرة المحامي قد أقبل.

ويستقبل السمسار المحامي باستقبال الأمراء ويوسّع له الطريق حتى يصل به إلى جانب الباشا بعد أن ألقى في أذن صاحبه ما ألقاه. ١٠،٣

المحامي (بصوت عال) أنا لا أستطيع قبول التوكيل عن أحد في هذه الأيام لتراكم الأعمال وتزاحم القضايا فلم يبق عندي وقت للطعام وللشراب (وربما كانت الحقيقة أنه لم يبق عنده شيء لا وقت) فكيف تكلفني أن أقبل التوكيل عن صاحبك في هذه القضية الصغيرة وقد رفضت في صباحي خمس قضايا ذات أهمية كبرى.

السمسار سألتك بحق الإنسانية وحرمة المروءة وبما جبلت عليه من الحنو للضعفاء أن تأذن لأحد موظفي مكتبك أن يباشر هذه القضية، إن لم تتنازل لقبولها بنفسك فإنّ الغرض هو تأثير اسمك على المحكمة.

المحامي لا أرى في ذلك بأساً عناية بك وشفقة بصاحبك (ثم يصافح الباشا وينصرف فينزوي عن عينه).

السمسار (للباشا) هلمّ فادفع عشرين جنيهاً مقدماً.

الباشا ليس عندي نقود.

السمسار اعطني تحويلاً على أحد أقاربك أو معارفك.

الباشا أنا لا أفهم لك كلاماً فاذهب عني فقد ضقت ذرعاً.

السمسار كيف أتركك وقد اتفقت مع حضرة المحامي؟

الباشا أنا لم أتفق مع أحد فاتركني.

السمسار كيف تنكر أنك اتفقت معه بعد أن وضعت يدك في يده؟

الباشا من يصبر على هذه الحال. أشرت بيدي في حديثي مع صاحبي فأوقعتني في حادثة المكاري وصافحت ذلك الرجل فصرت له مديوناً بعشرين جنيهاً ففي أي العوالم أنا؟

PĀSHĀ I know nothing about advance or arrears. My friend didn't mention this powerful arbiter you describe. So once I've asked him about it—

AGENT (*interrupting*) There's no need to ask anyone! Here comes the lawyer now.

3.10

(*The Agent greets the Lawyer with the lavish respect due to a prince. As he clears a path toward the Pāshā, he is whispering in the Lawyer's ear.*)

LAWYER (*raising his voice*) I cannot possibly take on anybody else's brief these days. I have piles of work and a colossal number of cases. There's no time left to eat and drink. (Maybe the truth of the matter was that he had nothing left at all, not just time.) How can you expect me to take on your friend's brief in such a trifling case, when I've already turned down five major cases this very morning?

AGENT For humanitarian reasons and in the name of the sanctity of chivalry and your inborn sympathy and pity for the weak, I beg you to allow one of your office staff to handle this case. Even if you cannot demean yourself so far as to handle it yourself, all that's needed is the influence that your name brings to the court.

LAWYER Out of regard for you and sympathy for your friend, I can see no objection.

(*The Lawyer shakes hands with the Pāshā, then turns away and leaves.*)

AGENT (*to the Pāshā*) Come on, that'll be twenty pounds.

PĀSHĀ I haven't a single dirham on me.

AGENT Then give me a check from a relative or acquaintance.

PĀSHĀ I don't understand what you mean. Go away, I'm fed up with you!

AGENT How can I leave when you have just reached an agreement with the Lawyer right in front of me?

PĀSHĀ I made no agreement with anyone. Go away!

AGENT How can you possibly deny shaking hands with the Lawyer and reaching an agreement with him?

PĀSHĀ How can anyone tolerate this situation? I gestured while talking to my friend, and that resulted in the disaster with the Donkeyman. Now I shake the Lawyer's hand, and I'm twenty pounds in debt! What kind of world am I in?

١١،٣ قال عيسى بن هشام: فلمّا رأيت لوائح الغضب بدت على وجهه خشيت أن يقع مع السمسار في ورطة أخرى فأدركته ووبخت الرجل على احتياله وتوعدته برفع الأمر إلى النائب العمومي فتخلصنا منه. ونادى الحاجب أرباب القضايا فدخلنا فوجدنا النائب لا زال مستمرًا في حديثه مع زائريه وأشاروا لنا بالتقدم إلى الكاتب فتقدمت بالنيابة عن صاحبي وشرعت في بسط القضية وسوء معاملة البوليس وافترائه فالتفت النائب إلى الكاتب وقال له لا تقبل كلاماً في البوليس واعتمد أقواله وتحقيقه ثم نظر في الساعة فوجد ميعاده حل فأخذ عصاه ونزل يجري مع صاحبيه. وقلت لصاحبي سأذهب للبحث لك عن أحد المحامين الصادقين من أصحابي.

١٢،٣ الباشا قل لي بالله ما هو المحامي عندكم؟

عيسى بن هشام هو الذي يتكلم عنك بما تعجز عنه ويدافع عنك بما لم تعلمه ولم يخطر على بالك وهي صناعة شريفة يمارسها كثير من الفضلاء، ولكن قد دخل فيها جماعة ليسوا بأهلها فاتخذوا طرق النصب والاحتيال بضاعة للتعيش منها كهذا المحامي وسمساره وهؤلاء هم الذين عناهم علاء الدين علي بن المظفر الكندي بقوله فيهم:

ما وكلاء الحكم إن خاصموا
إلا شياطين أولوا بأس
قوم غدا شرهم فاضلا
عنهم فباعوه على الناس.

3.11 ʿĪsā ibn Hishām said: I noticed signs of anger on the Pāshā's face and was afraid there would be another disaster, this time with the Agent. I rushed over. After reprimanding the Agent for his trickery, I proceeded to threaten him, saying that I would raise the matter with the Public Attorney. He went away and left us alone.

The usher who was supervising plaintiffs gave a shout. We went inside and found the Attorney still chatting merrily with his two visitors. They indicated that we should go to talk to his secretary, so I went along and began to explain the case on my companion's behalf. I told him about the bad treatment we had received from the police and the shocking way they had trumped up the charges. The Attorney turned to his secretary and told him not to allow any statement against the police; he should accept their statements and investigation. With that, he looked at his watch, found that it was the time for his appointment, grabbed his stick, put on his tarboosh, and left in a hurry with his two colleagues.

I must go now, I told my companion, and look for one of my friends who is an honest lawyer.

3.12 PĀSHĀ Tell me, what's a lawyer in this system of yours?

ʿĪSĀ He's the one who speaks on your behalf on matters in which you have no competence. He will defend you in areas you know nothing about, and testify for you about things which normally would not occur to you. His is a noble profession practiced today by many excellent people. However, certain other people have entered the profession who aren't worthy of it and who use deceit and trickery as a means of making a profit, like this lawyer and his agent. It is people like them whom ʿAlāʾ al-dīn ʿAlī ibn Muẓaffar al-Kindī has in mind when he says:

Whenever they litigate, legal attorneys
are simply all-powerful Satans.
They are a people who find they have evil to spare,
so they sell it off to mankind.

قال عيسى بن هشام: فلمّا حلّ يوم الجلسة رافقت صاحبي إلى المحكمة فوجدت في ساحتها أقواماً ذوي وجوه مكفهرة، وانقباض في الأسرّة، وأنفاس مقطوعة، وأكف مرفوعة، وباطلا يذكر، وحقّاً يستر، وشاكيًا يتوعد، وجانيًا يتودد، وشاهداً يتردد، وجنديًا يتمرد، وحاجبًا يستبد، ومحاميًا يستعد، وأمًّا تنوح، وطفلاً يصيح، وفتاة تتلهث، وشيخًا يتأفف، وسمعت أقوالاً متناقضة، وأحاديث متعارضة، ورأيت المحامين للخصمين، يشحذ كل منهما لسانه، ويقدح جنانه، استعداداً للنزول في ميادين المقال، والدفاع في مواقف النزاع، ليخرج كلاهما بغنيمة البراءة في الحكم، ورفع التهمة والجرم. وانزويت بصاحبي ومحامينا بجانبي، يذكر لنا أصولا مرعية، ومسائل فرعية، وظروفًا وأحوالاً، وشروحاً وأقوالاً، ومواد وفقرات في الجنح والمخالفات، ثم يتصفح محاضره، ويقلّب دفاتره، ويقسم بوكيد الأيمان، أنّ الباشا من تهمته في أمان، وأنا أجيب صاحبي عن كل سؤال بما يقتضيه الحال. ولمّا سألني عن هذه الملحمة قلت هي المحكمة. ١،٤

الباشا قد كان العهد بالمحكمة الشرعية وبيت القاضي على غير ما أرى فهل أصابها الدهر فيما أصاب بالتغيير والانقلاب. ٢،٤

عيسى بن هشام هذه المحكمة الأهلية لا الشرعية.

الباشا وهل القضاء بين الناس غير المحكمة الشرعية؟

عيسى بن هشام للقضاء في هذه البلاد على ما تشتهي، محاكم متعددة ومجالس مختلفة فمنها المحاكم الشرعية، والمحاكم الأهلية، والمحاكم المختلطة، والمجالس التأديبية، والمجالس الإدارية، والمجالس العسكرية، والمحاكم القنصلية دع المحكمة المخصوصة.

ʿĪsā ibn Hishām said: When the day of the court session arrived, I went to the court with my friend. In the courtyard outside I found people who looked pale; their expressions were grim. They breathed heavily and lifted their hands towards the heavens in despair. We watched in amazement as falsehood was passed off as truth and truths were denied. In all the commotion, we noticed some people complaining and making menacing remarks, a criminal currying favor, and a witness hesitating. A policeman kept uttering threats. Elsewhere, an orderly was taking matters into his own hands, and a lawyer was making his preparations. A mother was wailing, a baby crying, a girl fretting, and an old man grumbling. I heard people making incompatible and contradictory statements, and saw the lawyers who were about to defend the two parties sharpening their tongues and rousing their spirits, as they prepared to enter the arena of verbal combat and conduct the defense in cases of dispute, so that both of them could take away as their spoils from the legal battlefield an acquittal and the removal of suspicion and guilt. 4.1

With my friend I withdrew to a corner. At my side, the lawyer kept talking about the requisite principles, subsidiary issues, various other points and circumstances, and also mentioning the various phrases, articles, and sections dealing with misdemeanors and infractions. Then he thumbed through his notes, turned his files over, and gave us a solemn promise that the Pāshā need have no worries about being acquitted of the charge. Meanwhile, I was answering all my companion's questions as the situation demanded. When he asked me questions about this particular slaughterhouse, I informed him that it was actually the court itself.

PĀSHĀ The memories I have of the Shariah Court and the judge's residence are certainly different from what I see now. Has Time included it among the things on which it has wrought such a major transformation and upheaval? 4.2

ʿĪSĀ This is the Native Court, not the Shariah Court.

PĀSHĀ Is there some other form of jurisdiction besides the Shariah Court?

ʿĪSĀ In this country you can take your pick! The judiciary operates through numerous courts and a variety of committees. These include Shariah Courts, Native Courts, Mixed Courts, Disciplinary Tribunals, and Consular Courts, not to mention the Special Courts.

الباشا ما هذا الخلط وما هذا الخبط؟ سبحان الله هل أصبح المصريون فرقاً وأحزاباً، وقبائل وأفخاذاً، وأجناساً مختلفة، وفئات غير مؤتلفة، وطوائف متبددة، حتى جعلوا لكل واحدة محاكم على حده، ما عهدناهم كذلك منذ الأعصر الأول، ودولات الدول؟ وهل اندرست تلك الشريعة الغراء، وانهدمت بيوت الحكم والقضاء؟ اللّهم لا كفران، وأعوذ بالله من الشيطان.

عيسى بن هشام ليس الأمر على ما تظن وتحدس فلم يتوزع المصريون فرقاً بل هم أمّة واحدة وحكومة واحدة ونظام الأمور فيها يقضي بهذا الترتيب. وأنا أشرح لك الحال كعادتي معك:

٣،٤ أمّا المحاكم الشرعية فقد اقتصرت من الحكم الشرعي على الأحوال الشخصية يعني الزواج والطلاق وما يدخل في بابهما.

الباشا لقد فسد الحال وانحل النظام، كيف يعيش الناس بلا شرع وهل أصبحنا في الزمن الذي يقول فيه القائل:

قد نسخ الشرع في زمانهم.
فليتهم مثل شرعهم نسخوا؟

عيسى بن هشام لم يُنسخ الشرع الشريف بل هو باق على الدهر ما بقي إنصاف في الحكم وعدل في الأمم ولكنه كنز أهمله أهله وجوهرة أغفلها تاجرها.

أو درّة صدفية غواصها
بهج متى يرها يهل ويسجد

٤،٤ فلم يلتفتوا إلى تشييده وتمكينه وتمسكوا بالفروع دون الأصول واستغنوا عن اللب بالقشور واختلفوا في الأحكام وعكفوا على سفساف الأمور وحقيرها وأتعبوا العزائم وصرفوا الهمم إلى الإغماض في الحق الأبلج والتعقيد في الحنيفية السمحة والمحجة البيضاء ولم يفقهوا إلى ما تدعو إليه أحكام الزمن ولكل زمان حكم فيطبقوا الشرع

Pāshā What is this utter confusion? Have Egyptians divided into different sects and parties, tribes, and family groups? Have they turned into people of different species who live in discordant groups and divided classes, so that they've had to establish a special court for each one? This isn't how I remember them in days of old, even though dynasties may have changed. Is the noble Shariah extinct? Have the centers of judicial authority been eradicated? Oh God, forgive me and curse the devil!

ʿĪsā Things are not the way you think or surmise. Egyptians are not split into groups; they are a single people and a single government. It is the organization of things that demands this kind of arrangement. I'll explain it to you as I always do:

4.3 The role of the Shariah Court is now restricted to matters of personal status: marriage, divorce, and things like that.

Pāshā By God, things really have decayed; all semblance of organization has vanished! How can people live in stable surroundings without God's holy law? Are we really living in an age which the poet meant when he said:

In their time the holy law was abrogated.
If only they had been abrogated like their holy law![34]

ʿĪsā The noble Shariah has not been abrogated; on the contrary, it lasts for ever, as long as there is any justice in the world and honesty exists among peoples. But it is a treasure ignored by its own folk, a jewel neglected by its own merchants,

Or a precious pearl, no sooner did a diver see it
than he rejoiced and sank in prayer.[35]

4.4 Nowadays people pay no attention to the various aspects of its structure and formulation. Instead they prefer to adhere to the branches at the expense of the roots and to dispense with the kernel for the husks. They argue about regulations, concentrate assiduously on insignificant matters, and devote themselves to paltry and worthless matters. Their greatest aspiration and goal is to obscure the clear truth and complicate our liberal faith. They've never grasped what the laws of time demand. Every era has an order of its own which requires that the provisions of the Shariah be adjusted. Instead they are preoccupied with insignificant issues, in the apparent belief that that's the way of the

على مقتضى الأحوال، بل أقاموا في اشتغالهم بالمسائل الضعيفة الواهية معتقدين أنّ الدنيا على ذلك تكوّنت ودار الدهر دورة ثمّ وقف فلا أمل فيه ولا عمل. فكانوا سبباً في رمي الشرع الشريف – تطهر وتعالى – بخلل الحكم وهضم الحقوق وبعد الإنصاف، ورضوا بهذا العار واطمأنوا عليه وهم يتفكهون في الشرع ولا يتفقهون، وأصبح من أكبر همّهم فيه «هل المسح على الخف في الوضوء جائز إن كان الخف من زجاج». وما يماثل هذه الأمور الغريبة. وهكذا وقف بنا الأمر واستقر الحال وقامت المحاكم الأهلية مقام المحاكم الشرعية

٥،٤ الباشا لا بد أن يكون لهم عذر واضح في بلوغ هذه الحالة من نزاع منازع ومعارضة معارض وسلطة حاكم قاهر قسرهم على هذا المرعى الوبيل وصدهم عن سواء السبيل.

عيسى بن هشام لم يكن من ذلك شيء، فالإرادات مختارة والأفكار مطلقة والنفوس حرة والصدور مطمئنة والأرواح آمنة، وليس الفساد من أحكام الزمان وطوارق الحدثان ولكنه فساد في التربية والأخلاق سكنوا إليه وارتاحوا له ورضوا به وأقاموا عليه حتى صاروا يعدّون الخروج منه محنة والرجوع إلى السنّة بدعة وفشا فيهم داء التحاسد والتباغض والتنافر والتشاحن، ورسخ فيهم الجبن والخور والضعف والضجر والذهول والخمول والملل والكسل، فوصلنا بفضل هذا كله إلى الحال التي تراها ونحن الذين فعلنا ذلك أنفسنا بأنفسنا فمنّا الإثم والذنب وعلينا الملام والعتب.

الباشا أراك منذ اليوم تبالغ في الأمر وتغالي في الوصف، ولو فرضنا أنّ هذا الفساد عام، ألا يشذّ منه من ينبهكم إلى واجب شرعكم ويرشدكم إلى أصل دينكم «أليس منكم رجل رشيد؟»

عيسى بن هشام بلى فينا الرشيد والحصيف، وفينا العلماء والفضلاء والأذكياء والنبهاء والأتقياء والصلحاء، ولكن ما قام أحد إلّا ورموه بالخروج والشذوذ، واتهموه بالمروق والعقوق، وتلك أخلاق متأصلة في النفوس والناس في أسر التقليد، فيحجم المتقدم وتفتر العزائم ولم ترسخ لدينا الفضيلة إلى حد التهاون بأفكار الناس

world; Destiny and Time follow their course for a while and then come to a stop. As a result, they're a primary reason for the charge that's leveled against the noble Shariah—may it be purified and sanctified!—namely that its legal authority is deficient, its obligations are weakened, and it lacks fairness. They are all entirely happy with this appalling situation. Instead of upholding the law, they fool around with it. The kind of thing that they bother about now is: "During the ritual ablutions, is it legitimate to wipe your shoes if they are made of glass"—weird things like that. Everything has ground to a halt, whence the need to create the Native Court alongside the Shariah Court.

4.5

PĀSHĀ Shariah scholars must have an obvious excuse. They've been faced with either the objections and arguments of opponents or the oppressive tyranny of a powerful ruler. This has prevented them from following the right course and made them choose this pernicious path instead.

ʿĪSĀ It was nothing of the kind. People are free to choose and can form their own opinions independently. By so doing they may obtain peace of mind. The source of corruption is not the laws of time or unforeseen happenings. It's the consequence of faulty education and moral decline, something to which they're happily reconciled. It's reached such a stage now that any attempt to extricate themselves from this situation is regarded as a trial and any return to the genuine tenets of the religious law is seen as heresy. The diseases of mutual envy, hatred, discord, and rancor have spread among them; cowardice, lassitude, weakness, dissatisfaction, slackness, tedium, and laziness are now deeply ingrained inside them. As a result we've now reached the stage that you're witnessing. Since we've all done these things ourselves, the sin and responsibility is ours; we're the ones to blame.

PĀSHĀ I realize that you're exaggerating. But, even if we're to suppose that the corruption that you describe is widespread, isn't there some rare individual to point out to you the need for the law to be upheld and to guide you toward the true bases of your faith? Is there no one to offer you such guidance?

ʿĪSĀ Oh yes, we have such judicious counselors. There are scholars, men of virtue, intellectuals, true believers, and pious folk. But, whenever any of them takes a stand, he's immediately accused of being a deviant heretic. They call him a recalcitrant apostate. Such are the moral postures so deeply ingrained in the souls of people in the grip of conservative tradition. So the forward-looking person thinks twice, and ambitious ideas falter. Virtue is so lacking among us that people's ideas are scoffed at and their statements are

والازدراء بما يقولونه فينا، وفوق ذلك فإنّ السكون أسهل من الحركة، والراحة أهون من التعب. وأنا ما بالغت ولا غاليت وستطّلع بعينك فيما بعد على حقيقة ما أقول.

٦،٤ قال عيسى بن هشام: وبينا نحن في هذا الحديث إذ ارتجّ المكان وتماوج الزحام وأقبل القاضي وهو في عنفوان شبابه وصبا أيامه يتألق حسنا، ويشاكل في القد غصنا، وكأنه طائر في مشيته من نشاطه وخفته، يتّقد في وجهه الذكاء، وفي شمائله التيه والخيلاء. ولمّا دخل الجلسة ذهبت أسأل عن دور القضية ثم عدت إلى صاحبي فطلب مني أن أصل له ما كان انقطع من سلك الحديث بيننا فأجبت ولبيت.

عيسى بن هشام ... وأمّا المحاكم الأهلية فهي القضاء الذي يقضي على الأهالي في جميع الخصومات. وهذا الداخل هو من رجال تلك السلطة القضائية ووظيفته الحكم بين الأفراد على السواء طبقاً للقانون.

الباشا القانون الهمايوني؟

عيسى بن هشام القانون الإمبراطوري.

الباشا ما عهدت منك أن تعجم عليّ وتبهم.

عيسى بن هشام لا إعجام ولا إبهام، هو قانون نابوليون إمبراطور الفرنسويين.

الباشا وهل عاد الفرنسيس فأدخلوكم تحت حكمهم؟

عيسى بن هشام لا وإنما نحن الذين أدخلنا أنفسنا في حكمهم فاخترنا قانونهم ليقوم مقام شرعنا.

الباشا وهل هذا القانون مطابق للشرع وإلّا فإنهم يحكمون بغير ما أنزل الله؟

٧،٤ عيسى بن هشام هكذا يقول علماؤنا في سرّهم ونجواهم، ويظهر أنه مطابق للشرع بدليل ما أعلنه عالم من أكابر العلماء في الشريعة الإسلامية وأقسم الأيمان المغلظة على فتواه التي أفتاها لهم عند نشره بأنه غير مخالف للشرع. وإن كان لا عقاب فيه على الفسق واللواط مع رضا المفسوق به إن زاد عمره عن الثانية عشرة بيوم

despised. Not only that, but it's always easier to do nothing rather than take action; a life of ease is more convenient than one of exhaustion. I've not been exaggerating in my description, as you're about to see for yourself.

4.6 ʿĪsā ibn Hishām said: While we were conversing like this, the whole place was reverberating with the noise of people surging around in crowds. Then the Judge appeared. He was in the prime of his youth, still quite young, his face radiantly handsome. His stance made him look like a tree branch; with his light, energetic stride he seemed to be flying. When he entered the court, I went to ask when our case was coming up, then returned to my companion. He asked me to continue our conversation, and I duly responded to his request:

ʿĪsā The Native Court is the judicial authority that passes judgment on subjects today in all litigations in accordance with the stipulations of the law.

Pāshā Do you mean the Humāyūnī law code?[36]

ʿĪsā The Imperial Code.

Pāshā I don't remember you speaking in a foreign language or using obscure terms like that before!

ʿĪsā I'm doing neither. It's the Code of Napoleon who was Emperor of France.

Pāshā Have the French returned to Egypt and subjected you to their regime again?

ʿĪsā No. We're the ones who subjected ourselves to their authority. We chose their legal code to replace the Shariah in our country.

Pāshā Are this code's regulations consistent with those of the noble Shariah? If not, then you are being governed with something which was not sent down to earth by the Almighty.

4.7 ʿĪsā That's what Shariah scholars state in private confidential discussion. However, it seems that it is compatible with the holy law. As proof, one can cite the pronouncement made by a scholar of great eminence who swore a mighty oath on a legal decision which he'd given at the time of its promulgation to the effect that this French code was not at variance with the Islamic holy law, even though there's no punishment specified in the French code for adultery or homosexuality, provided that the object of affection agrees and is one day over twelve years of age; nor for anyone who commits incest with his

واحد. ولا عقاب على من يزني بأمه إذا رضيت به وكانت غير متزوجة، وهو يعد الأخ الذي يدافع عن عرض أخته ويحميه مجرماً جانياً، وكذلك بقية أهلها ما عدا الزوج. وهو الذي يحكم بإلزام المديونين بدفع الربا لمداينيهم. وهو الذي يقبل شهادة المرأة الواحدة على الرجل. وهو الذي لا يعاقب الزوج إذا سرق من امرأته، ولا المرأة من زوجها، ولا الولد من أبيه، ولا الأب من ابنه.

٨،٤ وأمّا المحاكم المختلطة ففيها القضاة الأجانب وهي تختص بالنظر فيما يقع من الخصومات بين الأهالي والأجانب، وبين الأجانب وبعضهم في الحقوق المدنية يعني في قضايا المال. ولمّا كان الأجانب هم أحق بالغنى لجدّهم ونشاطهم، وكان المصريون أحق بالفقر لإهمالهم وتراميهم على الأجنبي، كان معظم القضايا التي تحكم فيها هذه المحاكم ينتهي بسلخ المصري من عقاره وثروته.

وأمّا المجالس التأديبية فهي تختص بالنظر في عقاب الموظف الذي يخل بتأدية وظيفته وهي تؤلف في الغالب من نفس الرؤساء الذين يتهمونه وحدّها في العقاب الرفت والحرمان من المعاش وما بقي من درجات العقاب، فالنظر فيه للمحاكم الأهلية.

٩،٤ وأمّا المجالس الإدارية فهي تختص بعقاب من يخالف اللوائح والأوامر والمنشورات وشرح ذلك يطول.

وأمّا المحاكم العسكرية فهي تحكم على الضباط والعساكر والأهالي أيضاً في مسائل القرعة وغيرها.

والمحاكم القنصلية تختص بالنظر في الجنح التي تقع من الأجنبي على المصري ومن الأجنبي على الأجنبي من جنس واحد. امّا إذا وقعت جناية من أجنبي على مصري فليس لها في مصر من حكم أو عقاب ولا تختص محكمة من جميع هاتيك المحاكم التي عددتها لك بالنظر فيها بل يرتد الجاني بالقضية إلى وطنه ومسقط رأسه وديار قومه وأهله، فإذا نظر قضاته هناك فيما وقع منه من تلك الجناية لم يكن لهم بد من تبرئته «لعدم ثقتهم بتحقيق البوليس المصري ولضياع معالم القضية ولعدم توفر الشهود.»

mother, provided she assents and is unmarried. This is the legal code which considers a brother guilty of a criminal offense when he risks his life in the defense and protection of his sister's honor, and the same with the rest of her family beyond her husband; which decrees that debtors shall be compelled to pay interest to creditors; which is willing to accept the testimony of a single woman against a man; and which does not punish the husband who steals from his wife, nor the reverse, nor son from father, nor the reverse.

4.8 The Mixed Courts, which have foreign judges, specialize in investigating litigation between native people and foreigners, and amongst foreigners themselves on matters of civil rights, by which I mean cases involving money. Foreigners have a greater right to wealth because they are serious and work harder. Egyptians on the other hand deserve to be poor because they are negligent and leave everything to foreigners. As a result, the majority of cases in which these courts have competence to pass judgment inevitably result in Egyptians being deprived of their money and property.

Disciplinary Tribunals deal specifically with the punishment of officials who fail to carry out their job properly. They're usually made up of the same officials who charge the offenders. The severest sentences which they can impose are dismissal from office and loss of livelihood. The remaining degrees of sentence are referred back to be dealt with by the Native Courts.

4.9 Administrative Tribunals deal with the punishment of anyone who contravenes edicts, orders, and decrees. It would take ages to explain.

Military Courts are concerned with the punishment of officers and troops on a charge. They also have authority over people in questions of conscription and the like.

Consular Courts cover the supervision of misdemeanors committed by foreigners against Egyptians and by one foreigner against another of the same nationality. If a foreigner commits a felony against an Egyptian, the courts have no jurisdiction or power of punishment in Egypt; none of these courts which I have explained to you has any special authority in this matter. The offender is returned to his country of birth and homeland for trial. When judges there look into the case, they inevitably end up acquitting the criminal for "lack of confidence in the Egyptian police's investigation," "loss of data relevant to the case," and "lack of sufficient witnesses."

وأمّا المحكمة المخصوصة فهي تختص بمعاقبة الأهالي عند تعدّيهم على العساكر الأجنبية.

الباشا ما زلت تسمعني الغريب وتفهمني غير مفهوم، متى كان المصري يتعدّى على الجندي؟

١٠،٤ قال عيسى بن هشام: وفي أثناء هذا الكلام جاء دور قضيتنا فنودي الباشا فدخل مع المحامي في الجلسة وقام النائب فطلب الحكم على المتهم بمقتضى مادتي ١٢٤ و١٢٦ عقوبات لتعديه بالضرب على أحد رجال الضبطية القضائية في أثناء تأدية وظيفته، وبالمادة ٣٤٦ مخالفات لتعديه على المكاري بالإيذاء الخفيف.

القاضي (للمتهم) هل فعلت هذه التهمة؟

المحامي ما فعلنا.

١١،٤ قال عيسى بن هشام: واستحضروني شاهداً فسألني القاضي عمّا أعلمه في هذه المسألة فأجبته:

عيسى بن هشام إنّ لهذه الحادثة قصة عجيبة وحكاية غريبة وهي أنه . . .

القاضي (مقاطعاً) لا لزوم للقصة والتفصيل وقل لي عن معلوماتك.

عيسى بن هشام معلوماتي هي أنني كنت أزور القبور في فجر ليلة أطلب الموعظة وأنشد الاعتبار . . .

القاضي (مستثقلاً) لا لزوم لكثرة الكلام وأجبني على النقطة التي سألتك عنها فقط.

عيسى بن هشام بن هشام هذا ما أفعله من حكاية الواقعة وذلك أني رأيت رجلا خرج من . . .

القاضي (مشمئزاً) قلت لك إني لا أقبل التطويل ولا شرح الواقعة ولكن هل ضرب المتهم العسكري والحمار أم لا؟

عيسى بن هشام ما ضرب الحمار وإنما دفعه من شدة إلحاحه وما ضرب

Special Courts handle punishment for people who assault foreign troops.

PĀSHĀ You keep on giving me curious bits of information and explaining things I don't understand. When did Egyptians ever assault troops?!

4.10 While we were talking, our case was called. The Pāshā was summoned and entered the court with the Lawyer. The Attorney of the Parquet stood up and asked for a conviction against the accused, in accordance with articles 124 and 126 of the Penal Code, for an assault on a member of the judicial police during the execution of his duty, and with article 346, dealing with misdemeanors, for a minor assault on the Donkeyman.

JUDGE (*to the accused*) Did you commit the offence with which you have been charged?

LAWYER He did not.

4.11 ʿĪsā ibn Hishām said: They then brought me forward as a witness. The Judge proceeded to question me about my knowledge of the whole affair. I responded to his questions.

ʿĪSĀ The whole thing is a most peculiar tale. It started like this—

JUDGE (*interrupting*) There's no need to go into details. Just tell me what you know about it.

ʿĪSĀ What I know is that one night at daybreak I was visiting the graveyard in search of spiritual counsel and reflection.

JUDGE (*getting irritated*) There's no need to speak at length, just answer the point I asked you.

ʿĪSĀ That's what I was doing. I was telling you what happened. I saw a man coming out of—

JUDGE (*fidgeting*) I've just told you I won't accept any elaborate accounts of what happened. Did the accused strike the police officer and the Donkeyman?

ʿĪSĀ The accused did not strike the Donkeyman; he merely pushed him away because the Donkeyman was being so persistent. He didn't hit the

العسكري وإنما وقع عليه مما غشيه بغير عمد ولا قصد وهو يجهل . . .

القاضي يكفي. (ثم يلتفت ويقول) «النيابة.»

النائب إنّ هذا الباشا متهم بتعدّيه بالضرب على أحد رجال البوليس في أثناء تأدية وظيفته بالقسم وبالتعدّي بالإيذاء على مرسي الحمار والتهمة ثابتة من شهادة الشهود التي في الأوراق واطلاع المحكمة عليها كاف وبناء عليه فالنيابة تطلب الحكم على المتهم بالمادة ١٢٤ و١٢٦ عقوبات وبالفقرة الثانية من المادة ٣٤٦ مخالفات، وتطلب من عدالة المحكمة التشديد في العقوبة لأنّ حالة المتهم تستدعي ذلك فإنه يظن أن رتبته تجعله خارجاً عن سلطة القانون وتخوّله الحق في اعتبار بقية الناس أصغر منه فيؤدّبهم بنفسه مع عدم مراعاة حقوقهم وحرمة القانون. ولا شكّ أنّ تشديد العقوبة عليه واجب لاعتبار أمثاله به وللمساواة في العدالة وأفوّض الأمر إلى المحكمة. ١٢،٤

القاضي (للمحامي) المحاماة، مع الاختصار. ١٣،٤

المحامي (يتنحنح ويقلب في أوراقه) إننا نتعجب من أنّ النيابة العمومية استحضرتنا اليوم بصفة متهمين، ونقول إنّ أصل وقوع الجرائم في العالم والأصل في وضع الشرائع والقوانين منذ البداوة وعصور الهمجية. . .

القاضي (متأففاً) اختصر يا حضرة المحامي وادخل في الموضوع.

المحامي ومن المعلوم أنّ نظام الترتيب في طبقات الهيئة الاجتماعية. . .

القاضي (متضجراً) اختصر يا أفندي.

المحامي الموضوع يقتضي ذلك.

القاضي لا لزوم له.

المحامي (متحيراً) قالت النيابة العمومية (ويسرد شيئاً من أقوالها ثمّ يقول) ولو سلّمنا جدلاً. . .

القاضي (مغضباً) يكفي يا أفندي. الموضوع.

المحامي (متلعثماً) إنّ هذا المتهم الواقف بين يدي المحكمة هو رجل عظيم وأمير خطير من أهل الزمن القديم وله حديث منشور في الجرائد – وهذه أعداد جريدة

policeman either. He was feeling faint and simply fell on him by accident. He's quite unaware—

JUDGE All right, that's enough! Call the Attorney.

4.12 ATTORNEY This Pāshā stands accused of assaulting a member of the police during the course of his duties at the police station, and also of injuring Mursī the Donkeyman. The charge is substantiated by the witnesses' testimony in the dossier on the case. The court has enough information about all this. On that basis therefore, the Parquet demands that sentence be passed against the accused according to article 346 dealing with misdemeanors. It demands that the court must prove its integrity by showing no mercy in its sentence. The accused's attitude demands no less. He seems to be under the impression that his status exempts him from the authority of the law and gives him the right to regard the rest of the population as being less important than himself. So he disciplines them himself without regard to their rights and the sanctity of the law. He must undoubtedly be punished severely so as to provide an example and warning to people like him and to ensure that justice will be unbiased. I commit the case to the court.

4.13 JUDGE (*to the lawyer*) Now the defense, and make it brief.

LAWYER (*after clearing his throat and fumbling among his papers*) We are indeed amazed that the Attorney of the Parquet has summoned us here today describing us as the accused. What we say, your worship, is that, since desert civilization and the barbarian ages, the origin of the occurrence of crimes according to the law in this world was meant—

JUDGE (*in disgust*) Would my learned friend be brief and get to the point?

LAWYER It is well known, your worship, that the system of organization in the classes of human society demands—

JUDGE (*irritated*) My dear Sir, be brief.

LAWYER But the point at issue requires that—

JUDGE (*grumbling*) There is no need for all this.

LAWYER (*flustered*) The Attorney has said . . . (*here he quotes something from the Attorney's speech*), however, we claim that, were we to concede for argument's sake—

JUDGE (*annoyed*) That's enough, sir. Get to the point!

LAWYER (*stuttering and confused*) May it please the court, this accused man who now stands before the Judge is a man of importance and an amir of considerable standing in days of old. His story has been published in the

«مصباح الشرق» تطّلعون عليها - وقد اعترضه في طريقه أحد المكارين فدفعه عنه والناس يعلمون إلحاح الحمارة وسوء أدبهم ومثل هذه الطبقات ليس فيها تربية. . .

القاضي (وقد نفد صبره) قلنا اختصر يا أفندي.

المحامي (وهو يتصبب عرقًا) ولمّا توجه إلى القسم أغمي عليه فسقط بدون تعمّد على عسكري يكنس أرض القسم بغير ملابسه الرسمية وعدالة المحكمة تقضي بعدم الالتفات إلى دعوى البوليس ولا عقاب على المتهم البتة لأنه كان في زمان غير زماننا وفي نظام خلاف نظامنا، ولم تبلغه دعوة القانون فهو يجهل أحكامه وحضرة القاضي الفاضل أدرى بالأحوال وأنّ. . .

القاضي (منفعلاً ضاربًا بيده على المكتبة) المحكمة تنورت يا أفندي ولا لزوم للكلام فهلم طلباتك.

المحامي (ساخطًا في نفسه) طلباتنا هي أننا نطلب من باب أصلي الحكم ببراء المتهم وإن رأت المحكمة غير ذلك فنرجو استعمال الرأفة بالمادة ٣٥٢ عقوبات.

قال عيسى بن هشام: وبعد ذلك نطق القاضي بالحكم فحكم على المتهم بالحبس سنة ونصفًا بمقتضى المادتين المذكورتين من قانون العقوبات وبخمسة قروش والمصاريف بالمادة المذكورة أيضًا في المخالفات. فضاقت الأرض بي وأظلمت الدنيا في عيني وكدت أشترك مع صاحبي في الإغماء لولا أنّ المحامي أكّد لي أنه لا بدّ من البراءة في الاستئناف لعدالة رجاله وأنه يلزمنا أن نرفع عريضة شكوى إلى لجنة المراقبة لما في ذلك من حسن التأثير على القضية عند نظرها في الاستئناف، وأنه لو كان أحد أعضاء اللجنة حاضرًا في هذه الجلسة لما استطاع القاضي أن يأتي ما أتاه. ثمّ قال اعلم أنّ السبب في كل هذه المقاطعة والمعاكسة وطلب الاختصار والاستعجال وكل ما صدر من حضرة القاضي معنا هو لأنه مدعو إلى وليمة عند بعض أصحابه في الساعة الواحدة بعد الظهر، وأمامه في دور القضايا ثلاثون قضية يريد أن يأتي عليها كلها قبل حلول الميعاد. ١٤،٤

papers; here are the numbers of *Miṣbāḥ al-sharq* for you to examine.[37] While he was walking, a donkeyman kept blocking his path, so he pushed him aside. Now we're all well aware of how persistent and uncouth donkeymen and uneducated people like them can be—

JUDGE (*losing all patience*) Listen, my good Sir, I've told you to be brief!

LAWYER (*sweat pouring off him*) When the accused reached the police station, he fainted and fell unintentionally on a policeman out of uniform who was sweeping the station floor. The integrity of the court therefore demands that no attention be paid to the police claims. There can be no charge against the accused whatsoever. He lived in an age different from our own; in his day the whole system was different. He has never heard of the demands of the law, so he is unaware of its regulations. Your worship knows the situation best of all, and if—

JUDGE (*pounding the desk with his hand in annoyance*) The court has been enlightened, so there's absolutely no need for all this talk. Get on with your demands.

LAWYER (*suppressing his own anger*) We have two demands. We ask that the accused be acquitted as a matter of principle. If the court decides otherwise, then we hope that, in accordance with article 352 of the Penal Code, it will show due clemency.

4.14 ʿĪsā ibn Hishām said: The Judge proceeded to deliver his verdict. In accordance with the two articles of the Penal Code as cited, he condemned the Pāshā to a year and a half's imprisonment and fined him five piasters with costs as stipulated by the article on misdemeanors also mentioned above. I found this too much to bear; the world darkened before my eyes. I would certainly have joined my companion in a swoon of astonishment, had not the Lawyer given us every possible assurance that the Pāshā was bound to be acquitted at the Court of Appeal because of the fairness of its members. However, he told us that, besides that, we would have to raise a grievance with the Committee of Surveillance so as to present the case in a favorable light when it was considered at the appeal. "I want you to realize," he told me, "that the Judge kept interrupting and hurrying me on because he's been invited to the banquet of a friend of his at 1 p.m. He's got thirty cases on his agenda, and intends to pass sentence in all of them before his appointment."

عيسى بن هشام لا حول ولا قوّة إلا بالله العظيم. وماذا أقول إلا ما قاله ١٥،٤
الشاعر الحكيم؟:

أنهاك أن تلي الخصومة أو ترى
حلف الخطابة أو إمام المسجد
وذر الإمارة واتخاذك درة
في المصر تحسبها حسام المنجد
تلك الأمور كرهتها لأقارب
وأصادق فابخل بنفسك أوجد.

ʿĪsā ibn Hishām said: God Almighty alone is the possessor of power and might! What could I say other than quote the words of the wise poet, al-Maʿarrī: 4.15

I forbid you to pursue controversy or to be seen
as linked to preaching or mosque-imam.
Abandon princedom and using a whip in the city,
thinking it a champion's sword.
These things have I despised in relatives
and friends alike. It were better to stint your own self.

١٫٥ قال عيسى بن هشام: أشار علينا محامينا بعد أن قدّم العريضة إلى لجنة المراقبة بأن نتوجه للسؤال عنها وقال لنا أنه كان يود مرافقتنا إلى نظارة الحقانية ولكن يمنعه عن ذلك أنّ القاضي الذي هو موضوع الشكوى لمقاطعته علينا في الشهادة والمرافعة ربما تعمّد أذاه في المستقبل إذا علم أنه هو المباشر لشكايته إلى اللجنة أو المغري لموكله عليها وهو في حاجة دائمة إلى اجتناب غضبه ودوام رضاه. ولما استفززت الباشا إلى حيث أشار المحامي أعرض ونأى بجانبه واشتدّ في الأباء ولجّ في الامتناع وقال:

الباشا يكفيني ما قد وصلت إليه من الذل والهوان وحط الكرامة ونزول القدر وحلول الضيم بحكم القضاء من السماء وأنا أربأ بنفسي أن يجتمع عليها ذلان في سلك واحد، ذل المتحمّل للظلم الصابر على الإساءة وذل المشتكي الضارع والمتظلم الخاضع. فإليك عني ولا تكن عوناً للخطوب، ومفتاحاً للكروب، وإلى الله المشتكى وبه الانتصاف ﴿رَبِّ السِّجْنُ أَحَبُّ إِلَيَّ مِمَّا يَدْعُونَنِي إِلَيْهِ﴾. ويعلم الله أنه لولا عذاب النار لفرّجت عن همي بالانتحار، ولوددت لو كان ذلك القاضي استبدل حكم الحبس بالإعدام، وأراحني من هذه الآلام، وقد عشت في عصري ودهري ما علمت أنّ السجن يكون في عقاب الأمراء وإنما هو من جملة العقوبات لغوغاء الناس وسفلة العامة. وللأمراء الامتياز في كل حال، فإن كان ثمّ لنا عقاب، فضرب الرقاب، ولقاء المنون أهون لدينا من ظلمة السجون.

٢٫٥ عيسى بن هشام ما كنت أعهد من مثلك الجزع والفزع، والخور والهلع، وأنت الشجاع والبطل، وما الشجاعة إلا الصبر على المكروه ومقابلة الخطوب في إقدامها بالوجه الطلق والنفس المطمئنة.

Our Lawyer forwarded a petition to the Committee of Surveillance and suggested that we should go to inquire about it. He told us that he would like to deal with it himself, but he was prevented from so doing by the realization that the Judge who was the subject of the complaint because of his continuous interruptions during the evidence phase might well make a determined effort to do him some harm in the future. He would be aware that the Lawyer was the one who had lodged the complaint with the Committee or been its primary instigator. Lawyers, he told us, must always avoid annoying judges and foster their goodwill. 5.1

When I urged the Pāshā to follow the Lawyer's suggestion, he shied away, adamantly refusing to come and being persistently obstructive. This is what he kept saying:

PĀSHĀ I've had enough. The utter humiliation, injustice, damage, loss of honor, and lack of respect that I've endured as a result of the Creator's predestined decree are more than enough. I couldn't bear the thought of putting up with two humiliations at once: enduring oppression and submitting to injustice on the one hand, while making weak and humble complaints on the other. Just leave me alone! Don't give these misfortunes any more encouragement; don't serve as the key to open up any more troubles. One should complain to God alone, and through Him alone comes recompense. «Lord, I prefer prison to the thing to which they are summoning me.»[38] God knows, I would have sought release from my worries through suicide, were it not for the punishment of hellfire. I only wish that the prison sentence could be changed to one of death, so that I could escape from these dreadful misfortunes. Throughout my life I never heard of a prison sentence being given to any amir. In our time, it was only applied as a punishment to the plebs and lowest classes. At least amirs had this special privilege: if the question of sentence ever arose, it was execution. It would be far easier to face death rather than gloomy prisons.

ʿĪSĀ I've never noticed such panic and fear in a person like you, nor do I expect to encounter such cowardly resignation from you, the dauntless, courageous hero. Courage consists merely of showing endurance in the face of adversity, and confronting the circumstances in which you find yourself with a cheerful and calm equanimity. 5.2

رُبَّمَا تَجْزَعُ النُّفُوسُ مِنَ الأَمْـرِ
لَهُ فَـرْجَـةٌ كَحَـلِّ العِقَالِ

وأنت العاقل والحازم، وما العقل إلا نفاذ الرأي في كشف الملمة، وتسديد الحيلة في إزاحة الغمه. وأمامنا طرق شريفة ووسائل مشروعة لا غضاضة علينا في سلوكها ولا مضاضة في استعمالها. واعلم أنّ تبدل الأزمان وتحوّل الأحوال يغير من هيئة الأمور واعتبار الأشياء، فما كان يعتبر فضيلة في زمن مضى يعتبر رذيلة في زمن حدث، وما كان يعدّه الناس بالأمس نقصاً أصبح يعدّ اليوم كمالاً. وإن كان الشرف في السطوة والمنعة والبأس والبطش فيما غبر من الأيام فإنّ الشرف كل الشرف اليوم في الاستكانة للأحكام والخضوع للقانون فهلمّ نسلك سبيله ونأخذ طريقه عسانا أن ننتهي إلى الخلاص والنجاء ممّا وقعنا فيه من البلاء.

الباشا لطعم الموت الزؤام أهون عليّ من هذا الكلام، وللشرب من حميم آن آثر عندي من ورود هذا الذل الآن.

٣،٥ قال عيسى بن هشام: وبينا نحن في هذا الحديث والجدال وقد اعتلت عليّ وجوه الآراء في صرفه عن ذلك الأباء. وكدت أيأس من بلوغ الغاية في الهداية، إذ سمعنا منادياً ينادي من باعة الجرائد: المقطم والمؤيد ! الأهرام ومصر ! الأربعة بقرش صاغ.

الباشا ماذا أسمع من الأعاجيب! أأصبحت الجبال والجوامع والآثار والبلاد تباع على الناس بالمزاد؟:

لقد ضل الأنام بغير شك
فجدوا في الزمان أو العبوه

عيسى بن هشام ما هي بالبلاد ولا الآثار وإنما تلك أسماء انتحلت إعلاماً لهذه الجرائد اليومية.

Hearts will often panic because of something
which can be resolved like the untying of a cord.[39]

In my opinion, you're a man of the very soundest resolve and steadiest intellect. Intelligence involves the effective use of thought to rid oneself of misfortunes and devising a scheme to put an end to anxieties. At our disposal today we have a variety of sanctioned and prescribed courses of action. We will suffer no disgrace or harm by making use of them. You must realize that changing times and the fickle vicissitudes of life alter the basis of things and bring about modifications in the way in which one looks at them. What was considered a virtue in the past is regarded as depravity on the morrow; behavior which was regarded as a failing in past ages is now considered a virtue. In the past, nobility may indeed have derived its splendor from forceful authority and used brute strength to support itself, but today nobility in every sense demands submission to the regulations of the law. Come on then, and let's follow this course of action! We may eventually be rid of these misfortunes and escape safe and sound from the troubles we are experiencing.

PĀSHĀ The taste of violent death would be easier for me than what you suggest. I would rather drink boiling water than suffer such humiliation.

5.3 ʿĪsā ibn Hishām said: We continued this discussion, but the various suggestions I made to change my companion's stubbornly defiant attitude failed to achieve anything. I was on the point of giving up my attempt to carry out my intention of advising and guiding him. Just then, we heard a newspaper vendor shouting in a voice so hideous that it was even worse than a donkey braying: "*Al-Muʾayyad* and *Al-Muqaṭṭam*, *Al-Ahrām* and *Miṣr*, all four for a piaster."

PĀSHĀ What incredible things I keep hearing! Have mosques, mountains, monuments, and countries become things one can purchase by auction in the market?

Without a doubt mankind has been disturbed;
so be serious about time, or else make sport with it.[40]

ʿĪSĀ Those names aren't monuments or countries! They're used as titles for daily newspapers.

الباشا لعلك تعني جرائد الصيارف ويومياتهم أو جرائد الالتزام ولكن ما وجه هذه التعمية في التسمية؟

عيسى بن هشام ليس الأمر ما ذهبت إليه ولكن الجرائد عبارة عن أوراق تطبع كل يوم أو كل أسبوع أو كل شهر تجمع فيها الأحوال العمومية الجارية ليطلع الناس على أخبار الناس. وهي أثر من آثار المدنية الغربية انتقل إلينا فيما انتقل منها، والأصل في وظيفتها انتشار الحمد للفضيلة، والذم للرذيلة، والانتقاد على ما قبح من الأعمال، والحث على ما حسن من الأفعال، والتنبيه إلى موضع الخلل، والحض على إصلاح الزلل، وتعريف الأمّة بأعمال الحكومة فلا تجري بها إلى غير المصلحة، وتعريف الحكومة بحاجات الأمّة فتسعى في قضائها. وبالجملة فهي في مقام الآمرين بالمعروف الناهين عن المنكر الذين أشارت الشريعة الإسلامية إليهم.

٤،٥ الباشا قد كنّا نسمع في زماننا بشيء من هذا القبيل يقال له «غازيته» وكانت تصدر عندنا واحدة باسم «روزنامة وقائع» تذكر فيها المدائح والتهاني وانتقال الركاب العالي. ولكن إن كانت الجرائد اليوم على ما تزعم فلا بد أن يكون قد اشتغل بها وقام بأمرها جماعة العلماء الأعلام والمشايخ الكرام ونعمت الوسيلة وحسنت الطريقة في تبليغ الناس ما ينفعهم في معاشهم ومعادهم.

عيسى بن هشام علماؤنا ومشايخنا أبعد الناس عن اجتياز هذا الطريق، وهم يرون الاشتغال به بدعة من البدع وفضولاً تنهى الشريعة عنه وتداخلاً فيما لا يعني فيجتنبونها وربما اختلفوا في كراهة الاطّلاع على الجرائد أو إباحته. وقد مارس هذه الصناعة قوم آخرون فيهم الفاضل وغير الفاضل، واتخذها بعضهم حرفة للتعيش منها بأي طريقة كانت فلا تجد فرقاً بينهم وبين باعة الأسواق في الغش والخداع والكذب والنفاق والاحتيال للاغتيال.

Pāshā By newspapers do you perhaps mean the lists and daily sheets used by money changers, or are they lists of tax farms? But what's the point of these obscure titles?

ʿĪsā Things are not as you think. Newspapers are sheets of paper printed daily, weekly, or monthly, in which news and stories of public interest are collected and reported, so that people can find out about public affairs. They are one of the aspects of Western civilization that we've imported into our own society. The purpose of issuing papers is to publish articles which give due credit for value and merit; and to rebuke depravity, to criticize bad actions and encourage good ones, to draw attention to points of imperfection, and to urge people to correct mistakes. They are meant to tell people what the government is doing on their behalf, so that it doesn't drag them into anything against their interest, and also to let the government know about the people's needs so that it can endeavor to satisfy them. To sum up, those who run the press occupy the position of "those who command good deeds and prohibit bad deeds" as referred to in the Islamic Shariah.

5.4

Pāshā We used to hear about something of the kind in our time called "Gazette." One of them was published in Turkish called *The Daily Record of Events*. Eulogies and congratulations were recorded in them, and there were notes about movements of the Viceregal entourage. But, if the status of newspapers today has been raised to the level you claim, then the most eminent scholars and important shaykhs must be involved in their production. It is an excellent means of informing people about things which will benefit them in their present life and help them in the hereafter. So let me take a look at one of them.

ʿĪsā Our scholars and shaykhs are of all people the least likely to follow this course and pursue the journalistic profession. They consider working in it to be heresy. They've dubbed it innovation (which the Shariah forbids) and interference in matters of no concern to anyone. So they ignore newspapers and often disagree as to whether or not it's even permissible to read them. But other people have chosen it as a profession, some of them worthy, others unworthy. Some have used it as a means of earning a living by all possible means. So you'll find them no different from tradesmen and market vendors. They are all as fraudulent, treacherous, lying, hypocritical, cunning, and crafty as one another when it comes to looting and murdering:

عمّـروا موضـعَ التصنّع فيهـم
ومكانُ الإخـلاصِ منهـم خـرَابُ

فذهب الغرض المقصود منها وانحطّ شأنها في أعين العامة فما بال الخاصة، وأصبح ما يرجى فيها من النفع دون ما تجلبه من الضرر. والعقلاء لا يزالون يرجون من مرور الزمن أن يذهب من هذه الحال ويضع هذه الصناعة في الموضع اللائق بها من الشرف وعلو المكان. والحكم كله للقارئين في الإقبال على ما ينفع والإضراب عمّا يضر ﴿فَأَمَّا الزَّبَدُ فَيَذْهَبُ جُفَاءً ۖ وَأَمَّا مَا يَنفَعُ النَّاسَ فَيَمْكُثُ فِي الْأَرْضِ﴾.

٥،٥ ونادیت البائع فاشتريت منه وفتحت واحدة أقرأ على صاحبي نتفًا منها فإذا فيها كلام عن الحكم على أحمد سيف الدين واستعطاف للقلوب عليه وطلب للعفو عنه ووصف لما يقاسيه من خشونة الملبس والمطعم في سجنه واستدرار للدموع على حالة هذا الغلام من سلالة الولاة والأمراء، ولمّا انتهيت من قراءة ذلك التفت إلى الباشا وقلت له:

عيسى بن هشام انظر كيف وصل بنا الحال في المساواة في الحكم وقد سمعت ما جرى «للبرنس» أحمد سيف الدين فكيف تأبى بعد ذلك الخضوع للقانون والامتثال لأحكامه والتوسل بطرقه للخلاص ممّا وقعت فيه.

الباشا ما هو البرنس، ومن هو أحمد سيف الدين؟

٦،٥ عيسى بن هشام أمّا البرنس فهو لقب أجنبي كان يتلقب به رؤساء الدولة الرومانية قبل أن يجترؤوا على الأمّة بانتحال لقب «إمبراطور» ثم صار يطلق بعدهم في أوربا على بعض أعضاء بيت الملك ورؤساء الحكومات الصغيرة. واليوم يطلقه على أنفسهم أعضاء العائلة الخديوية ذكورًا وإناثًا، وإن كان لا ذِكر له في ألقاب الدولة الرسمية. وأمّا أحمد سيف الدين فهو أحمد بن إبراهيم بن أحمد بن إبراهيم بن محمد علي جد العائلة الخديوية وأساسها، وقد ارتكب جناية فسحبوه أمام المحاكم ونال العقاب الذي يوجبه القانون فحكمت عليه المحكمة الابتدائية بسجن سنوات سبع فاستأنف

They have peopled the site of hypocrisy among themselves,
but the haven of loyalty lies in ruins.[41]

The original intentions of the press and the respect which it commanded have foundered ever since its standing fell among the élite and the benefits expected from it proved to be less than the damage it caused. Some sensible people still hope that one day the situation can be rectified and the profession elevated to the noble and worthy position it deserves. The whole question lies in the hands of readers. They must focus on what is beneficial and reject what is harmful. «Dross metal disappears as rubbish; what benefits people remains on the earth.»[42]

5.5 I called out to the vendor and bought papers from him. I opened one of them to read some items of news to my friend. There was some news about the sentence passed on Aḥmad Sayf al-dīn, the sympathy people felt for him, and the attempts to obtain a pardon. It described the coarse clothing and poor food he was having to deal with in prison, enough to bring tears to the eyes when contemplating the fate of this young man, a scion of princes and rulers. Once I had finished reading, I turned to the Pāshā and said:

ʿĪsā Just observe how circumstances have made us equals. You've just heard about the sentence passed on Prince Aḥmad Sayf al-dīn by the court judge. Having heard that, how can you still refuse to submit to the law, conform with its regulations, and make use of its channels to get out of the situation in which you find yourself?

Pāshā What's this word "prince," and who's Aḥmad Sayf al-dīn?

5.6 ʿĪsā "Prince" is a foreign title given to heads of the Roman Empire before they had the audacity in the face of the populace to adopt the title of Emperor. Later on, it came to be used in Europe to apply to members of the royal family and to heads of petty governments. Today male and female members of the Khedive's family call themselves by it, even though it's not included in the list of official Ottoman titles. Aḥmad Sayf al-dīn is in fact Aḥmad ibn Ibrāhīm ibn Aḥmad ibn Ibrāhīm ibn Muḥammad ʿAlī, the latter the ancestor and founder of the present Khedive's family. He committed a felony, was dragged before the courts, and incurred the penalty laid down by the law. The Court of First Instance sentenced him to seven years' imprisonment. He appealed, asking the Court of Appeal judges for clemency. They reduced his sentence to five

يلتمس الرأفة والشفقة من قضاة الاستئناف فاستبدلوها بخمس ثم استغاث بمحكمة النقض والإبرام ولا تغيثه. وقد انصرفت المساعي لاتفاق أعضاء العائلة الخديوية على التماس العفو عنه وذهبت أمّه يميناً وشمالاً فلم تبق وسيلة من وسائل الاسترحام والاستعطاف إلا سلكتها، ولكن القانون فوق الكل. فهل يجوز لك الشموخ والأنفة والترفع عن التوسل والتظلم والسعي وراء لجنة المراقبة والاستئناف وقد علمت من تاريخ الأمراء ما علمت؟

الباشا كيف لا تخر الجبال الشم إذا استنزلوا منها الأراوي العصم؟ وكيف لا تنشق القبور وينفخ في الصور، لقد انحط المقام والقدر، وحقت كلمة ربك على مصر ﴿فَجَعَلْنَا عَالِيَهَا سَافِلَهَا﴾؟ وما دام حفيد محمد علي في السجن يخضع لهذا القانون ويتوسل بتلك الوسائل وتتشفع أمه بتلك الشفاعات فما عليَّ من عار فيما تدعوني إليه وليتهم يقبلونني فداء لابن سادتي، وأولياء نعمتي، فتضاف عقوبته إلى عقوبتي، فهلمّ بنا إلى حيث تريد.

٧،٥ قال عيسى بن هشام: فصحبني وهو مختنق بدمعه متعثر بقدمه حتى وصلنا نظارة الحقانية فدخلنا إلى محل لجنة المراقبة فهدونا إلى حجرة المفتشين فحاولنا الدخول فمنعنا الحاجب وطلب من الباشا «الكارت.»

الباشا ما هذا اللفظ الأعجمي؟

عيسى بن هشام هو عبارة عن وريقة يطبع فيها الزائر اسمه فيقدمها قبل الدخول ليكون المزور بالاختيار في قبول الزيادة أو التخلص منها.

الباشا قد كانت أبواب التظلم في أيامنا مفتوحة لمن يطرقها وكيف ينطبق هذا التضييق على ما تزعمه من المساواة والعدالة؟

عيسى بن هشام لا يسلم الحال من زيارة زائر بغير شغل أو إلحاح من صاحب شغل فوضعوا ذلك ليتفرغ الحكام لعملهم.

years. Then he asked the Court of Cassation for assistance, but obtained none. Efforts were made to arrange for members of the Khedive's family to request that he be pardoned. His mother went this way and that, trying every possible means of asking for clemency, but the law applies to everyone. So how can you deem it proper to hold yourself aloof by refusing to submit a grievance petition? Now that you have heard about the history of princes, are you still too proud to pursue your case with the Committee of Surveillance and the Court of Appeal?

PĀSHĀ Lofty mountains must inevitably crumble when the whitefooted mountain goats are brought down. Graves must be split asunder and the trumpet be blown when all ideas of dignity have vanished and all values have been debased. The words of the Almighty have come true with regard to Egypt: «And We have made its highest parts into its lowest parts.»[43] As long as you tell me that Muḥammad ʿAlī's descendant is in prison, is conforming with the law's regulations, and using these avenues for submitting a petition, while his mother tries to intercede on his behalf, then I can see no disgrace in what you're asking me to do. So take me wherever you wish. I only hope that they will accept my wish to act as ransom for the son of my masters and benefactors. Then his sentence can be added to mine.

5.7 ʿĪsā ibn Hishām said: The Pāshā accompanied me to the Ministry of Justice. He kept dragging his feet and choking back his tears. We entered the place where the Committee of Surveillance sat. They directed us to the inspectors' room and we tried to enter, but an orderly stopped us and asked the Pāshā for his "carte."

PĀSHĀ What does that foreign word mean?

ʿĪSĀ The "carte" is a small piece of paper on which visitors write their name. They're supposed to show it before entering an office. The person being visited can then decide whether to receive the visitor or avoid seeing him.

PĀSHĀ In our day, channels for complaint were open to anyone who wished to use them. How can this restriction be in keeping with the equality of rights and justice in matters of law that you've been talking about?

ʿĪSĀ That system provides no safeguards against visits from idle callers or importunate petitioners. So this method has been evolved to give authorities enough time to perform their duties.

الباشا ألم تكن هيبة الحكام وعظمتهم كافية في صد مثل هؤلاء عن تعطيلهم؟

٨،٥ قال عيسى بن هشام: وكتبت ورقة فيها اسم الباشا فجاءنا الحاجب بالإذن فدخلنا فوجدنا في الحجرة فتى من الشبان، قد التحى قبل الأوان، فترى ماء الشباب يتموّج في محيّاه تحت الشعر كما يتموّج الضوء في وسط هالة البدر. ولمّا اقتربنا منه كل الاقتراب رأيت في يده قائمة حساب يقلّبها، وأوراقاً يجمعها ويضربها، ثمّ يضع يده على جبهته كمن يتذكر رقماً ضاع من حسبته، وعن يمينه كتاب أعجمي، وعن شماله كتاب عربي، فتأملت فإذا كتاب اليمين لفولتير الفيلسوف الفرنسوي الملحد، وكتاب الشمال لمحي الدين بن العربي المتصوف الموحد.

ولمّا سألنا هذا المفتش عن حاجتنا قصصت عليه القصة وما عاملنا به القاضي من المقاطعة في الشهادة والمرافعة وذكرته بالعريضة التي قدّمناها فقاطع عليَّ الباشا في الكلام وقال له: وأعجب ما في النازلة وأدهى ما في القضية وأمرّ ما في الأمر أنّ الذي تسمّونه «النائب» اعتبر رتبتي سبباً لإهانتي وماكنت أتخيل في الأحلام أنّ الرتبة التي نلتها باقتحام الأخطار واحتمال المشاق تكون جريمة لا تغتفر وبرهاناً سديداً لديه يستند به في تشديد دعواه ويطالب به تشديد العقوبة، فقولوا لي بالله متى كانت الرتبة تستوجب العقاب والانتقام، ومن أي صنف أنتم بين صنوف الأنام. . . ؟

٩،٥ قال عيسى بن هشام: ودخل أحد الزائرين في هذه الأثناء فحمدت الله على انقطاع الكلام وإلّا فقد كان الباشا اندفع فيه بما يتعذر تلافيه، فسلّم الزائر وسأل عمّا حدث من الأخبار في وجه النهار، فناوله المفتش خطبة يتفكه بقراءتها بعد أن بالغ له في بلاغتها، وما كاد يلتفت إلينا حتى وافاه أحد المفتشين من الأجانب فأطلعه على رسم في ورقة زعم أنه رسمه في أثناء مناقشة قانونية كان مشتغلاً بالخصام والجدال فيها فضحك

PĀSHĀ But isn't the very prestige and kudos that people in authority have sufficient to prevent the kind of people you have mentioned from stopping in and bothering them?

5.8 ʿĪsā ibn Hishām said: I wrote a little slip with the Pāshā's name on it. The orderly came back to tell us we could go in. We entered and found in front of us a young man with a premature growth of beard; signs of his youth welled up like a spring beneath it just as light swells in the midst of the moon's halo. As we moved a little closer, I noticed that he had an account sheet in his hand which he turned over and other papers that he kept piling together and pounding. Then he put his hand to his forehead like someone trying to remember a figure which is missing from his calculations. On his right was a foreign book, on his left an Arabic book. I took a look at them: the former was by Voltaire, the French atheist philosopher; the latter by Muḥyī al-dīn Ibn ʿArabī, the monist Ṣūfī. When the Inspector asked us our business, I told him the whole story and mentioned the way the Judge had kept interrupting the testimony of the defense lawyer. I described for him the petition that we had presented. At this point the Pāshā interrupted me and spoke to the Inspector:

PĀSHĀ The worst thing at the trial, the bitterest stroke of all in the entire matter, was that the man whom you call the Attorney of the Parquet considered my rank to be sufficient cause to insult me. Never in my dreams did I imagine that the rank that I obtained by rushing without regard into perilous missions and enduring great hardships would turn out to be an unpardonable crime, something that would in his view provide a conclusive proof to support his claims, something to be used as a pretext for demanding that the sentence be more severe. Tell me, by God, since when has this noble rank of mine deserved punishment and vengeance? Furthermore, where do you belong within the various species of mankind?

5.9 ʿĪsā ibn Hishām said: At this point another visitor came in. I thanked God that his entrance had interrupted the Pāshā. But for that, he might well have said things that could not have been put right. Once the visitor had offered his greetings, he asked what news there was at the start of the day. The inspector expressed his great admiration for a speech he had been reading for amusement and handed it over to him. He had only just turned his attention to us again when a foreign inspector came to see him and showed him a drawing

الشاب من الرسم وأعجب بإتقان التصوير ثم تخلّص منه واشتغل بنا فتكلم مع الباشا كلاماً عذباً لطيفاً لتطييب خاطره بما ينبئ عن كرامة نسبه وحسن أدبه ثمّ قال له:

المفتش (للباشا) قد اطلعت على ظروف القضية في «مصباح الشرق» فأمّا القاضي فقد يكون له العذر في مقاطعة المحامي لأنّ منهم من تعوّد أن يأتي في مرافعاته بتاريخ نشأة الخليقة وتأليف الجمعية الإنسانية وما يجري هذا المجرى ممّا يطول شرحه ولا صلة له بجوهر القضية مطلقاً، وطالما استعملوه في أبسط القضايا وأهونها ليقتنع صاحب القضية أنّ محاميه لم يدّخر عنه كلاماً يقال في الدفاع عن حقه بقطع النظر عن ربح القضية أو خسرانها وكثير من أرباب القضايا يعتقدون أنّ المحامي لا يستحق أجره من المال إلّا بكثرة ما يقال كبضاعة التجار يكون تقدير ثمنها على قدر وزنها، وقد توقف أحدهم مرة عن دفع المتأخر من أتعاب المحامي بعد أن ربح له قضيته بدعوى أنه لم يسمع منه كلاماً مطوّلاً في المرافعة يستحق عليه الأجر سواء أفاد ذلك القضية أو أضرّ بها، ووقت القاضي ثمين قصير فلا يسعه إلا المقاطعة على المحامي المكثر في كلامه. وكذلك تكون المقاطعة على الشاهد لمجرد التنبيه إلى وقائع الحادثة لئلّا يفوتها بالخروج عنها. ولم يخالف القاضي القانون فيما أتاه.

الباشا ليت شعري إذا اعتذرت عن القاضي في مقاطعته بالقانون فما هو العذر في وضعه لي في قفص المتهمين وإلزامي بالقيام عند كل سؤال وأنا رجل كهل مسن قضيت عمري في وظائف الحكومة المصرية العالية وبذلت حياتي في خدمة العائلة الخديوية؟ فهلّا وقّرني لسنّي واحترمني لقدري وأيّ قانون في الدنيا يمنعه من ذلك؟ وتوقير السن قانون طبيعي واحترام المقامات أمر أصلي ﴿وَرَفَعْنَا بَعْضَهُمْ فَوْقَ بَعْضٍ دَرَجَاتٍ﴾. ١٠،٥

المفتش ذلك ما يقضي به القانون أيضاً فإنه قائم على المساواة بين الناس ولا فرق بين المقامات والأعمار وهذا عين ما يأمر به الشرع الشريف وعين ما يجري على أعضاء العائلة الخديوية وخاصة الحكام إذا ارتكب أحدهم ما يؤاخذه القانون

on a piece of paper which he claimed to have drawn during a legal discussion in which he had been involved in arguments and disputation. The young man looked at it and laughed, admiring the fine craftsmanship, then got rid of him so that he could attend to us. He addressed the Pāshā in a sympathetic tone that showed his noble background and good breeding. He finished by saying:

INSPECTOR (*to the Pāshā*) I've already studied the angles of the case in *Miṣbāḥ al-sharq*. The Judge may well have a good reason for interrupting the lawyer. Some of them make a habit of including the history of mankind's creation, the formation of human society, and other similar matters, into their defense speech. Such antics lead to lengthy expositions and have no relevance whatsoever to the point of the case. Such lawyers will often insist on using such devices in the simplest and most trifling cases in order to convince their client that no word has been left unsaid in his defense, regardless of whether the case is won or lost. Thus, one finds some clients who believe that the lawyer only earns his fee by the amount said, just like an article that is costed according to its weight. One of them once refused to pay his lawyer the fees in arrears even after winning his case, claiming that he had not heard him make a long enough defense speech to deserve the fee, regardless of whether it achieved good or bad results. The judge's time is both short and valuable, so the only thing he can do is to interrupt any lawyer who makes lengthy speeches. The judge will also interrupt the witness in order to direct his attention to the facts of the case so that he will not omit anything by getting off the point. In short, the judge in no way contravened the law in the way in which he treated you.

5.10

PĀSHĀ Now that you've explained away the Judge's interruptions, I wish I knew what excuse there can be for putting me in the prisoner's dock and making me stand for every question. I'm an old man who spent his life filling the highest positions in the Egyptian government and gave his blood freely in the service of the Khedive's family. Why did he show no consideration for my age and no respect for my position? What law is there in the world to prevent him from doing that? Reverence for age is something inborn; respect for people of high rank is something innate. God Almighty says in the Qur'an: «We have raised some of them above others in degrees.»[44]

INSPECTOR The law stipulates that as well. It's based on the concept of equality. In the eyes of the law, there's no difference in either age or status. This is exactly in accordance with the commands of the noble Shariah and applies in particular to members of the Khedive's family and people in authority when

عليه. ولا معرة عليك في وقوفك أمام القاضي فإنما تقف أمام النائب عن الحضرة الخديوية وهي أكبر الدرجات.

الباشا إن كان هذا حكمكم في القاضي فما هو الحكم في ذلك النائب وتعييره لي برتبتي؟

١١،٥ المفتش أنا لم أطّلع على أوراق القضية ولكن مرافعة النائب على ما جاء في «مصباح الشرق» لا يفهم منها معنى التعيير بالرتبة وإنما أراد بكلامه عنها أن يثبت أنّ الرتبة مهما عظم شأنها لا يكون من مستلزماتها هضم حقوق الضعيف والامتياز بها أمام القانون بل هي قاصرة على صاحبها لا تجعل على محروم منها سبيلا. ولا بأس على سعادتكم من ذلك فإنّ هذا الكلام جرى مجرى العادة في هذا العصر.

الباشا إذا كان للقاضي عذر وللنائب عذر فما هي فائدة حضوري هنا أمامكم وتظلمي بالعريضة لكم إلا أقل من استحضار النائب والقاضي وتوبيخهما ثم تفحصون القضية وتنظرون في تهمتي حتى إذا تبيّن لكم فسادها استرددتم ذلك الحكم أمامهما.

المفتش ليس ذلك من اختصاصنا وإذا حصل من أحد رجال المحاكم ما يخالف وظيفته فالنظر موكول في أمره إلى مجلس التأديب ولا سبيل لرئيس على مرؤوس إلا بحكم من المحكمة. وأنا أتأسف غاية الأسف لعدم القدرة على التصرف في قضيتك فالنظر فيها يتعلق بمحكمة الاستئناف لأنها هي الجهة الخاصة بتكسير الأحكام.

١٢،٥ قال عيسى بن هشام: وكنت أشاهد في هذه المحاورة شاباً آخر بجانبنا من المفتشين يسطع طربوشه احمراراً، ويقلب طرفه ازوراراً، تلوح على وجهه مخايل الإمارة، ولا تنفك يده على جبينه في رفع وخفض للنظارة، وتشهد عليه سيماه بالتفنن في التدبير، وقوة الدهاء في التفكير. فلمّا وصلنا إلى حيث وقف بنا الكلام نادى هذا المفتش على الحاجب فقال له وعلامات التأسف والإشفاق بادية على وجهه: ائتني بدالوز

one of them commits a crime indictable under the law. So you have suffered neither ignominy nor disgrace in standing up before the Judge. You merely stood before the representative of His Excellency the Khedive who holds the highest rank of all.

PĀSHĀ If that constitutes your opinion about the Judge, then what about the member of the Parquet who saw fit to reproach me for my noble rank?

5.11 INSPECTOR I haven't studied the files on the case and the details of the defense yet. But the part of the Attorney's speech which has been published in *Miṣbāḥ al-sharq* is not intended to convey any idea of reproach because of your rank. On the contrary, its aim is to make it clear that it is not the right of people of high rank, however important they may be, to completely override the rights of the weak and use it to claim precedence over other people before the law. The scope of rank is limited purely to its possessor, without giving him any advantages over those who do not have it. Thus you have no reason to complain about the things which the Attorney said on this point. That's the way things normally happen in this age.

PĀSHĀ Well then, if the Judge and Attorney can both be excused, what's the point of my coming to see you and submitting a petition of complaint? Wouldn't it be proper to summon the Judge and Attorney, reprimand them both, then examine the case, verify the falsity of the accusation, and on that basis quash the sentence in their presence?

INSPECTOR That's not within our sphere of jurisdiction. If a court official acts contrary to the dictates of his office, the investigation of the case is in the hands of the Disciplinary Committee. A senior person has no recourse against a subordinate except through a court decision. Thus, I'm extremely sorry to say that we can't act in your case. The decision rests with the Court of Appeal alone since it is the entity charged with annulling verdicts.

5.12 ʿĪsā ibn Hishām said: As this conversation proceeded, I was watching another young inspector at our side. His bright red tarboosh was tilted to one side. His expression showed signs of authority, and he kept raising and lowering his hand to and from his glasses. His appearance confirmed the fact that he was well organized and astute. When our conversation reached a certain point, he hailed the orderly, signs of regret and sympathy imprinted on his expression:

SECOND INSPECTOR Bring me Dalloz and Garraud.

وجارو، فالتفت الباشا إليّ قائلاً: هل هذان الاسمان هما اسما القاضي والنائب وهل آن أن ينتصفوا لي منهما؟

عيسى بن هشام هما اسمان لكتابين في فقه القانون بدل ابن عابدين والهداية في فقه الشرع الشريف.

ولمّا حضر حافظ الكتب بالكتابين أرجع المفتش له أحدهما وقال أنا ما طلبت «بودري» بل طلبت «جارو» ولمّا جاء له به أخذ يبحث فيهما ثمّ نظر نظرة اليائس ونادى الحاجب فقال له: عليّ بفوستن هيلي، فجاء له بكتاب آخر فخرج منه بعد النظرات الطويلة إلى المناقشة مع زميله باللغة الفرنساوية وانتهى الأمر بينهما أن قالا للباشا: ليس أمامك إلا الاستئناف في قضيتك، وأمّا ما يختص بالقاضي والنائب فسنعمل عنه نوتة (مذكرة) ونقدّمها إلى اللجنة عند انعقادها فإذا اتضح للجنة خلل في تصرّف القاضي والنائب أصدرت منشوراً للمحاكم بعدم اتباع ذلك في المستقبل، ثمّ ودّعانا بالاحترام والتعظيم وخرجنا والباشا يقول: ١٣،٥

كلما وضعت قدمي في دائرة من دوائر هذه الحكومة وجدت أمامي شباناً يتصرفون في أمورها فهل خلق المصريون خلقاً جديداً أم صرنا في الجنة استوت فيها الأعمار؟ وقد كاد ينفض بالي من الحزن اليوم فإنني كلما دخلت في حزن محاه حزن آخر.

فإنّي رأيت الحزن للحزن ماحياً
كما خُطّ في القِرطاسِ رسمٌ على رسمِ

عيسى بن هشام لا تعجب من تقلد الشبان لمناصب الحكومة فإنّ نظام العصر الحاضر يقضي بذلك وليس في استطاعة من تعهّدهم من أولئك الشيوخ أن يقوموا بأعباء الحكومة لخلوّهم عن علومها الجديدة. ١٤،٥

لو رأى الله أنّ في الشيب خيراً
جاوَرَتهُ الأبرارُ في الخلدِ شيبا

The Pāshā turned to me and asked: Are those the names of the Judge and Attorney? Has the time come for me to get fair treatment from them both?

'Īsā They're the titles of two books on civil jurisprudence, instead of Ibn 'Ābidīn and Al-Hidāyah on Shariah jurisprudence.

The librarian fetched the two books, but the Inspector gave one of them back to him. "Not Baudry," he said. "I asked for Garraud." When they brought him that book, he began to delve into the two works for a long time. He looked despairingly at the librarian. "Get me Faustin Hélie," he said, whereupon the librarian brought him another book. After studying this book for a while, he began to argue with his colleague in French. Eventually, when they finished, they spoke to the Pāshā:

5.13 Your only recourse in this case is the Court of Appeal. As far as the Judge and Attorney are concerned, we will make a note of it and refer it to the Board when it meets. If they find the slightest fault in their conduct, they will send out a circular to all courts ordering this practice to be discontinued in future.

With that, they both bade us farewell with reverence and respect.

As we left, the Pāshā spoke to me:

Pāshā Every time I've set foot in one of this government's departments, I've found myself faced with young people conducting its business. Have Egyptians been created afresh, or are they living in heaven where all ages are equal? My heart is almost completely exhausted from the way these worries and anxieties keep piling up against me.

I have seen sorrows obscuring sorrows
just as one line is written over another on paper.[45]

5.14 'Īsā Don't be surprised that young men are appointed to government positions; in this era the system requires it. They claim that men in middle and old age cannot bear the burdens of responsibility because they lack the necessary knowledge about modern sciences and the skills they demand.

Were God to see any good in old age,
The devout would abide near Him, old-aged for all eternity.[46]

الباشا كيف تدّعي أنّ العلم ينحصر في الشبّان دون الشيوخ وما عهدناه إلّا فيمن أحنت السنون ظهره وبيّضت التجارب مفارقه فابتسم فيها بياض الرأي والأدب؟

عيسى بن هشام لا يختص بالعلم عمر دون عمر ولا سن دون سن وربما كان الشاب أسرع جولانا في ميدان العلوم وأجمع لشتات المعارف لما لديه من حدة الذهن وقوة الإدراك واشتمال الذكاء، فإذا انصرف بهمته إليها لم يكن بأقل نصيباً فيها من الكهول والشيوخ وربما بلغ بسرعة الفهم ما بلغه الكهل بطول التجارب. فلا تنكر على الشبان علمهم ولا تبخسهم حقهم في توليهم معالي الأمور.

ليس الحداثة عن علمٍ بمانعةٍ
قد يُوجد العلمُ في الشبّان والشيبِ

الباشا قد تبعت آراءك وامتثلت نصائحك وعرضنا أمرنا للجنة المراقبة فخرجنا منها بالخيبة كما ترى فليس لنا بعد هذا التعب إلا راحة اليأس ولم يبق لك وجه في احتجاج وجيه عليّ تسحبني به للسعي والتظلم أمام الحكام. ١٥،٥

عيسى بن هشام لا تيأس فأمامنا محكمة الاستئناف ولي الأمل الوطيد في عدلها فإذا خاب أملنا فيها على الفرض فلنا أن نلتمس العفو يتوسط لنا في التماسه سعادة ناظر الحقانية.

الباشا لا تذكر لي بعد اليوم حاكما ولا ناظراً فقد سئمت من وقوفي أمام هؤلاء الشبان مهما بالغت في الوصف واستشهدت بالشعر.

عيسى بن هشام ليس ناظر الحقانية الذي أذكره لك من طبقة هؤلاء الشبان وطرزهم بل هو رجل عاكف على العبادة منكب على الأوراد مزاحم في حلقات الأذكار يظل ليله قائماً، ونهاره صائماً، وبين السبحة وأصابعه عهد وميثاق، وجبهته والسجادة ارتباط والتصاق، وبالجملة فهو رجل يذكّرنا في هذا العهد بعهدكم ١٦،٥

Pāshā How can they possibly claim that knowledge is the sole province of the young to the exclusion of older people? I've only encountered genuine learning in people whose backs have been bent by old age and whose hairline has been whitened by experience. It's only then that reason and culture shine forth in all their brilliance.

ʿĪsā Knowledge and learning are not the exclusive province of one age group or one period of life. Young men are often more effective in the scientific sphere and can gather more information on various subjects because of the sharp intellect and quick comprehension which is characteristic of people of their age. As a result, when they apply their energies to learning with determination, they can take in materials that are no less abundant than those possessed by men in middle and old age. Indeed their swift comprehension of things may enable them to achieve the same as older men have done after lengthier experience. You should not deny young people the knowledge they acquire nor challenge their right to assume high office.

Youth is not something to prevent one from learning;
learning may exist in both young and old.[47]

5.15 Pāshā So far I've followed your line of reasoning and taken your advice. We've presented our case to the Committee of Surveillance. But, as you can see, we've emerged without success. After going to all this trouble, we can only trust in despair. With today's events behind us, you have no plausible reason for dragging me into making any further efforts to lodge a complaint before the judges.

ʿĪsā Don't despair or lose heart. We still have the Court of Appeal before us. I've great faith in the fairness of its judgment. And, even supposing that our hopes were to be dashed there, the gate still remains open for us to try to obtain a pardon through the Minister of Justice.

Pāshā From now on, don't mention any ruler or minister. I've had enough of standing in front of these young men, however much you exaggerate and quote poetry to describe them.

5.16 ʿĪsā The Minister of Justice I'm describing is not at all like these young men. He prays devoutly, devotes all his attention to extra recitations and remembrances of God, and spends the night standing in prayer and the day fasting. There's a pact of understanding between his fingers and the rosary, and a firm connection between his forehead and the prayer mat. All in all, in

وأبوه رجل من رجالكم وهو إبراهيم باشا فؤاد ابن حسن باشا المناسترلي.

الباشا المناسترلي، ذاك خليلي وقريني وصاحبي وخديني ورفيقي في الخدمة، وأخي في الحكومة، ولماذا لم تخبرني عن ابن أخي من أوّل الأمر فتكون قد حقنت ماء وجهي وأنقذتني من كثير ممّا رأينا من الإهانات؟

عيسى بن هشام ما غاب عني أن أذكّرك به فإنه لم يكن له نفع فيما تقلبنا فيه وإنما نفعه في آخر الدرجات ولا عمل نرجوه منه إلّا بعد حكم الاستئناف للختم على التماس العفو.

this modern age he reminds us more than anyone else of the old times you knew. His father was in fact one of the great men of your day, Ḥasan Pāshā al-Manāstirlī.

Pāshā Al-Manāstirlī! He was my greatest friend and companion, my colleague in government service. Why didn't you tell me about the son of this companion of mine right from the very beginning? You'd have preserved the color in my cheeks and saved me this abuse and degradation.

ʿĪsā I didn't forget. It's just that he wouldn't have been of any help in avoiding the misfortunes in which we've been involved. He'll only be useful in the final stages of the process. We can't expect any assistance from him until after the decision of the appeal regarding the request for a pardon is published.

التزام حكومة السودان

مصباح الشرق ٤٠، ١٩ يناير ١٨٩٩

١،٦ حدثنا عيسى بن هشام قال: سمعت حديثاً عن أحد النظار، في المسألة التي تشغل اليوم الأفكار، إذ قصده مكاتب جريدة ليستنير بآرائه السديدة، ويستمد من أخباره المفيدة عن الحكومة الجديدة، حكومة آخر الزمان في بلاد السودان. فرأيت أن أعجل بنقله إلى القرّاء لغرابته، قبل الرجوع إلى حديث الباشا في محاكمته.

٢،٦ قال المكاتب: سألت عن الوقت الذي يكون فيه ناظر الحربية فارغ القلب فارغ البال، فارغ اليد من الأشغال والأعمال، فقالوا لي هكذا يكون الناظر عند تأدية وظيفته في نظارته ودست إمارته، ولكنهم بالغوا لي في حزمه وكتمانه، وقدرته على حفظ لسانه، وكم أعاد مثلي من قبل بالمنع والحرمان، والخيبة والخذلان، فلم ألتفت إلى مقالتهم، ولم أعبأ بإشارتهم، وذكرت في نفسي أنّ الرجل ربما كان يمتنع عن أرباب الجرائد الذين يخشى انتقادهم فيأبى مساعدتهم وإمدادهم. فأمّا من قصده متظاهراً بنية المطرئ المادح لينتصر له على المنتقد القادح، والصادق المخلص ليعينه على الكاذب المتخرص، فلا مكان لكتمانه عنه ما يغلي في صدره من باطن أمره وخفي سرّه ووجه عذره. ولكل امرئ ولع بعذر يبديه فيما يفعله ويأتيه.

٣،٦ فقصدت النظارة فاستأذنت على الناظر فرفع لي الحجاب، فدخلت فوجدته مستدبر الباب، مستقبل مستوقد النار للاصطلاء من برد الشتاء.

متى تأته تعشو إلى ضوء ناره
تجد خير نارٍ عندها خيرُ مُوقِدِ

فوقفت مكاني وهو ذاهل لا يراني، فرأيته يشير بيديه ويضرب الأرض برجليه ثمّ

Sudanese Government Monopoly

Miṣbāḥ al-sharq 40, January 19, 1899

ʿĪsā ibn Hishām told us: I heard a story about a minister concerned with the topic that is on everyone's mind at the moment. This happened when a newspaper reporter came to see him to try to get the benefit of his enlightened views and learn some accurate information about the new government in the Sudan. Because it seems to me so remarkable, I've decided to relay it to our readers immediately before we go back to the story of the Pāshā and his trial. 6.1

The Reporter said: I inquired when the Minister of War would have some free time from all his responsibilities. They told me that he was too busy carrying out his ministerial duties, but they also went to great lengths to explain how stubborn and secretive he was; he excelled at saying nothing. Many newspaper reporters like myself had tried in vain and had left frustrated and disappointed. However, I paid no attention to these statements and ignored their advice. I reminded myself that he might be reluctant to meet newspaper owners through fear of their criticisms; as a result he would regularly refuse to help them or give them information. On the other hand, any reporter who pretended to praise him to the very heavens as a way of offering him support against bitter critics, thus playing the role of a genuinely loyal helper in the face of slanderous falsehoods, would find that the minister had no cause to hide his innermost feelings and secret thoughts or offer the usual excuses. After all, people love making excuses for themselves, whatever they happen to be doing. 6.2

So I headed for the Ministry and asked for an audience with the Minister. The curtains were pulled back for me, and I went in. He was standing towards the door in welcome, lighting the fire to keep warm in the winter cold: 6.3

Approaching him, you glow in the warmth of his blazing fire;
there you find the best of fires, and to tend it, the finest kindler.[48]

I stood where I was. He seemed completely distracted and did not even notice me. I watched as he gestured with his hands and stamped on the ground,

يطرق رأسه ويخاطب نفسه ويصرف نابه مما نابه، وأمامه رمح طويل وسيف صقيل وبجانبه جبة وسبحة، وهو يقول بصوت فيه بحّة:

٤،٦ الناظر (لنفسه) لقد سفهت الأحلام، وضلت الأفهام، يتطلع إلينا المتطلعون، ويسعى وراءنا الساعون، ويكيد لنا الكائدون، ويمكر بنا الماكرون لينزلونا عن مراتبنا ويصعدوا بعدنا إلى مناصبنا، ولو علم هؤلاء الأغمار الأغرار بما نكابده ونقاسيه، ونمارسه ونعانيه، وأننا نقضي النهار في ذل وصغار، ونبيت الليل في هم وويل، لاستبدلوا الحسد والعدوان بالشفقة والحنان.

ذَلَّ من يغبط الذّليلَ بعيْشٍ
رُبَّ عيشٍ أخفُّ منه الحِمامُ

هذه البلاد السودانية فتحت باسمي، ودوّخها الجيش برسمي، ففاز كلّ بالسهم الرابح، وعادوا بالسنيح وعدت بالبارح، ولم يبق أحد دوني إلّا وله من الغنائم رزق مقسوم، ومن الجوائز والصلات نصيب معلوم، وبقيت وحدي في حالة اليائس المحروم.

وبدر أضاء الأرضَ شرقًا ومغربًا
وموضعُ رِجْلِي منه أسْودُ أقْتَمُ

٥،٦ نال كتشنر رتبة اللوردية وحق المدنية وناهيك بالخمسة والعشرين ألف جنيه والسيف المرصع، وبلغ من شهرة الصيت ما لم يكن يحلم به في عمره، ومن رفعة القدر ما لم يكن يتمناه على دهره. ونال اللورد كرومر رتبة الفيكونت، وبطرس باشا لقب سير (وما أبعد الخارجية من الحربية). ونال ونجت رتبة لواء بعد أن تأخرت عنه عشر سنوات. ونال الكولونيل رودس شرف العودة إلى الجيش البريطاني بعد أن أُبعد عنه تأديبًا على حملة ونجت في الترانسفال. ونال الزبير عودة أولاده أمراء في السودان بعد أن صدوه في وجوههم طول تلك الأزمان. ونال هنتر العثماني الثاني وجريفيث المجيدي الثالث وكذلك بقية إخوانه من الضباط، وأبيحت أم درمان للعساكر السودانية ثلاثة أيام. ونال جميع الذين حضروا الفتح مكافأة شهرين من مرتباتهم. ونال الذين لم يحضروه

then started banging his head and mumbling to himself about his sorry plight. In front of him was a long spear and gleaming sword while by his side was a coat and rosary. He spoke in a hoarse voice:

6.4 MINISTER (*talking to himself*) How futile are people's dreams, how erroneous their understanding! They keep watching me closely, hatching all kinds of plots, all in order to have me relieved of my post so they can step into it themselves. If only the silly fools knew the things I have to tolerate and suffer through! We spend the whole day being despised and looked down on, and then worry all through the night. They should feel pity and sympathy rather than envy and hatred!

He who envies a poor wretch his livelihood is himself despicable;
Death itself is less burdensome than many a life.[49]

The Sudan has been conquered in my name, subjugated by the Egyptian army under my authority. Now, everyone's earned their laurels and come home victorious. However, I'm out of luck. Everyone but me has their share of booty, a portion of the prizes and gifts:

To East and West, a full moon has lit up the earth;
but the place where my foot has stepped is as black as pitch.[50]

6.5 Kitchener has been given the title of Lord, and twenty-five thousand pounds to boot, not to mention an embossed sword. He's gained the kind of fame and prestige that he would never have dreamed of in his entire life. Lord Cromer has been made a Viscount, and Buṭrus Pāshā a Knight—and there's obviously a world of difference between the Foreign Ministry and the Ministry of War! Wingate has been promoted to Major-General after ten years of waiting, and Colonel Rhodes has been allowed the privilege of returning to the ranks of the British army after being cashiered for Wingate's campaign in the Transvaal. Zubayr has the reward of seeing his sons going back to the Sudan as amirs after being thwarted for so long. Hunter has got the Second Class 'Uthmānī decoration and Griffith the Third Majīdī. All their officer colleagues have been decorated, and Omdurman has been open to the Sudanese soldiery for three full days. Everyone who participated in the conquest has got two months' pay as a reward and those who didn't got one month's, right down to the military draft councils in the various provinces. But even though the Minister of War,

مكافئة شهر حتى مجالس القرعة العسكرية في المديريات. وناظر الحربية ورئيس الجيش الأعلى لم ينل خيرا ولم يصب حظا والأمر أمره والختم ختمه، بل أصبح يكرّر قول القائل:

أليس من العجائب أنّ مثلي
يرى مَا هانَ مُمْتَنِعًا عليه
وتُؤخذُ باسمه الدّنيا جميعًا
وما من ذاك شيءٌ في يديهِ

٦،٦ أستغفر الله إلا ما أراه أمامي من هذا السلاح وهذا اللباس الذي أهدوه لي من غنائمهم وكان نصيبي من فتحهم ونصرهم، وقسمي من مجدهم وفخرهم، وهذا ما كان يهديه المهدي من قبلهم لمن يدعوه إلى الهداية، والنزع عن الغواية. ذلك كل ما نلته من الأجر على ما أحمله من عبء المسئولية فوق عاتقي وما أثقل كاهلي من شدة اللوم وقبح الذم ورمي الأعداء لي بالتهاون في خدمتي والتقصير في عملي والإخلال بفروض الوطنية والإغضاء عن مصلحة الأمّة.

٧،٦ قال المكاتب: واشتدّت بالناظر الحال فأخذ ينهنه من دمعه ويكفكف من غربه وينشد بيت أبي الطيب متمثلا:

ماذا لقيتُ من الدّنيا وأعجبُها
أنّي بما أنا باكٍ منه محسودُ

وأخذتني الرقة، واعترتني الشفقة، فتنحنحت فالتفت الناظر إلى الباب مندهشاً مبهوتاً فاقتربت فسلمت فسألني عن مدة وقوفي بالباب، فحاولت وأغمضت عليه في الجواب حتى اعتقد أني لم أسترق السمع، ولم أشاهد استباق الدمع. ولمّا علم ذلك مني اضطجع على كرسيه الواسع المماثل لكرسي وليّ في نظارة الحربية الانكليزية وعضّ على سيجار من سجاير هفانا كالجنرال مايلس الأمريكي في دخوله إليها ثمّ وضع رجلا على رجل وأخرج من جيبه الختم مسلسلا وأخذ يلعب به فتلاً على أصابعه وتناول

the head of this splendid army, is in charge and signs the documents, he has no share in this bounty. All he can do is to repeat these lines of poetry:

Is it not incredible that someone in my position
watches as his inferiors stay aloof from him?
In his name the whole world is being subdued,
and yet none of it comes into his hands.[51]

I seek God's forgiveness! This weapon and these clothes they've given me as reward constitute my entire share in the spoils of victory, with all its glory and honor. They're the kind of thing that the Mahdī would previously give to those people whom he was encouraging to follow the path of true guidance and avoid temptation. This is all the reward I get for assuming so much responsibility and enduring so much blame and criticism. My foes have even accused me of neglecting my job, going against the canons of patriotism and disregarding the people's interests. 6.6

The Reporter went on to say: The Minister became quite upset and started sobbing. He quoted al-Mutanabbī's line to himself: 6.7

What have I ever got from the world? Most incredible of all
is that people envy me for something which makes me weep.[52]

I felt sorry for him so I coughed. The Minister turned towards the door with a jump. I went over to him and offered my greetings. He asked me how long I had been standing there; I hedged and gave an ambiguous answer so that he would think I had not been eavesdropping on him and not seen him sobbing. When he accepted that, he sat down in a chair which was an imitation of one in the English War Ministry and chewed a Havana cigar like the one the American general Miles had in his mouth when he entered that city. He put one foot on top of the other, brought the seal of office out of his pocket and started fiddling with it. He began counting his fingers and sifting papers on his desk in the pretence of being busy. All the while, he kept sneaking glances

من فوق مكتبته أوراقاً بيده يوهم الاشتغال بالنظر فيها ويلمحني من طرف خفي. وبعد برهة من هذه الهيئة سألني عن حاجتي فقلت له:

٨،٦ المكاتب لا يخفى على الناظر أن المسألة السودانية اليوم هي القطب الذي تدور عليه الرحى في مجرى الحوادث ونقطة الدائرة التي ترفرف حولها الأفكار وقد سئمت وسئم معي القرّاء من الخبط والخلط فيها والطعن والقدح فيكم فجئت لأقتبس من كنه علمك وفضل اختبارك ما أتحف به القرّاء، وأمتاز بنشره على القرناء من الأقوال الراجحة والأعذار الواضحة، فيذهب عنكم اللوم والتعيير، وما ينبئك مثل خبير.

٩،٦ الناظر الأمر بسيط والخطب هيّن ولا محل لاشتغال الخواطر وقلق الأفكار فالسودان أرض مشتركة بين الحكومة المصرية التي نحن نظارها وبين الحكومة الانكليزية التي ينوب عنها اللورد كرومر، ونحن نبحث الآن جميعاً في كيفية نظام الحكومة السودانية وإقامة الحضارة والمدنية الغربية فيها مقام الوحشية والهمجية غير مكترثين بما يتشدق به الجاهلون ويتنطع فيه ذوو الفضول والتقصير عن إدراك غوامض المستقبل، فإنّ هذا السودان سيكون جنة لمصر يأتيها رزقها رغداً وكما أنه منبع نيلها فسيصير منبع خيرها، ودعامة عزها وفخرها. وأهل السودان قوم لا يزالون على الفطرة والبداوة لم تتأصل فيهم عادات الحضارة الشرقية بأباطيلها وأضاليلها وترفها ورفهها، ولم ترسخ فيهم الأخلاق الفاسدة والسجايا الذميمة والرذائل المستحكمة في بلاد الشرق، بل أفكارهم كأرضهم بكر لا ينقصها إلا أن تمهر بحلي المدنية فيزهو جمالها ويتجلى حسنها على سائر الأفكار كما لو بذرت في أرضهم بذراً فاق ثمره سائر الأثمار والسودانيون غير المصريين أهل جد ونشاط وأصحاب عزيمة وإقدام مع مواظبة في العمل وقوة في الإرادة فلا يلبثون أن يبلغوا في زمن قليل مبلغاً عظيماً في المدنية فيصبحون في إفريقا كأهل الجنوب من أمريكا. وأي عمل في هذا العصر أعظم مجداً وأكبر فخراً وأجلّ قدراً وأخلد ذكراً من هذا العمل. وأجدني كلما تأملت في هذا المجد العظيم وتفكرت في هذا الأثر الفخيم هان عليَّ ما ألاقيه من سفاهة السفيه، وطعن

in my direction. After carrying on like this for some time, he asked me what I wanted. I responded as follows:

6.8 REPORTER You are well aware, Sir, that the Sudanese problem is the primary event of the day and the focus of everyone's attention. I'm fed up, and so are our readers, with all the confusion and bungling, not to mention the slanderous criticisms being leveled at you. I've come to get some idea of the situation from you since you have a complete mastery of the whole picture. I can then pass it on to our readers and claim distinction from my colleagues by providing plausible statements and clear rationales. That will rid you of all the criticisms and abuse. As the saying has it, if you want information, ask someone who knows.

6.9 MINISTER The whole thing is quite straightforward; there's no cause for concern and nothing for people to be worried about. The Sudan is being governed jointly by the Egyptian government in which we are ministers and the British government represented by Lord Cromer. At the moment, we are considering together ways of organizing the government there and introducing Western culture and civilization instead of the primitive barbarianism which subsists there at the moment. We are entirely unconcerned about the stupid prattle of those ignorant meddling fools who are unable to grasp what lies in the inscrutable future. Sudan is going to be a veritable garden for Egypt; it will provide us with all our wants. It is the place where we find the source of Egypt's Nile and so it will also be the source of its welfare and mainstay of its power and pride. The Sudanese people are still primitive; they don't have ingrained in them the customs of Oriental civilization with all its futilities, delusions, opulence, and luxury. The corrupt character and nasty traits which are so common in Oriental countries have not become so deeply rooted in their nature; in fact, quite the opposite, their thoughts are like their own land, virgin. All this bride lacks is a dowry made up of the jewels of civilization. The country will then reveal its true beauty and shine radiantly over all other ideas. It's as if you are planting a seed in their soil; the fruit it produces will be better than any other fruit.

The Sudanese are not like the Egyptians. They're serious and energetic; they have a sense of purpose and élan, they persevere with whatever they're doing and have a strong willpower. It won't take them long to reach a quite sophisticated level of civilization. In Africa their position will become like that of the people in South America. In this era of ours what project is more

الحسود، ونكران الجحود، ثمّ إنّ يدنا هناك مطلقة التصرف لا صندوق للدين يعاكس مشروعاتنا، ولا محاكم مختلطة تقوم في وجوهنا، ولا امتيازات للأجانب تصدّنا عن أعمالنا، ولا معاهدات دولية تقذف الرعب في قلوبنا، ولا جرائد معارضة تشوش علينا، ولا أدري بعد ذلك ممّ يشتكي الشاكون، ولِمَ يبكي الباكون، وعلام ينوح النائحون، وفيم يصيح الصائحون، وبم يعيب العائبون، وإلام يكذب الكاذبون، والسودان كله في يد الجنود المصرية وليس للاحتلال فيه أثر بغير مائتي عسكري انكليزي.

١٠،٦ المكاتب إذا كان الناظر بالدرجة التي أراها من الشغف بمستقبل السودان والاهتمام بتنظيم إدارته والاشتراك في ترتيب حكومته فلماذا لم يتوجه مع من توجه إلى الخرطوم ليطبق العلم على العمل ويؤيد ما سمع بما يرى.

الناظر ليس من الضرورة أن أتحمل المشاق وأتكبد الأسفار إلى بلد لم يقم فيه المرحوم سعيد باشا إلا نصف ساعة بعدما قضى في قصده أشهراً في السفر. وقد توجه إليه اللورد كرومر نائباً عن الحكومة الانكليزية ومستشار المالية نائباً عن الحكومة المصرية والسردار هناك نائب عني.

المكاتب وهل أعجبك وراقك ووافق هواك ما جاء في خطبة اللورد؟

الناظر نعم إنّ في ما ابتكره اللورد من وضع الحكومة السودانية تحت أمر السردار دون أمر الحكومة الانكليزية ودون أمر الحكومة المصرية دقيقة من دقائق السياسة ونكتة من نكات الدهاء فإنه أراد بذلك أن يخرج الحكومة السودانية عن قيود الامتيازات والمعاهدات والديون فلم يقدر أن يصرّح بإلحاقها بإنكلترا لأنّ فيه نقضاً لعقد الشركة ولم يرض أن يصرّح بإلحاقها بمصر فتدخل تحت محظورات حكومتها الحاضرة فجعلها قائمة تحت حكم السردار يعني تحت الإدارة العرفية ليتسنى لنا تنظيمها بلا معارض ولا معاكس وما أجملها طريقة وأحسنها وسيلة.

١١،٦ وأنت تعلم حديث القائد اليوناني الذي كان رئيساً على حكومة أثينا إذ حشد الأهالي يوماً كما هي عادتهم في جمهوريتهم وقال لهم: أتدرون من هو الحاكم على العالم، قالوا: لا، قال: هذا الطفل – وأشار إلى ابنه بجانبه – فإنه يحكم على أمه وأمه تحكم عليَّ وأنا

worthy, glorious, memorable, and long-lasting than this one? Every time I think about the enormous pride and prestige it brings, I find it easy to ignore the idiotic things people say, the envy that people feel, and the criticisms of my detractors. All the yelling and screaming, fault finding, and prevarications are of no import. The whole of the Sudan is in Egyptian hands; the only trace of the occupation is two hundred English soldiers.

6.10 REPORTER Since you seem to be so enthusiastic about the future of the Sudan, Sir, and so concerned about its administration and coordination of government arrangements, how is it that you haven't traveled to Khartoum along with the others to put your concern to work and confirm reports by seeing everything for yourself?

MINISTER I don't have to put up with the hard journey all the way up there. The late Saʿīd Pāshā only stayed there for half an hour even though it had taken him months to get there. Lord Cromer is representing the British government, the Financial Adviser is representing the Egyptian government, and the Sirdar is my personal representative.

REPORTER Were you happy about Lord Cromer's speech? Did it conform with your intentions?

MINISTER Certainly! The device Lord Cromer has come up with to put the Sudanese government under the control of the Sirdar instead of the British and Egyptian governments is a very subtle maneuver which shows considerable shrewdness. By so doing, his intention is that the Sudanese government will be rid of the fetters imposed by capitulations, treaties, and debts. He couldn't say it had been annexed by England because that would have involved the violation of company contracts, and he didn't want to have it declared as annexed to Egypt since that would put it under the same restrictions as our present government. So he put it under the Sirdar's control, or, in other words, under martial law. In that way, things can be organized without any opposition or objection—what a marvelous way of doing things!

6.11 You're aware of the story about the Greek general who was in charge of the Athenian government? One day, people met as was the custom in their republic. The general asked them if they knew who ruled the world. When they said they didn't, he told them that it was the little boy who was standing at his side, his son. He pointed out that the boy ruled his mother, his mother ruled him (the general), he ruled Athens, and Athens ruled the world. One day, I should ask the Egyptian people if they know who rules the world's great

أحكم على أثينا وأثينا تحكم على العالم. ولي أن أقول يوماً للمصريين: أتدرون من هو حاكم القارة الكبيرة في الكرة الأرضية، فإذا قالوا لا، قلت: أنا ناظر الحربية المصرية فإني أحكم على السردار والسردار يحكم على السودان والسودان يحكم على إفريقا.

المكاتب لو علم الناظر بأني كنت واقفاً بالباب وقت محادثته لنفسه أسمعه وأراه، لم يتكلف معي هذا التكلف، ولم يتصنّع معي هذا التصنّع.

الناظر لا حول ولا، ونضيف على الهموم أيضاً رذالة الحاجب وإهماله والحيلة في ترك الحيل، ولم يبق حينئذ إلا أن أستكتمك ما سمعته فلا تنشر منه شيئاً في الجرائد، ورجائي أن تسامح وتغض الطرف عن هذا التصنع والتحيل فذاك أمر قضى به عليَّ دست الوظيفة وهكذا شأننا مع المحتلين يفكرون ويديرون في سبك أعمالهم سبك الحديد وندبر ونتفكر نحن في نسج الأعذار نسج العنكبوت، وغيري من يتمتع بالمكافأة ويحظى بالصلات.

المكاتب لا تحزن ولا تذهب نفسك حسرات على ما اختصوا به من المكافئة دونك فقد انتحلوا لإسدائها إليهم أسباباً. فالسردار نال ما ناله بما تحمّله من المشاق والمتاعب في الحروب وبما سهر في تدبيره من الكيد للعدو وبتوفيره على دولته حشد الجنود الكثيرة في وقائع السودان إلّا بالعدد الذي يقتضيه التظاهر بوجودهم في الوقائع لإثبات الاشتراك وبجعله العمل كله على الجيش المصري. واللورد كرومر نال رتبته لأنه نصح لحكومته أن تقرض الحكومة المصرية الثمانمائة ألف جنيه وقت الحاجة والعوز ثم تتنازل عنها عند الفرصة اللائقة ليكون ذلك بمثابة رأس المال لعقد الشركة الانكليزية المصرية في امتلاك السودان. وبطرس باشا نال لقبه لأنه لم يناقش في قبول الهبة ليتم للورد فرصته. ونال الزبير عودة أولاده لأنه أرشد بما ينفع في الانتصار على البلاد السودانية. وكذلك ونجت نال رتبته لاجتهاده في الوقوف على أخبار العدو. وكلهم نالوها لأسباب ولم يجدوا لك سبباً انتفعوا به في الحركة السودانية. ١٢،٦

الناظر إذا صرفنا النظر عن المكافئات فهلا كانوا يحفظون معي ما لا يضرهم من مراعاة الظواهر فكانوا يأخذونني في صحبتهم إلى السودان ويعرضون تعيين ناظر ١٣،٦

continent. When they say they don't, I'll reply that I'm the Egyptian Minister of War, I have authority over the Sirdar, he rules the Sudan, and Sudan commands Africa.

Reporter If you realized, Sir, that I was standing by the door all the time you were talking to yourself, watching and listening to you, you wouldn't carry on pretending like this.

Minister All is lost! As if I didn't have enough to worry about! My chamberlain is so negligent and doesn't use his wits to keep people out of my office. In that case, I've no alternative but to ask you to keep everything you've heard a secret and not publish any part of it in the newspapers. I hope you'll be kind enough to turn a blind eye to my dissimulation. Such things are forced on me by the prestige of the office I hold. This is what happens when the occupying power does all the thinking and arranging. Their actions are all like cast iron whereas we keep weaving excuses for ourselves like a spider. Meanwhile, all the other people get the rewards and presents.

6.12 Reporter Don't be so sad and resentful that they're the ones getting rewards and not you. They can quote a number of reasons for their good fortune. The Sirdar has got his for putting up with so many troubles in the war, for the stratagems he's devised against the enemy, and for saving his country the need to gather a large force together for the battles in the Sudan. He's only been using a token number so as to give some semblance of their being there as part of a cooperative effort during the battle, whereas in fact it's Egyptian soldiers who do all the work. Lord Cromer has got his title for advising his government to lend the Egyptian government eight thousand pounds at a time of desperate need and then forgoing it at the right moment so that it could be used as capital for setting up the Anglo-Egyptian Company to control the Sudan. Buṭrus Pāshā got his title because he didn't object to receiving this gift from Cromer's government so that the latter could make full use of this opportunity. Zubair secured the return of his sons because he gave advice which proved useful in the conquest of the Sudan. Wingate got his promotion for his efforts to keep track of enemy information. They've all been rewarded for good reasons, but they couldn't come up with anything you've done to help them in the Sudanese campaign.

6.13 Minister Let's leave aside the question of rewards. Why didn't they at least maintain some semblance of form in their dealings with me? It wouldn't do them any harm. They could have taken me with them to the Sudan and

ماليته باقتراح مني على مجلس النظار بدل تعيينه من فوق رؤوسنا مباشرة من لوندره، ولكن أراد اللورد بجميع ما عمله وقاله وخطب به في السودان أن يأتي بعمل غريب يختم به القرن التاسع عشر وهو أن يعيد فيه بحكومة السودان إقطاعات البلاد والتزامها كما كانت المادة جارية به في حكومات القرون الوسطى وكأنه تعب من تنظيم الحكومة المصرية على طرز المدنية الغربية الحاضرة فأراد الإبداع بقلب ما كان مستقبحاً مذموماً مستحسناً ممدوحاً. ولا أقدر أن أعتقد بقلب الحقائق فإنّ ما أجمع الناس على ذمّه مذموم على الدوام والعاقبة على أي الأحوال لاحقة بنا داخلة في مسؤوليتنا، وعلى ذكر المسئولية. . . .

١٤،٦ قال المكاتب: وضغط الناظر بيده على زر الجرس فجاء الحاجب فأمره باستدعاء كاتب الحسابات فعاد إليه الحاجب يقول أنه مشتغل عند الأدجوتانت جنرال ولا يمكنه الحضور، فقال له الناظر أبلغه أنني أرجو حضوره لمسألة خصوصية لا لمسألة تتعلق بالديوان، ولما حضر الكاتب بعد أن أتمّ شغله مع الأدجوتانت قال الناظر له: أرجوك تحويل ماهيتي على البنك الأهلي الوطني. ثمّ التفت إليّ وقال: هذه الماهية هي كل مالي في مقابلة مسئوليتي الطويلة العريضة وأنا لا أزال أعلل النفس وأحلم بالأماني أنهم إذا عثروا على كنوز التعايشي أتحفوني بضروة المهدي أو جلد الأسد الذي كان يقعد عليه التعايشي للحكومة بين الناس. فقل لي بالله بعد إذ علمت ما علمت هل رأيت في أحوالنا ما نحسد عليه أو في وظائفنا ما يروق التطلع إليه.

قال المكاتب: وجاء الحاجب يخبر الناظر بانصراف الديوان فسلمت عليه وانصرفت.

suggested on my recommendation that the Minister of Finance be appointed to the cabinet, instead of appointing him over all our heads direct from London. In everything Lord Cromer has done, said, and projected regarding the Sudan he seems to have wanted to bring the nineteenth century to a strange end; namely to get the Sudanese government to reintroduce the feudal system and tax farming just as it was during the Middle Ages. It's as if he's tired of organizing the Egyptian government along the lines of contemporary Western civilization and is eager to try something new by turning a loathsome and objectionable concept into something commendable. But I can't believe in the inversion of basic truths. Something that people unanimously condemn continues to be unacceptable. In any case, the upshot of it all is my chief concern and that comes within my responsibility. Talking of responsibility. . .

6.14 The Reporter said: The Minister pressed his bell button, and the chamberlain came in. The Minister instructed him to call the accounts secretary. The chamberlain came back after a while and told him that the secretary was busy with the Adjutant General and could not come. The Minister told him to go back and inform the secretary that he very much hoped he would be able to come; it was a private matter, not government business. As soon as the secretary had finished his business with the Adjutant, he came in. The Minister told him that he wanted him to forward his salary to the National Bank. The Minister turned to me and told me that this salary was all he got in return for his considerable responsibilities. He told me that he still cherished the hope and continued to dream that, if they came across al-Taʿāyishī's treasure, they would make him a gift of the Mahdī's fur or the lion skin which al-Taʿāyishī used to sit on while carrying out his functions as governor. He asked me, in view of what I'd learned, whether I could envisage anyone casting an envious eye on his situation or thinking that his office was worthy of aspiration.

The chamberlain came in to say that the council had left. So I said farewell and left too.

١٫٧ قال عيسى بن هشام: آن أوان الجلسة في الاستئناف فسرنا نسلك طريقه ونؤم سبيله وكل واحد منا مشتغل بحاجته، لاهٍ بنازلته، فالباشا يفكر في مصيبته ويتألم من بليته، والمحامي يدبر في قضيته ويتطلع لأجرته، وأنا أسأل الله النجاة من مكائد الحياة. ولمّا وصلنا إلى الإسماعيلية ورأى الباشا قصورها ومبانيها وبيوتها ومغانيها ورياضها وحدائقها وازدهارها وشقائقها وطرقها وتنظيمها وأشجارها وتقويمها، استوقفنا مبهوتا، واستنطقنا بعد أن كنّا سكوتا، وسألنا ما موضع هذه الجنة الزاهرة من مدينة القاهرة، فوصفنا له وعرّفناه به فقال:

٢٫٧ **الباشا** سبحان الله ما أجله وأكبره، وأعظمه وأقدره، لقد كانت هذه الأرض خرابًا قفرًا، لا تحمل بيتًا ولا قصرًا، ولا ترى فيها من النبات غير الطلح والضال وشوك القتاد وشوك السيال، ولا من الطير إلّا البوم والغربان والرخم والعقبان، ومن الوحش الثعالب والذئاب والضباع والضباب، ولا تجد فيها من الإنس إلّا لصًا سالبًا ومغتالًا ناهبًا وفاتكًا متأهبًا وكامنًا مترقبًا. لله در المصريين، لقد ابتسم لهم الدهر، وأبدلهم بالشوك الزهر، وأسكنهم هذه القصور العالية بعد تلك الديار البالية.

المحامي أيها الأمير لا تغبط المصري على نعمته، وتعال فابك معنا على نقمته، فليس له في هذه البقعة من دار يقرّ له فيها قرار، وكل ما تراه في هذا الجانب هو ملك للأجانب.

الباشا لله أبوك كيف يختص الأجنبي دون أهل البلاد بالجنان الناضرة والمساكن الفاخرة، ولعلك تلغز وتحاجي وتعمي وتداجي.

٣٫٧ **المحامي** لا تحجية ولا تعمية، بل هكذا قدّر المصري لنفسه، واستبدل سعده بنحسه، واقتنع بالدون وبالطفيف، واقتصر على القسم الخسيس الضعيف، وبات المصري محرومًا تحت ظل إهماله وخموله، وسباته وذهوله، وما زال الأجنبي يسعى ويكد، ويجتهد ويجد، وينال ويطمع، ويدخر ويجمع. والمصري يبذر ويسرف ويبدد

Miṣbāḥ al-sharq 41, January 26, 1899[53]

ʿĪsā ibn Hishām said: The time came for the appeal. We went to the court to seek a fair hearing. Each one of us was intent on his own business and occupied with his own aspect of the judicial contest. The Pāshā was considering the misfortunes he had suffered and complaining about his tribulations; the Lawyer was arranging his material and keeping a mental note of his fee; for my part, I was asking God to deliver us from life's intrigues. We reached the Ismāʿīliyyah quarter.[54] When the Pāshā saw the mansions, houses, palaces, and villas, he was entranced by the gardens and bowers which had grown around them and the neat layout of the streets with their trees. He stopped us and broke the silence by asking in astonishment what place this gleaming paradise occupied in the city of Cairo! Once we had given him a description of it, he said: 7.1

PĀSHĀ All praise be to Almighty God, Glorious and Powerful! This district used to be in ruins; there were no houses or mansions in it. The only plant life was the barren acacia tree; the only flowers the tragacanth and sayal thorn; the only birds owls, crows, falcons, and eagles. Of wild beasts there would have been foxes, wolves, hyenas, jackals, and lizards. The only humans would have been plundering brigands, murderers, or lurking cutthroats. What wonders the Egyptians have accomplished! Fate has clearly smiled favorably on them by giving them these flowers in exchange for thorns and housing them in these lofty mansions instead of those shattered ruins. 7.2

LAWYER My dear Amir, don't envy the Egyptians their good fortune. Rather join us in bewailing their misfortune. They don't own any of the houses in this paradise where they could settle down. Everything you see in this area belongs to foreigners.

PĀSHĀ Heavens above! How can foreigners claim this beautiful paradise, such a superb residential area, for themselves and keep native Egyptians out? Are you speaking in riddles? Are you perhaps being deliberately vague in your explanation?

LAWYER There's no riddle involved, nor is anything vague. Egyptians have brought it on themselves by exchanging their happiness for misfortune. As their lot in life they're satisfied with whatever is paltry and inferior. Each one of them makes do with his meager, pathetic share. In the shadow of his own negligence, sloth and apathy, he remains deprived, leading a wretched life full of degradation and bewilderment. Meanwhile foreigners keep working 7.3

ويتلف، ويلعب ويلهو، ويعجز ثم يزهو، ويفتقر ثمّ يفتخر، وساداتنا وكبراؤنا ووزراؤنا وأمراؤنا يعاونون الأجانب بسلطتهم وسطوتهم، ويساعدونهم ببأسهم وقوّتهم، ويتخذونهم على المصريين أنصارًا وأعوانًا، فيسومونهم معهم ذلّا وهوانًا حتى وقعوا هم أيضًا بأسرهم في قبضة أسرهم، وتساوى السيد بالمسود، والحاسد بالمحسود، والمنيع الرفيع بالذليل الوضيع، واشتركا على السواء في الشدة والبلاء، وأصبح نصيب القوي المكين كنصيب الضعيف المستكين. وهكذا عاقبة من يلقي للطامع بيديه، «ومن أعان ظالمًا سلط عليه».

ومن يجعلِ الضِرّغامَ بَازًا لصيدهِ
تصيّده الضرغامُ فيما تصيّدا

٤،٧ قال عيسى بن هشام: وماكاد رفيقاي ينتهيان من خطابهما، ويفرغان من سؤالهما وجوابهما حتى مرّ بجانبنا راكب دراجة ينساب بها انسياب الصلال في بطون الرمال، ويتمايل بها تمايل النشوان، مالت به الخمر، ويتثنى تثني الأغصان عند نسيم الفجر، فامتلأ الباشا تعجبا واندهاشًا، وسألنا البيان عن أمر هذا البهلوان، فقلت له: هذه عجلة حادثة يختارها اليوم كبراء الناس على المركبات والأفراس، وممّا يرغّبهم فيها أنها لا تأكل ولا تشرب، ولا تسأم ولا تتعب، ويقصدون بها رياضة الأعضاء ليتوازن العقل بتوازن الجسم، وما أظنّ هذا الراكب إلّا أحد القضاة. ثمّ تتبعناه بالنظر فوجدناه قد سقط من فوق دراجته فانفرط عقد الهيئة إلى ثلاثة أقسام على الأرض: الراكب والعجلة والطربوش، ثمّ قام فلمّ شعثه وحاول أن يعلو الدراجة ثانية فلم يقدر عليها فسحبها بيده يماشيها وتماشيه.

٥،٧ الباشا يا حبذا لو عدنا من حيث أتينا، وكنا مطلقين لا لنا ولا علينا، وكيف يكون شأن الحاكم والقاضي إذا كان هذا منظرهما أمام أعين العامة، وهل حكمت

hard; they take their job seriously. They acquire goods and want more; they store and collect things. Alongside them, Egyptians squander and waste everything. They get distressed, then fritter their time away; they become helpless, then grow conceited; they become poor, and start boasting. Our rulers and men of influence, our governors and amirs, all of them help foreigners rule and dominate us. They use their power and authority to assist foreigners and use them as allies and helpers against Egyptians. In that way they can make use of them to humiliate the Egyptians even more. Eventually however, they too have fallen into the clutches of foreigners; now they too have become their prisoners. Masters and servants are now on equal footing, envier and envied are alike, and exalted and unapproachable people are on a par with the despicable and lowly. We are all participants in the varying degrees of hardship and suffering; a distinguished and powerful man now suffers the same fate as a weak and lowly person. Such are the consequences for anyone who gives in to the avaricious. "He who assists a tyrant will find himself oppressed":

If a hunter uses a lion as a falcon,
  the lion will surely count him amongst its prey.[55]

7.4 ʿĪsā ibn Hishām said: My two companions had only just finished their conversation, with its questions and answers, when a cyclist came speeding past us like a viper in the depths of the sand. He was swaying like a man intoxicated by wine and bending over like branches in the early morning breeze. The Pāshā was utterly flabbergasted and asked us about this acrobat. I informed him that it was a new bicycle, something that people chose to ride in preference to carriages and horses. What they liked about it was that it didn't eat or drink, nor did it become bored or tired. The intention of such riders was to exercise their limbs so that mind and body were in equilibrium. That particular rider, I surmised, was none other than one of the judges. We all stared after him, only to witness the rider fall off his bicycle. The ensemble had fractured into three separate entities which were lying on the ground; rider, bicycle, and tarboosh. He stood up again and brushed himself off. He tried to get back on the bicycle, but was unable to do so, so he started pushing it by hand and walking alongside it.

7.5 PĀSHĀ How I wish we could go back where we've come from, at liberty and with no encumbrances. How can judges or governors fare when this is the kind of image they project in full view of everyone? Were people ever judged

العامة يوماً بغير الأبهة والحجاب وتهويل المناظر. ولذلك كان الحاكم لا يركب في زماننا إلا في موكب تحف به الجنود والفرسان، وتتقدمه الخدم والحشم والأعوان، فتمتلئ النفوس رعباً، وترتجف القلوب رهباً، فلا يجترئ أحد أن يرتكب ما يوقفه أمام الحاكم في تلك الهيئة.

عيسى بن هشام   نعم نعم، لقد تفنّن الشعراء في وصف هذه الهيئة وأدخلوها في مخالصهم البديعة، قال أبو الطيب:

جمح الزّمانُ فما لذيذٌ خالصٌ
مـمّا يشوبُ ولا سـرورٌ كامـلُ
حتّى أبو الفضلِ ابن عبدِ اللهِ رُؤ
يتُـهُ المُـنى وهي المُـقامُ الهائـلُ

المحامي   دعونا من هذا فقد قربنا من المحكمة. ٦،٧

عيسى بن هشام   ولعلنا نجدها بإذن الله في مكانها فقد تعوّدت التنقل حتى أشبهت خيام العرب.

يومًا بجِزْوَى ويومًا بالعقيقِ وبالْ
عُـذَيْبِ يومـًا ويومًا بالخُـلَيْصَاءِ

ثمّ اقتربنا فوجدناها فدخلناها وأقمنا برهة ننتظر دورنا في الجلسة فنودي علينا فوقفنا أمام ثلاثة من القضاة فيهم شيخ عليه جلال القضاء ووقار الحكم فأعجب الباشا بهيئته واطمأنّ لرؤيته، ثمّ قام منهم أجنبي يقرأ ملخص القضية بلهجة أعجمية وحروف لم تستوف مخارجها.

قارئ التلخيص   إنّ هذا الرجل متهم بالتعدّي على العسكري فلان بالضرب في أثناء تأدية وظيفته في يوم كذا والمتهم أنكر وشهد المجني عليه ودلّ الكشف الطبي على وجود علامات فيه للضرب والمحكمة الابتدائية حكمت عليه بحبس سنة ونصف بالتطبيق لمادة ١٢٤ و١٢٦ عقوبات فاستأنف المحكوم عليه.

in court without pomp, chamberlains, and impressive displays? In our day, no judge or governor would ride anywhere without an escort of soldiers and cavalry, preceded by servants, retinue, and aides. People's hearts would shudder in awe and respect. No one would dare commit a crime which involved appearing before such a judge.

'Īsā Yes indeed! Poets have gone to great lengths to depict such status, weaving it into their figurative creations. Here is what al-Mutanabbī has to say:

Time is defiant, there exists no pleasure
that is unsullied, no complete joy,
Not even Abū l-Faḍl ibn 'Abdallāh. To see him may be one's dearest wish,
and yet it is also an awesome experience.[56]

7.6 Lawyer It's time to stop this chatter, we've reached the court.

'Īsā Let's hope, God willing, that we find it in its proper place. I'm getting so used to going from one place to another that they will seem like Bedouin's tents:

One day in Huzwa, another in al-'Aqīq, another
in al-'Uthyab, and another in al-Khulayṣā'.[57]

We approached the place where the building was supposed to be and actually found it! There we stood for a while awaiting our turn. Eventually we were summoned. We stood before three judges. One of them was a shaykh who displayed the august demeanor of a judge and the law. The Pāshā admired his appearance and took comfort from his aspect. The judge who was a foreigner stood up and began reading the summary of the case in a foreign accent, without bothering to articulate the consonants fully.

Reader of the Summary This man stands accused of an assault on X, the policeman, during the course of his duty on such and such a day of such and such a month. The accused denies this. The plaintiff has testified in person, and medical evidence has shown the existence of marks on his person from the assault. The Court of First Instance sentenced him to a year and a half in prison according to articles 124 and 126 of the Penal Code. The convicted person has appealed.

٧،٧ قال عيسى بن هشام – وسألت المحامي عن هذا التخليص الغريب فقال لي هكذا تجري العادة في الغالب أنّ مثل هذا القاضي الأجنبي يأخذ عبارة الديباجة المذكورة في الحكم الابتدائي فيجعلها تلخيصاً ثمّ يكتبها بعربيتها بحروف افرنكية ليقرأها أمام الجلسة. ثمّ التفت رئيس الجلسة إلى المتهم وسأله عن سنّه وصناعته ومحل إقامته حسب المعتاد وأشار إلى النيابة بقوله: «حضرة النائب».

٨،٧ فشرعت النيابة في شرح القضية على ما يوافق هواها ولم أسمع مقاطعة عليها من الرئيس في كلامها كما يقع في المحاكم الابتدائية لأنّ بعض القضاة الذين لم يكونوا قد اطّلعوا على أوراق القضية في الاستئناف هم في حاجة إلى الوقوف عليها من أقوال النيابة فيتركونها وشأنها في التطويل والإسهاب في التهمة. وبعد أن فرغت النيابة من الإسهاب والإطناب في أقوالها طلب الرئيس من المحامي الكلام عن المتهم بالإيجاز. فأخذ المحامي يسرد أقواله في أوجه الدفاع عن المتهم وكلما وصل إلى النقطة المهمة في دفاعه قال له الرئيس: «الموضوع»، «طلباتك» ولمّا تكرّر وقوع ذلك لحظت أحد القضاة ينبه الرئيس بإشارة خفيفة أنّ كلام المحامي في عين الموضوع (وللرئيس العذر لأنه لم يطّلع على القضية).

الرئيس سمعت القضية والحكم بعد المداولة.

٩،٧ قال عيسى بن هشام: فخرجنا ننتظر وانتقلت الجلسة إلى حجرة المداولة فسألت المحامي عن المسافة التي تقتضيها المداولة.

المحامي لا تزيد المداولة في الغالب عن ساعة واحدة.

عيسى بن هشام وما هو مقدار المتوسط من عدد القضايا في الجلسة.

المحامي متوسطها عشر قضايا.

عيسى بن هشام وهل تفي هذه المدة للاطلاع على ما تحتويه القضايا الجنائية من كثرة الأوراق.

المحامي نعم تكفي لكل القضايا ولو كان الاطلاع على إحدى القضايا الجنائية التي يكون الحكم فيها بالإعدام أو الأشغال الشاقة المؤبدة يستغرق ساعتين أو ثلاثاً.

ʿĪsā ibn Hishām said: I asked the Lawyer about this peculiar summary. "It's normal practice here," he replied. "Foreign judges like this one adopt the same style of preamble as was used in the initial trial, and turn it into a summary. They write it down in its Arabic form but in foreign characters, so that they can read it before the court." 7.7

The chief judge of the court now turned to the Pāshā. He asked him, as was customary, his name, age, profession, and place of residence. He then invited the Parquet Attorney to address the court.

The Attorney began to explain the case as suited his fancy. This time, however, I heard no interruptions from the chief judge as had happened in the Court of First Instance, the reason being that some of the judges who had not read up the notes of the case in the appeal needed to hear about it from the Attorney's speech. So they allowed him to go on with his accusations at length. Once the Parquet Attorney had finished his expatiations, the chief judge allowed the Lawyer to speak briefly. The latter began to go into details about the aspects of the accused's defense. Every time he reached the crucial point, the chief judge told him to get to the point and make his demands. When this happened again, I saw one of the judges make a cryptic gesture in order to inform the chief judge that the Lawyer was actually talking about the point. (However, one had to excuse the chief judge because he did not know the details of the case.) 7.8

Chief Judge The case has now been heard. Sentence will be passed after deliberation.

ʿĪsā ibn Hishām said: We went outside to wait while the session moved to the deliberation chamber. I asked the Lawyer how long the deliberation usually took. 7.9

Lawyer Usually no more than an hour.

ʿĪsā What's the average number of cases per session?

Lawyer Ten on average.

ʿĪsā Is that enough time to study all the papers which go into criminal cases?

Lawyer Certainly, although when a criminal case involves the possibility of a death sentence or hard labor, it may take two or three hours. I've often perused case files which have been returned from the judge who sums up to the secretary's office for the lawyer's perusal. We found a mark on them with

وطالما اطلعنا على القضايا التي تعود من عند الملخص إلى قلم الكتّاب تحت اطلاع المحامي فنجد عليها رمزًا بأحد هذه الحروف «ب. ع. ت» فالباء إشارة إلى البراءة، والعين إشارة إلى العقوبة، والتاء إشارة إلى تأييد الحكم الابتدائي. وإنما يضع القاضي هذه الرموز حتى لا ينسى رأيه في القضية عند عرضه على زملائه في المداولة فإذا عرضه عليهم لم يضع الوقت بينهم سدى.

١٠،٧ ولمّا كان القاضي الجنائي له الاستقلال المطلق في الحكم بما يرتاح إليه ضميره وتطمئن به نفسه كان الواجب عليه أن يفحص أدلة الثبوت وأدلة البراءة بنفسه فيعرضها على ضميره وهو خال من كل اعتقاد مخصوص بالبراءة أو التهمة، حتى إذا غلبت عليه الأدلة حكم بما يغلب عليه من الأدلة والبراهين، وهذا لا يأتي من طريق التسليم لرأي الغير والاكتفاء بحكمه وإلا أن يكون الحكم مبتوتًا في القضية بهذه الأحرف الثلاثة بعد أن مرّ عليها القاضي الملخص مرورًا وهو منفرد في بيته.

١١،٧ وبينما نحن في هذا الكلام إذ عادت الجلسة إلى انعقادها فدخلنا لسماع الحكم فنطق الرئيس ببراءة الباشا لعدم ثبوت التهمة عليه ولأنه قد حالت دونه ودون دعوة القانون قوة قاهرة. فخرجنا مسرورين بتلك البراءة ورأيناها نعمة من النعم بعد تلك النقم.

الباشا لا أنكر اليوم أنّ العدل موجود ولكنه بطيء، لا يتحمل أعباء بطئه البريء، وكان الأولى في هذه المحاكمات، وهذه المناقشات والمداولات أن تكون النهاية في البداية، فلم يلحق من كان مثلي هذا الهوان والصغار، والحبس والعار، والذهاب والإياب، والإذن والحجاب، وشهرة الاتهام، والوقوف موقف الذنب والإجرام. وأنا أفرح الآن بالبراءة لا لأنها لذة حقيقية وإنما لكونها رفعت عني الآلام.

المحامي إني أهنئك بهذه البراءة وأسأل لك دوام العافية من مصائب هذا الاتهام ولا زلت تخرج من كل قضية خروج السهم من قوسه والسيف من غمده، وقد مضى الدفاع وبقي عليكم الدفع.

one of these letters A, C, and E. A stood for acquittal, C for conviction, and E for endorsement of the verdict of the first court. The judge writes these signs so that he won't forget his opinion on the case when he presents it to his colleagues during the deliberation process. In that way, when he gives them his opinion, he doesn't waste time on discussion and argument.

7.10 But, since the criminal judge has absolute discretionary independence to decide on the verdict according to his own conscience, he has to check the proofs of confirmed guilt and innocence for himself. After that, he deliberates the entire matter for himself without any personal feeling about innocence or guilt. Once he's convinced of the proof, he passes sentence according to the weight of evidence. In so doing, he isn't giving way to someone else's opinion or making do with the verdict of another. However, the final verdict is settled based on one of those three letters which the summarizing judge skims over in the seclusion of his own home.

7.11 As we were talking, the court resumed its session. We went back in to hear the verdict. The chief judge pronounced the Pāshā innocent because the case against him was not proven and there were cogent mitigating circumstances which kept him apart from the claims of the law. With that we left, feeling overjoyed at this piece of good fortune after so much bad luck.

PĀSHĀ Today I cannot deny that justice still exists. But it's so slow. This slowness is an intolerable burden on the innocent. In these trials, with all their arguments and deliberations, it would be better for the conclusion of the case to be reached at the beginning. Then people like myself would not have to suffer the shame and degradation of imprisonment, comings and goings, permissions and chamberlains, all the while being labeled and treated like a criminal. If I'm happy to be found innocent, it's not because I feel any genuine pleasure, but rather that I feel relieved of real pain.

LAWYER I congratulate you on your acquittal. It is my hope that you may continue to be free from the trials of being under suspicion. May you emerge from every trial like an arrow from a bow and a sword from a scabbard! My defense of you is now complete, so it only remains for you to pay me.

مصباح الشرق ٤٢، ٢ فبراير ١٨٩٩

١،٨ قال عيسى بن هشام: ما زال المحامي عاكفاً علينا يطالبنا بالأجر والباشا يعده لآخر الشهر حتى يأتيه أحد حاشيته وأتباعه بمال من أملاكه وضياعه، والمحامي يأبى التسويف والإمهال، وإلّا الدفع في الحال، ويقول:

المحامي هل تقوم هذه الوعود مقام النقود في بلد كثر فيه الإنفاق وزادت الضرورات وقلّ فيه الربح كما قلت المرؤات، وصار الدرهم فيه أعز عند الأب من بنيه، وعند الابن من أبيه، ولقد تعبت في القضية تعبين بالبنان والجنان، ولا أستريح منهما إلا بعد الدراهم الآن، وإنك لا تصرفني وإن كنت محمود الخلق بالوعد، ولكنك تصرفني وأنا أحمد بالنقد، وإني لا أريد أن أسكن في بيت المتنبي - أنا الغنيّ وأموالي المواعيد - فلا تجعل الخلاص من قضية بقضية، والفكاك من بليّة ببليّة، فهذا ما لا يأتيه العقلاء، ولا يقدم عليه الفهماء.

٢،٨ قال عيسى بن هشام: ولمّا رأيت الباشا لا يقدر على الكلام والتلفظ من شدة الحنق والتغيّظ، تداخلت بينهما تداخل الأريب، وتوسطت بينهما توسط اللبيب، ولم أدع في التنازل باباً إلّا ولجته، وفي لطف الالتماس وجهاً إلّا كشفته، حتى نلت ببركة الخضوع والرجاء رضاء المحامي بالمهلة والإرجاء، إلى أن ينتقل الباشا من العسر إلى اليسر، ويتحلى بغناه بعد الفقر، وقلت للمحامي ما يقال في باب المروءة والهمة، من وجوب الحنو على من يقع في مصيبة وملمّة، وأنّ من تذكر الدهر وغيره، والزمان وعبره، لانت عريكته، وطاوعت شكيمته، وليس بين صعود المرء ونزوله، وإشراق سعده وأفوله، وغناه وفقره، وصفوه وكدره، إلا مسافة انقضاض القضاء من السماء.

Miṣbāḥ al-sharq 42, February 2, 1899[58]

'Īsā ibn Hishām said: The Lawyer kept on nagging us to give him his fee. The Pāshā promised it to him by the end of the month, by which time one of his servants and retainers would be able to bring him some money from his estates and property. But the Lawyer rejected the idea of deferred payment and demanded payment on the spot. 8.1

LAWYER (*to the Pāshā*) Do you imagine such promises can take the place of cash in a country where there are so many expenses and daily needs keep increasing, a place where profits are as scarce as common decency, and the dirham is more valuable to a father than his own son and vice versa? This case has exhausted me in two ways: fingers and heart. The only relief I can get from such exhaustion is for you to pay me with some of that ringing gold stuff. Don't dismiss me with promises, even though you are a man of integrity; but rather with cash—then I'll be grateful. I don't want to be in the position that the poet al-Mutanabbī describes in his line:

I'm rich, but my wealth is all in promises.[59]

Don't get to the end of one case simply to start another and be rid of one misfortune only to fall into another. That's not the kind of thing for intelligent men to do; people of discretion should not embark upon such a course.

'Īsā ibn Hishām said: I noticed the Pāshā was rapidly losing his temper, so much so that he could hardly speak. At this point I prudently intervened between the two of them. There was no form of humble petition that I did not try, no kind of polite request that I did not essay. Eventually my pleadings and fawnings persuaded the Lawyer to agree to a deferment of payment till the Pāshā's circumstances changed from difficulty to ease and from crippling poverty to wealth and affluence. I told him all the usual things about generosity and magnanimity: how one should show consideration to people in trouble; that, whenever anyone pauses to consider the role of fate and the lessons of time, his temper calms down and his obstinacy gives way. Between a man's ascent and descent, the rising and setting of his fortunes, his wealth and poverty, his happiness and grief, there lies only the distance of that fatal judgment from the heavens. 8.2

٣،٨ الباشا لبئس الصاحب والقرين أنت، كيف تسمني بسمة الفقراء، وتستعطف عليّ قلوب الضعفاء، وأنا المثري الغني، والأمير السري، وأين ما ادخرته في عمري واكتنزته في عصري من مال وعقار وفضة ونضار وأملاك وضياع وزخرف ومتاع، وكان يضرب بغناي المثل، فإن كنت جاهلاً بي فسل، اذهب فأتني بخبر ما ادخرت، وأثر ما اكتنزت، وكيف يخفى عليك وعلى المحامي ما لي من الأموال والعقار، وما قضيت فيه العمر من الجمع والادخار، فإني ما تركت حيلة، ولا أغفلت وسيلة في الحصول على الغنى، حتى جمعت كثيرًا ممّا تفرّق على الورى، فجعلته عدة لشدة أزري، وأمانًا من مصائب دهري، وذخيرة لأبنائي وحفدتي، وأعقابي وذريتي، ليأمنوا من بعدي ويكونوا في جنة من ذل الحاجة وجنة من رغد العيش، ونجوة من الافتقار، ونجوة عن التلبس بالعار، فإذا تركتهم تركتهم مطمئن القلب مستريح الفؤاد باقي الذكر دائم المجد رفيع عماد البيت.

٤،٨ عيسى بن هشام نعم نحن نعلم يا معشر الأمراء والحكام أنكم قضيتم الأعمار في جمع الحطام واتخذتم وظيفة الحكم تجارة من التجارات تربحون منها الإثراء ولم تكونوا تعلمون للحكم من مزية سوى اكتناز الأموال واستلاب الحقوق وابتزاز الأقوات من أفواه الأرامل واليتامى، والأطفال والأيامى، وسواء عليكم حزتم المال من حله ومن غير حله لم تبالوا في طريقكم بالضعيف المسكين، ولم ترثوا للعاجز والمستكين، بل ظلمتم البريء وبرّأتم الظالم فجمعتم لديكم ما فرّقه الله على العباد من رزق وما قسمه لهم من قوت ورضيتم بالوزر، وطوّقتم أعناقكم بالإصر، ثمّ حرمتم أنفسكم من التمتع بما جمعتموه، وبخلتم عليها بما حزتموه، ولم تكونوا من الذين في أموالهم حق معلوم للسائل والمحروم، ولم تؤدوا ما فرض الله فيها من الحقوق ولم تطهروها بزكاة ولا صدقة ولا إحسان، وأطربكم منها رنين الدرهم فوق الدرهم وصمت الدينار مع الدينار،

8.3 PĀSHĀ A fine friend and companion you've turned out to be! How dare you label me "poor" and try to win me the sympathy of weak people? I'm a high ranking amir, a man of great wealth. Where are the things I treasured and stored up in my lifetime, my money and real estate, the silver and gold, mansions and farms, ornaments and belongings that I owned? My wealth was proverbial. If you haven't got any information about me, then simply ask people. Go and bring me news of all the other things I collected and hoarded. How can it be that you and the Lawyer have no idea about the money and estates I possessed and about the time I spent collecting and treasuring objects? I left no ruse untried and no means neglected in order to gain wealth. Eventually I had amassed a huge store of the things which are divided up amongst mankind. I used it to support myself, a safeguard against the misfortunes that my destiny might bring down upon me, and as a treasure for my sons and grandsons, an inheritance for my descendants. Then, after my demise, they could be protected against the humiliation of need and could live comfortably in an earthly paradise, free of poverty and involvement in wrongdoing. When I left them, it was with a feeling of security and self-satisfaction, because in people's memories I would remain exalted and revered.

8.4 ʿĪSĀ IBN HISHĀM Oh yes, you amirs, members of the ruling class, we're all too well aware of how you spent your lives collecting ephemeral objects. You plied power and authority as your trade, using them to gain riches. The only point you could see in having authority was in order to amass money, to deprive people of their rights, and to snatch food out of the mouths of widows and orphans. It didn't matter whether you obtained the money by fair means or foul; it was all the same to you. You showed no concern for the wretched weakling and felt no pity for the humble disabled person. Instead you wronged the innocent and set guilty people free. As a result, you amassed for yourselves whatever bounty God had apportioned to His servants and whatever nourishment He had divided among them. You condoned all kinds of sin and took the burden of guilt on yourselves. Afterwards, you deprived yourselves of any enjoyment of what you had collected and acted like misers. You did not number among those people to whose wealth beggars and the needy have an acknowledged right. You failed to carry out the duties which God has enjoined regarding your wealth or to render it pure by giving alms and charity.[60] It was the ringing of dirham against dirham and the hushed sound of dinars clinking against each other that thrilled you.

٥،٨ واخترعتم وسائل وطرائق يأباها الله لعباده ويمقتها ويستبشعها الإنسان ويستفظعها لجمع ما جمعتموه، وكنز ما كنزتموه، وسلب ما سلبتموه، ونهب ما نهبتموه بالإثم والعدوان ومعصية الرسول، وتجاسرتم على الله في أوامره ونواهيه وكلفتم العلماء بتأويلها على أهوائكم فأوّلوها لكم لانحصار الأرزاق في أيديكم واحتياجهم إلى ما يقتاتون به من فضلاتكم، فالوزر عليهم وعليكم ولكنه عليكم أعظم وفوقكم أثقل، حتى إذا انقضى العمر وحلّ الأجل تركتم ما خلفتموه لغلمة من ذريتكم وصبية من جواريكم ربيتموهم على الحرمان ولم تثقفوهم بالتعليم ولم تتركوهم للزمن يؤدّبهم وللأيام والليالي تهذبهم فصرتم في أعينهم كالرصد الذي يكون على باب الكنز يحتالون لنقله بقتله فإذا استراحوا منكم بالقتل أو الموت مزقوا أموالكم انتقاماً منكم ومنها، فما هو إلا أن يتسابق الدود والورثة في أحشائكم المدفونة والمخزونة فتسبق الورثة الدود في الصدور والورود، فتذهب البدرة إثر البدرة والضيعة إثر الضيعة والعمارة إثر العمارة حتى إذا لم يبق إلا بيت السكن أتوا على ما فيه من الأثاث بيعاً وما في أعناق الجواري من الجواهر والقلائد رهناً ولا يزالون يشغلون حجرة إثر حجرة والدائنون يدخلون فيه خطوة إثر خطوة حتى يندك أثره ويعفى خبره ويزول اسم بانيه الذي ارتكب ما ارتكب لبقائه فلم يبق له إلّا اللعنتين في الحالتين، حالة الخلاص منه بالتشييع إلى قبره وحالة أسفهم بعد فقرهم على إهماله لتعليمهم في صباهم بما كان ينفعهم في معاشهم.

٦،٨ هذه عاقبة ما صارت إليه أموالكم أيها الأمراء من بعدكم، ويا ليت أولادكم وأحفادكم ووارثيكم خففوا عليكم من الإثم في جمعها من دماء المصريين بتبذيرها فيهم وإنفاقها بينهم فيكون ذلك منهم كردّ بعض الشيء لصاحبه ولكن البلاء كل البلاء أنها ذهبت جميعاً إلى يد الأجنبي الغريب. وكأنّ الدهر سلّط المماليك على المصريين ينهبون أموالهم ويسلبون أملاكهم ثمّ سلّط الله على المماليك من سلبهم ما جمعوه

In order to rob, despoil, and hoard as you did, you devised all sorts of ways abhorred by God and utterly condemned by mankind. In so doing, you acted in sin and willfully disobeyed the Prophet's injunctions. You dared to flout the commands and prohibitions of God Almighty and forced religious scholars to interpret His authority as you fancied. They fulfilled that role for you because you had exclusive control over their salaries; they needed the surplus from your way of life to provide food for themselves. So the burden of guilt is on you and on them, but it is greater and heavier on you. Eventually when your life came to an end when the moment of death arrived, you bequeathed what you had left behind to your young sons and daughters who had grown up in your midst in a state of deprivation. You didn't enlighten them with any kind of education, nor did you allow them to be taught and instructed by the inexorable passing of days and nights. In their eyes, you were like a watchdog in front of the door of a treasure chamber, and they were forever making schemes to get rid of it by killing it—as the saying goes. When death or murder finally relieved them of your presence, they tore your wealth apart out of vengeance on it and you. So it happened that worms and inheritors had a race over your buried remains as well as over your hoarded ones, and the inheritors beat the worms coming and going. More and more money disappeared, estate after estate, mansion after mansion, till only the house in which they were living was left. Then they started selling off the furniture, and pawning the jewels and necklaces off the girls' very necks. They kept working on the house, room by room, and creditors entered step by step until all vestiges of it and every detail about it disappeared. The name of the original builder who had committed so many crimes in order to keep it standing was forever lost, and all that remained was a separate curse for each of two circumstances: the first for being rid of him by committing him to the grave; the second for their regret that he'd failed to teach them anything when they were still young that would help them live useful lives. 8.5

This then was the way, you amirs, that your money and property came to nought after your death. If only your children and grandchildren had mitigated the crime you had committed in amassing this wealth from the blood of Egyptians by spending and squandering it in their midst. That at least would have been akin to restoring some rights to the proper owner. But the worst misfortune of all is that all this wealth has fallen into the hands of foreigners and aliens. It seems as if fate put the Mamluks in authority over the Egyptians in 8.6

ثمّ سلّط على هؤلاء أعقابهم فسلموا مجامع ذلك للأجانب يتمتعون به أمام المصريين وهم أولى بالقليل منه. وما دفعهم إلى هذا التسليم إلا ما ورثوه عنكم من احترام الأجنبي واحتقار المصري، فإنكم لم تكتفوا أن تكونوا أرباباً للمصريين حتى شاركتم الأجنبي في تلك الربوبية فغلبكم عليها وأشركم مع المصريين في العبودية.

٧.٨ واعلم أيها الأمير أنّ أقرانك وأخدانك وأصحابك من ذوي الثروة والغنى الذين كنتم تعدّونهم بالألوف أصبحت بيوتهم خاوية على عروشها وأبصار أعقابهم شاخصة إليها فإن تبحث عن أموالك وضياعك اليوم فابحث عنها تحت ثقال تلك الرحى.

فيا عبث المدخر الجامع، والمكتنز الطامع، ما كان أغناكم عن الجمع والادخار، وحرمان نفوسكم في الدنيا وعرضها في الآخرة على النار.

يقولُ الفتَى ثَمّرتُ مالي وإنّما
لوارثهِ ما ثمّر المالَ كاسبُهُ
يُحاسبُ فيه نفسَهُ في حياتهِ
ويتركُهُ نهباً لمن لا يحاسبُهُ

الباشا أراك قد تجاوزت الحد في اللوم والتعنيف واللوم والتوبيخ والعذل والتعزير وما أظنّك إلّا صادقاً فإنني لم أتعوّد منك منذ صحبتي على مثل هذه الجرأة في القول كذباً وباطلاً، فكيف التدبير في اكتساب المعيشة وسد الحاجة بعد أن ضاعت الأموال وذهبت من أيدينا الأحكام، ولم يبق إلا أن أورد نفسي حمامها، وأسكنها رجامها، فما أروح ما كنت فيه بالأمس، وأشرحه للنفس، وما أحسن ظلام ذلك الرمس، وأقبح ضياء هذه الشمس.

٨.٨ عيسى بن هشام ليس لمثل حالتكم غير الأسف منّا والتوجع لكم، فقد اعتقدتم أيها الحاكم أنّ ما يقع بالاتفاق والصدفة بين أحايين الدهر في ولاية الأحكام قياس مطرد تبنى عليه المعيشة لاعتباره آلة كآلات الصناعة في الارتزاق بها، فإذا

order to rob them of their wealth and deprive them of their properties, then God put other people in command in order to rob the Mamluks of what they had collected. He then put their descendants in control, and they've proceeded to hand it all over to foreigners to enjoy in front of the very eyes of Egyptians who have more right to at least part of it. The only thing which has led your descendants to submit like this is their reverence for foreigners and the utter contempt for the Egyptian people which they've inherited from you. You weren't satisfied just to be masters of the Egyptians! You had to bring in foreigners as your partners in this domination. The result was that they beat you at your own game and forced you to join the Egyptians in their subjection.

8.7 You need to know, Amir, that the mansions of your wealthy friends and companions from your era whom you used to count in the thousands are all in ruins. Their descendants just stare at them. If you want to find out about your wealth and estates today, then inquire under the surface of that millstone. Oh the sheer futility of those who collect and hoard with such relish! You had no need to indulge in such avarice, depriving yourselves in this world and earning hellfire in the next.

Man says: "I have invested my wealth," and to the heir alone
belongs the money which the earner has invested.
He holds himself to account for it in his lifetime, then bequeaths it
as booty for those whom he cannot hold to account.[61]

Pāshā In my opinion you've exceeded all reasonable bounds in your opprobrium and hypercritical comments. I have thought of you as a friend; ever since we have been together, I have never made such a series of rash and deceitful statements. How am I supposed to earn a living now that all the money has disappeared and, as you point out, we no longer have any authority? The only way out of my difficulties which I can see is to allow my soul to return to the grave and rest in deathly peace again. How serene everything felt just yesterday, how soothing to the soul! How fair is the shadow of the tomb, and how foul the light of this sun!

8.8 'Īsā Someone in your circumstances can only expect sorrow and pity from us. You members of the ruling class have come to believe that the power to exert authority which you happened to have at one time is a general phenomenon on which to base existence, in that it provides an instrument for earning a living wage, just like any other craft or job. But, once authority falls

أصابكم العزل تقطعت بكم الأسباب كما يصيب الشلل يد الصانع فيتعطل عن عمله ويبقى كلّاً على كاهل الكل فيرجو الموت كما رجوت، وكأنكم أيها الحكام صنف من الناس لكم نصيب من العيش دونهم فلا تكونون إلا فوق العرش، أو على النعش، وقد قال مسكين من رؤساء صناعتكم وهو في ضيق الحبس، كما أنك في ضيق النفس:

ونحن أناس لا توسط عندنا
لنا الصدور دون العالمين أو القبر

ومعلوم لك ما في هذه الصناعة، صناعة الحكم، من قلة ما يرفعه الصدر، وكثرة ما يضمه القبر، وكان الأولى بكم أن تكونوا كالناس في معايشهم لكل واحد وسيلة وصناعة وحرفة وآلة يحسن الارتزاق بها، فإذا نزلتم عن تلك العروش بقيتم أحياء بين أفراد الجمعية تنفعون وتنتفعون.

الباشا لك الله، إنّ كل ما قاسيته من البوليس والنيابة والمحكمتين واللجنة كان أقل همّاً وأدون شجناً من مرارة وعظك هذا، ولكن ما الرأي وقد مضى العمر إلا الأقل، ولم يبق وقت للصناعة ولا العمل، وموعظتك نافعة لمن يجيء لا لمن يمضي.

٩،٨ قال عيسى بن هشام: وأحزنتني حالة الرجل وكدت أذوب عليه أسفاً فأخذت أتدبر له وأتفكر في طريقة يحيى بها. وكلما خطر لي رأي تخيلت فيه نجاحاً عدت بالخيبة بعد الإمعان فيه وصاحبي ينظر إليّ في تفكيري مرّة ويطرق لتفكيره أخرى. وما زلنا على هذا الوجه حتى انتفض من مكانه آخذاً بثوبي قائلاً لي:

الباشا قد وجدت ما يشد العوز ويكفي الشيخوخة.

عيسى بن هشام ماذا وجدت؟

الباشا كان من عادات الحكام في الأزمان السالفة أن يفتدوا أنفسهم من

from your grasp, you lose the means of earning a living, just as a craftsman becomes unemployed when his hand is paralyzed. He can no longer function and becomes a weight on everyone's shoulders. Like you, his only wish is to die. It's as though you members of the ruling class are a group apart, with a guaranteed share of some form of livelihood to the exclusion of everyone else. You have to be on top, either of a golden throne or a bier. A poor chap who was one of the leaders in your profession wrote the following line while he was in low spirits in prison:

> We are a people for whom there's no middle course:
> For us it is either the forefront over others or the grave.[62]

In the profession of authority and order, you know full well how little is raised to prominence and how much is left to be contained in the grave. It would be more appropriate if you were to behave like other people by earning a living. Everyone has a particular method, trade, profession, and machine which enables him to earn a decent living wage. If you step down from your thrones, you can join the other members of our society doing something useful and also gaining some rewards.

PĀSHĀ By God, all the harm I have suffered at the hands of the police, Parquet, the two courts, and the Committee is far less worrying and distressing than this bitter advice of yours. What's to be done? My life has long since passed, save for a very little. I've no time left for crafts and hard work. The moral you draw may be sound enough, but it's meant for somebody who's on the way up rather than passing on.

8.9 ʿĪsā ibn Hishām said: The Pāshā's mood saddened me, and I started feeling sorry for him. I tried to think of ways he could earn a living. Every time an idea occurred to me that might work, my hopes were dashed when I thought about it more carefully. Sometimes the Pāshā stared at me as I was thinking, at others he thought for himself. We stayed like that, but then he suddenly leapt to his feet and grabbed my coat.

PĀSHĀ I've come up with a way to ward off poverty and suffice for my old age.

ʿĪSĀ What have you thought of?

PĀSHĀ In former times rulers used to save their necks from hellfire and purchase a place in heaven by building a public fountain, mosque, and Qurʾan

النار ويشتروا الجنة ببناء سبيل وجامع وكتّاب، وإيقاف ما يكفي ريعه لذلك من عمارة أو أراض، وقد سلكت مسلكهم واتبعت سنّتهم وشيّدت مثلهم «مجلبة للغفران» فهلمّ معي نبحث على ما بنيت وأوقفت.

school. To cover the costs they would use a building or lands to provide an endowment. I followed the same plan and copied their precedent; like them I erected a "forgiveness factor." Come with me, and let's find out what I built and endowed.

مصباح الشرق ٤٣، ٩ فبراير ١٨٩٩

١،٩ قال عيسى بن هشام: فظللت أنا والباشا نواصل الطواف بالطواف للوقوف على تلك الأوقاف، ونسائل العابر وابن السبيل عن المسجد والسبيل، سؤال المجدب عن الروض، والظمآن عن الحوض، فلم نجد من يرشد إلى ما ننشد. وأخذ الباشا يتذكر الطرق وأماكنها، والأزقة ومساكنها، ويقول كان هنا وكان هنا، وجل ما يقضي به الهنا، وما زال يقاصر خطواته، ويطاول آهاته، فتبكيه رسوم الديار بكاء صاحب عزة أو صاحب نوار:

فَاسْأَلَنْهَا واجعَلْ بُكَاءَ جَوَابًا
تَجِدِ الدّمعَ سائِلًا ومُجيبًا

٢،٩ حتى وصلنا بعد طول التجوال والتجواب، وترداد الجيئة والذهاب إلى مضيق في منتهى الطريق، فوقف الباشا قبالة دور مهدّمة، وجدران محطّمة، ومسجد في فجوة منه حانوت خمار، وفي زاوية منه دكان عطّار، وبجانبهما حوانيت مختلفة الأصناف، متباينة الأوصاف. فطفق الباشا يصعد فيها نظره ويصوّبه، ويخطئ حدسه تارة ويصوّبه، فهداه طول النظر والتدقيق، ودوام الإمعان والتحقيق، أن رأى شيخًا فانيًا متربعًا في دكانه، متحيّزًا بمكانه، عليه علامات الانحلال والسقوط، وشارات الانخذال والقنوط، وسيما الرضاء بالمقسوم، والتسليم للقضاء المحتوم، فترى جبهته كأنها من ورق البرديّ العتيق، تقرأ فيها ما دوّنه الدهر من آيات الشدة والضيق، فخرج الباشا من حال المتحيّر المتردد إلى حال الواثق المعتمد، فناداه من بعد، نداء السيد للعبد، فانتفض الرجل انتفاضًا عجيبًا وقصده ملبيًا ومجيبًا، فما شككت من جلال النداء وأدب التلبية إلّا أنّ أميرًا ينادي من فوق دسته أحد الحاشية، ولمّا وصل صاحب الحانوت وقف أمام الباشا وقفة الممتثل الخاضع، والطائع الخشع، ثمّ بدأ يراجع فكره، ويحدّد نظره، فقال له الباشا:

Miṣbāḥ al-sharq 43, February 9, 1899[63]

9.1 ʿĪsā ibn Hishām said: The Pāshā and I kept on going round in circles, trying one course after another in an attempt to find these endowments. We questioned passersby and travelers about mosques and fountains; it was like seeking verdant meadows in an arid desert or a thirsty man in quest of a pool of water. We could not find anyone to guide us to the object of our search. At this point the Pāshā began to remember the location of streets, alleyways, and houses; he would say that the endowment was here and then there, and that what the Almighty brings about is glorious. He kept shortening his pace and prolonging his sighs as he wept at the sight of the ruins and old houses, like the lovers of ʿAzza or Nawār:

> Question these ruins and make your weeping an answer;
> in tears you find both question and answer.[64]

9.2 After spending ages wandering around and walking hither and yon, we eventually reached a narrow lane at the end of the road. The Pāshā came to a halt in front of some ruined dwellings, derelict walls, and a small mosque. The front part consisted of a wine shop, and there was a perfumer's shop in one corner. Alongside these two were some other shops of various shapes and sizes. The Pāshā looked up and stared at them intently, but was not sure whether he was right or wrong. A long close scrutiny led him to see an old man sitting cross-legged by himself on a bench. He looked weak and timeworn, and seemed very despondent, as though he had resigned himself to his lot. His forehead looked like an old papyrus sheet, showing signs of dreadful hardship that time had inscribed on it. The Pāshā's uncertainty now changed to conviction. From a distance he yelled over to the man as a master would to his slave. The man leapt to his feet remarkably quickly and ran towards him in answer to his summons. From the fearsome yell and the manner of response I assumed a prince seated on his throne was summoning one of his courtiers. When the Shop Owner reached us, he stood humbly in front of the Pāshā. After collecting his thoughts and staring intently at the man, the Pāshā spoke to him:

٣،٩ الباشا ألست أنت أحمد أغا الركبدار الذي كنت من المعدودين في حاشيتي، ألم تعرفني من أنا.

صاحب الحانوت لولا أنّ الموت حجاب كثيف وحجاز منيع بين ظهر الأرض وبطنها لقلت أنك سيدي وأميري ويشهد الله أنني كلما نظرت إلى مخائلك وسمعت صوتك في كلامك كاد يطير عقلي ويندهش لبي لاستحكام الشبه بينك وبين المرحوم.

الباشا إني أنا هو وهذه العلامة التي تعلمها في جسمي من اللعب بالجريد على مشهد منك في ذلك اليوم المشهود.

وكشف الباشا عن ساقه فأراه العلامة فوقع الرجل منكبّاً على الأرض من دهشة ما رأى ثمّ أخذ يقبّل قدمي الباشا والدموع تنحدر من عينيه ويقول.

صاحب الحانوت كيف الحياة بعد الممات، لحق أنت إحدى المعجزات، وليس بغريب ما أرى، فقد شاهدت في هذا العمر الموجز ما لا تحيط به الأقلام والمحابر، ولا تسعه بطون الدفاتر من عجائب الانتقال وغرائب المحال، ولا يبعد بعد ذلك أن تشرق الشمس من مغربها وتُخرج الأرض أمواتها من مقابرها.

٤،٩ عيسى بن هشام

هيَ الأيّامُ قد صِرنَا كُلُّها
عجائبَ حتّى ليس فيها عجائبُ

اعلم أيها الرجل أنّ القدرة لا تعجز عن شيء. وقصصت عليه قصة الباشا منذ البداية، فصاح الرجل يبكي ويتأسف ويقول ليت أمّي لم تلدني وليت شعري. لو كانت القدرة التي أحيت الباشا أحيت معه زمنه ووقته وإلا فكيف له بالعيش في مثل هذا الزمن؟ وما أجدره بالعودة إلى أدراج الكفن.

٥،٩ قال عيسى بن هشام: وقصّ لنا الرجل قصته وما جرى عليه بعد موت الباشا وما جرى على بيت الباشا وأهل طبقته من إخوانه وأصحابه، ثمّ التفت إليه فقال:

9.3 Pāshā Aren't you Aḥmad Aghā, the groom? Weren't you a member of my entourage? Don't you know who I am?

Shop Owner If it weren't for the fact that death is a thick and impenetrable screen separating the surface from interior of the earth, I would have said that you were my master and amir. God is my witness that, every time I look at your face and hear your voice, my mind almost takes flight. I am utterly bewildered, so closely do you resemble my late master.

Pāshā I am indeed your master. Here's the mark on my body that you'll recognize. I got it as a result of a javelin contest you saw on that notable games day.

The Pāshā uncovered his leg and showed him the mark. The man was so amazed that he fell to the ground. He started kissing the Pāshā's foot, tears cascading from his eyes.

Shop Owner How can there be life after death? You're a miracle indeed! Even so, I'm not surprised by what I see. In my lifespan I've witnessed remarkable transformations and alterations which pens cannot describe nor notebooks contain within their covers. From now onward the sun may well start rising in the West and the earth release the dead from its graves!

9.4 ʿĪsā ibn Hishām said:

Every day is an object of wonder
so that nothing it brings forth can amaze.[65]

"You must realize," I said, "that all things are possible." I then told him the Pāshā's story from the very beginning. With that he uttered a cry and started weeping and moaning:

Shop Owner If only my mother had never borne me! Would that I knew whether the force that resurrected the Pāshā after his death would also bring back the era in which he lived as well. Failing that, how can he possibly make a living in this age? It would be far better for him to retrace his steps to the shrouds of the grave.

9.5 ʿĪsā ibn Hishām said: He started telling us his own story, what had happened to him after the Pāshā's death and what had befallen the Pāshā's house and his peers who were both colleagues and friends. Turning to face the Pāshā he went on:

صاحب الحانوت اعلم أيها المولى أنه لم يبق لك من أثر يذكر في ضياعك وأموالك وثروتك ومتاعك، وقد عشت زماناً وأنا متمتع بريع ما أوقفته أيها الأمير على حاشيتك وأتباعك مع هذا المسجد والسبيل الذين أقمتهما لتخليد ذكرك فما لبث الوقف أن تخرّب بقوة الإهمال فوقعنا في الاحتياج، وصار السبيل خمارة والماء خمرا والمسجد مصبغة والكتّاب مخزناً كما تشاهد وترى، وصرتُ أنا بيطاراً بعد أن كنت ركبداراً، وأخذت هذه الحانوت من أرض الوقف للتعيش منها.

الباشا ألم يبق من ذريتي أحد يباشر هذا الوقف بنظره.

البيطار آخر العهد عندي كان بواحد منهم ذهبت إليه لأجل هذه الحانوت وأعلمته بمكاني منك فلم يلتفت إلى حاجتي وانتهرني وطردني وأبعدني وزجرني، ولكن الحاجة دفعتني إلى الإلحاح فترددت عليه مرارا فتخلص من ثقل إلحاحي عليه بإحالتي على خواجة عنده يدبر له ما بقي لديه من ثروة نضبت عينها ونزحت بئرها فأحالني الخواجة على صاحب الخمارة لأنه المستولي على هذه القطعة بوضع اليد عليها ولا يجسر أحد أن يعمل فيها شيئاً بغير هواه خوف من تشكيه إلى المحاكم فقصدت الخمّار واتفقت معه على أجرة، وأقمت في هذه الحانوت أصرع الدهر ويصرعني، وأطلب القوت ويعوزني، وأتعجل الأجل ويمهلني، وسبحان المنفرد بعزته المبدع في حكمته.

الباشا وأين مكان هذا العاق المخالف لإرادتي وشرط الواقف كنص الشارع. ٦،٩

البيطار هو مقيم الآن في الأوتيل.

الباشا وما هو الأوتيل.

البيطار اللوكاندة.

الباشا وما هو اللوكاندة.

عيسى بن هشام الأوتيل بيت معروف يعدّونه لنزول من لا مكان له بالأجرة من الغرباء والأجانب وطراق المسافرين، وهو في المعنى كالخان الذي تعرفونه في زمانكم.

Shop Owner Master, not a single trace of your wealth remains. Lands, money, wealth, and possessions—they're all gone. For a long time I was able to live on the profits of the endowment that you bequeathed to your household and retinue, along with this mosque and fountain, both of which you established to perpetuate your memory. But before too long, the endowment collapsed through prolonged neglect. We were all left in dire need. As you can see for yourself, the fountain has turned into a wine shop, its water into wine, the mosque is now a dye works, and the Qur'an school is a storehouse. I became a farrier after being a groom, and took over this shop from the endowment's property as a way of earning a living.

Pāshā But aren't there any of my descendants left to supervise the endowment?

Groom The last I heard of them was when I went to see one of them about this shop. I mentioned to him the position I'd held in your entourage, but he paid me no attention, upbraided me, proceeded to throw me out, and sent me away with a rebuke. However, my desperate needs forced me to persist, so I went to see him several times. He rid himself of my tiresome and persistent pleas by sending me to a European he had with him who had taken control of what was left of his wealth after the cash had dwindled and the well had run dry. The European sent me to the wine-shop owner. He had purloined the endowed property and taken it over. No one dared to do anything about it without his sanction for fear of litigation at court. So I went to the owner of the wine shop and agreed on a fixed rent with him. I've stayed in this shop struggling against a fate which in turn struggles with me, as I search for food that I can't find and crave the hour of my death which keeps delaying me. God is almighty, alone in His might and outstanding in His wisdom.

9.6

Pāshā Where's this disobedient child who's acting contrary to my wishes? The stipulations of the endower are as fixed as the text of the giver of the Shariah itself.

Groom At present, he's staying at the "Hotel."

Pāshā What's a "hotel?"

Groom The locanda.

Pāshā And what's the "locanda?"

'Īsā ibn Hishām The hotel is a residence available to strangers, foreigners, and travelers with no home of their own to stay in for a fixed price. It's like the hostel that you'd recognize from your times.

الباشا هل وصل النزول بهذا الخائن إلى سكن الخان، وسبحان من لا تهتدي إلى كنه أفعاله الفهوم والأذهان. وكيف يعيش المسكين في هذه الحال بعد عز النعمة والإقبال، أكان رجوعي إلى الحياة بما حكم به القدر عليّ وقضاه، تعذيباً لي على ما فرّطت في جنب الله، ألم يكن عنده سبحانه التعذيب في الآخرة بالنار، وذلك أحب لديّ من التعذيب بالعار في هذه الدار، ربّ إنّ الجحيم لأهون في النكال ممّا أسمعه من الرزية في المال والعيال:

فليتَ وليداً مات ساعةَ وضعِهِ
ولم يرتَضِعْ من أمّهِ النُّفَسَاءَ

٧،٩ عيسى بن هشام ليست السكنى في الأوتيل عن فقر وانحطاط، بل هي منتهى الغنى والعلو في هذا العصر، فإنّ النفقة على الإقامة فيه أياماً تكفي شهراً لنفقة قصر بجواريه وخدمه وأتباعه وحشمه، وقد دعاهم إلى ذلك كمال التقليد للأجانب فانتشر هذا الداء بين أولاد الأمراء حتى صاروا يقترضون بالربا الفاحش ويرهنون الأملاك والأطيان للسكنى في هذا الخان، وصار من يلزم بيته لخوفه في تهتكه أن تحكك فيه الأجانب بدعاوٍ يلفقونها ويقيمونها عليه يأتي بالطعام من الأوتيل إلى البيت وعنده الطباخ في أسفله والجواري الطاهيات في أعلاه.

الباشا (للبيطار) أرجوك أن تصف لصاحبي هذا الأوتيل حتى نتوجه إلى مقابلة ذلك الغلام فإنّ بي حاجة إلى لقائه.

البيطار أستغفر الله كيف ترجو مني وصف المكان، وهل تتصور أني أزايل خدمتك أو أفارق معيتك مهما تقلبت بك الحال، فدونك فأمر بما تريد.

٨،٩ قال عيسى بن هشام: وجذبني الباشا نقصد وجهة الأوتيل وأخذنا نسير والرجل يمشي معنا بخطاه الثقيلة، وعصاه الصقيلة، فقد صقلتها كثرة التوكأ والاستعمال إلى أن وصلنا إلى أحد الأوتيلات العالية الشهيرة فهال الباشا ما رأى عند دخوله من جمال البناء وحسن الرياش وبهاء الزينة وأدب الخدم، وظنّ أننا أخطأنا فدخلنا

Pāshā Has this reprobate now stooped so low as to stay in a hostel? Praise be to the One whose deeds human minds cannot comprehend! How can the poor man lead an agreeable life under such conditions after living a life of great luxury and prosperity? Was this resurrection of mine, something decreed upon me by fate, meant to serve as a form of torture for the excessive offences I committed against God? May He be praised! Isn't there something in the punishment of hellfire in the world to come? To me that's preferable to shame in this world! O Lord, Hell is an easier punishment to endure than what I'm hearing about loss of both money and family.

If only a child died at the hour of its birth
and never suckled from its mother in childbed.[66]

9.7 'Īsā ibn Hishām Today it's not a sign of poverty and humiliation to live in a hotel. Quite the contrary, it's an indication of considerable importance and wealth. The expenses for a few days spent there would be enough for a month's stay in the very largest mansions, complete with maids, servants, courtiers, and retinue. Your children were attracted to this trend by their crazy desire to copy foreigners exactly and imitate everything they do as precisely as possible. Today fortunate and wealthy children of amirs sell their property and pawn their estates in order to afford a stay in this hostel. Some of them stay at home because they are scared that foreigners will raise cases against them, so they have food brought to their house from the hotel even though they have cooks downstairs and cooking maids upstairs.

Pāshā (*to the Groom*) I hope you'll give my friend directions to this hotel so we can go there and meet this fellow. I must meet him.

Groom God forbid, my dear Amir! How can you talk to me about giving directions? Do you imagine that I'd leave your retinue or desert your company whatever changes may have been brought about by the vicissitudes of time? So come! It's your prerogative to give instructions.

9.8 'Īsā ibn Hishām said:[67] The Pāshā asked me to go with him, and we set off with the Groom plodding along behind us. He had a smooth walking stick that he had used so much that it looked quite polished. Eventually we stopped by the lofty structure of one of the best-known hotels. As the Pāshā went in, he was amazed by the beautiful building itself, the lovely furniture, the splendid

بيت أحد القناصل في زمانه ففصّلت له ما يخفى عليه من أمر الأوتيل، وسألنا عن الضالة المنشودة بعد أن تركنا البيطار خارجاً فأخبرنا أحد الخدم بثمرة الحجرة فقصدناها ولم يلتفت الباشا إلى طلب الإذن ورجع الجواب، بل فتح الباب مفاجئاً فدخلنا فوجدنا فيها جماعة من الشبان من أولاد الأمراء متقسمين أقساماً في اجتماعهم، فمنهم جماعة معتكفون على طاولة لاهون في لعب القمار. وطائفة أخرى في يد كل واحد منهم رسم لخيول المضمار، ومنهم فئة محيطون بامرأة نصف، لا عجوز شوهاء ولا فتاة حسناء تحاول اجتلاب الحسن بإفراط التصنّع والتزيّن، والتأنّق والتفنّن. ويكاد يضيء وجهها بسنا العقود والقلائد ولمعان الجواهر والفرائد، وفي وسط المكان طاولة عليها صنوف الراح في الأباريق والأقداح تختلط بآنية غالية الأثمان، مختلفة الأشكال والألوان، مع دواة وقرطاس، ويراعة منضدة بالألماس، وكتب مجلدة بالذهب، معدودة للزخرفة لا للعلم والأدب، وعلى الأرض أوراق أحكام، وجرائد منشورة تحت النعال والأقدام، لم يفض عنها ختام، ولم يقرأ منها إلا العنوان، أو ما اختص بأخبار السبق والرهان. ورؤوس الحاضرين كلها عريانة مكشوفة، وأيديهم مكسوة مكفوفة، وهم يتراطنون بلغات مختلفات أجنبية، ويجتنبون النطق بينهم بالعربية، إلا ما كان من أسماء الأفراس العربية، بعد إبدال القاف بالكاف، والحاء بالهاء.

٩،٩ ولمّا رأونا ظهر فيهم العبوس والقطوب، وتكدير الصدور والقلوب، وانخرط من فئة المرأة شابّ، فقصدنا نحو الباب، وقال لنا بلسان فرنسوي:

كيف ساغ لكم الدخول بغير إذن.

فقلت له: دعا إليه شوق الوالد إلى لقاء بضعته وآخر ذريته.

وسألني الإفصاح.

فقلت: فلان يسأل عن فلان.

فقال أنا فلان ومن هو فلان.

فبدأت أقص عليه مجمل القصة ومحصل القضية، فقطعها عليّ ساخرًا هازئًا وقال:

decorations, and the politeness of the waiters. He imagined we had made a mistake and entered a consular residence from his own era. I gave him details about the hotel and, after leaving the Groom outside, we inquired about his long-lost descendant. One of the waiters gave us the number of the suite. The Pāshā did not bother to ask for permission to enter or even wait for a response. He simply pushed the door open, and we entered. In front of us we discovered a group of amirs' sons, divided up into different groups. Some were playing dice while others were looking at pictures of racing horses. A group of them were clustered round a middle-aged woman neither old and ugly nor young and beautiful; she made full use of what little beauty she possessed by embellishing herself to the maximum extent possible with all kinds of makeup and finery. Her face was almost aglow with the glint of necklaces and ornaments, while her forehead sparkled with the pearly glimmer of jewels and gems. The middle of the room was occupied by a table with different types of wine in flagons and glasses, along with various expensive vessels. Laid out on top were an inkwell and paper, a pen inlaid with diamonds, and foreign books adorned with gold—all prepared for display, not for learning or culture. Sheets of regulations were scattered all over the floor, and newspapers were strewn about under people's feet still intact and unread save for the title or racing news. They all had their heads uncovered, and their hands were gloved. They were all jabbering away in foreign languages, making sure not to speak Arabic unless it involved the names of Arab horses, in which case the *kāf* sound was used instead of *qāf* and *hā'* instead of *ḥā'*.[68]

When they noticed us, they started frowning and scowling and looked put out. A young boy left the woman's side, hurried over to the door, and addressed us in French: 9.9

Young boy How dare you enter without permission!

'Īsā ibn Hishām We were prompted by a father's desire to see his offspring.

The youth asked me to explain.

'Īsā ibn Hishām A is enquiring after B.

Young boy The latter is my name, but who is this other person who is enquiring after me?

I started telling him the entire story and the issues it raised, but he interrupted me with a scoff.

اذهبا عني فليس لي والد ولا والدة، ولا بعيد ولا قريب، ولست ممّن يصدّق هذه الخرافات، ويؤمن بهذه المفتريات، وأنا ممّن تعلّم إنكار البعث بعد الممات، فكيف التصديق به في الحياة.

والتفت إلى بعض إخوانه منادياً ومقهقهاً، فقال لهم والضحك ينضغ كلامه ويقطع حروفه:

تعالوا فاسمعوا العجيب الغريب وانظروا إلى هذا الباشبوزق الغليظ (مشيراً إلى الباشا) يدّعي أنه من آبائي وأقربائي ويطالبني بشيء من ميراثه وحساب أوقافه، فهل سمعتم بأعجب ممّا أصبحنا فيه، لم يكتف الدهر بما نحن فيه بتكدير عيشنا وتعكير صفائنا بمطالبة أرباب الديون لنا حتى بعث الأموات من قبورها للمطالبة بميراثهم وأملاكهم وأوقافهم، ألا ترون أيها الخلان أنها آخر نكتة في ختام هذا القرن، فاستغرقوا ضحكاً عند هذه الكلمة.

١٠،٩ وكان كلما سألني الباشا عن وريثه، استمهلته لتمام حديثه، وهو لا يفهم شيئاً ممّا يقال، ولا يحس بوقع تلك النبال. ولمّا انتهوا من ضحكهم نادوا بالخادم ليخرجنا ويطردنا، وحانت من الوريث التفاتة في دوراته وحركاته فلمح قريناً من خاصة خلانه ونخبة إخوانه قد انزوى بتلك الخليلة التي هي عندهم كالحليلة، يلاعبها وتلاعبه، وينازلها وتداعبه، فانقضّ عليهما كالصقر الأجدل فاستعر بينهما الخصام واشتدّ النزاع والتفّ عليهم الجمع وسمعت الوارث يعتب والصديق يعتذر والمرأة تبكت وتؤنب وتقول لعشيقها: ليس لك مثل هذه الجرأة في العتاب، ولا يأتي ما تأتيه من التهوّر في الغيرة إلا من كان قائماً بكل شؤوني مجيباً لجميع رغباتي وقد طلبت منك أمس أن تشتري لي ذلك العقد الذي حضر لتاجر الجوهر من أوربا في البريد الأخير فأبيت بعد الوعد معتذراً بعسر الدراهم ثمّ بلغني اليوم أنك اشتريت فرساً جواداً فكيف تطلب مني الاقتصار عليك والاختصاص بك دون بقية من يجيب طلبي من المتولعين بي.

YOUNG BOY Get out of here! I don't have to listen to such childish lies. I have no father or mother, and no relatives close or otherwise. I am certainly not one of those people who's going to believe such fairy stories or give credence to made-up tales. I'm someone who's learned to deny the possibility of resurrection after death, so how am I supposed to believe in it when I'm still alive?

With that he turned and addressed his brothers, interrupting his words with frequent guffaws:

Come on, brothers, just listen to this weird tale! Just take a look at this scruffy bashibozuk beside him.[69] (*He points at the Pāshā.*) He's claiming to be one of my ancestors and relatives; he's demanding that I give him part of his bequeathed wealth and payment for his endowment. Have you ever heard anything more peculiar than the events of this morning? Fate isn't satisfied any more merely to disturb our lives with creditors' claims. Now it's started raising the dead from their graves to demand back their wealth, inheritance, and endowments. My friends, isn't that the best joke of all at the end of this century!

And with that, the entire assembly burst out laughing.

9.10 When the Pāshā kept questioning me about his grandchild, I asked him to wait till the talking stopped. He had no idea of what was being said and could not feel the impact of the sarcastic barbs. Once the laughter came to an end, they yelled to the servant to eject us. At this point the Pāshā's descendant turned round to discover that one of his closest friends and brothers had slunk off with the girl whom they were treating as though she was their wife. The two of them kept flirting, the brother making advances while she toyed with him. He swooped down on the two of them like a hawk, and a fierce quarrel broke out that turned more and more bitter. Everyone gathered round. I listened as the Pāshā's descendant scolded the woman while the woman's friend kept offering excuses. But the woman herself would have none of it:

"How dare you scold anyone like that?" she yelled in rebuke. "Only men who take care of me and respond to my wishes and needs are permitted such rash displays of temper. Only yesterday, I asked you to buy me that necklace that the jewelers received from Paris in the last post. At first you promised to buy it, but then you refused claiming you were hard up. Then today I find out you've bought a stallion for a huge sum of money. How can you expect me to keep myself only for you, when other men who are infatuated by me are eager to respond to my demands?"

١١،٩ ثمّ سمعت الوارث يجاوبها بقوله والعرق يتقطر من جبينه والوجد يقطع أنفاسه: تالله ما اشتريت شيئاً، بل بعت أشياء لا تشتري لك العقد بثمنها وإن كنت اغتررت بما يقال لك عن ثروة هذا الصاحب الدنيء الخائن وعن قلة المحصول في أطياني ورهن أملاكي فأنت تعلمين مقدار المبالغ التي ستأتيني من اكتساب القضايا المعلقة لي في المحاكم كما ينبئك به المحامي في كل حين.

وما سمع ذلك الصاحب وصفه بهذين النعتين حتى ثارت به سورة الغضب فلطم صاحبه بكساء اليد فوعده الملطوم بتعيين الشهود. وعلا صياح آخر عند طاولة القمار بين صديق وآخر، ورابح وخاسر، وأخ يطلب الاقتراض من أخيه، ومفلس يطالب مثريا بدين لا يؤديه، وانتهى هذا الجدال أيضاً باللكم واللطم وتعيين الشهود. واشتبك خصام آخر في الجماعة المجتمعة على رسوم الخيل والسباق أحدهم يقول فرسي سابق، والثاني يقول فرسك لاحق، وركبداري حاذق وابن حاذق، وجوادك قصير وجوادي شاهق، وأنت الآن مقر معترف بأنّ الوزن بينهما مختلف، واشتدت المنافسة والمنابزة، وجرى بينهم حديث المبارزة. كل هذا والمرأة تنسحب في الجمعية من حلقة إلى أخرى، تسحب الحية والأفعى، فتطفئ نار الجدال مرة على حسب بغيتها، وتشعلها طوراً لخبث نيتها،

١٢،٩ فجذبت بضبع الباشا خارجاً من هذا المكان، متأسفاً على ما وصل إليه جهل الإنسان، وأسرعت به منحدراً إلى الطريق وترجمت له شرح الحال والمآل فاضطرم غيظه واشتدّ حنقه فلم يطفئه إلا ما سمعه في آخر الحديث من عزم القوم على المبارزة فيما بينهم فقال لعلّ القدرة تكشف عني هذا البلاء وتريحني المبارزة من الأعقاب والأبناء. فقلت في نفسي إنّ أبناءكم لم يرثوا منكم أخلاقكم كما ورثوا عنكم أموالكم، وليس عندهم من الشجاعة ما يقتحمون به الأخطار لكشف العار، والمبارزة عندهم كلمة تقال بالليل وتمحى بالنهار.

I listened now as the Pāshā's descendant replied, with sweat pouring off his brow and panic cutting short his breaths: 9.11

"I swear by God," he said, "I haven't bought anything. In fact, I've had to sell some things to get enough cash to buy you the necklace. Don't be deceived by the things they're saying about how wealthy this vile and treacherous friend is or by rumors about my poverty and my lands being in pawn. You know very well how much money is coming to me from the profits of the court cases I have pending. The lawyer keeps telling you all about it."

No sooner had his colleague heard him call him by those two epithets than he flew into a terrible rage and gave him a resounding slap. The target of his curses promised in his turn to appoint seconds. Now a further commotion arose at the gaming table between two friends, one of whom had won and the other lost. Elsewhere one of them was asking his brother for a loan, and another who was bankrupt was asking a wealthy man for a loan that he would not be repaying. The quarrel eventually resorted to fisticuffs and yet again ended up with the appointment of witnesses. Still another dispute occurred in the corner of the room where people were looking at pictures of racing horses. One of them kept saying his horse had won and the other man's came next; his groom was intelligent and was the son of an intelligent father; the other man's stallion was short whereas his was tall; you have to admit, one of them claimed, that there's a clear difference in their weights. The quarrels and insults kept getting worse, and the conversation degenerated into a fight. All the while the woman was flitting from one circle to another like a slinky viper. At her whim, the fire of discord was put out, but then she would rekindle it again for her own vicious intentions.

I dragged the Pāshā out by the arm and left the room. As we hurried toward the street, I felt sad to see the degree of sheer ignorance mankind had reached. I gave him a version of what had transpired, and that made him even more annoyed. The only thing that managed to calm him down was to hear that they had decided in the end to resolve their differences by fighting each other. 9.12

"Maybe fate can remove this misfortune from me," he said with a sigh. "The duels may at least relieve me of sons and descendants."

"Unfortunately," I told myself, "your sons inherited neither your money nor your ethics. They don't possess enough courage to embrace danger so as to expose what's wrong. For them, dueling's a word spoken at night and forgotten about the next day."

وتذكّر الباشا حاجته إلى تسديد ما عليه للمحامي فالتفت إلى البيطار يسأله:

الباشا هل بقي ممّن كنت أعرفهم أحد من الخلطاء والأصحاب.

البيطار لم يبق إلّا فلان وفلان وفلان.

الباشا ابدأ بالذهاب معنا إلى بيت الأوّل منهم.

قال عيسى بن هشام: فسرنا إلى حيث أشار والهموم تفرسنا، والغموم تخرسنا، والأقدار لا توافقنا، والأكدار لا تفارقنا. ١٣،٩

The Pāshā now remembered that he needed to pay the Lawyer's fees. Turning to the Groom, he asked:

PĀSHĀ What about my close friends? Are any of them still alive?

GROOM Only X, Y, and Z are left.

PĀSHĀ Well, take us to X's house first!

ʿĪsā ibn Hishām said: So we went where he indicated. We were beset by anxieties, and constant worry reduced us all to silence. The Fates were not working in our favor, and problems would not let us be. 9.13

١،١٠ قال عيسى بن هشام: وسرنا نقصد أحد الثلاثة من قرناء الباشا ورفقائه ممّن بقي من أخلائه وأصدقائه، فانتهى بنا المسير إلى بيت ذلك الأمير وكأنه ميدان في اتساعه وحصن في ارتفاعه. ووقف بنا الركبدار عند باب الدار، فسلّم على الخدم وحيّاهم، وسألهم عن سيدهم ومولاهم فأجابوه بالتجهّم والعبوس إنه في قاعة الجلوس، فخطونا في بحبوحة الميدان، فرأينا في وسطه شجرة ملتفة الأغصان حنا قوامها تقادم الأزمان، فهي كالثكلى حلت شعورها في مأتم للأحزان، وتحت ظلها فرس في قيده قد جنّ من النشاط والمراح وبجانبه كبش للنطاح، وحولهما ديكة ضراب ظنابيبها مسنونة كالحراب.

فَحُمْرٌ وَسُودٌ حالكاتٌ كأنّها
سَوَامُ بني السِّيدِ ازْدَهَتْهُ القَوَائِمُ
يُزَانُ لديها الطّعنُ في حَوْمَةِ الوَغَى
إذا زُيّنَتْ للعاجزين الهزائمُ
وفيها إذا ضيّعَ النّكسُ غَيْرَةً
تُصانُ بها المُسْتَصْحَبَاتُ الكَرَائِمُ

٢،١٠ ثمّ وصلنا إلى قاعة مشيّدة البنيان فسيحة الأركان، في أحد جوانبها سلسبيل يرسل الماء من أفواه التماثيل، والأرض مفروشة بالبسط الفارسيّة، وجلود الضواري الوحشية، والحيطان مستورة بأنواع السلاح، من خناجر وسيوف ورماح، بين عدّة صفوف من الرفوف، تحمل الطرائف الكريمة والأواني الصينية القديمة مع عيدان للتدخين من أغصان الياسمين. فخلعنا نعالنا وتقدمنا أمامنا، فوجدنا الأمير في صدر القاعة ومن معه جلوساً متربعين، منصتين سامعين، يضيء في وجوههم نور المشيب والوقار، وتزدهيهم هيئة العزة والاستكبار، فانقطع الحديث عند دخولنا بردّ سلامنا، ولكن ما لبث أن اتّصل ما انقطع بينهم من الكلام بعد رجع التحية والسلام.

Miṣbāḥ al-sharq 44, February 16, 1899[70]

10.1 ʿĪsā ibn Hishām said: So we set out to look for one of the Pāshā's three friends and companions who were still alive. After a long walk, we reached the amir's house. Its grounds were so extensive that it looked like a square in its own right; looking at its height you would have said it was a fortress. The Groom stopped us at the door, greeted the servants and asked them about their master. With a frown they replied in a surly fashion that he could be found in the reception hall. We proceeded across the central courtyard. In the middle we noticed a tree with thick branches. Time's relentless progress had bent it over, and it now looked like a bereaved woman who in sheer grief lets down her hair at a funeral. In its shade a horse was tethered but clearly full of energy; beside it was a ram with thrusting horns. Strutting around them was a fighting cock with talons as sharp as spears:

Red and pitch black; nimble as the legs
of the herd of the Banū al-Sayyid.
In the heat of the battle, attack is glorious in their eyes,
where the weak would find flight more attractive.
And when the weak would be useless, defiance is there,
keeping honorable women protected.[71]

10.2 We reached a lofty hall with spacious alcoves. On one side was a spring with water flowing from the mouths of statues. The ground was covered with Persian carpets and the skins of wild animals, while the walls were hung with arms of various sorts: daggers, swords, and spears. Above these were a number of rows of shelves supporting precious objets d'art and ancient Chinese vessels along with pipes made of jasmine branches. We removed our shoes and moved forward. We found the amir with a group of people sitting cross-legged around him listening. Their faces gleamed with the light of age and dignity, and a splendid and proud bearing irradiated from them. When we entered, the conversation stopped while they greeted us. Once greetings had been exchanged, the conversation picked up from where they had left off.

٣،١٠ ولمّا استقرّ بنا المجلس همست في أذن الركبدار فسألته أن ينبئني بأسماء من أراهم، فقال لي: أمّا المتصدر فيهم فهو فلان رب الدار وهو رفيق صاحبنا في خدمة البيت الكريم الخديوي وتراه قد اعتكف في آخر عمره الآن يتعبّد ويتهجّد، ويسلك طريقة النسك والتزهد، ويتقرّب إلى الله بدوام القيام والقعود وطول القنوت والسجود، وله مال عريض ينفق منه على قعدة المشايخ وقوّام أهل الطريق وطوّاف الآفاق من سكان الأماكن المقدّسة ليغفر الله له ما تقدّم من ذنبه ويلحقه بالصالحين من أوليائه. وأمّا الذي عن يمينه فهو فلان، كان عضواً من الأعضاء الكرام في مجلس الأحكام أيام جنتمكان. والذي بجانبه عالم من جملة العلماء الأعلام والمشايخ العظام. وأمّا الجالس عن شماله فهو فلان الفريق الجهادي المشهور في الفتوحات والوقائع. والذي بجانبه أحد كبار المديرين السابقين. وأمّا الذي تراه في أخريات المجلس فتاجر من تجار خان الخليلي.

٤،١٠ قال عيسى بن هشام: ولمّا وقفت على ما أوقفني عليه الركبدار وأدركت من الباشا أنه لا يبغي المبادرة إلى كشف أمره لهم قبل انتهائهم من حديثهم أنصت مع المنصتين فسمعت الفريق يقول في اتصال حكايته وروايته:

الفريق الجهادي وكان جنتمكان محمد علي باشا الكبير معجزة دهره وآية زمانه في الدهاء وعلو الهمّة وبعد النظر وإحكام عقدة التدبير وجذب القلوب وتربية النفوس على الأمانة في خدمته، فكان له من الكفاة من خدموه بالصداقة وفدوه بالنفوس، وأذكر منهم المرحوم محمد بك لاظ أوغلي، فهو الذي دبر له قطع دابر المماليك في ساعة واحدة، وقد حكى لي أخي وكان حاضراً في تلك الواقعة المهولة أنّ المماليك لمّا رأوا المكيدة في استئصالهم قد استحكم عقدها واشتدّ رباطها وأُحيط

When we were settled in our places, I whispered in the Groom's ear and asked him to tell me the names of the people I was looking at. 10.3

GROOM The person presiding is X, the owner of this mansion. He was a great friend of my master, the Pāshā, in the Khedive's esteemed household. As you can see, in his later years he has devoted himself entirely to the pious observance of prayer to God and a life of abstinence and asceticism. He seeks favor with God through continual rituals of prayer and renunciation of the world through prolonged periods of piety and prostration. He has vast resources at his disposal which he spends on shaykhs, Ṣūfīs, and dwellers in holy places who tour around various parts of the country. By so doing, he hopes that God will forgive him the sins he has committed and will add his name to the company of His blessed saints. To his right is C who used to be a distinguished member of the Judicial Committee in Muḥammad ʿAlī's time. Next to him is one of the most eminent religious scholars and shaykhs. The person on his left is General Y, famous for his battles and victories, and next to him is Z, the retired governor. At the back of the gathering, the person you can see is A, a merchant in Khān al-Khalīlī.

ʿĪsā ibn Hishām said: Once I had taken in what the Groom told me, I looked at the Pāshā and realized that he was in no hurry to reveal his business until the people present had finished their conversation. So I sat there listening along with the other people present. Here is part of what the General had to say: 10.4

GENERAL Muḥammad ʿAlī Pāshā the great (whose place is in heaven) was the marvel of his age. He was a shrewd man possessed of a lofty ambition, farsightedness and firm grasp of management, added to which was a unique ability to win over people's hearts and train their minds to serve him faithfully. He had at his disposal capable men who served him loyally and were prepared to risk their lives for him. From among their number I would single out Muḥammad Bey Lāẓoghly who masterminded the annihilation of the Mamluks in the space of a single hour. My late brother who witnessed this dire event told me that the Mamluks realized that there was a plot to wipe them out, that everything had been fixed, and that they were surrounded on all sides. So they set about looking for Muḥammad ʿAlī in every nook and cranny of the palace, but they could find no trace of him because Lāẓoghly had taken enormous precautions to keep him hidden. At the time in fact he

بهم من كل مكان أقبلوا للبحث عن محمد علي في كل حجرة وزاوية من زوايا القصر فلم يجدوه، لأنّ لاظ أوغلي أخفاه عنهم شديد الإخفاء وقام له في ذلك الوقت - لو جاز التشبيه والتمثيل - قيام علي بن أبي طالب مقام الرسول عليه السلام ليلة الهجرة. وقد اعترت المرحوم جنتمكان تلك الصيحة المزعجة المشهورة منذ ذلك الحين لم تفارقه فكان يزأر أحيانًا في مجلسه بزأرة كزئير الأسد يتقطع منها نياط القلوب وقد مات منها رجل مصوّر افرنكي كان يقعد له المرحوم لرسم صورته وكانوا قد نبّهوه إليها فلم يستطعها مع ذلك لشدتها ومات أمامه من ساعته. فأين مثل لاظ أوغلي لمثله وأين مثل تلك الصيحة في مثله من الرجال.

٥،١٠ العضو في مجلس الأحكام نعم كان محمد علي فوق ما يقال وما يتصوّر في دقة سياسته في تربية الرجال لخدمته، وكان من مقدرته أن يشتري أمانة من يخدمه منهم طول عمره بكلمة واحدة، فمن ذلك ما حكاه لي أخونا المرحوم راغب باشا، قال:

«كنت أقرأ أوراقًا عن المغفور له فدخل علينا سامي باشا في أثناء قراءتي ووقف معنا فسأله محمد علي عمّا يريد فتلعثم تلعثم المتطلّع لخروجي حتى ينفرد به فيقول له ما عنده فقال له: قل ما عندك فإني لا أخفي عن راغب سرًّا من أسراري، وكتبة معيتي كأولادي».

فهل يقوم يا قوم مقام هذه الكلمة في جلب النفوس وارتباط القلوب على النصح والأمانة في الخدمة إنعام بضياع أو إحسان بأموال؟ وقد كان المرحوم راغب باشا يقابل بين هذه الكلمة وبين ما كان يفعل معه إسماعيل باشا فإنه كان يتركه وهو ناظر مالية ويدخل مع بقال أو سمسار في حجرة أخرى ليناجيه فتمضي ساعة أو أكثر على راغب باشا وهو جالس وحده وأشغال الحكومة المهمة في يده ينتظر انتهاء المناجاة ويقيس تلك بهذه فكانت هذه تذهب بالإحسان والإنعام وتبقى بجانب أختها السابقة تشك الصدر وتحز في الفؤاد.

occupied the same position—if this comparison is permissible—as ʿAlī ibn Abī Ṭalib did for the Prophet of God (peace be upon him) on the night of the hijra.[72] It was from that same period that Muḥammad ʿAlī inherited the unnerving shout which never deserted him thereafter. In his council chamber he used to roar like a lion; the effect was enough to stop your heart beating. It caused the death of a European painter for whom the late master was sitting for a portrait. They had warned him in advance, but it was so loud that the poor man could not stand it and died on the spot. Where are there governors like Lāẓoghly today, and where will you encounter shouts of such a kind in other men like him?

10.5

MEMBER OF THE JUDICIAL COMMITTEE Yes indeed! The procedures used by the late Muḥammad ʿAlī to train men to serve him were too subtle for mere words and concepts. Some of them were even won over by him with a single word which impressed them so much that they served him faithfully for the rest of their lives. Such was the case in the story which our late friend Rāghib Pāshā told me:

"When I was one of the secretaries in the late Pāshā's entourage, I was reading over some pages with him. While I was reading, Sāmī Pāshā came in and stood beside us. Muḥammad ʿAlī asked him what he wanted, but he hesitated, as though he wanted me to leave so that he could be alone with the Pāshā and then tell him his news. 'Tell me your news immediately,' the Pāshā ordered him. 'I keep nothing from Rāghib. The secretaries in my entourage are like my own children.'"

Now tell me, gentlemen, in your experience can gifts of estates, distributing money as bounty, or the award of titles and decorations serve as an appropriate substitute for words such as those when it comes to persuading people to serve you faithfully and reliably?

The late Rāghib Pāshā often used to compare these words with the kind of thing he witnessed when he was serving Muḥammad ʿAlī's successors, Ismāʿīl Pāshā for example. When Rāghib was Egyptian Minister of Finance, Ismāʿīl would leave him with papers in front of him and go into another room for a private conversation with some grocer or moneylender. Rāghib would be left there waiting hour after hour with pressing government business in his hands until the private conversation came to an end. Naturally enough, when it came to comparing the two experiences, one brought him a beneficial reward while the other merely exasperated him.[73]

٦،١٠ فانظروا إلى الرجل كيف أتقن صناعة الألفة وما للملوك صناعة غيرها، فإذا أتقنها أحدهم فاز بالتسلط على النفوس واحتكر مودات القلوب. وسمعت فيما سمعته من التاريخ القديم أنّ المنصور العباسي له واحدة في هذا الباب تدلّ على براعته ومهارته في صناعة الملك، وذلك أنه كان يأكل مع قائد من أكابر قواد جيشه وعلى المائدة ابناه، وكان القائد قد ذهبت أسنانه لكبر سنه فكان يقع من فمه بعض الفتات وهو يأكل والأميران يتغامزان عليه فحانت من المنصور التفاتة فرأى ما بينهما فمدّ يده فجمع ما وقع من ذلك الفتات فأكله فقام القائد يقول «لم يبق إلّا ديني أقدّمه لك يا أمير المؤمنين فامرني بما تريد».

٧،١٠ المدير السابق وأنا أقص عليكم واحدة أخرى من لطيف سياسته وجميل نكاته في شفقته على الرعية وعطفه على الأهالي وهي أنّ أحد المديرين أراد أن يفوق إخوانه ويبلغ مكانة عالية من أميره فجدّ في تحصيل الأموال وتعالى في طريقته وأخذ ما عند الأهالي من المال جملة واحدة فضجّ ضجيجهم واشتدّ صياحهم وعلا صراخهم حتى بلغ مسامع ولي النعم فأمر بإحضار المدير فوقف في حضرته، فقال له: أُدن مني، فلمّا دنا منه أخذ بعنقه في قبضة يده وصار ينتزع من رأسه شعرة ومن عارضه شعرة ومن قفاه شعرة ومن حاجبة شعرة حتى جمع في قبضته خصلة من الشعر والمدير لا يجد من ذلك إلا ألماً خفيفاً لا يكاد يشعر به، ثمّ إنّ الأمير انتقل إلى لحية الرجل فانتزع منها خصلة مثل تلك نزعة واحدة من جهة واحدة فنبع من تحتها الدم وصرخ المدير من الألم، فقال له محمد علي: «هكذا تكون المعاملة مع الرعية في تحصيل الأموال، إذا أنت أخذت من هنا درهماً ومن هنا درهماً آناً بعد آن خفّ الوقع على الأهالي ولم يدركوا الألم وتحصلت منهم على مثل المقدار الذي تأخذه جملة واحدة في وقت واحد كما رأيت الفرق بين نزع الشعرات متفرقات ونزعها

10.6 Just consider how Muḥammad ʿAlī perfected the art of geniality. Kings need not possess any other skill. If they can perfect just this one, then their subjects' goodwill and affections will be under their exclusive control. I heard of another instance from history involving the Abbasid Caliph, al-Manṣūr, which shows how skilful and adroit he was in the art of monarchy. One day he was eating with a shaykh who was one of his generals. His two sons were at his side. Being an old man, the shaykh had lost all his teeth. While he was eating, bits of food kept falling out of the side of his mouth. The two young princes kept winking at each other at his expense. When the Caliph looked in their direction and saw what was causing their amusement, he stretched out his hand, gathered up the bits that had dropped to the floor and ate them. The general stood up. "My fealty is all I have to offer you, Commander of the Faithful," he said, "so command me to do as you wish."

10.7 Retired Governor Let me tell you another story about the late Muḥammad ʿAlī. This one will show you how gentle his policies were and how sympathetic he was towards the common people. One particular governor wanted to outdo his colleagues in a display of dutiful service in order to gain his amir's esteem. He proceeded to collect money from his province with great zeal and exceeded all normal bounds in the methods he used. By such means he managed to collect in one fell swoop everything people owned. The hue and cry grew ever louder, and the people's complaints became increasingly vociferous. Eventually there came the day when they reached the ears of Muḥammad ʿAlī, the dispenser of bounty. He ordered the governor to appear before him. When the governor came into his presence, Muḥammad ʿAlī told him to come closer. When the governor came up to him, Muḥammad ʿAlī grabbed him by the neck and started pulling out one hair at a time from his head, neck, cheek, and eyebrow until he had collected a little tuft; all of which caused the governor little pain—he hardly felt it. Then the amir turned to his beard and from one side pulled out all at once a tuft as large as the other tuft of separate hairs, which caused blood to well up beneath it. The governor let out a yell of pain. "Let that serve as a demonstration," Muḥammad ʿAlī told him, "of the different ways of dealing with people when you're taxing them. When you take a dirham at one moment and then another dirham at a later date, people can tolerate it and don't notice any hardship. But when you demand this large amount all at once in one lump sum, it causes them a lot of suffering. In the same way, you can see the difference between pulling hairs out individually and pulling them

مجتمعات والكمية واحدة والألم بينهما مختلف فإيّاك أن تعامل الأهالي بعد اليوم بما يلجئهم إلى الصراخ ويجرؤهم على الاستغاثة».

٨،١٠ وأعرف له واحدة أخرى في حسن الإجمال والإدماج في إدارة الأمور، وذلك أنه صدر أمره إلى حسن باشا الأنجيركويلي بتعيينه حاكما في السودان فامتنع الرجل لجهله باللغة العربية، وقال: كيف يمكن لي أن أدير أمور أقوام لا أعرف حرفًا واحدًا من لغتهم، فدعاه محمد علي وقال له: ليست معرفة اللغة ممّا يقتضيه الحكم ولا هي أداة لازمة له يخلّ به فقدها وما عليك في مأموريتك هذه إلا أن تردّد كلمتين عربيتين في لسانك وهما «فلوس، وكرباج».

ولو تأمل حسن باشا إلى أنّ محمد علي حكم الأمّة المصرية الدهر الطويل وفتح البلاد العربية ولم يكن ينطق باللغة العربية في حياته ولم يمنعه ذلك من استقامة الحكم ونظام الأمور وتشييد الملك لم يعتذر بمثل ذلك الاعتذار.

٩،١٠ ومن النوادر التي تروى في هذا الباب أنّ محمد علي أمر بأن يكون أهل العاصمة رديفًا عسكريًا وعيّن منهم ضباطًا عليهم بالرتب العسكرية، فدخل عليه يومًا ضباط من أهالي بولاق وكان الذي يترجم بينه وبينهم صبحي باشا فقال لهم محمد علي كلامًا يجب أن يشكره عليه فقال واحد منهم «نأشك يا أفندينا» وهي كلمة عامية منتشرة متداولة في ذلك الوقت يقولها الرعاع عند الاستحسان والإعجاب فظهر الغضب على وجه محمد علي لأنه فهمها بلفظها التركي «نه أشك» فأسرع صبحي باشا بتفسيرها له فاستلقى محمد علي على ظهره من الضحك. فأي فائدة من معرفة اللغة إذا كان أهلها يستعملون مثل هذه الألفاظ السافلة الساقطة في مخاطبة أميرهم. والذين حكم المصريين ممّن لا يعرف لغتهم عدد ليس بقليل منهم نوبار وغيره.

١٠،١٠ الشيخ

فلا تُكثروا ذكرَ الزّمان الذي مَضَى
فذلك عصرٌ قد تقضّى وذا عصرُ

out in a clump. In both cases the amount is the same, but the suffering involved is completely different. From now on, make sure you don't treat people in such a way that they resort to complaints and begin sending pleas for help."

I can cite you yet another example of his talent for succinctness. He gave orders that Ḥasan Pāshā al-Injirköylü was to be appointed governor of the Sudan. The latter declined the post, pointing out that he couldn't speak Arabic. "How can I govern and regulate the affairs of a people," he asked, "when I don't know a single letter of their language?" "You don't need to know the language in order to supervise the laws," Muḥammad ʿAlī retorted. "It's not a requirement for sound government; the regime can be quite effective without it. For your job, you only need to know two Arabic words to keep on the tip of your tongue, *fulūs* and *kurbāj*."[74] Had Ḥasan Pāshā bothered to recollect that Muḥammad ʿAlī himself managed to rule the Egyptian people for a long time and to conquer Arab lands without ever speaking Arabic or being prevented thereby from running government affairs efficiently and maintaining his authority, he would never have invoked such an excuse. 10.8

On this particular topic, one of the most incredible stories tells how Muḥammad ʿAlī ordered the citizens of the capital to form a military reserve, and appointed officers of military rank to command them. One day, some officers from Būlāq came in; at the time, Ṣubḥī Pāshā was acting as interpreter. Muḥammad ʿAlī addressed some words to them in a manner which demanded some expression of appreciation. One of them said: "Thanking you kindly, Sire," an expression which was commonly used by the populace at that time to express pleasure and approval. Muḥammad ʿAlī looked very angry; he'd taken it in its Turkish sense, "What an ass!" Ṣubḥī Pāshā hastened to interpret, then Muḥammad ʿAlī fell flat on his back laughing. 10.9

So tell me, what's the point of knowing Arabic when Arabs use these low and uncouth phrases when addressing their amir? Actually, quite a few people have governed the Egyptian people without knowing their language, Nūbār Pāshā and others among them.[75]

SHAYKH (*quoting*) 10.10

Spend not too long recalling times long past.
That is an age gone by; this is another.[76]

ورحم الله الماضي وأعاذنا من الحاضر وأجارنا من المستقبل، وأراكم أيها الأمراء مهما أسهبتم وأطنبتم في محاسن المغفور له وأفضاله، وحميد أخلاقه وخصاله، فلستم ببالغي حق الشكر، ولا موفين بجميل الذكر، ومن حسناته التي يغنيكم ذكرها عن الإجمال والتفصيل، وتحكم له بالسبق والتفضيل، أنه كان يقرّب العلماء ويعظمهم ويحترمهم ويكرّمهم، ويقضي جميع حوائجهم ويتبرك بدعائهم، ولقد رأيت له رؤيا صالحة تحكم له في أخراه بأنّ له جانباً مع الله وأنّه نال جزاء الإحسان بسكنى الجنان.

١١،١٠ قال عيسى بن هشام: وأقبل رجل مكيّ في أثناء هذا الحديث من أولئك المطوفين المزورين فتقدم إلى الأمير صاحب الدار ووضع بين يديه بعد أن قبلهما مع يد الشيخ العالم صرة من حرير خضراء وعلبة من التمر ومكحلة وأمشاطاً وسبحا وحناء خضاب وقال للأمير بعد قراءة الفاتحة:

المكّي قد جئتك أيها الأمير بالقطعة التي أمرتني بإحضارها من الكسوة المباركة وأتيتك بعلبة من تمر النخلة التي غرستها السيدة الزهراء بيدها الشريفة.

الأمير (للخدم) عليَّ بالمعلم مسيحه باشكاتب الديرة ومعه الكيس لنعطي هذا المسافر جائزته.

قال عيسى بن هشام ودخل المعلم مسيحة ودنا من الأمير فلمّا بصر بتلك الآثار المباركة التي بين يدي الأمير انكب وجهه يقبلها تبركًا بها ويقول:

المعلم مسيحه تالله ما نفع ابني من عماه إلا هذا الكحل ولا شفا أمه من داء الرعشة إلا هذه الحناء.

الشيخ (بعد أن ذاق التمر وتمطق) صدقت أيها الرجل ومن كان صائماً فأفطر على تمر المدينة كتبت له الجنة.

١٢،١٠ قال عيسى بن هشام: فتأفف الباشا بجانبي وزمجر، وتململ وتضجّر، وهمّ بأن يتكلم فالتفت صاحب الدار إلى الركبدار يسأله عن هذا المتعرض المتأفف فبدأت بشرح

May God have mercy on what is past, may He protect us from the present, and give us a safe refuge against the future! Amirs, however far you've gone in describing his virtues and enumerating his good qualities to fulfill all the obligations of dutiful remembrance, I still feel that you've failed to do full justice to our late master. Of all his good works, which need neither summary nor explanation, showing both his expertise and sense of priorities, it's enough to remember that he always fostered and revered the religious scholars, kept them close to him, and showed them great respect. He answered their needs and asked for the blessing of their prayers. I myself had a genuine vision about him which gave him the promise of a place with God in the next world and a residence in paradise as a reward for his good deeds.

10.11 ʿĪsā ibn Hishām said: During this conversation one of the people from Mecca (known as the Circumambulators or Guides) came up to the owner of the house.[77] After kissing his hands, he handed over a purse of green silk, along with some dates, a comb, a jar of kohl, a rosary, and some henna. He recited the Fātiḥah and then spoke to the Amir:

MECCAN Amir, I've brought the piece of the holy *kiswah* as you requested, and also some dates from the blessed palm tree that Fāṭima planted with her noble hand.

AMIR (*to the attendants*) Fetch the chief clerk, Master Masīḥih, for me and get him to bring the purse so that we can give this traveler his reward.

ʿĪsā ibn Hishām said: Master Masīḥih came in and approached the amir. When he set eyes on the blessed gift in front of the Amir, he prostrated himself face to the ground, kissed the gifts one after the other, and then spoke to the Amir:

MASTER MASĪḤIH By God, it was this blessed kohl which saved my son from going blind. Only this pure henna managed to cure his mother of malaria.

SHAYKH (*after testing the dates and registering approval*) Yes indeed, my dear man, you are right. Heaven is assured to anyone who fasts and then breaks the fast with dates from Medina.

10.12 ʿĪsā ibn Hishām said: The Pāshā was seated at my side muttering and fuming, and I could tell that he was getting furious. He was about to speak, but just then the owner of the house turned to the Groom to ask what was causing all the angry muttering. I stepped forward to tell them the story. I explained how

قصته وذكر خروجه من قبره فمنهم من صدّق ومنهم من أنكر فتنحنح الشيخ وقال لهم:

الشيخ ايه ايه ليس للمعجزات حد ولا للخوارق حصر ولا تنكروا على الرجل حياته بعد موته وليس من حسن اليقين أن ننكر بعث الدفين، والرجوع إلى الدنيا بعد الفناء أمر معلوم بلا مراء تخص القدرة به من تشاء على يد الأصفياء الأولياء، وأقرب ما أستشهد لكم به على ذلك ما هو مذكور مسطور في مناقب سيدي الغوث عبد القادر الكيلاني وأرويه لكم بنصه:

١٣،١٠ «ذكر في رسالة حقيقة الحقائق أنّ امرأة غرق ولدها في اليمّ وجاءت إلى الغوث الأعظم وقالت أنّ ولدي غرق في البحر واعتقادي جازم بأنك تقدر على رد ولدي إليّ حيًّا فقال لها رضي الله عنه: ارجعي إلى بيتك تجدي ولدك فراحت ولم تجده فجاءت ثانية وتضرّعت فقال لها الغوث أيضاً: ارجعي إلى بيتك تجدي ولدك في بيتك فراحت ولم تجده فجاءت ثالثة بالبكاء والتضرّع فراقب الغوث وانحنى برأسه ثمّ رفع رأسه فقال لها: ارجعي إلى بيتك تجدي ولدك في البيت فراحت ووجدت ولدها في البيت فقال الغوث الأعظم بطريق المحبوبية: يا رب لمَ أخجلتني مرتين عند تلك المرأة فجاءه الخطاب من الملك الوهاب أنّ كلامك حين قلت لها كان صدقاً، ففي المرة الأولى جمعت الملائكة أجزاءه المتفرّقة وفي المرة الثانية أحييته وفي الثالثة أخرجته من اليمّ وأوصلته إلى دارها فقال الغوث: يا رب خلقت الأكوان بأمر (كن) ولم يسبق زمان ولا آن ووقت البعث تجمع أجزاءها المتفرقة التي لا نهاية لها وتحشرهم في طرفة عين وجمع أجزاء جسد واحد وإحياؤه وبعثه إلى دارها شيء جزئي , ما الحكمة في هذا التأخير فجاءه الخطاب من الرب القدير: اطلب ما تطاب , فقد أعطيناك عوضاً عن انكسار قلبك فتضرّع الغوث ووضع وجهه على التراب وقال: يا رب أنا مخلوق فبقدر مخلوقيتي يليق بي الطلب وأنت خالق فبقدر عظمتك وخالقيتك يليق بك العطاء فجاءه

the Pāshā had emerged from the grave. Some of them believed me, others did not. With that, the Shaykh cleared his throat and spoke to them:

SHAYKH Indeed, there are no limits to miracles and supernatural phenomena, nor should you entertain any doubts about man's return to life after death; to do so is to display a lack of conviction concerning the resurrection of buried men. It's an incontrovertible fact that one returns to life after disappearing into oblivion; that is something which God in His omnipotence accords to those people whom He wishes with the blessing of holy men and saints. The closest thing I can quote to you on this subject comes from the books of *Glorious Deeds of the Crown of Saints and Proof of Holy Men* by the divine leader and everlasting refuge al-Sayyid ʿAbd al-Qādir al-Jīlānī. Let me quote you his text word for word:

10.13 In the *Treatise on the True Nature of Realities*, he tells the story of how a woman's son was drowned in the sea. She came to the Mightiest Refuge[78] and said to him: "My son has drowned in the sea, and I'm utterly convinced that you can bring my son back to life." "Return to your house," he replied (God be pleased with him), "and you'll find your son there." So she went home but didn't find him there. She came back again and begged him. "Return to your house," he told her again, "and you'll find your son there." She went home again but failed to find her son. Yet again she came back and entreated him in tears to bring her son back to her. This time he watched closely and bowed his head. Then he raised it again. "Go to your house," he said, "and you'll find your son there." She went home again and found her son. The Mightiest Refuge addressed God in the manner of those who are beloved to Him: "Lord, why did You embarrass me twice in dealing with that woman?" Back came the word from the Almighty Provider: "When you spoke to her, it was the truth. On the first occasion, the angels collected his different parts; on the second, I brought him back to life; and on the third, I extracted him from the sea and brought him to her house." To this the Refuge replied: "But Lord, with the command 'Be!' You created worlds before which there was neither time nor epoch. At the moment of resurrection You gather and muster the infinite different parts of these beings in the flash of an eye. It's a trivial matter for You to collect the parts of a single body, revive them, and then send them to this woman's house. So what was the point of this delay?" From God Almighty came the reply: "Ask anything you wish. We bestow it on you as a recompense for breaking your heart." At that, the Mightiest Refuge placed his face to the

الخطاب: كل من يراك يوم الجمعة يكون وليًا مقربًا وإذا نظرت إلى التراب يكون ذهبًا فقال: يا رب ليس لي نفع من هذين، أعطني شيئًا أعظم منهما ويبقى بعدي لينفع في الدارين فجاء الخطاب من الله العزيز القدير: جعلت أسماءك مثل أسمائي في الثواب والتأثير ومن قرأ اسما من أسمائك فهو كمن قرأ اسما من أسمائي».

١٤،١٠ ورُوِيَ عن السيد الشيخ الكبير أبي العباس أحمد الرفاعي رضي الله تعالى عنه أنه قال توفي أحد خدام الغوث الأعظم وجاءت زوجته إلى الغوث فتضرّعت والتجأت إليه وطلبت حياة زوجها فتوجه الغوث إلى المراقبة فرأى في عالم الباطن أنّ ملك الموت عليه السلام يصعد إلى السماء ومعه الأرواح المقبوضة في ذلك اليوم فقال: يا ملك الموت قف واعطني روح خادمي فلان وسمّاه باسمه فقال ملك الموت: إني أقبض الأرواح بأمر إلهي وأؤديها إلى باب عظمته كيف يمكنني أن أعطيك روح الذي قبضته بأمر ربي فكرّر الغوث عليه إعطاء روح خادمه إليه فامتنع من إعطائه وفي يده ظرف معنوي كهيئة الزنبيل فيه الأرواح المقبوضة في ذلك اليوم فبقوة المحبوبية جر الزنبيل وأخذه من يده فتفرقت الأرواح ورجعت إلى أبدانها فناجى ملك الموت عليه السلام ربه وقال: يا رب أنت أعلم بما جرى بيني وبين محبوبك ووليك عبد القادر فبقوة السلطنة والصولة أخذ مني ما قبضته من الأرواح في هذا اليوم فخاطبه الحق جل جلاله: «يا ملك الموت» إنّ الغوث الأعظم محبوبي ومطلوبي «لمَ لا أعطيته روح خادمه وقد راحت الأرواح الكثيرة من قبضتك بسبب روح واحد فتندم هذا الوقت.»

(انتهى بحرفه من الكتاب المنتشر المسمى بمناقب تاج الأولياء وبرهان الأصفياء القطب الرباني والغوث الصمداني السيد عبد القادر الكيلاني المطبوع بنفقة الشيخ عبد الرحمن نيازي شيخ تكية القادرية بثغر الإسكندرية من صحيفة ٢٠ إلى ٢٢).

ground and replied in supplication: "Lord, I am created, and so it is fitting for me to make requests by virtue of my createdness. You are a Creator, and so it is right that You should give in proportion to Your might and being Creator." "Everyone who sees you on the day of communal prayer will be a close friend," God replied. "Whenever you look at the ground, it will turn into gold." "But these things are of no use to me," the Refuge replied. "Give me something of greater worth to leave behind, something which can serve in both worlds." "I have made your names as meritorious and influential as My own," God replied. "Anyone who recites one of your names is doing exactly the same thing as someone who recites one of Mine."

10.14 There is another story in this book from al-Sayyid the great Shaykh Abū l-ʿAbbās Aḥmad al-Rifāʿī (may God be pleased with him). One of the servants of the Mightiest Refuge died. His wife came to the Refuge and begged him to help get her husband's life back. The Refuge turned to observe and consulted the world of the unseen. He saw the Angel of Death (blessings upon him) going up to heaven with the souls which he had snatched away that day. The Refuge said: "Angel of Death, stop and give me the spirit of my servant." (He gave his name.) "I take away spirits by divine decree," replied the Angel of Death, "and conduct them to the gate of His glory. How can I give you back a soul which I've snatched away at my Lord's command?" The Refuge repeated his request to be given back the spirit of his servant and was again refused. The Angel of Death had a spiritual container in his hands which looked like a palm-leaf basket. In it were the souls he had snatched that day. By the power invested in him as a beloved of God, the Refuge tugged the basket and snatched it from the Angel's hand. All the souls were scattered and returned to their bodies. The Angel of Death (blessings upon him) confided in his Lord: "Lord," he said, "you know best of all what has occurred between myself and your beloved associate, ʿAbd al-Qādir. He forcibly removed the souls that I snatched today." "Angel of Death," God (may His splendor be exalted) replied, "the Mightiest Refuge is My beloved and My desire. Why didn't you give him his servant's soul? Because of your actions many souls have escaped your grasp for the sake of just one. On this occasion, you are the loser."

(Here ends the quotation from *Manāqib tāj al-awliyāʾ wa-burhān al-aṣfiyāʾ al-quṭb al-rabbānī wa-al-ghawth al-ṣamdānī al-Sayyid ʿAbd al-Qādir al-Jīlānī*, printed at the expense of Shaykh ʿAbd al-Raḥmān al-Niyāzi, Shaykh of the Qādiriyya House in Alexandria, pp. 20–22.)

قال عيسى بن هشام: وانتفض الباشا صاحبي قائماً والغضب باد على وجهه والحزن والأسف ملء صدره وقال لهم: ١٠،١٥

الباشا اعلموا أيها الإخوان أنّ المغفرة وسكنى الجنان لا تنال بمجرد الصوم وأكل التمر والتبرك بالآثار ولا تكتسب الدرجة الرفيعة في الآخرة إلا باجتناب الشر وفعل الخير وإسداء الجميل وحسن الصنيع والرحمة بالضعفاء والمساكين من عباد الله وقد غرّني في دنياي ما يغرّكم الآن فكنت أسمع قبل الممات من مثل هذا الشيخ العالم ما يهوّن عليَّ ارتكاب المخزيات وفضائح الشرور في معاملة عباد الله ارتكاناً على نهار أصومه، وليل أقومه، وحرز أحمله، وأثر أقبّله، واتكلت على مثل ذلك ونمت عن الخير والمعروف فلمّا توفاني القدير العليم وسكنت في حفرة القبر علمت ما لم أكن أعلم فلم تغنني صلاتي وصيامي وأدعيتي وقيامي وحدها من الله شيئاً وما خفّفت عني أهوال القبر وهوّن عليَّ سؤال الملكين إلا حسنة واحدة أتيتها في إغاثة مظلوم استجارني فأجرته من يد الجلاد وهو بين النطع والسيف. فعليكم بالعدل والإحسان وتقوى الله في عباده وإفشاء البر والمعروف، ولا تطيعوا النفس الأمّارة بالسوء في فعل الشر واجتناب الخير والارتكان على الغفران بلا عمل. قال الله تعالى: ﴿فَمَن يَعۡمَلۡ مِثۡقَالَ ذَرَّةٍ خَيۡرٗا يَرَهُۥ﴾ وقال علي رضي الله عنه: «كم من صائم ليس له من صيامه إلا الجوع والظمأ وكم من قائم ليس له من قيامه إلا السهر والعناء» وقال حكيم الشعراء:

ما الخير صومٌ يذوب الصائمون له
ولا صلاة ولا صوف على الجسد

ʿĪsa ibn Hishām said: Barely had the Shaykh finished talking before the Pāshā leapt up before my very eyes, anger, sorrow, and regret written all over his face. This is what he had to say: 10.15

PĀSHĀ My brothers, pardon from God the merciful and a place in heaven, you should realize, are not to be gained by prolonged fasting, eating dates, seeking blessings from relics, or by protecting oneself with pious recitations. The only way to win an exalted position in God's eyes is to be just and charitable, to practice good and avoid evil, and to show mercy towards those of God's creatures who are weak and poor. During my own life here on earth, I too was deceived by the very same things which are now deceiving you. Before I died, I too used to listen to the kind of things this Shaykh has been saying; all of which made me think nothing of committing the most outrageous acts and condoning terrible wrongs in the way I treated people. I felt I could rely on a day of fasting and a night spent performing prayers, or on an amulet I would carry around with me and some relic or other which I would kiss, as a way of atoning for all these wrongs. As a result, I put my trust in such beliefs and slept with a clear conscience. However, when the mighty omniscient God sent me to my death and I became an inhabitant of the grave, I learned things which I didn't know before. All my prayers, fasts, and supplications did not spare me from God's judgment at all. The only thing which alleviated the terrors of the grave and made the angels' interrogation easier to bear was a single act of charity which I'd performed when someone who had been wronged asked for my protection when he was almost under the executioner's sword, and I'd given it to him. My advice to you then is to make sure that you all behave in a just and charitable manner. Show fear of God in the way you treat mankind and spread kindness and goodwill among His creatures. Don't follow that side of your nature which suggests an evil course of action; in that case, you'll rely on being deluded by vain hopes and will have to ask for forgiveness without having done anything worthwhile. God Almighty has said in the Qur'an: «Whoever does one atom's weight of good, God sees it.»[79] Also bear in mind ʿAlī's words (may God be pleased with him): "Many people who fast only get hunger and thirst from their fasting; many a man who performs prayers at night merely loses sleep and wears himself out." Here is what the wise poet has to say:

Doing good is not just a fast that makes fasters waste away,
nor prayer, nor wearing wool on the body.

وإنّما هو ترك الشرّ مُطّرحًا
ونفضُكَ الصّدرَ من غلٍّ ومن حسد

١٦،١٠ الشيخ إني لأخالك أيها الرجل شيطاناً في زيّ إنسان وزنديقاً يتستر بدعوى النشور من القبور تعساً وبؤساً لهذا الزمن ما أكثر أضاليله وأعظم أباطيله، ولم يبق علينا من مدّخرات عجائبه إلا أن يخرج الميت من قبره فيخبرنا بما رأى وما سمع.

الأمير صاحب الدار سألتك بالله أن تخبرني بأي لغة كان سؤال الملكين لك أبالعربية أو التركية أم السريانية.

الشيخ ناشدتكم الله أن لا تكلموا هذا الرجل فإنه فتنة من فتن إبليس اللعين.

١٧،١٠ قال عيسى بن هشام فاحتدّ الباشا واضطرم وولّى عنهم وجهه وخرج مهرولاً يهدر ويغلي ويستعيذ ويستعدي وانخرطت وراءه وتركنا المجلس وذلك الشيخ البدين الذي قال في مثله عمر رضي الله عنه «إنّ الله يبغض الحبر السمين» وما زلت أردّد ما قاله علي كرّم الله وجهه ودويّ كلام الشيخ في أذني «أشكو إلى الله من معشر يعيشون جهالاً ويموتون ضلالاً ليس فيهم سلعة أبور من كتاب الله إذا تلي حق تلاوته ولا سلعة أنفق بيعاً وثمناً من الكتاب إذا حرّف عن مواضعه ولا عندهم أنكر من المعروف ولا أعرف من المنكر».

ولحق بنا في طريقنا الركبدار والتاجر الذي كان في المجلس يناديانا فوقفنا لهما فتقدّم التاجر إلى الباشا ومال إلى تقبيل يده وقال له:

التاجر (للباشا) اعلم أيها المولى أني مصدق بأمرك وقد حكى لي أحمد أنما هذا عمّا أنت فيه وعن حاجتك التي جاءت بك إلى هذا المجلس وعلمت أنك أنفت من ذكرها عندما غضبت لله، وأنا رجل غني ولله الحمد ولك عليَّ فضل لا أنساه وما أنا فيه من نعمة فمن فضلك وإحسانك وبركة يمنك فلست أنسى أنّ أصل شهرتي التي أكسبتني هذه الثروة هو أنك ركزت في دكاني برهة في ذات يوم عندما عثرت بك

It involves utterly rejecting all evil
and ridding your heart of malice and envy.[80]

10.16 Shaykh I think you must be Satan in human form, or else a heretic masquerading as someone who has risen from the dead. A curse on this age with its enormous follies, a plague on its utter trivialities! There's only one other miracle still in store for us: for a dead person to come out of his grave and tell us the things he's seen and heard!

Owner of the House (*to the Pāshā*) I beg you to tell us, by God, in which language did the two angels interrogate you? Was it Arabic, Turkish, or Syriac?

Shaykh I implore you in God's name not to talk to this man alone! He's one of the accursed Devil's temptations.

10.17 ʿĪsā ibn Hishām said: The Pāshā was in a seething temper. He turned his back on them and rushed out in a fury, asking God for help and protection. As I departed the assembly and rushed out after him, I left behind the fat Shaykh about whose type the Caliph ʿUmar ibn al-Khaṭṭāb once said: "God hates fat men of religion." I repeated to myself Abū Turāb's words (may God honor his aspect): "I complain to God about a community living in ignorance and dying in error. In this community nothing is as hard to sell as the Book of God when it is recited properly, and no article is a more saleable commodity than God's book once its meaning has been distorted. Nothing is less well-known than what is approved, nothing more well-known than what is abhorred."[81]

As we left, the Groom and Merchant who had been with us in the assembly called out to us and so we waited for them. The Merchant came up to the Pāshā and leaned over to kiss his hand.

Merchant Master, I call God to witness that I believe your story. Aḥmad here has told me about your situation and the needs that brought you to this assembly. You refused to draw attention to it while you were standing up for God. I'm a wealthy man, and I owe it to God and yourself for a favor that I'll never forget. The prosperity that I now enjoy comes from your generosity, kindness, and blessed fortune. I can never forget that the fame that has brought me this wealth came as a consequence of your spending a short while sitting in my shop one day after you had tripped during a visit to the al-Husayn mosque. As a result, my own fortune and reputation both grew, and people

رجلك في قصدك زيارة الحسين فارتفع بذلك قدري واشتهر أمري وأقبل عليَّ الناس بتنازلك للجلوس في دكاني وأنا أسألك بحق الله أن تقبل مني ما تسدّ به حاجتك ويخلصك من مطالبة المحامي.

١٨،١٠ قال عيسى بن هشام: وأخرج الرجل كيساً مملوءاً فقدّمه إلى الباشا وهو يرتعش من الخجل وخوف الرد فأخذه الباشا وقال له:

الباشا إني أشكرك على مرؤتك وأسأل الله لك حسن الجزاء عليها فهلمّ أكتب لك صكا بالمال لأردّه إليك عند استيلائي على أوقافي.

التاجر حاشا لله أن أكون من أهل هذا الزمن في المعاملات الذين أصبحوا لا يثقون ببعضهم فلا يأمن الأخ أخاه ولا الأب ابنه ولا القريب قريبه ولا الصاحب صاحبه على فلس واحد إلا بعقود وشهود وصكوك مسجلات، بل أنا من أهل ذلك الزمن الذي لم يكن يتعامل التجار فيما بينهم بغير الأمانة دون احتياج إلى هذه الأوراق وهذا الضمان، فكانت الأمانة عامة بينهم، فلا أحد يخون ولا أحد يحتيل، وما يكون الاستيثاق إلا عند توهّم الخيانة ونعوذ بالله من هذه الأحوال.

١٩،١٠ قال عيسى بن هشام: فأعاد الباشا شكره للتاجر وقال لي هلمّ بنا إلى المحامي نستنقذ رقابنا منه فتوجهنا إليه وتخلصنا منه بعد طول العناء. وقال لي الباشا عند نزولنا من مكتب المحامي: لم يبق إلّا أن نشرع في إقامة دعوى بالمحكمة الشرعية للاستيلاء على أوقافي.

فقلت له: لا بدّ لنا أوّلاً من محام شرعي فطلب مني أن نتوجّه إلى أحد المضطلعين من المحامين، فخرجنا من قبضة محام للدخول في قبضة محام. ونسأل الله العافية في الختام.

flocked to my place because you had deigned to sit there for a while. They assumed that I'd some personal connection with you and your vast influence. So, in the name of God, I beg you to accept enough money from me to satisfy your needs and rid yourself of the claims of this Lawyer.

ʿĪsā ibn Hishām said: The Merchant now produced a full purse and offered it to the Pāshā, shaking all the while in case he refused his offer. The Pāshā took it and said: **10.18**

PĀSHĀ I'm deeply grateful to you for your kindness, and I ask God to give you a worthy reward. Come now, write yourself a check for the amount. I'll repay you when I get my endowments back.

MERCHANT God forbid that I should be one of those people these days who don't trust anyone. Brothers no longer trust each other, a father will distrust his own son, and relatives and friends will not rely on one another. People will squabble over a mere dirham, and everyone insists on legal transactions, witnesses, and checks. I'm still one of those people from that age when no merchant would do business without trust and confidence, and there was no need to write notes or demand guarantees. Everyone trusted everyone else, and there was no deceit or trickery. Checking is only necessary when one suspects dishonesty. We all seek refuge in God from such circumstances!

ʿĪsā ibn Hishām said: So the Pāshā repeated his thanks to the Merchant. "Come on," he said to me, "let's go to the Lawyer and get him off our backs after so much trouble." **10.19**

As we left the Lawyer's office, the Pāshā told me that now the time had come to bring a case in the Shariah Court to recover his endowments.

"What we need first," I replied, "is to find a Shariah Court lawyer."

He then asked me to take him to consult a competent lawyer. So we were now out the clutches of one lawyer, only to fall into another's. We ask God to deliver us in the end.

مصباح الشرق ٤٨، ٢٣ مارس ١٨٩٩

١٫١١ قال عيسى بن هشام: وسرت في طريقي مع رفيقي أنشد صاحباً أسترشده في محام شرعي أعتمده، وبينا نحن نسير في طلب هذا الأمر العسير إذا بصاحب لي عرفته فاستوقفته، قال ما خطبكما، قلت قضية في المحكمة الشرعية، فما طرق الخبر سمعه حتى أجرى دمعه، وحوقل وحوقلت، واستعاذ واستعذت، ثمّ قال: لقد وقعت في هذا البلاء، ولمّا تتم لي النقاهة من هذا الداء العيناء، وأنا أنصح لك إن كنت مدعياً أن تترك دعواك، وتصبر على بلواك، وإن كانت الدعوى عليك، فالخيار ليس إليك، ولا مردّ للقضاء بتدبير الآراء، فقلت: للضرورة أحكام، وأنا أستصبح برأيك في انتخاب محام يكون مشهوداً بعدالته، مشهوراً بطهارته، بعيداً عن خلف الوعد، وخلق الوغد، لا يتفق مع الخصم، ولا يسرق من الرسم.

قال: اطلب من أنواع المحال، أن يحمل الذر الجبال، ولا تطلب في محام اجتماع هذه الشروط فينتهي الأمر بك إلى اليأس والقنوط ومحاولة الارتقاء فوق متن العنقاء أيسر مطلبا، وأوسع مذهبا، والمحامون الشرعيون حماك الله يستوون لدى الاختيار كأسنان المشط أو أسنان الحمار، بل هم أجمعهم كحماري العبادي قيل له أي حماريك شر قال هذا ثمّ هذا. وأقسم لك بخالص الود أني لا أثق منهم بأحد، وكيف تكلفني أن أنتقي لك ذئباً من الذئاب، وأحمل على كاهلي عبء التأنيب والعتاب، فاعفني من هذا الانتقاء عافاك الله من كل الأسواء.

٢٫١١ ثمّ ما لبث أن سلّم ومضى وخلفني على جمر الغضا، فسرت كئيباً حزيناً أبغي سواه مرشداً ومعيناً. ولمّا لم أجد من أصحابي من يأخذ على عهدته اختيار محام يثق بذمّته قصدت أحد المعلومين عندي بكثرة الخصومات في المعاملات فكاشفته بطلبتنا لكشف مصيبتنا، فقال: اعلم أنّ المحامين الشرعيين أشكال وصنوف، فمنهم المبصر

Miṣbāḥ al-sharq 48, March 23, 1899[82]

11.1 ʿĪsā ibn Hishām said: I went with my friend to look for an acquaintance whom I could ask for advice in our search for a Shariah Court lawyer. While we were proceeding on this difficult quest, I spotted a friend of mine and asked for a minute of his time.

"What's the problem?" he asked.

"A court case," I replied, "in the Shariah Court."

Barely had he heard the words before he started weeping. We both bewailed the situation and realized how hopeless it was. "I've already suffered such a misfortune," he said, "and I've yet to recover. If you're the litigant, my advice to you is to drop your summons and accept your sufferings with patience. If you're the defendant, then you've no choice since prescient planning is of no avail against the course of fate."

"Even necessity has its own rules," I replied. "I'm asking you for guidance in choosing a lawyer who is highly regarded for his impartiality and famous for his honesty. We need someone who will not break promises, a person who has not the slightest trace of a crooked character in him and who will not make agreements with the opposition or ask for extortionate fees."

"Of all kinds of impossibility," he replied, "ask rather that ants carry mountains, but don't look for such a collection of qualities in a lawyer! You'll only finish up in despair and despondency. Try climbing on the back of the Phoenix instead; that's a much easier task, one that allows you more scope than what you're asking! When it comes to choosing Shariah Court lawyers—God protect you! They're like the teeth in a comb or a donkey's molars. In fact, they're just like al-ʿIbādī's two donkeys: to the question as to which one was worse, he responded: 'This one, then that one.' On the basis of sincerest affection I can swear to you that I don't trust any one of them. How can you ask me to choose one wolf from among a whole pack? Were I to do so, I would have to shoulder the burden of blame. Please absolve me from making such a choice, and may God protect you from all misfortunes!"

11.2 Soon after he said farewell and went on his way, leaving me on tenterhooks. I moved on too, feeling sad and discouraged. I continued to look for someone else to advise and help us. When I discovered that none of my friends was prepared to select a lawyer whom we could trust, I went to see someone who was known to me because of the many litigations he had undertaken. I told him

ومنهم المكفوف، وفيهم كتب الله لك منهم السلامة صاحب الطربوش وصاحب العمامة، وأنا أدلّك على أهونهم شرّاً وأقلّهم ضرّاً وأخفهم بليّة وأوسعهم اطلاعاً على الحيل الشرعية، فعليك بفلان ودلني على بيته ثمّ ذهب لطيته.

فأخذنا نشقّ طرقاً معوجّة، ونخترق ثنيات مزدوجة وأسواقاً مزدحمة بأقوام ملتحمة إلى أن انتهينا إلى دار حلّت بساحتها الأقذار واكتنفتها الأوساخ والأوضار، فأمست كأنها مطلية بالقار، وعلى الباب صبية يلعبون بالتراب وبينهم صغيرة على وجهها من الذباب برقع لبسته قبل أوان النقاب. ولمّا خطوناهم غشيتنا رائحة المرحاض فوقعنا هناك على أنقاض بجانبها معتلف أتان تزاحمها عليه بطتان، ووجدنا حجرة في جهة اليمين ورأينا فرانًا ينادي العجين العجين،

٣،١١ فسألناه عن رب الدار فأشار إلى الحجرة فدخلنا فوجدنا حصيراً تغطى بالغبار والحصباء ومتكأ تعرّى من الفرش والغطاء، وفي زاوية من الأركان سراج لا ينفذ نوره من تكاثف الدخان، وعلى رف في ذلك الرواق كتب وأوراق قام لها نسيج العناكب مقام الوقاية والتجليد، وألصقتها الرطوبة فحفظتها من التوزيع والتبديد، وفوق الأرض زجاجات فارغة من المداد، وفي الحائط تخطيط من لعب الأولاد، وبصرنا برجل:

تُغيّـرُ حِـنّاؤُهُ شَيْبَـهُ
فهل غيّرَ الظهرَ لمّا انحنى

لم يزل جالساً على سجادة الصلاة يسبّح مرة ويكلم امرأة عن يساره مرات، فيقول لها: أتستكثرين - أدرّ الله عليك خيره وأبدلك زوجاً غيره - ما أخذته منك للتطليق، واستنباط الحيلة في التفريق، فأبعدتُ عنك زوجاً تكرهينه لتستبدلي به زوجاً تحبينه.

of our search for a lawyer who could get us out of our unfortunate situation. "You should realize," he told us, "that there are various types of Shariah Court lawyer. Some can see, others are blind. In their ranks one finds wearers of the tarboosh and wearers of the turban—may God give you protection![83] I'll direct you to one whose evil ways are the easiest to contend with and who will cause you the least harm. He knows more than anyone else about the ruses of the Shariah. Go and see X." With that he gave me directions to the lawyer's house and went on his way.

We made our way along twisting roads and winding alleyways crowded with people. Eventually we came to the door of a house which looked as though it was tarred with pitch. It was blocked up with mounds of filth and surrounded by piles of rubbish. At the entrance we noticed some children playing with the earth. Among them was a little girl whose face was covered with so many flies that it looked as though she had donned the veil before her time. As we walked past them, we were hit by the stench of the lavatory, and rested for a moment on a pile of debris. Alongside it there was a mule's feeding trough with ducks and geese crowding round it. We found our way to a room to the right, and saw a baker in front of us shouting out his wares.

11.3 We asked for the owner of the house, and he pointed to the room. We went inside and found a carpet covered with dust and small stones, a couch without any padding or covering left. In one of the corners was a lamp which was too weak to pierce through the thick smoke. On the topmost shelves were piles of books and scrolls; a spider's web acted as their protective covering and binding, and the mildew which clung to them stopped them from splitting and falling apart. On the floor were discarded bottles of ink, while the white walls had been covered by the black scribblings of children at play. There we saw a man:

Henna had altered his grey locks;
but can it change his back once bent?[84]

The Lawyer was still sitting on his prayer mat; at times he was praying, while at others he would keep talking to a woman. He was speaking to her as follows: "May God shower His blessings on you and find you another husband! How can you claim that I've overcharged you for the divorce and for devising a strategy for getting you a legal separation? Haven't I rid you of a husband you loathed, so that you could marry a man you love instead?" Just then he noticed that we had entered behind his back and started reciting

ولمّا استحس بدخولنا من ورائه ارتدّ إلى صلاته ودعائه، وانتفضت المرأة فتلفت بإزارها وتنقبت بخمارها، وخرجت وتركتنا مع رجل يخدع بصلاته الأنام، ويصلي بسورة البقرة والأنعام.

إذا رامَ كيداً بالصّلاة مُقيمُها
فتاركها عمداً إلى الله أقربُ

٤،١١ وأقمنا ننتظر خلاصنا من هذا العناء، وخلاصه من هذا الرياء، وخلاص الملكين من صحيفته السوداء، وهو مغذ في سيره ليصل المغرب بالعشاء، وما زلنا نشاهد له في خلال ذلك نظرات مختلسات نحو الباب كأنه هو أيضاً في انتظار وارتقاب، إلى أن خرج علينا خارج يصيح به: إلى متى هذه العبادة، فقد بَليَتْ السجادة والناس في حاجة إليك، وقضاء مصالحهم في يديك، وهذا البرنس ينتظرك في القصر منذ العصر، ومدير الأوقاف يقول لك نجّنا ممّا نخاف، فلم يعبأ المصلي بهذا الكلام، بل جهر بالآية التي وصل إليها من سورة الأنعام: ﴿وَكَذَٰلِكَ فَتَنَّا بَعۡضَهُم بِبَعۡضٍ لِّيَقُولُوٓاْ أَهَٰٓؤُلَآءِ مَنَّ ٱللَّهُ عَلَيۡهِم مِّنۢ بَيۡنِنَآۗ أَلَيۡسَ ٱللَّهُ بِأَعۡلَمَ بِٱلشَّٰكِرِينَ﴾ فجلس الغلام وهو يمسح العرق، وهممنا بالقيام من شدة القلق، وقلنا من يضمن بعد ذلك لصلاته انتهاء، ولتسبيحه انقضاء، فلم نشعر به إلا وقد طوى الصلاة بالتحيات والتسليمات، والتفت إلينا فقال: أهلا بكم بارك الله فيكم فيم تختصمون، قلنا في قضية في وقف، قال الغلام: تريدون ريعه أو بيعه، قلنا: وهل تباع الأوقاف، قال: نعم ويباع جبل قاف.

٥،١١ المحامي (بعد أن تنحنح وسعل، وبصق وتفل، وتسعط ثمّ تمخّط) دعكما من هذا

his prayers all over again. The woman jumped up, put up her veil, wrapped her shawl round herself and departed. We were left with a man who was deceiving people with his long prayers, and reciting the Surahs of the Cow and the Sheep during his prostrations.

> Should he who prays wish to deceive,
> the one who intentionally stops praying is closer to God.[85]

11.4 For a while we just sat there; we were waiting for ourselves to be rid of this trouble, for him to stop this hypocrisy, and for the two questioning angels to finish with his black list. All the while he was fussing about and hurrying to perform the evening prayer. Meanwhile, we noticed that he kept glancing furtively towards the door as though he too were waiting for someone. Eventually an Assistant came in. "How long are these devotions going to take?" he shouted. "You've already worn out the prayer mat. People have put their cases in your hands, leaving it to you to carry out what is in their best interests. His Highness the Prince has been waiting for you since the afternoon prayer, not to mention the Director of Religious Endowments who is asking you to rescue him from his plight." The praying Lawyer paid no attention to all this. Instead he recited the verse from the Surah of the Sheep: «And thus have we tested some of them with others so that they may say: Are these the ones among us to whom God has been gracious? Is not God most knowledgeable about the thankful?»[86]

His Assistant sat down, wiping the sweat from his brow. Who, we asked ourselves, could guarantee that this praying and glorification would ever come to an end? We were so upset that we were on the point of getting up and leaving. Just then the Lawyer Shaykh completed his prayers with the necessary concluding phrases. He then turned toward us. "Greetings to you," he said. "What is the cause of your litigation?"

"It concerns a religious endowment," we replied.

"Are you seeking the income from it," the Assistant asked, "or do you wish to sell it?"

"Can religious endowments be sold?" we asked.

"Certainly," he replied, "Mount Jabal Qāf itself is on the market!"

11.5 The Shaykh cleared his throat, coughed, spat, took some snuff, and blew his nose.

الغلام وقولا لي ما هو الحق في الوقف وما هو شرط الواقف وكم يقدّر ثمن العين لتقدّر الأتعاب بحسبه.

عيسى بن هشام إنّ لصاحبي هذا وقفاً عاقته العوائق عنه فوضع سواه عليه يده ونريد الآن رفع الدعوى لرفع تلك اليد.

المحامي سألتك ما هي قيمته.

عيسى بن هشام ربما بلغت قيمته كذا ديناراً.

المحامي فتكون قيمة الأتعاب كذا جنيهاً، وعليكما دفع نصفها مقدماً.

عيسى بن هشام ألا ترى أيها الشيخ أنّ هذه القيمة عالية وإنه ليتعذّر علينا نقدها.

الغلام كيف تقول هذا الكلام وتعتذر بتعذر النقد، ألم تعلم أنّ هذا شغل له اشتراكات وللكتبة والمحضرين تطلعات، وإني لكما بغير مولانا الشيخ يضمن ربح الدعوى وكسب القضية بما يهون معه دفع كل قيمة في أتعابه، وهل يوجد مثله في علم الحيل الشرعية حتى فاق فيها جميع الواضعين لكتبها، ومن سواه يقدر على استمالة محامي الخصم.

عيسى بن هشام هذا والله كل ما معنا الآن ونكتب بما بقي صكا لحين كسب القضية ولا ضرر من هذا التأجيل ما دامت الثقة في الربح على ما ترى (وناول الشيخ كيساً من الدراهم).

المحامي (بعد أن عدّها) أنا أقبل منكما هذا القدر القليل الآن وأبتغي ما ادّخره الله لعباده من حسن الثواب والأجر في خدمة المسلمين ونفعهم وعليكما بشاهدين للتوكيل. ٦،١١

عيسى بن هشام وكيف يكون التوكيل.

المحامي يجب عليكما أن تستحضرا معكما شاهدين يشهدان في المحكمة بأنّ فلاناً ابن فلان وكّل فلاناً ابن فلان ابن فلان في المرافعات والمدافعات والمخاصمات والمصالحات والقبض والاستلام والتسليم وفي المطالبة والدفع والإقرار وفي كل ما

Lawyer Don't take any notice of my Assistant. Tell me what right you have to the endowment. What's the circumstance of the endowment's donor? What's its current cash value so that the fees can be calculated accordingly?

ʿĪsā The endowment belongs to my friend here, but certain factors are preventing him from obtaining it. Other people have laid their hands on it. We want to initiate a suit to reclaim it from them.

Lawyer I asked you what its cash value was.

ʿĪsā I don't know exactly; certainly in thousands.

Lawyer Then the advanced charges will certainly be X pounds. You need to pay half in advance.

ʿĪsā My dear Shaykh, isn't that too much. We can't possibly pay it.

Assistant How can you say such a thing and refuse to pay? Don't you realize that this business involves subscriptions, and that secretaries and clerks all charge search fees? Apart from my master, the Shaykh, how do you expect to find anyone else who can guarantee you success in the case and profit from the suit? That should make it easy to pay all the fees he asks for? Is there anyone else so knowledgeable about the ruses of the Shariah? He stands head and shoulders above everyone who's written on the subject. Other than he who else can win over the opposition lawyer?

ʿĪsā This is all the money we have with us now. We'll write you a check when the case is won. The delay won't be a problem as long as you're prepared to guarantee the success of the trial at all events.

The Lawyer now took the purse and counted the money.

11.6 Lawyer (*after counting the money*) I accept this paltry sum from you now, desiring that great reward which God reserves for His servants who act in the service of Muslims. But you're responsible for providing two witnesses for the warrant of attorney.

ʿĪsā And how, pray, do we obtain a warrant of attorney?

Lawyer You need to produce two witnesses to testify before the court that "A, son of B, son of C, appoints D as attorney for the purposes of proceeding at law, making defense speeches, conducting cross examinations, settlements, payments, receipts and consignments; for appeals, expenditures, undertakings, in fact anything in which the warrant of attorney is permissible according to the Shariah law; and to subcontract the suit to someone else

يصح فيه التوكيل شرعاً، وفي أن يوكّل عنه في هذه الدعوى غيره وأن يعزله وأن يفعل ذلك مراراً وتكراراً كلما بدا له فعله المرة بعد المرة والكرة بعد الكرة، وفي غد إن شاء الله تحضران مع الشاهدين ومستند الوقف.

عيسى بن هشام ليس لدينا الآن إلا شاهد واحد يعرف أصل صاحبي ونسبه.

الغلام هذه أول خطوة في كلف القضية ومشاقها، ولعلك تعرف قيمتها ونحن نجد لك عندنا من يعرف صاحبك ونسبه ويشهد به بين يدي الله.

عيسى بن هشام كما أنه ليس في يدنا مستند للوقف.

المحامي أمّا من جهة المستند فينبغي استخراج صورة من السجل «المصان» (بهذا اللحن) وهذه الخطوة الثانية في متاعب القضية.

٧،١١ قال عيسى بن هشام: وعند ذلك قطع الشيخ كلامه واستقبل القبلة بوجهه ووضع يمينه فوق جبينه وقام لصلاة العشاء فخرجت مع الباشا وأنا أعجب ممّا رأيت من سكونه وسكوته وحسن صبره على ما نقاسيه وأقول في نفسي لا شيء أسرع في تهذيب النفوس وتربيتها وحملها على التخلق بالأخلاق الفاضلة مثل ممارسة الخطوب ومصارعة الرزايا، ولقد كان هذا الباشا شديد الحدّة سريع الغضب قليل الصبر يرى القتل واجباً عند كل هفوة فأصبح بفضل وقوعه في هذه الخطوب المتتالية والرزايا العامة واسع الصدر لين العريكة عظيم الحلم موطأ الكنف كثير الاحتمال حتى إنه لم يأنف ولم يتأفف من كل ما رأيناه في يومنا هذا، ولم ينطق بحرف، بل كانت حالته حالة الفيلسوف الذي يجعل دأبه في كل معاملاته مع الناس البحث في الأخلاق، وازدادت يقيناً بأنّ أسوأ الناس أخلاقاً وأنكدهم عيشاً وأنغصهم حياة هؤلاء الأغمار المترفون المنعمون الذين لم يأخذوا العيش عن تجارب الحدثان ولم تهذبهم صروف الأزمان،

٨،١١ ولم يزد الباشا في كلامه لي عند سيرنا في طريقنا على أن قال:

and dismiss him, to do this repeatedly whenever he deems it fit, time after time." So tomorrow, God willing, you'll appear with the two witnesses and the record of the endowment.

'Īsā At this point, we've only one witness who knows about the Pāshā's origins and lineage.

Lawyer's Assistant This is stage one in the expenses of the case and its various difficulties. You'll probably realize the cost involved. We'll find someone for you who knows your friend and his origins and can witness to that effect before God.

'Īsā We don't possess the record of the endowment either.

Lawyer In that regard one has to produce a copy of the "official" record (said in a particular tone of voice). This is stage two in the expenses of the case.

11.7 'Īsā ibn Hishām said: At this point, the Lawyer brought his conversation with us to a close. Facing the qiblah, he placed his right hand on his brow and started praying the evening prayer. My companion and I got up to leave and walked out. I was amazed at the subdued calmness and patient resignation I had noticed in the Pāshā. I told myself that nothing educates and trains the soul in the paths of virtue so quickly as the experience of misfortune and a struggle with disaster. It was only a short time ago that he had been cantankerous and quick-tempered, finding it necessary to kill someone for the most trifling lapse and the least pretext. After succumbing to this series of calamities, he had become meek-tempered, magnanimous, approachable, and patient; so much so that he no longer scorned and grumbled about everything we saw that day. He had nothing to say, but had instead turned into a wise philosopher who habitually observes people's manners and customs in the course of his dealings with them. I became further convinced that the people with the worst natures who lead the most miserable lives are those gullible fools who are pampered and spoilt by their luxurious existence and who have never been taught how to live by the bitter experience of adversity nor learned any lessons from the misfortunes of time.

11.8 As we walked, the Pāshā merely said the following to me:

الباشا   اعلم أيها الخل الصديق أنه لولا ما أشربته في قلبي من تبجيل المشايخ وألفته من احترام أرباب العمائم الحاملين لكتاب الله لما صبرت على هذا المحامي هذا الصبر ولطلبت منك أن تذهب بي إلى صنف الطرابيش من هؤلاء المحامين الشرعيين.

عيسى بن هشام   اعلم أنّ الخيرة في الواقع والحمد لله على كل حال وربما كان فيهم تحت الطربوش من هو أشد فتكاً من ضواري الوحوش، وأعرف طربوشاً منهم أقسم أمامي بالطلاق ثلاثا من زوجته ومن كل زوجة يتزوجها في مستقبل دهره على إنكار كلام نطق به في مجلس كنتُ حاضراً فيه وسمعته يقول بأذني هذه فأقدم هذا المحامي الشرعي على الاستهانة بحكم الشارع وعمل بقول الشاعر:

وإن حلّفوني بالطلاق أتيتها
على خير ما كنّا ولمّا نتفرّقِ
وإن حلّفوني بالعتاق فقد درى
عبيد غلامي أنّه غير معتقِ

ومضت علينا الأيام بعد ذلك ونحن نقصد الشيخ في كل يوم فلا نجده، فإن ذهبنا إليه في البيت قيل لنا إنه في المحكمة، وإن سألنا عنه في المحكمة قيل لنا إنه في القصر العالي أو غيره من قصور الكبر، حتى حفيت الأقدام ونفد الصبر فاخترنا أن نربط له أمام بيته عند الثلث الأخير من الليل فنصطاده قبل خروجه منه. وقعدنا بعيداً عن الباب حتى خرج علينا الشيخ فأتانا راكباً أتاناً وقال: أرجو المسامحة في هذا التأخير والذنب في ذلك لكثرة مشاكل الأمراء ودعاويهم، فقبلنا عذره وتوجهنا معه إلى المحكمة فذهب بنا إلى كاتب الإشهادات والله ينجيك من مثل هذه المواقف فوجدناه يلمع في ثيابه من حمرة الحذاء تحت فخذه وزرقة الجبة على كتفه وصفرة الحزام في وسطه وبياض العمامة على رأسه.

٩،١١

Pāshā I want you to know, my dear friend, that, were it not for the great respect and veneration which I have for shaykhs and wearers of the turban who are the bearers of God's holy book, I would have asked you to take me to a Shariah Court lawyer who wears a tarboosh.

ʿĪsā One must take things as they come, you should realize, and in any case it's all God's will! Beneath the tarboosh you'll often find some people more ferociously destructive than wild beasts. I myself know a tarboosh wearer who swore in my presence that he would pronounce the threefold divorce on his current wife and every wife he would marry in the future, all that in order to deny something which he had in fact said in a company at which I was myself present. By so doing, he was mocking the lawgiver's authority, relying instead on the words of the poet who said:

If they make me swear to divorce my wife,
  I will return to her, our relationship better than before we separated.
Should they make me swear to free a slave,
  my slave ʿUbayd knows he will not be freed.[87]

11.9 ʿĪsā ibn Hishām said: The days went by. Every day we went to see the Lawyer Shaykh, but never found him. If we went to his house, we were told he was in court; and if we went to court, we learned that he was at the royal palace or a mansion owned by some important personage. Eventually our feet were sore, and we grew tired of waiting. We decided to lie in wait for him in front of his house during the last hours of darkness, so that we could catch him before he left. We sat at a distance from the door. Eventually he emerged riding a donkey. "Please forgive this delay," he said. "The real fault lies with the numerous problems and lawsuits involving princes with which I'm dealing." We accepted his excuse and accompanied him to the court. He went with us to the testification clerk—and may God preserve you from such circumstances! We found him sitting there in resplendent attire: red shoes on his feet, blue coat on his shoulders, yellow belt around his waist, and a white turban around his head:

تعــدّدت ألوانــه كأنّه قوسُ قُزح

وكان تركنا الشيخ مع الغلام، فلمّا نظر الكاتب إلى أحد الشاهدين توقف وقال أنه شاب صغير السن وأنه وأنه. . . . فمال عليه غلام المحامي وألقى في أذنه كلاماً فقام الكاتب معنا إلى قاضي الجلسة لسماع الإشهاد بعد أن قال الغلام: وهذه الخطوة الثالثة في متاعب القضية. ثمّ انتهى الإشهاد بحمد الله وحسن العناية في مسافة يوم واحد فقط، وعند الانصراف قيل لنا ينبغي تقديم عريضة لحضرة القاضي بطلب الكشف من الدفترخانة عن الوقفية في السجل وأن نوضّح فيها نمرة الوقفية وتاريخها وعملية من (يعني اسم الكاتب الذي كتبها في ذلك الزمان) فخرجنا نبحث عن الركبدار لعله يعرف طريقة للحصول بها على هذا المطلوب. وبعد أن عثرنا عليه وأعلمناه بغرضنا قال إنّ عندي ورقة فيها نمرة الوقفية تحصلت عليها بطرق مختلفة بعد الجهد الجهيد والزمن المديد لإثبات حقي في الريع. وذهب إلى بيته وعاد إلينا بها فوجدناها قاصرة على النمرة والتاريخ لم يُذكر فيها اسم الكاتب الذي عمل العملية. ١٠،١١

ثمّ توجّهنا إلى المحكمة مع غلام الشيخ فكتبنا العريضة وقدّمناها إلى حضرة القاضي فوضع عليها إشارة للباشكاتب ليتولى التحرّي عن مسألة الشأن، ثمّ طلبوا منّا شهوداً يشترط أن يكونوا من جيل الباشا يثبتون شخصيته ويشهدون بأنه صاحب هذا الوقف وأنّ غيره وضع يده عليه فاحترنا في الأمر فتكفّل الغلام باستحضار هؤلاء الشهود بعد أن قال وهذه هي الخطوة الرابعة في متاعب القضية. ولمّا نظروا في العريضة وجدوا أننا لم نبيّن اسم صاحب العملية في الوقفية وقيل لنا إنه لا يمكن الاهتداء في الدفترخانة إلا بها وإنه لا بدّ لنا من انتظار السنين والأعوام حتى يمكن العثور على صورة الوقفية في السجل بالنمرة والتاريخ وحدهما فنزلت بنا الأكدار والأحزان فقال لنا غلام الشيخ لا تحزنا فأنا أساعد على سرعة الإنجاز وأتوجه معكما ١١،١١

His colors were so numerous, he looked like a rainbow.[88]

11.10 The Lawyer Shaykh had left us with his Assistant. The clerk gave one of the witnesses a doubtful look. "He's young and under age," he told us. "He's this and that." The Lawyer's Assistant leaned over and whispered something in his ear, whereupon he immediately accompanied us to the assize judge to hear the testification. The Assistant meanwhile let us know that this was stage three in the expenses of the case. Through God's grace and concern for us, the testification was completed in a single day. As we were leaving, we were told that we would have to submit a petition to his honor the judge requesting permission to investigate the original charter of the endowment in the archives of the Public Records Office. That would show the number and date of the original charter, and from whose agency it came (implying the name of the scribe who had originally drawn it up). So we went looking for the groom, who might conceivably know a way of getting hold of what we needed. Once we found him and told him what we needed, he told us that he had a scroll with the number of the original charter on it. He had obtained it by various means after a good deal of time and effort in order to confirm his rights to the endowment's proceeds. He went to his house and came back with the scroll, but we discovered that it only mentioned the number and date; the name of the scribe who executed the document was not recorded on it.

11.11 We accompanied the Lawyer's Assistant to the court once again. We wrote the petition and presented it to his honor the judge. On the page he wrote instructions to the chief clerk to investigate the problem of the case. They asked for witnesses, stipulating that they had to be from the Pāshā's generation in order to confirm his personal identity, to testify that he was the possessor of the endowment, and that other people had laid their hands on it. The entire process left us completely baffled, but the Assistant undertook to produce such witnesses as well, not before he had informed us that this was stage four in the expenses of the case. They looked at the petition and noticed that we had not given the name of the clerk of the agency in it. We were informed that, without that information, it would be impossible to look into the records at the Registry Office. With only the number and date, we'd have to wait for years and years till we came across a copy of the original endowment. This information distressed us greatly, but the Assistant told to us not to give up hope. "I'll help you to complete the business quickly," he told us, "and God willing,

إلى الدفترخانة إن شاء الله وهذه هي الخطوة الخامسة في متاعب القضية، وما يزال الخبيث يعدّ لنا الخطوات. ونعدّ له في كل خطوة دريهمات، ونسأل الله أن ينقذنا ممّا أوقعنا فيه حكم الدهر، وأن يعجّل بقضاء قضيتنا في المحكمة الشرعية قبل انقضاء العمر.

I'll come to the Registry Office with you, that being, of course, stage five in the expenses of the case." The wretch continued to count out the stages for our benefit. At each stage, we counted out some dirhams for him, asking God, as we did so, to rescue us from fate's decree which had struck us so hard and to bring the case to a speedy conclusion before our very lives came to an end.

مصباح الشرق ٤٩، ٣٠ مارس ١٨٩٩

١،١٢ قال عيسى بن هشام: وعكفنا نشتد في الطلب والمحامي يشتد في الهرب، فلمّا طال علينا الأمد في ارتياده، ويئسنا من لحاقه واصطياده، انتقلنا للبحث عن غلامه حتى قبضنا على زمامه بعد كثرة البحث والتنقيب، فقيّدناه بقيود الترغيب والترهيب، فقال لنا: أقول لكما الحق والحق أقول، إنه ليس من المتصور المعقول أن نهتدي في هذه القضية إلى صورة الوقفية بنمرتها وتاريخها واسم صاحبها دون الوقوف على اسم كاتبها، ولا يجول في الأفكار والأوهام أنّ كاتب السجل يعثر عليها بين تلك التلال والآكام من غير وحي أو إلهام إلا بعد كر الأيام ومر الأعوام، وإن لم تصدّقاني بظهر الغيب وأبيتما إلا الشك والريب فهلمّا معي أطلعكما على ما يزول معه اللبس وتقتنع به النفس. ثمّ انطلق أمامنا يثب ويجل إلى بيت السجل.

٢،١٢ فلمّا جاوزنا الباب حيث يجلس الكتّاب ألفينا خشبا مسندة على خشب موطدة، وهياكل تفترش الأديم على الأديم والفراء على الثرى، لا تميز منهم وجه إنسان من إنسان لزوغ البصر من عشوة المكان، فتذكر الباشا ظلمة الزمن وكرّ راجعاً إلى ضوء الشمس، ومال الغلام إلى أذن أحدهم يكلمه بما لا أسمعه فأفهمه، فبادر الرجل بالقيام والغلام خلفه وأنا خلف الغلام، فما خطونا خطوات حتى أسدل علينا من الظلمة ستار، وحيل بيننا وبين ضوء النهار، فوقفت لا أبصر ولا أهتدي حتى أخذ الغلام بيدي وقد عميت عليَّ المسالك في هذه المهالك، وكنت أحسّ بشيء تحت قدميَّ يهش ويلين كالهشيم تلبّد في الطين، وما زلنا نمشي على هذه الصورة في تلك المطمورة حتى تخيلت أني أجول في أحد قبور القدماء من المصريين، أو في هياكل الأسرار في معابد الرومانيين، أو في طريق الامتحان عند أحرار البنائين.

٣،١٢ وقد داخلني الرعب ووجب القلب خشية أحبولة نصبت أو مكيدة رُتّبت فوجمت ثمّ أجمت، وقلت للغلام: ماذا تريد بي في هذا الغيهب وليس من فضة معي

ʿĪsā ibn Hishām said: We applied ourselves eagerly to the search, and the Lawyer was just as assiduous in keeping out of our way. We spent ages trying to visit him, but eventually we gave up and tried instead to look for his Assistant. After a good deal of searching we eventually got hold of him and used both incitements and threats to keep him with us. "I'll tell you the truth," he said, "and nothing but the truth. Knowing only the date and name of its owner, it's absolutely out of the question to find the text of the endowment in this case. We also need to know the name of the scribe who wrote it out. One just cannot envisage the Records Clerk coming across it amongst all these piles of papers. He would need to be inspired, and days and years would have to pass. If you don't believe me and still doubt my word, come with me. I'll show you things which will dispel any uncertainty you may have and convince you of what I'm saying." And with that, he set off, jumping and skipping his way to the Records Office. 12.1

Once we had passed through the doorway where all the clerks were sitting, we found piles of timber propped up against other blocks of strong wood, and trestles with goatskin rugs spread out over the filth and dust. It was so dark in this gloomy place that you could not distinguish one man from another. The darkness was so intense that it reminded the Pāshā of the grave which he had only just left, and so he turned back and decided to wait for us in the daylight outside. The Assistant leaned over and whispered something in the ear of one of them. I could not make out what it was he said, but in any case the man got up hurriedly and went away with the Assistant. I tagged along behind them. After just a few steps, a veil of darkness descended and daylight vanished. I could not see where I was going and stopped where I was. The Assistant grabbed me by the hand; I had no idea where I was going in this terrifying and dangerous place. I kept feeling something under my feet that crunched and sagged like chaff trodden into the soil. We made our way through this cellar until I imagined that I was either in the midst of the graves of ancient Egyptians, involved in the sacred mysteries in Roman temples, or else in the course of examination by Freemasons.[90] 12.2

My heart leapt. I was panic-stricken and scared in case a trap had been set or some sort of trick arranged. I was so frightened at first that I could not say a word, but then I plucked up my courage and spoke to the Assistant: 12.3

ولا ذهب، وليس بيننا ما يوجب الاحتيال لتدبير الاغتيال، فقهقه الفاجر ثمّ حلف بالطلاق أننا إنما نسير بين غرائر الدفاتر ولفائف الأوراق، وقال: كن مطمئنًا على نفسك، فسترى الحقيقة الآن بعيني رأسك.

ولم يكد يتم هذه العبارة حتى عثرت في لفافة فسقطت على غراره، وإذا بصائح يصيح من تحتها متأففا، ويقول متغطرساً متعجرفًا: ما هذه العشاوة يا عديم الإبصار في ضحوة النهار، فقمت متساندا وقلت في نفسي منشدا:

دُجى تتشابه الأشياءُ فيه
فيُجهَلُ جنسُها حتّى يصيحا

وقد رأيت خيالاً ينفض الغبار عن رأسه ولحيته بفضل جبته، فذعرت وأخذني الوجل وقلت مَنِ الرّجل، فقال الغلام: هذا أحد كتبة السجلات ينبش عن ورقة في سجل الأيلولات، فقلت: وكيف يهتدي إلى ذلك في هذا الظلام الحالك، فقال: إنّ تعوّدهم على العمل مع احتجاب الضياء جعلهم يبصرون في الظلماء، ومن اعتاد استرشد، ولكل امرئ من دهره ما تعوّد:

ولو سارَ كلُّ الوَرَى هكذَا
لما حسدَ العُميُ منْ يُبْصِرُونْ

٤،١٢ ثمّ انعطفنا من ذات اليمين إلى قاعة يلوح فيها من الضوء مثل جناح اليراعة، وإذا هو لعاب الشمس تمجه من ثقب في سقف ذلك الجب، وقد تموّج بأنواع الجراثيم تموّج الماء بالهشيم، أو كأنّ الشمس تريد اجتياب هذا المكان واجتيازه، فخشيت ظلمته فجاءت متوكئة على عكازه فمسحت على بصري وأحدقت بنظري فأبصرت وماذا أبصرت، ونظرت وماذا نظرت.

ما إنْ سمعتُ ولا أُراني سامعًا
أبدًا بصحراءٍ عليها بابُ

"What do you want by bringing me into this gloom? I don't have any silver or gold. There's no reason why you should be planning to commit murder."

The blackguard guffawed and then swore to divorce his wife, all in order to assure me that we were simply walking between the sacks of ledgers and bundles of scrolls. "Just remain calm," he told me. "You'll see the truth with your own eyes." The wretch had barely finished explaining things to me when I tripped over a package and fell over on to a pile of scrolls. All of a sudden, someone started shouting from underneath them.

"What's the matter with you, you blind idiot?" this personage yelled at me in haughty disdain. "Can't you see straight? After all, we're still in broad daylight."

I pulled myself up again and recited to myself the following line of poetry:

A gloom in which everything is alike
and people's sex is unknown until they shout.[91]

As I looked again, a specter suddenly appeared, wiping the dust off his head and beard with the edge of his cloak or gown. I was seized with panic. "Who's this man?" I asked. "Just one of the records clerks," the Assistant replied, "unearthing a scroll in the records of title deeds."

"But how can he find such things in this pitch darkness?" I asked."These are people," he replied, "who are used to working without any light; they can see in complete darkness. With habit comes guidance; every mortal gets his accustomed due from fate.

If all mankind walked like this,
then the blind would not envy those who can see."[92]

12.4 Turning to our right we noticed the outline of a hall. Patches of light gleamed in it like fireflies' wings, the rays of the sun as they poured in through a hole in the roof of this pit. Various types of microbe kept making ripples, like straw on water or as if the sun were trying to penetrate and traverse this space but was scared of the dark, so it was leaning on a cane. I rubbed my eyes and looked carefully. What did I see, you ask?

I have never heard, and I cannot see myself ever hearing
of a desert with a gate.

نظرت متسعاً قام فيه ما تراكم من الأوراق الرثيثة والدفاتر البالية مكان الهضبات الشاهقة والأكمات العالية، غير أنّ هذه تمر وتكلا، وتلك تعث وتبلى، هذه مخضرة مخصبة أن جادها الحيا أينعت بالنبات، وتلك سوداء مجدبة إذا سقتها الرطوبة أثمرت بالحشرات:

والأرضُ تبسطُ في خدِ الثّرى وَرَقًا
كما تنشرُ في حافاتها البُسُطُ
والرّيح تبعثُ أنفاسًا مُعَطّرَةً
مثلَ العبيرِ بماءِ الوردِ مختلِطُ
وهذه بسطتْ فوق الثّرى وَرَقًا
لكنّه للبلَى والعثّ مُنبَسِطُ
وريحُها تُورثُ الأسقامَ ناشِقَهَا
كأنّه من ترابِ القبْرِ يستَعِطُ

٥،١٢ ثمّ استبان لي في ذلك السنا وجه الكاتب المرافق لنا فرأيته قصير القامة كبير العمامة، له وجه تبرقع بالاصفرار، وعينان تكحلتا بالإحمرار، قد طوى من خلفه الجبة ورفعها على ظهره كالجعبة، وفي حزامه دواة من نحاس أصفر، وفي دائرة العمامة أوراق مرتشقة للتواريخ والنِمَر، فالتفت إلى الغلام وقلت له:

عيسى بن هشام هلمّ بنا إلى الباب لنعود إلى ضوء الحياة فقد يئست من أمري وصدقتك فيما قلت وأنّى لهذا الشيخ الكاتب أن يهتدي إلى تمييز هذه الأوراق المشتتة البالية في هذه الظلماء الداجية، ولوكان معنا ألف تاريخ وألف اسم للكاتب.

الغلام لا تنكرعليه الاهتداء في الظلماء، ولا يهولنك تشتيت الأوراق فهي مرتبة في ذهنه يعلم بمواقعها من طريق الوراثة عن أبيه وعن جده كما يتوارث رؤساء البوغاز في الإسكندرية هداية المراكب في دخولها بما علموه عن آبائهم من مواقع الأرض تحت لج البحر ولوكان معنا اسم الكاتب لسهل البحث ولوصلنا إلى الغرض.

In front of me I saw an area piled high with old scrolls and frayed ledgers, looking for all the world like towering hills and lofty mounds. The difference was that, whereas the latter bear fruit and are productive, these were moth-eaten and threadbare; while the latter are verdant and fertile, and, if watered by plenty of rain, will produce lush plants, these were black and arid; dampened by moisture they would produce insects:

The earth spreads leaves on the earth's cheek
as carpets are spread on the edge of the soil.
The wind emits perfumed breaths
like scent mixed with rose water.
But these scatter paper over the earth,
but only for moths and decay to consume.
Whoever inhales their scent is only left with disease,
as though he were inhaling the grave's own soil.[93]

12.5 After a while I managed to make out the face of the clerk who was accompanying us. He was short and wore a large turban. His face was masked by a pale coloring, and his eyes were bloodshot. He had wrapped up his coat behind him and pulled it up on his back like a quiver. In his belt he was carrying a brass inkwell, while between the folds of his turban were scrolls with dates and numbers on them. I turned and spoke to the Assistant:

'Īsā Come on! Take us back to the door so that we can return to the light of day. I've given up. Now I believe what you've been telling me. Even supposing we had a thousand dates and numbers for the original scribe, how on earth would this clerk be able to make out all these crumbling manuscripts in such pitch darkness?

Lawyer's Assistant Don't assume that people like him cannot find things in total darkness! Don't be put off by the scattered ledgers and piles of scrolls. They're all arranged and codified in his memory. Thanks to his father and grandfather he knows the whereabouts of every one of them. It is just like pilots in Alexandria who inherit the ability to guide ships at the entrance to the harbor on the basis of information about the shape of the sea bed that they've learned from their fathers. If only we knew the name of the scribe, the search would be easy, and we'd get what we wanted.

٦،١٢ **الشيخ** نعم لا تنكر علينا الاهتداء بارك الله فيك بين هذه الأوراق والله يعلم أنّ هذه الدفترخانة مرسومة في ذهني منذ الصغر على أحسن ترتيب وأجمل تبويب، فهي مقسّمة إلى عدة سجلات، فمنها سجل الباب العالي: تسجل فيه الأعيان المباعة غير الموروثة، ومنها سجل القسمة العسكرية: تسجل فيه الأعيان المباعة الموروثة، ومنها سجل الأيلولات: تسجل فيه الأعيان المحصورة من تركة وتباع بالمزاد أو تخصص، ومنها سجل الإعلامات: تسجل فيه المواد التي تصدر فيها أحكام من المحاكم الشرعية من أي نوع كان، ومنها سجل التقارير: تسجل فيه تقارير النظار وقفاً وغيره، ومنها سجل الوقفيات: تسجل فيه نفس الوقفيات ويدخل فيه التوكيلات والوصايا والتصادق.

عيسى بن هشام سبحان الفاتح الوهاب، وهلمّ بنا إلى الباب.

الشيخ ومنها سجل الديوان العالي: تسجل فيه الفرمانات المتعلقة بتولية القناصل وعزلهم والإعلامات الصادرة من مجلس استئناف مصر في الهيئة التي يحضر فيها القاضي الشرعي أو نائبه وجملة من كبار العلماء من المذاهب، ومنها سجل القسمة العربية: تسجل فيه الأعيان الموروثة المختصة بالذميين.

عيسى بن هشام قد صدّقتُ ما قلت ويكفي فقد ضاق الوقت.

٧،١٢ **الشيخ** (مسترسلاً) .... ومنها سجل إسقاط القرى: تسجل فيه الأطيان ويتعلق بتسجيل ما يأخذه الأمراء وما يعطونه من الأطيان في القرى. وقد كانت في مدينة مصر محاكم نيابية وكانت السيطرة عليها للقاضي الذي يُعيَّن من قبل السلطان، وكان لكل واحدة من هذه المحاكم سجل تسجّل فيه جميع الأنواع وحفظت هذه السجلات بهذه الدفترخانة وكانت مراكزها في باب الشعرية، وقناطر السباع، وجامع طولون وقيسون.

عيسى بن هشام كفى أيها الشيخ فلا حاجة لنا في هذا التطويل فقد آن الرحيل.

الشيخ ... ودرب سعادة، وباب الخلق، والصالحية، والنجمية، وأحمد الزاهد، والبرشمية، ومصر القديمة وبولاق.

Clerk Yes indeed! God bless you—please don't assume that I can't find things in my search through the scrolls. God knows that this Records Office has been imprinted on my mind from earliest childhood according to the very best methods of arrangement and description. They are subdivided into a number of records. There is firstly the record of the Sublime Porte in which saleable objects which have not been inherited are written down; the record of the military division in which saleable inherited chattels are recorded; the record of title deeds in which defined properties are recorded (such as a bequest which is specially allotted or sold by auction); the record of notifications detailing those articles in which all kinds of regulations of the Shariah Courts are published; the record of accounts, in which the accounts of trustees in matters of endowment and other things are put down; the record of the endowment system, where the original endowment charters are recorded, and the warrants of attorney, wills, and authentification are entered. 12.6

ʿĪsā All glory be to the Opener and Provider! Let's go back to the door!

Clerk Then there's the record of the High Committee, recording the decrees dealing with the appointment and dismissal of consuls, and the proclamations published by the Egyptian Appeals Committee in the form in which it is presented by the Shariah Court judge or his deputy together with all the great religious scholars from all sects; the record of the Arab division, where the inherited chattels particular to *dhimmī*s are noted down.[94]

ʿĪsā I believe you! But that's enough. We're short of time...

Clerk (*enlarging on the subject*) Then there's the record of confiscation of villages, in which lands and villages seized by amirs are registered. In the city of Cairo, there were District Courts in which the ruling authority was the judge appointed by the Sultān. Each court kept a record (and they've all been kept in this Records Office) in which all kinds of things were written down. They had offices in various areas: Bāb al-Shaʿriyyah, Qanāṭir al-Sibāʿ, Ibn Ṭulūn's mosque, and Qayṣūn's mosque.[95] 12.7

ʿĪsā Enough Sir! There's no need to go to such lengths in your explanation. We have to leave.

Clerk (*continuing with his list*) In Darb Saʿādah, Bāb al-Khalq, Ṣaliḥiyyah, Najmiyyah, Aḥmad al-Zāhid, al-Barshamiyyah, old Cairo, and Būlāq.

عيسى بن هشام قلت لك لست في حاجة إلى هذا التطويل.

الشيخ ... وجامع الصالح، وجامع الحاكم، ومحكمة الباب العالي، وهي المحكمة الكبرى وقاضيها هو المسيطر على الكل والمولى من القسطنطينية، ومحكمة القسمة العسكرية وقاضيها يُعيَّن كل سنة من دار السعادة كقاضي المحكمة الكبرى ويسمّى القسام العسكري وشغله المواريث بأنواعها فقط و...

٨،١٢ قال عيسى بن هشام: فجذبت بدرع الغلام ناحية لأخرج من هذا الموقف فقد ضقتُ نفساً من هواء هذا المكان وضقت ذرعاً من ثرثرة هذا الشيخ. وليس لنا في الوقوف من فائدة بعد أن يئسنا من حاجتنا.

الغلام لا تيأس ولا تقنط وأنظرني قليلاً حتى أستنير برأي الشيخ لعلنا نجد عنده حلا للعقدة وفرجا للكربة.

ومال على الشيخ منفردا به فسمعت فيما يقوله له:

الغلام ... وأنت لا تأبى لنا الربح وأصحاب هذه القضية من كبار الناس ومن أهل العطاء والبذل.

الشيخ مهلا فقد كدت أتذكر اسم كاتب الوقفية من ذكر العطاء والبذل فإنّ لكاتبها حكاية مشهورة في الجود والكرم وإنّ الخلع التي خلعت على كاتبها لا يزال إلى اليوم منها آثار عند بنيه وذريته وهو المرحوم الشيخ فلان، فدونك وأصحابك فاتفق معهم لوضع هذا الاسم في ورقة النمرة والتاريخ كأنك جئت به من عندك والله ينفعنا بنفع المسلمين.

قال عيسى بن هشام: وخطا الغلام نحوي خطوة وقال:

الغلام قد تيسرت الحالة بإذن الله فقد تذكرت طريقة للوصول إلى اسم الكاتب ولم يبق علينا إلا اتخاذها لنخطو الخطوة السادسة.

٩،١٢ قال عيسى بن هشام: ثمّ انطلق الغلام أمامي يسحبني وراءه حتى خرجنا بحسن صنع

ʿĪsā I've told you that we don't need all this detail!

Clerk The Mosque of Al-Ṣaliḥ, the Mosque of Al-Ḥākim, and the Court of the Sublime Porte. That is the most important court of all, and the judge has authority over every one and is appointed from Constantinople. The court of the army division, the judge of which is appointed every year from Dār al-Saʿādah, as is the judge of the Supreme Court—he is known as "The Ordainer," and his function is restricted to various kinds of legacies, and—

ʿĪsā ibn Hishām said: I grabbed the Assistant by the arm so we could escape from this predicament. I had totally lost patience with this place and this prattling clerk. We had no hope of getting what we needed, so there was no point in hanging around. 12.8

Assistant Don't give up or lose your temper! Wait a bit till I've consulted the Shaykh. He may be able to help us solve our problem and help us escape from our misfortunes.

With that, he leaned over and had a word with the Shaykh. I heard him say:

Assistant Surely you wouldn't turn down a chance for all of us to make a profit. After all, the influential people involved in this case are full of kindness and generosity.

Clerk Just a minute! The mention of that word "generosity" almost permits me to recall the name of the scribe of the endowment. The drafting process provided a story which is still famous because of the munificence of the gifts involved. Even today, the family and descendants of the clerk who wrote it still own some remnants of the robes of honor which were presented to them. His name was the late Shaykh X. It's up to you to deal with the people involved in the case. Come to an agreement with them to write the scribe's name on the document with the date and number as though it came from you. By helping Muslims we all gain benefit from God.

The Assistant came over to me and said:

Assistant (*to ʿĪsā*) Things are now becoming easier through God's sanction. We've found the way to get the name of the scribe who produced the copy. All we have to do is to act on it as the sixth phase in the case.

ʿĪsā ibn Hishām said: The Assistant went on in front and pulled me along behind him till we emerged from darkness into the light of day—through God's 12.9

الله من الظلمات إلى النور فجهرت عيني فلم أبصر في الشمس إلا بعد التردد بينها وبين الباب. ولمّا التقيت بصاحبي سألني عن هذا الغياب فلم أرد أن أضيف إلى مصائبه وصف ما قاسيته من الأهوال، بل أخبرته بتيسير الأمر واتفقنا مع الغلام أن يباشر وضع اسم الكاتب في الورقة ويسعى وراءها حتى يأتينا بصورة الوقفية وننقدناه ما نقدناه. ودارت علينا الأيام ومضت الشهور ونحن نتردد على الدفترخانة تارة في صحبة الغلام وتارة من غيره إلى أن آن الأوان وحل الأجل فجاءنا الغلام ذات يوم يبشرنا بالعثور على الوقفية ففرحنا فرح الغواص بدرة التاج تحت تلاطم الأمواج، ونهضنا معه إلى الدفترخانة فقابلنا الكاتب فوجدناه يتيه إعجاباً بمهارته في الاهتداء عليها في مثل هذا الزمن القصير فحمدنا الله على حسن الطالع وعناية البخت وحمدناه على همته العالية وصنعه الجميل فأخرج لنا من تحت إبطه أوراقاً بالية متشذرة متآكلة لا تستوي منها ورقة على أخرى فيها خطوط مخرمشة لا يحلها إلا من كان عريقاً في فن الرموز ووجدنا أواخر السطور متقطعة .

١٠،١٢ فقلت له: إنّ الاهتداء إلى نقل صورة من هذه الأوراق أعظم مشقة وأكبر بلية من الاهتداء إلى موضعها من تلك الصحراء فقال لي: نعم ولكن التعوّد ييسّر كل أمر عسير، وقد ورثت عن والدي قراءة هذه الخطوط ووصل ما انقطع من عبارة السطور فإنّ العبارة واحدة تقريباً في كل باب.

ثمّ انصرفنا وعاد إلينا الغلام بعد أسابيع يخبرنا بانتهاء الصورة ويطلب منا أن ندفع الرسم وأن نستحضر شاهدين يشهدان لنا باستلام تلك الصورة من المحكمة ووعدنا بإحضارهما بعد أن سمّى هذه الخطوة سابعة خطواته وقمنا له بمرضاته.

bounty. I was blinded by the sunlight and couldn't see anything till I had gone backwards and forwards between the light and darkness several times. When I met my friend the Pāshā, he asked why I had been away for so long. I did not want to add any more misfortunes to his troubles by recounting the terrors I had faced, so I told him how the situation had improved. We reached an agreement with the Assistant that he would deal with the recording of the scribe's name on the document and then return next day to the clerk in the Records Office to bring us the copy of the endowment document. We then paid him some more money.

Now, days and months went by. We kept going back to the Records Office, sometimes with the Assistant, other times without him. At last one day the Assistant brought us the news that the text of the endowment had been found. We were overjoyed; our feelings were the same as those of a diver who beneath the buffeting waves finds a pearl fit to be used in a royal diadem. We accompanied him to the Records Office and found the clerk congratulating himself on his skill at finding the document in such a short time. We offered praise to God for our good fortune and happy outcome, and then congratulated him for his outstanding zeal and splendid work. From underneath his armpit he produced some ragged, tattered, and torn documents; no one sheet was level with the one next to it. The writings on them were disjointed and could only be deciphered by someone with a profound knowledge of the techniques for solving riddles. Not only that, but we discovered that the ends of lines were cut off.

12.10 I told the clerk that it would be even trickier and more complicated to translate the documents than it had been to unearth them in this murky desert. To which he responded that such problems were solvable through constant practice. He went on to tell me that he had also inherited from his late father the ability to read these scripts and to supply endings for lines which had been erased. Only one form of expression is used almost without variation in every type of record.

We said farewell and went on our way. After several weeks the Lawyer's Assistant came back and told us that the copy of the endowment had been completed. He asked us to pay the fee and to bring two witnesses to testify to its receipt. He promised to bring two of them after notifying us that this was the seventh phase in the trial's expenses. We duly conformed with his wishes.

١،١٣ ولمّا صارت في يدنا الصورة بعد تلك المواقف المذكورة خطا الغلام خطوته الثامنة بعد طول المعاكسة والمشاحنة، وذهب إلى كاتب الطلبات لتحديد إحدى الجلسات، واستخراج طلب لحضور الخصوم في يوم معلوم، ثمّ عاد إلينا يبشرنا بأنّ الكاتب اتفق مع المجلس واتحد على أن تكون جلستنا يوم الأحد، فأقمنا نعلل النفس بالأمل حتى حلّ هذا الأجل، وسمح لنا الدهر بقرب المحامي ودنوّه بعد اختفائه منا في رواحه وغدوّه:

وقد يجمع الله الشَّتيتينِ بعدما
يظنّان كلّ الظنّ أن لا تلاقيا

٢،١٣ فقصد معنا قصد المحكمة ليكشف عنا بهمته تلك المظلمة، فسرنا إلى بيت القضاء الشرعي والحكم المرضي والعدل المقضي بوحي الله وسنّة النبي - إلى حيث تقام منابر الهدى، وترتفع منائر التقى، ويتبلج نور الحق والعدالة، وتتضأل ظلمة البدعة والضلالة، وتتشيّد أركان الإسلام بتسديد الأحكام، واتباع الصراط السويّ في الحكم بين الضعيف والقويّ، والأخذ من الظالم للمظلوم، والانتصاف من الحاكم للمحكوم - نعم إلى حيث تتساوى مواقف الأقدام، وتتلاشى الأباطيل والأوهام، وتغتدي الأرملة الضعيفة ربة الأيتام، منتصرة في الحق على المدجج رب الرمح والحسام، ويضحي الأعزل الشاكي متغلباً على الفاتك الشاكي، ويمسي العاجز الفقير أعز من صاحب التاج والسرير، ورب الشويهة والبعير فوق رب الخورنق والسدير - نعم إلى ذلك المقعد الموروث عن الرسول المبعوث حيث يعمل بالسنّة وآي الكتاب، فينتصر للذليل من العزيز، ويؤخذ بسيرة عمر بن الخطاب وعمر بن عبد العزيز، وحيث يكون مقر الهيبة والجلال، والوقار والكمال، ومحل الطهارة والأمانة، والعفة والصيانة، وموضع السكون والخشوع، وحسن الطاعة والخضوع.

Miṣbāḥ al-sharq 50, April 6, 1899[96]

13.1 ʿĪsā ibn Hisham said: As a result of the events described in the previous chapter, we now had a copy of the endowment in our hands. After a good deal of argument and opposition, the Assistant proceeded with the eighth phase. He went to the Petitions Clerk to make an appointment for one of the sessions and to draw up a subpoena calling for the presence of the opposing parties on a particular day. He returned with the good news that the clerk had agreed with the session Judge; our session would take place on Sunday. With that we kept nursing our hopes, until the appointed day dawned. Good fortune willed that the Lawyer Shaykh should be close by; he had been staying out of our way for some time as he went to and fro:

> Perhaps God had brought the two pieces together
> after they had become convinced that they would never meet again.[97]

13.2 He accompanied us to the court where he could use his expertise to rid us of the wrongs we had suffered. We all made our way to the Shariah Court, haven of law and fair judgment, where justice would be dispensed in accordance with divine inspiration and the Prophet's own practice. This was the place where the pulpits of divine guidance are located; there the minarets of piety are established, and the light of truth and justice shines forth. In it, the murky paths of heresy and error are exposed, the oppressed person gets back the things which are taken away from the oppressor, and the ruled receive justice from their ruler. Yes indeed, this is the place where all are equal and frivolity and fancy vanish into thin air; the poor widow with her orphaned children is considered more important than the knight with his spear and sword, and the defenseless plaintiff has more power than someone bristling with arms. In the court's eyes, the indigent weakling has more power than any monarch seated in a throne; the owner of a tiny sheep and a camel stands above the lord of Al-Khwarnaq and Al-Sadīr.[98] Yes indeed, this is the seat inherited from the Prophet who was sent to us, and where matters are conducted according to the Sunna and verses of the Qur'an. It always aids the lowly against the powerful, sometimes following the practice of ʿUmar ibn al-Khaṭṭāb, and at other times the practice of ʿUmar ibn ʿAbd al-ʿAzīz.[99] It is also regarded as the residence of all awe and majesty, the font of piety and perfection, the seat of purity and fidelity, the source of decency and respectability, the focal point of all devoutness and humility, and the place where obedience and submission are to be found.

٣،١٣ ولمّا وصلنا إلى تلك المحكمة رأينا ساحتها مزدحمة بالمركبات، تجرّها الجرد المطهمات، وبجانبها الراقصات من البغال والحمير، عليها سرج الفضة والحرير، فتخيلناها مراكب للأمراء في مواكب الزينة والبهاء، وسألنا لمن هذي الركاب، فقال الغلام إنها لجماعة الكتّاب، فقلنا سبحان الملك الوهاب، ومن يرزق عباده بغير حساب. وصعدنا إلى الباب، فوجدنا عنده كهلا حنت ظهره السنون فتخطته يد المنون، قد اجتمع عليه العمه والصمم، والبله والبكم، وقيل لنا إنه حارس بيت القضاء من نوازل القضاء. وصعدنا في السلم فوجدناه مزدحماً بجملة أناس، مختلفي الأشكال والأجناس، يتسابّون ويتشاتمون، ويتلاكمون ويتلاطمون، ويتقاذفون ويتلاعنون، ويبرقون ويرعدون، ويتربصون ويتوعدون، وأكثرهم آخذ بعضهم بتلابيب بعض، يترامون على الحيطان ويتساقطون على الأرض.

٤،١٣ وما زلنا نزاحم على الصعود في هذا الدرج، والعمائم تهوي فوقه وتتدحرج، حتى منّ الله علينا بالفرج، وتسنّى لنا المخرج من هذا الزحام المتلاصق، والمأزق المتضايق، فما دخلنا القاعة السفلى حتى رأينا على بابها امرأة حبلى، تتقلب على الأرض كالثعبان، وتستشهد من حولها من الأهل والجيران بأنّ بعلها أسقط حملها. فخطونا خطوة إلى الأمام وسط الزحام، فلم نستطع التقدّم في عباب موج ملتطم، وسيل مرتطم من نساء صائحات مولولات، ونائحات معولات، ونادبات باكيات، ومتضرعات شاكيات كأنهنّ قائمات في مأتم على مدافن الأموات، تقرّحت فيه العيون وبحّت الأصوات، فيهنّ المسفرة والمتقنّعة، والمضطجعة والمتربعة، والحاسرة عن الرأس، تفليها أختها في حر الشمس، والكاشفة عن ثدييها ترضع طفلا في يديها، وأخرى يتقدّمها طليقها، ويتبعها عشيقها، تشيع الأولى بألفاظ السباب، وتشير إلى الثاني بكف تحلت بالخضاب، وأخرى ترضع طفلين في حذاء، وزوجها يضربها على رأسها بالحذاء، وغيرها آخذة بضفيرة ضرّتها، ورضيعها يتلهف على درتها، ورأينا المخدرة مع الأغا، لا يكاد يحميها

When we reached the court, we found the courtyard crowded with carriages pulled by rearing steeds. At their sides stood prancing mules and asses with silver and silk trappings on them. We thought these must be the mounts of important men and amirs in splendidly decorated retinues. But, when we inquired to whom these carriages belonged, we were told that they belonged to the group of secretaries, to which our only reaction was: Praise to the Lord, the Almighty provider, who gives unlimited benefits. We went up to the door; alongside it we found a Shaykh bowed down by age; the hand of fate seemed to have passed him by. He was both deaf and nearsighted, and plagued by senility and disease. We were told that his job was to guard the court against the adversities of Fate. After climbing the stairs, we found the whole place teeming with people of various shapes and sizes. They kept exchanging insults and abuse, punching and walloping one another, flashing and fulminating, and cursing and swearing at each other. The majority of them were grabbing other people by the collar, pounding them against the walls and falling over each other on the floor. 13.3

With turbans tumbling and rolling around us, we kept pushing our way up the stairs until God graciously released us and enabled us to escape from this mass of people crammed together in such a crushing bottleneck. Once we had reached the lower hall, we found a pregnant woman by the door writhing around on the floor like a snake. She kept asking the people around her to witness to the fact that her husband refused to acknowledge her pregnancy. We endeavored to move forward a step, but were unable to do so, faced with a torrent of clashing waves. A headlong flood of women kept shouting and screaming, howling and wailing laments; with all their screeching and complaining it was as though they were performing the last rites for the dead, an occasion when their eyes would normally become sore and their voices hoarse. Among them was a woman with her face partly uncovered and arms and head exposed, sitting cross-legged in the heat of the sun, while her sister deloused her. She had bared her breasts and was suckling an infant in her arms. Another woman was preceded by her divorced husband and followed by her lover; she was wishing the former good riddance with curses and abuse, and beckoning the latter with her hand which was decorated with dye. Yet another was suckling two children facing each other while her husband kept hitting her on the head with his shoe. Still another kept clutching the hair of her husband's second wife while her child was yearning for her milk. We noticed a cloistered 13.4

في حومة هذا الوغى، وشاهدنا بين الجمع جماعة من فجار الخلعاء، وتباع النساء، ينازلون كل غانية هيفاء، ويتعرضون لكل غادة غيداء، ويتزاحمون على حسم النزاع بين ذوات القناع، وفصل الشقاق، بين الطاعنات بالإحداق، فتختلط غمزات الطرف بإشارات الكف، وينتهي الخلاف والخصام إلى الحسنى والرقيق من الكلام.

٥،١٣ ورأينا فيما رأينا من غرائب البشاعة، وعجائب الشناعة رجلا وامرأته يتسابقان في ألفاظ الفحش والهجر، ويتباذان في أقوال البذاءة والنكر، ويتجاذبان في أيديهما غلاما، ويشدانه كأنما يحاولان له اقتساما، ليأخذ كل منهما من أعضائه بنصيب، والولد مغمى عليه من شدة الألم والتعذيب، فاستعذنا بالله السميع العليم من هذا العذاب الأليم. وسمعنا من أفظع ما سمعنا امرأة تنتحب وتقول والنقاب بماء العين مطلول مبلول لوكان للنساء قضاة من النساء لما وصلنا إلى هذه الحالة التعساء، فإنّ الرجال يميلون لجنس الرجال، وينتصرون للبعولة من أمهات العيال، فاستعنا برب المثالث والمثاني، وصعدنا في السلم الثاني، فإذا هوكالأوّل يتموّج بالصاعدين والنازلين كبيوت النمل، وخلايا النحل، فانتهينا منه إلى قاعة ممتلئة بأصناف الباعة، أحدهم يصيح الخبز والجبن، والثاني ينادي الدخان والبن، وهذا يقول الزبدة والعسل، وذاك ينادي الفول والبصل، وآخر يصفق بأكواز العرقسوس، وبائع الضأن يضرب بسكينه جماجم الرؤوس، وهناك قهوة يستريح فيها أرباب الخصومات، ويحيط بكل واحد منهم شهود يعدّون بالعشرات، ووجدنا الزحام هنا أوسع وأعم، والخصام أكبر وأعظم، وغلمان المحامين يروحون بين هذه الجموع ويغدون، ويمكرون ويكيدون، ويتقلبون بين الخصوم ويحتالون، ويخدعون ويغتالون، يعيشون مع الذئب ويبكون مع الراعي.

٦،١٣ ودخلنا حجرة ضيّقة من حجرات الكتّاب، فدفعنا عنها ما على أطباق الباعة من جيش الذباب، فجذبنا غلام المحامي إلى حجرة أخرى وسيعة الساحة، وقال اجلسوا هنا للاستراحة، وأقعدنا بين كاتبين وغلامين، ولكل كاتب هناك غلام يقوم مقامه في إنجاز الدعاوى وتنسيق الأحكام، فسمعت الكاتب الجالس عن اليمين يقسم على أقواله

wife walking with her eunuch, but he could hardly keep her protected in the thick of such a fray. Among the mob we spotted a whole crowd of wanton lechers and girl-chasers, flirting with every lithe maiden and hassling every pretty girl who passed by. They tried to settle the arguments and disagreements between the women and girls whose glances had bowled them over. Thus it happened that winks became intermingled with urging hands, all argument and controversy ceased, and everyone began talking amicably.

13.5 One of the most incredibly awful things we saw was a man and woman challenging each other to produce more obscene language and going to utter extremes in vulgarity. They were dragging a boy along by the hand, almost as though they both wanted to divide him up and keep part of his limbs for themselves. The boy was in severe pain and kept crying. For our part, we asked God who hears and knows everything to rescue us from this Hellish torture. Among the utterly dreadful things we heard was something spoken by a weeping woman with tears sprinkling her veil. "If we women had female judges," she said, "we would never have reached this miserable state. Men always favor the members of their own sex and help each other against women." With that, we asked the Lord of the Holy Book to help us. We climbed the next flight of stairs, but found that it was just like the first floor, seething with people going up and down like an ant's nest or bee hive. Eventually we finished up in a hall filled with various types of salesmen. One was shouting "bread and cheese," another "tobacco and coffee," another "butter and honey," and another "beans and onions." An ice vendor was clanging liquorice juice cups together while a sheep seller was cutting open the animals' skulls. There was a café where people with cases could relax, each one of them surrounded by witnesses in scores like insects. The crowds here were even bigger and the arguments were that much fiercer than before. Lawyers' assistants ran to and fro between the litigants, using every trick they knew to dupe people and play false with them. They were living with the wolves and crying with the shepherds.

13.6 We went into a small secretarial room, but were driven out by the army of flies on the vendors' trays. The Lawyer's Assistant now took us to another large room. He told us to sit down and have a rest, and found us some seats between two clerks and assistants; every clerk here had an assistant who deputized for him in implementing lawsuits and recording sentences. I heard the clerk to my right swear a solemn oath that his donkey would never have lagged behind A's donkey during the race if he had not been hampered by the tramcars and

بكل يمين بأنه لولا اعتراض مركبات الكهرباء وضيق الميدان لما تأخر حماره عن حمار فلان، وسمعت صاحبه بجانبه يحلف بجدّه وأعز أقاربه أنه لولا حبسه للعنان لسبق بقية الحمير وقبض الرهان، ويقول له: اعلم أيها السيد أنّ فيما سمعناه عن الأجداد والآباء أنه إذا صحت الشعرة الخضراء لم يتعلق بذيل الحمار الهواء، ولطار بصاحبه إلى عنان السماء، ثم التفت ذات الشمال فوجدت سيداً ظريفاً غض الشباب يتألق في نضرة الثياب، ويلمع ويبرق في سندس واستبرق كأنهم خاطوا له قباء من أزهار بستان مختلفة الأشكال والألوان، فقد فغم الأنوف بعطره، وعبق الجو بطيب نشره، وأمامه رجل في يده صرة ثياب ينشرها ويطويها، فيأخذها منه السيد ويرميها، ويقول له:

٧،١٣ السيد هذه ثياب لا أرضاها ولا أقبلها، وبئس المفصل مفصلها.

الخياط كيف تقول ذلك أيها السيد وأنا أقسم لك بالقرآن المجيد، أنها أوسع من ثياب السيدين عبد العزيز وعبد الحميد.

السيد كذبت ورب الكعبة، فإنّ استدارة الكم والرقبة صغيرة ضيّقة لا تنطبق على الزي الحاضر.

الخياط ماذا أصنع وذلك كل عرض القماش، ولوكنّا على الزي القديم لدخل مع السيد اثنان أو ثلاثة من أصحابه في طي ثيابه.

أحد أصحاب القضايا صبح الله السيد بالخير والإنعام.

أحد الكتبة المنكتين لا، بل بالخيل والأنعام.

صاحب القضية أرجو من سيدي أن يعطيني الإعلام.

السيد اذهب حتى يأتي الغلام.

الكاتب المنكت عليك به في شارع أم الغلام تجده جالساً نصاً تحت الاعلام.

٨،١٣ قال عيسى بن هشام: واقشعرّ جسدي من هذه النكت الباردة والمعاني الساقطة

the narrowness of the square, while his companion at his side swore by his grandfather and most revered relatives that, if he had not tightened the reins, he would have beaten every other donkey and won the bet. "You should know, dear sir," the companion said, "that we have it from our ancestors that, when the grey hair is in good trim, even air cannot grasp the donkey's tail. It will fly its owner to the highest heavens." Turning now to my left, I spotted another posh gentleman in the prime of his youth whose clothes exhibited the most exquisite taste. He positively glistened in silk brocade; such was their profusion of shapes and sizes, he looked as though his clothes had been assembled from a montage of all the flowers in the garden. The scent he was wearing inundated everyone's noses and permeated the air all around. In front of him, a man was spreading out and folding a pile of clothes which he had in his hand, while the gentleman was taking them from him, then discarding them. He was speaking to him:

13.7 GENTLEMAN I don't like these clothes at all I won't accept any of them. Whoever cut them is no good.

TAILOR My dear Sir, how can you possibly say such a thing? I swear to you on the noble Qur'an that they are larger than the suits being worn by those two gentlemen, ʿAbd al-ʿAzīz and ʿAbd al-Ḥamīd.

GENTLEMAN By the Lord of the Kaaba, you're lying. The curve of the sleeve is too narrow, and the neck is completely out of fashion.

TAILOR What am I supposed to do? That's the width of the fabric. If we were dealing with the old style, my dear Sir, you could have put two or three of your friends into the folds of your present clothes.

LITIGANT May God bless the gentleman with kindness and generosity.

WITTY CLERK (*making a pun*) No, but rather with horses and livestock.[100]

LITIGANT May I ask you, Sir, to give me the notification of the judge's verdict.

GENTLEMAN Go away till the assistant comes.

WITTY CLERK (*punning yet again*) Go and look him out in Umm al-Ghulām street; you'll find him sitting there, literally under the signposts.

13.8 ʿĪsā ibn Hishām said: These stupid jokes and vulgarities set me all aquiver, so I stopped listening and looked round in other directions. I saw all the clerks

فأعرضت عن الإصغاء، وسرحت طرفي في بقية الأنحاء، فرأيت الكتبة كلهم يتسامرون ويتحادثون، هذا يلت في يده أفيونة، وذاك يكور بين أصابعه معجونة، والغلمان يشتغلون تارة ويتضاحكون أخرى، وأرباب الحاجات بين أيديهم ينهرونهم ويطردونهم ويعدونهم ويمطلونهم، ورأيت كاتباً يتشاحن مع صاحب قضية ويقول له: كيف تعطي الغلام هذا المبلغ الزهيد، أتظنه كان لك من العبيد، أتريد أن يكتب لك ويتعب بغير ربح ولا مكسب، وليس له في الحكومة أجرة ولا مرتب، إنّ هذا لمن أعجب العجب. وجاء رسول القاضي يطلب أحدهم فتفقدوه بينهم فوجدوه راقداً فبعضهم أشار بإيقاظه وبعضهم عارض بقوله أتركوه في رقدته، ألم تعلموا قديم عادته، إنه لا يتمالك نفسه إلا إذا سال الأفيون مع الدم في دورته، ثمّ اتفقوا مع الرسول أن يرجع فيقول أنه لم يجده مكانه، فقد نزل إلى الدفترخانة، ثمّ قام الراقد بعد مدة يتثاءب ويتمطى، ثم يتدثر ويتغطى، ويعود ثانية إلى لذيذ الرقاد والسبات، وينشد للمعري من أبيات:

وفضيلة النّومِ الخروج بأهلهِ
عن عالمٍ هو بالأذى مَجْبُولُ

ولمّا أفاق من منامه وجد بجانبه بائع كتب ينتظره فقال له: ٩.١٣

الكاتب هل أحضرت ما طلبته منك.

البائع نعم عثرت لك على كتب قديمة، لا تقدّر لها قيمة، منها كتاب «حل الرموز لفتح الكنوز» ومنها «أصول المراسم في فك الطلاسم» و«إرشاد الناس إلى استخراج الذهب من النحاس» و«القول المشهور في تأثير البخور».

الكاتب ألم تعثر لي على كتاب في الاستحضار.

البائع نعم معي كتابان أحدهما «قلائد اللؤلؤ والمرجان في استحضار الجان» و«خير المواقيت لرؤية العفاريت».

الكاتب بارك الله فيك عندي نسخة مخرومة من هذا الكتاب فهلمّ بنا إلى البيت لنقابلها ونصحّحها.

talking and joking with one another. One was crushing opium in his hand, another rolling his majoon between his fingers. Sometimes the assistants busied themselves with their papers, at others they shared jokes. Meanwhile the poor people who had entrusted their affairs to them were being upbraided and pushed aside with promises and delays. I overheard one clerk arguing with a litigant about terms: "How can you give the assistant such a paltry sum?" he asked. "Do you think he's your slave? Do you expect him to record and work for you when he has no wage or salary from the court and gets no profit from it? How utterly incredible!" When the judge's messenger came in searching for one of the head clerks, he found him sound asleep. Some of them suggested waking him up, but others advocated letting him be, pointing out that for a long time the clerk in question had made a habit of staying asleep till the opium was circulating in his veins alongside the blood. They all agreed that the messenger should go back and say he hadn't been able to find the Shaykh where he was supposed to be, but then he had heard that he'd gone down to the Records Office. A while later, the sleeping clerk woke up, yawned, and stretched himself. He then resumed his slumber, reciting the lines of al-Maʿarrī as he did so:

The primary virtue of sleep is that it takes the sleeper
out of this world, one molded in suffering.[101]

When he finally woke up, it was to find a bookseller waiting for him. 13.9

CLERK Have you brought the books I requested?

VENDOR Yes. I've managed to get you some priceless old volumes, including *The Solution of Riddles for Opening Treasure Chests*, *The Principles of Ritual in Unraveling Mysteries*, *The Perfect Guide for People to Extract Gold from Copper*, *The Proverbial Truth about the Effects of Incense*, and...

CLERK Didn't you find any books on the invocation of spirits?

VENDOR Yes, I've brought you two: *Jewels of Pearl and Coral Concerning the Invocation of Demons*, and *The Best Times for Seeing Devils*.[102]

CLERK May God bless you and reward you well! I've got a defective copy of the latter work. Come home with me and we'll compare them and make corrections.

١٠،١٣ وقام الكاتب مع البائع، وأقمت أسخط على هذا الجهل الشائع. وبينا نحن على هذا الحال إذ أشار إلينا غلام المحامي بأنّ أوان الجلسة قد آن فخرجنا فوقفنا على باب الحجرة التي تنعقد فيها الجلسة. فرأينا الزحام داخلها وخارجها في أشد ما يكون عليه، وسمعنا الحاجب ينادي تارة بصوت عالٍ وتارة بصوت منخفض، فسألت الغلام عن السبب فقال إنه يخفض الصوت حتى لا يسمع المدعي النداء فتشطب القضية رأفة بالمدعى عليه، وللحجاب أن يدخلوا الجلسة من أرادوا ويحجبوا من أرادوا. ونودي علينا فدخلنا الجلسة مع شهود المعرفة الذين استحضرهم الغلام في بعض خطواته فوجدنا فيها ثلاثة أعضاء ورئيسهم كل واحد منهم في ناحية بعيداً عن الآخر وأنت لا تكاد تسمع حديث من بجانبك لشدة الضوضاء وعلو الأصوات، ودخل الكاتب يرقص في مشيته كأنه الطاوس في حسن هيئته، وجلس ووقفت بجانبه بحيث أرى ما يكتبه، فتناول القلم بأطراف أصابعه يضعه في الدواة تارة ثم يتركه ويشتغل بتصليح ثيابه أخرى.

١١،١٣ وتقدّم الباشا والمحامي والشهود فلم أسمع ما قالوه ولا ما قيل لهم من شدة الجلبة والصياح، وإنما رأيت الكاتب يكتب في دفتر الضبط ما يأتي:

«استحضر أمام الجلسة المدعي والمحامي والشهود فتقدّم المدعي وعرف أنه فلان ابن فلان ابن فلان وسمّى شاهدي معرفته وهما فلان ابن فلان ابن فلان وفلان ابن فلان ابن فلان الساكنان بجهة كذا شياخة فلان ابن فلان ابن فلان وشهد كل منهما على انفراده بأنه يعرف المدعي المذكور وأشار إليه بيده وهو فلان ابن فلان ابن فلان المذكورين، ثمّ قال المدّعي المذكور أنّ لي قبل فلان ابن فلان ابن فلان دعوى نظر على وقف ومعي مستند دعواي والمدعى عليه لم يحضر مع استلامه علم الطلب المحدد له فيه الحضور في هذه الجلسة».

ʿĪsā ibn Hishām said: With that, the clerk got up and went off with the vendor. I got up too, feeling utterly disgusted at such rampant ignorance. Meanwhile, the Lawyer's Assistant beckoned us to get up as our case was about to be heard. We went out and stood by the door of the room where the session was being conducted. Both inside and out we saw the most appalling crowds of people, and heard the orderly shouting loudly sometimes and softly at others. I asked the Assistant about this. He replied that the orderly lowered his voice so that the litigant would not hear all the shouting; if that happened, the entire case would have to be annulled out of sympathy and consideration for the defendant. In addition to this, the orderlies could bring in and keep out people as they saw fit. Our turn was called. We went inside, accompanied by the witnesses to our acquaintance whom the Assistant had brought for us as one of the stages he kept counting out for us. The session, we discovered, consisted of three members along with the chairman, each one of whom sat apart from the others. There was so much noise from people shouting and raising their voices that you could barely hear what someone next to you was saying. The clerk of the session who was dressed up like a peacock now pranced his way in and sat down. I stood in a position where I could see what he was writing. He took the pen in his fingertips, put it in the inkwell at one moment and then put it down. He kept on fussing with his clothes. 13.10

The Pāshā now moved forward with the lawyer and witnesses. I could not hear anything being said to them because there was so much noise and shouting. I could only see the clerk writing in the minutes book. I quote it word for word: 13.11

The plaintiff, lawyer, and witnesses appeared before the session. The plaintiff stepped forward and introduced himself as A, son of B son of C. He then identified two witnesses to tesify to knowing him, they being P son of Q son of R son of S resident in such and such an area and ward. Each one of them testified separately to the effect that he knew the aforementioned plaintiff and pointed him out, as being the aforementioned A. Then the plaintiff said: "I have a claim to make against B son of C son of D son of E concerning the administration of an endowment. I have the documents concerning my claim with me." The defendant did not appear even though he had received notification of the application which clearly laid down that he should appear before this session.

١٢،١٣ ثمّ أمرت المحكمة بانصرافنا للمداولة والنظر في المستند، فوقفنا ناحية ننتظر في هذه الحجرة مع من ينتظر من أرباب القضايا، وبعد برهة يسيرة نودي علينا فقالوا لنا أنّ المحكمة تعلمنا بمضمون المادة ٧٢ من اللائحة وهي تقضي على ما قال لنا المحامي بالإعذار إلى المدعى عليه وأننا لا بدّ أن نطلب ذلك من المحكمة لأنه لا يسوغ لها أن تعذر من نفسها إلا بناء على طلب المحامي وطلبناه فقررته، وسيتبع الإعذار الإعذار، والله يكفيك مكروه الأقضية والأقدار، ويقيك شر هذه الدار، ويرفع عنك ما تحتويه من الهموم والأكدار.

The court then ordered us to leave so that they could discuss the case and inspect the documents. We stood in a corner of the room waiting along with the other people. After a while we were summoned. They told us that the court wished to acquaint us with the contents of article 72 of the code which stipulates (so the Lawyer informed us) that the defendant shall be granted a statutory deferment of the hearing. The Lawyer informed us that we were obliged to submit such a request to the court, since it could only authorize such a deferral if the Lawyer made such a request. Once we had such a request and the court had granted it, there would follow one deferral after another. And may God suffice you against the misfortunes of fate, protect you from the evils of this building, and rid you of every trial and tribulation that it involves! 13.12

١٫١٤ قال عيسى بن هشام: ودخلنا - لا أدخل الله عليك طوارق النقم، ولا أخرجك من طرائق النعم - في دور الإنذار يتبعه الإنذار، والإعذار يتلوه الإعذار، ومندوب المحكمة لا يعود إلا بالخيبة عند كل أبوابه زاعماً أنّ خدم الخصم لا يقابلونه إلا بالازدراء كغيرهم من خول أبناء الأمراء حتى وصلنا إلى حد الإعذار الأخير، ولم نعتقد في المندوب غير الإهمال والتقصير، فرأينا أن نخبر خبره، ونقتفي أثره، وننظر بأعيننا كيف يتسع الذرع للاستخفاف برسول الشرع، وسرنا وراء المندوب ومعه الشاهدان يشهدان بأنه أعذر فلاناً ابن فلان ابن فلان، وقد أمسك الواحد منهم بكتف الآخر على هيئة تضحك كل هازئ وساخر وكل منهم يخد الأرض بحذائه ثم يعفي الأثر بذيل ردائه، وهم يسيرون الذميل والرسيم والوخيد كأنهم منطلقون إلى جفنة ثريد، ونحن من خلفهم نخب ونهرول، ونحسبل ونحوقل إلى أن كادوا يغيبون عن البصر،

٢٫١٤ وكدنا نفقد منهم الأثر لولا أن عثر أحدهم بشريط الكهرباء فطاحت عمامته وانفلت من رجله الحذاء فانفتل يلتمسها ويلتمسه فلم يرعه إلا السائق وجرسه، فما فطن له وما أبه حتى أدركته المركبة وكاد يقضي عليه لولا أن اجتذبه رفيق إليه، فحيل بين الرجل وبين عمامته ونعله، ووقف لا برأسه ولا برجله وهو يستغيث فلا يغاث حتى مرّت عليهما مركبات الكهرباء الثلاث فأدركناه وهو ممتقع اللون من اليأس والوجل، فبشّرناه بسلامتهما فاعتمّ وانتعل، وقد حمد الله على هذا اللطف في القضاء، وحمدنا ما أتيح من التعويق والإبطاء إذ تمكنا من اللحاق بهم واستئناف السير في عقبهم.

٣٫١٤ ووصلنا إلى قصر في سرة بستان، يزري حسنه بقصور بغداد وغمدان،

ʿĪsā ibn Hishām said: May God never afflict you with disaster or lead you away from the road to abundance! We now started on a round of warnings and deferments one after another. On each occasion, the court representative kept returning with the same news of failure. He informed us that the servants of our opponent in this case had only received him with contempt as did other servants of amirs' children. Eventually the time limit of the last deferment was reached. We assumed that it was merely a case of the representative's negligence and inefficiency, and decided to check his story by going with him to find out for ourselves how it was possible to treat the messenger of Muslim Holy Law with such contempt. We followed the representative, along with two witnesses to testify that he had issued a deferment to A son of B son of C. One of them had clasped the other by the shoulder in a manner enough to incite the wit of any sarcastic mocker; they were scuffing the ground with their shoes and then rubbing out the marks with their cloaks. They kept loitering and then speeding up, as if they were hurrying to get a bowl of meat broth. We sauntered along behind them at a reasonable pace, but then hurried along, with prayers to the all-powerful God, in quiet resignation until they were almost out of sight. 14.1

We might well have lost track of them altogether, if one of them had not tripped over the tram lines and lost his turban and shoes. He turned around to look for them, but before he knew it, along came a tram with the driver ringing the bell for all he was worth. The man was not even aware of it till the tram had almost reached him. It would almost certainly have killed him if his companion had not dragged him back. His turban and shoes were lost, and he was left standing there with nothing to cover his head or feet. He asked someone to help him save them, but without any success; and so the three carriages passed over them. Meanwhile we had caught up with them. The poor man looked pale with fright and was in despair, but we were able to give him the good news that his clothes had in fact been saved. He put his turban and shoes on again, praising God for this happy outcome. We in turn offered our own praises since this delay had slowed them down, and we had been able to catch up and could now carry on walking behind them. 14.2

This brought us to a mansion in the centre of a garden, the beauty of which belittled the very mansions of Baghdad and Ghumdān. It was bedecked with 14.3

والبستان قد تحلى بأنواع من الأزاهر، كأنها اليواقيت والجواهر، والقصر بينهما اليتيمة العصماء أو البدر بين نجوم السماء، أو

كأنّـه جيدٌ وبسـتانُـهُ
من حولِهِ عقدٌ بديعُ النّظام

وماذا نقول في روض نسجته الأرض حلة ليوم زخرفها و زينتها، ونمنمته رداء تختال به في ميدان حسنها وبهجتها:

موزّرة من صنعـة الوَبْـلِ والنّـدَى
بوشْيٍ ولا وشْيٌ وعصبٍ ولا عصب

قد أغنى الغواني نسيمه العليل، عن ملامسة المسك الأذفر وكفاها ريحه البليل تضمخها بالطيب والعنبر:

بغـرسٍ كأبكار الجواري وتُربـة
كأنّ ثراها مـاء وردٍ على مسكِ

٤،١٤ ومناها أن لو اتخذت من أزرار الأزهار فصوصاً للخواتم، ومن أكمام الأشجار معاقد للتمائم، وودها أن لو تأزرت من سندس أرضه بأبهى إزار وصرط، وتحلت من جوهر نباته بأزهى شنف وقرط:

إذا ما النّدى وافاه صُبحًا تمايلت
أعـاليـه من دُرٍ نثـيرٍ وجوهـرِ
إذا قـابلته الشـمس ردَّ ضياءَهـا
عليهـا صِقـالُ الأُقْحُوان المـنوّرِ

قامت فيه بنات الأغصان قيام الكواعب الأتراب، ساقيات بالأباريق والأكواب، ساكبات سؤر الطل من تلك الأقداح، مائسات من رحيق النّدى ومداعبة الرياح:

different kinds of flowers which looked like sapphires and other jewels. In the center was the mansion itself which looked like a white pearl or the full moon among the stars in the sky:

As though it were a neck, and its garden around it
a beautifully arranged necklace.[103]

What can we say about a garden so decorously woven by the earth's hand for the day of its festive decoration: a place garlanded in a cloak through which to relish its own radiant beauty?

It is clothed in a garment made by downpour and dew;
needlework, though not real, and striped cloth, though not such.[104]

In its wafting breezes, girls could dispense with the scent of musk, while the cool winds could save them the bother of perfuming themselves with ambergris:

With plants like young virgins, and soil
whose surface seemed rose water on musk.[105]

14.4 Their dearest wish would be to make ring-stones from the flower blossoms and amulet chains from the tree buds; they would long to be clothed in a glittering gown made from the silken brocade of its earth, and to be adorned with brilliant earrings from the jewels of its plants:

Whenever morning rain falls, its top parts
sway with scattered pearls and jewels of dew.
When greeted by the sun, the shining surface
of a gleaming marguerite reflects its light.[106]

In this garden fruit-laden branches took the place of buxom companions; flowers like serving maids with pitchers and cups who were pouring the remains of the dew from those cups and carrying the moisture's nectar as they swayed from side to side in the winds' flirtatious breezes:

شقـائقُ يحمـلن النّـدى فكأنّـه
دموعَ التصـابي في خدود الخرائـدِ

٥،١٤ وما تخيلنا في هذا الروض مذ نظرناه إلا أننا في حفلة عرس جمعت أسباب اللّهو وأطراف الأنس، فنصب الدجن عليه سرادقه، ومد ملتف النبات فيه نمارقه، وأشرقت في أغصانه الأنوار إشراق مصابيح الأنوار، وقامت الأطيار على الأعواد للتغريد والإنشاد فتأتي بألحان يقطع لها السامع من الطرب حبل النفس، ويبهت عندها الوحش المفترس:

رأتْ زهرًا غضًا فهاجتْ بمِزْهَـرِ
مـثانيهِ أحشـاءٌ لطُفْن وأوْصَـالُ

وللنسيم نغمات من ثقيل وخفيف، بالهينمة والحفيف، فتصفق أكف الأوراق، وتقوم الأفنان للرقص على ساق، مترنحة الأعطاف للصبا بخمر الندى، وتبسم عن أقاحها النضيد بما يرخص ثنايا الغيد ثمّ تميل برشيق القوام لالتقاط ما نقطها به الغمام، والجدول تحت أذيالها يجري ويتعثر، وينساب في ظلالها ويتكسر كأنّ حصباءه اللؤلؤ والمرجان أو قلائد العقيان في أجياد القيان:

ترُوعُ حصـاهُ حاليـةَ العـذَارَى
فـتلمسُ جـانبَ العـقدِ النّظِيـمِ

٦،١٤ ولمّا ملئنا من هذه الجنة طربا وقضينا عجبا، قلنا ما شاء الله لا قوة إلا بالله، ما أعجز الخلق عن شكر فضله وحمد نعماه، وإذا بقوم عند باب القصر قد امتلأت نفوسهم بالغم والقهر، تعلو وجوههم قترة، ترهقها غبرة، وهم بين باك ومنتحب، وصارخ ومصطخب.

فتفرست في هيئاتهم وهم يذكرون حاجاتهم فإذا هم جميعاً في يأس وقنوط، وخيبة وحبوط، وإذا اليهودي يقول بصوت المقهور المخذول.

Anemones carrying dew, as though they were
childhood tears on young girls' cheeks.[107]

14.5 Seeing this garden, we could only imagine that we were at some wedding feast where all means of arousing pleasurable and delightful sensations were gathered. Here the clouds had erected their pavilion and the intertwined plants had laid out their cushion. Flowers bloomed in the branches gleaming like lights, and birds perched on the trees vied with each other in their songs and chants, warbling melodies enough to sever the listener's heartstrings and attract even the wary beast of prey to hear them:

They saw the blooming flowers, and were roused by a lute,
the strings of which were delicate sinews and limbs.[108]

As the breeze rustled and blew, it played its own tunes in beats both light and heavy. The leaves clapped their hands, and the branches stood up to dance, swaying to the moisture's intoxicating effect and showing a smile that revealed a well-ordered daisy to put to shame the teeth of young girls. Swaying on their slim figures, they collected drops of rain. Beneath their garments, the brook trickled and flowed falteringly. Water coursed along in their shade and was channeled in different directions; it was as though its pebbles were pearl and coral on beauties' necks or golden necklaces on the finest singing girls:

Its stones so amaze bejeweled virgins,
they touch the edge of the well-strung necklace.[109]

14.6 Once we felt completely sated and overwhelmed by this earthly paradise, we intoned our praises to the only all powerful God, realizing as we did so how incapable mankind is of expressing its gratitude for His bounty. Just then, we noticed some people at the door of the mansion. They seemed both desperate and despondent, their expressions were gloomy, and their faces were covered in dust. All of them were either weeping, sobbing, or shouting angrily. As each one announced his purpose, I took a closer look: they all seemed utterly frustrated, thwarted, and discouraged. A Jew was talking with a sense of total failure:

٧،١٤ **اليهودي** تعساً لي لقد ضاع مالي وذهبت آمالي.

التاجر لي البؤس لو كنت أعلم بهذا المآل لم أقع في تلك الحبال.

البائع يا ويح نفسي اغتررت بالمقام العالي فخسرت رزق عيالي.

الجوهري ويل لمن خدعته الظواهر فضاعت عليه الجواهر.

الصيدلاني أقسمت لا يضيع عنده ثمن الدواء ولو تعلق بأطراف السماء.

الخمار سقيا له من محتال مال على دني ثم اختفى عن عيني.

القصاب أنا لا يضيع حقي ولو وضعوا السكين على حلقي.

الخياط وأنا لا أترك هذا الباب حتى أمزق ما عليه من الثياب.

الإسكاف ورأس أبيه وجده لآخذنّ ثمن أحذيتي من جلده.

الحلاق أنا ابن جلا وطلاع الثنايا، وكم لصنعتي من منافع ومزايا، فليتني شوهت خلقته، ومسخت سحنته فنتفت شاربه، وحلقت حاجبه، تالله لآخذنّ بناصية هذا الثقيل البارد، ولأسدّنّ عليه المصادر والموارد، ولألزمنه صباح مساء ولو حلق في الهواء.

٨،١٤ كل هذا والخدم ينكرون وجود صاحب الدار، ويقسمون أنه لم يبق عنده درهم ولا دينار، وإذا همّ أحد الغرماء بالدخول منعوه، أو غافلهم واحد منهم أرجعوه، وبينما نحن نتأمل ونتعجب ونتقلى على مثل الجمر ونتقلب، ونقابل بين سعد المكان ونحس السكان إذا بأجنبي قد خرج من بيت الحرم وهو يلتهب ويضطرم ويقول للبواب: لقد طالبته فأبان الإفلاس والعجز، فأوقفت عليه الحجز، وإليك قائمة البيان، وحذار من النقصان. وما كاد محضر المختلطة ينتهي ويذهب، حتى حضر محضر الأهلية يلهث من التعب فسلّم للبواب ورقة إنذار فقبلها بعد أن كرّر له الإفلاس والإعسار.

JEW Woe is me! My money is all gone, and I've lost all hope. 14.7

MERCHANT What misery! If I'd known this was going to happen, I would never have fallen into such a trap.

VENDOR Too bad for me! I've been duped by high rank, and now I've lost the means of supporting my family.

JEWELER Woe to anyone who lets himself be deceived by superficialities and loses his jewels as a result!

PHARMACIST I'm prepared to swear that I'm not going to lose the costs of his medicine, even though he be suspended from the outermost limits of the heavens.

WINE SELLER A plague on this swindler who takes a fancy to my wine bottle and then disappears.

BUTCHER I'm not giving up my rights even if they put a knife to my throat.

TAILOR I won't quit this door till I've torn the clothes off him.

SHOEMAKER By the head of his father and grandfather, I'm going to get the cost of his shoes from his own skin.

BARBER "I'm someone well known and ambitious."[110] My trade brings with it many privileges and benefits. If only I could have marred his face and spoiled his features, I would have torn his moustache off and shaved his eyebrows. By God, I'm going to tackle this unpleasant dunderhead, block all the entrances and exits, and stick to him morning and evening even if he takes off into the sky.

14.8 While all this was going on, the servants were refusing to acknowledge that the owner was at home. They kept swearing he did not have a dirham or dinar left. If a creditor tried to enter, the servants stopped him; if someone simply ignored them, they pushed him away. We observed the scene in amazement. Contrasting the beauty of the place with the misfortunes of its inhabitants, we felt we were being roasted and turned on the embers of our own worries. Just then a European man emerged from the inner sanctum; he was seething with anger. He addressed the Doorkeeper: "I have made my demands, but he has explained that he is bankrupt and unable to pay. There is no alternative but to impose distraint on the property. Here is a detailed list. Make sure nothing is lost or damaged." Barely had this usher of the Mixed Courts finished and left before the usher from the Native Courts arrived, panting with

وبعد ذلك انصرف المحضر وتبعه جميع من حضر لاشتداد حر الظهيرة وأوارها، واضطرام نارها. ثمّ انتهزنا هذه الفرصة فتقدّم مندوب المحكمة وأعلم البوّاب بصفته وقدّم له الإعذار فدفعه في صدره وأبى أن يستلمه منه وقال له: لم يكن ينقصنا إلّا هذه المحكمة ثمّ ولّاه ظهره وأغلق الباب، فأخذ المندوب بين الشاهدين ووقف بينهما ينادي بهذا النداء المقرّر:

٩،١٤ «يا فلان ابن فلان ابن فلان إنّ مولانا قاضي مصر يأمرك بأن تحضر إلى المحكمة في يوم الأحد للنظر في دعوى اغتصاب الوقف الموجهة عليك من قبل فلان ابن فلان ابن فلان وإن لم تحضر في اليوم المذكور ينصّب عنك وكيلاً ويسمع الدعوى في وجهه ويحكم عليك غيابياً.»

ثمّ ودّعنا المندوب والشاهدان بعد ذلك وانصرفوا إلى سبيلهم وبقيت أنا مع الباشا في دهشة وذهول وحزن وأسف فاستند الباشا إلى سور البستان وقال لي:

الباشا ما زالت بواطن الأمور وحقائق الأشياء تتجلى لدي وتتبيّن منذ وقوعي في هذه الخطوب والمشكلات حتى ظهر لي اليوم أنّ أمور هذه الدنيا كلها بهتان وتضليل وبطلان وتمويه وغش وتدليس، فبالله عليك من ذا الذي يرى هذا القصر بزينته وخدمه وحشمه ولا يلعب بلبه الحسد لمن يسكنه وتتلطع نفسه إلى غبطته فيسخط على حظه من الدنيا ويندب نصيبه من الحياة وقسمه في العالم.

١٠،١٤ عيسى بن هشام نعم لا زالت تسلك سبل الحكمة والهداية، إنك لترى الحق وتقول الصدق، فأكثر من ترى من المنعمين المترفين، والأغنياء والموسرين، لو كشفت عن باطن أحوالهم، وخبايا معيشتهم، لرأيت ما يوجب الرحمة والشفقة، لا ما يدفع إلى الحسد والغبطة، ولعلمت أنّ الرجل الذي يستخرج قوته منغمساً بعرق جبينه

fatigue. He handed a warning notice to the Doorkeeper who took it from him while repeating the same story about bankruptcy and inability to pay. That usher departed too. By now the midday heat was intense and the sun's rays were scorching their faces, so everyone present followed him. We seized this opportunity. Our court official moved forward, informed the Doorkeeper of his status at the Shariah Court, and handed him the warning notice. The Doorkeeper pushed him in the chest and refused to take the notice. "This is the only court we haven't heard from!" So saying, he turned his back on us and closed the gate. The court official now took the two witnesses by the hand and stood between them as he shouted the following statement in an official tone:

14.9 "The Qadi of Egypt orders you, A son of B son of C, to present yourself at the court on Sunday next, the purpose being to investigate a claim of unlawful seizure of the endowment now filed against you by X son of Y son of Z. Should you not be present on the specified day, then a deputy will be appointed on your behalf to hear the claim in his presence and judgment will be passed upon you *in absentia*."

With that, we bade the official and the two witnesses farewell, and they went on their way. The Pāshā and I were still utterly staggered by the things we had seen and heard. We both felt very despondent. The Pāshā leaned on the garden wall and spoke to me:

PĀSHĀ Ever since Fate has placed me in such difficulties and misfortunes, I've begun to see more clearly the inner significance of things as they really are. So much so that I've become convinced today that worldly matters work on the basis of deception and untruth; they all involve the use of falsehood, fabrication, fraud, and swindling. Try to find anyone, for Heaven's sake, who can look at this mansion—with its glittering decorations and its retinue of servants—without being overwhelmed by a feeling of jealousy toward the people who live there and by a desire to enjoy the same good fortune and happy life as they do. As a result, such a person will resent the lot he has in life and his particular fate in this world!

14.10 ʿĪSĀ Yes indeed, you're still pursuing the path of prudence and good judgment; you speak the truth as you see it. If you discovered what the situation is really like for the majority of wealthy people you're seeing and the kind of life they lead, you'd discover something that demands compassion and sympathy rather than envy and jealousy. You'd realize that any employee

أحسن منهم حالاً، وأنعم بالاً، وكلما كان الظاهر زاهياً زاهراً، كلما كان الباطن معتماً مظلماً، وأعرف واحداً من أولئك أشد ما يكون محزوناً مهموماً، أكثر ما تراه متصنعاً للانشراح متكلفاً للضحك، وأعظم ما تراه متضايقاً مفلساً، أقرب ما تراه متعرضاً للإنفاق.

الباشا لقد كان الأمر في أيامنا على العكس، فكان الرجل أوسع ما يكون ثروة إذا أظهر الاحتياج، وأبلغ ما يكون سروراً إذا أظهر الكدر والكمد.

١١،١٤ قال عيسى بن هشام: وما زلنا في مثل هذا الحديث وأنا مبتهج بما وصل إليه الباشا من تعوده الأبحاث العقلية، واهتدائه إلى قواعد الحكمة، واستنباط الحقائق من ثنايا الأخلاق، ورأيت أنّ الرجل المرتفع لا يزال غافلاً، فإذا وقع في حبالة المصائب يوماً علم ببطلان ما كان فيه بحقيقة ما وصل إليه. وحانت منّا التفاتة إلى ما وراء سياج السور فرأينا الخدم مجتمعين حلقة وهم يتحاورون ويتجادلون ويتباحثون ويتناقشون، وسمعنا البوّاب يقول:

البوّاب ليت أمي لم تلدني وليت أبي لم يعلمني الخط فقد كلّت يدي من التوقيع على تلك الإنذارات والمحاضر، فقلما يمضي يوم إلا ولي فيه إمضاء واستلام، وبئست هذه المعيشة وبئس ما وصلت إليه حالي فليتني كنت في زمرة هؤلاء الغرماء لأخلص بشيء مما هو متراكم لي من أجرة الأشهر المتأخرة ومن لي بالفرار من هذا البيت الذي انتشر في أثاثه جراد الحجز، وأزعجت من فيه أصوات الغرماء حتى لقد خفت من المحضرين على صندوق ثيابي.

١٢،١٤ الكاتب لست أدري ماذا يصنع هذا الشاب في حالته وكيف لنا المعيشة معه ولم يبق عنده كثير ولا قليل وإن صدق ظني كانت عاقبته من أفظع ما تصوّرون فقد أحسست من حركاته واضطرابه أنه يدبر لنفسه خلاصاً من هذه الحالة، ولكن بئس الخلاص وبئست الخاتمة خاتمة السوء، ويعلم الله أنني لولا ما التقطته في أشغاله من هنا وهناك لما تيسّر لي القيام بقوت عيالي بعد أن تعسّر عليّ الحصول على مرتبي،

who earns his daily livelihood through the sweat of his brow is happier and more comfortable than these people are. The more flashy and splendid the exterior, the gloomier and darker the interior. I know one of them personally who may actually be extremely worried and anxious. And yet, the more that's the case, the more you'll see him pretending to be happy and faking laughter. The poorer and more bankrupt he is, the more he risks lavish expenditure.

PĀSHĀ In my day, it was exactly the opposite. The richer someone was, the more needy he appeared; he was never as happy as when he made a display of his grief and misfortune.

14.11 ʿĪsā ibn Hishām said: We went on talking like this for quite a while. I was delighted to notice that the Pāshā was now regularly applying rational investigation and logical principles to obtain insight into the inner aspects of character. I became more than ever convinced that men in important positions remain totally inexperienced and ignorant; it is only when they happen one day to fall into the snares of misfortune that from the realities of their current situation they come to realize how futile their past way of life has been.

At this point we happened to glimpse over the wall and noticed the retinue of servants gathered round in a circle, chattering and arguing with each other. We heard the Doorkeeper start by saying:

DOORKEEPER How I wish my mother had never given birth to me and my father had never taught me how to write! My hand's sore from signing all these warning notices and statements. Hardly a day passes without my signing signatures and receiving papers. I've despaired of this life and the sorry state in which I find myself. How I wish I could be included in these clusters of creditors! Then at least I'd be able to escape with part of my salary which has been piling up for months. Who can help me get away from this house where distraint spreads like a plague of locusts? The people who live here are being constantly harassed by the voices of creditors. I myself am scared of court ushers who keep perching themselves on my clothes trunk.

14.12 CLERK I've no idea what the young man is going to do. How can we earn a living with him when he has absolutely nothing left? If I'm right, then the outcome will be the worst imaginable. He's been very restless of late, and I've the impression that he's devising some escape from this situation, but it'll be a poor way out and a vile end. God knows that, if it weren't for the things I pick

ولقد أرسلني أمس بخاتم ياقوت لبيعه كان ثمنه عليه مائة جنيه فلم يعطني فيه بائعه إلّا خمسة وعشرين جنيهاً فقط.

أحد الخدم كشفت لي ما كان عليّ غامضاً، فقد كان معه أمس مقدار من الذهب وكنت لا أهتدي إلى مورده، وقد أعطاني منه عشرة جنيهات فابتعت له بها من أخيه هذا الكلب الذي تراه مولعاً به منذ الصباح. ١٣،١٤

خادم ثان وأنا أعطاني ثمانية جنيهات فاشتريت له بها من صهره تلك البيغاء وأخذت له ورقة غرفة في الأوبيرا.

خادم ثالث وأنا اشتريت له من «جاكان» علبة أعطار بجنيه ونصف.

الكاتب فعلى هذا لم يبق معه إلا جنيه ونصف فإني أخذت منه في هذا الصباح أربعة جنيهات لأربط بها قلم صاحبنا صاحب الجريدة المعهود الذي يتهدده كل يوم بكشف الستر عن حالته وتسويد صحيفته بين أقرانه.

سائق المركبة إذن أذهب إليه الآن وأطلب ما وعدني به من ثمن الريش والإسفنج ما دام قد بقي معه من الدراهم باقية.

خادم رابع إنكم والله لمغبوطون بما تنالونه من وراء هذا البيع وهذا الشراء، ولكننا بقية الخدم قد اقتنعنا من أجرنا على الخدمة بالأكل والشرب وصبرنا على هذه الحال وفاء بالعهد لمجد هذا البيت، ويا ليت هذه النعمة تدوم فقد سمعتم اليوم تهديد القصاب كما سمعتم أمس تهديد رسول البك الخباز.

خادم خامس لم يبق حينئذ أمامنا من سبيل نطمئنّ به سوى إحالة أرزاقنا على إيراد الوقف الذي سلم من كل حجز وإنذار.

البواب لقد خاب ظنك وضاع أملك فإنّ هذا الوقف الذي ترتكنون عليه فقد دخل أيضاً في دور الدعاوى وجاء مندوب المحكمة الشرعية بإعذاره الثالث ولم يبق إلّا الحكم بنزع الوقف من يد سيدكم.

الجميع واويلاه واحرباه.

ثمّ ينادون من الداخل بأنّ سيدهم استيقظ من نومه يطلب الركوب.

up here and there while doing jobs for him, I couldn't afford to provide food for my family now that I've had difficulty getting my monthly salary. Yesterday he sent me off to sell a sapphire ring. It was valued at a hundred pounds, but the jeweler would only give me twenty-five for it.

14.13 SERVANT Now I can see things clearly. Yesterday I noticed that he had some gold with him, but I'd no idea of where he'd got it from. He gave me ten pounds. I used it to purchase from his brother the dog which you've seen him playing with since this morning.

SECOND SERVANT And he gave me eight pounds that I used to buy him the parrot from his son-in-law. I also bought him a ticket for a box at the Opera.

THIRD SERVANT And I spent one and a half pounds on perfumes from Jacquin.

CLERK If that's the case, then he has only a pound and a half left. Only this morning I took four pounds to pay the owner of a well-known newspaper to keep quiet. He's been threatening every day to expose the young man's true situation and blacken his name.

DRIVER While he still has some cash left, I'll go to see him as well to collect the cost of the bristles and sponge he promised me.

FOURTH SERVANT You're well off now thanks to the profit you've made from these purchases and sales. But we other servants have to make do with food and drink as our only salary. We've put up with this situation out of a sense of loyalty to this illustrious house. If only this prosperity would last! You've heard the butcher's threats today, and only yesterday you heard the baker's messenger issue a warning too.

FIFTH SERVANT I think our only course of action is to ask him to transfer our wages to the profits of the endowment, which is the only thing which has escaped confiscation and court notices so far!

DOORKEEPER Your thoughts and hopes are all in vain. The endowment on which you were all relying has now been taken to court as part of legal proceedings. The representative of the Shariah Court came today with the third notice of deferment. All that remains is for a verdict to be reached removing the endowment from your master's possession.

EVERYONE What a calamity!

A shout came from inside the house, to the effect that the master had woken up and wanted to take a ride.

١٤،١٤ قال عيسى بن هشام: فانفضوا فانصرفنا نحن أيضاً بعذاب لا يعذّبه أحد، على أن نذهب إلى المحكمة يوم الأحد.

وحلّ اليوم الموعود فتوجهنا إلى المحكمة وفُتحت الجلسة ونودي على المتخاصمين فأجبنا مع وكيلنا ولم يحضر المدعى عليه. ولمّا أخذ كلّ مجلسه طلبت الجلسة شهود المعرفة فاستحضر غلام المحامي شاهدين يشهدان بمعرفة المدّعي اسماً ولقباً وعيناً، ثمّ اطّلع المجلس على الإعذارات الثلاثة فوجدها جامعة للشروط المطلوبة، واختار وكيلا ممّن يثق بهم ويعلم فيه المحافظة على حقوق النائب، وطلب من المدّعي شرح دعواه كما لو كان المدّعى عليه حاضراً، وهناك أخذ محامينا في البحث في الصورة التي استخرجناها من الدفترخانة عن أعيان الوقف فلم يجد فيها إلا النزر اليسير من تلك الأوقاف الكثيرة التي عددناها له، وخشي أنه لا يحكم له إلا في ما يختص بما في تلك الصورة من الأعيان وهي لا تساوي شيئاً من تلك المشاق والمتاعب فطلب من المجلس تأجيل سماع الدعوى زماناً طويلاً يتمكن فيه من البحث عن بقية تلك الأعيان الموقوفة، فوافق الوكيل المنصوب من القاضي عن الغائب فتأجلت الجلسة إلى ما بعد العطلة القضائية من هذا العام.

١٥،١٤ وخرجنا مع محامينا وقد فتح له ولعيني غلامه باب رزق جديد، فسألنا المحامي عن المظان التي يمكن العثور فيها على تلك الأعيان الموقوفة، فتنحنح ثمّ سكت، ولمّا سرنا مع الغلام خطوات قال لنا لا مظنة لها أقرب من ديوان الأوقاف لأنه يوجد بهذا الديوان سجلات تسجل فيها تلك الأعيان وغيرها وخصوصاً إذا كان المدّعى عليه الآن قد أضاع بعض الموقوف ووضع الديوان يده عليه فإنه يكون قد سجّلها بغير شكّ في سجلاته. ثمّ أشار علينا بالاتفاق مع المحامي اتفاقاً جديداً وهو يأخذ على عهدته الحصول على هذا المطلب الجديد، فأجبناه والله يفعل بنا في الأوقاف ما يريد.

ʿĪsā ibn Hishām said: They all leapt to their feet. For our part, we left feeling deeply unsettled by what we had heard, inasmuch as we were going to court on Sunday. 14.14

The day appointed for our session in the Shariah Court arrived, so we went there once again. When the session opened, the contestants were summoned as usual. We duly responded with our agent, but the defendant was not present. Once everyone was seated, the session asked for the witnesses of cognizance. The Lawyer's Assistant produced two witnesses who gave their testimony regarding the defendant's particulars. The session then asked about the three deferments, and they were found to conform with all the established requirements. A deputy was now chosen for the defendant, someone reliable and well-known for protecting the rights of those not present. They asked him to explain the defendant's claims in his place. Our Lawyer began to check the text of the endowment which we had obtained from the Records Office concerning the endowment's assets. However, he could only identify a small fraction of the many assets we had enumerated for him. He was afraid that the court would only adjudicate the assets detailed in this copy of the document which was not worth all the trouble. With that in mind, he asked the court to postpone the hearing for a significant amount of time, so that in the intervening period it would be possible to investigate the rest of the endowed property. The deputy acting on behalf of the absent defendant agreed to this, and so the case was adjourned until after the year's judicial vacation.

We now left the session with the Lawyer. Both he and his Assistant now saw further scope for trickery opening up before them. When we asked him where we might find out about the rest of the endowment property, he cleared his throat and said nothing. As we walked a short distance with his Assistant, he told us that the only likely place was the Department of Endowments since it had records in which such properties are registered. That would be particularly true if the defendant in this case had lost some of the endowed property and the Department of Endowments had taken it over. Almost certainly it would have recorded this endowment in its records. 14.15

He now asked us to come to a new agreement with the Lawyer, while he committed himself to carrying out this new plan. We agreed to this latest request. God deals with us on matters of endowment as He wishes.

مصباح الشرق ٥٥، ١٨ مايو ١٨٩٩

١٫١٥ قال عيسى بن هشام: وبينما نحن على رجاء الإسعاد والإسعاف، فيما بين المحكمة والأوقاف، مبتهلين إلى الله أن يكفينا هول الموقف في هذا الديوان، وأن يحفظنا فيه من تقلب الحدثان لما امتلأت به الأسماع، ووقع عليه الإجماع من وصفه بالاختلال، ونعته بالاعتلال، واختلاف الوجوه في مهالجة دائه، ونفاد الحيل في محاوله شفائه، واتفاق الجمهور على وجوب الإصلاح فيه، وتدارك الخلل وتلافيه قبل أن يتفاقم الخطب، ويتعاظم الكرب، ويسوء المآل بدوام الإهمال والإغفال، إذ نزل بصاحبي الباشا ما ينزل بمثله ممّن يطيل تفكيره فيما يوجب تكديره، فأصبح مريضا عليلاً، وغدا جسمه نحيلا ضئيلا:

والهم يخترق الجسيم نحـافة
ويشيب ناصية الصبي ويـهرم

٢٫١٥ وكلما أشرت عليه بالأطباء قابلني بالتكره والأباء، قائلا ماذا ينفع الطبيب وماذا يفيد، وللآجال توقيت وتحديد، فأقنعه بأنّ الاعتقاد بتحديد الأجل لا يمنع من مداواة العلل، وكم من مريض طالت مدته دون أن تفارقه علّته، وكم من صحيح عاجله الحمام ولم يتناوله السقام. فقال لي: إن كان لا بد من الاحتياج إلى التماس العلاج فليكن الطبيب ممّن يعتمد في علاجه على البخور والتمائم، وكتابة الأوفاق والطلاسم، لا من أولئك الذين يعتمدون على العقاقير والنبات، ويصفون البسائط والمركّبات، ولقد كنت في الزمن السالف أعرف كثيرًا من المغاربة أهل العرافة، وأرباب العيافة، فلو التمستَ لي واحدًا منهم أعوّل في معالجتي عليه، لرجوت شفائي على يده.

فسعيت أنقّب عن طلبته، وأجتهد في إدراك رغبته حتى عثرت بعد طول البحث والاستقصاء على رجل من أهل الغرب الأقصى، فأخبرته الخبر، فطلب أوّلا أن يقيس الأثر، وهو في اصطلاحهم قطعة من ثياب المريض، تعقد على شيء من الصفر أو البيض، ويزعمون أنهم يصلون بها إلى الغرض من كشف المرض، فلمّا

Miṣbāḥ al-sharq 55, May 18, 1899[111]

ʿĪsā ibn Hishām said: At this point we were hoping for some help and good news as we hovered between the court and the Department of Endowments. It was our fervent prayer that God would suffice us as we confronted the dire situation with this particular department and that He would preserve us from the vicissitudes of fate. Our ears had been filled with grim reports about this particular administration; there seemed to be a consensus on its incompetence and dysfunction.[112] No one could agree on the diagnosis of its ills, and people had run out of ideas as to how to cure them. Everyone agreed on the need for reform; the faults had to be acknowledged and addressed before things got worse, the entire situation deteriorated, and a prolonged period of neglect and indifference led to the direst consequences. It was at this point that my friend the Pāshā suffered the fate of people who go through a prolonged period of tension and worry; he fell ill and kept on losing weight and energy. 15.1

Anxieties can render even the portly man thin,
and turn the youngster into a grey-haired old man.[113]

But every time I suggested seeing a doctor, he kept balking and refusing. What is the point of doctors, he would say, when the fates have their schedule and appointed time. I managed to convince him that a belief in the inevitability of fate need not stand in the way of a cure to illness. How many sick people have waited for ages, but the illness has lingered on; on the other hand, how many healthy folk have died young without ever being sick? To that the Pāshā replied that, if indeed there was a need to undergo treatment, then let it be a doctor who relied for his treatment on incense and amulets, writing charms and talismans, but not those types who rely on medicaments and plants and keep talking about herbs and compounds. In olden times, he told me, I used to know a lot of people from the Maghrib, fortune tellers and diviners. If you could find me one of them, I would entrust my treatment to them and trust them to cure me. 15.2

So I set about responding to his request and did my utmost to meet his wishes. After a prolonged search I came across someone from Morocco. After I had told him the Pāshā's story, the first thing he asked was to "measure a sample": in their practice that meant a piece of the invalid's clothing—something white or yellow which, they claim, can point to the origins of the patient's

حصل على المرام قال: أنظرني إلى ثلاثة أيام.

٣،١٥ فجئته في اليوم الموعود، فطلب مني ثمن البخور من الند والعود، وثمن المداد من الزعفران والصندل لضرب الزايرجة وفتح المندل. قال: إنّ صاحبك به مس وخبل من بنت الملك السمندل، ولا بدّ لإحضارها من أن تكون الملوك السبعة حاضرة مجتمعة، ومعهم ميمونة وعاقصة، ودهنش وواقصة، وجلجال بن المجلجل، وزلزال بن المزلزل، وزوبعة وبرقان، وغيرهم من الأوهاط والأعوان، وكل غواص وطيار من سكان التخوم وعمار القفار. ولا بدّ لكل واحد من بخوره المألوف بثمنه المعروف، وأنا أدلك على بائعيه إن كنت ممّن يدرك الوصف ويعيه، أو تعطيني الثمن الوافي وأنا الكافل الكافي. فرأيت أنّ الحصول على ما طلب ممّا يتعذر عليّ ويتعسّر، فنقدته في الحال ما تقدّر بيننا وتقرّر، ثمّ استمهلني أيضاً أياماً معدودة ليذهب معي إلى المريض في ساعة محدودة.

٤،١٥ فلمّا حان الوقت حضر ثمّ استحضر، ورقّم وسطّر، وعزم وبخّر، وهمهم وزمجر، ورطن وبربر، ثمّ هلل وكبّر، ثمّ نزع خصلة من شعر العليل فتألم، وتأوّه دون أن يتكلم، ثمّ أخذ يقلّبه ذات اليمين وذات الشمال حتى كاد يفتت الأعصاب والأوصال، وأوشك أن يدرك المريض الغرق في بحر من العرق، ثمّ محا بالماء ما خطّه في الإناء، وناوله ليشرب من ذلك المداد، فأخذ يتجرعه ولا يكاد، ثمّ طلب ماء من بئر لم ترها الشمس، وطفق يقرأ عليه بين جهر وهمس، وهو يديره بكفه ثمّ يبصق فيه بملء فيه. وبعد أن انتهى من تلاوة العزيمة والزجر، وضاق مني الصدر وفني الصبر، شرع يقذف وجه العليل بذلك الماء البارد، وهو يقول باسم الله أوقيك من كل شيطان مارد، فقام الباشا وقعد، وارتعش وارتعد، ثمّ أغمي عليه فهذى وهجر، فقال المغربي: الله أكبر، لقد أشرق النجاح وأسفر، وتخلصنا من بنت الملك الأحمر، وقد كان يغشى عليّ أيضاً من الجزع والوجل، فصحت به: ماذا فعلت أيها الرجل؟ فقال: لا توجل

illness. Once he had acquired what he was looking for, he told me to come back in three days.

15.3 So I kept the assigned appointment. He asked me to pay for the necessary fumigants: musk and ambergris, to which was added the cost of saffron and sandalwood, so as to afford a gaze into the unseen. He told me that my companion had been "touched" and was afflicted by a madness induced by the daughter of the Salamander King. In order to invoke her, all seven kings had to be gathered together in the same place. Not only that, but there also had to be present Maymūnah and ʿĀqiṣah, Dahnish and Wāqiṣah, Rattler son of Shaker, Quaker son of Shocker, Storm and Flasher, along with other rowdies and assistants. They would also need every diver and flying beast from the boundless climes and the denizens of desert wastes. Each one of these would need to have their particular vapors, each with its acknowledged cost. I can point you, he told me, to the vendor who knows the potion and can reproduce it exactly; either that or else you can give me the full amount, and I'll take care of the whole thing for you. I now realized that what was being demanded was beyond my ability to pay, so I immediately gave him an agreed-upon amount, and he in turn asked me to delay for a few days until he could visit the invalid at a specified time of day.

15.4 He did indeed come at the appointed time and invoked the spirits. He now proceeded to count and record, to resolve and cense, to mutter and growl, to rant and babble. With praises and prayers to God he pulled out one of the sick man's hairs and moaned and groaned without saying a word. He then started turning the patient over to left and right till his joints and nerves almost fell apart. The poor sick Pāshā was on the point of drowning in a sea of sweat. Using water he wiped off the design he had made in the basin, then handed it to the invalid to quaff some of its contents. He started to swallow, but could hardly manage it. This "doctor" then demanded some water from a well untouched by sunlight and started chanting over it, sometimes loud, sometimes in a whisper. He kept turning it in his hands and then spitting a whole mouthful of saliva into it. Eventually he finished reciting this mumbo jumbo, while I was getting more and more aggravated and impatient. He now started spraying the invalid's face with this cold water, all the while chanting that in the name of God he was protecting him from all fiendish devils. The Pāshā stood up, then sat down, shivering and shaking; he then fainted clear away, whimpering as

ولا تجزع، فلم يبق بين مريضك وبين الشفاء سوى أن يفيق من هذا الإغماء، وهكذا إذا خرجت الشياطين من الجسد، خار من الضعف وخمد، فإذا خلا بالمريض المكان عاد إلى الصحة كما كان، إذ يتولاه الأعوان من الأمناء والحفظة، فيعيدونه إلى الإدراك واليقظة، وهم لا يقومون بهذا العلاج الخفيّ ومعهم في المكان إنسيّ، فهلمّ بنا إلى خارج الدار، وإياك والعودة إلّا في آخر النهار.

٥،١٥ فامتثلت ما أمر به، وخرجت في عقبه، ثمّ تركني هذا المشعوذ وانصرف، وخلفني حليف أسى وأسف، وبقيت منتظرًا بين همّ وويل، إلى أن أدبر النهار وأقبل الليل، وما كان صبري علم الله على هذا الدجال وبهتانه إلّا احتراما لبساطة الباشا في اعتقاده وسرعة إيمانه. فأسرعت إلى البيت لا ألوي على شيء، فألفيت صاحبي بين ميت وحي، ووجدته لم يفق بعد من غشيانه، ولم يزل في هذر المرض وهذيانه، فعلمت أنّ الأمر عسير عصيب، وأنه لا بد من استدعاء الطبيب، وتحققت ما أدخله علينا المغربي من الاحتيال حتى ابتزّ ما ابتزه من المال، وأوقع الباشا فيما أوقعه فيه من شدة الاعتلال وسوء العقبى والمآل. فذهبت مسرعا إلى صيدلية قريبة من هناك، وأنا على أشد ما يكون من الاضطراب والارتباك، وسألت عن طبيب يتدارك العليل في شدته، ويخفض من صورة المرض وحدته، فأشار الصيدلاني إلى رجل بجانبه يلعب بالنرد، وقال دونكه فقد أصبت الفرصة وخدمك السعد، فاعتذر الطبيب وتعلّل، وامتنع وتدلل، ثمّ قال لي وهو يتمطى ويتثاءب، ويمزح مع اللاعب:

٦،١٥ **الطبيب** دعني فليست تسمح لي الأشغال بإجابة السؤال.

الصيدلاني مثلك أيها الدكتور لا يخيب لديه الرجاء والالتماس، ولا يذهب العرف بين الله والناس.

الطبيب قل لي من الذي كان يباشر علاجه من قبل.

عيسى بن هشام لم يباشره أحد قبلك ولم أعلم أنه مرض قبل اليوم.

الطبيب لو فرضنا أني قمت معك فأين المركبة.

he did so. The Maghribi doctor now proclaimed: "God is Almighty! Success! We are now rid of the red king's daughter."

I too was close to fainting out of sheer panic and fright. "What have you done?" I shouted at him.

"Don't be afraid!" he replied. "Don't panic! It only remains for your sick friend to come round from his fainting spell. Now that the devils have left his body, he's feeling feeble and weak. Once the space is completely clear again, he'll be just as healthy as he was. Once he is in the hands of the righteous and devout helpers, they'll soon wake him up and restore him to consciousness. But they never perform this cryptic cure if there are human beings in the room. So we need to leave the house. Make sure you don't go back inside till day's end."

15.5 So I obeyed his instructions and followed him out of the house. This total phony now left me and went on his way, leaving me prey to sorrow and regret. I waited on tenterhooks till nightfall. God is my witness that the only reason I put up with this trickster's routine was out of respect for the Pāshā's naïveté when it came to traditional beliefs. Rushing headlong back to the house, I found my friend lying there between life and death and still unconscious as he ranted and raved. I immediately realized that the situation was very grave, and we needed to find a doctor. I was now certain that this Maghribi so-called doctor had tricked us simply in order to extort money from us and had left the Pāshā in this serious condition with its uncertain consequences. In a total panic I rushed over to a nearby pharmacy and asked for a doctor who could take on a severely sick patient and alleviate the symptoms of his illness. The pharmacist pointed to a man sitting beside him playing backgammon. "There you are!" he said. "What a lucky chance; the fates have smiled on you!" But the doctor kept making excuses and coyly refusing to cooperate. He stretched and yawned and then spoke to me:

15.6 DOCTOR Leave me alone! I'm far too busy to answer your request.

PHARMACIST But, my dear Doctor, the likes of you will surely not dash the hopes of one who asks for help. The traditional bond between God and mankind still exists.

DOCTOR Tell me, who's been treating him up till now.

ʿĪSĀ IBN HISHĀM No one. I didn't realize he was sick till today.

DOCTOR Assuming I agree to go with you, where's the carriage?

عيسى بن هشام نحن من البيت على مقربة.

الصيدلاني (لغلامه) اذهب فأتنا بمركبة فلا بد منها على أي حال.

اللاعب (للطبيب) اعلم أنك إذا قمت من قبل أن تتم الدور ضاع عليك الرهان.

الطبيب كيف تقول ذلك وقد انتظرتك أمس ثلاث ساعات طوال والدور منصوب أمامي حتى عدت وأتممته.

اللاعب كان ذلك لأنّ الغلبة في الدور كانت محققة لجانبك.

الصيدلاني اركب أيها الدكتور واذهب وأنا أقوم مقامك في لعب الدور وأتكفل ببذل الرهان من عندي إن وقعت الغلبة عليك.

٧،١٥ قال عيسى بن هشام: فتمّ على ذلك الاتفاق، وانفض الخلاف والشقاق، وركبت وركب الطبيب معي، وأنا من الحزن لا أبصر ولا أعي. ولمّا صرنا في حضرة المريض وجدناه قد أفاق من غيبوبته، وخلص من نوبته، فتقدّم إليه الطبيب وجسّ نبضه وقرع صدره، ثمّ وضع يده على جبينه كالقادح فكره، ثمّ قطب وعبس، وهزّ رأسه دون أن ينطق بحرف أو ينبس، ثمّ أدخل يده في جيبه فأخرج منه ورقة بالية مطوية، ففتحها فإذا فيها أسطر فرنسوية، وأخذ القلم فنقش به ورقة على مثلها، ثمّ زاد عليها الإمضاء في ذيلها، وقال لنا دونكم صفة الدواء، يؤخذ منه ملعقة في الصباح وملعقة في المساء، والحذر الحذر من التأخير والتواني، وإياكم إياكم أن تشتروا هذا الدواء من غير ذلك الصيدلاني، فإنه رجل صادق مؤتمن، لا يغش في الأصناف ولا يغش في الثمن. ولمّا همّ بالانصراف خاطبته باللغة الفرنسوية دون اللغة العربية لأقف منه على كنه المرض خشية أن يدرك المريض معنى الخطاب، فلم ينطق بحرف في الجواب، فعلمت أنه لا يدرك من تلك اللغة غير رسم الأسماء في وصف الدواء. ولمّا أعطيته أجرة الزيارة على حسب ما قدّر وعدنا أن يعود المريض كل يوم حتى ينجو من الخطر. وما زال الطبيب يذهب ويحضر، والدواء يتجدد ويتكرر، والمريض يتألم

ʿĪsā ibn Hishām The house is close by.

Pharmacist (*to his assistant*) Go and get a carriage. We need it at once.

Backgammon Player (*to the Doctor*) You realize that, if you leave before the game's over, the bet will be forfeited.

Doctor How can you say that when I had to wait three long hours yesterday with everything set up in front of me before you came back and finished?

Backgammon Player That was because you were bound to win that particular game.

Pharmacist My dear Doctor, get in the carriage and go. I'll take your place in this game and guarantee to pay the bet myself if you happen to lose.

15.7 ʿĪsā ibn Hishām said: And with that we reached an agreement; there was no further cause for argument. The doctor and I got into the carriage. In my misery I was barely conscious and aware of my surroundings. Once we reached the sick Pāshā, we found that he had come round from his fainting spell and had no more spasms. The doctor went over, felt his pulse, tapped his chest, then put his hand on his forehead like someone deep in thought. The doctor frowned and shook his head, but did not utter a single syllable. Putting his hand in his pocket, he brought out a ragged folded piece of paper and opened it up. On it were some phrases in French. Taking a pen, he copied them exactly on to another sheet of paper, added his own signature at the bottom, and told me that this was the prescription. The Pāshā was to take one spoonful in the morning and another in the evening. Great care needed to be taken to make sure that there were no lapses and the medicine was taken on time. It was also essential that the medicine be bought from the very same pharmacy; the pharmacist was an honest, devout man, who would not adulterate the medicine or charge an exorbitant amount. Just as he was leaving, I spoke to him in French instead of Arabic in order to find out what exactly the sickness was without the Pāshā understanding how serious his condition was. The doctor did not respond, which made it clear to me that the only French he knew were the precise words needed for the prescription. Once I had handed over the agreed amount for the visit, he promised to come back every day until the danger was

وتضجر، والمرض على حاله لا يتغير، وكلما سألنا الطبيب عن سبب ازدياد المرض واشتداد الآلام، قال لا بدّ أن تكونوا خالفتم أمري في الحمية عن الشراب والطعام.

٨،١٥ فشكوت النازلة إلى أحد الأصدقاء، فقال لي عليك بسواه من الأطباء، من تلقى صناعة الطب في مدارس الغرب فوقف منه على القديم والحديث، ومن الدواء على الطيب والخبيث، فعملت برأيه وإشارته، وقصدت أحدهم في محل استشارته، فوجدت الخادم ينتهر الزائرين، ويقول لهم: ما لكم تأتون مبكرين، وقد علمتم أنّ الدكتور لا تفوته نومة الضحى، ولو فتكت سهام الردى بجميع المرضى، والناس يحتملون ويصبرون، ويعتذرون وينتظرون، إلى أن بزغت شمس الطبيب من وراء الحجاب، وخرج في أبهج زينة وأبهى ثياب، فانتظرته حتى خلص من ذلك السواد المتجمع، فتقدمت إليه بهيئة المتوسل المتضرع، وتلطفت له ما شئت في العبارة، وسألته أن يتخير وقتاً للزيارة.

٩،١٥ الطبيب ما هذا التزاحم وما هذا الإلحاح وما مزية هذه المعيشة التي لم يكن لي فيها وقت للأكل ولا للشرب ولا للراحة ولا للنوم، وهل فُقِدَت الأطباء من البلد حتى لم يبق فيها من طبيب غيري، أم وقع الناس كلهم في الأمراض فاشتغل جميع الأطباء بهم وتوزعوا فيما بينهم، واعلم يا عزيزي أنه ليس في تقويم أوقاتي وقت أزورك فيه إلا بعد يومين.

عيسى بن هشام أقسمت عليك بحق الإنسانية ألا ما أجبت رجائي فقد دلتني شهرتك عليك، واعتقدت شفاء المريض على يديك.

الطبيب اعلم أنني لا أباشر معالجة مريض اعتورته أيدي الأطباء، فإن كان مريضك في أوّل مرضه ولم يتقلب بين أيديهم قبلت منك الرجاء، وحضرت لعيادته في هذا المساء.

عيسى بن هشام لم يره إلا طبيب واحد ولم ينجع فيه علاجه ولا دواؤه.

الطبيب أولى لك أن ترجع إليه وأن تتركني وشأني فلست ممّن ينتظرون بأس المرضى من أطبائهم حتى أسارع إلى استدراك غلطهم في علاجهم، وما أظن

past. The doctor did continue to come and go, and the same prescription kept being renewed and repeated, but the patient was still suffering and groaning; and the disease stayed the same. Every time we asked the doctor why the disease and pain seemed to be getting worse, he replied that we must not have been following his instructions about food and drink.

15.8 I now complained to a friend of mine about this terrible situation. He told me that I needed to look for another doctor, someone who had been trained in Europe, who knew about both modern and ancient medicine, and treatments that were good or bad. I followed his advice and sought out such a doctor at his consulting office. I found one of his servants upbraiding visitors for coming so early. He told them that they were supposed to know that the doctor was always asleep in the morning. It made no difference whether death's arrows were carrying away the sick and people were suffering in patience, apologizing and waiting, till the time came when the sun emerged from behind the veil and showed itself in its finest garb. With that in mind, I waited till this mob had been dealt with, and then approached the doctor. I acted as a humble postulant and made use of the politest possible language to ask him to choose his own time for a visit.

15.9 Doctor Why are there these mobs of people? Why is everyone so insistent? What's the value of this kind of life when I've no time to eat and drink, let alone to relax and get some sleep? Are there no other doctors in this country, such that I'm the only one left? Or is it that everyone is sick now, and all the doctors are busy caring for them and sharing the burden. My dear Sir, please realize that my schedule only permits me to pay you a call in two days' time.

ʿĪsā ibn Hishām I beseech you by in the name of humanity not to reject my request. It is your repute that has led me to you, and I'm sure that at your hands the invalid can be cured.

Doctor You need to know that I won't take on a patient who has been sullied by the hands of other doctors. Provided that your sick friend is in the initial stages of his illness and hasn't been treated by them, then I can respond to your request. I'll come to see him tonight.

ʿĪsā ibn Hishām He's only been seen by one other doctor, but he's failed to treat him properly or cure him.

Doctor Then you should go back to him and leave me alone. I'm not one of those doctors who wait till other doctors have failed the sick, only to

طبيبكم إلا من أولئك الذين لم يفارقوا مصر، ولم يتعلموا في سوى القصر، ولم يقفوا على محدثات هذا العصر، واكتفوا بالقليل من الأجر.

عيسى بن هشام أظنه كذلك وما قصدتك إلا لما سمعته من اتصافك بنقيض ما ذكرت، وبضدها نتبيّن الأشياء.

الطبيب وأظنك سمعت أيضاً بالتفاوت في الأجرة بين أمثالنا وأمثالهم.

عيسى بن هشام نعم ولك ما تحب وتريد.

الطبيب إذن لا أرى في عيادتكم من بأس.

١٠،١٥ قال عيسى بن هشام: فتركته على ميعاد وعدت إلى الباشا. ولمّا حضر في المساء دخل على المريض حاسرًا عن رأسه واضعاً يده في أنفه ثمّ اقترب من الفراش ويده اليمنى تصلح مفرقه واليسرى على يد المريض يحس بها نبضه ونظره شارد نحو الباب كأنه يحاول أن يرى من يكون في البيت وراء الحجاب، وما لبث أن كتب الدواء وأسرع بالرجوع من حيث أتى، وبعد يومين حضر إلينا شخص يسأل عن حالة المريض وقال أنه مساعد ذاك الطبيب، فلم أملك نفسي عند ذلك من الحنق والغيظ لما رأيته من سوء المعاملة وقلة الاعتناء وأغلقت الباب في وجهه وقلت له: اذهب فلا حاجة لنا بك ولا بمن أرسلك، ثمّ خرجت وأنا على تلك الحال تبدو على وجهي علاماتها، فأدرك ذلك مني أحد الجيران وسألني عن النازلة فقصصتها عليه وكان قريب عهد بالبلاد الأجنبية، فقال لي: لا غرو وإذا أصابكم ما أصابكم لاعتمادكم على الأطباء الوطنيين وأنّ من أشار عليك بهم لغير ناصح لك، وأعرف طبيباً من أطباء باريس حضر معي في باخرة واحدة لا أشك في شفاء مريضك على يديه، وهو يسكن في المكان الفلاني وهلمّ معي لأدلّك عليه.

١١،١٥ فلمّا وصلنا إلى حيث يسكن ذلك الطبيب قابلنا باللطف والإيناس وأخذ يتكلم معنا بأحاديث شتى لا مناسبة بينها وبين حاجتنا، ثمّ قام معنا، ولمّا صرنا عند المريض أخذ يقلبه ويفحصه ويقيس حرارته ويعدّ ضربات نبضه على ثواني ساعته، وبعد طول الفحص والإمعان كتب ورقة الدواء وانصرف على أن يعود في المساء، وأقام على ذلك

rush over and correct the mistakes they've made. I assume that this doctor was someone who has never left Egypt; he has only studied locally, has no idea about modern developments, and accepts a paltry wage.

ʿĪsā ibn Hishām I think that's right. But I've only come to see you because I've heard that you're the exact opposite of that. Things always become clear through their opposites.

Doctor And I suppose you've also heard about the different prices charged by them and us.

ʿĪsā ibn Hishām Yes. You'll get whatever you wish to charge.

Doctor In that case I see no reason why I shouldn't pay you a visit.

15.10 After fixing the appointment, I left him and returned to the Pāshā. When the doctor arrived in the evening, he went in to see the patient with his head uncovered and holding his nose. As he approached the bed, he was adjusting his hair-parting with his right hand and holding the patient's hand with his left as he felt his pulse. He kept looking distractedly toward the door as though he were trying to see what might be in the private quarters. It was not long before he wrote out a prescription and hurried away as quickly as he had come. Two days later another person arrived to ask how the patient was doing, saying that he was the doctor's assistant. This poor treatment and general lack of concern was enough to make me lose my temper. I slammed the door in his face, but not before telling him to go away: we have no need of you, I told him, or of the person who sent you. That done, I went out again, the signs of my state of mind clearly visible on my face. One of my neighbors spotted my angry mood and asked me what the problem was. I told him the whole story. This neighbor had recently been abroad. He told me that what had happened was no surprise. You have been relying, he told me, on local doctors; whoever suggested using them was giving you bad advice. I happen to know a Parisian doctor, he said, who came here on the same boat as myself. I'm sure he can cure your sick friend. He lives in such-and-such a place, and I can show you where it is.

15.11 Once we reached this doctor's residence, he gave us a friendly welcome and started using a variety of verbiage that had nothing to do with what we needed. He came to the house with us. Approaching the invalid, he proceeded to turn him over, examine him, take his temperature, and count his pulse beats with the second hand on his watch. After a lengthy examination, he wrote out a prescription and left, saying that he would come back in the evening. That is

أياماً وإذا بالمرض قد اشتد بما أفزعنا وأزعجنا فلم يسعني إلا أن أعود باللائمة على من أشار علينا بهذا الطبيب، فلمّا قابلته وكان أحد أصحابه حاضراً قلت له:

عيسى بن هشام هلمّ وانظر ماذا فعل طبيبك الأجنبي.

الجار وماذا فعل، ألم يشف مريضكم.

عيسى بن هشام بل الأمر بالعكس، فقد اشتد المرض وازداد الداء بما لم يكن في الحسبان.

الجار كيف هذا والدكتور فلان من أشهر أطباء باريس وممّن امتلكوا ثقة الجمهور بهم واتفاق الناس على صدقهم وأمانتهم.

الصاحب لصاحبه ألا تزال على غرورك في شغفك بكل من كان غريباً أجنبياً وتفضيلك إيّاه على أبناء جنسك وأهل بلدك وإنّ في أطبائنا لرجالا يفوقون الأجنبي بسعة اختبارهم وطول تجربتهم.

الجار إنني لم أشر عليه بالأجنبي إلا بعد أن شكا إليّ ما ذاقه من الأطباء الوطنيين.

الصاحب مثل من؟

الجار مثل فلان وفلان.

الصاحب وأين أنت من مثل فلان وفلان من فحول الطب ورجاله، وما على صاحبك إلّا أن ينتخب واحداً منهم وأنا الضمين له بقرب الشفاء.

١٢،١٥ قال له عيسى بن هشام: ووقع الاختيار على أحدهم فتوجهت إليه وأحضرته، ولمّا انتهى من فصح جسم المريض أخذ يسألني عن حالته الأدبية في ماضيه وحاضره وعن أشغاله الفكرية، فقصصت له مجملا من تاريخه فقال:

الطبيب اعلم أنّ ليس بصاحبك داء دفين أو مرض عضال، وما هي إلا الانفعالات النفسانية من تأثير الحوادث، فهزل جسمه ووهنت قوته من ألم النفس

the way things stayed for several days, and the illness only got worse, sending us into a further panic. All I could do was to blame the person who had sent me to this particular doctor. When I met my neighbor, he had one of his friends with him.

ʿĪsā ibn Hishām Come with me and see what your foreign doctor has managed to do.

Neighbor What's he done? Hasn't he cured your friend's illness?

ʿĪsā ibn Hishām Just the opposite! The condition is even worse than it was, something that we never expected.

Neighbor How can that be? That doctor is one of the most famous doctors in Paris. Everyone trusts him and people regard him as being honest and reliable.

Neighbor's Friend (*talking to him*) Are you still so infatuated with everything Western and foreign. Do you still prefer such people to your own folk, your fellow countrymen? We have doctors in Egypt who are far superior to any foreigner in the breadth of their expertise and their long experience.

Neighbor I only recommended the foreigner to him after he had complained about the experiences he had had with local doctors.

Friend Such as who?

Neighbor Doctors X and Y.

Friend How can you possibly consider X and Y proper doctors? All your friend needs to do is to choose a truly competent local doctor, and I'll guarantee you that the patient will be cured in short order.

15.12 ʿĪsā ibn Hishām said: So I chose one of them, went to his house, and brought him back. Once he had completed his physical examination, he asked me about his cultural background, both present and past and his intellectual concerns. I told him the Pāshā's entire history. He then spoke to me as follows:

Doctor You should know that your companion doesn't have some hidden disease or chronic illness. It is the events that have happened to him that have had a negative psychological effect on him. The reason why he's grown so thin and lost his energy is that his mind has been suffering. In order

وليس له من دواء إلا تبديل الهواء والتسلي عن الهموم مع تناول الأغذية النافعة والأشربة المنعشة.

عيسى بن هشام إذن فما بال أولئك الأطباء الذين ملؤوا البيت علينا زجاجات وعقاقير.

١٣،١٥ الطبيب (بعد أن وقف على قصتهم واطلع على أنواع أدويتهم) إنّ في كل صناعة صالحاً وطالحاً وعالماً وجاهلاً ونبيهاً وغبيّاً. وقد ظهر لي أنّ الطبيب الأوّل ممّن لا عناية لهم بصناعتهم فلم يقف على حقيقة المرض ورأى أن يستحل الأجر بوصف دواء بسيط لا يضر إذا لم ينفع، وأن يترك المرض للطبيعة فإذا طال أمده كانت الفائدة عائدة عليه. أمّا الطبيب الثاني فيظهر أنّ أعراض المرض التبست عليه فشخصه على غير حقيقته ووصف الدواء على حسب تشخيصه فوقع في الخطأ من حيث لا يدري. والطبيب الأجنبي عرف العلة ولكنه وصف الدواء كما يصفه لأحد أهل بلده بغير تمييز بين هواء البلدين واختلاف الأمزجة في سكانهما فأخطأ أيضاً.

١٤،١٥ واعلم أنّ أي صناعة في العالم لا تعادل صناعة الطب شرفاً وقدراً ومجداً، وفخراً وجمالاً وجلالاً، ومن تأمّل من الأطباء في هذه الصناعة وهداه الله إلى معرفة مقدارها شرفت عنده نفسه واعتلى في نظره قدره فنبت عينه عن سفاسف الأطماع وزهدت نفسه التطلع إلى الغنى من طريق التكسب بهذه الصناعة الجليلة واتخاذها وسيلة من وسائل اكتناز المال وادخار الذهب، وتبيّن له أنّ لذة الصنعة في حدّ ذاتها لا توازيها لذة في العالم من مال وبنين وما شئت من متاع الحياة وزخرف الدنيا، وأي رتبة تصل إلى رتبة الطبيب وهو القيم على صلاح الأبدان والمتكفل بصحة الأجسام، والرقيب على اعتدال الأمزجة وسلامة الجوارح، وأي صناعة تفضل صناعته وتطولها وهي أقرب الصناعات إلى خلقة الصانع وتكوين المنشئ القادر؟ وإذا كان ذلك المصوّر ازدهته صناعته في تمثال إنسان صنعه من رخام، فلمّا وقف يشاهد إتقانه التهبت نفسه غراماً لحسن الصنع حتى ذهل لبه

to recover what he needs is a complete change of air and a release from his troubles, along with some healthy food and refreshing drink.

ʿĪSĀ IBN HISHĀM But what about all the doctors who have filled the house with bottles and drugs?

15.13 DOCTOR (*once he has been told about the various doctors and their medicines*) Every profession has its practitioners, both useful and useless; there are those who know and those who don't, people who are honest and others who are crooked. It is clear to me that the first doctor could not care less about the medical profession. He failed to diagnose the illness and decided that he could justify his fee by prescribing a medicine that was neither harmful nor beneficial and then leaving the entire illness to nature to cure. As long as the illness persisted, he would benefit from it. The second doctor found the symptoms of the illness too complicated, so he misdiagnosed it and chose a medicine in line with his own misdiagnosis. He didn't even realize the mistake he'd made. The third doctor realized what the problem was, but he chose to write out a prescription as he would do for someone from his own country without taking into account the difference in climate and the variations in physical constitution. So he too was wrong.

15.14 You should realize that there is no profession in the world that can rival that of medicine when it comes to honor, respect, esteem, pride, beauty, and significance. Medical practitioners who contemplate the nature of their profession and are guided by God to an awareness of its scope will feel their souls ennobled and their worth enhanced. As a result they'll eschew the trivialities of cupidity and abstain from all thought of wealth gained by exploiting this noble profession and making use of it to acquire money and hoard gold. It will be clear to them that the pleasure of it all lies in the profession itself. No other pleasures in the world, be they money, children, or whatever of life's delights and fripperies you wish to mention, can rival it. What status can possibly compare with that of a doctor who is responsible for people's bodily health and the guardian of well-balanced constitutions? Which other profession is preferable to the one that is closely modeled on the very creation of God, the Maker and Originator? There is the story of that famous Greek sculptor whose craft led him to boast about the image of man that he had created in marble. When he stood there contemplating the marvel that he had made, its very beauty made him fall in love with it, to such an extent that he lost his mind and started

وغاب رشده فانحنى على التمثال يضربه بمنحاته حتى كسر أجزاءه وأتلف صنعه انفعالا لعجز الصورة عن النطق مع تمام التمثيل في الخلقة.

١٥،١٥ فما عسى أن يكون مقدار هذه اللذة التي ذهبت باللب وأذهلت العقل؟ وما بالك بالطبيب الذي يشاهد أجسام الأحياء وقد استخلصها من شوائب الأمراض وطهرها من آفاق العاهات، وردّ نظام الخلقة إلى أصله وأعاد التركيب إلى حسن شكله؟ لكن الذين يذهلون عن فضل صناعتهم وينحطون بها إلى درجة الباعة والمكارين لا يرون فيها إلا أحبولة لصيد الدرهم واقتناء الدينار بقطع النظر عن إيفائها حقها والسعي وراء اتقانها، وما أرى فرقا بين نظرة الطبيب إلى مريضه يتمنى له طول المرض ليزداد أجره وبين المرتزقين من دفن الموتى الذين يتمنون كثرة الموت لتيسير الرزق. وممّا يدلّك على أنّ أمثال هؤلاء لا يهمهم إلا منافعهم الخاصة ما تراه من محاولتهم الاشتغال بكثير من أعمال الدنيا دون الاقتصار على ممارسة الطب المنتسبين إليه، وما ذلك إلا لتوسيع موارد الرزق وشدة الطمع فيُهملون صناعتهم ولا يهتدون إلى ما فيها من تلك اللذة العالية فيغلطون ويخطئون ويجعلون الطب والأطباء مضغة في الأفواه. وتالله ما يحزنني في الدنيا شيء هو أصدق ما يكون وأشد ما يؤلم مثل قولهم «كثيرًا ما يكون مرض المريض من طب الطبيب».

١٦،١٥ قال عيسى بن هشام: فاقتنعت بكلام هذا الطبيب وتوسمت فيه الخير لصاحبي. وتمنيت أن لو كان كل أطبائنا على شاكلته، وقد أرشدني إلى المكان الذي يجب أن يذهب إليه المريض لتغيير الهواء فيه وأوضح أنواع الأغذية والأشربة وترتيب أوقاتها ثمّ انصرف على أن لا نقطع عنه أخبار المريض إلى تمام الشفاء.

smashing it with his chisel till it fell in pieces. His wonderful creation ceased to exist because he was so upset that his perfect creation was unable to speak.

What must have been the level of pleasure that led this man to lose his mind and destroy his common sense? Compare that with the feelings a doctor will have as he watches human bodies being cured of diseases and purged of all kinds of malady; things will have been returned to their normal condition and the person's constitution restored to balance. However those doctors who ignore the nobility of their profession and reduce it to the level of mere vendors and tricksters simply regard it as a means to make money with no consideration of the obligation to fulfill its mission and to perform its tasks as well as possible. I can see no essential difference between the doctor who examines a patient and decides to prolong the treatment as a means of making more money, and gravediggers who hope for as many dead people as possible in order to increase their revenue. One of the things that illustrates the behavior of such doctors and their exclusive concern with their own interests is that they spend a lot of time on worldly matters to the exclusion of the practice of their own specialized field in medicine. The only reason is that they want to broaden their revenue sources and earn more money. As a result they ignore their own profession and fail to trace a path toward its loftier compensations. They are wrong, and all they manage to do is to turn medicine and doctors into something to chew on. By God, there is nothing in this world that saddens me as much as what is both utterly true and at the same time painful, namely when people say that "when a patient's ill, it's often the doctor's treatment that's at fault." 15.15

ʿĪsā ibn Hishām said: I was completely convinced by what this doctor had to say and was optimistic about his treatment of my friend. I only wished that all doctors could be like him. He had advised me about the best place for the invalid to go to get a change of air and had designated the most appropriate food and drink and the best times to consume them. He then departed, but not before asking to stay in touch with the Pāshā until he was completely cured. 15.16

مصباح الشرق ٥٧، ١ يوليو ١٨٩٩

١،١٦ قال عيسى بن هشام: فاستخرت الله في السفر كما وصف الطبيب وأمر نلتمس برء الداء بتبديل الهواء ونيل الشفاء باعتزال مواقف القضاء. واخترت للباشا من مدينة الإسكندرية قصرًا ذا روضة غناء، في بقعة فيحاء، لا تسمع فيها إلا هديل الورقاء، إيقاعا على هدير الماء، إذا ابتل هناك بالماء جناح النسيم، ورفرف به على ذلك الروض البسيم، نثره دارا على تيجان الأزاهر، ورقرقه دموعا في أحداق العباهر، فيتمنى العاشق لو استعار هذه لمحاجره، يستلين بها قلب هاجره، وتود الغانية لو نظمت ذاك عقدًا لنحرها أو نطاقا لخصرها:

إنّ هذا المكان شيء عجيب
تضحك الأرض من بكاء السماء
ذهب حيث ما ذهبنا ودر
حيث درنا وفضة في الفضاء

٢،١٦ أو هو المجرة قامت فيه زواهر الزهر، مقام الكواكب الزهر، وعناقيد الكروم، مقام ثريا النجوم، وأنوار الأثمار، مقام الشموس والأقمار. فأقمنا هناك في راحة وإيناس، معتزلين عن الناس، ولا راحة في الدنيا إلا لمن تزهّد، ولا سلامة من الخلق إلا لمن اعتزل وتوحد، وأقرب الناس إلى كرم السجايا أبعدهم من معاشرة البرايا:

بعدي عن الناس برء من سقامهم
وقربهم للحجى والدين أدواء
كالبيت أفرد لا إيطاء يدركه
ولا سناد ولا في اللفظ أقواء

٣،١٦ وما كاد طيب الإقامة يعيد إلى الباشا العافية والسلامة حتى راعنا شيطان من الإنس بخبر الطاعون، فقلنا إنا لله وإنا إليه راجعون، ما زلنا نعلل النفس بزوال النحس والنكس، وما زالت تناوحنا النوائب والأحزان عند كل منزل ومكان، وقلنا

Miṣbāḥ al-sharq 57, June 1, 1899[114]

16.1 ʿĪsā ibn Hishām said: So in compliance with the decree of Fate, we decided to take a trip. The idea was to give the Pāshā a chance to recover from his illness by having a change of air. We stayed in a mansion in the suburbs of Alexandria with lush gardens. It was set in a sweet-smelling district. The only sound to be heard was the cooing of wood pigeons; when they sang, their song was in harmony with the rippling water. When the billows moistened the edge of the breeze and hovered over that smiling meadow, they scattered drops of water like pearls on the flowery diadems and bathed the eyes of the narcissus in tears. Lovers would have craved to borrow those tears and put them on their own eyelids so that they could soften the heart of their coy and distant beloved. Young girls would love to use pearls to make a necklace for their neckline or a belt for their waists.

This place is an object of wonder;
the earth laughs at heaven's tears.
Gold wherever we go, pearls
wherever we turn, and silver in the sky.[115]

16.2 Rather liken it to the Milky Way, where bright flowers have taken the place of glittering stars, clusters of vines the place of the Pleiades, and gleaming fruits the place of suns and moons.

So we stayed in this place, secluded from the world of people; for in this world there can be no peace save in the ascetic life, no escape from mankind except through seclusion and privacy. The most noble of people are those furthest from contact with mankind.

My very separation from people saves me contamination
whereas their proximity infects both mind and faith.
Just as a line of poetry, if left on its own,
cannot be affected by common faults.[116]

16.3 This pleasant sojourn would have led to my friend's complete recovery if the very devil in human form had not terrified us with the news of a plague. We reflected that all God's creatures are in His hands (glory and praise to Him). We kept nursing our soul's ills through an avoidance of disaster and misfortune, and yet calamities and griefs seemed to beset us wherever we went.

قد وجب الفرار من قدر الله إلى قدر الله، وسبحان من إذا أراد الحسنى بعبده امتحنه وابتلاه. فقفلنا للرجوع، وودّعنا محاسن تلك الربوع، وعدنا إلى حيث يطمئن علينا الصاحب والقريب، ولا يرجف بنا الحاسد والمريب. وكان مكاننا من القطار بجانب مكان النظار وقد حجبنا الليل عن الأنظار، فكشف لنا عن مكنون الأسرار، فسمعنا قائلاً منهم يقول بلسان غير عضب ولا مصقول:

٤،١٦ «تالله ليس ينفع التوقي من المخاوف والتحرز من الأخطار، لقد عشت زمناً وأنا بين خوف ورعب من ذكر حرب السودان حتى وضعت أوزارها، والحمد لله وأنا سليم الجسم معافى البدن، وقضيت مدتها متسلياً مستريضاً في منازه أوربا، متروحاً متشمّماً في حمامات كرلسباد، ولم يزعجني فيها من شيء سوى ذلك المكاتب الذي سألني ما ليس لي به علم حتى إذا اطمأنّ منا الخاطر في هذا العام من كل حادث فظيع وخطب مريع جاءنا هذا الطاعون في أوقات لا تمكننا حوادثها من المسارعة إلى الرحيل من هذه الديار حتى ولا من الابتعاد عن مهبطه في مدينة الإسكندرية. فلولا نازلة القضاء الشرعي ما أصبحنا مثل مكوك الحائك يزج بنا بين البلدين جيئة وذهابا، ويشهد الله أنني أفضل الآن أن أكون قائداً للجيش في السودان أروح وأغدو فوق ظهر الجواد بين الصفوف تحت سعير الحرب على هذا الترامي على هذا الموت في أيام السلم، فإنّ في ذلك من الفخر والمجد واكتساب الحمد واغتنام الغنائم ما يهوّن على النفس من هول الوقف، ولكن ما الذي يهوّن علينا اليوم موقفنا في مشروع المحكمة الشرعية ورمينا بأنفسنا في مخالب الطاعون وإن كان فيه شيء من الفخر فقد غلبنا عليه ناظر الخارجية واستبدّ به دوننا وتركنا منه صفر اليدين».

٥،١٦ ناظر الخارجية تعالى الله، ما هذا الفخر الذي يزعم ناظر الحربية أني نلته، وما أعلم إلا أنني خسرت بهذا المشروع جميع ما صرفت عمري في ادخاره من اجتلاب مودة المسلمين نحوي وائتلاف قلوبهم عليّ وحسن ثقتهم بي، وأصبحوا يرمونني بالتعرض لأمورهم الشرعية وتلك التي كنت أحاذرها وأتقيها منذ مبدأ أمري إلى اليوم، وما كان أغناني عن مثل هذا الموقف لو أنّ ناظر الحقانية أنصفني من نفسه

We told ourselves that we had to flee from one of God's decrees to another, He being the One who tests His servants when He wishes for them a good outcome.

So we set out to return to Cairo after saying farewell to this beautiful spot. We knew that we could trust our friends and relatives who lived in the capital and that no jealous snoopers would be able to spread any false rumors there. We sat down in the train compartment next to some ministers, but, as it was nighttime, it was very dark and so we were able to hear their innermost secrets. As the train took us back to Cairo, we listened to their conversation. One of them was saying things neither contentious nor polished.

16.4

MINISTER OF WAR By God, in the face of these worries and dangers all precautions are useless! I've been living on my nerves throughout the Sudanese campaign till it came to an end. Thank God I'm still safe and sound. I've spent the entire time in Europe, taking exercise and having a wonderfully relaxing time in Karlsbad. That aggravating newspaper reporter who kept asking me questions about things I knew nothing about was the only thing that bothered me while I was there.[117] But now, just when I've recovered from such dreadful perils, the plague has struck at a time when we can't leave the country or even get out of Alexandria where it's struck. If it weren't for this terrible judicial situation, we wouldn't find ourselves being shunted backwards and forwards between two towns like some weaver's shuttle. God is my witness that at this point I'd rather be in command of the army in the Sudan, riding to and fro along the ranks in the heat of battle, than be subjected to death by the plague in peacetime. At least in war, there is pride and glory to be won, not to mention decorations and booty, all of which lessens the impact of the dangerous situation. But what is there to make our situation with regard to this Shariah Court project easier to swallow? How can the risk of catching the plague be made even bearable? If there's any prestige to be gained, then it's the Foreign Minister who has got it all for himself while leaving us all empty-handed.

16.5

FOREIGN MINISTER By God Almighty, tell me, what's this prestige I'm supposed to have acquired? All I know is that I've lost everything I've spent my entire life cultivating, namely the trust and affections of Muslims and their continuing favor towards me. Now they've started accusing me of interfering in their judicial affairs, something I was careful to avoid from the moment I took office. I could have avoided the entire situation if the Minister of Justice

فتحمّل العبء كله على عاتقه، ولا عتب للمسلمين عليه لما هو مشهور به بينهم من الورع والتقوى والصلاح والنسك.

ناظر الحربية إن لم يكن في الأمر إلا أنك قمت في آخر أمرك خطيباً مفوهاً في مجلس الأمة المصرية لم يرتج عليك ولم تحصر ولم تتوقف ولم تتلعثم لكفاك ذلك فخراً في دنياك.

ناظر الخارجية وهل ترى من فخر لمن يقوم متكلماً بين أعضاء مجلس شورى القوانين.

ناظر الخارجية أرى في هذا الموقف موقف الخطيب منتهى الفخر ومجتمع المجد وكثيراً ما يشبّهونه بموقف الحرب لشدة أهواله، وأنا وإن لم أجرّب الحرب فقد جرّبت ما يشيب له الوليد يوم اندفعت أتكلم في الجمعية العمومية بكلمتين عن مشروع الضرائب فلا أدري وأيم الله إلى الآن من شدة ما اعتراني من الذهول إن كنت تكلمت في الموضوع أو خرجت عنه وانصرفت عن ذلك المكان وأنا أشد ما سخط إنسان على نفسه لولا أن خفض علي من أمري أحد الذين يتفرغون للقراءة والاطّلاع على نوادر الأزمان الماضية فقصّ عليَّ عدة وقائع مضحكة لأكابر الخطباء في هذا الباب أذكرها لك لتعلم مقدار نعمة الله عليك إذ نجّاك وأنقذك من الوقوع في مثلها يوم كنت أنت تخطب وأنا أشفق عليك وأعرق لك. ٦،١٦

لمّا حصر عبد الله بن عامر بن كريز على المنبر بالبصرة وكان خطيباً مشهوراً شقّ عليه ذلك فقال له زياد ابن أبيه وكان خلفه: «أيها الأمير لا تجزع فلو أقمت على المنبر عامة من ترى من الناس أصابهم أكثر ممّا أصابك» فلمّا كانت الجمعة تأخر عبد الله بن عامر وقال زياد للناس: إنّ الأمير اليوم موعوك، فقيل لرجل من وجوه أمراء القبائل قم فاصعد المنبر، فلمّا صعد حصر فقال الحمد لله الذي يرزق هؤلاء وبقي ساكتاً فأنزلوه وأصعدوا آخر من الوجوه، فلمّا استوى قائماً قابل بوجهه الناس فوقعت عينه على صلعة رجل فقال: «أيها الناس إنّ هذا الأصلع قد منعني الكلام اللّٰهم فالعن هذه الصلعة» فأنزلوه وقالوا لوازع اليشكري: قم إلى المنبر فتكلم، فلمّا صعد ٧،١٦

had treated me fairly. He could have taken the entire burden on his shoulders. Such is his piety, devoutness, probity, and asceticism that no Muslim would ever think of criticizing him.

MINISTER OF WAR If all you did was to stand up at the conclusion of your period in office and speak eloquently in the Egyptian parliament without being at a loss for something to say or faltering, then that alone would be enough to satisfy your quest for prestige during your earthly life.

FOREIGN MINISTER What kudos can you see in getting up to speak in front of the members of the Legislative Council?

16.6 MINISTER OF WAR I regard the art of oration as being a very glorious and praiseworthy profession. People often associate it with war because of the perilous situations both involve. Even though I've never had any experience of war myself, I've still gone through things which would turn your hair grey. When I was saying a few words in the general assembly about taxes, I got so completely distracted that, to this day, I don't know whether I kept to the point or not. As I left the building, I would have been thoroughly annoyed with myself if someone who specializes in the study of anecdotes from past eras had not provided some consolation by telling me a number of amusing tales about great orators. I'll tell you some of them now, and then you'll realize God's kindness to you in saving you from similar situations when you got up to make a speech and I felt so sorry for you.

16.7 When ʿAbdallāh ibn ʿĀmir ibn Karīz, a renowned homilist, faltered while standing in the minbar in Basra, he was upset. Ziyād ibn Abīhi who was standing behind him told him, "Do not worry, amir. If I put some of the ordinary folk up there first, they would be even worse off than you." When Friday came, ʿAbdallāh was late, and so Ziyād told the people that he was indisposed. One of the prominent tribal amirs was told to go up; when he reached the top, he was lost for words and said, "Praise be to God who feeds these folk," and then stood there in silence. They brought him down and sent up another prominent person. Once he was finally in place, he turned towards the people and spotted a bald head. "People," he said, "this bald-headed man has prevented me from speaking, so God curse his bald pate!" So they brought him down too and told Wāziʿ al-Yashkurī to go up and address the assembly. When he got up there and saw all the people, he said, "People, I was reluctant to come to the Friday prayer today, but my wife forced me to do so; I call you to witness that she is

ورأى الناس قال: «أيها الناس إني كنت اليوم كارهاً لحضور الجمعة ولكن امرأتي حملتني على إتيانها وأنا أشهدكم أنها طالق ثلاثا» فقال زياد لعبد الله بن عامر: كيف رأيت؟ قم فاخطب الناس.

٨،١٦ وخطب مصعب بن حيان خطبة زواج فحصر فقال: «لقنوا موتاكم لا إله إلا الله» فقالت له أم الجارية: «عجّل الله موتك» وخطب مروان بن الحكم فحصر فقال: «اللّهم إنا نحمدك ونستعينك ونشكرك بك».

فكيف تنكر أيها الناظر ما نلته من الفخر والمجد ولم تقع في مثل ما وقع فيه أشياخ العرب أرباب الفصاحة وملوك الكلام؟ وما أخال إلا أنّ مومياء الملوك من أجدادك الفراعنة كانت تهتز في المتحف طربا يوم وقوفك ذلك الموقف، فإنهم إن كانوا امتازوا عن العالم بجر الأثقال في تشييد الجبال فما كانوا يتصورون أنهم يفوقون أمّة العرب بمثلك في فن الخطابة فوق أعواد المنابر.

ناظر الخارجية دعنا بالله من هذا الهزل وخذ بنا في الجد ولنلتفت إلى ما يقوله ناظر الحقانية.

٩،١٦ ناظر الحقانية وإني لأعجب والله من الأستاذ شيخ الجامع كيف ينكر عليّ ما أتيته في هذا المشروع ويرميني بمخالفة الشرع، وما وقفت على الشرع إلا منه وما تلقيت دروسي فيه إلا عنه ولست أحمل له مع ذلك ضغناً في صدري فإنّ انحرافه اليوم عني أشبه بما كان يتكلفه معنا معاشر تلامذته لتأديبنا في الدرس ثمّ لا يلبث أن ينكشف غضبه ويذهب انحرافه ويعود معنا إلى أحسن ما كان من الرضا. وكلما تذكرت تلك الأيام أيام الصبا والدرس في حضرته شغلني الحنو إليها عن التكدر الآن منه، على أنني لم آت شيئاً فرياً، فهذه شروط القضاء بين أيديهم أقرأها عليكم كما نقلتها من كتبهم لتحكموا إن كنت خالفت الشرع كما يزعمون.

١٠،١٦ إنّ أهله (أي القضاء) أهل الشهادة «كذا في الحواشي السعدية» وشروط الشهادة هي الإسلام والعقل والبلوغ والحرية وعدم العمى والحد في قذف، كلها شروط لصحة توليته ولصحة حكمه بعدها.

divorced three times." At that, Ziyād turned to ʿAbdallāh ibn ʿĀmir. "Do you see what I mean?" he said. "Now go up there and address the people."

16.8 Muṣʿab ibn Ḥayyān was giving a wedding sermon when he faltered. "Remember your dead; there is no God but He," he said on the spur of the moment. "May God hasten your death too," the bride's mother retorted. Similarly, when Marwān ibn al-Ḥakam faltered while delivering a sermon, he said: "O God, we praise You, seek refuge with You, and we offer You thanks."

And so, Minister, since you haven't encountered the same kind of problems as these prominent figures from Arab history who were masters of rhetoric and the spoken word, how can you deny that you've achieved a good deal of prestige and distinction. On the day you adopted your position on this matter, I can only imagine that the mummies of the Pharaohs, your ancestors, were quivering with delight. And even though their fame may have rested on getting people to drag huge stones around and erect artificial mountains, I'm sure they never imagined that, with someone like your eminent self in mind, they could surpass the Arabs in the rhetorical art delivered from the wooden portals of the minbar.

Foreign Minister Stop this sarcasm and let's be serious. What about what the Minister of Justice was saying?

16.9 Minister of Justice I'm amazed that the Shaykh Professor of al-Azhar has rejected the ideas I've put forward for this project and accused me of acting contrary to the Shariah. Everything I know about the subject I've learned from him; I studied with him and bear him no grudge. After all, the way he's behaving now is just like the way he behaved when we were students as a way of reprimanding us. It wasn't long before his anger and disapproval disappeared, and he was kind and sympathetic to us again. Every time I recall those days of my youth and the lessons I took with him, I long to be back there; and that takes my mind off his feelings towards me at the moment. Even so, I've done nothing unprecedented. I'll read out to you now the stipulations for the office of judge just as I've copied them directly from their books. Then you can decide whether or not I've contravened the Shariah as they claim I have:

16.10 "People eligible for the position of judge are those who are entitled to testify as witnesses as it says in *al-Ḥawāshī al-Saʿdiyyah*; other qualifications for such people are adherence to Islam, intelligence, eloquence, freedom, non-blindness, and avoidance of slander.[118] These are all conditions for the acceptability of his appointment and also of his jurisdiction thereafter."

هذه هي شروط القضاء، ولا ينكر أحد وجودها في قضاء الاستئناف، ومن الذي يدّعي أنّ القاضيين المنتدبين منه أحدهما مشرك أو مجنون مثلا والآخر عبد أو أعمى حتى لا يتم فيه شرط القضاء.

فإن أبوا إلا أن يحكموا عليهما بالفسق مع ذلك رددنا عليهم بما جاء في كتب الشرع وهو «أنّ الفاسق أهلها (للشهادة) فيكون أهلّه (للقضاء) لكنه لا يقلد وجوبًا ويأثم مقلده وقيده في القاعدية بما إذا غلب على ظنه صدقه فليحفظ (در)».

وأنا مستعد لقبول ذلك الإثم راض به لنفسي فما لهم وللمعارضة وما لهم وللفضول بعد ذلك على أنهم إذا قلبوا الصحيفة من هذا الكتاب وجدوا فيه ما نصه «واستثنى الثاني الفاسق ذا الجاه والمروة فإنه يجب قبول شهادته بزازيه قال في النهر وعليه فلا يأثم أيضاً بتوليته القضاء حيث كان كذلك».

ومن يقول أنّ قضاة الاستئناف ليسوا بذوي جاه ولا مروة، فإن اعترضوا علينا ١١،١٦ بأنّ المحكمة العليا ليس اختصاصها القضاء وحده بل الإفتاء أيضاً، ويجب على المفتي أن يكون عالما بالراجح والمرجوح والقوي والضعيف من القول المشهور في مذهب أبي حنيفة، وأنّ هذه الشروط لا تتوفر في قضاة الاستئناف لا سيما وهم يرمونهم بالفسق ويستشهدون على ذلك بقولهم «والفاسق لا يصلح مفتيا لأنّ الفتوى من أمور الدين والفاسق لا يقبل قوله في الديانات قاله ابن مالك وزاد العيني واختاره كثير من المتأخرين وجزم به صاحب المجمع في متنه» وفاتهم أنّ صاحب الدر المختار زاد بعد ذكره لهذه العبارة قوله «وقيل نعم يصلح وبه جزم في الكنز لأنه يجتهد حذار نسبة الخطأ ولا خلاف في اشتراط إسلامه وعقله وشرط بعضهم تيقظه لا حريته وذكورته ونطقه فيصح إفتاء الأخرس»؟

No one denies that Court of Appeal judges fulfill these stipulations regarding the qualifications for judge. Who can claim that either of the two representative judges from that court is either a polytheist, insane, a slave, or blind, or anything else which would disqualify him from holding the office of judge? While they have insisted on accusing the two judges of immorality, our retort has come from the very same law books, namely that "the immoral person is still qualified to testify, so he is also qualified to be a judge. However, it should not be compulsory, and anyone who installs a judge in that way commits a sin. The *al-Qāʿidiyyah* chooses to restrict this point to a situation in which the appointer deems him to be truthful. So let this be memorized. [*Al-Durr*]."[119]

I am personally quite happy to accept this notion of sin, but why are they so opposed to the general idea? Why do they keep fussing when, if they turn the page in the very same volume, they'll find the following passage: "The second authority makes an exception for the immoral person who has both status and virtue. His testimony must be accepted." From the *Bazzāziyyah*, while in the *Nahr* we find "accordingly, he is not considered to be committing a crime if he appoints a person judge in such a condition."[120]

16.11 The people who keep arguing that the judges of the Court of Appeal are neither prestigious nor courteous object that the highest court in the land does not just pass judgments but also issues fatwas. They note that the mufti must be well versed in both the preferable and the acceptable, the weak and the strong, principles well known in the Ḥanafī school of law. These stipulations, they say, are not satisfied by the Court of Appeal judges, particularly since they're accusing them of depravity and backing up their statements with the following text: "The sinner will not be a good mufti because fatwas are religious matters and the sinner's word cannot be accepted on such matters," as Ibn Malak duly noted, amplified by Al-ʿAynī, followed by a number of recent scholars, and specifically stipulated by the author of *Al-Majmaʿ*.

However, these people fail to recall that the author of *Al-Durr al-mukhtār* cites this phrase and then goes on to say: "Yes indeed, it is valid. In the *Kanz* there is an authoritative statement that offers an individual judgment on the relative nature of the fault involved.[121] There can be no disagreement about such a person's Islamic faith nor his intellect. Some scholars make alertness a criterion, but not freedom, being male, or ability to speak. Thus a speech-impaired person may issue a fatwa."

وأنتم تعلمون والحمد لله أنّ قضاة الاستئناف كلهم يفضلون الخرس فكيف لا يصح إفتاؤهم إن صحّ إفتاء الأخراس.

١٢،١٦ إلى أن يقول صاحب الدر «ويفتي القاضي ولو في مجلس القضاء وهو الصحيح ويأخذ القاضي كالمفتي بقول أبي حنيفة على الإطلاق ثمّ بقول أبي يوسف ثمّ بقول محمد ثمّ بقول زفر والحسن بن زياد وهو الأصح منية وسراجية» انتهى منقولاً من شرح الدر.

فيتضح من جميع ما قرأته عليكم أنهم إذا كانوا قد جعلوا لشروط القضاء هي شروط الشهادة المذكورة آنفاً فإنها متوفرة في أهل الاستئناف ولا يعارضهم فيها معارض، وإن كانوا أباحوا للقاضي الفتوى كالمفتي بقول أبي حنيفة على الإطلاق فقد خرج بهذا الإطلاق الراجح والمرجوح والقوي والضعيف. وأظنّ أنّ قضاة الاستئناف هم أوّل الناس محاذرة من الوقوع في الخطأ، والمرجح في عدم الخطأ هو مراجعة كتب الفقه، وقد تعوّد أهل الاستئناف كثرة الرجوع إليها في حكمهم بالقوانين الوضعية حتى لقد تجاوز بعضهم مذهب أبي حنيفة إلى مذهب مالك والشافعي وابن حنبل، فإذا تقيدوا في المحكمة الشرعية بمذهب أبي حنيفة وحده توفر عليهم تعدد المراجعة في المذاهب الأخرى وتفرغوا للتمكن من مذهب أبي حنيفة والتعمق فيه.

١٣،١٦ ومع ذلك فما لنا ولهذا كله بعد أن كانوا يكتفون منذ زمن غير بعيد بتلقين من يتولى القضاء من الجاهلين بأحكام الشرع هذه العبارة «البيّنة على من ادّعى واليمين على من أنكر» ويعتبرونها شرطاً جامعاً لصحة توليته ويعتذرون عن جهله للأحكام بأنّ العمدة فيها على المفتي، فإذا كان المفتي عالماً جاز التجاوز عندهم عن جهل القاضي وعدم توفر شروط القضاء فيه ونسوا أنّ المرحوم إبراهيم باشا ولّى المرحوم الشيخ العباسي وظيفة الإفتاء وهو في حلقة الدرس غير متجاوز السابعة عشرة من عمره، واعتذروا إذ ذاك بأنّ أمين الفتوى عالم متضلع من المذهب يقوم له بتنسيق الفتوى وما عليه إلا ختمها. وهم لا ينكرون علينا أنّ القاضيين المنتدبين حرسهما الله قد تجاوزا هذا السن وهما ليسا بمنفردين بالفتوى في انتدابهما بل معهما ثلاثة من فحول العلماء الشرعيين

Now, thanks be to God, you are all aware that the judges of the Court of Appeal all prefer to be dumb. So how can their fatwas have no validity if such people are allowed to pronounce them?

16.12 The author of *Al-Durr* goes on to say: "The judge can issue a fatwa even in a court of law, and it is still valid. In so doing, the judge in his role as mufti is exactly following the dictum of Abū Ḥanīfah, then Abū Yūsuf, then Muḥammad al-Shaybānī, then Zufar and al-Ḥasan ibn Ziyād who is the most authoritative and enlightened." Here ends the extract from *Al-Durr*.

It seems abundantly clear from what I've just read to you that, if these people are using such passages as those I have just read to you as criteria, then the Court of Appeal judges are fully qualified and no one can object. If they have authorized the judge to issue fatwas as a mufti, following the dictum of Abū Ḥanīfah without exception, then the criteria of "preferable and acceptable, weak and strong" have to be subsumed as well. Of all judges, I am inclined to believe that those of the Court of Appeal are the most cautious about committing errors. In avoiding mistakes, the most plausible method is to consult books on law. The Court of Appeal judges are so completely accustomed to basing their judgments on positive law that they go beyond the Ḥanafī school by itself and also consult works of the Malakī, Shāfiʿī, and Ḥanbalī schools too. And so, if they find themselves restricted to the Ḥanafī code in the Shariah Court, they'll be able to make use of their knowledge of the other schools and devote their attentions to mastering the Ḥanafī code.

16.13 But even apart from such considerations as these, what is the point of all this fuss? Not long ago, when they were training people who had no familiarity with the Shariah yet were to be appointed judge, they were quite happy to make use of the following phrase: "Evidence is required of a claimant; oaths are needed in a case of denial." They would regard that phrase as an all-encompassing rubric to justify the appointment and then excuse his ignorance of the Shariah by saying that the onus was on the mufti. If the mufti was learned, they said, one could overlook the fact that the judge was ignorant and didn't meet the criteria needed for his judicial position. In saying this, they apparently forgot that the late Ibrāhīm Pāshā appointed Shaykh al-ʿAbbāsī as mufti when that latter was still a student and was only seventeen. On that occasion, the excuse they gave was that the mufti's secretary was a scholar who was completely familiar with Ḥanafī legal practice and could draw up the fatwas; all the mufti himself had to do was put his seal on it. They can't deny that the

يزدان بهم صدر المحكمة الشرعية وهم يقومون للقاضيين المنتدبين مقام أمين الفتوى لدى المرحوم الشيخ العباسي حتى ينبغا بينهم في الشرع كما نبغ هذا العلامة فصار من أعظم العلماء الذين يعز بهم الدين وتفتخر البلاد بذكرهم.

١٤،١٦ ناظر الخارجية تبارك اسم الله الفتاح الوهاب، من أين لك هذا العلم وهذه الحجج الدامغة؟ لقد كدت والله تزري بنفسي في عيني، وأين كانت منك هذه الأدلة الساطعة يوم كنّا نجادل أعضاء مجلس شورى

القوانين في المشروع؟

ناظر الحقانية ليس لي فيها من فضل معدود، وغاية ما في الأمر أني رجعت إلى دروسي أمام الأستاذ شيخ الجامع فألقيتها إليكم كما تلقيتها عنه.

ناظر المالية شهد الله أنني ما فهمت شيئاً ممّا تقولون إلا بمقدار ما أفهم العبرانية واللاتينية، وجل ما أعلمه في باب المشروع أنّ القاضي عظم في عيني حتى تخيلته أكبر زاهد في العالم لما أقدم عليه من الاستهانة بالمال والرضا بالخسارة في اعتزال المنصب، ولا شك أنكم تدهشون معي إذا حسبت لكم مبلغ خسارته فأقول أنّ مرتبه ١٨٠٠ جنيه في السنة، وقد بلغت مدة خدمته إلى الآن تسع سنوات ادّخر فيها ١٦٢٠٠، وإذا فرضنا أنه يبقى ست سنوات في الخدمة كان مجموع ما يكتنزه ٢٧٠٠٠ جنيه، فإذا أضفنا إلى ذلك ربع المعاش الذي يستحقه بعد تلك المدة وهو ٤٥٠ جنيهاً في السنة، وفرضنا أنه استبدله على سن ٧٥ سنة يكون ما يخصه ٦٧٥٠ جنيهاً وحينئذ يجتمع لديه من المال بعد تلك الست سنوات ٣٣٧٥٠ جنيهاً. إذا اشترى بها أطياناً واستغلها عشر سنوات تحصل لديه مثل ثمنها فإذا باعها أصبح صاحب مائة ألف جنيه تقريباً، يشتغل بها في مشترى الأسهم، وأنتم تعلمون ما ربح الأسهم، فلا يمضي عليه بضع سنوات حتى يصبح صاحب مليون من الجنيهات. فقولوا لي بالله من ذا الذي يجود في دنياه بمليون لبخله بتحريك شفتيه بكلمة يقولها للقاضيين المنتدبين مثل قولك «أذنتكما».

two judges from the Court of Appeal—may God watch over them!—who have been delegated are certainly over seventeen years old and aren't the only ones who will be giving fatwas; indeed they will have with them three paragons of Shariah scholarship whose presence embellishes the bench of the Shariah Court. These luminaries can fulfill the same function with their Court of Appeal colleagues as the secretary did with Shaykh al-ʿAbbāsī. Then the two judges will be able to show their prowess in legal matters just as this great sage did in earlier times, becoming one of the most illustrious religious scholars, someone to be respected in his religion and celebrated by his countrymen.

MINISTER OF WAR Blessed be the name of God the Opener, the Provider! Where have you acquired such learning and such an impressive array of arguments? By God, you've put me to shame. But where were these trenchant arguments on the day when we were arguing before the Legislative Council about this project? 16.14

MINISTER OF JUSTICE There's nothing particularly extraordinary about it. I simply went back to my studies with the Shaykh of al-Azhar. I conveyed it to you just as he did.

MINISTER OF FINANCE God is my witness that it might just as well have been in Hebrew or Latin for all I understood of it. Here's the gist of what I know about this project: judges have a revered position, so much so that I looked on them as the world's greatest ascetics for the way in which they belittled money and were prepared to take a loss when they retired. I'm sure you'll be as amazed as I was when I tell you what it is that they lose. The judge's salary is 1,800 pounds a year; with nine years' service, he can make 16,200 pounds. Supposing that he stays in the service for six years more, he can save 27,000 pounds. Add to that a quarter of his salary to which he's entitled after this length of service (450 pounds a year) and assume that he'll convert it at the age of seventy-five, his share will be 6,750 pounds. Thus, in those six years, he'll collect a total of 33,750 pounds. If he uses that to buy land and invests it for ten years, he should get a similar amount in return. If he sells the land, he has almost one hundred thousand pounds which he can use to buy shares. You all know what profits can be made there; within a few years, he can have a million pounds. Tell me, by God, how can anyone who owns a million be so stingy when it comes to saying one simple word to the two nominated judges: "Admitted"?

قال عيسى بن هشام: وما وقف عند هذه الكلمة حتى وقف بنا الوابور في محطة القاهرة. ١٦،١٥

وذهبت بالباشا إلى البيت فتركته هناك وتوجهت إلى أحد أصحابي لبعض أشغالي فوجدته يتأهب للخروج، فلمّا بدأت بمفاتحته في ما حضرت لأجله أغلظ عليّ بالتوجه معه أوّلاً إلى المحفل الماسوني لحضور احتفال فيه، فاضطررت إلى مطاوعته فوصلنا فوجدت جمعاً عظيماً، وفي وسطه حلقة من قضاة الاستئناف يتذاكرون حديث المشروع والانتداب فأصغيت لهم فسمعت أحدهم يقول:

أحد القضاة إلى متى الصبر على هؤلاء الشرعيين وطعنهم علينا ورميهم لنا بالكفر تارة والفسق أخرى كأنهم احتكروا دين الله على أنفسهم يخرجون منه من شاؤوا ويدخلون فيه من أرادوا، وما علمنا أنّ في الإسلام ما في غيره من الأديان من تحريم قوم لقوم وإمساك المغفرة عن آخرين ووسعت رحمة ربك كل شيء. وهم يشترطون اليوم على من يقبلونه منا بينهم أن يبادر إلى التوبة وأن يجدّد إسلامه وأن يلبس العمامة ويرسل اللحية ولا يحمل ساعة من ذهب ولا يشرب في إناء من فضة، وفي أمثالهم يقول القائل:

يحرم شرب الماء في فضة
ويشرب الفضة إن نالها

وإنّا لنحمد الله على نور العلم الذي أخرجنا من زمرتهم وكشف عنّا غطاءنا فبصرنا اليوم حديد.

قاض ثان وأعجب ما في الأمر أنّ هؤلاء الذين يكفّروننا ويفسقوننا ولا يقبلون شهادتنا ويقولون عنّا أنّا نحكم بغير ما أنزل الله هم أنفسهم الذين يصدّعوننا في كل حين بالرجاء والالتماس للفصل في قضاياهم وقضايا ذويهم بنفس هذا القانون الذي يكفّروننا من أجله فيقبلون قضاءه داعين شاكرين. ١٦،١٦

ʿĪsā ibn Hishām said: At this point, the train reached Cairo Station. I went home with the Pāshā and left him there. I went to see one of my friends on some business, but found him just on the point of going out. When I began to explain to him my reasons for coming to see him, he told me brusquely to go with him first to a Masonic meeting to attend a party there. I was forced to do as he asked. Eventually we reached the place and found a lot of people there. In the middle of the group was a circle of Court of Appeal judges who were discussing the project and their proposed secondment to the Shariah Court. I listened to what they were talking about and heard one of them say: 16.15

FIRST JUDGE How long are we going to put up with these Shariah Court people? Here they are slandering us and accusing us of apostasy at one moment and immorality at another; it's as if they've got some kind of monopoly on religion and can insert and extract whatever aspects of the law they feel like. As far as I know, Islam is unlike other religions, in that no one's allowed to proscribe other people or to withhold forgiveness from others. God's mercy is wide enough to encompass everything. Today they require those whom they are willing to accept to repent in a hurry, renew their adherence to Islam, put on a turban, grow a beard and not wear a gold watch or drink from a silver vessel. People like them are described in this verse:

He forbids people to drink water from a silver container;
but, if he acquires any silver, he consumes it.[122]

The knowledge which we have allows us to stand apart from their group, thank God. The blinkers have been removed from our eyes and so we can see things in sharper focus.

SECOND JUDGE What amazes me is that the people who keep calling us infidels and sinners, who refuse to accept our testimony and are claiming that, in making judgments, we are not using God's transmitted message, are the very same people who keep bothering us all the time with requests to make categorical decisions on judgments which they and their colleagues have already made, decisions based on the very same law that they're now using to call us infidels. In those cases they're very willing and grateful to accept our judgments! 16.16

قاض ثالث   ولا يفوتنّك أنّ الحق عندنا واحد والقول في الحكم واحد وهم بما أدخلوه على الشرع الشريف الإسلامي الذي لا يتعدد فيه الحق صاروا يحكمون بالأقوال المختلفة من الراجح والمرجوح والقوي والضعيف والمشهور وغير المشهور والقول الذي عليه الفتوى والذي لا يفتى به والخلاف بين الإمام والصاحبين، واختلاف الشارحين وواضعي الحواشي، وحاشا للشرع ثمّ حاشا أن يكون قائماً على هذا التشتيت في الأحكام.

قاض رابع   أشهدكم أيها الإخوان المحترمون أنني لا أقبل انتداب الحكومة لي في المحكمة الشرعية فإنهم سيشيعون عني وعن المنتدب الثاني أنواع الإشاعات من ترك الصلاة وحضور الملاهي والجلوس في القهاوي وما يدخل تحت طي ذلك من سوء السمعة وفساد السيرة.

قاض خامس   أمّا أنا فإذا عرضت الحكومة عليّ الانتداب فلا بدّ أن أشترط عليها أن لا تسمع فيّ قولاً يقال من هذا القبيل.

قاض سادس   أقول لكم الحق أيها الإخوان، إنّ انتداب قاضيين منا ليس من ورائه أقل فائدة لإصلاح المحكمة الشرعية، وما عسانا أن نصلح فيها وعملنا كله هناك في القضاء، ولا عمل لنا في الإدارة، والفساد كل الفساد في الإدارة، وأقرب الطرق عندي في إصلاح المحكمة ليس هو في توجهنا إليها ولكن في انضمامها إلينا.

١٦، ١٧ قال عيسى بن هشام: وضاق عليّ التنفس من الحر وشدة الزحام في المحفل فانتهزت فرصة دخولهم إلى هيكل الاحتفال ونزلت مع أحد أصحابي من أرباب العمائم، ولمّا صرنا في الطريق قال لي: هل لك في أن نقضي جزء من الليل عند الشيخ فلان فقد طال عهدك بزيارته وعنده جمعية من المشايخ مجتمعين في ساحة بيته في مطلق الهواء فرأيت مطاوعته لعلي أقف من المجلس على شيء يطمئن له خاطري في هذا المشروع الذي ما وضعت قدمي في محل إلا ورأيت الأفكار فيه متضاربة والآراء مختلفة. فسرنا حتى وصلنا إليه فوجدنا البيت غاصّاً بجمهور من العلماء الأعلام والمشايخ

THIRD JUDGE Don't forget too that talking about rights is one thing, but judicial authority is something else. They have introduced a number of new concepts into Islamic law where the concept of rights is not quantified. They have started making judgments on the basis of new criteria—probable and preferable, weak and strong, famous and obscure, statements based on a fatwa and others without such a basis, a disagreement between the Imam and the two people bringing the case, or even an inconsistency between the commentators and writers of the marginal notes. Heaven forbid that the Shariah should have to function amid such judicial chaos!

FOURTH JUDGE I hereby vouch to you, my revered colleagues, that I won't accept the nomination to the Shariah Court which the government has offered me. People are spreading all kinds of rumors about me and the other nominees to the position—that we never pray, that we go to nightclubs and sit around in cafés, and indulge in other kinds of debauchery, all of which suggest immoral conduct and ruin our reputation.

FIFTH JUDGE If I'm offered the job, I will certainly stipulate that no such rumors are to be circulated about me.

SIXTH JUDGE My friends, I'm going to tell you the truth: two judges from our court won't be able to do anything about reforming the Shariah Court. What are we supposed to do by way of reform when we already know that everything about it is in a hopeless mess and its administration is rampant with corruption. In my opinion the easiest way to reform the Shariah Court is not for us to move over but rather for the whole court to be incorporated into ours.

16.17 ʿĪsā ibn Hishām told us: It was so hot and crowded in the room that I found it difficult to breathe. When they all left to go into this shrine for socializing, I took the opportunity to leave with one of my turbaned friends.[123] As we were walking along the road, he asked me whether I would like to spend some time that night at a shaykh's house. He reminded me that it was a long time since I had last seen him and that, in any case, he would have a group of shaykhs with him who would be sitting out in the open air in the courtyard of his home. I decided to accept his invitation in case I might hear what the group had to say to ease my anxieties about this project. Wherever I went, people seemed to have different ideas and viewpoints about it. When we reached the house, we found that it was overflowing with shaykhs and religious scholars who

الكرام، والحديث مستفيض بينهم في المشروع، فأخذت مجلسي على ما يقتضيه المجلس من الاحترام، وإذا أحد المتصدرين من العلماء يقول:

١٨،١٦ أحد العلماء رضي الله عن الشيخ شيخ الجامع فقد أحيا السنّة وأمات البدعة وباع الدنيا لأجل الدين، ولم يخسر آخرته بدنياه، ولم تأخذه في الله لومة لائم، ولم يزده الترغيب والترهيب إلا رسوخ قدم في الدفاع عن الشرع الشريف، ولله درّه فقد نفض عنه غبار الوهم فلم يحجم به عن موقفه ذكرى ذلك اليوم المشهور الذي تساقط فيه وبل الرصاص وطله بين محابر الطلبة وكراريسهم. ونحن متحدون معه بحمد الله متضافرون على نصرته، وكلنا في عونه والله في عون العبد ما دام العبد في عون أخيه، وكلنا يد واحدة ويد الله مع الجماعة، والمؤمنون كالبنيان المرصوص يشدّ بعضه بعضاً، قال الله تعالى ﴿إِن تَنصُرُوا اللَّهَ يَنصُرْكُمْ وَيُثَبِّتْ أَقْدَامَكُمْ﴾ وجزى الله الشيخ عن الإسلام خير الجزاء، فقد جدّد فينا ما اندثر من سيرة السلف الصالح، ووقف في الحق أمام ناظر الحقانية المناسترلي موقف أبي حنيفة أمام الخليفة العباسي، والعز بن عبد السلام أمام السلطان الأيوبي، والشيخ المهدي العباسي أمام عباس الأوّل. ولا شكّ أنّ الحكومة ستنتهي بالعجز عن تنفيذ مشروعها لأنها لا تجد بيننا من يستهويه زخرف الدنيا فيبيع آخرته بدنياه، ويقبل منها منصب القضاء.

عالم ثان بخ بخ لك أيها الأستاذ وصدقت فيما تقول فكلنا عند حد قولك في الائتلاف والاتحاد والتعاون على الحكومة حتى يقعد بها العجز دون ما نبتغيه من مصادمة الشرع.

١٩،١٦ قال عيسى بن هشام: ودخل أحد الزائرين وأظنه من كبار المحامين فأخذ يحدق ببصره بين الجالسين كمن ينشد ضالته فاشرأب أحد المشايخ عند رؤيته فاهتدى الزائر إليه فسقط جالساً بجانبه يقول له في أذنه وأنا على مسمع منه:

were discussing the project at great length. I took my place with all the deference which the company demanded. One of the more prominent scholars was talking:

First Scholar God bless the Shaykh of al-Azhar! He's revived the practice of the Prophet and put an end to heresy! He has dispensed with all worldly considerations for the sake of his religion, and by so doing he's not sacrificed the life to come! No one can possibly censure his conduct. Any attempt to prod or intimidate him only reinforces his stance in defense of the Shariah. How wonderful that he's managed to shake off the dust of illusion. He's never flinched, even with the memory in mind of that infamous day when a hail of bullets fell on al-Azhar students with their notebooks and inkwells. Thank God, we're all united and rallying for his success. All of us support him, and God will support his servants as long as they in turn support their brothers. We're all a single hand, and the hand of God is with the community. Believers are like a buttressed building where one part strengthens another. As God Almighty says in the Qur'an: «If you help God, He will help you and plant your feet firmly.»[124] May God give the Shaykh a good reward on behalf of Islam. He's reinvigorated the practices of our pious ancestors that had become defunct. In his stance toward the Minister of Justice al-Manāstirlī he is behaving like Abū Ḥanīfah confronting the Abbasid Caliph, like al-ʿIzz ibn ʿAbd al-Salām with the Ayyūbid Sultan, and like Shaykh al-Mahdī al-ʿAbbāsī with ʿAbbās the First. Undoubtedly, the government won't be able to implement this project because they won't find any among us who's so attracted by the superficialities of this life that he's prepared to sell his life in the hereafter and accept the position of judge in this new court. 16.18

Second Scholar Well said, Sir! We are all with you! We'll stick together and help each other against the government, and then they'll be unable to carry on with their plan to fight the Shariah.

ʿĪsā ibn Hishām told us: At this point, a visitor came in; I think he was an important lawyer. He started looking around the company as though searching for something he had lost. When one of the scholars spotted him, he craned his neck and beckoned him over. The lawyer sat down beside him and whispered in his ear, but I could make it out: 16.19

الزائر أبشرك أيها الأستاذ البشارة المنتظرة فقد تأكدت أنّ اسمك معروض الآن على هيئة النظار وذكرت بين المترشحين لمنصب القضاء إن لم تكن أوّلهم، وأشهد أنّ صاحبنا عمل بالرجاء فلم يقصر جهده في إقناع إخوانه بتفضيلك على سواك.

الشيخ المرشح وهل لم يزل التصميم باقياً على ترشيح فلان وفلان.

الزائر نعم، ولكن لكل منهما موانع تمنعه إن شاء الله عن الوقوف في طريقنا ولك البخت السعيد والجد الصاعد إن شاء الله.

اللشيخ (مجاهرًا بالقول متوجهاً به إلى العالم المتكلم داخلا في حديثه) لا حول ولا قوة إلا بالله العلي العظيم ذكروا من أشراط الساعة أنّ الشمس تطلع من مغربها وأنا أقول إنّ من أشراطها أيضاً أن يكون قاضي المسلمين هذا الذي رشّحوه اليوم في هيئة النظار على ما جاء يخبرني به صاحبي هذا فما أقبحه من مشروع وما أضره على الشرع وما أبرده على قلب إبليس. ٢٠،١٦

عالم شافعي نعم، قد قيل إنّ عيسى عليه السلام لا يظهر إلا بعد أن تدرس معالم الشريعة في الأرض، ولا شبهة في أنّ مشروع اليوم هو علامة ظهور الدجال قبل عيسى عليه السلام. ولكن سبحان الله إذا كان ولا بد من تعيين قاض من مصر فهلا تجد الحكومة طريقاً لعدم اختصاص السادة الحنفية بالوظائف الكبرى دون سواهم أو لم يكفهم أنّ جراياتهم في رواق الحنفية تفوق غيرها مع ما يصيبهم فوق ذلك في توزيع الجرايات من أوقاف زينب هانم وراتب باشا.

عالم مالكي إني أعرف عالماً شيخاً جليلاً مضى عليه تسع سنوات في تدريس حاشية البناني على السعد مستصحباً تقرير الأنبابي عليها وهو لا يأخذ إلى الآن إلا نصف جراية، ولا يزال ينتظر الدور مثل كثير من أمثاله لاتساع مرتب الرواق فيحصل على جراية كاملة ولو كان المسكين حنفياً لامتلأ بيته خبزًا فباع منه ما زاد عن حاجته فادخره مالاً.

العالم الأوّل إنما الدنيا لعب ولهو وما عند الله خير وأبقى، وإني أشهدكم أنني لا أقبل منصب القضاء ولو أعطوني ما أعطوني لأنّ يقيني غير مرتاح إلى ما ادعاه

VISITOR I've brought the news you've been waiting for. I've confirmed that your name has been forwarded to the cabinet. You're being mentioned as one of the candidates for the post of judge, if you're not actually the first name on the list. Our friend is doing all he can to convince his colleagues to give you preference over the others.

NOMINEE SHAYKH Do they still intend to nominate X and Y ?

VISITOR Yes, but there are a number of factors which will prevent them, God willing, from getting in our way. We hope you'll be the lucky one.

16.20 NOMINEE SHAYKH (*now raising his voice, addressing the scholar who has been talking, and joining in the conversation*) God alone has the power and judgment! They say that one of the signs of the Day of Judgment is that the sun will rise in the West. To that I would add that another sign would be that, according to information which my friend has brought me, a Muslim judge has been nominated today to the cabinet to fill the post. The whole project is disgusting and will have a terrible effect on the Shariah. How it must soothe the devil's heart!

SHĀFĪʿĪ SCHOLAR Yes indeed! They say that Jesus (peace be upon him) will only appear when all traces of the Shariah on earth have disappeared. Today this project is undoubtedly a sign of the appearance of the Anti-Christ before Jesus himself appears. Thank God nevertheless that they've got to appoint a judge from Egypt. Wouldn't it be possible for the government to find some way of seeing that all the major positions don't keep going just to Ḥanafīs? Isn't it enough that the salaries Ḥanafīs get are much higher than anyone else's, quite apart from the stipends they get from the endowments of Lady Zaynab and Rātib Pāshā.

MALAKĪ SCHOLAR I know of a venerable Shaykh who has spent nine years teaching Al-Bannānī's *Abridgment* of al-Saʿd's *Commentary* together with the *Account* of Al-Anbābī.[125] So far, he has been on half salary and, like so many of his colleagues, is still waiting for salaries to be raised so he'll receive the full amount. If the poor man were a Ḥanafī, his home would be full of bread to eat and he'd be able to sell the left-overs and keep the cash.

FIRST SCHOLAR All this world is just a game; the next world with God is better and more lasting. I make you all witnesses to the fact that I won't accept the nomination for the post of judge even if they offer it to me.

النظار من أنّ ولاية القضاء لمصر.

الشيخ المرشح كيف فعلتم أيها الأستاذ في تعيين المرحوم الشيخ عبد الرحمن نافذ وتركتم المغفور له إسماعيل باشا يذكر في الأمر الصادر بتوليته بناء على انتخابكم «بما لي من الولاية العامة».

العالم الأوّل إنني تمارضت ذلك اليوم فلم أحضر المجلس، ومع ذلك فمن الذي كان يجرأ على معارضة إسماعيل باشا في رغائبه أو يتظاهر بالشك والارتياب فيما يفعله ويأتيه، هو أمرنا بالانتخاب فانتخبنا اتقاء للشر وعملا بالقول الكريم ﴿وَلَا تُلْقُوا بِأَيْدِيكُمْ إِلَى التَّهْلُكَةِ﴾ أمّا الآن فإنّ الخديو لم يأمرنا بأمر ومن الواجب علينا إذن المحافظة على الشرع الشريف وحاشا أن نرضى بمخالفة أحكامه، ونعيم الدنيا ظل زائل، وبماذا نلقى وجه الله إذا أخفينا في أنفسنا ما تلقيناه عن مشايخنا وليس ثمّ ما يمنعنا عن المجاهرة به. ٢١،١٦

الشيخ المرشح يقولون إنّ مرتب القاضي لا يطرقه نقص بل يبقى مائة وخمسين جنيهاً على ما هو عليه، وأنا الحمد لله في غنى عن هذا المرتب الذي يزري بالدين وما أرضى بقبول المنصب ولو راودتني عن نفسها الجبال الشم من ذهب، وهم يقولون أيضاً في تحليل مشروعهم أنّ الأمر الذي يصدر بتعيين القاضي سيذكر فيه العبارة التي قالها إسماعيل باشا «بما لي من الولاية العامة» وربما أضافوا إليها «والتفويض الشرعي أيضاً» ولا شك أنّ بعد ذكر هاتين العبارتين لا يبقى شك في أنّ الخديو له حق التولية، ومع ذلك فالحكومة تعلم أنه لا يقبلها منا أحد. وقد أشيع أنّ القاضيين المنتدبين من الاستئناف لا يكتفيان بترك محكمتهما وقوانينها الوضعية بل إنهما سيتوبان إلى الله توبة نصوحاً عمّا فرط منهما، وبذلك يمكن للقاضي أن يأذن لهما بالحكم.

العالم الأوّل ولكن يلزم أن يمر على التوبة ستة أشهر على الأقل قبل جواز الإذن لهما بالحكم الشرعي، ألم تر أنّ السكّير إذا تاب فإنّ توبته تقبل عند الله، ولكن القاضي لا يقبل شهادته ما لم يمر على توبته مدة كافية من الزمن يتبيّن له فيها صدق توبته.

I'm not comfortable with the ministers' assertion that "judicial supervision is over Egypt."

Nominee Shaykh How was it possible, Sir, for you to appoint the late Shaykh ʿAbd al-Raḥmān, and then let the late Ismāʿīl Pāshā state in the decree, which publicized his appointment on the basis of your nomination, that it was made "through the general authority invested in me"?

16.21 First Scholar I was actually ill that day and didn't attend the meeting. Furthermore, who would dare go against anything which Khedive Ismāʿīl wanted or even show any misgivings or signs of doubt about the things he did? He told us to select someone, and we did so for fear that something terrible might happen. We were acting in accordance with the Qur'anic text: «Do not give yourselves up to destruction.»[126] These days we don't get any instructions at all from the Khedive, so it's entirely up to us to uphold the Shariah; God forbid that we should ever willingly go against its tenets. After all, this world is just a vanishing shadow. How will we be able to look God in the face if we keep the things which our shaykhs have taught hidden inside us when there is nothing to stop us proclaiming them?

Nominee Shaykh They say the judge's salary will not be reduced; it'll stay at one hundred and fifty pounds. Fortunately, I don't need the salary they're offering for a post which disparages the very name of our religion, and I wouldn't accept it even if they tried to tempt me with mountains of gold. They say too in their analysis of the project that the decree authorizing the appointment of these judges will contain mention of this same phrase that Ismāʿīl Pāshā used, "through the general authority vested in me," and they may also add to that "Shariah authority as well." From the terminology of these two expressions, it's quite obvious that the Khedive has the right to make these appointments. However, the government is well aware that none of us will accept it. We've heard that the two judges to be appointed from the Court of Appeal are not content simply to leave their court and its positive law approach; they are offering their total repentance to God for their shortcomings. In that way the Shariah Court judge will be able to allow them to pass judgments.

First Scholar There must be at least a six-month period after their repentance before it's permissible for them to exercise canonical judgment. Surely you can appreciate that a drunkard can repent and God will forgive him. But when a judge repents, some time must go by so that his repentance can be shown to be genuine.

٢٢،١٦ **الشيخ المرشح** ومع هذا كله فطاعة أولي الأمر واجبة، قال الله تعالى ﴿يَا أَيُّهَا الَّذِينَ آمَنُوا أَطِيعُوا اللَّهَ وَأَطِيعُوا الرَّسُولَ وَأُولِي الْأَمْرِ مِنكُمْ﴾ وما علينا إلا الإرشاد والبلاغ ﴿فَمَن شَاءَ فَلْيُؤْمِن وَمَن شَاءَ فَلْيَكْفُرْ﴾ ﴿لَا إِكْرَاهَ فِي الدِّينِ ۖ قَد تَّبَيَّنَ الرُّشْدُ مِنَ الْغَيِّ﴾ ﴿إِنَّكَ لَا تَهْدِي مَنْ أَحْبَبْتَ﴾ ﴿فَمَنِ اهْتَدَىٰ فَإِنَّمَا يَهْتَدِي لِنَفْسِهِ ۖ وَمَن ضَلَّ فَإِنَّمَا يَضِلُّ عَلَيْهَا﴾ ﴿قُلْ كُلٌّ يَعْمَلُ عَلَىٰ شَاكِلَتِهِ﴾ وقاعدة الأشباه في ارتكاب أخف الضررين مشهورة وقد جوّزوا إتلاف الثلث لإصلاح الثلثين، ومن لنا إذا تركناهم وشأنهم وبقينا على أبائنا للمنصب بمن يمنعهم عن استحضار قاض من الهند - وتلك التي تستك منها المسامع - ولا يزال سميع الله خان يذكر بيننا إلى اليوم.

العالم الأوّل أراك أيها الأستاذ تدخل من باب وتخرج من باب وتضرب قولا بقول كأنّ حاجة في نفس يعقوب.

الشيخ المرشح حاشا لله أن أكون مبطناً خلاف ما أظهر، وذو الوجهين لا يكون عند الله وجيهاً، وأنا لا أزال على رأيي القديم أنصح به في نبذ المشروع ومقاومة من يدخل في الشرع من غير أهله، ولا أزال أتمثل في كل صبح ومساء بقول أحد الشعراء:

ضلّ الذين قضوا بغير شريعة
وتحكموا في الناس حكم ثمود
نبذوا كتاب الله خلف ظهورهم
وتصدوا للحكم بالتلمود

٢٣،١٦ قال عيسى بن هشام: وعلى هذا انفض المجلس وقام الشيخ المرشح يجر المحامي وراءه وسمعته يخاطبه في منصرفه بقوله «هلمّ بنا إلى صاحبنا نكرّر عليه الاستنجاد به عسى أن يصدق معي لبخت ويساعدني الحظ فأرتقي سنام ذلك المنصب والله يرزق من يشاء بغير حساب».

NOMINEE SHAYKH In spite of all that, compliance remains the major factor. God Almighty has said: «You who believe, obey God, the prophets, and those among you who are in command.»[127] All we can do is to guide people and proclaim the truth. «Let whosoever wishes be a believer, and whosoever does not, be an unbeliever»; «there is no compulsion in religion; the difference between sin and rectitude has been made clear»; «you do not guide those whom you love»; «whoever follows the right path, it is to his own benefit—whoever goes astray, it is to his own disadvantage»; «say, everyone acts in their own way.»[128] The analogy of adopting the lesser of two evils is well known; they're allowing one third to be destroyed in order to preserve the other two thirds. If we ignore them and have nothing to do with their project, how can we stop them bringing in an Indian judge?—perish the thought! After all, the name Samīʿ Allāh Khān is still mentioned in our midst right up to today. 16.22

FIRST SCHOLAR My dear Sir, I can see that you're going in one door and out of another. Your statements are contradicting each other like "a need in Jacob's soul."[129]

NOMINEE SHAYKH God forbid that my thoughts should seem to contradict what I've been saying; hypocrites cannot gain God's respect. I still stick to my original opinion in which I advised that the project be rejected and objections be raised to the imposition of any unqualified person in the domain of the Shariah. Every morning and evening, I repeat these verses to myself:

Those who pass judgment without the Shariah are in error;
their judgment is like that of Thamūd.
They have thrust God's book behind their backs
and publish judgments based on the Talmud.

ʿĪsā ibn Hishām told us: At this point the company broke up and left. The Nominee Shaykh got up and took the lawyer along with him. I heard the Shaykh talking as they were leaving: "Let's go and see our friend again. We'll ask him to help us again, and then I may be lucky enough to mount the hump of this judicial post. 'God gives to whoever he wishes without reckoning.'"[130] 16.23

١،١٧ قال عيسى بن هشام: ولمّا أتمّ الله للباشا العافية في جسمه، وأبل من علته وسقمه، أخذت أهنئه بالشفاء والإبلال من المرض والاعتلال، وأذكر له أنّ صحة الأبدان هي ملاك السعادة للإنسان، وأنك لو جمعت نِعَمَ العالم للمريض من المال الواسع والجاه العريض لانصرفت نفسه عنها انصراف الضب عن الماء، والأرمد عن الضياء، والممعود عن شهي الغذاء، وأنّ خاتم الياقوت في إصبع أصابها دمل، لا يساوي عند صاحبه حبة من خردل، وأنّ ما اجتمع في سرير الملك وتاجه من الجبرية والبأس يهون عند مفقور الظهر أو مصدوع الرأس:

ومن يكون ذا فم مرّ مريض
يجد مراً به الماء الزلالا

٢،١٧ وكلما زدته من هذه الموعظة والحكمة زاد في الإعراض عن شكر تلك النعمة، والمرء يذكر النعيم في البؤس ولا يذكر البؤس في النعيم، وينسى المرض في الصحة ولا ينسى الصحة وهو سقيم، فلا يحسب أنّ له يداً تعمل إلا متى أصابها الشلل، وقلّ من يجد النعمة في لبسها، ويدرك سعادة الحياة إلا في نحسها، ﴿وَإِذَا مَسَّ الْإِنسَانَ الضُّرُّ دَعَانَا لِجَنبِهِ أَوْ قَاعِدًا أَوْ قَائِمًا فَلَمَّا كَشَفْنَا عَنْهُ ضُرَّهُ مَرَّ كَأَن لَّمْ يَدْعُنَا إِلَىٰ ضُرٍّ مَّسَّهُ﴾. كان ذلك يمرّ بي والباشا يقول لي فيم الهناء بكشف الضرر وما قمت من خطر إلا إلى خطر؟

فإن أسلم فلا أبقى ولكن
سلمت من الحمام إلى الحمام

وانبرى يسألني عن الطاعون وأخباره، وعن ما حدث من آثاره، فعلمت أنه لم يزل كأمثاله من الناس يغلب عليه الوهم والوساوس، وإن كان جرّب في الحياة شدة الألم وذاق في القبر راحة العدم، وأنّ ما كان يتمناه على دهره من الرجوع إلى قبره عند اشتداد الكروب من وقع الخطوب. لم يكن لشجاعة في النفس تستهين بسكنى

ʿĪsā ibn Hishām said: Once the Pāshā had recuperated his bodily strength and been cured of his illness, I congratulated him on his recovery. Reminding him that bodily health is the basis of man's happiness, I observed that, even if you offered a sick man all the riches in the world, money in plenty, and a lofty status, he would recoil like a lizard from water, like a man with an eye condition from bright sunlight, and like someone with stomach conditions from rich food. Someone who has a sore on their finger does not value the emerald ring as much as a grain of mustard seed. You may gather together all the might, power, and authority of a royal throne, but it will be of little value to someone with a crooked back or fractured skull. 17.1

One who has a bitter taste in his mouth
will still find fresh water bitter.[131]

Whenever I offered him more of this sensible advice, his reluctance to show any gratitude for the boon of good health only increased. I came to realize then that humans only recall periods of happiness when they are in trouble. When a human being is content, he forgets his worries; when he is healthy, he forgets about ill health, but he never forgets about good health when he's sick. He only realizes that his hand functions so well when it is struck by paralysis. Few indeed are the people who acknowledge their good fortune at the time or appreciate life's happiness until misfortune strikes. «When some injury befalls man, he summons us to his side sitting or standing. When we have removed his injury, he passes on as though he had never summoned us to an injury that afflicted him.»[132] 17.2

As I was thus engaged, the Pāshā asked me why I was congratulating him on his recovery when he kept shifting from one problem to another:

If I escape safely, I will not abide;
but I have avoided one fate only to fall into another.[133]

The Pāshā now started asking me about the plague and its effects. I could tell that he was still behaving like everyone else, influenced by rumor and illusion; and that was in spite of the fact that he had experienced real pain during his life and savored the serenity of oblivion in the grave. That would explain his reasons for wanting to return to the grave when the onset of disasters increased

الرمس، وإنما كان لضعفه وخوره عن احتمال الآلام من نوازل الأيام، والناس عاملون على إضاعة الحياة بالتخوف من الممات.

وخوف الردى آوى إلى الكهف أهله
وعلم نوحًا وابنه عمل السفن
وما استعذبته روح موسى وآدم
وقد وُعِدا من بعده جنتي عدن

٣،١٧ فقلت له كاد يصبح الطاعون أثرًا بعد عين، وما أصاب إلا عدد أصابع اليدين، وفرّ هذا العدو المبارز، وأنشدته قول الراجز:

قد رفع الله رماح الجن
وأذهب التعذيب والتجني

٤،١٧ الباشا كيف تدّعي ذلك وتزعمه، وما عهدت منك إخفاء للحقائق ولا تمويهًا للوقائع، وللطاعون في مصر أفاعيل تذوب لها المآقي والأحداق، وتنفطر منها القلوب والأكباد، وهو من أمراض مصر الموضعية التي تحدث عند اختلاف الفصول في كل عام، والمصريون يتوقعونه لكل ربيع حتى أطلقوا عليه كلمة (الفصل) فيقولون جاء الفصل عند ظهور الطاعون، فترتاع النفوس وتنخلع القلوب وتخار القوى وتذهل العقول، ثمّ يصول صولته ويفتك فتكته فلا يقف سيله عند حاجز، ولا يمنع اندفاعه مانع، ولا تفيض قرارته حتى يخرّب القصور، ويعمّر القبور، فتصبح الأطفال يتامى، والنساء أيامى، ويمسي الناس بين ثاكل ومثكول، وحامل ومحمول، هذا يبكي أباه، وذلك يندب أخاه، وهذه تولول على أهلها، وتلك تنوح على بعلها، وقد سمعت عنه في زماني من أحد المعمّرين يقول في وصفه عند وقوعه في سنة ١٢٠٥:

٥،١٧ «ابتدأ الطاعون في شهر رجب سنة ١٢٠٥ وداخل الناس منه وهو عظيم، واشتدّ بطشه وقوي بأسه في رجب وشعبان، ومات به ما لا يحصى من الأطفال

the level of anxiety. Residing in the grave was not easier for him because of any courage he might possess; rather the cause was a weakness and inability to endure the agonies brought about by the vicissitudes of fate. People waste so much time in life worrying themselves about death:

Fear of death led the People of the Cave to shelter there
and taught Noah and his son how to construct boats.
The spirits of Moses and Adam did not relish the experience,
and both had been promised the Garden of Eden thereafter.[134]

I went on to tell him that these days the plague was a shadow of its former self, affecting only a handful of people. The dogged enemy has now disappeared. And I quoted for him the line of *rajaz* poetry: 17.3

God has taken away the spear of the jinn
and forever banished torture and criminality.[135]

Pāshā I've not found you to be someone who conceals the truth or falsifies things, so how on earth can you make such a claim? The plague wreaks tremendous havoc in Egypt; it's enough to melt your very eyelids and split your heart in two. It's one of Egypt's endemic diseases, one that occurs each year with the changing seasons. Egyptians expect it every spring, so much so that they've given it the nickname "Season"; they say, for example, the "Season" has come when the plague appears. People become alarmed and start panicking. Their faculties dwindle, and they become utterly confused. It attacks and destroys, its course unhampered and unimpeded by any obstacle. It only abates when palaces are in ruins and graves have been filled. It turns children into orphans and women into widows; people are either mourning or being mourned, carrying someone to the grave or being carried themselves. One person will weep for his father, another will mourn his brother; one woman laments for her family, another for her husband. In my own time I heard about it from an old man who gave me the following account of the epidemic in the year 1205 [1791]:[136] 17.4

"The plague began in Rajab 1205, causing a huge panic among the populace. It increased in intensity during the months of Rajab and Shaʿban. Countless people died—babies, young men, girls, slaves, Mamluks, soldiers, scouts, and amirs. The governors of twelve provinces died, among them Ismāʿīl Bey the Elder. It wiped out the marine contingent and Albanians living in Old Cairo, 17.5

والشبان والجواري والعبيد والمماليك والأجناد والكشاف والأمراء، ومات من الصناجق أمراء الألوف اثنا عشر صنجقاً منهم إسماعيل بك الكبير، وأفنى عسكر القليونجية والأرنؤوط المقيمين ببولاق ومصر القديمة والجيزة، وكانوا لكثرة الموتى يحفرون حفراً بالجيزة بالقرب من مسجد أبي هريرة ويلقونهم فيها، وكان يخرج من بيت الأمير في الجنازة الواحدة الخمسة والستة والعشرة، وازدحم الناس على الحوانيت يلتمسون ما يجهّزون به موتاهم، ويطلبون من يحمل النعوش فلا يجدونهم، ويقف الناس يتشاحنون ويتضاربون على ذلك، ولم يبق للناس شغل إلا الموت وأسبابه، فلا تجد إلا مريضاً أو ميتاً أو عائداً أو معزّياً أو مشيّعاً أو راجعاً من صلاة جنازة أو دفن أو مشغولاً بتجهيز ميّت أو باكياً على نفسه موهوماً، ولا تنقطع صلاة الجنازة من المساجد والمصليات، ولا تقام الصلاة إلا على أربعة أو خمسة، وندر من يصاب ولا يموت، وقلّ ظهور الطعن على الجسم فيكون الإنسان جالساً فيرتعش من البرد فيندثر فلا يفيق إلا مخلطاً أو يموت في غده إن لم يمت في نهاره، واستمرّ فتكه إلى أوائل رمضان، فمات الآغا والوالي في أثناء ذلك فولوا خلافهما فماتا أيضاً واتفق أنّ الميراث انتقل ثلاث مرت في سبعة أيام وأغلق بالمفتاح بيت أمير كان فيه مائة وعشرون نفساً ماتوا جميعاً» .

٦،١٧ وما كان الأمر ليقتصر في الطاعون على فتكه بعد ذلك، بل كان يزيد عليه من البلاء ما دسه الإفرنج للولاة من وجوب إزعاج الناس بأمور تشق على نفوسهم يزعمون أنها تدفع الطاعون فيفصلون بين الناس وبعضهم، ويفرّقون بين الأب وابنه، والأخ وأخيه، والمرء وزوجه، ويهدمون الدور ويحرقون الثياب، وينشرون البخور كأنهم لجهلهم يظنون أنّ هذه الأعمال التي تؤذي النفوس، وتعطل مصالح العباد، تشتت شمل الجن، وتكسر ألسنة رماحهم فيزداد الناس ويلاً على ويل وحزناً على حزن وخراباً فوق خراب، وقد شاهدت بعيني من ذلك ما تشيب له النواصي في

Būlāq, and Giza. So many people died that they used to dig pits in Giza near Abū Hurayrah's mosque and throw all the bodies into them; out of the amir's house would come five, six, and ten in a single funeral procession.

"People crowded into shops looking for things with which to prepare the dead for burial, and asking people to carry their coffins; but without success. So they fell to quarrelling and fighting each other about it. Death and everything connected with it were the only thing on people's minds. Everyone you met was either sick, dead, visiting or consoling someone, attending funerals, returning from a funeral service or a burial, busy with the preparation of a dead person or else weeping apprehensively for himself. In mosques and places of prayer, funeral services never ceased, and on each occasion the prayers were pronounced over four or five people at once. Only in rare cases did anyone who contracted the disease not die. The attack would appear quite insignificantly on the body. A man might be sitting somewhere, then he would suddenly shiver with cold and wrap himself up. If he ever came round, he would be delirious; otherwise he died the next day, if not that actual day itself.

"The plague continued to strike people down until the beginning of Ramadan, when the Āghā and Governor both died. Their two successors were appointed, and both died within three days, so others were appointed to succeed them as well. The legacy was passed on three times in seven days. An amir's house was locked up with a hundred and twenty people inside, and they all perished."

17.6

'Īsā The scene you've been describing sounds to me like one of the halting spots on the Day of Judgment, or one of the horrors of the Day of Resurrection which you yourself have witnessed.[137]

Pāshā During the course of the plague, people's miseries were not confined to the epidemic itself. The schemes which the Europeans imposed on the rulers were even worse. They forced them to harass people with distressing regulations which, they claimed, would prevent the spread of the plague. So they separated people from one another, splitting up father and son, brother and brother, husband and wife. They tore down houses, burned clothes, and scattered incense, as though, in their ignorance, they imagined that these measures which only hurt people's feelings and thwarted their best interests would scatter the assembled jinn and break the tips of their spears. People went from one misery and grief to another, from one kind of destruction to another. In 1260 [1844], I saw with my own eyes things which would turn your hair

سنة ١٢٦٠، وقصّ عليّ أخي ما رآه منها في سنة ١٢٢٨ وكان في خدمة المرحوم محمد علي، قال:

٧،١٧ «أمر جنتمكان محمد علي بعمل كورنتيلة بالجيزة في اليوم العاشر من شهر ربيع الثاني، وعزم على الإقامة بها إذ اشتدّ عليه الوهم والخوف من الطاعون لوقوع القليل منه بمصر، ومات به الطبيب الفرنسوي وبعض من نصارى الأروام، وهم يعتقدون صحة الكورنتيلة وأنها تمنع الطاعون، وقاضي الشريعة الذي هو قاضي العسكر يحقق قولهم ويسير على مذهبهم، وكان الباشا لشغفه بالحياة، وحرصه على الدنيا يصدّق هذا الزعم ويغرسه في نفوس حاشيته وأهل دائرته، واتفق أن مات بالطاعون شخص بالمحكمة من أتباع القاضي فأمر بحرق ثيابه وغسل المكان الذي فيه وتبخيره بالأبخرة المتنوعة، وكذلك الأواني التي كان يمسّها، وأمروا أصحاب الشرطة أنهم يأمرون الناس وأصحاب الأسواق بالكنس والرش والتنظيف، ونشر الثياب في كل وقت، وإذا وردت عليهم مكاتبات خرقوها بالسكاكين ودخنوها بالبخور قبل تسليمها إليهم.

٨،١٧ «ولمّا عزم الباشا على كورنتيلة الجيزة أمر في ذلك اليوم أن ينادوا بها على سكانها بأنّ من كان يملك قوته وقوت عياله ستين يوماً، واختار الإقامة فليمكث بالبلدة وإلا فليخرج منها ويذهب فيسكن حيث أراد، وأعطوا لهم مهلة أربع ساعات، فانزعج سكان الجيزة وخرج من خرج وأقام منهم من أقام، وكان ذلك في وقت الحصاد، وللناس مزارع ومرافق مع مجاوريهم من أهل القرى، ولا يخفى احتياج الإنسان لبيته وأهله وعياله وأسباب رزقه، فيحرمونه من ذلك كله، حتى لقد سدّوا خروق السور والأبواب، ومنعوا مراكب المعادي من السير. وأقام الباشا ببيت الأزبكية لا يجتمع بأحد من الناس إلى يوم الجمعة، ثمّ قصد الجيزة في وقت الفجر من ذلك اليوم، وصعد إلى قصره، وأوقف مركبين، الأولى ببر الجيزة والأخرى في مقابلتها ببر مصر القديمة، فإذا أرسل الكتخدا أو المعلم غالي إليه مراسلة ناولها المرسل للمقيد بذلك في طرف مزراق بعد تبخير الورقة بالشيح واللبان والكبريت فيتناولها منه الآخر بمزراق آخر على بعد منهما، ويعود راجعاً، فإذا قرب من البر تناولها المنتظر له أيضاً بمزراق

grey. My brother recounted to me what he saw in 1228 [1813] while he was in the service of the late Muḥammad ʿAlī the Great, in which he said:

17.7 "On the tenth day of Rabiʿ al-Thani, Muḥammad ʿAlī, whose place is in heaven, ordered a quarantine to be put into effect in Giza, and decided to stay there himself. He had severe misgivings about the plague because a few cases had already occurred in Egypt. A French doctor and some Greek Christians had died of it, convinced that the quarantine was effective and would stop the plague. The Shariah judge who served as judge for the military ratified their statement and went along with their plan. It happened that one of the judge's followers in the court died, so he ordered his clothes to be burned and the place he lived in to be scrubbed and fumigated with various disinfectant vapors. The same thing was done to the vessels he had been using. They gave orders to the police to tell the public and stall owners to sweep, spray, and clean on every possible occasion and also to spread out their clothing. When they received written a message, they pierced the paper with knives and fumigated it before handing it over.

17.8 "On the day the Pāshā decided to impose quarantine on Giza, he issued instructions that the people who lived there were to be told that anyone who had enough food for himself and his family for sixty days and who chose to stay could remain in the district. Otherwise he would have to leave and go to live where he wished. They were granted four hours' grace. The inhabitants of Giza were very alarmed; some left and others stayed. This was at harvest time, and the folk there owned pastures and had various forms of traffic with their neighbors in the village. Man's need of his home, family, dependents, and means of sustenance is well known. But, in spite of all that, they deprived these people of all these things, and even went so far as to block up cracks in walls and doors and stop the ferry boats running. The Pāshā meanwhile stayed in the Ezbekiyyah Palace and only met people in public on Fridays. On that day he went to Giza at dawn and entered the palace there. Two boats were posted, one on the Giza bank, and the other opposite it on the Old Cairo bank. When the town clerk or Muʿallim Ghālī sent a dispatch, the sender handed it to the designated receiver on the end of a javelin after fumigating the paper with wormwood, incense, and sulphur.[138] The other person received it from him on another javelin standing at a distance from them both, and then recrossed the river. When he approached the other bank, the person waiting for him also took it from him on yet another javelin and immersed it in vinegar and

وغمسها في الخل وبخرها بالبخور المذكور، ثمّ يوصلها إلى حضرة المشار إليه بكيفية أخرى، وأقام الباشا على ذلك أياماً، وسافر إلى الفيوم، ثمّ عاد وأرسل مماليكه ومن يخاف عليه من الموت إلى أسيوط».

٩،١٧ عيسى بن هشام اعلم أنّ ما كان يعترض عليه عامة الناس في الأزمان الغابرة (ولا يزال بيننا إلى اليوم بقية منهم) من الأخذ بأسباب التوقي والاحتياط لدفع غائلة الطاعون لجهلهم بماهيته وأسباب انتشاره هو الذي يحمينا اليوم من فتكاته وسطواته التي قصصت عليّ منها طرفاً، وكان الناس في أزمانكم ينكرون هذه الوقاية ويسخرون منها.

الباشا قل لي بالله، أيّ علاقة بين إحراق الثياب وتلك الوخزة التي تأتي بالأجل، وأي ارتباط بين هذا البخور وحمى الطاعون، اللّهم إلا أن يراد به تلطيف أمزجة الجن.

عيسى بن هشام لا يفوتنك أنّ كثيراً من الماهيات والحقائق كانت مكنونة في خفاء الجهل عند عامة الناس لاختصاص الأفراد بالعلم والبحث، وبعد تناوله على بقية الطبقات، فلمّا انتشر العلم وأضاء برهانه، كشف للكل ما كان مخفياً عنهم، وأظهر من العلل والأسباب ما كانت تقف دونه الأفكار حيرى، فإن كان الناس في زمانكم يعتقدون أنّ الطاعون من رماح الجن، وأن لا شيء يقوى على رد تلك الرماح الخفية عن العيون، فإنّ البحث أوصلهم اليوم إلى اليقين بأنّ للطاعون جنوداً لا تدركها العيون المجردة، ولها وخز خفي دونه وخز الرماح وعوالي الأسنة، ولكنهم استعانوا بالعلم، فصنعوا آلة تجسم الأشياء الدقيقة، وتبرزها مرئية للعين، فوقفوا بها على حقيقة تلك الجنود، واستنبطوا طرق الوقاية منها فتدرعوا بها لدفع أذاها.

١٠،١٧ الباشا وماذا تجدي الوقاية والحذر من القضاء والقدر.

عيسى بن هشام حفظت شيئاً وغابت عنك أشياء، إنّ الوقاية من السنّة الشريفة، فقد ظاهر عليه الصلاة والسلام بين درعين في الحرب، وقال الله تعالى

fumigated it with the above-mentioned vapours. He then gave it to his Eminence the Pāshā by some other method. The Pāshā continued this practice for some days, and then travelled to al-Fayyūm. Later he came back and sent his Mamluks and those who he feared might die to Asyūt."[139]

17.9 ʿĪsā You need to know that in days gone by people didn't understand the true facts about the plague and the reasons why it spreads (in fact there are still people like them around today). Those very same precautions to which people were exposed with the goal of preventing its lethal infection are today the very things which protect us from violent epidemics, some of which you've just been describing for me. In your time people refused to acknowledge this type of protection and even ridiculed it.

Pāshā Tell me, by God, what's the connection between burning clothes and those stings which carry death; or between these vapors and plague fever? For the life of me I cannot understand, unless the aim is to placate the jinn's foul moods.

ʿĪsā You shouldn't forget that the common people's ignorance has meant that they were unaware of many facts. Very few people have specialized in science, and it has remained beyond the reach of other classes of society. However, when science began to spread and the facts which it could prove became evident, it began to show people things which they hadn't comprehended before and factors which had previously baffled them. In your time, people may well have believed that plague was the jinn pricking them with their spears and that there was nothing capable of staving off these invisible spears. But today, research has convinced them that the plague does indeed have armies which are invisible to the naked eye and a prick far worse than the kind caused by the tip of any sword or spear. However, with the aid of science, they have produced an instrument which magnifies minute objects and shows them up clearly. By using this instrument, they have discovered the facts about these armies, devised ways of guarding against them, and equipped themselves to rid people of the pain they cause.

17.10 Pāshā How can careful precautions be of any use against predestined fate?

ʿĪsā "Some things you have remembered, but there are others that have escaped your notice."[140] Precaution is enjoined by the tenets of our revealed faith. The Prophet of God (peace and blessings be upon him) always fought between two pieces of chain mail in wartime. In the Qur'an, God Almighty

﴿وَأَعِدُّوا لَهُم مَّا اسْتَطَعْتُم مِّن قُوَّةٍ﴾ وطرق الوقاية عندهم اليوم مختلفة الأنواع لدفع هذا العدو الخفي الذي يسمّونه بالمكروب، وهو حيوان دقيق من عالم الذر ينطبق عليه وصف من أوصاف الجن في سرعة التولد وكثرة التعدد في أيسر برهة من الزمن، وللتوقي منه طريقتان، إفناؤه بالبخورات التي تحل تركيبه وإيقاف عدواه وانتقاله بإحراق الثياب وكل ما اختلط به.

الباشا لقد كشفت لي معنى دقيقاً في رماح الجن المسمومة، ما كنت أخال أنّ أحداً من الناس يدركه في عصرنا، وأين منّا هذه الآلة العجيبة المجسّمة للأشياء الدقيقة لأزداد يقيناً بالنظر إلى عجائب المخلوقات.

١١،١٧ قال عيسى بن هشام: فأخذته إلى المعمل الكيماوي وأطلعته على نقطة من الماء تحت المكرسكوب، فلمّا رآها غديراً ورأى ألوف الألوف من الحيوانات سابحة فيها سجد سجدة التقديس لقدرة الخالق والتمجيد لعظمة الصانع، فحمدت الله إذ آمن بالرهان الساطع، ولم يفعل ما فعله ذلك الهندي الذي أراه الألماني مثل هذه النقطة وما فيها من الحيوانات ليقنعه بأنّ ماء الشرب مشحون بما يحرّم الهندي قتله وأكله، فكسر النظارة إصراراً على الباطل وعناداً للحق.

ولمّا أيقن الباشا بصدق ما قلته له، وأنّ العلم هزم جنود الطاعون وحطّم رماحه، ولولاه لمات اليوم مكان العشرة مئات من الألوف سألني يقول:

١٢،١٧ الباشا لا شك أنّ الذي بحث حتى اخترع هذه الآلة التي تدلّ بلا واسطة على عظمة الخالق وقدرته هو شيخ من مشايخ الموحدين وعالم من علماء المسلمين يجب له الشكر والحمد في كل آن.

عيسى بن هشام أحلف لك بالله وملائكته وكتبه أنّ مشايخنا لا يزالون كعهدك بهم في معزل عن هذه العلوم النافعة والمخترعات المفيدة، ولم يروا إلى

says: «Prepare as much power for them as you are able.»[141] Today there's a whole variety of precautions one can take to ward off this unseen enemy. They call it the microbe, a tiny creature from the world of the atom. One can apply at least one of the jinn's attributes to it, namely the speed of its procreation and the broad scale of its onslaught in a very short space of time. There are two ways of protecting against it: using fumigants that dissolve its structure; and burning clothes and anything it has come into contact with as a means of stopping the spread of the infection.

PĀSHĀ You've provided me with a precise definition of the jinn's poisoned spears, one which I don't think anyone could have comprehended in the age in which I lived. Can we take a look at this remarkable instrument which can magnify tiny objects? Then I can increase my conviction by looking at the marvels of God's creatures.

17.11 ʿĪsā ibn Hishām said: So I took him to a chemical laboratory where I showed him a speck of water under a microscope. When he saw that it looked like a huge pool and noticed the thousands of thousands of creatures swimming around in it, he prostrated himself in reverence to the power of the Creator and in praise to the greatness of the Maker. For my part I praised God because the Pāshā was convinced by this clear proof and did not behave as a Hindu once did with a German scholar. When the latter showed the former a speck similar to this one and the creatures which it contained so as to convince him that drinking water is full of creatures which Hindus are forbidden to kill and eat, the Hindu smashed his instrument because he sullenly persisted in his beliefs and refused to accept the truth.

The Pāshā was now convinced of what I had told him: science had defeated the plague's cohorts and destroyed its spears. But for that, people would be dying today in hundreds of thousands instead of in tens. Turning to me he asked:

17.12 PĀSHĀ No doubt the person who invented this instrument that can demonstrate so effectively the might and power of the Creator without recourse to an intermediary was a devout shaykh and learned doctor of the faith. We owe him our praise and gratitude for all time.

ʿĪSĀ IBN HISHĀM By God, His angels, and His books, I swear to you that, as was the case in your own time, our shaykhs know absolutely nothing

الآن هذه الآلة، ولم يسمع بها أكثرهم، وهم يفضلون التعرض لنيران الرصاص على الإذعان لوجوب الوقاية من هذه الحيوانات الدقيقة، ولا يعرفون منها إلا ما نخر كتبهم من الأرضة وإلا ما سبح في حلقات دروسهم من البق والنمل والقمل و «أكلوني البراغيث.»

about this instrument. As is their wont, they remain isolated from all these useful sciences and helpful inventions. None of them have seen this instrument, and most of them have never even heard of it. They would rather face bullet fire than submit to the necessity of taking precautions against these tiny microbes.[142] Their knowledge comes entirely from their termite-ridden books and their study groups where bugs, ants, lice, and fleas float around, and their grammatical examples in which the phrase "the fleas have eaten me" does the rounds.[143]

١٫١٨ قال عيسى بن هشام: وخشيت على الباشا إن أنا تركته غريق أفكاره، وأسير همومه وأكداره، أن ينتويه الانتكاس، ويعتريه الارتكاس، والنكسة بعد البله شر أدوار العلة. فطفقت أتنقل به من مكان إلى مكان، ومن بستان إلى بستان، لأقاطع بينه وبين أحزانه، وأباعد بينه وبين أشجانه، إلى أن وصلنا إلى قصر الجيزة ومتحف الآثار، وملتقى السيارة من سائر الأقطار، فرأينا روضة تجري الأنهار من بينها، كأنها الجنة بعينها، وقصرًا يقصرعنه الطرف، كما يقصرعنه الوصف، فأخذنا نرتاد خلاله، ونتفيأ ظلاله، وقد نظرنا الأسود مقصورات في المقاصير، والأساود مكفوفات في القوارير، ورأينا النمور في الخدور، والرئال في الحجال، والذئاب في القباب، والظباء في الخباء.

٢٫١٨ ولمّا رأى الباشا الأرض منضدة، مرصعة مزردة حسبها أرضاً مفروشة ببسط منقوشة، وأشكل الأمرعليه، فهمّ بخلع نعليه، فقلت له طريق معبّد، لا فرش منجد، وحصباء ومرو، لا بساط وفرو، قال: لمن هذه الجنان؟ وكيف يسكنها الحيوان؟ وما علمت أنّ الأسد الضواري تسكن مغاني الجواري، وأنّ ساكنات البيد تلعب في ملاعب الغيد، فقلت بيت إسماعيل طالما كانت حجراته مطالع للأقمار، ودرجاته منازل للأقدار، كان إذا نادى صاحبه يا غلام، شقيت أقوام وسعدت أقوام، ولبى نداءه البؤس والندى بأسرع من رجع الصدى. هنا كان يفصل الأمر ويحكم، وينقض الحكم ويبرم، وكان من احتمى بظل هذا الجدار، تحامته غوائل الأقدار، هنا كانت فرائد القلائد، من أجياد الخرائد، تختلط بمنثور أزهاره فترصع لجين أنهاره، هنا كانت تتناثر الجواهر من قدود الحسان فتشتبه بأثمار الأغصان، هنا كانت تصدح القيان على المزهر والأعواد، فتجاوبها الورق على الأفنان والأعواد، فأصبح حديقة عامة، وموطئاً للخاصة والعامة، وأصبحت أرضه تكترى، وجني أشجاره يباع ويشترى، ودوّى فيه صياح النسور وزئير الأسود، وعواء الذئاب وهمهمة الفهود، وزال ما

Miṣbāḥ al-sharq 59, June 15, 1899[144]

18.1 ʿĪsā ibn Hishām said: I was afraid that, if I left the Pāshā deep in reflection and a prisoner of his own anxieties, he might have a relapse and become ill again. A relapse after convalescence is the very worst thing that can happen with an illness. So I set about moving from one place to another, from garden to garden, as a way of putting a distance between him and his worries. Eventually we reached the Giza Palace and antiquities museum where tourists from all countries in the world can be seen. We saw a park with streams flowing through it as though it were heaven itself, and took in the sheer beauty of the palace itself, a building so staggeringly beautiful that it beggared description. We proceeded to explore it, seeking shade beneath its eaves. We found lions kept in private compartments and snakes locked up in bottles; tigers in separate quarters, baby ostriches in alcoves, jackals kept in domed buildings, and gazelles in tents.

18.2 When the Pāshā looked at the ground, neatly laid out and paved, he assumed that whole area was carpeted. He did not know what to do and was on the point of removing his shoes. I told him that it was just an ordinary path, not an upholstered carpet; mere stones and pebbles, not rugs and skins. He asked me who these gardens belong to, and how was it possible for animals to live there? He told me that he had never heard of wild lions being kept in girls' quarters before, nor of desert animals playing in secluded apartments. In reply I told him that the house belonged to Khedive Ismāʿīl. In former times its chambers would often serve as the starting point on the path to the very moons in the sky; its stairs were stages on the way to lofty status. When the owner yelled "Servant," some people would be miserable, others happy. In fact, misery and generosity were both at his beck and call and responded quicker than the echo's rebound. Here decisions were made, rules were formulated, and orders cancelled and confirmed. The person who sought shelter in the shade of this wall was shunned by adverse fate. Necklaces of previous stones would mingle with scattered flowers and decorate silver streams. Here trinkets dropped from the bodies of beautiful girls were likened to fruit on tree branches. To the sound of lute and mandolin songstresses used to sing, and their songs would be answered by the cooing of turtle doves on the tree branches. But now it's been turned into a public garden, ground to be trodden by upper- and lower-class feet alike. The grounds are hired out, and the produce of the trees is bought

كان فيه من عز وطول، ومجد وصول، وأيد وحول، وصدق الكتاب فحق القول:

في هذه الدار في هـذا المكان على
هذا السرير ورأيت الملك قد سقطا

٣،١٨ وقصصت على الباشا قصة صاحب القصر، ومليك ذلك العصر، وما كان فيه من الجد الصاعد، والبخت المساعد، وما صار إليه من نحوسة سعده، ثمّ سكنى لحده، بعد أن ذاق في هذه الدار دار الفناء، مثل عذاب تلك الدار دار البقاء.

نالوا قليلاً من اللذات وارتحلوا
برغمهم فإذا النعماء بأساء

فقال الباشا لقد رددت إليّ صبري، وهوّنت عليّ من أمري، ولكني دعني أبكي هذه الدمن، وأفكر في صروف الزمن، واتركني أسكب العبرة بعد العبرة، وأزداد عبرة إلى عبرة، وأتأمل في المبدأ والمآل، وأشكر الله على كل حال. ومال إلى ظل الشجر، فتوسّد الحجر، ثمّ أخذ كأنه يخاطب الجد القديم، ويستبكيه فعل الدهر الذميم إلى أن اعتراه الوهن، فأخذه الوسن.

٤،١٨ فتركته في منامه، يستريح من أوصابه وآلامه. وملت ناحية فإذا أنا بشابين يتشابهان رشاقة وظرفا، ويتماثلان رقة ولطفا، عرفتهما وهما وإن اتفقا في الجنسية والمذهب، فقد اختلفا في السياسة والمشرب، لأنّ أحدهما تربى في أنكلترا والآخر في فرنسا، فدنوت منهما وسلمت عليهما، وكان الحديث بينهما يجري في مضمار السباق، ورهان الجرد العتاق، ويقول أحدهما أمّا فلان صاحبك فقد رهن ما يمتلك من العقار والأفدنة ليقتني المركبات والأحصنة، وأمّا فلان فقد باع ما لزوجته من الأساور والخواتم ليشتري السروج والشكائم، فيتفاخران بالخيل المسومة، والمركبات المعلمة، كأن لم يبق من سمات الأقدار الخطيرة إلا أن يقال ما أحسن خيل فلان في ركب الجزيرة.

٥،١٨ فقال الآخر دعنا من هذا وهلمّ بنا نسمع ما يدور الآن على ألسنة العوام من حوادث

and sold. The place resounds with the cries of vultures, the roars of lions, the howls of wolves, and the snarls of lynxes. All glory and esteem, all splendor, might, power, and authority have vanished. It has been truly spoken:

In this house, in this place,
on this throne, I saw that the king had fallen.[145]

18.3 I told the Pāshā about the former owner of the palace, the monarch of that age, also about the good fortune that he had initially enjoyed, the bad luck that beset him thereafter, and the great suffering he had endured in exile until his death:

They enjoyed a small amount of pleasure and went away
against their will; days of grace became that much worse.[146]

The Pāshā said to me, “I have recovered my endurance and now regard my own affairs as somewhat trivial. But allow me to weep over these ruins and contemplate the vicissitudes of time. Let me learn from one lesson after another and consider both beginning and end. At all events I thank God.”

And with that he leaned his head against a rock in the shade of a tree and seemed to start talking to his ancient ancestor, invoking his tears at the doings of unjust fate. After a while, he became drowsy and fell asleep.

18.4 I left him asleep, trying to relieve his anxieties and hardships. Moving to one side, I spotted two elegant and suave young men who both seemed quite amiable. In fact I already knew both of them; they were both Egyptians and adhered to the principles of the same school of law, but their political views and tastes differed. One of them had been educated in England, the other in France. As I approached them and offered my greetings, the conversation involved discussion of horse racing and pawning old clothing. One of them was saying, “That friend of yours has pawned all his lands and estates so that he can spend the money on horses and carriages. Someone else has sold all his wife’s jewellery to buy himself saddles and bridles. They both keep boasting about their horses and carriages; it’s as though the only sign of prestige left is to hear people saying what a wonderful horse someone had at the Gezīra race track.”

18.5 “Forget about that,” his colleague replied. “Let’s hear what everyone’s talking about these days.” He pointed to two turbaned men, both of whom I knew. I informed them that one of them was a merchant and the other a

هذه الأيام. وأشار إلى رجلين من ذوي العمائم، فعرفتهما فقلت أمّا أحدهما فتاجر وأمّا الآخر فعالم، وكانا جالسين على الأرض، فوق نباتها الغض، وقد وضع كل منهما عن رأسه العمامة، وبين يديه سكين وشهامة، وكان بجانبهما مقاعد فسلمنا وجلسنا، وفتحنا باب الحديث معهما وأنسنا، ودارت بينهم المحاورة على الأحوال الحاضرة:

التاجر ما هي أخبار الطاعون في علمكم اليوم؟

الوطني الفرنسوي انظر إلى هذه البساطة والسذاجة ودخول الحيلة الانكليزية على الناس، وتصديقهم بمفتريات أهل السياسة وأباطيلهم، وما الأوبئة والطواعين إلا شباك يصيدون بها الأغراض والمآرب، أما علمتم أنهم كلما أرادوا مكيدة بالمسلمين وإهانة لهم جلبوا إليهم من الهند جرثومة من جراثيمه ليزعجوا الناس ويوقعوهم في الهياج، ويتذرعوا بذلك إلى فعل تلك الإهانة شفاء لما في صدورهم؟ أرادوا إهانة الجامع الأزهر فاتخذوا الوباء وسيلة إلى إطلاق الرصاص عليه، أرادوا إبطال الحج فجعلوا أخبار الوباء حجة على المنع سنة بعد أخرى، أرادوا خلط الشرع بالوضع فلم يفلحوا فأرادوا الانتقام فاستنجدوا بهذا الطاعون.

التاجر تالله إنك لصادق في ما قلت وإنه لكلام معقول وإلا فما معنى حدوث الأوبئة في مصر آنًا بعد آن في زمن هذا الاحتلال بعد أن كنا لا نسمع ذكر الوباء إلا حكاية من الجد عن الجد، ولا يفوتنّك ما في ذلك من تعطيل تجارة الغير وترويج تجارتهم. ٦،١٨

العالم ﴿وَضَرَبَ اللَّهُ مَثَلًا قَرْيَةً كَانَتْ آمِنَةً مُطْمَئِنَّةً يَأْتِيهَا رِزْقُهَا رَغَدًا مِنْ كُلِّ مَكَانٍ فَكَفَرَتْ بِأَنْعُمِ اللَّهِ فَأَذَاقَهَا اللَّهُ لِبَاسَ الْجُوعِ وَالْخَوْفِ بِمَا كَانُوا يَصْنَعُونَ﴾ واعلموا أنّ ما نزل بكم من هذه المحن إنما هو لتهاونكم بالعلماء وازدرائكم بأقوالهم واستخفافكم بأقدارهم وميلكم عن علومهم النافعة في الأولى والآخرة إلى تلك العلوم الحديثة الضارة بالدنيا والدين، المخلة بقواعد اليقين، مع ما يضاف إلى ذلك من انحرافكم عن الاسترشاد بنا عند الوقوع في الملمات فخالفتم قوله تعالى ﴿فَاسْأَلُوا أَهْلَ الذِّكْرِ إِنْ كُنْتُمْ لَا تَعْلَمُونَ﴾ وهل غير العلماء يدفع عنكم الخطوب ويكشف النوازل ويصادم النكبات،

religious scholar. The two of them had removed their turbans and were sitting on the lush grass with a knife and melon in their hands. There were some chairs beside them, so we greeted them and sat down beside them. They were discussing current affairs:

MERCHANT What's today's news about the plague?

FRENCH-EDUCATED NATIONALIST Just look at this utter stupidity! See how the English are working their trickery and believing the futile lies and falsehoods of politicians. The plague is simply a trap which they're using to contain people's desires and aspirations. Surely you all realize that every time they want to trick and belittle Muslims, they simply bring in some germs from India with which to pester them and make them agitated. They then use it as an excuse for the way they insult us just to gratify their own feelings. They wanted to insult the al-Azhar mosque, so they used the epidemic as an excuse for firing bullets at it.[147] They've wanted to cancel the pilgrimage, so they've used the epidemic as an excuse for stopping it year after year. They wanted to mix canon law with positive law, but there they didn't succeed. Because of that, they were out for vengeance, so they've used this plague as a device to help them.

18.6 MERCHANT By God, what you're saying is quite right; it makes good sense. If that were not so, how come it keeps reappearing in Egypt time after time under British Occupation when for years we've never heard it mentioned except for some stories passed on from one generation to the next. You're well aware, of course, of the negative effect it has on trade with the outside world and commercial prosperity.

RELIGIOUS SCHOLAR «God has made an example of a town which was safe and peaceful. Its provisions came in abundance from every place; but its people denied the favours of God, and so he made them taste famine and fear for what they had done.»[148] You should realise that these troubles all stem from the way you have shown your contempt for religious scholars and their teachings. You show contempt for their status and keep ignoring the useful sciences concerning all things, preferring to rely instead on modern sciences which are harmful to both worldly life and religion and contrary to the basic principles of belief. Not only that, but now you've turned away and no longer ask us for our guidance in times of trouble. In so doing, you've gone against the words of God Himself: «Ask the people of the remembrance if you do not know.»[149] Can anyone other than religious scholars ward off

وهذا شيخنا الأكبر لولاه لقضي على الشرع، ولولا دفاعه ونضاله عن الدين وشريعته لأصبحت أثرًا بعد عين.

٧،١٨ التاجر يا لها من همّة عالية، ويا لها من عزيمة ماضية، ويا له من ثبات عظيم وموقف جليل قد ردّ الدين إلى نصابه، وحفظ للشريعة مقامها، وعلم الله أني قضيت الليالي الطوال لم يغمض لي جفن، ولم يرقأ لي دمع، ولم يهدأ لي فكر، ولم أتمتع فيها بأهلي وعيالي حتى لقد هانت عليّ نفسي، وجازفت بوضع اسمي ولا فخر مع الذين أمضوا على تلغراف الشكوى من هذه النازلة، وإني أحمد الله على حسن العواقب ونيل هذا الفخر، وجزى الله ذلك الشيخ الجليل عن الإسلام خير الجزاء.

٨،١٨ العالم بارك الله فيك وفي أمثالك، وليت كل الناس يحفظون للشيخ هذا الجميل ويعرفون له هذا الفضل لا سيما العلماء منهم ولكنهم لم يذكروا له ذلك إلا ريثما قام به ثمّ قعد في بيته فانحبست ألسنتهم عن الشكر، وانطلقت في ذكر ما يأخذونه عليه من سيرته الماضية في إدارته فأصبحوا يقولون إنه كان رجلا متهورًا بعيدًا عن التقيد بروابط النظام في أعماله تاركًا لقواعد الأهلية والاستحقاق، فكم قدّم من يستحق التأخير وأخّر من يستحق التقديم، وسار في طريق المحاباة والمراعاة والأخذ بالوسائط.

الوطني الفرنسوي قاتل الله الانكليز، هل سمعتم بمثل هذه الأفعال في تونس أو الجزائر، وهل علمتم هناك بوقوع مثل هذه الخدع وهذه الحيل التي يتخذها الانكليز أسبابًا لتنفيذ مآربهم؟ ولو فقه المصريون هذه المكائد وتنبهوا إلى هذه الدسائس لما أصابهم من الدهاء الانكليزي ما أصابهم، ولما رسخت قدم الاحتلال في أرضهم.

٩،١٨ الوطني الانكليزي نعوذ بالله من أمراض الأغراض ومن أدواء الأهواء، يا ويحكم أفكلما طرق طارق من السماء، أو طرأ طارئ في الأرض، أو عرض عارض من الجو، أو حدث حادث من الدهر قلتم شبكة انكليزية وحيلة بريطانية، وجعلتم الأقدار مسخرة لأمر الانكليز يستخرجون من مواقعها ما صغر وما كبر من أغراضهم؟ ولو كانوا من القوة الخارقة على ما تصورونهم به لما احتاجوا لنصب الشباك وتحيل

such perils, remove all disasters, and confront calamities? If it weren't for our great Shaykh, the Shariah would have been abolished. Had he not mounted a steadfast defense on behalf of the faith and its law, they would have vanished without trace.

MERCHANT Yes indeed, what lofty ambition, what superb determination, what wonderful persistence, and what a splendid stand he took! Our religion's underpinnings have been restored and the Shariah law has retained its status. God is my witness that I spent many sleepless nights weeping and disconcerted. I was unable to enjoy the company of my family and dependents. Eventually I decided to take a risk and, with no desire for fanfare, signed my name to the telegram in which we complained about this dreadful calamity. Now I thank God that things have worked out well, and I've acquired some prestige. May He reward the Shaykh in every way possible on Islam's behalf! 18.7

RELIGIOUS SCHOLAR May God bless you and everyone who did the same. If only everyone respected the Shaykh as you do and recognised the qualities he has, especially the religious scholars themselves. The only time they say anything is when he does something they approve of, but then they start accusing him about his past conduct in office. They've started claiming that he's reckless and feels in no way bound by the rules of order in anything he does. He's supposed to have abandoned the principles of eligibility and merit, and brought forward many people who did not deserve such advancement. According to them, his methods involve favoritism, compliance, and graft. 18.8

FRENCH-EDUCATED NATIONALIST God fight the English! Have you ever heard of anything like this happening in Tunis or Algeria? Do the French ever use the kind of ruses and deceits which the English employ here to get their own way? If only the Egyptians would appreciate these machinations and kept a closer eye on these ruses, they would not have been so adversely affected by English cunning, and the occupation forces would not be so firmly implanted in our country.

ENGLISH-EDUCATED NATIONALIST Heaven protect us against such sickly motives and caprices! Why is it that, every time some occurrence comes down from on high, there is an emergency of some kind, a weather event happens, or some other unforeseen event takes place, you always talk in terms of British tricks and cunning? You have made the fates themselves subservient to British commands; as a result they can achieve their goals, big or small. If they did in fact possess the amazing power you attribute to them, they'd certainly 18.9

الحيل على أنّ الانكليز قوم من البساطة وسلامة النية بمكان عظيم، وهم كغيرهم من الناس يحتاجون إلى الهداية والإرشاد في ما يجهلونه من الأعمال، وكان الأولى بكم أن تنزلوهم منزلتهم من هذه البساطة وتحفظوا لهم سلامة نيتهم نحوكم فتسيروا أمامهم وتقودوهم في طريق ما يرمونه لكم من الإصلاح وتنتفعوا بذلك أعظم النفع لا أن تضعوهم كلما راموا إصلاح مختل أو تقويم معوج موضع المحتلين المدلسين والمخادعين الماكرين فتسيئوا بهم الظن فيسيئوه بكم وتسقط الثقة بينكم وبينهم فيضيع النصح والرشد فيما بين الجانبين فتضطروهم إلى ابتكار المشروعات التي تبلغها أفكارهم في مصالحكم ويحملوكم على تنفيذها والأخذ بها. وما أحوجهم إلى عقلاء منكم يعرفون سلامة نيتهم ويعتقد الانكليز فيهم الصدق في القول والعمل وبعدهم عن الأغراض والمؤثرات التي تنأى عن الحق جانباً فيبادلونهم الثقة ويأخذون بإرشادهم ويعملون برأيهم ولكنهم لم يروا منكم في جميع أعمالهم إلا العكس من ذلك،

١٠،١٨ هذا شيخ الجامع أقام زمنا في وظيفته لا يرى منه إلا اللين ولا يعرف بغير التساهل في الأمور شخصية كانت أو متعلقة بوظيفته الدينية، هجمت العساكر بنيران البنادق وظبى السيوف على الأزهر الشريف كعبة المسلمين في علوم الدين وصوبوها إلى صدور ملؤها العلم وحشوها كتاب الله فاختلط سواد المداد بحمرة الدماء فما راعنا إلا تقرير الشيخ يعتذر به عن القاتل ويهدر به دم القتيل ويسترضي به القوي مكان الغضب للضعيف.

أرضى ويغضب قاتلي فتعجبوا
يرضى القتيل وليس يرضى القاتل

١١،١٨ وكان الشيخ حاضرا في الجلسة التي قال فيها تلميذه ناظر الحقانية عند الكلام في توحيد حسابات الأوقاف «إذا كان الشرع الإسلامي كما تصفون فإننا لا نعمل به» فابتلع الشيخ هذه الكلمة وطوى عنها كشحاً ولم ينطق بكلمة تقتضيها حمية الدفاع عن الدين.

not need to use any tricks or cunning. The fact is that the English are an uncomplicated and amazingly peaceful people; like everyone else, they need guidance in order to deal with things about which they know nothing. Things would go much better for you if you complied with their peaceful intentions and accepted them for the simple people they really are. Then you would be able to move forward and provide them with leadership as they aspire to initiate reforms, something from which we could all benefit. Far better that way than to call them arrogant forces of occupation and cunning tricksters every time they try to improve something that is wrong or put something faulty to rights. That only makes them think badly of you, and then any trust and cooperation between both sides is lost. They then have to devise projects which they have to think up for themselves as being in your best interests and force you to adopt and implement them. What they really need are some intelligent people from among you who realize their good intentions and can convince them that they are sincere in both word and deed. The English will then come to realise that there are no ulterior motives or influences to divert them from the truth and they'll come to trust each other. Then the English will begin to listen to their advice and act on their opinions. But now, whatever they do, all they see from your side is the very opposite.

18.10 The Shaykh of al-Azhar has held his post for some time and all he has done in that time is to comply and show leniency whether in his personal life or as part of his religious function. Now soldiers have attacked the noble al-Azhar with rifles and swords, the very Kaaba of Islamic learning. Rifles were aimed at men whose heads were filled with scholarship and whose very marrow was the book of God. Ink was mixed with blood. Then, lo and behold, the Shaykh's report exonerates the killer and the victim's blood is shed in vain; and all to appease the people in power instead of venting his wrath on behalf of the weak:

I am content and my killer is angry, so be amazed;
the victim is happy but the killer is not.[150]

18.11 The Shaykh himself was at the meeting at which the Minister of Justice (a pupil of his) was talking about unifying the accounts of the endowments. He said that, if the Shariah was really as he had described it, then he would not act by it. The Shaykh simply swallowed the pill and said nothing; he said nothing to defend the religion as he was bound to do. He has been much too indulgent in the way he has handled the duties of his position, not bothering about

تساهل في حقوق وظيفته فلم يكترث بتواتر وقوع الغبن على ما يتعلق منها بديوان الأوقاف ودأب في إرضاء غابنيه في الأمور المشتركة بينه وبينهم وفي ماله حق التصرف فيه. تساهل في حفظ كرامته إلى درجة أنه رضي لنفسه بما كتبه إليه أحد المحامين مما يحط بقدره وغض الطرف عنه وسكت عليه على أن كلمة واحدة منه لنظارة الحقانية كافية لتأديب المستهين به. تساهل الشيخ في هذا وفي كثير من أمثاله حتى اشتهر ذلك عنه.

١٢،١٨ وطالما نادى المحتلون بوجوب إصلاح المحكمة الشرعية سائلين أهل الشرع عن وجوه ذلك الإصلاح محرضين لهم على فتح بابه وسلوك طريقه فلم يروا منهم إلا الامتناع والأباء مع اقتناعهم بوجوب الإصلاح فلما أعياهم النداء اندفعوا لفتح باب الإصلاح بيدهم على قدر علمهم وما يرشدهم إليه حسن نيتهم فما يشعرون إلا وقام الشيخ في وجوههم على خلاف سيرته ونقيض عادته يدافع ويناضل ويعارض ويجادل ويتهور تهورا لم يعهد فيه من قبل في كثير من المواقف التي كانت أعظم تعلقا بالدين من مشروع المحكمة وقد قام قومته في مجلس شورى القوانين و رفض المشروع باسم الدين فأيقنت الحكومة أنه أمر بيت بليل وأن الشيخ متأثر بمؤثرات خارجة عن كنه المشروع وموافقته للشرع أو مخالفته له ولذلك لم يثقوا برأيه وتأكدوا من عمله أن المقصود خذلان الحكومة وقضاء حاجات في النفوس.

١٣،١٨ ولو أنّ الشيخ قال للحكومة قبل عرض المشروع على المجلس أن لي في هذا المشروع بحثا أو كلاما يخلو به المشروع مما عساه أن يخالف الشرع لبادرت الحكومة إلى إجابته ولأخذت برأيه ومشورته ولاستفادت منه تصحيحا للمشروع أو استرشدت منه إلى مشروع آخر تدخل به الإصلاح المطلوب، ولا يعتذر له معتذر بأنّ الحكومة لم تدعه بادئ الأمر لأخذ رأيه في المشروع لأنه مفتي الديار المصرية وعليه أن يقوم من نفسه بمقتضى وظيفته لإرشاد الحكومة بما يراه أو يسمعه في ما يختص بالشرع الشريف، ولو أن بعض الوقت الذي قضاه في تحرير المذكرة قبل عرض المشروع على

the continuous incidents of fraud connected with the Department of Endowments and actually placating those committing these swindles in matters concerning both parties and his obligations to handle the monies properly. He has also been far too negligent about preserving the dignity of his office, to such an extent that he was prepared to overlook the way a lawyer wrote to him in an insulting and denigrating fashion, whereas a single word spoken to the Minister of Justice would be quite sufficient when it came to punishing anyone who shows the Shaykh such contempt. In summary he has been negligent in these and other similar matters.

18.12 The occupying power has been calling for a reform of the Shariah Court for ages and asking experts about ways of implementing such a proposal. They have been urging these experts to open the court's doors and let progress in. But, even though those experts were convinced of the need for reform, all the English have encountered has been obstruction and rejection. When they got tired of talking about it, they started opening the doors of reform with their own hands, relying entirely on their own knowledge and good intentions. But, before they could turn round, there was the Shaykh of al-Azhar standing up to defend Islam in complete contrast with his normal behavior. He started arguing, protesting, and expressing his opposition with a rashness that he's never shown before in any number of other situations which were far more relevant to Islam than this court-reform project. He made his point at the Legislative Council and rejected the project in the name of Islam. However, the government is convinced that there's more in it than meets the eye; the Shaykh is governed by factors beyond the project per se or whether or not he agrees with it. So they've lost all confidence in his opinions and assumed that his aim is simply to frustrate the government and give people some gratification.

18.13 After all, if, before the project was presented to the Council, he'd said that he was looking into it and that he had certain things to point out which ran contrary to the Shariah, the government would have accepted his suggestion with alacrity and would have taken his advice and counsel. They would then have benefitted from his learning in the process of improving the project or might even have asked him to advise them in drawing up another project to incorporate the desired reforms. Let no one claim that the Shaykh didn't have an early opportunity to state his opinion on the subject. He's the Mufti of Egypt and, according to the requirements of his office, it's his duty to give the government guidance in any matter which has any relevance to the Shariah.

مجلس شورى القوانين كان قضاه في ذهابه إلى بعض رجال الحكومة يبحث معهم فيه لأخذوا برأيه ولم يقع ما وقع من ذلك الاضطراب والارتباك وتشعب المشاكل.

١٤،١٨ ولا يقال إن الشيخ بطيء الحركة في قصد رجال الحكومة فإنه طالما قصدهم في جزئيات الأمور التي تدور على توزيع الجرايات والأرغفة وقد نزل بجلالة قدره إلى الذهاب إلى بعض عمال مجلس النظار يستنجز ما لديهم من الأوراق التي تختص بزيادة مرتبه عشرة جنيهات ولكن الشيخ لم يعمل بواجب وظيفته في إرشاد الحكومة وآثر أن ينتظر المشروع في مجلس الشورى انتظار الخصم المعارض والعدو المعاند والباحث على خذلان الحكومة في أعين الناس ليحكم عليها بالخروج عن الشرع ويسجل بانحرافها عن الدين.

١٥،١٨ وأنتم تعلمون أن النظار قوم مسلمون وأن الانكليز قوم اشتهروا باحترام الأديان والابتعاد عن مس المعتقدات فلا يعقل أنهم كانوا يصرون على المشروع أن سلك الشيخ بهم طريق الإرشاد والتنوير. وأما ما يقال من أن للمحتلين غرضا مخصوصاً في مشروع للحط من سلطة الشرع وخلط المحكمة الشرعية بالمحاكم الوضعية فذلك باطل في باطل لم يوجبه إلا سوء الظن واعتقاد السوء فيهم وهو من قبيل اتهامهم بتسخير الأوبئة والطواعين واختلاق الحوادث العظيمة لخدمة أغراضهم، وما أطوع الحكومة للعمل بكلمة الدين لتظهر للملأ أنها محافظة على الشريعة خروجا عن وصمة الاستسلام للأجنبي، وما طوع الانكليز لسماع كلمة الحق من أهل العلم في الدين يبادرون إلى العمل بها ليزيدوا الناس برهانا على برهان بأنهم لا يقصدون النكاية بالأديان في كل أرض احتلوها لأن مدنيتهم في الوقت الحاضر سلخت من صدورهم ماكان في صدور آبائهم من أهل القرون الوسطى. ولا أجد أفضل للعالم المتقي من إرشاد قوم ديدنهم احترام الأديان فهو يقول وهم يفعلون إذا ثبت عندهم خلوه عن الغرض وصدقه في خدمة الحق وإخلاصه في النصح.

If only he'd taken some of the time he spent composing his memorandum in going to see some members of the government and discussing it with them, they would have accepted his advice and none of this confusion and complication would have arisen.

18.14 No one should claim either that the Shaykh is slow when it comes to going to see members of the government. He often goes to visit them on trivial matters like the distribution of salaries and loaves of bread. He has even debased his position to the extent of going to see certain cabinet staff members and asking them to expedite documents concerning the raising of his own salary by ten pounds. The Shaykh is not offering the government advice in the way that he should. He's preferred for the project to linger in the Legislative Council, like some dogged adversary whose aim is to frustrate the government so he can then claim that it's deviating from the Shariah and turning from the true path of Islam.

18.15 As you're well aware, the ministers are all Muslims. The English are renowned for their respect for religions and their unwillingness to violate other people's beliefs in any way. It's quite inconceivable that they would insist on implementing the project if the Shaykh had given them some guiding counsel. Furthermore, anyone who claims that the occupying power has an ulterior motive in introducing this project—namely of reducing the Shariah's authority by joining its court to the secular courts—is talking rubbish. Their only motivation for saying so is their poor opinion of the British and an assumption of evil intent. To say that they exploit plague epidemics and use such disasters to serve their own purposes falls into the same category. This government is more prepared than anyone else to act in accordance with the dicta of Islam to show that it's adhering to the tenets of the Sharīʿa and not succumbing to the interests of foreigners. The English are most cooperative when it comes to listening to religious authorities; they implement their advice immediately so as to give people as much proof as possible of the fact that they're not trying to damage the religion of every country they occupy, because at this moment in time their own civilization has plucked from their hearts the spirit which their forebears had in the middle ages. There can be nothing more virtuous for a pious scholar than to give guidance to a people whose nature it is to respect religions. When they're sure that he has no ulterior motives, he can speak and they will act. He can prove his sincerity by serving the truth and providing reliable counsel.

١٦،١٨ العالم (للتاجر) لقد أصاب الأول ولم يخطئ الثاني والله در شبابنا في سعة اطلاعهم وقدرتهم على إقامة البرهان لخدمة أوطانهم.

التاجر دع الخلق للخالق ونسأل الله أن يحفظ علينا السلامة ويحسن لنا العاقبة وأن يقينا شر الدخول في ما لا يعني.

الوطني الفرنسوي يا خيبة الأمل وضيعة العمل ماذا أسمع منكما وأنتما من أهم أجزاء هذا الوطن ومحبة الوطن من الإيمان وكان الأجدر بكما وبأمثالكما أن تتألموا معنا بما نتألم منه وأن تثبتوا على مبدأ واحد تجعلونه نصب أعينكم ووجهة أفكاركم وأعمالكم فتتحدوا معنا على الكلمة العالية كلمة الوطن التي لا تقاوم بشقشقة اللسان وبلاغة البيان وإحكام البرهان وما عداها فألفاظ وهي المعنى وكفى بالتعذيب في حب الوطن فخرا فقد استعذبته النفوس العظيمة، وأين أنتم من ذلك الروماني الذي أسرته قرطاجنة ثم أرادت مبادلة الأسرى بينها وبين الحكومة الرومانية فبعثته إلى حكومته ليخابرها في ذلك واعتمدت على كلمته في الرجوع فذهب إلى رومية فأشار على مجلس السناتو بأن ليس من مصلحة الجمهورية الرومانية أن تستبدل الأسرى وهو الأسير- وكر راجعا إلى مقر أسره وهو على يقين بما سيلاقيه من التعذيب على بذل هذه النصيحة التي رآها نافعة لحكومته وتحمل تعذيب الجسم للذة الروح؟

١٧،١٨ وأين أنت أيها الشيخ العالم من ذلك العربي وقد حاصر التتار مدينة من أعمال أزربيجان حصارا شديداً واستضعفوها وكادوا يملكونها وتوجه إليها لمعونتها سعيد الحرشي من قبل هشام بن عبد الملك في جيوش كثيفة فأرسل واحدا من أصحابه إلى أهلها سراً يعرفهم وصوله ويأمرهم بالصبر خوفا أن لا يدركهم فسار الرجل فلقيه قوم من التتار فسألوه من حاله فكتمهم فعذبوه فأخبرهم وصدقهم فقالوا إن فعلت ما نأمرك به أطلقناك فقال ما تريدون قالوا أنت عارف بأصحابك بالمدينة وهم يعرفونك فإذا وصلت تحت السور فنادهم أن ليس خلفي مدد ولا من يكشف ما بكم وإنما بعثت جاسوساً فأجابهم إلى ذلك فلما صار تحت سورها وقف حيث يسمع أهلها كلامه

Religious Scholar (*to the Merchant*) They have both made their point, haven't they? Young people today read so widely and can serve their country well by giving us such powerful arguments. 18.16

Merchant Leave mankind to its Creator. We ask God to preserve us all in safety and to grant us a happy outcome! Certainties are the worst possible intrusion into something which has no meaning.

French-Educated Nationalist How disappointing! How frustrating! What is this that I hear you saying? You two represent some of the most important segments of our population. Patriotism is a matter of faith. You and your peers should be complaining about the same things as we are. You need to make one principle the focus of your attentions and the fulcrum of your ideas and actions. Then you can join us in supporting that sublime word "homeland," something that no amount of prattling and eloquence can resist. Everything else is simply empty words. People have been tortured for love of their homeland as a matter of pride. Some of their stories are famous. Take for example the Roman who was taken prisoner by the Carthaginians. They sent him to Rome to arrange an exchange of prisoners, relying on his word of honor that he would return. When he arrived in Rome, he advised the Senate that it wasn't in their best interest to exchange prisoners, he being one of them. He then returned to Carthage, knowing full well the punishment which awaited him because of the sound advice he'd given his own governing body. Bodily torture was compensated by a spirit's delight.

Esteemed Shaykh, how about the Arab hero whose city in Azerbaijan was besieged by the Tartars; they had weakened it considerably and almost captured it. The Caliph Hishām ibn ʿAbd al-Malik sent Saʿīd al-Ḥarashī with a large troop of soldiers to relieve the beseiged city. The commander sent one of his companions ahead in secret to inform the people in the city that he was on his way and they were to wait patiently; he was afraid that he might not reach the city in time. The man left, but was captured by a group of Tartars. They interrogated him, but he told them nothing. They then tortured him, so he told them and made them believe him. The Tartars told him: "If you do as we ask, we'll release you." "What do you want me to do?" he asked. "You know your friends in the city," they said, "and they know you. When you arrive at the city walls, shout out that there is no help on the way and no one can save you. I've been sent as a spy." He told the Tatars that he'd do as they asked. Once he arrived at the walls, he stood where the people inside could hear him. 18.17

وقال لهم أتعرفوني قالوا نعم قال فإن سعيد الحرشي قد وصل إلى مكان كذا في مائة ألف سيف وهو يأمركم بالصبر وحفظ البلد وهو مصبحكم أو ممسيكم فرفع أهل البلدة أصواتهم بالتكبير وقتل التتار ذلك الرجل ورحلوا عنها ووصل سعيد فوجد أبوابها مفتوحة وأهلها سالمين، ﴿لِمِثْلِ هَـٰذَا فَلْيَعْمَلِ الْعَامِلُونَ﴾.

قال عيسى بن هشام: وقام الباشا ينادي من رقدته، فأسرعت لإجابة دعوته. ١٨،١٨

"Do you know me?" he asked. They replied that they did. "Saʿīd al-Ḥarashī has reached such-and-such a place," he told them, "He has a thousand men with him. He orders you to stay steadfast and hold the city; he'll be with you either in the morning or evening." With that the people inside the city raised paeans of praise to Almighty God. The Tartars killed the man and abandoned their siege. When Saʿīd arrived, he found the city gates open and the people inside safe and sound. «May people learn to do likewise.»[151]

ʿĪsā ibn Hishām told us: The Pāshā had woken up by now and was shouting for me. So I hurried over to him in response to his call. **18.18**

مصباح الشرق ٦٣، ١٣ يوليو ١٨٩٩

١،١٩ قال عيسى بن هشام: إذا استأنست من الإنسان العين، بمنظر واضح الشين تضاءل قبحه لتواتر الرؤية، وامتنع فيه أعمال الفكرة والروية، وشبت عليه النفس في نمائها شب الشجرة في انحنائها وائتلاف العادة يحيل السماجة سماحة، ويخيل البدعة السيئة حسنة مباحة، يستحسنها من يألفها، ويأنفها من لا يعرفها:

إذا ألف الشيء استهان به الفتى
ولم يره بؤسى تعدّ ولا نعمى
كاتفاقه من عمره ومذاقه
من الريق عذبا لا يحس له طعما

٢،١٩ واضرب لذلك مثلا أمة وكعاء، تسوم الإبل والشاء، في عرض الفلاء، ووهاد البيداء، يمر من فوقها فتاك الغارات، وطلاب الثارات، وبغاة السبي والسلب، من كماة الطعن والضرب، يرعف في أيديهم الحديد الأخضر، بالنجيع الأحمر، وهي كامنة بالسرح، في بطن السفح - نقلتها من تلك الأرض المخيفة القفراء، إلى أرض الحضارة الزهراء. . . وأشهدتها حفلة رقص غربي فرأت هناك مصابيح الكهرباء، ترسل ساطع الضياء، على وجوه يشرق فيها الجمال، إشراق الشمس في وجه الهلال، وقدود ينحني أمامها كل قد، وخدود إذا وردت خجل منها الورد، وصدور تبرز منها كواعب النهود، وتغوص فيها لآلىء العقود، وأكباد عارية ونحور، في نقاء الجبين وصفاء البلور، ومعاصم بضة غضه، كأنها شماريخ الفضة، وشعور كسلوك الذهب، يتقد فيها الجوهر اتقاد اللّهب، وكأن ما تناثر على فضة الجبين من ذهب الشعر أشعة الشمس تفرعت على صفحة الفجر،

٣،١٩ ثم رأت الشيوخ والشبان والكهول والفتيان، يختالون بين هذه البيض الحسان، متألقين في حسن سمتهم وزيهم، متأنقين في حللهم ووشيهم يمشي الشاب منهم مشية الطالب المرتاد، إلى حيث يقوده الجمال فينقاد، فيقف بين يدي ربة

19.1 ʿĪsā ibn Hishām said: When the human eye becomes acquainted with a scenario that is manifestly shameful, the disturbance to that person's vision will lessen his evil intent. Both thought and vision will play a preventitive role. His soul will grow like a tree that bends. Habit will replace what is loathsome with what is kindly. Malicious heresy will now be seen as something permissible and good, approved by those familiar with it and rejected by those who are unaware.

When man is familiar with something, he despises it,
seeing in it neither bad nor good.
He can find nothing to savor in a reconciled life
nor in the taste of his own saliva.[153]

19.2 In such a context let me use the simile of a wretched woman dealing in sheep and camels in the dunes and depressions of the desert. All around her are raids and revenge missions, men seeking prisoners and spoils, fearsome warriors armed to the teeth—the grey of their swords stained with the red blood of victims. She meanwhile continues to cower on the hillside grazing her flocks. People then transport her from this fearful desert environment to the gleaming city. There they show her a Western dance party. She can see electric lights emitting brilliant beams on beautiful people, their faces gleaming like the sun on the moon's surface; lovely figures before which all others bow; cheeks whose very blush puts the rose to shame; bosoms revealing buxom breasts on which float pearl necklets; shoulders and necks exposed, as smooth as brows and peerless as crystal; lustrous wrists like date-clusters made of silver; hair like golden threads with jewels that glow like flame—as though the golden hair spread across the silvered brow were the very rays of the sun branching out across the vista of dawn.

19.3 Then she spots men of all ages—old, middle-aged, young, and boys—strutting their way amid these beauties, bedecked in all their personal finery and relishing their fancy clothes. A young man acts like an aspiring student as he goes wherever beauty leads him. Standing in front of a beautiful woman, he bows like a tree branch, as though he were freeing a lovely cow from the

الحسن، وينحني أمامها كالغصن، فيستخلص المهاة من حجر أبيها، ويقتنص الظبية من جانب أخيها، ويجتني الغادة من يد بعلها، ويختطف الخريدة من وسط أهلها، فإذا ترنمت الألحان، ترنحت الأغصان فانعطفت القدود على القدود، والتصقت الخدود بالخدود، وصارت الأيادي مناطق للخصور، ومساند للظهور، ورسفت الأقدام كما ترسف في القيد، واضطربت الأجسام، كالقطا في شباك الصيد:

يميل بها ميل النزيفة مسندا
إلى الصدر منها ناعم الصدر قد نجم

٤،١٩ ثم تحين فترة عند انقطاع الأنغام، فيهرعون إلى شرب المدام، فتلعب الكؤوس بالرؤوس وتعبث الشمول بالعقول، هنالك تلتقي الأشواق، في معترك القلوب والأحداق، وتعود سوق الرقص قائمة على ساق تحت جوّ عبق بالطيب والعبير، عبق الزهر في الروض النضير، يتناثر فيه العرق من أجياد الغيد، كما يتناثر بينهن الدر النضيد، من كل عقد فريد، عند ذلك تستر الأمة البدوية وجهها بعصابها، وتتقلص خيوط أعصابها، من شدة ما يعتريها من الخجل، وينتابها من الوجل، وتفر راجعة تطلب منزلها ببطن الوادي، في منقطع البوادي، تراه بالنسبة لما تراه آمن فناء وجنابا، وأصون سترا وحجابا، وأنقى حياء لها وأقل عابا.

٥،١٩ ولو نقلت غادة من أولئك الغربيات، إلى مجلس نسوة من المصريات، في بيت استدار به الحراس والحجاب، وسدت منه المنافذ وغلقت الأبواب، وقام عليه الخصي، في شدة الجندي، وغلظة الشرطي، فسمعت ما يدور بينهن من المقال، مقصورا على ذكر ما يكون من الرجال، يتسامرون وأبكارهن في حجورهن وصبيانهن بين أيديهن بفاضح القول وفاحش اللفظ وخبيث الكلام ورفث الحديث، ورأتهن إذا دخل أحد أقاربهن يقوده الخصي وراءه ويكثر صياحه ونداءه، إنذارا لهن بالاختفاء تحت الغطاء، وقد سترن الوجوه بأذيالهن وأبقين فيها منفذا لأبصارهن- لفزعت الغربية، فزع تلك الأعرابية ولعدت نفسها في مثل ذلك المرقص أحسن أخلاقا وأجمل آدابا وأكمل احتشاما.

protection of her father or a gazelle from beside her brother—plucking the girl from her lord and snatching the virgin maid from her family. As the melodies swell, the branches begin to sway; figures draw closer together and cheek touches cheek. Now hands are clasping waists and supporting backs. Feet are constrained as though in chains, and bodies are in turmoil like sandgrouse caught in a trap:

> He leans over her like a welt, pressing
> on her breast that appears in all its smoothness.[154]

19.4 Once the music comes to an end, they rush over to get a drink of wine; the glasses toy with people's heads, and the entire blend plays with their minds. In a joust of hearts and glances passions now come together. The dancing recommences, people pirouetting to the scents of fragrant perfume, the sweet smell of flowers in a verdant meadow. Sweat now drops from the necks of beauties like rows of pearls scattered among them from rare and costly necklaces. Seeing all this, the Bedouin woman covers her face with her shawl, her nerves in a tangle in sheer embarassment at what she has witnesed. She runs away as fast as she can, needing to go back to her home in the depths of the valley at the desert crossroads. Bearing in mind what she has now seen, she sees her home as a safe haven, offering more seclusion and protection, more modesty and less shame.

19.5 On the other hand, if one of these Western lovelies was transported to an Egyptian women's gathering in a household where guards and chamberlains did the rounds, passageways were blocked, and doors were kept locked—the kind of place where a eunuch held sway with all the force of a soldier and gruffness of a policeman—she might hear the kind of chatter the women indulged in, usually restricted to talk about men. With their young daughters sitting in their laps and their sons in front of them, they would resort to the lewdest and foulest of verbiage. And, if a male relative should happen to be brought in by the eunuch, this Western women would watch as he yelled at them all to cover themselves up; and they would all duly wrap their faces in the hems of their garments and leave just a slit so they could see. Confronted with such behavior, the Western woman would be just as alarmed as the Arab woman was. In this dance hall she would consider herself to be behaving immaculately and showing the best of manners and the most seemly modesty.

٦،١٩ وكذلك كان الحال بيني وبين الباشا دائرًا على هذا المثال كلما أريته شيئًا لم يعرفه في زمانه ولم يألفه في عصره ولم يعهد مثله من قبل نفرت نفسه منه ونبت عينه عنه وأراني فيه ما لم أكن أراه ونبهني إلى ما هو كامن فيه من القبح تحت غطاء العادة ومحجوب بحجاب الإئتلاف والاستئناس فتراني أنتقل به منذ نقه من علته في الأماكن التي يرتاح فيها الخاطر والمجالس التي يتسلى فيها الفكر لأشغله عن هواجس المنازعات والخصومات وذكرى النعيم الغابر والبؤس الحاضر فأراه يحدث لي من كل شيء ذكرا ويستخرج لي من كل ما كنت أتوهمه من أسباب الارتياح وجمام النفس همًا وكدرا حتى وصل بنا الدور إلى دعوة في عرس فأجبنا الداعي وبادرنا إلى المكان بعد الغروب فرأينا في حفظ الباب جنديين يمنعان الناس من الدخول بالنهر والطرد وسوء الدفع فجذبني الباشا وقال:

٧،١٩ الباشا على رسلك أيها الصديق فلست ضللت الطريق وأخطأت الغرض إن لم تكن أردت الذهاب بي مرة أخرى إلى دار الشرطة وأبواب المحاكم.

عيسى بن هشام لا شرطة ولا محاكم وإنما هذا باب بيت العرس وأما الشرطيان فإنهما مؤجران لمنع من لم يكن مدعوًا عن الدخول خشية الغوغاء وضوضاء الزحام وهي عادة متحسنة يجري كبراء الناس اليوم عليها.

الباشا بئست العادة، وما كانت الولائم تقام في أيامنا إلا يجتمع فيها كل من قصدها ولا يمنع منها فقير ولا محروم وكانت تمد فيها الأسمطة لهم فيأكلون ويشربون ويتفرجون على ما يقام من الألعاب الشائقة والمناظر البديعة من مطاردة الفرسان ومسابقة الخيول وحركات الفروسية من المصارعة ولعب السيف وسماع المرتلين للقرآن والمنشدين بجميل الذكر وكان ما في نفوس الناس من احترام الكبراء وتبجيلهم ورفعة مكانتهم وجلالة هيبتهم كافيا في الردع عن لغط الزحام وضوضاء الجموع وكان على كل نفس رقيب منها، فهل انحطت عندكم الأقدار وانخفضت المقامات وجهل الكبير قدر نفسه فلم يحافظ على مقامه ولم يسلك في سبيل ما يجعله محترما موقرًا حتى ذهبت هيبته من نفس الصغير وزال الأدب والحياء من الأصاغر

This is the way things were between the Pāshā and me. Every time I showed him something with which he had not been familiar in his own lifetime and had never encountered before, he would object and turn away, showing me as he did so things that I had not previously noticed and making me aware of the evil underpinnings that lurk beneath the surface cover of habit and are shrouded by the veil of familiarity and acceptance. Once he had recovered from his period of illness, I would take him to a number of places that would delight the heart and to assemblies that would distract his attention from the succession of troubles and anxieties that had beset him, not to mention the good times in the past and the miseries of the present. I found that he would talk to me about everything; for each idea that I thought of to provide a serene setting he would produce some issue or concern. Eventually our routine involved an invitation to a wedding. Accepting the offer we hastened to the location after sunset and discovered two policemen guarding the door. They kept shouting and shoving people away to stop them getting inside. The Pāshā pulled me aside. 19.6

PĀSHĀ Wait a minute, my friend! Are you sure you haven't gone the wrong way and mistaken the intention here? Unless, that is, you plan to go to the police station with me again and through the entire court system. 19.7

ʿĪSĀ IBN HISHĀM No, there'll be no police and no courts! This is the door of the house where the wedding is being held. The two policemen have been hired to keep out people who haven't been invited. They don't want crowds of noisy people. These days important people have adopted this practice.

PĀSHĀ It's a very bad one! In our day wedding celebrations were specifically intended for everyone to attend who wished to do so. Poor and indigent people were never excluded. People would spread out tablecloths for them; they would eat and drink and then watch the amazing games that were put on for the occasion: horse races, displays of horsemanship, wrestling, and sword drills. They would listen to people chanting the Qur'an and singing lovely Sufi liturgies. The respect that everyone felt for important people, their lofty status, and their august demeanor were all sufficient to prevent any likelihood of rowdiness and noise. Every person had their own internal monitor. Has high rank and status now sunk that low with you? Does the man of influence no longer appreciate his own status, so he is neither capable of maintaining his prestige nor of behaving in a way that will earn him respect? It seems that now the common people have lost their sense of reverence and no longer behave with

فاستهانوا بمقامات الأكابر فاحتاجوا إلى الشرطي في نظام أعراسهم كما احتاجوا إلى الجنود والحجاب في دوائر حكمهم.

قال عيسى بن هشام: فقلت في نفسي يا سبحان الله لقد بدأنا في استخراج الأكدار حتى من الأعراس. وجاوزنا الباب فرأينا في المدخل أربعة من الشبان في أبهى ما يكون من الحلي والحلل فاستوقفني الباشا وقال لي: ٨،١٩

الباشا عجبا هل أصبح من العادة عندكم أن يزف أربعة في عرس واحد وهل هم لأب واحد أم هم أجانب مشتركون وكيف حازوا هذه النياشين التي تتألق في صدورهم على صغر سنهم.

عيسى بن هشام ليس في هؤلاء الأربعة عروس ولا يقال لهذه العلامات نياشين بل هم أصحاب العروس يخدمونه في استقبال الوافدين وإجلاسهم مجالسهم وميزوهم بهذه العلامة يستدل بها الناس عليهم لقضاء حاجاتهم.

الباشا فما بالهم إذن لم يلتفتوا إلى استقبالنا ولم يهدونا إلى مجالسنا.

عيسى بن هشام لأنهم لم يعرفونا ولم تبهرهم ملابسنا.

الباشا وهذه المادة أيضا قبيحة فقد كان عهدنا أن يقف كبير البيت وأقاربه لاستقبال الزائرين حتى لا يجهل واحد منهم ولم يترك وشأنه كما وقع معنا الآن.

عيسى بن هشام لصاحب البيت في ذلك عذر فإن أكثر أرباب الأعراس اعتادوا التفاخر بالباطل والتظاهر بالمباهاة وحب السمعة فيدعون الوزراء والكبراء والعلماء ممن لا يعرفون أشخاصهم ولم تقع أعينهم قط عليهم فيضطرون إلى انتداب مثل هؤلاء الأغراب لمقابلتهم. وأعرف رجلا تاجرا أنفق نصف ثروته في عرس ليدعو إليه بعض كبار الوزراء فأصبحت دفاتر تجارته شطرين شطرا محتوي على بيان أنواع التجارة وأصنافها والآخر على بيان أسماء من حضر عرسه من أولئك الوزراء. ٩،١٩

قال عيسى بن هشام: فوجم الباشا وهز رأسه متأسفا متعجبا ثم صرنا في ساحة الدار ١٠،١٩

any kind of modesty. As a result they despise the status of influential people, and that requires them to have policemen when they organize weddings just as they need soldiers and chamberlains in government departments.

'Īsā ibn Hishām said: Good heavens, I told myself, now we're finding things to grumble about even at weddings. Once we passed through the front door, we noticed four young flashily dressed men. The Pāshā stopped me and asked: 19.8

PĀSHĀ Incredible! Is it a custom among you now for four men to be married at one ceremony? Do they all have a single father, or is it that they're foreigners? How have they managed to earn those medals on their chests when they're so young?

'ĪSĀ IBN HISHĀM Those four men are not the bridegrooms, nor are the things on their chests medals. They're simply friends of the groom who are helping welcome the guests and seating them in their places. They're wearing those pendants on their chests to let people know what their function is.

PĀSHĀ Then how come they didn't bother to welcome us and take us to our seats?

'ĪSĀ IBN HISHĀM They don't know us, and our clothes didn't impress them enough.

PĀSHĀ That's a bad custom too. In my day the head of the household and his relatives stood by the door to welcome visitors. That way no one was ignored and left to his own devices as we have been here.

'ĪSĀ IBN HISHĀM The person putting on this wedding ceremony has an excuse. The majority of such people want to put on stupid displays and demonstrate how famous they really are. So they send invitations to government ministers, important social figures, and religious scholars—people they don't know and have never even met. As a result they have to get people like these complete strangers to welcome guests. I know a merchant who spent half of his entire fortune on a wedding so he could invite senior ministers to attend. Afterwards his own ledgers were divided into two parts: one contained the various types of merchandise that he had; the other was a list of ministers who'd attended the wedding. 19.9

'Īsā ibn Hishām said: The Pāshā stared at the ground shaking his head in regret. We made our way into the courtyard. It was brightly illuminated and decked 19.10

فإذا هي مشرقة بالأنوار مكللة بالأزهار، مزدانة بالأعلام محلاة بالبسط المفروشة والستائر المنقوشة، فجلسنا حيث وجدنا مكانا خاليا بجانب صاحب لي من ظرفاء الأصحاب ثم أخذ الباشا يسرح الطرف يمينا وشمالا ويسألني بقوله:

الباشا قل لي بالله من هؤلاء المضطجعون على الأسرة في صدر المكان، كأنهم آل كسرى وآل ساسان، جلوسا في صدر الإيوان، ومالي أراهم في سكون، لا ينطقون ولا يتحركون؟ أهؤلاء عندكم أيضا من محدثات الزينة في الأعراس، أم هم من متممات الزخرفة في مجالس الائتناس؟

الصاحب الظريف (داخلا معنا في الحديث) ﴿فَاسْأَلُوهُمْ إِن كَانُوا يَنطِقُونَ﴾.

عيسى بن هشام (عيسى بن هشام) هؤلاء هم حكام القطر وأولياء الأمر.

١١،١٩ الباشا وهل الحكام عندكم حكام في مجالس الأنس ووليمة العرس، يتخذونها دستا للأبهة والعظمة ويترددون فيها برداء الكبرياء والخيلاء كما يتكلفه الحكام في مجالس الحكم لما تقتضيه من الهيبة في النفوس والتوقير في الصدور وإني لأتذكر ما كنت أتكلفه لذلك في زمان حكمنا فأتنغص به وما أعلم معيشة سوء هي أنكد وأنكى من معيشة دائمة التكلف والتصنع ولقد كان الحاكم منا إذا انتهى من دائرة حكمه وأخذ مجلسه في بيته انبسط وجهه للناس وانحلت منه عقدة التقطيب وترقرق فيه ماء البشر. والناس أعداء للحكم والحكام فليس من الحكمة أن تجمع عليهم بين مضاضة الحكم وغضاضة التكبر والتغطرس ومقابلتهم بوجه دائم التجهم والتقطيب في كل الأطوار واختلاف المجلس ولذلك كنت ترى الناس أكثر ما يقصدون الحكام لحاجاتهم وهم في بيوتهم لخوفهم وانكماشهم أمام هيبة الحاكم في دست حكمه ولاعتماد نفوسهم على سهولة جانبه وسكون قلوبهم إلى انطلاق وجهه وانبساط نفسه وهو بعيد عن محل حكمه.

١٢،١٩ الصاحب الظريف نعم إن الأمر لدينا على ضد ما تقول وعكس ما تصف فالحكم عندنا حكام في بيوتهم أمراء في بيوت الناس ورعية في دواوينهم فترى

with floral arrangements; there were flags, woven carpets, and colorful drapes. We took a seat where we found an empty space; it was right alongside one of my more fashionable friends. The Pāshā started looking around him.

PĀSHĀ Tell me, who are those people lounging on couches in the center? They're behaving like Persian monarchs in some royal enclave. How come they're doing nothing, neither talking nor moving? Are they too some kind of new-fangled embellishment to weddings, or are they instead a final touch to the decoration in these social soirées?

SUAVE FRIEND (*entering the conversation*) «Question them if they are able to speak.»[155]

ʿĪSĀ IBN HISHĀM They're provincial governors and local authority figures.

19.11 PĀSHĀ So do these governors of yours now exert their authority at soirées and wedding celebrations and use them as a means of showing how important and powerful they are? Do they don the same garments of arrogance and pride as they do in government chambers as a necessary way to inspire people's awe and respect? I can clearly recall the effort I used to put into such things when I was part of the government. How I used to hate it! I cannot imagine a life more wretched than one in which you're constantly having to put on airs and act a part. In our times when a government official finished his period in office and returned to the evening gatherings in his own home, he greeted everyone with a smile, unknitted his frowning brow, and showed a joyful countenance. People are the foes of government and its governors. When the grind of government, the arrogance of power, and the adoption of phony airs are all combined into one, it makes no sense to greet everyone with the same gloomy visage, no matter what the occasion or the venue. That's why in the past you would notice people going to see government officials in their own homes, for the simple reason that people were afraid of dealing with the officials' august demeanor when they were in their seat of authority. Once the official was far removed from his government offices, they could place more faith in his indulgent side and calm their fears by observing his more relaxed and open expression.

19.12 SUAVE FRIEND Yes indeed, these days things are the exact opposite of what you've been describing. Now government officials are in their homes, princes are at other people's houses, and the populace is in their offices. You can

الواحد منهم في مكان حكمه ودولة إقباله حذرا وجلا متضائلا منكمشا يخشى عين المراقب وإن كان دونه في الرتبة ويفرق من لحظة المترصد وإن كان تحته في الدرجة فهو كالطالب في حلقة الدرس والتلميذ في صف الامتحان. إذا قصدت الحاكم هناك وقلّ من يقصده وجدت لديه من البشر والترحيب وحسن التخلص ولطف الاعتذار وجميل الرد وبساطة النفس مثل الذي تصف به أمراء زمانكم في بيوتهم وبيوت غيرهم فإذا تخلص من عقال منصبه وانطلق في مجالس الناس ومحافل أنديتهم انقلب البشر اكفهرارا والترحيب ازورارا وغدا السهل صعبا والذلول جموحا. وحكامنا أعزك الله لصغر نفوسهم في أنظارهم وشدة هوانها في أعينهم وحذرهم من انكشافها للناس واطلاعهم عليها يحاولون تغطيتها بغطاء الكبر ويدأبون في سترها بستائر التيه ويتصنعون الظهور بمخائل الاختيال وشمائل العجب فيتفننون في تعظيم هيآتهم عند مشيهم وتهويل صورهم عند جلوسهم، ولبعضهم دروس أمام المرآة في الحركات التي يرضونها لأجسامهم يتمرنون عليها جانبا من وقتهم، وما مثلهم إلا مثل رجل من أعيان المصريين كان معروفا بالبلاهة وكان يهوي غادة في حانة خمار فيدخلها ويحاول الاختفاء عن أعين الجالسين من العامة حفظا لمقامه وصونا لكرامته فيجلس مسندا ظهره إلى عمود في وسط الحانة متوهما أنه توارى عن أعين الخلق أو كالنعامة إذا أزعجها زئير الأسد أو أفزعها صوت الصائد طوت رأسها تحت جناحها وأيقنت أنها توارت عن الأعين بجميع جسمها.

١٣،١٩ على أنهم في الواقع ونفس الأمر قد انخفضوا من حيث أرادوا الاعتلاء وانكشفوا من حيث أرادوا الاستتار فإن إفراطهم في كبريائهم ومبالغتهم في كبريائهم ومبالغتهم في خيلائهم دفع بالناس إلى البحث عن مبلغ قدرتهم والتنقيب عن منتهى سلطتهم ليطابقوا بين ذلك وبين ما يتكلفونه من الإيهام بعظمتهم والتهويل بمناصبهم فظهر للناس ما بطن وكان سقوطهم من أعينهم بمقدار تعاليهم في تعاليهم أستغفر الله إلا ما يكون من هؤلاء الذين تراهم بجانبنا لا يستقرون على هيئة في جلوسهم كأنهم جالسون على شوك القتاد.

see any one of them in his government office where he is supposed to hold sway, but he's a picture of apprehension, caution, and diminished authority, all because he's afraid he's being watched and spied on even if it's by someone who's his junior in rank. He's just like a student in the classroom or taking an exam. If you were to visit such an official—and few people do so—you'd discover that he'd welcome you with open arms, respond nicely to your requests, apologize profusely, and send you away content, just the way you have been describing the rulers in your day inside their own homes and those of others. Once he casts off the chains of office and is free to return to people's normal assemblies and clubs, his open smile becomes a frown and his welcome turns into avoidance; what was easy is now difficult, and what was pliable now becomes defiant. May God bolster you! Today our government officials have such a low opinion of themselves and are so scared to reveal their sentiments in public that they make every effort to cover it all up with boasts and displays of pride. They fabricate phony illusions of conceit and arrogance and go to enormous lengths to enhance their dignity in the way they walk and make their image that much more daunting in the way they sit. Some of them even take lessons in front of a mirror on bodily movements that they like and spend some time perfecting them. They can all be compared with the illustrious Egyptian who was renowned for his stupidity. He was in love with a girl in a wine seller's shop. He went in and tried to hide from the other people sitting there so that his status and honor would not be affected. As he sat down, he leaned his back against a pillar in the middle of the store, assuming that he was out of sight, or like the proverbial ostrich: when it hears a lion roar or is startled by the hunter's voice, it puts its head under its wing and assumes that its entire body is now hidden.

19.13 In actual fact, however, they've sunk low instead of aspiring to be seen on high; what they hoped to keep concealed is now revealed. The absurd lengths to which they've gone in their pride and arrogance has now led people to investigate quite how much power they really have and what are the precise limits of their authority. That's allowing people to make comparisons between these realities and the efforts they make to claim an illusory greatness and to use their positions to frighten people. Now everything that was concealed is out in the open, and their decline is in direct proportion to the exaggerated assertion of prestige that they claimed for themselves. But, seeking God's forgiveness, I wonder what's the matter with these people alongside us; they keep fidgeting as though they're sitting on a bed of thorns.

الباشا صدقت فإني أراهم على ما تقول فمن هم وما سبب اضطرابهم؟

الصاحب هؤلاء فئة من أعيان المصريين وتجارهم لم تزل عندهم بقية مما ترك في نفوسهم الحكم السابق من وجوب التزاف إلى الحكام والتفاخر بأدنى صلة بهم فتراهم يتحفزون للقيام لكل داخل فإن علموا إنه كبير أو حاكم قاموا تعظيما له وإجلالا ليتفخروا على أقرانهم بإشارة سلام منه نحوهم وإن علموا أنه على خلاف ذلك عادوا إلى جلوسهم بعد اهتزازهم، وانظر الآن كيف تشرئب أعناقهم ويحدقون بأبصارهم نحو مجلس الكبراء علهم يتلفتون إليهم من أخطأهم سلامه منهم عند دخوله.

١٤،١٩ قال عيسى بن هشام: فنبهنا هذا الانتقاد اللطيف إلى توجيه النظر ناحيتهم والاتصال لما يجري به الحديث بينهم ولله در صاحبنا إذ كشف عن غمتنا وروح عن أنفسنا فإنه كلما دخل من الباب داخل وتحرك منهم متحرك وقام منهم قائم استغربنا في الضحك ولم يتمالك الباشا نفسه من التبسم فيواري فمه بمنديله. ومر صاحب البيت فسمعنا قائلا منهم ويقول:

أحدهم كم تقدرون ما أنفق صاحب العرس على هذا الاحتفال؟

آخر منهم أنفق عليه كل ما كان لديه من الثروة وسيخرج منه صفر اليدين خالي الوطاب.

آخر لا حول ولا قوة إلا بالله، وما الذي اضطره إلى هذا السفه ومن أين يرتزق وينفق على بيته بعد ذلك.

آخر تنفق عليه عرسه فقد سمعنا أن لها متاعا تنفق منه من سعة ووقاك الله شر الرياء والسمعة فما اضطره إلى ذلك إلا حب التفاخر على الأقران.

١٥،١٩ قال عيسى بن هشام: وما كادت تحين نظرة من صاحب العرس إليهم حتى قطعوا

Pāshā You're right. They're acting just as you describe. Who are they and what's their problem?

Friend They're a group of Egyptian notables and merchants. They still base their behavior on vestiges left from the previous regime, namely of ingratiating themselves with members of the government and boasting about the very least connection they may have with such people. You can watch as they leap up with every new arrival. If they realize that the person is a senior official or a member of the government, they make a big display of awe and respect, all with the goal of boasting to their colleagues whenever they happen to receive a greeting of some kind from such people. On the other hand, if they discover that the person is not important, they sit down again. Just look at the way they're straining their necks and staring at the group of government officials in case someone who didn't greet them when they entered happens to look in their direction.

19.14 ʿĪsā ibn Hishām said: This subtle criticism made us look in their direction and pick up bits of their conversation. Our Friend was truly amazing in the way he was helping us relieve our problems and calm our worries. Every time someone came in, and some of the company stood up to greet them, we dissolved in laughter. The Pāshā himself could not avoid smiling and hid his face in a handkerchief. The owner of the residence swept past us, and we heard someone ask:

An Attendee How much do you think the sponsor of the wedding has spent on this celebration?

Another Attendee He's spent all the money he has. When it's over, he'll be completely penniless.

Still Another Attendee God alone possesses the power and strength! Whatever made him go to such absurd lengths. When this is all over, how's he going to earn enough to support his household?

Yet Another Attendee May God protect you from the veils of hypocrisy and ill repute! We've heard that a truly lavish amount is being spent on this wedding. The only reason is so that he can boast to his colleagues.

19.15 ʿĪsā ibn Hishām said: No sooner had the host of the wedding celebration looked in their direction than the conversations ceased. They all stood up

الكلام ونهضوا على الأقدام يستعدون لتحيته وسلامه واشتغلوا به فاشتغلنا عنهم بالنظر إلى فئة أخرى من الشبان يضحكون ويقهقهون ويدور حديثهم على النساء والغلمان فيقولون بنت فلان وابن فلان فغضضنا النظر عنهم وأنفنا السماع منهم والتفتنا ناحية فإذا بالأصوات قد علت من بين فئة أخرى وإذا هم يتجادلون ويتناقشون في القضايا والأحكام والقوانين واللوائح فعلمنا أنهم جماعة من القضاة والمحامين، وبينا نحن كذلك إذا بجماعة من المشايخ والعلماء خارجين من جوف البيت مسرعين مهرولين لا يلوون على شيء وخدمة الموائد في أعقابهم يحملون فوارغ الآنية وبقايا الطعام فقال الباشا:

١٦،١٩ الباشا من هؤلاء المسرعين في مشيهم؟

عيسى بن هشام هم جماعة من علمائنا ومشايخنا.

الباشا هل نزل بالدين أمر حملهم على مغادرة هذا المجلس بهذه السرعة؟

الصاحب لا ولكن هذه عادتهم إذا انتهوا من طعام وليمة خرجوا على الفور مرتلين ﴿فَإِذَا طَعِمْتُمْ فَانتَشِرُوا﴾ ويعتذرون عن المبادرة في خروجهم عقب الطعام بأنه لا يليق بهم الجلوس في مجالس اللّٰهو وسماع الألحان والغناء المكروه.

الباشا لنعم ما فعلوا وهم الأجدر بذلك والأولى فهم حفظة الدين وقدوة المسلمين.

١٧،١٩ الصاحب لا وحقك إنما هي التخمة يحذرونهم لكثرة ما أكلوا من الألوان المختلفة التي ملؤوا بها بطونهم وليس ذلك منهم من كره السماع واتقاء هذه المجالس فقد شاهدت أحدهم منذ ليال غير بعيدة في بيت أحد أعيان القبط ليلة الاحتفال بزفاف قد لبث فيه إلى ما بعد نصف الليل داخلا خارجا وراء أحد النظار في حجرات الطعام والشراب والألحان فهو وأمثاله يتمسكون بأهداب الدين على حسب ما يستحسنونه وما يستقبحونه فيحللون لأنفسهم هناك ما يحرّمونه عليها هنا ويبحون السماع في مكان ويقولون بكراهته في آخر.

ready to greet him and pay him some attention. However he ignored them, preferring to pay attention to a group of young men who were cackling and joking as they conversed about women and other young men. "We're totally ignoring X's daughter and Y's son," they were saying, "and we don't even want to hear about them."

We looked round just in time to hear voices raised in yet another group; they were yelling and screaming about court cases, laws, and decrees. We discovered that they were a group of judges and lawyers. While we were listening to them, a cluster of religious scholars came rushing out of the inner parts of the house, ignoring everything going on around them and leaving the meal service behind. They were carrying some empty plates and leftovers with them.

19.16

PĀSHĀ Who are these people rushing away?

ʿĪSĀ IBN HISHĀM They're a group of religious scholars.

PĀSHĀ Has some disaster befallen our faith which requires them to leave in such a hurry?

FRIEND It's not that. What usually happens is that when they've eaten as much food as they want, they leave, reciting the Qur'anic injunction «Once you have eaten, then scatter» as they do so.[156] They justify their hasty departure after they've eaten by saying that it's inappropriate for them to sit in a company where there's to be entertainment and singing, which is considered loathsome.

PĀSHĀ That's an admirable thing that they are doing! After all, they are the preservers of our faith and the living example for all Muslims.

19.17

FRIEND No, it's not like that. It's simply that they're worried about indigestion because of the wide variety of food with which they've stuffed their stomachs. It has nothing to do with a disapproval of singing or steering clear of gatherings like this. A few nights ago I saw with my own eyes a religious scholar in a Coptic house where a wedding was being celebrated. He stayed there till well past midnight, going in and out of the dining rooms behind a minister, eating, drinking, and listening to the singing. Scholars like him cling to the fringes of their faith in accordance with their personal likes and dislikes. They'll make a personal judgment as to what they consider forbidden, what one is allowed to hear in one place, and what's to be declared abhorrent in another.

الباشا وما هو أصح الأقوال في ذلك وهل يجوز لنا أن نمكث هنا حتى نسمع الغناء؟

قال عيسى بن هشام: فما كدت أبدأ بشرح ما أعلمه في هذا الباب حتى حانت صلاة العشاء فقمنا إلى الفرض نقضيه على أن نعود إلى ما كنا فيه . ١٨،١٩

Pāshā What's the truth about this issue. Is it permissible for us to stay here and listen to the singing?

ʿĪsā ibn Hishām said: No sooner had I started to explain the doctrine on this topic than the evening prayer was called. We all stood up to fulfil the obligation before returning to the topic. 19.18

مصباح الشرق ٦٤، ٢٠ يوليو ١٨٩٩

١،٢٠ قال عيسى بن هشام: ولما عدنا إلى مجالسنا بعد صلاة العشاء، عدنا إلى ما كنا فيه من كلام على الغناء، في كراهته وإباحته فقلت:

عيسى بن هشام أعلم أن الطرب والغناء أمر طبيعي راسخ في غريزة الحيوانات العجم تحن إليه وترتاح له وتنشط به فترى الوحوش النافرة إذا سمعت الغناء أنست به وسكنت إليه و زالت قسوتها وضعفت حدتها و رقت طباعها وذلت رقابها وسكنت حركاتها وخفتت أصواتها، وهذه الفيلة أعظم الحيوان أجساما إذا سمعت صوتا مرنما أو كلاما منغما فلا يلبث هذا الجسم العظيم أن يهتز طربا وهو في مواقف النيران اهتزاز المطوقة على فنن من الأفنان وهذه الإبل أغلظ الحيوان أكبادا يبريها السرى ويضنيها السير وينضيها الاين وينكزها التعب ويهلكها الظلماء إذا تغنى لها الحادي نسيت ما نابها وذهلت عما أصابها وألفتها عن حياض الماء وهي على الخمس في ظمئها والعشر ونشطت تستعيد القوى وتستأنف السرى.

٢،٢٠ وطالما شاهد المشاهدون هوام الأرض تجتمع من بطون الأودية وشقوق الجبال وخروقها جيوشا تتبع الجيوش، في مسيرها فبحث أحد علماء الطبيعة في علة ذلك فظهر له أن صوت الموسيقى في مسير الجيش هو الذي اجتذبها من مآويها إلى السير خلفه، ومن الروايات المشهورة أن أحد الموسيقيين من الفلاسفة كان بمنقطع من الأرض على شاطئ البحر يبغي الشاطئ الآخر ولا يجد لذلك سبيلا فخطر له الغناء وبينما هو كذلك إذا بدرفيل قد شق إليه البحر يتدنى منه فلم يزل الرجل في تغنيه والدرفيل في تدنيه حتى حاذاه في الشاطئ وسكن يستمع إليه فعلم الفيلسوف أنه استهواه بالغناء ولما استيقن ذلك منه استهون ركوبه فاتخذه بسحر الغناء مركبا ذلولا إلى حيث مبتغاه، وحكاية إبراهيم بن المهدي في اجتذاب الوحوش الضارية بغنائه مشهورة مذكورة، هذا شأن الحيوانات في سماع الغناء على ضعف إدراكها وبساطة

Miṣbāḥ al-sharq 64, July 20, 1899[157]

20.1 ʿĪsā ibn Hishām said: Once we had come back to the wedding, regathering after performing the evening prayer, we returned to the topic of singing and whether it is permitted in Islam or not:

ʿĪsā ibn Hishām You should realize that the enjoyment of singing is something innate, deeply rooted in the makeup of all animals. They will become fond of it, relax to it, and be invigorated by it. When untamed wild animals hear music, they calm down, get used to it, and lose their more violent traits. Their natures are softened, their movements become less frenzied, their voices soften, and they can often be tethered. Take the elephant for instance, the biggest of all animals. When it hears a voice singing or melodious speech, its huge body starts shaking with pleasure even in the face of fire—just like a ringdove on a branch. When a camel, the animal with the hardiest disposition, is exhausted by a long journey and is expiring from thirst, the camel driver will sing to it. That makes it forget all its afflictions and takes its mind off the thought of water wells, even though it may be the animal's fifth or even tenth day without water. It'll then resume the journey with renewed energy.

20.2 People have often observed how the earth's reptiles leave valley depths and mountain passes and congregate in great hordes to follow armies on the march. A naturalist scholar who was investigating the reasons why these creatures behaved this way determined that they were attracted by the sound of music at the head of the column and felt compelled to leave their habitats and follow the army. There's also a well-known tale about a philosopher musician who was standing on a promontory by the seashore. He wanted to get to the far shore, but couldn't find anything to take him there. It occurred to him to start singing. All of a sudden a dolphin came ploughing through the sea towards him. As he sang, it kept coming closer until it was alongside the shore and stopped to listen. The philosopher realized that he had charmed it with his singing. Once he was certain of that, he had no qualms about climbing on its back and through the magic of singing using it as a willing vessel to take him wherever he wished. Another story tells how Ibrāhīm ibn al-Mahdī was able to control wild beasts through his singing for which he was renowned. This then is the situation regarding the effect that songs have on animals, and all that in spite of their weak powers of comprehension and their crude sensitivities. How much greater then will be the effect on mankind, which represents

إحساسها فما بالك بالإنسان وهو أسمى الحيوانات وجودا وأكملها خلقة وأعظمها تميزا بشدة الإدراك وقوة النطق وصفاء الجوهر ولطافة الروح.

٣،٢٠ لا جرم كان الغناء فيه أطبع وأطبع والطرب ألصق به وألصق، والغناء في تعريف جماعة من الفلاسفة فن يقصد به تحريك النفس بتنسيق الأصوات وتأليفها على طريقة ترتاح لها الأذن. وفي تعريف جماعة آخرين هو فن لتحريك النفوس من أرباب المدارك العالية وأصحاب الأمزجة الصافية فإنه المساعد للنطق في قوة التأثير على السامع وكان الأقدمون يعتبرونه لغة عامة للناس على اختلاف لغاتهم وكان طالب علم الفلسفة لا بد له من فن الموسيقى مع الرياضيات لإعداد نفسه لدروس الفلسفة، وعبر عنه كل من هرمز وفيثاغورس أنه علم التنسيق لكل شيء ولذلك أطلقوا عليه لفظ (أرمونيا) أي التنسيق أو الترتيب ومنه الغناء في تهيئة الأرواح وتوطئة النفوس لقبول الفضائل ومكارم الأخلاق والارتفاع إلى أوج الكمالات وعندهم أن الذي لا يتأثر بالغناء لا بد أن يكون به نقص. والغناء مغروس في طينة الإنسان منذ نشأ في حجر الطبيعة متأصل في فطرته منذ استهل في الدنيا باكيا فلا يسكن إلا به.

٤،٢٠ وفضل تأثير الغناء في النفوس على تأثير الكلام كفضل الشعر البليغ في لغة عليه إذا ترجم كلاما غير موزون في لغة أخرى. والشواهد على قوة تأثير الغناء كثيرة جمة ومنها أنّ أهل سويسرا كانوا يحكمون بالإعدام على كل من تغنى منهم في مجتمع الجنود المتجمعة من رؤوس الجبال بلحن خاص يتغنى به الرعاة في تلك الجبال لما نشأ عن ذلك المرة بعد المرة من تأثير على نفوس الجنود فيلهب فيها نار الحنين إلى منازلها فيلقون أسلحتهم من أيديهم ويهمون على وجوههم إلى مرابعهم، ومنها أن فتنة وقعت في اسبرطه فلم تخمد نارها ولم يكن شرها إلا بفعل الغناء في نفوس الذين قاموا بأمرها فلم يسعهم عند سماعه إلا أن استبدلوا صياح الشغب بصياح الطرب، ومنها حكاية أبي نصر

the highest level of animal life, possessing the most perfect disposition and distingushed by the greatest powers of comprehension, the power of speech, the purest essences, and the gentlest spirit of all?

20.3 Singing has always been something completely natural and most closely associated with the emotions. A group of philosophers has defined singing as the process of affecting the heart by subtle control of the voice and by use of the vocal chords in a manner that is soothing to the ear. Others have defined it as the stimulation of the souls of people who are endowed with higher faculties and serene temperaments. It's a force which can buttress the powerful effect of speech in influencing the listener. The ancients regarded it as a general language medium for all people to understand in spite of their linguistic differences. In their opinion, the student of philosophy needed a thorough grasp of the art of music in addition to mathematics. The two great philosophers, Pythagoras and Hermes, declared that the science of musical arrangement is universally applicable, and so they gave it the name *harmonia* which means "order," "arrangement," and from which was derived "singing." They all agree that, when it comes to instilling in man various qualities and virtues and aspiring to the acme of perfection, nothing in the world can rival the effect of music. Anyone who isn't affected by it must, in their view, have some defect in his nature. Singing was implanted in man from the moment of his creation within nature's confines and his first bawling moments on earth. Nothing else can afford him rest.

20.4 In fact, the way in which singing moves people more than the spoken word is analogous to the superiority of eloquent poetry in its original language to unrhyming translation into another language. There are many events in history that demonstrate the powerful effect of singing. One story tells how the people of Switzerland used to condemn to death anyone who sang a particular tune when soldiers used to come down from the mountain peaks to enroll in the army. This song was one that shepherds used to sing in the mountains, and it would always provoke feelings of intense nostalgia for home in the soldiers' minds. They would lay down their arms and make their way back to their home pastures. A similar story tells about a revolt in Sparta which flared up and could not be quelled until singing had its usual effect on the instigators. When they heard the singing, all they could do was to shout for joy instead of in rancor. Yet another story tells of Abū Naṣr al-Fārābī and Sayf al-Dawlah ibn Ḥamdān. The philosopher began by making the ruler's council laugh, and then

الفارابي مع سيف الدولة بن حمدان حيث أضحك مجلسه بالأوتار وأبكاه ثم نومه وتركه، وقد استعمل تأثير الغناء لكثير من المنافع .

٥،٢٠ وقلّ أن تجد دينا من الأديان إلا ويستعان فيه على العبادة والترتيل والترنيم والتنغيم لما في ذلك من نشاط النفوس وانتعاش الأرواح. وذكر أحد مشايخ الصوفية عن بعض السلف رضي الله عنهم أنهم كانوا يدخلون إلى خلوتهم فمن عجز منهم عن تمام المدة التي دخل عليها خرج لحضر السماع ثم رجع إلى خلوته نشيطا، كما أنك لا تجد أمة من الأمم باديها وحاضرها متوحشها ومتمدنها إلا والغناء في الجيش آلة من آلات الحرب تعين على ممارسة الأهوال ومصافحة المنايا ومنازلة الحتوف ومشارفة المهالك. ولقد كان الخطباء الرومانيون يتغالون في تنسيق أصواتهم في الخطابة وعدم الخروج عن أصل النغم لزيادة التأثير على النفوس وشدة التمكن من القلوب حتى أن أحد مشاهيرهم كان يتخذ له منبها من الموسيقيين وهو يخطب فإذا شد عن النغم نبهه بإحدى الآلات فرجع إلى الأصل، وآخر عناية أهل هذا العصر بفن الغناء أن حكومة ألمانيا قررت أن يكون الغناء من الدروس الأساسية في المدارس يبتدئ به التلامذة ابتداءهم في دروس الهجاء وينتهون منه انتهائهم من دروس الفلسفة.

٦،٢٠ هذا ما يقال عن الغناء من طريق البحث وإذا نظرنا إلى الوجه الشرعي وجدناه غير منكر ولا مكروه وناهيك بما ورد عن النبي صلى الله عليه وسلم أنه سمع نسوة يتغنين في وليمة عرس فلم ينكر ذلك عليهن وما جاء من نسوة الأنصار استقبلنه عند مقدمه من إحدى الغزوات بالدفوف والمزاهر وهن يتغنين على الإيقاع بقولهن:

طلع البدر علينا
من ثنيات الوداع
وجب الشكر علينا
ما دعا لله داع

فلم ينكر ذلك عليهن أيضا، وقد درج السلف الصالح والخلفاء على سماع الغناء

he made them cry. Afterwards he put them all to sleep and departed. He made use of the effects of singing for a number of useful purposes.

20.5 It is rare to find any belief system in any part of the world that doesn't use recitation, chanting, and singing in its liturgies. That is because of the way music invigorates man's soul and nourishes the spirit. A Sufi shaykh recalls from one of his forebears—God be pleased with them!—that, when they went into seclusion, if one of them was unable to complete the entire period, he would go outside, listen to some singing, and then return invigorated. You'll not be able to locate a single people, whether in the desert or urban society, primitive or civilized, and possessing armed forces, that doesn't make use of music as a weapon in wartime. It is used to confront danger, handle what fate decrees, and deal with the perilous situations that ensue. Roman orators used to compete with each other to make their voices sound more melodious when they were making speeches and to maintain a tuneful pitch so that the words would have a greater effect on people. One of the more famous orators used to make use of a musician while he was speaking. If he happened to go off pitch, the musician could notify him by using one of his instruments and bring him back to the original pitch. And in our own era the latest concern people have shown with the art of singing is that the government of Germany has decided that singing will be one of the basic subjects in schools beginning at the earliest stages when pupils are learning the alphabet and continuing until they finish studying philosophy.

20.6 This then is what research can tell us about singing. If we look at it from a legal perspective, we discover that there is nothing reprehensible or hateful about it. Just take for example what is reported concerning the Prophet (peace and blessings be upon him). He heard women singing at a wedding feast and didn't stop them. Once, when he arrived back from a raid, some women of the Anṣār[158] came up to him with lutes and tambourines, singing in rhythm to the words:

The full moon has risen over us,
  from the folds of departure.
We should show our thanks
  as long as one still prays to God.[159]

He didn't stop them singing. Our pious forebears and Caliphs regularly listened to singing and attended musical sessions, and neither category denied themselves the pleasure nor proscribed it for other people. Consider the

وحضور مجلسه لم ينكروه على أنفسهم ولم ينكر عليهم منكر وهذا عمر بن الخطاب على غلظته وشدته في الدين سمع الغناء فما أنكره وحكى أسلم مولاه قال مر بي عمر وأنا وعاصم نغني فوقف وقال: أعيدا علي فأعدنا عليه وقلنا: أينا أحسن صنعة يا أمير المؤمنين فقال: مثلكما كحماري العبادي قيل له: أي حماريك شر فقال: هذا ثم هذا فقلت له: أنا الأول من الحمارين قال: أنت الثاني منهما، وكان عبد الله بن جعفر على قرابته من رسول الله صلى الله عليه وسلم وصحبته له يجلس للسماع ويحتفل له وذلك مشهور عنه.

٧،٢٠ الصاحب لقد أحسنت في الشرح وأجدت في السرد وإن كنت طولت وأسهبت وكان يغنيك عن بعض هذا أن تقول إن الله جلت عظمته جعل من فضله ونعمته على الإنسان لكل حاسة لذّة فكما أن لذة العين في تناسق الأجزاء وترتيبها وذلك هو الجمال ولذة اللسان في إتلاف الطعوم وذلك هو العذوبة ولذة الأنف في عدم تنافر الرائحة وذلك هو الطيب ولذة اليد في تناسب دقائق الملموس وذلك هو النعومة كذلك لذة الأذن في تناسق الأصوات وترتيبها وذلك هو الغناء، فكأن القائل بتحريمه أو بكراهته يريد أن يحول بين الناس وبين التمتع بنعمة أنعمها الله عليهم.

الباشا ما أسهب صاحبي وما أطنب ولكنه جرى على ما ألزم به نفسه الشريفة معي مما أنا محتاج إليه من حسن التفهيم وبيان التعبير ووضوح الحجة بما يجعل المسائل راسخة في صدري لا تزعزعها الشكوك ولا تحللها الأوهام فهو لي في الكبر كالمعلم الناقش على الحجر في الصغر.

٨،٢٠ قال عيسى بن هشام: وما انتهينا من هذا المبحث إلا وقد اعتلى المغنون منصتهم وأخذوا فيها مجالسهم وقد لاحظ الباشا عليهم عند جلوسهم أمرا استلفتني إليها وهو يقول:

case of ʿUmar ibn al-Khaṭṭāb, who was well known for his rigid conformity in religious matters. When he heard singing, he did not disapprove. The following story is told on the authority of his most devoted follower, Aslam, who recounts how ʿUmar walked by as ʿĀṣim and he were singing. "ʿUmar stopped and asked us to sing it again," Aslam says, "so we repeated it. 'Tell us, Commander of the Faithful,' we asked him when we'd finished, 'which one of us is the better singer?' 'You're like al-ʿIbādī's two asses,' he replied. 'When he was asked which of his two asses was worse, he replied: "This one, then that one!"' 'Am I the first of the two?' I asked. 'No,' the Commander of the Faithful replied, 'you're the second.'" And in spite of ʿAbdallāh ibn Jaʿfar's close association and friendship with the Prophet of God, he's famous for frequently sitting down to listen to singing and enjoying it.

20.7 FRIEND That's a wonderful explanation and description, although you have gone into more detail than seems necessary; we could have made do with noting that God—may His greatness be exalted—out of His great virtue and beneficence assigned to every sense of mankind its own pleasure. For the eye, the pleasure of observing comes from the symmetry of visible objects and the arrangement of their components, namely beauty; for the tongue, the pleasure of tasting in the blending of food, which is sweetness; for the nose, the pleasure of sniffing a pleasant odor, which is perfume; for the hand, the pleasure of touch in the proportions of the parts of what is touched, which is smoothness; and for the ear, the pleasure of hearing in the harmony of the voice and the pulses of its rhythm, which is singing. It's almost as though those who would either forbid singing or declare it objectionable have it in mind to place a barrier between people and the enjoyment of a blessing that God himself has ordained.

PĀSHĀ Yes indeed, my friend has certainly expatiated at some length. However he's also engaged his noble soul so as to provide me with the lucid understanding, clear expression, and cogent evidence that I've needed. The issues are now firmly implanted in my mind, and there's no room for doubt or fanciful notions. Now that I'm old, for me he's been serving the same kind of role as a teacher who would draw on a slate when I was very young.

20.8 ʿĪsā ibn Hishām said: No sooner had we finished our discussion than the singers mounted their dais and took their seats. The Pāshā noticed something about them which he drew to my attention:

الباشا ما لي أرى هؤلاء إن كانوا هم المغنين ليسوا من الحشمة والوقار على ما يجب أن يكونوا عليه مما ينطبق على ما وصفته وعبرت به من جلال هذا الفن ورفعته فإني أرى أحدهم يبصق ويمخط يمينا وشمالا وأرى الآخر يهزل ويمزح ويقهقه مع الجالسين لسماعه وأرى الثالث ينادي بطلب القهوة بأعلى صوته وأرى الواحد منهم يقف في المنصة على النعل في وجوه الناس وكلهم في سنة لا نشاط بهم ولا ارتياح عندهم وكأنما هم من المسحوبين بين التسخير في عمل شاق على رغم الأنوف فيقابلونه بالصدر المنقبض والوجه المقطب.

عيسى بن هشام ازدرى الناس بالغناء وعدّوا ممارسته من النقائص والمثالب فهانت على المغنين نفوسهم واحتقروا فنهم الشريف في أعينهم فانكسرت قلوبهم ولم يعبأوا بالأخذ بأسباب آداب الفن والترقي في العلم به.

قال عيسى بن هشام: وفيما نحن في هذا الكلام وإذا بالأربعة المستقبلين يخترقون صفوف الجالسين رائحين وغادين في طلب صاحب العرس فلما عثروا به جذبوه فتبعهم مهرولا ينفض العرق عن جبينه ويصلح ما اختل من زي لباسه فشخصنا نحوه فرأيناه عائدا ممتلئ الوجه بشرا مبتسم الثغر ابتسام الاختيال والفخر وأخذ يدفع في صدور الناس لإخلاء الطريق لمن وراءه وكانوا جماعة من الأجانب بين الرجال والنساء فدخلوا قاصدين باب الحرم فالتفت إلى الباشا متعجبا: ٩،٢٠

الباشا من هؤلاء الأفرنج، أترى صاحب العرس يريد أن يقيم أيضا أمام الحاضرين ألعابا افرنجية؟

الصاحب هؤلاء جماعة من السياح الذين يترقبون الاحتفالات الشرقية لمشاهدتها والتفرج على ما يحدث فيها وقد جرت العادة أن بعض التراجمة يحصلون على ورقة دعوة إلى عرس فيبيعونها لهم بقيمة غالية ويوهمونهم أن هذه من عادة الشرقيين فإذا حضروا إلى العرس استقبلهم صاحبه أحسن استقبال وأكرمهم أعظم إكرام ونسي كل من كان ذا قدر في الاحتفال وأجلسهم فوق رؤوس

Pāshā How is it that these singers aren't behaving in the serious and dignified way that they're supposed to, at least if we bear in mind the nobility and status of the art as you've just been describing it? One of them is spitting and blowing his nose left and right, while another is guffawing and making jokes to the people sitting to listen to him. A third is yelling for coffee at the top of his voice, and still another is standing on the dais in sandals right in front of everybody. They're all of an age when they seem to have little energy or get minimal pleasure out of their art. It's as though they've been dragged into forced labor against their will, so they approach the task with gloomy expressions and sagging spirits.

ʿĪsā ibn Hishām People now look down on singing and regard its practice as something reprehensible and blameworthy. Singers themselves despise it too and disparage their noble art. They've become disheartened and don't bother about adopting the lofty standards and exalted learning that are associated with it.

20.9 ʿĪsā ibn Hishām said: While we were talking, four people made their way back and forth through the rows of listeners looking for the wedding host. Once they found him, they pulled him away. He rushed out after them, wiping the sweat from his brow as he did so and adjusting his clothing. When we looked in the direction where he had gone, we saw that he was coming back, his face beaming with pleasure and pride. He started pushing people in the chest to make way for the people entering behind him. They turned out to be a group of foreigners, men and women. Once they had all come inside, they made their way to the harem. The Pāshā turned to me in utter amazement:

Pāshā Who are these foreigners? Do you suppose the wedding host plans to put on some European entertainments for the attendees?

Friend No. This is a group of European tourists who attend Eastern celebrations to see what goes on. What usually happens now is that some dragomen obtain letters of invitation to a wedding, and they sell them for a very high price to tourists, who get the impression that this is an oriental custom. When they arrive at the wedding celebration, the owner gives them a lavish welcome, assigns them places of honor, and neglects everyone else of any repute who's at the reception. Once he's esorted the women into the harem, he makes sure to give the foreigners the best seats and devotes all his attention

الجالسين بعد أن يدخل نساءهم إلى دار الحرم ثم يقصرهمه على خدمتهم إلى أن يحين انصرافهم فيدعوهم مشيعا إلى الباب بأجمل توديع. كل هذا وهو لا يعرفهم ولا يعرفونه وكثيرا ما يكون مع نسائهم آلة رسم يأخذون بها رسم ما وراء الجدار وما تكون عليه حالة النساء في حفلة الزفاف وصاحب العرس يقبل كل ما يكون منهم فرحا منشرحا لاعتقاده أن زيارتهم له تعلي قدره وتزيده اعتبارا في أعين الناس.

الباشا إذا كان ذلك من عادات أعراسهم فبؤسا وتعسا.

قال عيسى بن هشام: وسمعنا عزف الموسيقى من الخارج تتقدم العروس في زفافه فسكت المغنون وضج المكان ووقف من كان قاعدا وتطاول الناس بالوقوف على الكراسي فدخل العروس بين زمرة من أصحابه فتوسطوا المكان ورقى أحدهم منصة المغنين وشرع يخطب فقال: ١٠،٢٠

«هذه ليلة قامت فيها أعواد السرور على منابر الحبور، وأشرقت فيها أهلة المسرة والبدور، في سماء القلوب وأرض الصدور وطلعت فيها كواكب السعود في أفق العيون، فأجلت عن وجوهنا عمائم الأحزان وسحائب الشجون،

«ولو أني لست من فرسان هذا الميدان، الراكبين فيه لحيازة قصب الرهان، ولا من المجردين لسيوف الخطب وخطب السيوف، ولا الطاغين مضمار الأدب، بحروف الرماح ورماح الحروف، ولا من الراكبين في شروح البلاغة متون الضوامر ولا من السابحين في بحور النظم من كل كامل ووافر ولا من الساحلين حلة سحبان ولا من المتحصنين بدروع المعاني والبيان، وقد حيل بين العير والنزوان , الا أن ما أعرفه في العروس من العلم والأقدام، وما له في حسن التربية من رسوخ الأقدام، وما اعتقده فيه من محبة الأوطان، ومصادقة الإخوان وما هو مشهور عن هذه الشمس التي تزف إلى البدر والغزالة المصونة بدل الكناس في الخدر ربيبة بيت المجد والمعارف، والشرف التالد والطارف وما أراه على وجوه الحاضرين من الكرم والسماح وعلائم الفرح والانشراح كل ذلك جرأني على الوقوف في هذا الموقف الحرج، وسط

to them until it's time for them to leave. He then escorts them back to the door and bids them a fond farewell. All this happens even though he neither knows them nor they him. The foreign women often bring a camera with them and take a picture behind the harem screen showing what the women are doing during a wedding celebration. The wedding host happily accepts whatever the foreigners choose to do because he's convinced that their visit will enhance his status and increase people's respect for him.

PĀSHĀ If this is now a custom at weddings, then it's a very bad one!

ʿĪsā ibn Hishām said: We now heard the sound of music outside, and the groom's procession came in. The singers fell silent, and noise filled the entire place. People who had been seated stood up, and others stood on chairs. The groom entered with a group of his friends, and they stood in the center. One of them now mounted the singers' dais and started his speech: **20.10**

"Tonight is a time when paeans of joy rise over pulpits of delight, and kinsfolk of happiness and new moons rise upward from these heavens that are hearts and the earth that is the soul; a time when stars of good luck rise from the horizon of the eyes, and clouds of grief and downpouring rains of anxiety are swept out of our sight.

"I may be no gallant cavalier in this arena, riding to win the stakes of the wager; nor am I one to unsheathe swords of lectures and speeches with the edges of spears and the javelins of letters; not for me either the backs of the lean to ride in expounding eloquence, nor to swim in the seas of poetry and prose with every *kāmil* and *wāfir*, to withdraw anything in the garments of Saḥbān,[160] or to arm myself with the twin fortresses of concepts and eloquence when both entrenchment and advance are impossible. And yet I know that the groom is a man of learning and initiative; he possesses a firm foothold in the field of education, a love for his homeland, and a devotion towards his brothers. I am also aware of what is known about this gleaming sun who tonight is marrying the full moon in all its glory, the lovely gazelle well protected in the women's quarters, mistress in a house of prestige and learning, one honored then and now. I can also see all the kind, friendly expressions and the delighted looks on the faces of the people present. It is all this that has encouraged me to stand up in this cramped space amidst the surging sea of this wedding feast. I now beg you all to turn a blind eye to my shortcomings and excuse my gaffes.

بحر هذا الأنس المتموج، وإني أطلب منكم أن تضربوا عن تقصيري صفحا وتطووا عن هفواتي كشحا، وأن تشربوا معي نخب الكؤوس، في نخب العروس ليحيي في سرور وهناء وحبور، متمتعا بالرفاء والبنين ما ناح القمري في رياض البساتين آمين آمين.»

١١،٢٠ قال عيسى بن هشام: فكان الخطيب يخطب ونحن نكاد نتميز من كتم الضحك عند كل فاصلة وسمعت بجانبي اثنين يتحاوران فيقول أحدهما لصاحبه:

الأول ما أبلغ هذا الكلام وما أفصحه فلله در هذا الخطيب فإنه مما يفتخر به كل وطني.

الثاني لعلك تظن أن مثل هذه البلاغة تكون لمثل هذا الشاب.

الأول فلمن هذه الخطبة إذن؟

الثاني لا شك أنه استخرجها من بعض كتب الإنشاء.

الأول لم نقرأ فيها مثل هذه الخطبة في مثل هذه الفصاحة.

الثاني نعم لم نقرأ في الكتب القديمة مثلها ولكنني طالما رأيت هذا الخطيب يقرأ في كتاب حديث العهد فلعله استمد هذه الخطبة من نفثات بيان واضعه الموري باسمه في عنوان كتابه (مفتاح الأفكار في النثر المختار).

الأول لا بد أن يكون الأمر كذلك فإن هذا النفس من ذلك النفس.

١٢،٢٠ قال عيسى بن هشام: وبعد أن حملوا العروس إلى بيت الحرم جاء رب الدار يدعوا الجالسين للقيام وراءه فقمنا في أعقابهم فأدخلونا قاعة للطعام والشراب بعد أن قدموا أكبر الموجودين مقاما لافتتاحها فافتتحها ولا افتتاح المعتصم عمورية والفاتح القسطنطينية وازدحم الناس بعده عليها ازدحام العفاة على الصلات والأتقياء على الصلاة. ووقفوا على المائدة وقوف المجدبين على الكلاء فهمّ الباشا بالرجوع وقال:

I ask you all to join me in raising your glasses to the groom's health: may he live in health and happiness, prosperity, and joy; may he enjoy marital bliss and produce many sons, so long as wood pigeons coo in garden meadows. Amen, Amen!"[161]

ʿĪsā ibn Hishām said: As we listened to this speech, we could barely suppress our laughter as one phrase followed another. I listened to two people standing beside me: **20.11**

FIRST How eloquent he is! What a wonderful speech. Every Egyptian should be proud of him.

SECOND Do you really imagine that this young man produced such eloquence?

FIRST Then where did he get it from?

SECOND He obviously got it from some composition books.

FIRST We don't get such eloquent discourse from reading books like that.

SECOND You're right! We've never read anything like that in books from the past. But I've often observed this particular orator reading from more recent tomes. Maybe he prepared this speech based on the section "examples of eloquence" by an author named al-Mawrī in a book entitled *Keys as Openings to Thought, Selected from Prose Extracts Wrought.*

FIRST That must be it. It has to be from there.

ʿĪsā ibn Hishām said: Once they had taken the groom to the bride's harem, the host came back and invited everyone to get up and accompany him. We followed his lead. After he had asked the senior person present to open the ceremonies and he had done so, we entered a room where food and drink was served. This was no conquest such as al-Muʿtaṣim at the Battle of Amorium, or Muḥammad the Conqueror at Constantinople. People crowded around like the chaste receiving gifts and devout going to prayer; they were standing close to the tables like sufferers from drought who have just found lush pasture. The Pāshā was on the point of going back. **20.12**

الباشا ويلك ما هذا الاحتقار وهل وصل الأمر بصاحب العرس أن يدخل الناس إلى الكيلار ليأكلوا فيه وهم وقوف على عجل؟

الصاحب ليس بكيلار وإنما هو مكان تباح فيه الأطعمة والأشربة ينتقي منها كل إنسان ما يوافق هواه ويناسب ذوقه ويسمونه (البوفيه).

١٣،٢٠ قال عيسى بن هشام: فقال الباشا وقد رأى الزحام يشتد والأقدام تتزاحم والمناكب تتلاصق والرؤوس تتصادم والأيادي تتسابق وتمتد الأصوات تعلو وتشتد وهذا يأكل من كل لون لقمة ويشرب من كل زجاجة قداحا وذاك يحمل قدحا في يد وقطعة من ديك في أخرى ويلوك في فيه قطعة من ضأن ويطلب من الخادم قطعة من السمك وغيره لم يسعفه الخادم بملء الأقداح فتأبط زجاجة وقبض على كأس وآخر يمسح ويمزح وسواه يتهته ويقهقه وواحداً يتجمل ويتلطف وصاحبه يتضجر ويتأفف.

الباشا لقد علمت من أحوال الناس ما لم أكن أعلم ونظرت ما لم أكن أنظر وأنا أقسم أنّ هول هذا المكان في نظري أشد وقعا على نفسي من أهوال ما شاهدته في الحروب وكابدته من الوقائع.

١٤،٢٠ قال عيسى بن هشام: وما زالوا كذلك يزدادون ازدحاما والتحاما فلا يقدر أحد أن يلتفت يمينا ولا شمالا إلا ويقع بجانبه أو على ملابسه قدح خمر أو صحفة طعام حتى امتلأت البطون واحمرت الوجوه ومالت الأعناق وحملقت الأحداق، واشتعلت الشهوات في النفوس ونفضت الصدور ما تكنه من سر وزال ما على الرذيلة من ستر فصار أحدهم يقيء كلاما والآخر يقيء طعاما وما لم يبق على الموائد شيء من فضلات الزائد وبقايا الشراب وصاحوا بصاحب المنزل يطلبون منه شرابا فسأل الخدم عنه فقالوا له لم يبق عندنا إلا صندوق واحد من الخمر كان آخر ما طلبوه في الحرم فلم نتمكن من منعه بعد أن أوسعنا الأغا سبا وشتما فاعتذر صاحب الدار

Pāshā Good grief, what an insult! Have things with the wedding host now reached the point that he makes people go into the scullery to eat, and on the run at that?

Friend It's not the scullery. This is a place designated for eating and drinking. People can choose the things that suit their fancy and satisfy their tastes. They call it a "buffet."

ʿĪsā ibn Hishām said: The Pāshā watched as the crowding got worse. Feet were cramped, shoulders clashed, heads collided, hands competed, and voices were raised and got louder. One person was grabbing a bite to eat from every plate and a glass of wine from every bottle, while someone else was holding a glass in one hand and a piece of turkey in the other while at the same time chewing on a piece of lamb and asking the waiter to bring him some fish and other things as well. The waiter did not offer to fill the glasses, so the man simply put a whole bottle under his armpit and grabbed a glass. Still another person was sweeping things up and cracking jokes, while his companion stood there stuttering and cackling. Some people were trading compliments while others were complaining and grousing. **20.13**

Pāshā I've now learned things about people that I didn't know before and seen things I've never seen in my life. I can only vouch for the fact that in my opinion this place is more horrifying to me than anything I've ever witnessed in war or on the battlefield.

ʿĪsā ibn Hishām said: The crowd and crush kept getting worse. No one could turn either to left or right without finding a glass of wine or a slice of meat either beside him or on his clothing. Eventually stomachs were filled, eyes turned red, necks began to droop, and people began to stare. Passions were roused, hearts abandoned all inner secrets, and the covers came off every kind of vice. While one person vomited words, another did the same with food. There was no food or drink left on the tables, so people began shouting to the wedding host to bring more drink. When he asked the servants, they told him that all they had left was a single case of wine which had just been requested in the harem. Even when the eunuch had cursed and sworn at them, they could not stop it going there. Hearing that, the wedding host **20.14**

للطالبين وصفق على يديه علامة لإقفال المكان وانصرف الناس إلى مجالسهم فخرجوا يتمايلون ويتساندون وبصرت بصاحبين يتنازعان عند الباب من شدة السكر فلطم أحدهما الآخر بيده فعثر برجله فسقط إلى الأرض وهو يقول:

١٥،٢٠

شربت الخمر حتى قال صحبي
ألست عن السفاه بمستفيق
وحتى ما أوسد في مبيت
أنام به سوى الترب السحيق
وحتى أغلق (البوفيه) دوني
وآنست الهوان من الصديق

ورأيت آخر ينتفخ عجبا ويتبختر تيها ويلوي عنقه صلفا ويسهر خده كبرا ويردد متلعثما:

شربت الخمر حتى خلت أني
أبو قابوس أو عبد المدان

١٦،٢٠

ولما جلس الناس للسماع قال الصاحب للباشا:

الصاحب انظر الآن إلى جماعة الحكام والأمراء الذين كانوا كالأصنام لا يتحركون في جلوسهم كيف تغيرت هيآتهم وأخذوا يتنقلون من مكان إلى مكان.

الباشا نعم صدقت وما لي أراهم يشتغلون بالنظر إلى السماء ويكثرون من الإشارة كأنما هم يتضرعون بالدعاء لدفع نازلة أو طلب رغيبة؟

الصاحب سكر الرجال وثملت النساء ففتحت النوافذ وأشرقت منها الشموس فأرسلت خيوط المغازلة لاصطياد حبات القلوب فترى الكبير من الرجال يحملق إلى النوافذ ببصره ويغمز بحاجبيه ويشير بيده ويعبث بشاربه وينشر منديله ويطويه ثم يضعه على أجفانه ليسترق ذات الدل بريق دموعه وكل واحد منهم يرى في نفسه أنه جذب قلوب الغانيات بحسنه وخلع أفئدتهن بلطف شمائله وخلب الألباب بسحر

apologized to everyone and clapped his hands to show that the dining room was now closed. People now went back to their seats. As they left the room, everyone was swaying and leaning on their neighbors. I spotted two friends who were so completely drunk that they started arguing by the door. One of them slapped the other, which made him trip and fall to the ground, reciting these lines as he did so:

20.15

I have drunk wine till my friends ask:
"Won't you come round after your foolish behavior?"
Till the only place to lay my head
is the dusty earth.
And till the buffet is shut in my face,
and I encounter contempt from my friends.[162]

I watched as the other one, puffed up with pride and strutting his way out, turned his head and stumbled his way through this line:

I have drunk wine till I imagined
I was Abū Qābūs or ʿAbd al-Madān.[163]

20.16

Once everyone had sat down to listen to the music, the Friend spoke to the Pāshā:

Friend Just look at the group of government officials and princes now. Before they were sitting motionless like idols, but now everything's changed and they're moving from one spot to another.

Pāshā You're right. I can see them looking up into the sky and making a lot of gestures. It looks as though they're praying for some disaster to be averted or some wish to be granted.

Friend The men are all drunk, and so are the women. Windows have been opened and gleaming suns are now shining bright. Flirtatious threads have been dispatched to ensnare heartstrings below. You can see the oldest man looking up at the windows, raising his eyebrows, waving his hand, toying with his mustache, unwrapping and folding his handkerchief, then putting it to his eyelids so as to use his fake tears to entice the woman above. Down below everyone is utterly convinced that he's managed to win over the hearts of the beauties above with his handsome mien; he's plucked at their heartstrings with his suave appearance, and attracted their attention with his magical

لحظاته ورقة إشارته. وانظر إلى النساء من فوقنا تراهن قد أسفرن عن وجوههن وأضاء حليهن على ما حولهن وترى الواحدة منهن تشير بمروحتها والأخرى تغازل بزهرتها وغيرها تلاعب بسجارتها وأختها تخايل بالكأس كالقبس في يدها. وانظر إلى المغني يغني ووجهه إلى النوافذ يرسل إليها عبارة الأدوار في شكوى العشق وحر الغرام وانظر إلى الأغوات يصعدون وينزلون إليه بطلب الأدوار المختارة عن لسان السيدات بما يوافق الهوى ويصادف الغرض واحكم لي أيها الباشا إن كان بقي لظهر الأرض فضل على بطنها.

١٧،٢٠ قال عيسى بن هشام: فالتهب وجه الباشا من حمرة الخجل وبدت عليه علامات السخط لا سيما عندما سكت المغنون ووقف المنكت يسرد بذيء القول وفحش الكلام وألفاظ السوآت والنساء يتناغين ويتضاحكن والرجال من تحتهن يصيحون ويقهقهون فعمد الباشا إلى الانصراف وهو يقول:

الباشا يكفيني من الهم والغم ما قد أحاط بي فقد وجب الانصراف ولست أرضى لنفسي بهذه المواطن الشنعاء.

١٨،٢٠ قال عيسى بن هشام: فقمنا على أثره للخروج فوجدنا قوما يتشاتمون ويتضاربون وصاحب العرس يستغيث بالبوليس حتى انقلبت الأفراح أتراحاً والغناء نواحا وتداخل البوليس لحسم المنازعات ودخل الناس في دور المحاكمات وهكذا عاقبة المسرات.

glances and subtle gestures. And just look up at the women above us, showing their faces and flashing their jewelry. One of them is waving with her fan, while another is flirting with her rosette; still another is toying with her cigarette while her sister is brandishing her glass like a bow. Then take a look at the way the singer is looking up at the windows as he sings about passion's complaints and the fiery heat of love. Notice the way eunuchs are going up and down with requests from the women for particular songs that fit the mood of love and serve their purpose. Having now witnessed all this, Pāshā, pray tell me if there can any longer exist any virtue on the earth's surface?

ʿĪsā ibn Hishām said: The Pāshā blushed scarlet in sheer embarrassment. Signs of fury began to show on his face, especially when the singer finished and a comedian of some kind started telling dirty stories and using the foulest possible language. The women kept laughing and asking for more, while the men below them were shouting and guffawing. The Pāshā made to leave, saying: 20.17

PĀSHĀ I've had more than enough grief here. It's high time we left. I can never find any pleasure in such a disgusting place.

ʿĪsā ibn Hishām said: We left behind him. Once outside we found people cursing and punching each other. The wedding host was asking for police assistance. All joy now turned to sorrow, and songs of celebration were replaced by lamentations. The police arrived to put an end to the fights, and people found themselves on the way to the courts. Thus end all joyous occasions. 20.18

مصباح الشرق ٦٨، ١٧ أغسطس ١٨٩٩

١،٢١ قال عيسى بن هشام: واعتزلت بالباشا برهة من الدهر نستملح العزلة ونستعذب الصبر، ونعيش فيها عيش الحكماء، من حسن الرضاء بحسن الأكتفاء ونستروح راحة البعد عن هذا العالم وأذاه، وإغماض الجفون على قذاه، مؤتنسين كل الائتناس بالوحشة من الناس، بعد أن شاهدنا من أعمالهم ورأينا وسمعنا من أقوالهم ووعينا، وعانينا من معاشرتهم ما عانينا وقاسينا من معاملتهم ما قاسينا، مما قل أن يخلو من التنفيذ أو العذل، سواه في الجد كان أو في الهزل، إذا سألتهم حاربوك، وإذا وادعتهم ناصبوك، وإذا عاملتهم عادوك، وإذا اتقيتهم كادوك وإذا خالطتهم لا تأمن الاعتداء، وإن مازجتهم لا تعدم الافتراء وإن طالبتهم بحق لا تسمع الصم الدعاء.

٢،٢١ ثم الويل لك من مواقف القضاء، فإن انتقلت إلى مجالس صفوهم ومعاهد لهوهم جنيت منها كل ما يبعد وينفر وينغص ويكدر، تدخلها مستروحا مستبشرا، فتخرج منها مستقبحا مستنكرا،

فعيشتهم في كلتا الحالتين قرارة معائب، ومجتمع مثالب، وينابيع أكدار ومنابت أضرار.

فلو خبرتهم الجوزاء خبري
لما طلعت مخافة أن تكادا

وكنت في عزلتنا أذهب بالباشا كل مذهب، وأنتقل به من مطلب إلى مطلب، فتارة اجتاز به عباب البحار، وطورا أخوض معه سراب القفار فنرى من يحرق في البحر مراكبه ليحمل على اقتحام المنايا في البر كتائبه، ونرى الحادي في القفر يحدو بناقته، ويثبت بمعشوقته فلا يقعد به ذل الغرام عن التفاخر بعز الكرام، ولا ينسيه

ʿĪsā ibn Hishām said: So the Pāshā and I spent some time in seclusion. We both relished the privacy it provided and were quite content to persevere with it. Like philosophers we lived in complete contentment and satisfaction, and enjoyed the feeling of release which came with being apart from the world and all its wrongs, avoiding all the tribulations that it forces us to endure. Now that we had seen some of the things people did, had heard and remembered some of the words they used, and had suffered discomfort from keeping company with them, it became second nature for us to live apart from them. Whether the matter was serious or in jest, it was rare for there to be no implications and no reproof involved. If you make a request, they attack you; if you come to terms with them, they oppose you; if you cooperate with them, they are hostile; if you make an agreement with them, they trick you; if you associate with them, you are not safe from attack; if you mix with them, you will find no lack of falsehood; and, if you demand your rights, how can your requests be heard by the deaf? 21.1

Then too bad for you if you go to the venues where judges are to be found! If you go to their gaming and sporting clubs, your harvest from this effort will be everything that is repulsive, loathsome, and annoying. When you go in, you will be happy and at ease; when you leave, you will be disgusted and appalled. In both situations, their way of life represents the very depth of sin and combines all conceivable faults and defects. It is the origin of all trickery and the source of all harm. 21.2

Had the Gemini experienced what I have,
they would not rise at all for fear of being tricked.[164]

So the Pāshā and I continued to live in seclusion. We broached all kinds of topics and moved from one subject to another. Sometimes in our readings I waded through the waves of the sea with him; at other times we traversed desert mirages together. We would see someone burning his boats so that he could induce his squadrons to hurtle headlong into the very face of death. We heard the cameleteer-poet in the desert wastes spurring on his camel and rhapsodizing about his beloved. His humble infatuation could not prevent him from boasting about the might of his noble colleagues or lead him to forget the mention of his passion when slaughter and death were in the air. And so

ذكر الهوى، مواقف الحتف ومواطن الردى، فيخلط بالعزل الفخر، ويخاطب خلته من جوف ذلك القفر:

٣،٢١

إنا محيوك يا سلمى فحيينا
وإن سقيت كرام الناس فاسقينا
وإن دعوت إلى جلي ومكرمة
يوما سراة كرام الناس فادعينا
أن تبتدر غاية يوما لمكرمة
تلق السوابق منا والمصلينا
وليس يهلك منا سيدا أبدا
إلا افتلينا غلاما سيدا فينا
إنا لنرخص يوم الروع أنفسنا
ولو نسام بها في الأمن أغلينا
بيض مفارقنا تغلي مراجلنا
نأسو بأموالنا آثار أيدينا
إني لمن معشر أفنى أوائلهم
قيل الكماة ألا أين المحامونا
إذا الكماة تنحوا أن يصيبهم
حد الظباة وصلنا بأيدينا

٤،٢١ وتطرب الناقة أيضا إلى مواطنها وتشتاق إلى مواطنها فتحن حنينه. وتئن أنينه، وكلما رآها تشكو شكواه، وتصغي إلى نجواه، وتردد برغائها صداه وتسعده في هواه تأوه وتنهد وترنم فأنشد:

he would mix boasting with love poetry and address his lady from the depths of the desert:

21.3

Hail to thee, Salmā! Respond to our greetings!
    If you give water to noble people, then do so for us!
If you call the leader of noble men
    to great and noble deeds one day, then call upon us!
If one day some objective spurs us to a noble deed,
    then in our number it will meet both leaders and runners-up.
No chieftain of ours ever perishes
    without our producing a young chieftain from among us.
On the day of battle, we place little value on our lives;
    should we bargain for safety, then we raise the price.
With our white hair and our pots simmering,
    we use our wealth to remedy the deeds done by our hands.
I am from a tribe whose chieftains were killed
    by the cries of heroes asking: "Where are the defenders?"
When warriors in armour swerve to avoid being hit
    by sword-tips, we grasp them with our hands.[165]

21.4 Beneath him you would see the camel relishing its own domain and yearning for a resting place. How it yearns, how it groans! He would hear its complaint as it pricked up its ears to listen to his conversation, responded to the echo of his voice with its bellowing, and delighted him in his passion with its replies. With a moan and sigh he would recite:

لقد زارني طيف الخيال فهاجني
فهل زار هذي الإبل طيف خيال
لعل كراها قد أراها جذبها
ذوائب طلح بالعقيق وضال
ومسرحها في ظل أحوى كأنها
إذا أظهرت فيه ذوات جمال
تلون زبورا في الحنين منزلا
عليهن فيه الصبر غير حلال
وأنشدن من شعر المطايا قصيدة
وأودعنها في الشوق كل مقال

٥.٢١ ثم انتقل الباشا إلى مشاهدة المعامع المشهورة، والمعارك المذكورة، فترى الدماء تجري أنهارا في الوديان، والمهج تسيل من مسايل الأبدان، والموت واقفا يحصد الرؤوس ويجني نفائس النفوس والفارس يمشي مشية الخيلاء ويطعن الطعنة النجلاء وينشد في وصف أثرها وبعد غورها:

طعنت ابن عبد القيس طعنة ثائر
لها نفذ لولا الشعاع أضاءها
ملكت بها كفي فأنهرت فتقها
يرى قائم من دونها ما وراءها
يهون عليّ أن ترد جراحها
عيون الأواسي إذ حمدت بلاءها

٦.٢١ فلا تنطفئ نارها ولا يخمد أوارها إلا وقد أصبحت النساء أيامي والأطفال يتامى والأموال نهبا منهوبا والأعلاق سلبا مسلوبا، والمدائن خالية خاوية، والقصور بائدة بالية، والحرب خدعة يخذل فيها القوي لأوهن سبب وينتصر فيها الضعيف من

A phantom vision has visited and spurred me on.
Has a similar spectre visited this camel?
Perhaps sleep showed it the way in which it tugs
at the top of the acacia and lotus trees in al-ʿAqīq
and its grazing ground in dark green shade, as though
it were to reveal canopied ladies.
In longing they have recited psalmody sent down to them
in which patience is never permitted,
and sung an ode of animal poetry; in their passion
they have imbued it with every kind of speech.[166]

Then we would turn our attention to descriptions of famous battles and conflicts. Blood would be cascading in the valleys and lives ebbed away as the blood flowed from dying bodies. Death would stand there gathering up heads and collecting precious souls. Cavaliers would walk haughtily among the ranks piercing every gaping wound with their spear. Then they would recite the following verses to describe its effects and depth: 21.5

I stabbed Ibn ʿAbd al-Qays with a vengeful, penetrating thrust;
but for the spattered blood, the very wound would illumine it.
I have given my hand free rein, opening its gash still further;
whoever stands on this side of it can glimpse what lies beyond.
It matters not to me that the wounds may repulse
nursing women's eyes, for I have lauded its dreadful effect.[167]

Up would flare the flames of war. The fiery heat would not abate till women were widowed and children orphaned. Money was plundered; booty and precious trinkets became stolen loot. Cities were rendered desolate, castles derelict and in ruins. Within them war remained dominant for the feeblest of pretexts. The weak were triumphant for reasons they did not even consider. War has caused dynasties to change and authority patterns to be altered. Thrones have been toppled and kingdoms have fallen even when their regime was well founded and their prestige extended far and wide. Their power may well have reached the heights and lasted for a long time. But, just when no one 21.6

حيث لا يحتسب، فكم دالت بها الدول ودارت الدوائر وانثلت العروش وسقطت الممالك بعد لواء العز المعقود وبساط المجد الممدود والتناهي في العظمات، والتمادي في الجبروت وبعد أن لم يكن يدور في الوهم سقوطها، ويخطر في الخيال هبوطها، كل ذلك يكون أسرع من لمح البصر إذا نزل القضاء وحم القدر فوقعت من قائد هفوة، فتقدم بالجيش خطوة أو تأخر خطوة، وكل ملك وإن امتد ظله زائل، وعند التناهي يقصر المتطاول.

٧،٢١ ثم أنتهي به إلى حلقة واعظ يسلب الألباب بقوة بيانه، وينير العقول بضوء برهانه، ويسترق النفوس بطلاقة لسانه، ويقول : أيها الناس والله لدنياكم هذه أهون عندي من عراق كلب في يد مجذوم، ويقول: المخير بين أن يستغني عن الدنيا وبين أن يستغني بالدنيا كالمخير بين أن يكون مالكا أو مملوكا.

من سره أن لا يرى ما يسوؤه
فلا يتخذ شيئا يخاف له فقدان

ويقول: الحياة الطيبة هي حياة الغنى والغنى هو القنوع لأنه إذا كان الغنى عدم الحاجة إلى الناس فأغنى الناس أقلهم حاجة إلى الناس، ولذلك كان الله أغنى الأغنياء.

غنى النفس ما يكفيك من سد خلة
فإن زاد شيئًا عاد ذاك الغنى فقرا

٨،٢١ ويقول: الجود حارس الأعراض والحلم فدام السفيه والعفو زكاة الظفر والاستشارة عين الهداية وأشرف الغنى ترك المنى، وكم من عقل أسير، عند هوى أمير، ومن التوفيق حفظ التجربة، ويقول: من لان عوده كثفت أغصانه ومن لانت كلمته وجبت محبته والخلاف يهدم الرأي ويقول: إنما المرء في الدنيا غرض تنتضل فيه المنايا ونهب تبادره المصائب ومع كل جرعة شرق وفي كل أكلة غصص ولا ينال العبد نعمة إلا بفراق أخرى، ولا يستقبل يوما من عمره إلا بفراق آخر من أجله فنحن أعوان المنون

could conceive of the possibility of its collapse and decline, Fate descended and executed its decree. With that, the whole episode happened in the twinkling of an eye, when a commander committed an error and led an army one step forward or backward. However far its shadow stretches, every dominion is ephemeral and its reach is eventually limited.

21.7 Later I took him to visit the circle of a learned preacher whose forceful explanations attracted our attention. He managed to coax our minds with his clear proofs and captivate our hearts with his unrestrained tongue. His topic was the baseness and ignominy of wealth: "O you people, I esteem this world of yours less than that of a dog's bone in a leper's hand." He would also say: "The ability to choose between eschewing the world altogether and using it to enrich oneself is like having the choice between being ruler or ruled:

Whoever is happy never to see things that distress him
should not acquire anything he is afraid to lose."[168]

He would also say: "A pleasant life is one full of riches. Rich people are content because their wealth means that they don't have to rely on other people. Thus the richest people are the least in need of other people. That is why Almighty God is the richest of all!

Wealth of spirit does not spare you the need to stave off want;
should it increase, that same wealth turns into poverty."[169]

21.8 He also talked about character traits: "Generosity is honor's sentinel, reason is the filter of the foolish, and forgiveness is the best justification for victory. To seek advice is the source of guidance, and to abandon one's desires is the finest wealth of all. Many a mind has been the prisoner of an amir's whim. Part of the road to success involves remembering one's experiences. Anyone with pliant wood has thick branches; anyone who uses gentle words must earn affection. Discord is the destroyer of reason." He then stated: "In this world mankind is a target for a struggle between fates, a helpless prey with misfortune hurtling headlong in its direction. In every gulp of liquid and mouthful of food there is something to choke him. No man receives a single act of kindness without losing another; no one is afforded a day in his life without losing another from his appointed time of death. We are all the fates' helpers; our lives are merely a signpost for death. How can we expect to be immortal? Day and

وأنفسنا نصب الحتوف فمن أين نرجو البقاء وهذا الليل والنهار لم يرفعا من شيء شرفا إلا إسراعا الكرة في هدم ما بنيا وتفريق ما جمعا.

٩،٢١ ويقول: الكاذب في نهاية البعد من الفضل والمرائي أسوأ حالا من الكاذب لأنه يكذب فعلا وذلك يكذب قولا والفعل آكد من القول فأما المعجب بنفسه أسوأ حالا منهما لأنهما يريان نقص أنفسهما ويريدان إخفاءه والمعجب بنفسه قد عمي عن عيوب نفسه فيراها محاسن ويبديها، ثم يقول: عجبت للبخيل يستعجل الفقر الذي منه هرب، ويفوته الذي إياه طلب، فيعيش في الدنيا عيش الفقراء ويحاسب في الآخرة حساب الأغنياء، وعجبت للمتكبر الذي كان بالأمس نطفة وفي الغد جيفة وعجبت لمن نسي الموت وهو يرى من يموت، ويقول أيضا: لا تشكون إلى أحد فإن كان عدوا سره وإن كان صديقا ساءه وليس مسرة العدو ولا مساءة الصديق بمحمودة.

١٠،٢١
ولا تشك إلى خلق فتشمته
شكوى الجريح إلى العقبان والرخم

ويقول: العجز عجزان أحدهما عجز التقصير وقد أمكن الأمر والثاني الجد في طلبه وقد فات والخير من العلماء من يرى الجاهل بمنزلة الطفل الذي هو بالرحمة أحق منه بالغلظة ويعذره بنقصه في ما فرط منه ولا يعذر نفسه في التأخير عن هدايته.
ويقول:

الدين إنصافك الأقوام كلهم
وأي دين لآبي الحق إن وجبا
والمرء يعييه قود النفس مصحبة
للخير وهو يقود العسكر اللجبا

ويختم وعظه بهذا الدعاء: اللّٰهم اكفني بواق الثقات ومكائد الأصدقاء.

١١،٢١ ثم أعوج مع الباشا بآثار أقوام أخنى عليها الزمان، ولعبت بها أيادي الحدثان، وقد كانوا يظنون أنه لا يبلغ مداهم أحد سواهم، فصبحهم الدهر بغارة من غيره وتركهم

night have never elevated anything without immediately rushing to destroy what they have built and to break up what they have gathered together."

21.9 He goes on: "The liar is as far removed from virtue as one can be and the hypocrite is even worse. The latter lies in his actions whereas the former merely lies in what he says—and actions are more definite than words. The self-satisfied person is worse than both of them. For, while the first two can see their own shortcomings and are prepared to conceal them, the self-satisfied person is blind to his faults and will even regard them as virtues and flaunt them." He continues: "I am always amazed at the way misers accelerate the very poverty they are trying to avoid. By so doing, they lose the things they want and live like poor men in this world while still being called to account like the rich in the next. I am equally surprised by the arrogant man who yesterday was just a sperm and tomorrow will be a corpse; by the person who forgets about death when he can see people dying all around him." He notes: "Never complain to anyone; if they are your enemies, they will gloat, and if they are your friends, they will feel sad. It is not a good idea either to delight one's enemies or sadden one's friends:

21.10 Do not complain to people, you will make them gloat,
like a wounded man complaining to eagles and vultures."[170]

He says: "The weakness is, in fact, twofold: firstly that of inadequacy when the thing was attainable, and the second is an eager, yet futile search for it once it has disappeared. The best kind of scholar is one who regards the ignorant person as a baby deserving sympathy rather than anger. As a result, he will excuse him when he makes an error but will never forgive himself for hesitating to give him guidance." He goes on to recite:

Religion involves being just to all peoples.
And what religion exists for the denier of truth when compelled?
Man cannot control his heart when it imparts good,
even though he be in command of a huge army.[171]

He finished his homily with the following prayer: "O God, protect me from the outrages of trustworthy people and the tricks that friends play."

21.11 At this point I turned away with the Pāshā in order to examine the traces of people obliterated by time and toyed with by the vicious hands of history. They had assumed that no one else could ever match their achievements, but destiny brought others to overrun them and left them as an object lesson for

لمن بعدهم عبرة من عبره، على أن هؤلاء اللاحقين لم يعتبروا بأولئك السابقين فساروا على طريقة سيرهم، واغتروا بمثل غرورهم، ﴿وَلَقَدْ جَاءَهُم مِّنَ الْأَنبَاءِ مَا فِيهِ مُزْدَجَرٌ * حِكْمَةٌ بَالِغَةٌ ۖ فَمَا تُغْنِ النُّذُرُ﴾ .

ثم أنتحي به مجلس محاضرات بين الأدباء ومفاكهات بين الندماء فنسمع من لطيف بوادرهم، ورقيق نوادرهم، ومحاسن أشعارهم، ولطيف أخبارهم، ما ينير ظلمة الفهوم، ويجلو صدأ الهموم.

١٢،٢١

لفظ كأن معاني السكر تسكته
فمن تحفظ بيتا منه لم يفق
جزل يشجع من وافي له أندا
فهو الدواء لداء الجبن والقلق
إذا ترنم شاد للجبان به
لاقى المنايا بلا خوف ولا فرق
وإن تمثل صاد للصخور به
جادت عليه بعذب غير ذي رنق

١٣،٢١

هكذا كنت أنتقل بالباشا من كتاب إلى كتاب، وأخرج من فصل فيها إلى باب، وأجتني معه نفائس الأعلاق، من حدائق الأوراق، وأقتطف له زواهر الأزهار، من صفحات الدفاتر، وألتقط درر الأدب، من سطور الكتب، إلى أن قال لي ذات يوم:

الباشا إن أعظم ما آسف عليه اليوم تلك الأيام التي أضعتها من عمري في ما لا يجدي ولا يفيد من مشاغل الدهر وملاهي العيش ويا ليتني كنت قصرت همي منذ صباي على مثل هذه المعيشة وهذا التفرغ لاكتساب الفوائد مغتبطا سعيدا لا حاسدا ولا محسودا أنتقل من مطالعة الكتب إلى مذاكرة العلماء ومن مذاكرة العلماء إلى مطارحة الأدباء، ومن مطارحة الأدباء إلى مسامرة الفضلاء، ويعلم الله أنه ليزيد أسفي كلما تذكرت ما كانوا يحدثونني عنه في أيام دولتي عن تلك المجالس, مجالس العلماء

those who came after. However, these younger people had learned no lessons from their forebears; they were behaving in exactly the same way and were similarly deluded. «There came to them news as a warning, sound advice, yet it was of no avail.»[172]

Later I accompanied the Pāshā as we went to listen to talks given in literary circles and to joke with some close friends. We read enough of their pleasant inclinations and subtle anecdotes to brighten the gloom and clear anxiety's rust from our minds:

21.12

Words seemingly vested with the ability to make you drunk;
anyone memorizing a verse never regains consciousness.
They are eloquent and hearten whoever lends an ear;
a cure for the disease of cowardice and anxiety.
When a singer chants them to a coward,
he will face the fates without fear or terror.
If a thirsty man quotes them to rocks,
they will gush with sweet, clear water.[173]

21.13

In this way, I led the Pāshā from one book to another, and from one chapter to the next. With him I would pluck the most priceless gems from the bowers of pages, pick the choicest buds from fragrant texts, and choose pearls of literature from volumes. Then one day he told me:

PĀSHĀ My greatest regret today is that I wasted so much of my life on totally useless and unprofitable diversions and amusements. If only I had had the foresight from my younger days to limit my aspirations to leading a life like this, and had concentrated on getting some benefit from learning, happy and content rather than jealous and envied. I could have read books, then moved on to confer with scholars, hold discussions with men of letters, and consort with men of virtue. Only God knows, every time I remember the things they used to tell me about learned societies and literary circles in the days of my period in office, how much I regret what I missed. I took no notice of such people and thought that the members of those circles were people of leisure, mere lazy idlers who sat down to study their books and journals, just as women

والأدب فما كنت آبه بها ولا ألتفت إليها وكنت أظنهم قوما من أهل الفراغ والكسل يجلسون للدفاتر والكتب كما تجلس النساء للغزل والردن. والحمد لله الذي أرشدني إلى ذلك آخر الدهر فعلمت مقدار هذه النعمة التي حببت إليّ الحياة وهونت عليّ متاعبها وما أخالك تبخل عليّ بعد الآن وقد علمت نفع ذلك لي بمداومة السير معي في هذا الطريق والتنقل بي في مجالس الأدباء ومجامع الفضلاء وأندية العلماء فأشكر لك هذه اليد البيضاء أولى من ضياع الوقت في الذهاب إلى المنتزهات والأعراس التي لم تزدني إلا هما ولم ترثني إلا غما.

١٤،٢١ عيسى بن هشام لا تطمعن أيها الأمير دفع الله عنك المكاره في مثل تلك المجالس فقد ذهب بها الأيام وطوتها الليالي ولم يبق بيننا من يأنس إليها وينافس فيها.

الباشا وكيف يكون ذلك وأنا لا أزال أسمع ما تزعمونه من كثرة المدارس الآن وتقدم العلوم وتعدد الطالبين وسهولة الحصول على الكتب ووفرة المطابع وحرية النشر فإذا قابلنا بين ذلك وبين ما كان عليه ذلك الزمن من تعسر الوصول إلى الكتب وتعذر استنساخها وضن أربابها بها كأنها خفايا الكنوز يفخر الواحد منهم كان بالكتاب الفلاني في مكتبته كما يفخر القائد المنتصر بسلاح عدوه المنهزم في بيت ذخائره حتى كان الجهلاء الذين لا ينتفعون بالكتب ولا يفقهون ما شأنها يعتبرون اقتناءها من أقصى ما يفخر به المفتخرون من ضروب الزخرفة وأنواع التجمل كأنها اليواقيت والجواهر يعجز عنها من يروم الانتفاع بها ممن لم يكن ذا ثروة واسعة تمكنه من استنساخها أو ابتياعها- لا بدع أن تخيلنا أن كل مصري في يده كتاب وكل واحد منهم أليف محاضرة وحليف مناقشة وتزهو مجالس الفضل وتزهر أندية الآداب وكيف لا يكون ذلك وقد أذقتني من ثمرة المطالعة في هذه المدة الوجيزة ما عفت معه كل لذة سواه؟

١٥،٢١ عيسى بن هشام نعم ترقت العلوم في هذا العصر وتقدمت المعارف وزاد عدد الطالبين وكثرت المطابع ورخصت الكتب وسهل على الناس تناولها وتيسر لهم اقتنائها ولكن قلّ بيننا عدد الراغبين فيها والمطالعين لها فكسد سوقها وبارت تجارتها وتلاهى عنها من ينتفع بها ورغب عنها من كان يدخرها للزينة لسبب كثرتها

do to their spinning and crochet. Now at the end of my days I can thank God who has revealed the truth to me. I can appreciate the extent of this blessing which has revived my love of life and made its difficulties easier to bear. Now that you know the help that this is to me, I don't imagine you will refuse to pursue this commendable course in my company. You can take me to literary circles, erudite communities, and scholars' clubs. I'll be that much more grateful for this favor than wasting time going to parks and wedding receptions. Such things have only increased my anxieties and left my nerves shattered.

21.14 ʿĪsā ibn Hishām My dear Amir (may God keep all misfortunes away from you), you shouldn't place any confidence in circles like these. Time has enveloped and buried them. No one alive today has any experience of them or displays the slightest interest.

Pāshā How can that be? I keep on hearing you talk about the large number of schools, the progress of sciences, the number of students, the ease of access to books, the abundance of printing presses, and the freedom to publish. If we compare all that to previous times, books were difficult to get hold of; not only that, but it was impossible to copy them because their owners were so miserly. It was as though they were the secret contents of treasure chests; an owner could be just as proud of having such-and-such a tome in his library as a victorious general would at having his enemy's weapons in his armory. In fact, even ignorant people, the kind who wouldn't get any benefit from books or understand their significance, would regard their acquisition as the ultimate form of luxury item and decoration they could boast about—as if they were sapphires and gems. Anyone who wanted to benefit from reading them couldn't do so unless he had enough wealth to either copy or purchase them. So it shouldn't come as a surprise that every Egyptian today should have a book to read; each one of them should be quite used to listening to talks and discussing things with other people. Learned circles and literary clubs would be proud to have such people as members. How can this happen, when the benefits of reading that you have let me savor during this short period have made me forget all other pleasures that the world has to offer?

21.15 ʿĪsā ibn Hishām It's perfectly true that in recent years sciences have indeed spread, the number of students has increased, printing presses have increased in number, and people can easily get hold of books. But in fact, few of us show any interest in buying and reading them. As a result, there's no market, and business is bad. The people who could benefit the most by

وتبذلها. والناس اليوم في حركة لا هي شرقية ولا غربية قد اشتغل بعضهم ببعض واكتفوا من دهرهم بحوادث يومهم فتعطلت مجالس العلم واندرست أندية الفضل وغاضت ينابيع المعارف وجفت عيون الآداب واقتصروا من المطالعة في مجالسهم على قراءة الجرائد وما تحتويه من أخبارهم اليومية الوقتية، وأنى لهم الاستقرار في المجالس وهم لا يستقرون في مكان ولا يهدأون من حركة فتراهم رائحين غادين متنقلين متشتتين وأكثر ما يكون جلوسهم في مركبات البخار ومركبات الكهرباء ومركبات الخيول ودراجات الرجل. والجانب الأعلى منهم يقضون جزءا عظيما من السنة مترجلين في بلاد الأجانب وديار الغربة ومطارح النوى؟

١٦،٢١ وقصارى العلم عندهم اليوم أن يتلقى الطالب أشتاتا منه في المدارس وهو في السن الذي لم يصل فيه إلى تمام التعقل وكمال الإدراك فيحفظ ما يحفظه الفونوغراف صوت المتكلم ويؤديه كما هو. فإذا أدى الطالب ما حفظه من تلك الأشتات عند الامتحان وأسعده البخت بنيله صك الشهادة تأبط ذلك الصك ونفض يده من العلم وتخلص من أثقاله ومتاعبه وطرحه عنه طرح الثوب الخلق ونبذه نبذ القادم على أهله وبلاده ما أسن من ماءه وما جف من زاده فإذا تنصب وتوظف أصبح صانعا من الصناع لا عالما من العلماء يحن إلى العلم وأهله ويتشوق إلى الأدب وكتبه فإن كان ممن قدر الله لهم بالمطالعة فإنه لا يتجاوز فيها حد الكتب التي تتعلق بأصول وظيفته ولذلك أصبحت كتب العلوم والآداب مستقلة مملولة ورأيت من هؤلاء الناس من إذا قوي على قراءة صحيفة في كتاب فإنه ينتهي منها والعرق يتصبب من جبينه لشدة الملل والسأم والضجر وضيق العطن فيلقي الكتاب عن يده كما يلقي الثقل حامله.

١٧،٢١ وقد بلغ بهم العجز عن حصر فكرهم في تفهم ما في الكتب إلى أن سرى ذلك العجز والملل إلى الحديث فتراهم لا يصغون فيه إلا إلى ما يكون منه متقطعا مبتورا ومختطفا مجذوما وأثقل ما يكون على نفوسهم في مجالس بحث طويل أو حديث ضاف أو قصة مسهبة.

reading books ignore them. Those who used to buy them as decoration now detest them because they are in such wide circulation and have become quite common. Today everyone is caught up in a movement which is neither Eastern nor Western; they are all involved in each other's business. By way of destiny they are content with everyday occurrences, and so their learned circles and gatherings have become defunct, sources of knowledge have diminished, and literary springs have run dry. Instead they devote all their attention in their gatherings to reading newspapers and their ephemeral daily reports. How can they establish for themselves a place in a learned circle when they never stay in one place and are always moving around. You see them coming and going, traveling here, there, and everywhere. The one place where they spend the most time sitting down is in vehicles: steamboats, tramcars, horse carriages, and bicycles. Affluent people spend months of the year traveling abroad and wandering through Western lands and distant locations.

21.16 For them learning consists solely in the student's studying various types of science in school at an age when he's not yet reached maturity in either intelligence or comprehension, then memorizing it all like a gramophone recording and repeating it like a parrot. If the student puts all this scattered information that he has memorized together when he takes an exam and is lucky to leave with a degree under his arm, he'll then proceed to wash his hands of all that information and the burdens and problems it brings, and discard it all like so much tattered clothing. He'll abandon it like someone who offers his family brackish water and dry food. After finding a job and taking a post, he becomes yet another working man rather than a scholar who appreciates learning and its practitioners and loves literature and its works. If one of them has a God-given capacity for reading, it only goes as far as books that cover the principles relevant to their position. Scholarly and literary works are now considered something out of the ordinary and tedious. You'll find that, if any of these people can read a single page of a book, he finishes up with sweat pouring from his brow and feeling utterly exhausted, angry, and bored. He tosses the book aside like someone gratefully shedding a heavy load he has been carrying.

21.17 This inability to put ideas together in their comprehension of books and their sense of boredom has now infected their ability to converse. The only things that they're prepared to listen to are disconnected and fragmentary, or else brief and in extracts. For them the most bothersome things about gatherings are lengthy research essays, complex conversations, or elaborate stories.

الباشا أراك أيها الصديق تغلو في الأمر فما أتخيل أن زمانا يخلو من مثل المجالس الأدبية التي كانت في أيامنا فإنها من لوازم المجتمعات في البداوة أو الحضارة وكانت لدينا أمرا لازما تكون المعيشة ناقصة بدونه حتى رأينا كثيرا من الأمراء والكبراء ممن ليس لهم حفظ في العلم أو نصيب من الأدب لا يخلو مجلسهم من عالم جليل أو شاعر بليغ أو فاضل أريب أو نديم أديب أو محدث ظريف أو راوية خبير تتفكه بهم النفوس في المجالس وترتاح إليهم القلوب من عناء الأعمال هذا والكتب نادرة وأسباب التعليم ضعيفة فما بالكم اليوم.

عيسى بن هشام قد استغنى كبراؤنا وأمراؤنا اليوم عن كل ما ذكرته بما يخترعه لهم الأجانب من آلات الزخرفة وأدوات الزينة وغيرها من ضروب الملاهي وإنك لتجد مثلا العصا التي تضيء بالكهرباء في يد الكبير والعظيم أكبر عنده نفعا من جميع أولئك الذين ينيرون العقول ويضيؤون الأذهان ويشرحون الصدور. ١٨،٢١

ولقد ذكرتني الآن بما فاتني من وجوب اطلاعك على بعض مجالس اليوم وأنديته لتعلم الفرق بينهما وبين مجالس أيامكم وستحكم لي بعدم الغلو في ما قصصته عليك.

Pāshā My friend, you're clearly exaggerating. I cannot conceive that this era can be devoid of the kind of literary circles that existed in our times. Whether we are talking about a desert or civilized culture, they constitute one of the requirements of society. For us they were a necessity, something without which life was lacking something; so much so that we noticed that amirs and important people who may have had no knowledge of sciences and literature would always include an illustrious religious scholar, an eloquent poet, a well-read sage, an amusing storyteller, a witty raconteur, or an experienced bard in their circle, people whose task it would be to entertain people and refresh their spirits after a hard day's work. And all this was in spite of the fact that books were scarce and scholarship was not easy to come by. So what's the matter with you people today?

21.18 ʿĪsā ibn Hishām I would include our important men and amirs in everything that I've already said. Foreigners have provided them with all kinds of ornamental devices, fancy goods, and other forms of entertainment. For example, you can find an important person carrying a stick that emits an electric beam. He will reckon that much more useful than all the people who offer enlightening ideas to people who need to be informed.

You have just reminded me of something I'd forgotten: I need to show you some of today's gatherings so that you can get an idea about the difference between the ones in existence today and the ones in your own time. Then you'll be able to judge for yourself quite how much my account has been exaggerated.

١،٢٢ قال عيسى بن هشام: فتخيرت من مجتمعات القوم، في منتديات اليوم، ما يقوم به وفاء العهد، وإنجاز الوعد من وقوف الباشا على ما يجري فيها من ظواهرها وخوافيها، واستقر في عزمي أن أزور به أربعة مجامع، مختلفة المشارب والمنازع، فندخل منتدى السادة الأعلام من علماء الإسلام مصابيح الدين، ونباريس اليقين، ونجوم الإرشاد، ورجوم الإلحاد، ونصراء الحق، وحلفاء الصدق، وهداة كل ضال ومارق، وأسباب الوصلة بين المخلوق والخالق، حيث يعلم الباشا ما مدار محاضرتهم، وما مغزى مسامرتهم.

ثمّ نلج مجتمع الأعيان والتجار، زينة المدائن وبهجة الأمصار، وعماد العمران والحضارة، ودعائم الصناعة والتجارة، ومواضع الصدق والأمانة، ومواطن الحزم والرزانة، ووسائل الثروة للدول والممالك، وذرائع النجح في تمهيد السبل والمسالك، فيقف الباشا على مبلغ أحوالهم بما يسمعه من أقوالهم.

٢،٢٢ ثمّ نحضر محضر أرباب المراتب، من ذوي الوظائف والمناصب، ممّن تقام بهم الأحكام، وتفتخر بهم الدفاتر والأقلام، ويستقيم بهم قوام الأمور، ويتوقف عليهم نظام الجمهور، وتشرق بهم أنوار العدل، وتحلى بآدابهم أندية الفضل، معادن العفة والاستقامة، ومصادر النزاهة والكرامة، فيخبر الباشا خبرهم، ويسبر غورهم.

ثمّ نشهد مجلس الأمراء من العظماء والكبراء، سادة الأقطار، وقادة الأفكار، وساسة الأمم، وأرباب السيف والقلم، وذوي النعمة والترف، وأصحاب العظمة والشرف، وأهل الرئاسة والزعامة، وأولي العزة والشهامة، فيستطلع الباشا طلع أمورهم من خلال قصورهم.

٣،٢٢ وبدأنا فقصدنا ناديًا يجمع جملة من ذوي العلم وطلابه، وأهل الفضل وأربابه ممّن تعرفت بهم، واتصلت بأسبابهم، فاستأذنا واستأنسنا، وسلّمنا وجلسنا، وإذا بهم يخوضون في حديث يبعد عن المرام، ويتشدقون بكلام لا يطفئ الأوام، ولا ينقع صدى الأسماع والأفهام، وقد توسدوا الوسائد، وتوركوا المقاعد، ووضعت أمامهم

ʿĪsā ibn Hishām said: I now chose some contemporary clubs and public meeting places of various sorts to fulfil my pledge and let the Pāshā find out for himself what went on there, whether obvious to the eye or beneath the surface. I decided to take him to four separate meeting places where we would encounter people with different ideas and inclinations.[175] We would start by visiting those distinguished gentlemen, the Islamic religious scholars, those lights of our religion, luminaries of our faith, stars of spiritual guidance, and scourgers of apostasy. As upholders of truth and sincerity, they guide all those who wander from the path and renounce the faith. They call mankind to the knowledge of their Creator. That way the Pāshā would learn about the contents of their lectures and the goals of their conversations. Next we would pay a visit to a meeting of notables and merchants, glorious ornaments of cities, supporters of civilized society, upholders of industry and commerce, seats of truth and reliability, havens of resolve and poise, conveyors of wealth to states and kingdoms, modes of success in the preparation of ways and means. By listening to their talk the Pāshā could assess the true extent of their circumstances. 22.1

Then we would attend a session involving civil servants and government employees, people involved in the passage of laws and celebrated by pens and dossiers. Through them affairs are put on a straight path; on them depends the right functioning of the people's welfare. From them emanates the gleam of justice, and with their literary erudition cultural clubs find themselves adorned. They are indeed veritable mines of decency and integrity, sources of probity and honor. The Pāshā could thus learn about them and probe their depths. Finally we would attend a meeting of royal princes and other members of the ruling class, lords of territories, leaders of thought, controllers of peoples, masters of both sword and pen, dispensers of beneficence and gifts, possessors of prestige and honor, people associated with command and leadership, glorious and proud. By visiting their palaces the Pāshā could assess their state of affairs. 22.2

We began by heading for a meeting where all the most unique and highly respected scholars used to gather with their students, a group of virtuous people with whom I had an acquaintance and remained in touch. We asked permission to join them, and they welcomed us. After greeting them we sat down. We found them involved in a conversation which was far removed from 22.3

المساعط والمجامر، مكان المقالم والمحابر، وقد عادوا إلى ما انقطع عند دخولنا من المقال، على هذا التفصيل والإجمال:

٤،٢٢ شيخ لقد وهمت يا مولانا في ظنك أنّ الطين في العقار خير من الدور والأماكن في هذه الأيام، وقد جربت كلا الموردين فوجدت البناء أكثر دخلا من غيره لا سيما إذا كان الصقع جيداً والموقع حسناً والساكن من أولئك الإفرنجة الذين هم أقل من المسلمين عيالاً، وأخف منهم على البناء وطأة، فلا يدقون ولا يطحنون، ولا يعجنون ولا يخبزون، ولا يغسلون ولا يكثرون من الاستحمام، ولا يسعون ضيفاً أو نزيلاً، ولا يستكثرون من الخدم والغلمان، وبهذا ينتفي ما قررته من أنّ البناء سريع العطب.

شيخ ثان ولكنك أيها الأستاذ حفظت شيئاً وغابت عنك أشياء، وأسرعت بالحكم على المسألة، فأين أنت من الحريق والزلازل والعواصف وغيرها من الآفات.

الشيخ الأول وأين أنت أيضاً في الأطيان من الدود والندى، والشرق والغرق وما أشبه ذلك.

الشيخ الثاني إنّ الأطيان وإن طرأ عليها شيء مما ذكرته وأفصحت عنه فالعين باقية ويرجى فيها أن تعوّض سنة خسارة أختها، أمّا البناء فيزول بنكبة من تلك النكبات التي تأتيك بغتة، وتكون خسارتك بها عظيمة، ولا يصيبك منه نفع بعد ذلك إلا بإنشائه وتجديده، ولذلك فقد عولت على بيع ذلك المنزل وشراء الفدانين المجاورين في الناحية لأطياني فتكون كل أطيانها خالصة لي.

الشيخ الأول ﴿لَكُمْ دِينُكُمْ وَلِيَ دِينِ﴾، فإني لا أتحول عن فكري، ولا أنزل عن رأيي.

٥،٢٢ شيخ ثالث التجارة خير من هذا ومن هذا، فهي الربح المستتر عن الأعين وسوء العينة، وهو محفوف دائما بالبركة والنمو، ومن منكم بلغ بأطيانه وأملاكه ما بلغه من الثروة مثل المرحوم الشيخ فلان رحمة الله على الجميع.

what we were seeking and bragging about things that neither quenched our thirst nor made for profitable listening. Having abandoned their chairs, they were all reclining on cushions; in front of them were snuffboxes and braziers instead of penholders and inkwells. They now went back to the conversation they were engaged in before we came in. Here is a summary:

22.4 FIRST SHAYKH My dear Sir, you are quite wrong to claim that these days, ownership of land and dykes is better than that of buildings and houses. I've tried both as sources of income and have found that the returns from buildings are more profitable, especially if they are in a pleasant district, the site is good, and the householders are Europeans who have smaller families than Muslims and thus exert less pressure and weight on the building's structure. They don't bang, grind, pound, bake, wash, or take a lot of baths; nor do they welcome strangers and guests in their homes or fill the house with butlers and servants. All this refutes your previous assertion that buildings disintegrate quickly.

SECOND SHAYKH My good Sir, as the saying goes, "For everything you know, there are several things you don't know."[176] You're making a hasty judgment on this matter. What about fires, earthquakes, storms, and other disasters?

FIRST SKAYKH But when it comes to land, what about worms, damp, flooding, and inundation?

SECOND SKAYKH I'll grant you that land can be affected by some of the things you've mentioned and identified. However, its value is permanent, and one can expect a loss one year to be compensated for by the following year. A building on the other hand can be destroyed by any natural calamity, something that can happen suddenly and catch you unawares. You suffer huge loss, and the only benefit you can get thereafter is by rebuilding it. That's why I've decided to sell my house here and buy the acreage next to the lands I already own. Then all the land'll be mine.

FIRST SKAYKH «You've your beliefs, and I've mine.»[177] My view remains unaltered, and I'm not going to change my mind.

22.5 THIRD SKAYKH Commercial profits are better than either of these other two. They can be kept out of sight and free of unwanted interference. They're veritably encircled by prosperity and growth all the time. Which of you has ever made as much from lands and buildings as the late Shaykh X (may God have mercy on all people)?

الشيخ الثاني نعم، إنّ التجارة على ما ذكرت لولا ما فيها من المشاغل والمتاعب والتلهي عن الدرس ومباشرة العلم.

الشيخ الثالث لقد كان الشيخ رحمه الله من أكابر التجار، فلم يمنعه ذلك من المناصب العالية والدرجات العلمية الرفيعة، وإفادة الطلبة بدروسه وتقاريره وشروحه وحواشيه، وهؤلاء تلامذته ممّن تزدان بهم حلقات التدريس وتفتخر بهم مجالس العلم.

شيخ رابع (متحسرًا متنهدًا)

وإذا السعادة لاحظتك عيونها

نم فالمخاوف كلهن أمان

شيخ خامس عندي أنّ الأربح والأستر والأضمن والأوثق أن يضع المرء ما لديه من العين والورق عند من يثق به، ويعتمد عليه من خيرة التجار، فيشتغل له بها وينميها ويضاعف له الربح فيأتيه عفوا صفوا بلا اشتغال فكر وتعب جسم. ٦،٢٢

شيخ سادس سمعت فلان باشا يقول إنّ الربح كل الربح اليوم في مشترى أسهم الشركات، ولذلك قصرهمّه عليها وأصبح قليل العناية بغيرها. ولكن ما قولكم في هذه الأسهم هل تحل المعاملة بها أو تحرم.

شيخ سابع هذه مسألة خلافية والكلام فيها يطول، وليس عندي أوفق من وضع ذهبي في صندوقي أمام عيني وتحت يدي، وعلى ذكر الباشا الذي تحدثت عنه أيها الشيخ أسألك هل سمعت منه أنّ كريمته خطبها فلان لابنه؟

الشيخ السادس نعم، سمعت أنّ أمر الخطبة قد تمّ بينهما.

الشيخ السابع ومتى يكون العقد؟

الشيخ السادس لا تطمعن أيها الأستاذ في هدية العقد ولا يطمعن فيها أحد منا فقد علمت أنّ جماعة الكبراء والعظماء لتناهيهم في الشغف بالفخفخة وحب السمعة قد جعلوا عقود الزواج محتكرة على الشيخ فلان والشيخ فلان للمنصب والوظيفة

SECOND SKAYKH You're right. Commerce is just the way you describe it. If only there weren't so much effort and trouble involved. It takes up time which should really be devoted to study and involvement in scholarship.

THIRD SKAYKH The late Shaykh—God have mercy on him!—was a merchant of great importance. That didn't stop him from achieving high office and ascending the ladder of scholarship. He helped students with his classes, his confirmations, his explanations, and commentaries. Pupils of his now adorn study circles and are an object of pride in learned gatherings.

FOURTH SKAYKH (*sighing regretfully*)

When the eyes of happiness look at you,
go to sleep; for all anxieties offer protection.[178]

22.6 FIFTH SKAYKH In situations like this, I think it's safer and more reliable to deposit cash and paper with a really good, trustworthy merchant one can rely on. He'll act on one's behalf in commerce, invest it, and double the profits. In that way one gets the whole thing without using brain power or tiring oneself out.

SIXTH SKAYKH I've heard Y Pāshā say that these days the best profits come from buying company shares. That's why he's restricting his involvement to that sector and is hardly bothering with anything else. What's your view on these shares? Are people allowed to deal in them or is it forbidden?

SEVENTH SHAYKH The issue is controversial, and there's a lot of discussion on the subject. For my part, I know of no safer place to store my gold than the chest which I keep in my own possession; then it's under my own eyes and control. Speaking of Y Pāshā, do any of you have news about his daughter's marriage to Z's son?

SIXTH SKAYKH Yes, I've heard that their engagement has been arranged.

SEVENTH SHAYKH When's the marriage ceremony?

SIXTH SKAYKH My dear fellow, don't expect to get presents from wedding ceremonies any longer. I've heard that a group of important and influential men have given two of our number who hold high offices exclusive rights to perform marriage ceremonies because they want to show off and enhance their reputation. Nobody else will gain anything even though they need such

فلا ينتفع بها غيرهما ممّن هم أحوج إليها منهما فلم يبق لسواهما إلا من لا تغني هديتهم شيئاً.

٧،٢٢ **الشيخ الخامس** الشيء بالشيء يذكر، هل بلغتكم الدعوة إلى عرس فلان؟

الجميع نعم، بلغتنا جميعاً.

السابع للخامس إذا ينبغي أن نؤجّل سفرنا إلى الريف إلى ما بعد ليلة الوليمة.

الشيخ الخامس لا بأس من ذلك والمجاملة تقضي به.

الشيخ الثالث لولا أنّ فلان باشا دعاني إلى العشاء معه في الليلة الموعودة لكنت معكم وقد علمت من سائق مركبته أنّ عنده حصاناً عتيقاً هو في غنى عنه، وأراه مشابهاً لحصاني في الطول والشعرة كما أخبرني سائس مركبتي، فلعلي أشتريه من سعادة الباشا بارك الله فيه بما خف من الثمن وطف.

وعسى الله أن يكون مجلسه خالياً من ذلك السفيه الذي شوّش علينا مجلسنا بسوء المجادلة فإنه خيّبه الله كان يحتجّ عليّ في تحليل التحلي بمصوغات الذهب بأنّ فلاناً من العلماء يحمل ساعة من ذهب غير ملتفت إلى اختلاف المذاهب في هذا الباب، ولوكان ذلك الشيخ ممّن يهتدي بنور العلم لما جعل إلينا سبيلا لمثل هذا السفيه في الاحتجاج علينا به.

٨،٢٢ **الشيخ الأول** قل ما شئت في هذه الأيام التي اجترأ فيها أرباب الطرابيش على أرباب العمائم من مباحثتهم ومجادلتهم ومناقشتهم ومزاحمتهم العلماء في علومهم، ولقد ذهبت تلك الأيام بعزة العلم و رفعة أهله و وقوف الناس أمام العلماء عند حدهم، والتزامهم الصمت في مجالسهم، وحسن الإذعان والتسليم لهم، وطلب الرضا منهم بما يقتضيه المقام من التوقير والتعظيم، والإجلال والإكرام، حتى كأنه قد كتب على صدر كل واحد منهم النص الشريف «العلماء ورثة الأنبياء» و«علماء أمتي كأنبياء بني إسرائيل» وكيف لا يكون الخطب أليماً والمصيبة عظيمة، أم كيف لا تنهل العين بالدم دون الدمع وهم في هذه الأيام لم يكتفوا بالإقدام على مجادلة العلماء حتى أقدموا على تجهيلهم في العلم وإدخال بعض علومهم المحدثة في هذا الزمن بين العلماء وفي

largesse much more than those two do. The only weddings left will be those whose gifts aren't worth anything.

FIFTH SKAYKH Duly noted. Have you all received invitations to A's wedding? 22.7

EVERYONE We all acknowledge receipt of the invitation.

SEVENTH SHAYKH Yes, I must postpone my trip to the country till after the wedding banquet.

FIFTH SKAYKH That's a good idea. Courtesy demands that.

THIRD SKAYKH If B Pāshā hadn't invited me to dinner that same night, I'd be there with you. I've heard from the Pāshā's carriage driver that he has an old stallion which he doesn't need. My own carriage driver's told me that it's of similar stature and coloring to my own stallion. Maybe I can buy it from the Pāshā—God bless him!—for a reasonable sum. But let's hope that this time he doesn't have anyone at his meeting like that fool who spoiled our gathering with his contentiousness. God thwart him, he was arguing with us about whether people were allowed to wear gold jewellery as ornaments. As his basis was citing the fact that one of our fellow religious scholars was wearing a gold watch without taking into consideration the fact that schools of law differ on this point. If the scholar he was citing were someone guided by the light of genuine scholarship, then fools like this man would have no way of arguing with us.

FIRST SKAYKH You can say whatever you like about these times when tarboosh wearers have the absolute effrontery to discuss, argue, disagree, and compete with turbaned shaykhs about their area of scholarship. Long gone are the good old days when scholarship and exalted religious scholars held a position of power and esteem. People used to follow their injunctions and keep quiet during their meetings. They would seek our favor—only to be expected in view of the reverence, respect, and honor that were our due. It was as if each one of them had the text of the following two noble hadith inscribed on his chest: "Religious scholars are heirs of the prophets," and "Religious scholars live long like the prophets of the Children of Israel." How can it be anything but a disaster of major proportions, how can eyes avoid shedding blood with no tears, when these braggarts are not content just to argue with religious scholars, but even go so far as to try to prove such scholars ignorant in their own field of learning? These days they introduce modern scientific ideas into scholarly circles so as to make religious scholars look like some of their 22.8

حلقات دروسهم ليجعلوهم كالتلامذة لهم؟ فانظروا إلى أين وصلت بهم الجرأة والوقاحة، على أنّ علومهم هذه ليست بنافعة في الواقع ونفس الأمر، وما هي والعياذ بالله إلا مدرجة للزيغ، ومزلقة عن الصراط، يستدرجهم بها الشيطان من حيث لا يشعرون، وفي معرفة قواعد الحساب الأربع ما يغني عن التبحر والتعمق كما يفعلون في علم الحساب بما يتدرج بصاحبه إلى علوم الفلسفة الممقوتة ويفضي به إلى الزندقة والإلحاد وقانا الله شر ذلك.

٩،٢٢ الشيخ الثالث وعندك من هذه العلوم علم التاريخ فإنه فضلا عن كونه من الأقاصيص والأساطير فإنه يجبر صاحبه إلى الخوض في حديث الصحابة رضي الله عنهم وما وقع بينهم من الحروب وهو ممّا نهى الشرع عنه بنص «إذا أفضيتم إلى ذكر أصحابي فأمسكوا» ويكفي منه أن يحيط المرء بما جاء في السيرة الحلبية.

الشيخ الثاني وما هذا العلم الذي يسمّونه بالجغرافيا؟

الشيخ الثالث هذا الذي يقال له عندنا علم تخطيط البلدان، ولو كان قاصراً على ذلك لما كان ضاراً ولا نافعاً ولكن ضرره عظيم ومغبته وخيمة بما امتزج به من نسبة الدوران للأرض والوقوف للشمس وتعليل حوادث الجو بتلك العلل المبتدعة التي يكذبها العيان ولا يقوم عليها البرهان، مثل قولهم إنّ مطر السماء من جوف البحر، وأنّ السحاب أبخرة متكافئة، ويكفي لبطلان هذا القول ما رواه كعب الأحبار من أنّ السحاب من ورق الجنّة، ومثله زعمهم أنّ الرعد والبرق حادثان من احتكاك السحب بضغط الهواء، ويفند هذا الزعم أيضاً ما روي من أنّ الرعد صوت ملك يسوق السحاب، وأنّ البرق لمعان حربة بيده.

١٠،٢٢ الشيخ الثاني وماذا تقولون في زعمهم أنّ الأرض معلقة في الهواء؟

الشيخ الرابع لقد ضلوا حسبهم الله ضلالاً بعيداً فأين هم ممّا روي من أنّ الأرض محمولة على قرن ثور، والثور محمول على صخرة، والصخرة على ظهر حوت، والحوت سابح في الماء، وأنّ أوّل ما يأكل أهل الجنة من كبد ذلك الحوت؟

students. Just see how far their sheer impertinence has led them, even though these sciences of theirs are utterly useless. God protect us! Such subjects are merely one stage on the road to error, a slippery slope that veers away from the straight path. It is Satan who entices them down it without their even being aware. For example a knowledge of the four principles of calculation dispenses with the need for thorough and detailed investigation. And yet, that is precisely what they do in arithmetic, the purpose being to gradually introduce the student to the hated science of philosophy and incite him to commit heresy and disbelief. May God protect us from such evil!

THIRD SKAYKH You can add history to the list of such subjects. Quite apart from the fact that it's based on tales and myths, it requires its practitioners to delve into hadith accounts of the Prophet's companions (God be pleased with them!) and the wars which broke out among them. That is something specifically forbidden by the Shariah in the text of the hadith: "When you come to mention my companions, then stop." For the purposes of this subject, it is enough just to understand the contents of *Al-Sīrah al-Ḥalabiyyah*. 22.9

SECOND SKAYKH What's the subject they call "geography"?

THIRD SKAYKH It's what we call country mapping. If that's all that was involved, it would be neither harmful nor useful. However, as it is, it does great harm and brings about disastrous consequences. It combines such things as the degrees of the earth's rotation and the sun's static position. Weather events are explained through contrived reasoning, something easily disproved by what the eye can clearly see is completely unfounded. They claim, for example, that rain from the skies comes from the depths of the sea and clouds are simply dense vapor. Such ideas can be easily dismissed by reference to the statement of Kaʿb al-Aḥbār, namely that clouds are the leaves of paradise. They also claim that thunder and lightning are caused by the clashing of clouds due to atmospheric pressure, something that can also be refuted by reference to the fact that thunder is the sound made by an angel pushing clouds while lightning is a spear flashing in his hand.

SECOND SKAYKH And what do you say about their claim that the earth is suspended in space? 22.10

FOURTH SKAYKH They're totally wrong—may God suffice them in their egregious error! How can they argue with the fact that the earth is supported on a bull's horn, and the bull in turn is supported on a rock which is supported on the back of a fish. The fish is swimming in water, and the very first thing that

على أننا لو طالعنا كتبهم التي زعموا أنهم فاقوا بها الأوائل والأواخر ووصلوا بها في علم تخطيط البلدان إلى ما لم يصل إليه سواهم بدعواهم لوجدناها لا تبلغ في الإحاطة والإفادة ما بلغته «خريدة العجائب» للإمام ابن الوردي فإننا لم نسمع أنه ذكر في تلك الكتب من عجائب المخلوقات ما ذكرته الخريدة من مثل بلاد واق الواق التي يثمر شجرها لكواعب الأتراب والغيد الحسان معلقة من شعورها في ذوائب الأغصان، ومتى أشرقت عليها الشمس صاحت واق واق، فسبحان الخلاق.

١١،٢٢ ومن مثل ما ذكر في «بدائع الزهور ووقائع الدهور» عن الشيخ حامد أنه بلغ منبع النيل وقد عبر إليه البحر الأسود على ظهر دابة تعبد الشمس، فإذا أشرقت على أحد شاطئيه أتت إلى ذلك الشاطئ ولا تزال دائرة مع الشمس حتى تصل إلى الشاطئ الآخر، وقد رأى الشيخ حامد النيل يجري في ذلك البحر كالخيط الأبيض في الثوب الأسود، ووجده يخرج من قبة من ياقوتة حمراء وراء جبل قاف، وأنه هناك أبيض من الثلج وأحلى من العسل، وهذه القبة يخرج منها أيضاً ثلاثة أنهار وهي سيحون وجيحون والفرات، فهل وصلوا إلى معرفة مثل هذه الحقائق في كتبهم؟

الشيخ الرابع تالله إننا لفي زمان أصبح القابض فيه على دينه كالقابض على الجمر في جانب هذه العلوم المحدثة علوم البدعة والوضع ﴿وَمَن يُضۡلِلِ ٱللَّهُ فَمَا لَهُۥ مِنۡ هَادٖ﴾.

١٢،٢٢ الشيخ الأول خبروني بالله ماذا حصل طلاب هذه العلوم منها،؟ وماذا أفادوا؟ وهل سمعتم يوماً أنّ أحدهم وضع شرحاً على متن أو حاشية على شرح، أو تقريرًا على حاشية، أو اختصر مطولاً أو طوّل مختصرًا؟

الشيخ الثاني ما أضعفهم عن ذلك وأعجزهم، وإنك لتراهم لعجزهم يعيروننا بإضاعة العمر في هذه الأعمال النافعة، ويسعون في إبطال ما ندرسه، وهل لعمرك قام دين، أو رسخ يقين، أو استقام شرع إلا على هذه الشروح والحواشي، ولكنهم لمّا قصرت أفهامهم، وضاقت قرائحهم عن استيعابها ومعرفتها حسدونا عليها فأرادوا أن يسلبونا هذه المزية العظمى والفضيلة الكبرى:

people in paradise eat is from that fish's liver. Were we to peruse their books, which they claim to be superior to anything else before or since and to have achieved an unprecedented level of knowledge of country mapping, we would discover that they lack the comprehensive and useful information to be found in *The Pearl of Wonders* by the Imām Ibn al-Wardī. We never hear any mention of the remarkable things to be found in *The Pearl*—the land of Wāq al-Wāq, for example, where the trees grow buxom beauties and lovely maids who hang down by their tresses from the branches. When the sun shines on them, they cry "Wāq Wāq, all praise to the Creator!"[179]

22.11 The same sort of thing is mentioned in the work, *Remarkable Blooms and Occurrences of Dooms,*[180] which tells how Shaykh Ḥāmid crossed the Black Sea on the back of a donkey that worshipped the sun and reached the source of the River Nile. When the sun shone on one of the riverbanks, the donkey headed for that bank and kept revolving with the sun until it reached the other bank. Shaykh Ḥāmid noticed that the river's flow in the sea was just like a white thread in a black gown. He discovered that it emerged from a red ruby dome beyond the mountain of Qāf and the water was whiter than snow and sweeter than honey. From this same dome emerged three rivers, the Sayḥūn, the Jayḥūn, and the Euphrates. Have they collected such information in any of their books?

FOURTH SKAYKH By God, we live in an age when adhering to one's faith in the face of these modern heretical sciences is like clasping red-hot coals. «He whom God leads astray will have no guide.»[181]

22.12 FIRST SKAYKH Tell me, by God, have the students of these new sciences learned anything or gained any benefit from them? Have you ever heard of one of them composing a commentary on a text, a marginal note on a commentary, or a report on a marginal note, let alone providing a lengthy precis or expatiating in brief?

SECOND SKAYKH They are quite incapable of such things. That is why you'll see them accusing us of wasting our time on such useful activities and striving to invalidate our studies. By your life, has any religion existed, has any faith become established, has any legal system been effective without the availability of commentaries and marginalia such as these? They are incapable of understanding them and are not gifted enough to comprehend and acquire them, and that's why they envy us so much and are determined to rob us of this greatest of all qualities and virtues:

حسدوا الفتى إذ لم ينالوا سعيه
فالكل أعداء له وخصوم

الشيخ الثالث صدقت صدقت.

وكم من عائب قولاً صحيحاً
وآفته من الفهم السقيم

١٣،٢٢ الشيخ السادس لا تشغلوا أوقاتنا بالله عليكم بمثل هذا الكلام في أولئك الثرثارين المتفيهقين المتشدقين، فلهم كتبهم ومدارسهم، ولنا علومنا ودروسنا، والله يحكم بيننا وبينهم يوم القيامة.

الشيخ الخامس كان يجوز لنا السكوت عن منكرهم لو لم يتعرضوا لنا ويعرضوا بنا في ما يسمونه بالجرائد فيملأوها بالانتقاد علينا والقدح فينا، ويتطفلوا على موائد اللغة والإنشاء، ثمّ يفخروا بأنهم برعوا فيها وسبقونا إليها، وإنما الجرائد فتنة من الفتن ولو أردنا لكتبنا.

الشيخ الرابع ومع ذلك ففي كثير ممّن طلب علينا العلم وسوّلت له نفسه الكتابة في الجرائد من قد فاقهم وبذهم في صناعتهم، وهذا الشيخ فلان ذلك النابغة عرض عليّ بالأمس مقالة لأمرّ عليها ثمّ يطبعها في الجرائد، وهي بديعة بليغة لا تزال في جيبي إلى الآن، فإذا أردتم أن أتلوها عليكم فعلت لتعلموا أنه ليس لأولئك المتشدقين من فضل علينا ولا مزية يمتازون بها دوننا.

الجميع أسمعنا أسمعنا.

١٤،٢٢ الشيخ الرابع (يقرأ):

«عوامل الفتح الإلهي طراءة التأثير محكم باعث اعتدال راع في رعيته ومرعى مع راعيه، ولما كانت القوانين الطباعية تدعو إلى حفظ مزاج الجامعة من طوارئ الكوارث الدهرية التي إذا دعاها داعي التفرق والانقسام تلبيه حيث هي النتيجة من مقدمات الاعتساف الذي هو مهد التخالف وبساط عدم التآلف، وكان الإنسان

They envied the man when they could not match his efforts
All were his enemies and foes.[182]

THIRD SKAYKH How right you are!

Many a true word comes from a critic,
His ruin is faulty understanding.[183]

SIXTH SKAYKH Let's not waste our time, by God, talking about these babbling would-be chatterboxes. They have their books and academies, and we have our sciences and schools too. On Judgment Day, God will decide between us. **22.13**

FIFTH SKAYKH We could overlook their reprehensible conduct if they did not object to our views and publish them in the things they call newspapers. As it is, they fill them with critical attacks on us and gatecrash on matters of language and proper composition. Then they brag about how wonderful their writings are and how easily they've bested us. In fact, newspapers are themselves a grievous source of temptation. We could be writing such things if we so wished.

FOURTH SKAYKH Even so, some of our own students who have been tempted to write in newspapers have actually beaten them at their own game. Yesterday Shaykh X, the illustrious scholar, showed me an article. He's since published it in the newspapers. It's an eloquent piece of writing, and I still have it in my pocket. If you like, I'll read it for you. Then you'll realize that those conceited idiots are in no way superior to us, nor do they have any distinctive qualities.

EVERYONE Let us hear it! By all means, let us hear it!

FOURTH SKAYKH (*reading*)[184] "The factors of divine inspiration take immediate effect by virtue of the moderation of a ruler toward his people and a people toward its ruler. Since natural laws lead to the protection of society's constitution from inroads of fate that respond to the call made to them by disunity and disruption (resulting from the premises of deviation, itself the very cradle of dissension and the breeding ground for disharmony), and since human beings incline by virtue of their upbringing to that factor which has the more immediate effect, every nation must have two things. The nation is the haven of perfection, the origin of beauty, and the meadow of authority. It constitutes the very source of sustenance, the basis of discourse, the point of **22.14**

بحكم نشأته ميلا إلى أقرب العوامل تأثيراً، فقد وجب أنّ كل أمّة لا بدّ لها من أمرين، فالأمة هي منزلة الكمال، ومحتد الجمال، ومربع الإمارة، ومطمح الإشارة، ومقصد العبارة، ومورد المحافظة، ومسند المحاضرة، وسجل المناظرة، وكمال النقص، ومرتغب الشاخص، وهي الرباط الأقوم، والحفاظ الأنظم، فيها كل خير، ولها كل نفع، وعليها كل ضير ذات الحق، وحليفة الصدق.

١٥،٢٢ «وإني ليدهشني وقعاً ويذهلني صدعاً أصل جامع وأثر نافع ما نطقت به ألسن الحكمة من سوالف العقلاء المفكرين، وذوي الدراية المتوغلين، وهو أنّ (مبادي تلاشي الأمم تخاذل عقلائها) أجل أجل، إنّ هذا الأمر أدعى إلى لمح السوانح الفكرية والمسابقة في مضمارها حتى يتبيّن طريق التلافي لأضرار التلاشي، وذلك أنّ تخاذل العقلاء يفضي إلى انقسام الوجهة، وبانقسام وجهتهم تنقسم أمّة البساطة فيسود الإيغار، وتحف مراكز العمران بالأخطار، ويتنفس فيها مصدور الأكدار بزفرات هي مبدأ كل دمار، وتتولد الضغائن بين الحميم والخليل، والوكيل والأصيل، فيمسي الحال بخيبة المآل إن لم تتوفر شرائط الاعتدال،

١٦،٢٢ «ثمّ والعقلاء في كل أمّة هم أركان مجدها، وأعمدة قوامها، وسراج سبجها، ومفتاح أقفالها، ومعيار أقدارها، ومصفاة أدرانها، ومشكاة أفراحها، فالاتحاد بينهم أقرب منه فيما بين غيرهم لأنهم على بصيرة من صيرورة المتساهل فيه إلى حد التخاذل الذي هو أس المبادئ العقيمة، والمواجيد السقيمة، والعوامل الكليمة، والضربات الأليمة، والبسطاء تباع فيما يسنّوه لهم من قوانين التزلف والإزلال والخرف إن كانوا متخاذلين، والحكمة والمدنية إن كانوا متعاقدين متحدين، وللناس قلوب يفعلون بها سوانح الفكر في سبحات الذكر، وشطط النظر ونول الوطر، ولهم آذان يسمعون بها منادي الحق في نادي الخلق بنشر الرق الذي هو لوح الاعتبار، ونظرة النظار، وصفوة الأخبار، ومرتغب السباق، ومصطبر الأشواق، وبرنامج الماجريات، وممثل الأحقاب للأعقاب، وحافظ ما مضى لما هو آت.

١٧،٢٢ «بني وطني من الأسف والاستغراب أنّ الأجانب أصبحت وأمست تدعي أنها

debate, the perfection of the faulty, and the object of the gazer's eyes. It is the firmest bond and the most organized defense, possessing every good quality; every good is its gain, every wrong its loss. It stands for what is right and is a confederate of truth.

22.15 "I am struck by a universal principle and useful statement from the past, one uttered by thoughtful men of intellect and acumen in olden times, to the effect that the decline of nations originates in the enfeeblement of its intellectuals. How true, how very true! This demands that we take a look at certain intellectual principles that have outlasted their rivals so that the way to eliminate the damage caused by decline can be clearly delineated. That enfeeblement of intellectuals leads to a disruption of objectives, and that leads in turn to fragmentation among ordinary people. Bitterness prevails, the centers of civilization are enveloped in danger, and consumptive calamities breathe in them with sighs which are the beginning of all destruction and the origin of hatred between lover and beloved and steward and master. Furthermore, if the condition of moderation does not prevail, then dire consequences ensue.

22.16 "In every nation it is the intelligentsia who are the pillars of its glory, the supports of its structure, the gleams of its jet, the key of its locks, the measure of its status, the purge of its dross, and the lamp of its joys. Unity among such luminaries can provide a closer insight than it does among other people into the way that slackness proceeds to the limit of decline, which is the origin of futile principles, of sickly emotions, of damaged elements, and of dire plight. Simple folk merely follow the example that they provide. If they are in decline, then it involves flattery, humiliation, and feeblemindedness; whereas, if they are united and in agreement, prudence and civilization are invoked.

"People make use of their hearts and minds to produce flashes of thought in praise of God's name, through unorthodox ideas and in attainment of their desires. They make use of their ears to listen to the herald of truth in the realm of mankind through the publication of newspapers. They represent the tablet of admonition, the views of the observer, the cream of information, and the finishing line in the race. They are expected with patient longing, they are the program of events and mirror an age for the benefits of later generations, and they preserve what is past for what is to come.

22.17 "My fellow countrymen, it seems both regrettable and peculiar that foreigners are continually claiming that they are following the practice of the previous generation by respecting the tenets of the Shariah in all circumstances,

متأسية بهيع السلف من مراعاة الشريعة في جميع الأطوار، وأنّ بيننا وبين التأسي بها بونًا بعيدًا وأمدًا مديدًا. نعم هذا الادعاء وإن كان ليس بواقعي إلا أنه أجدى ثمرة وأمرًا يجب علينا أن نتنحى عنه وإن كان ليس مقصودًا للأجنبي وحقًا له أن يدّعي ذلك لأننا معاشر الوطنيين لو لم نتصف بهذا الوصف حقيقة لما تفرّقت كلمتنا، وضعفت قوانا، وساءت حالتنا وأصبحنا في حالة يرثيها الراثون، فلا حول ولا قوة إلا بالله، أين المتمسكون بالشريعة؟ أين الغائرون؟ أين الوطنيون المحبون لبلادهم الذين تربوا من خيرها وجعلوها مرتعًا ومحطًا لرحال الأجنبيين؟ أي فرق بيننا والحالة هذه وبين العجم إذا لم نتأثر من هذه الأحوال والدواعي التي تصادمنا كل حين، وأي داع يدعونا للانتقاد على الأجنبيين في أعمالهم التي يحدثونها لغرض سياسي من الأغرا؟

١٨،٢٢ «كلا ثمّ كلا، إننا مذ تنائينا عن الجري على النمط الشرعي ألمّت بنا الشوائب اللأواء من كل صوب وفج، وصرنا كمن بسط كفيه إلى الماء ليبلغ فاه وما هو ببالغه، أو كرجل أعمى ألقي به في الفلوات فأمته الأسود. . . فهذه حالتنا المأثورة التي بها تقاعسنا وتقدم الأجانب.

«إنني بهذا الصدد أقول أنّ الاتحاد هو حفظ الأمّة من أيدي الغير عندما يريد المساس بها والدخول في أحوالها الشخصية التي لا تعلق له بها بأي حال من الأحوال، وإليكم بيان، المسألتان اللتان مضتا ورفت بسببهما أستاذنا المفضل حينما قام يساعد صاحب السماحة لخدمة الوطن الحقة فاتحدا، ولولا ذلك لحل ما حلّ بأهل الأندلس وزاد الطنبور نغمة، فسبحان مدبر الأحوال والله أعلم.»

١٩،٢٢ <u>الشيخ الأول</u> ما شاء الله لا قوة إلا بالله، لقد أحسن وأجاد، وأدمى عيون الحساد.

whereas in fact a huge gap separates us from an adherence to it ourselves. What a fine claim that is! Unfortunately it is one that cannot be substantiated. Nevertheless it has brought forth fruit and produced a state of affairs that we must abandon, even though foreigners have never countenanced such a thing. Yet they actually have the right to make such a claim. For if this were not the way we have been characterized, our influence would not have been so diffused, nor would our authority have been weakened and our status worsened, such that we have now reached a lamentable state of affairs. But then it is God alone who wields power and influence! So where are we to find people who are devoted to the Shariah law? Where are those zealots, patriots devoted to their country, raised on the good things that she provided for them, people who have converted her into a rich pasture for foreigners? In such circumstances if we are not moved to action by these exigencies which confront us all the time, are we any different from dumb animals? What factors will allow us to criticize foreigners over the courses of action that they keep taking to suit their own political purposes?

“No, and again no! Ever since we ceased adhering to the example of the Shariah code, we have been beset from every quarter by deficiencies, until we have now reached the stage when we see a man stretching his hand out to water so he can transfer it to his mouth but without it ever actually getting there; or even like a blind man abandoned in the desert where lions come and attack him. This is our traditional posture, one that has now led to our own backwardness and the foreigners’ advancement. **22.18**

“In such a context I would suggest that unity implies the protection of the nation from the clutches of other people when they aspire to encroach upon its interests and interfere in its particular situation, something that is of no concern to them under any circumstances. I refer you all, for example, to two recent issues as a result of which our revered professor has been dismissed. As a genuine service to his country he stood up in support of the Khedive, and as a result they took concerted action against him. But for that, the same thing would have happened as occurred to the people of Muslim Spain, and matters would have gone from bad to worse. So all praise be to God, the arranger of circumstances, and He knows best!”

First Skaykh How amazing! God alone has the power and might! Superb! He has made the eyes of the envious bleed! **22.19**

الشيخ الثاني صدق رسول الله صلى الله عليه سلم «إن من البيان لسحرًا»
الشيخ الثالث نعم إن هذا لهو السحر الحلال والعذب الزلال
الشيخ السابع تبارك الله ما أبلغ وأفصح وأبين وأوضح
الشسيخ الخامس بارك الله فيه فلقد نثر الدر من فيه
الشيخ السابع ألم أقل لكم إننا لو أردنا لكتبنا ولو عمدنا إلى الكشف عما تكنه الصدور من أنوار العلوم لأخرسنا كل ناطق وأزرينا بكل كاتب ولكن ليس من الرأي ولا من الحكمة أن نبذل الجوهر لمن لا يعرف قيمته ولا يقدر قدره.

٢٠،٢٢ قال عيسى بن هشام: كان الباشا لا يزال يتململ ويتضجر بجانبي طول المجلس فلما انتهينا منه إلى هذا الحد انتف قائما وجذبني بالخروج ساخطا فخرجت معه وهو يوالي الحسرات ويتابع الزفرات وينشد معي في أهل هذا المجلس الأول قول الأول:

ما فيهم بر ولا ناسك
إلا إلى نفع له يجذب
أفضل من أفضلهم صخرة
لا يخدع الناس ولا تكذب.

Second Skaykh The Prophet of God—God's prayers and blessings be upon him!—was right when he said "There is magic in eloquence."

Third Skaykh Yes indeed, this really is legitimate sorcery and the sweetest running water!

Seventh Shaykh God be blessed! What eloquence, what clarity, what pellucid discourse!

Fifth Skaykh God bless him! His mouth has produced a precious pearl!

Seventh Shaykh Didn't I tell you that we could write such things if we really wanted to do so? If we were to start revealing the glimpses of learning concealed within us, we'd strike any other speaker dumb and belittle every writer. But there's no point in wasting such jewels on people who don't realize their value or appreciate their true worth.

22.20 ʿĪsā ibn Hishām said: Throughout this session the Pāshā had kept on muttering and grumbling beside me. But at this point he leapt to his feet and dragged me out in fury. As we left, he was sighing and groaning. He joined me in reciting this comment on the people at this, our first gathering:

There is among them no one either pious or ascetic,
who does not entice to his own advantage;
A rock is worthier than the worthiest among them,
it neither deceives nor lies.[185]

١،٢٣ قال عيسى بن هشام: واستنهضت الباشا أزور به مجلساً من تلك المجالس المعدودة والاندية المعقوده مجلس الاعيان والتجار بعد مجلس العلماء والاحبار فآنست منه ازورارًا وانقباضا ووجدت فيه انحرافًا واعراضا ورأيته يعول في نفسه على التأخر والتخلف ويفضل مواصلة التوحد والتعكف ويقول ما عهدت منك منذ صاحبتك الا الخير لي تريده والضر تكشفه وتبيده والنفع تبدؤه تعيده والشر ترفعه وتذوده وما أزال أشكر لك تلك اليد البيضاء في التفرغ هونًا ما من مواقف القضاء دفعاً لما كنت تحذر وتخشى من شر الخاتمة وسوء العقبى بتراكم الاشجان . وتزاحم الاحزان وما تورثه من السقم والاعتلال وسوء النكسة بعد الابلال. فما بالك تجد في سحبي الى تلك المجالس والمعاهد وهي على خلوها من العوائد والفوائد وبعدها عن علو المطالب وسمو المقاصد ينقبض منها الصدر ويفقد عندها الصبر . ويكسف لها البال ويكثر فيها الهم والبلبال؟

٢،٢٣ فقلت له: عمرك الله ما أبغي لك الا الرشد والتوفيق في كل مذهب وطريق وقد رأيت التجارب أوسعتك كرماً وحلما وممارسة الامورا كسبتك معرفة وعلما بعد خشونة الملمس وشموخ الانف وضيق العطن وصلف الرأي وبعد طول الاغترار وقلة الاختبار وسوء الابتدار في الايراد والاصدار وما أحب لك ان ترى في أمور الناس الا مشهداً يفرج من كربك وملعباً يزيل الهم من قلبك فلا يكون نظرك الى اعمال اهل الدنيا في غدوهم ورواحهم وافراحهم واتراحهم ونعيمهم وبؤسهم وكدرهم وانسهم نظر الحكيم هيراقليط بل الحكيم ديموقريطكان الاول منهما يشاهد أمور الدنيا فيبكي ويتحسر ويراها الثاني فيضحك منها ويسخر فاذا انشد أولها في نصرة مذهبه:

الناس من دنياهم في مأتم
فالسحب تبكي والرواعد تندب

أنشد ثانيهما في تأيد مشربه:

ʿĪsā ibn Hishām said: I tried coaxing the Pāshā into visiting one of the numerous clubs and associations where notables and merchants would gather, following our visit to the religious scholars. However, all I encountered was avoidance and dislike; he kept on resisting the idea and preferring to procrastinate. What he wanted instead was for us to stay by ourselves and avoid company. "Ever since I've joined up with you," he said, "I've always found you to have the best intentions. Any harm, you have uncovered and eradicated; any benefit, you have initiated and continued; any evil, you have removed and fended off. I remain grateful to you for your kindness during our seclusion and the way you rescued us from the situations that Fate brought about, all so as to fend off the terrible consequences you were anxious to avoid, not to mention the illness caused by such an accumulation of worries and the inevitable relapse that would have followed. With all that in mind, why are you even bothering to coax me into visiting clubs and meetings like these? They are all completely useless and lacking in benefit, far removed from any exalted purpose. They're enough to make the heart shrink, exhaust one's patience, and depress one—quite apart from the anxieties they cause." 23.1

"God grant you long life!" I replied, "My intentions were good; I only wished you well. I've watched the way these experiences have enhanced your generosity and discernment. Real exposure to things has given you an understanding and knowledge that replaces the gruffness, arrogance, narrow-mindedness, and pomposity you used to display. You would approach things in a brash and boorish fashion, with little expertise whether listening or speaking. My aim is for you to be able to look at those aspects of people's lives which would take your mind off your misfortunes and at scenes which would let you relax. The way you're studying people's actions, their comings and goings, their joys and griefs, their comforts and sufferings, their hopes and despairs, is not like that of the philosopher Heraclitus, but rather Democritus. The former saw the way people behaved and wept in grief. The latter looked at them and then scoffed with laughter. To back up his views, the former wrote: 23.2

> Funerals distract people from their world;
> clouds weep and thunder laments.

"While to support his point of view, the latter said:

هذي الحياة رواية لمشخص
فالليل ستر والنهار الملعب

فلا تذهب نفسك عليهم حسرات ولا تذب مهجتك عليهم زفرات وهلم معي امتعك بزيارة مجلس يؤنس من وحشتك ويكشف عنك من غمتك

٣،٢٣ فوضح له بذلك طريق السداد فأسلس مصحباً في القياد فيممنا داراً عالية الجدران فسيحة الاركان مزخرفة البنيان تجمع مجلساً من خاصة التجار والاعيان فزاحمنا عند الباب سائس يحمل على كتفه طفلا ويسحب بيده من ورائه خيلا يقول وقد أظهر الغيظ بواطنه وابرز الغضب حسراته الكامنه «والله لست أدرى أسائس أنا أم حاضنه؟» ووراءه فتى يحمل صفحة مخلل قد تلوث بمائها وتبلل يقول «على ما اتعب في هذا البيت وأشقى والى ما يدوم هذا الشقاء ويبقى؟ ولست أدري والله أسائق أنا أم سقا؟» ولما ولجنا الباب رأينا في يد البواب صرة من الثياب وهو يقول: «لا مرد للقدر المقضي ولا أمل في العيش المرضي ووالله لست أدري أبواب أنا أم خصي؟»

٤،٢٣ وما جاوزنا دهليز المكان الى باب الايوان حتى رأينا عنده غلاماً فتي السن يتنهد ويئن وبين يديه دخان وورق وبجانبه كتاب مطبق وهو يقول: «عجباً والله يشغل الوالد ابنه بسجارات يحشوها فيلهيه بها عن دروس يتلوها ولاغرو ان فاضت العيون بسواكبها واحترقت القلوب بلواهبها فما أدري والله أفراش الدار أنا ام ابن صاحبها.»

ولما أحس بنا انتفض للقيام وتقدم للسلام ثم تقدمنا ونحن على الاثر فسأله أبوه عن الخبر فلم يكد الغلام يفصح في عبارته حتى اقبل علينا الوالد يتكفأ في مشيته ويهرول في جبته فقابلنا بلطف سلامه وحسن تحيته ثم جلسنا نسمع ما تجري به المسامرة وتدور عليه المحاورة بين قوم مختلفي الازياء والهيئات متبايني الاشكال والسمات فمن صاحب عمه قد قصر عليها همه فهو دائب يعيد رصفها ويجدد لفها وآخر يشبك بالابر اهداب العمامه ثم يأخذها بيده ويديرها امامه ومن صاحب طربوش قد أماله

This life is a drama for the actor;
night is a curtain and day is the stage.

"So don't allow yourself to feel sorry for them or shed any tears on their behalf. Come with me, and I'll make sure you enjoy your visit to a meeting that'll relieve your solitude and calm your fears."

23.3 With that he agreed that this was clearly the most satisfactory plan and he followed my lead obediently. We made our way to an imposing, highly decorated building with high walls and wide pillars. At the door, a groom pushed past us carrying a baby on his shoulders and leading an obedient horse behind him. The anger on his face showed clearly what he was really thinking. "My God," he said, "I don't know, am I a groom or a wet nurse?" Behind him came another person carrying a tray piled high with pickled vegetables, the juice of which had soiled his clothing. "Why on earth should I have to slave and suffer in this house?" he was saying. "How long will this hardship continue? I don't know, am I a driver or mere excrement?" Once we got past the door, there was the doorkeeper with a bundle of clothes in his hand. "There's no way of stopping Fate's decrees," he said, "and no hope for a comfortable life. I don't know, am I a doorkeeper or eunuch?"

23.4 Passing through the vestibule, we entered the alcove where we encountered a young servant sighing and moaning, tobacco and paper in front of him and an embossed book by his side. "By God, it's incredible," he was saying. "My father makes his son work at filling cigarettes and keeps him away from the lessons he's supposed to be studying. No wonder people's eyes overflow with floods of tears and their hearts are charred by agonizing flames. I don't know, by God, am I the house's valet or the owner's son?"

No sooner had he noticed our arrival than he sprang to his feet and came over to greet us. He went on in front to announce that we had arrived. The father asked who had come. No sooner had the boy explained things, than the father came over to us, swaying as he walked and stumbling over his coat. He bade us welcome, greeted us elaborately, and sat us down so we could listen to the conversation and hear what was being discussed. There we found a variety of people: they all looked different and were wearing a varied assortment of clothing. A turban wearer for instance was making sure his turban was tight, while another was refolding his and fastening the edge of it with a pin; he would then take hold of it and swivel it on his head. Elsewhere a tarboosh

على جبينه فاذا خشي انحراف وضعه أصلحه يمينه فترى يده لا تسكن ولا تستقر كانما هو في سلام مستمر والكل قد كثر بينهم اللفظ ووجدنا محاورتهم دائرة على هذا النمط:

٥،٢٣ أحدهم نعم لا بد من تلك ان يسر الله وتم الاتفاق مع الخواجه سوارس فان اقامة عمارة أخرى بجانب تلك العمارة مما يأتي بارباح لا تأتي بها الاشغال التجارية وأنا أنصحك يا فلان أن تترك التجارة جانباً فقد أصبحت الآن ولا نفع يرجى منها وتوكل على الله في الاشتغال معنا بالعمارات فهي أنجح واربح.

آخر ومن أين لي سيدي زادك الله نعمة ما يساعدني على هذا التوسع والحال ضعيفة على ما نعلم والحمد لله على نعمة الستر فهي الغنى الكامل؟

الأول لا لا أيها السيد ﴿وَأَمَّا بِنِعْمَةِ رَبِّكَ فَحَدِّثْ﴾. ودعواك ضعف الحال ان هي الا تواضع منك والا فالله يزيدك فضلا على فضل.

الثاني استغفر الله يا سيدي هذا حسن ظن منك والا فالحقيقة غير ما ظننت وقد قلت لك ان الستر هو الغنى الكامل على ان البركة في التجارة فمنها كان رزق الآباء والاجداد وربح مستور أبرك من ربح مشهور.

٦،٢٣ ثالث تالله انكم لفي ضلالكم القديم وهل بقي في هذه التجارة التي زاحمكم عليها الاجانب ربح أو رزق فاتركوا هذه السفاسف وعليكم باشغال الاقطان والمضاربات في البورصة فهي الربح المضاعف والرزق الحاضر يأتيك رغيداً بلا تعب ولا نصب فكم رأينا فقيراً ولج البورصة فأثرى وقد كان لا يملك نقيرا. وهذا صاحبنا فلان اليهودي وفيكم من أدرك والدته تبيع الخبز والفول بحارة اليهود قد مارس تلك الاشغال فاصبح أرفع الناس حالا وأكثرهم مالا. ونحن لا نزال على ما تركه لنا الآباء والاعمام رحمة الله عليهم.

wearer had tilted his tarboosh over his forehead. Whenever he was afraid it might slip, he would raise his right hand to adjust it. As a result his hand never stopped moving, and he looked as though he were continually greeting people. We noticed that they were all deeply involved in conversation. Here is what they were talking about:

23.5 ONE OF THEM Yes, God has facilitated things and agreement has been reached with Mr. Suarez. Putting up another building alongside the current one will bring you the kind of profit you couldn't possibly make in commercial dealings. I advise you to give up being a merchant; nowadays there's no hope of gain from it. Trust in God, and work with us on buildings; they're much more profitable.

ANOTHER May God increase my good fortune and blessing! Where can I find the wherewithal to back such an enlargement? You know full well how weak my position is. Thank God for the boon of concealment; that's the most complete wealth of all!

FIRST My dear Sir, don't say such a thing! Instead you should say: «And as for your Lord's blessing, talk about it.»[186] You're just being modest when you claim you're in a weak position. God lavishes favors on you one after another.

SECOND My dear fellow, I beg God's forgiveness, but that's mere flattery on your part. The truth is that my affairs are not as prosperous as you imagine. I've told you that concealment is the most perfect kind of wealth. In any case, there's good fortune in commerce. My forefathers and ancestors earned their living that way, and concealed profits bring more luck than those which are public knowledge.

23.6 THIRD You're still sticking to your old erroneous ways! How can you get any revenue or profit from commerce when you're competing with foreigners? Abandon such apathy and start operating with cotton in the Stock Exchange; your profits will be doubled, and you'll always have a livelihood at your disposal, one that'll provide you with a carefree life without trouble or hardship. How many poor people we've seen enter the Stock Exchange only to emerge rich and influential as a result of speculation! Take our friend, Mr. X the Jew, for example; some of you will remember his mother selling bread in the street and beans in the Jewish quarter. He went in for transactions like these and as a result he's become a really wealthy and important person. Meanwhile we keep on relying on what our fathers and uncles left us (God's mercy be upon them).

رابع   ولكن فاتك أيها السيد انه كان يشتغل باشغال السماسرة وفيها ما لا يخفاك. وهل تريد ان ننزل الى هذه الاشغال بعد ان عشنا هذا العمر؟

الثالث   حاشا لله يا سيد أنا لا أقصد هذا ولكنك ترى ان هذا اليهودي قد دخل البورصة سمسارًا لا يمتلك شيئًا من المال فاصبح من كبار الاغنياء. فما بالك بمن يدخلها غنيًا فانه يصبح في مدة قصيرة قارون زمانه؟

خامس   ما وراء الربح الكثير الا الخسران الكبير وقد شاهدنا بأعيننا ما تخرب من البيوت العامرة وما اندثر من الغنى الواسع وما اختل من البناء القديم وما انحط من العماد الرفيع وأرى ان من سوء الرأي الاقدام على هذه المهالك ﴿فَاللَّهُ خَيْرٌ حَافِظًا﴾.

سادس   أما أنا، «فلا يلدغ المؤمن من جحر مرتين.» وكفاني مؤدبًا ما تكبدته من الخسائر فيها والحمد لله على النجاة منها.   ٧،٢٣

الثالث   لا حول ولا قوة الا بالله، ﴿إِنَّكَ لَا تَهْدِي مَنْ أَحْبَبْتَ﴾. كيف تخشون الخسارة في أشغال الاقطان بالبورصة والربح فيها مضمون وأنا أحسب لكم حسبة صغيرة تقنعكم بكثرة الارباح وتأكيدها كما تقتنعون بان الواحد نصف الاثنين فاذا فرضنا مثلا ان محصول القطن في العام يبلغ كذا قنطارًا والمطلوب تسليمه كذا قنطارًا اتت النتيجة بالعجز عن التغطية فتعلو الاسعار. وعلى أي حال فما دامت هذه الوزارة في مركزها وأمور الحكومة في أيدي من هي في أيديهم وبقي قدم الاصلاح ثابتا راسخا بيننا فلا يخشى مطلقًا من نزول الاسعار.

رابع   كيف تقول ذلك حفظك الله وهذا فلان امامنا أخذ بمثل هذه الحسبة وتورط في هذه الاشغال واستهواه الطمع؟ فتراه لا يزال الى اليوم يهوي في مهاوي البورصة حتى وصل في الخسارة الى القرار وان كان لا يزال في أعينكم من أغنى الاغنياء مشهورًا باتساع الثروة.   ٨،٢٣

FOURTH You've forgotten, Sir, that this friend of ours whom you mention only attained such heights by working as a broker. You know full well the indignity that involves. Are you suggesting that one of us should stoop so low as to take that type of work after living our kind of life?

THIRD God forbid, Sir! That isn't what I meant. But you've noticed that this Jew entered the Stock Exchange as a broker without any money to his name, and has now become a very rich man. How much more do you imagine someone will earn when he's already wealthy at the start? After only a short while he's bound to emerge as the Croesus of his era.

FIFTH The only thing that can follow huge profits is huge loss. I've seen the results of working in the Stock Exchange with my own eyes: destruction of homes people live in, squandering of vast wealth and the collapse of ancient properties and lofty pillars. I think it's sheer idiocy to venture into such perilous undertakings. «God is the best guardian».[187]

23.7 SIXTH I'm following the Prophet's own statement: "No believer is ever stung twice from the same hole."[188] The lessons I've learned from the losses I suffered speculating on cotton are quite enough for me. All praise to God for saving me from ruin.

THIRD To God alone belongs the power and might! «You will not guide those you love.»[189] How can you worry about suffering a loss or have any qualms about dealings in cotton on the Stock Exchange? I'll do a little calculation for you which should satisfy your concerns about profitability just as surely as one is half of two. Suppose for example that the cotton yield is so many qanṭars a year, and you want to invest it at so many qanṭars. The return you'll get won't even cover your expenses; and then shares go up in price. In any case, as long as this ministry remains in power, the government is still in the hands of people who are in complete control of things; the road to reform is firmly established in our midst. So there's absolutely no need to be afraid of a collapse in share prices.

23.8 FOURTH How can you possibly claim any such thing? May God preserve you! We have before us the example of A who made such a calculation and concentrated on such things. He was tempted by greed, and now you can see him continuing to fall into the Stock Exchange abyss until his losses have plunged to the very depths. And all that although, as far as you're concerned, he's still regarded as being immensely rich.

ثامن سبحان الله ألا تعجبون معي من كذب الشهرة بيننا بالغنى وانكشاف المبالغة في الثروة عن القلة. فكم سمعنا بأن فلانا صاحب ثروة تقدر بألوف الالوف ثم لا يلبث ان يظهر الخفي ويتضح الباطن عن ما لا يبلغ معشار تلك الشهرة؟

الخامس نعم صدقت. ألم تر الى المرحوم فلان لما قام به الحسد وقعد عند ما أخذت الرتبة كيف كان يفخر علي في كل مجلس بانه اوسع مني غنى واكثر ثروة وان مقامه بذلك ارفع وقدره أعظم فلما توفاه الله لم يترك لاولاده من الثروة ما يكفي لبقاء بيته مفتوحا وبقاء اسمه مذكوراً وقس على ذلك فسبحان الدائم؟

الرابع دعونا بالله من ذكر الأولاد والمواريث، فإنني كلما تأملت في أخلاق أولادنا في هذا الزمن ورأيت ما وصلت إليه ثروة فلان وما انتهى عنده حال أولاده من الفقر والاحتياج بعد تبذير تلك الأموال الطائلة ونسيانهم لاسم والدهم في موته بعد سخطهم عليه في حياته، فلا يزورون له قبراً ولا يطلبون له رحمة، هان عليّ أن أنفق ما في حوزتي في حياتي وأتمتع به في آخر عمري.

الخامس لا تقل هذا فإنه ما فائدتنا في هذه الدنيا إذا لم نترك لأولادنا ما يغنيهم بعدنا عن سؤال اللئيم؟ وليس الذنب على الأولاد في تبديد المواريث، بل الخطأ كل الخطأ من الآباء فإنهم يتركون أموالهم هملا بعد موتهم يتصرف فيها الأولاد حسب أهوائهم، ويغفلون عن وقف الملك، فينتفع الأولاد بالريع وتبقى العين لا يندثر معها اسم البيت، ولا تحتاج الذرية وذرية الذرية مع وجودها و. . . .

٩،٢٣

السادس لا مؤاخذة في قطع حديث سعادة البك، ألم تسمع بما حصل في وقف فلان وفلان وفلان؟ وكيف أنّ النظار التهموا حقوق بقية المستحقين، وذهب الوقف ضياعاً بين القضايا والدعاوى، وبين تراكم الديون حتى آل النظر والاستحقاق فيها لليهود، واندثرت البيوت، وعفت الآثار، وذهبت أسماء أصحابها كما ذهب أمس قبل اليوم؟

السابع نعم، ينفع الوقف، ويحفظ الميراث من أيدي الضياع والخراب على شرط أن يكون بمثل الشروط التي وقف بها المرحوم فلان، فإنه اشترط بعد أن

EIGHTH God be praised! Don't you all share my amazement at the false renown some people have for being wealthy, whereas that same wealth turns out to be poverty? How often have we heard that X the man of means is worth many thousands! Soon afterward the secret's revealed and hidden facts come to light; his actual wealth doesn't equal even a tenth of that false renown.

FIFTH You're absolutely right! Just consider the late Y. He was so envious when I attained my post that at every meeting where I had any standing he used to brag that he was wealthier than I and thus had a loftier status. However when he died, he didn't bequeathe enough to his children to keep his house open and for his name to be remembered. But that didn't stop him doing it. Praise be to God, the Everlasting!

FOURTH I beg you, for God's sake, stop talking about sons and inheritances. Every time I think about our children's morality in the current age and see what's happened to Y's wealth, how his sons have ended up in desperate poverty after squandering riches galore, in the process forgetting their own father's name in death after their anger at him while he was still alive—never visiting his grave or asking God to have mercy on him—I think nothing of spending all the money I have and enjoying myself while I'm still alive.

23.9

FIFTH Don't even say such a thing! What use are we in this world if we don't leave our children an inheritance that will spare them the need to beg once we're dead? Don't put all the blame for squandering inheritances on the sons. In fact, the biggest fault of all lies with fathers who leave their wealth untended when they die. As a result the children can then spend the money as they see fit, totally ignorant of the realities of ownership which would enable them to benefit from the proceeds, keep the capital secure, and prevent the house's name from being obliterated. In that way none of the sons or the sons' sons would have any need to—

SIXTH My dear Sir, forgive me for interrupting you. Didn't you hear what happened to the endowment of A, B, and others? The supervisors grabbed the rights of the claimants, and the endowment fell into ruin during the course of all the court cases and claims. Debts kept piling up until eventually the supervision and claim to it were given to Jews. The houses involved fell into ruins, all trace of it disappeared, and the owners' names vanished just as yesterday precedes today.

SEVENTH Yes, endowments have their uses. Inheritances can be preserved from loss and destruction provided they contain stipulations like those

خصص لذريته جزءاً من الريع أنّ كل ما يبقى منه يحفظ ويدخر، وكلما تكوّن منه مبلغ عظيم يشتري به أملاك توقف مضافة إلى الوقف الأصلي، وهكذا يكون التصرف في الريع دائماً حتى يكون الوقف في نمو متواصل على توالي الأيام سالماً من صروف الحدثان، وبذلك يبقى البيت في درجة عالية من الغنى بعد وفاة صاحبه فوق ما كان أيام حياته، فأنعم بها من طريقة وأحسن بها من وسيلة.

الثالث ليس ذلك من الحزم في شيء ولكنه التغالي في الشح ومحبة الادخار في الحياة وبعد الممات، ولقد حرم المرحوم نفسه من ماله في حياته وحرم أولاده منه بهذه الطريقة الغريبة بعد مماته. ١٠،٢٣

الأول أرجو منك العفو والسماح وعدم المؤاخذة، فمن يقول أنّ المرحوم كان شحيحاً مقتراً في حياته قد والله عاشرته فرأيته لا يحرم نفسه من شيء ولا يقتر عليها طول عمره ولطالما شاهدت الحمام والدجاج وجدك يا أبا هاشم على مائدته؟ وإنما كان الرجل حازماً لا ينفق ماله إلا في الوجوه النافعة.

الثاني لا تقل وقف ولا ملك، وإنما أحسن ما يدخره الإنسان لأبنائه هو أن يحسن تعليمهم وتهذيبهم في المدارس، وأن لا يعوّدهم في حياته على التبذير والإنفاق، بل يروّضهم على التوفير والتقتير ومعرفتهم قيمة المال وقدر الدرهم.

الأول وهل جاءتنا المصائب يا مولانا في أولادنا إلا من هذه المدارس وهذا التهذيب؟ وما زادهم ذلك إلا وقوحة وسوء أدب وكبرياء نفس ومكابرة ولقد أضحكني فلان في شكواه لي أمس من ابنه إذ قال لي إنّ هذا الولد يزيد كل يوم في تعذيبي بعد خروجه من المدرسة، وأصبح لا يعجبه شيء في البيت، ولا يكلم أهله إلا بالرطانة، فإذا جاؤوا له بالماء قال فيه المكروب، وإذا أتوه بالخبز والجبن قال عليّ بالمكرسكوب، ثمّ ترى الخبيث يقسم الأطعمة أقساماً فيقول البيض واللبن غذاء كامل، والخضار (البقول) غذاء ناقص لا ينفع ولا يمري، إنّ الأرز وسائر المواد النشائية لا تستفيد منها المعدة سوى أن تحرقها كالوقيد وما زاد منها عن حاجتها فهو شحم على البدن ضرره أكثر من نفعه، وإنّ البطيخ إذا قطع لا بدّ أن يؤكل من ساعته لأنه أسرع الفواكه ١١،٢٣

under which the late D made an endowment. He detailed part of the revenues for his children and stipulated that the remainder should be saved and deposited. Each time a large sum accrued from it, an estate was to be bought. This was then to be endowed and added to the original endowment. In that way the profits were always disposable since the endowment itself was continually growing as time and fate's misfortunes passed. That explains how the family possessed considerable wealth after its owner's death, far more in fact than it ever did in his own lifetime. This is clearly an excellent way of doing such things.

THIRD That doesn't make sense at all! Rather it shows extreme niggardliness, a mere delight in storing things away after one's death. The late gentleman didn't permit himself the enjoyment of his own money during his lifetime and then deprived his children of it after his death. 23.10

FIRST I beg your pardon, Sir, and I trust I give no offence. Who says that the late gentleman was stingy and niggardly? By God, I was a close friend of his for a long time, and never saw him deprive himself of anything or be tightfisted throughout his lifetime. His table always had mutton, pigeon, or chicken on it—by your grandfather's right! He was merely a prudent man who only spent money on useful ventures.

SECOND Don't keep talking about endowments or possessions. The best thing which a father can reserve for sons is a good school education. In his own lifetime, he shouldn't let them get into the habit of spending money extravagantly, but instead should train them to economize and teach them the value of money and coin.

FIRST But, my dear Sir, aren't these schools and the education they offer primarily responsible for all the troubles we're having with our sons? All it does is to make them boorish, discourteous, arrogant, and supercilious? Someone made me laugh yesterday when he complained bitterly about his son. Here's what he had to say: 23.11

"Ever since this boy finished school, he's been torturing me every day. He doesn't approve of anything in the house and talks gibberish to his family. When they bring him some water, he says it contains microbes; when they bring him bread and cheese, he tells them to bring the microscope. Then you'll see the wretch cutting up food into sections. Then he'll start giving you a lecture. He'll tell you that eggs and yogurt are excellent food, but vegetables are rotten and unbeneficial. The only useful purpose that rice and other grown

قبولاً لتولد الحيوانات السامة، وهلمّ جرا، حتى حيّر الشقي أهل البيت في طعامه وشرابه فوق ما حيّر والده في اختلاف ملابسه وتعدّد أزيائه، وكلما عارضه والده في شيء شمخ بأنفه وسخر به وعيّره بالجهل وافتخر عليه بعلمههذا هو الأدب الذي يكسبه لهم التعليم، يتعالون على آبائهم بعد أن كان الولد في الزمن الماضي كالبنت البكر لا يرفع بصره في وجه والده ولا يكلمه إلا مجيباً عن سؤال من صغره إلى كبره.

الثاني ولكن فاتك أنّ في تعليم العلوم لأولادنا فائدة مادية يغتفر لها كل ذنب، وهي خدمتهم في الحكومة، وارتقاء المراتب والمناصب، ويا ليت آباءنا كانوا التفتوا إلى تعليمنا العلوم فكنا استغنينا عن عناء التجارة، ووقفة الحال في الأشغال - بلا قافية - وذل البيع والشراء وملاطفة العملاء وكساد السوق، وترويج السلعة بالأقسام والأيمان، فما العيش إلا عيش الموظفين الذين يأخذون مرتبهم في آخر كل شهر نقداً ذهباً عيناً خالصاً دفعة واحدة سالمة لأيديهم بلا مطل أو تسويف أو تجزيء في مقابلة أن يقعدوا أمام أقلامهم ومحابرهم على مساند إمارتهم ثلاث ساعات من كل يوم يقضون بعضها في نكات ومفاكهات، وتفنيد وانتقاد، ثم ناهيك بمثلهم في النفوس من الاحترام والتعظيم والتوقير والإجلال، وما لهم من القدرة على مساعدة الأصحاب، وتعطيل ما يشاؤون تعطيله أعواماً ودهوراً، ولا رأس مال لذلك كله إلا قراءة بضعة كتب في المدرسة فقل لي بالله عليك أي تجارة وأي ربح يوازي خدمة الحكومة وسبحان من قسّم الحظوظ فلا عتاب ولا ملامة. ١٢،٢٣

الرابع كل هذا معلوم مسلّم، ولكن من أين لك أن تنال الشهادة لابنك وأنت تعلم حال القابضين على زمام المدارس، فقد خرج أكثر أولادنا منها بلا شهادة، ومن صادفته العناية منهم ونالها فإنه لم يزل إلى الآن بلا خدمة لما تعلمه أيضاً من حالة القابضين على زمام الحكومة. ١٣،٢٣

commodities serve in the stomach is to burn like fuel. Any foods which exceed one's needs constitute fat, and that does more harm than good. Once watermelons are cut, they have to be eaten immediately because they produce poisonous bacteria so quickly. The wretch goes on like this till he has the whole house in a dither over his tastes in food and drink; to say nothing of the way he bewilders me with his various styles of dress and adornment. Every time his father disagrees with him, he gives a haughty look, pokes fun at him, and accuses him of being ignorant and brags about his own learning. So this is the kind of behavior that he has gained through this system of education. Children now look down on their fathers; and all this after times of old when the sons of the family were like young virgin girls who would never even look up at their father's face or speak to him except to respond to a question, and that from early childhood into their adult lives."

Second But you're forgetting that by educating our sons in schools we get one material benefit, one that compensates for every wrong, namely that they can enter government service and thus rise in rank and prestige. If only our fathers had bothered to have us educated in schools, we could have avoided the drudgery of commerce and the demands of hard work—the humiliation involved in buying and selling, being nice to customers, unsettled markets, and the need to market things in instalments and on trust. Being a civil servant is the only decent way to earn a living. They get their salary in cash and pure gold coin at the end of each month; it comes as a lump sum safe in their hands with no delay, postponement, or partial payment. All this is as compensation for spending three hours a day sitting in various government departments; and part of that time is spent talking, joking, disputing, and carping. And that's to say nothing of the respect and veneration they command and the power they have to help their friends and to hold up anything they wish for years and ages upon ages. The only capital involved in all this is reading a few books in school. So tell me, by God, what commerce and what profit can possibly rival government service? Praise be to Him who divides the lots, may there be no blame or reproach! 23.12

Fourth All this we know full well and acknowledge. But how do you foresee your son getting his certificate? You know the situation regarding the people in charge of schools. Most of our sons leave school without a certificate. Those who take the trouble to get a degree still don't get employed because of the people who, as you well know, control the government. 23.13

السادس عسى الله أن يغيّر الأحوال وتسقط هذه الوزارة ويبدلنا منها بوزارة وطنية فترى حينئذ كيف يكون تقدّم أبنائنا الذين تنعى اليوم حالهم.

الخامس (للسادس) حقاً، إذا تغيرت هذه الوزارة وجاء صاحبك أقبل السعد، وانجلت سماء المستقبل، وصفا الزمان، فإذا جاء هذا الوقت فلا تنس ابني مع أنجالك، فقد كان معهم في مدرسة واحدة، وهو دائما يطالع الجرائد، ويترقب الحوادث التي يكون من ورائها سقوط هذه الوزارة.

الثامن أراكم تخبطون في أمر أولادكم في حياتكم وبعد مماتكم، وتذهبون إلى غير الصواب، والصواب عندي أن نعلّمهم العلوم، ونربيهم في المدارس لا لانتظار التوظف في الحكومة، بل ليكونوا أسوة أهل زمانهم معرفة واطلاعا، وأمّا من جهة حفظ أموالنا في أيديهم بعدنا فهي أن لا نقتر عليهم في النفقة، وأن لا نتركهم بمعزل عن أشغالنا، بل نخصص لهم قسما منها يشتغلون به على حدة تحت أعيننا، فيتعلمون الأخذ والإعطاء، ويدركون لذة المكسب بأنفسهم، فتربى لهم ملكة الحرص على المنافع، وينتفعون بعلومهم في اتساع تجارتهم، وقد جربت ذلك في أولادي وأنا أرجو فيهم إن شاء الله حسن الخلف.

السادس وعلى ذكر الجرائد، ما هي أخبارها اليوم؟ ١٤،٢٣

صاحب البيت (مناديا لابنه) ائتنا بجريدة اليوم واقرأها علينا.

(الغلام ينشر الجريدة)

الأول اقرأ لنا من الأوّل.

الغلام «الحرب بين انكلترا والترنسفال».

السادس هل وقعت الحرب؟

الغلام ليس يتبيّن ذلك من أول المقالة.

السادس اقرأها من آخرها.

الخامس ما هي فائدتنا من قراءتها ومن وقوع الحرب؟

السادس غفر الله لي ولك، ألم تعلم أنّ فائدتنا منها عظيمة، فقد سمعت عنها ١٥،٢٣

SIXTH Perhaps God will bring about a change. Then this government administration will fall and be replaced by a nationalist one. Then you'll see how our sons whose circumstances you're bemoaning move up in rank.

FIFTH (*to the Sixth*) How true! If there's a change of government and your friend returns to the administration, we'll be in luck. The skies of the future will gleam bright, and carefree times will be with us again. Should such times ensue, don't forget my son along with your own children. He was at the same school with them. He's always reading the papers and watching for the events which will bring about the downfall of this ministry.

EIGHTH I think you're misguided regarding your children in this life and after your death. Your ideas are wrong. For me the best course involves teaching them various subjects and sending them to schools, but not in order to wait for appointments to government service but rather to be models of knowledge and learning for their contemporaries. As regards keeping inheritances in their possession once we are gone, the best plan is not to restrict their spending when we are alive or to distance them from our own business; but rather to set aside a sum of money for them to invest by themselves under our supervision. They can then learn how to give and take and come to appreciate the pleasure of earning for themselves. They'll thus have instilled in them the desire for profit and will benefit from their learning in expanding their commercial reach. I've implemented this plan with my sons and hope, God willing, that they'll prove to be worthy descendants.

23.14

SIXTH Has today's newspaper arrived?

OWNER OF THE HOUSE (*shouting to his son*) Get us the newspaper and read it to us.

(*The boy opens the newspaper.*)

FIRST Read the front page.

BOY The war between England and the Transvaal.

SIXTH Is there a war?

BOY It's not clear from the beginning of the article.

SIXTH Then read from the end.

FIFTH What's the point of reading that, or whether there's a war or not?

23.15

SIXTH God pardon us both! Don't you realize that we get an enormous benefit? I've heard a great deal about it in the High Council. They concluded

كلاماً كثيراً في المجلس العالي، ويستنتج من أنّ وقوعَ هذه الحرب يشغل الأجانب عنا وتضعف يدهم عن الضغط على حكومتنا، فتنطلق الأيدي وتتقلب الأحوال وتأتينا الوزارة الوطنية.

الرابع إذا كان الأمر كذلك فأرجو أن لا يذهب من فكرك مشروع الشركة الوطنية التي كنا تكلمنا في انعقادها لمشترى أطيان وأخذ امتياز بمساعدة هذه الوزارة المنتظرة.

الخامس إن شاء الله يكون لنا معكم نصيب في هذه الشركة.

الثالث من أعضاؤها ومن رئيسها؟

السادس أعضاؤها فلان وفلان و رئيسها فلان.

الثالث معاذ الله أن أقبل الدخول مع فلان وهل نسينا ما وقع منه؟

الخامس وأنا لا أقبل أن يكون فلان رئيساً عليّ في شركة.

الثاني وأنا لا أقبل الدخول فيها إلا إذا كانت أسهمي في التأسيس أكثر من أسهم فلان.

السابع وأنا لا أقبل الدخول في شركة بعد تلك الشركة المشهورة إلا إذا كنت أنا الواسطة في مقابلة الحكام والاتفاق معهم.

١٦،٢٣ قال عيسى بن هشام: واشتد الجدال واللجاج بين الجميع، فحملقت العيون، وعبست الوجوه، وتحركت الضغائن، وبدت الأحقاد، وظهر على كل واحد منهم أنه يتمنى لأخيه أن تسقط السماء عليه كسفاً أو تخسف به الأرض، فانصرفنا عنهم وتركنا بعضهم يومئذ يموج في بعض.

that this war will preoccupy the foreigners and reduce the pressures they're putting on our government. As a result, we'll have a free hand. Everything will be changed, and we'll get a Nationalist Ministry.

FOURTH If that's the case, then I hope you'll not forget about the idea we've discussed, the project to establish a national company to purchase recognized plots of land and get monopoly control with this new government's help.

FIFTH God willing, I might have a part share in this company.

THIRD Who's on the board, and who's the chairman?

SIXTH The board members are A, B, and C and the chairman is D.

THIRD God forbid I should ever join a company with B! Have we all forgotten the mess he made of things?

FIFTH And I won't accept D being my chairman in a company.

SECOND I'll never consent to participate unless my share in the foundation is larger than A's.

SEVENTH After what happened with that other notorious company, I won't agree to participate in any company unless I'm the one to mediate and come to agreements with government authorities.

ʿĪsā ibn Hishām said: They started a furious argument. Eyes bulged, and they all kept glowering at each other. They seemed to be nursing a whole store of grudges and hatred against one another. Every one of them seemed to be longing for the heavens to fall on his colleague or the earth to swallow him up. Leaving them raging at one another, we took our leave. 23.16

مصباح الشرق ٧٢، ١٤ سبتمبر ١٨٩٩

١،٢٤ قال عيسى بن هشام: وعزمنا على زيارة ثالث المحافل، ومجتمع الأكابر والأماثل من أرباب الحكم والحكم، ورجال السيف والقلم، ومن بيدهم حل الأمور وعقدها، وشقاء الأمّة وسعدها، الناشئين في مهاد المعارف والعلوم، والجامعين بين أشتات المنطوق والمفهوم، والمتفردين بأصالة الرأي وحسن التدبير، وقوة الفطنة وجودة التفكيرفقصدنا دارًا يزهر بياضها، ويبهر أيماضها، قد أنبتت العز أرضها، وأينع بالنعيم روضها، وضربت عليها المحاسن أطنابها، وكستها يد الزخارف جلبابها، فتجلت في أجمل شكل وأبدع مثال، كالغادة تتبرج يوم زينتها وتختال، فألفينا الخدم لدى الباب في أزياء تأخذ بالنواظر والألباب، فقابلونا بالترحيب والتأهيل، وحيونا بالتعظيم والتبجيل، ونحوا بنا ناحية في جانب الساحة، أعدّت للانتظار والاستراحة، وإذا بها رجل يهتز بين يقظان ووسنان، فرأسه كرة والكرى صولجان، فما دنونا منه وأقبلنا عليه حتى انتبه يزيح النعاس بأصابعه عن عينيه، فسلمنا فسلم، وهو يتثاءب ويتلعثم، فتخيلناه من ظاهرجملته، ورثاثة حلته أنه صانع من الصناع، أو تابع من الأتباع، ولكن ما لبث أن ظهر لنا من مخاطبته للغلام أنه ذومكانة في البيت وذو مقام وبعد أن ذهب الغلام ليأتينا بإذن الدخول التفت الرجل إلينا يقول:

٢،٢٤ «قبّح الله الخدم، فهم نقمة من النقم، شرهم حاضر، وخيرهم نادر، والعنا بهم ليس له آخر، فكم أغضبوا حليما، وكم آذوا كريما، وكم كسروا الصحيح، وخلطوا الصريح، وكم ارتكبوا جرماً وإثماً، وكم جاؤوا إفكاً وظلماً، وكم فتحوا الأغلاق، وسرقوا الأعلاق، وكم أذهبوا الوفاق، وأحدثوا الشقاق، وكم فرّقوا بين المرء وأهله، والفرع وأصله، فهم جراثيم الفساد، وشرر الأحقاد، ولعنة الله عليهم في الدارين، فقد لقيت منهم الأمرّين، وكادت تصل بنا أفعالهم الشنيعة إلى الجفاء والقطيعة، وأخي ينظر إليها ويغضي،

24.1 ʿĪsā ibn Hishām said: Next we decided to visit the third meeting, this one involving major figures and exemplars of government and wisdom, people of both sword and pen, possessed of absolute power, and capable of making people either miserable or content. Being brought up in the cradle of learning and possessing extraordinary talents in all categories of expression and concept, they are characterized by their authentic ideas and fine organizational skills, the power of their perspicacity and the quality of their intellect.

We headed for a house of gleaming whiteness that dazzled us with its brilliance. Its very grounds exuded prestige and its gardens fostered felicity. Sheer loveliness had taken root there, and its garments had been decorated by finery's hand. As a result it showed itself in the most beautiful of guises, the most perfect of forms, like a lovely girl displaying all her charms on the day where she is bedecked in jewels. At the gate we were met by servants wearing eye-catching clothes. They welcomed us warmly and showed us great respect, then took us to a room on one side of the courtyard where people could wait at their leisure. Inside was a man who was only half awake; his head was a ball, one might say, and slumber was the polo mallet. No sooner had we approached him than he roused himself and started using his fingertips to rub sleep from his eyes. We gave him our greetings which he reciprocated, yawning and stammering as he did so. From his general appearance and dirty clothes, we gathered that he was a workman or servant of some kind. However, before long, it became clear to us from his remarks to the servant that he was a relative of some importance in this household. When the servant went away to ask permission for us to go in, he turned in our direction:

24.2 "May God wreak havoc on all servants!" he said. "They are a kind of affliction. The damage they inflict is ever present, whereas the benefits they bring are often lacking; and one has to tolerate them ad nauseam. They've aggravated many a patient man and irritated generous people. Many times they've destroyed something genuine and muddled up something which is quite clear! Many are the crimes and sins they've committed, and many the lies and wrongs they've perpetrated. How many locks have they opened, how many jewels have they pilfered, how often have they caused discord between people and thwarted an agreement, separating people from their families in the process, and stepping in between the branch and its root! They're parasites of corruption

ويتحمل منها ما لا يرضي، وهم يتجنون عليه وينتصرون، وإذا أمرهم باحترام حرمتي فلا يأتمرون، ويشهد الله أنني كلما رأيت مال أخي في أيديهم يتبدد، وثقته بهم تتضاعف وتتجدد، ذاب الفؤاد فسال من العيون، مشوباً بماء الشؤون، وأمّا وكيل البيت وما أدراك ما الوكيل، ﴿حَسْبُنَا اللَّهُ وَنِعْمَ الْوَكِيلُ﴾، فتى لا تخطئ في النفاق مخيلته، ولا تطيش في البيت حيلته، دأبه المكر والخداع، وإلقاء الشقاق والنزاع، يرضي طفلا ليسخط كهلا، ويتملق الجارية بالطفيف التافه، ليدوم له الحال الناعم والعيش الرافه».

٣،٢٤ هذا وما زال الرجل يشكو ويتضجر، ويتأفف ويتحسر، فلم ينقذنا من هذه الشكوى التي تصم الآذان إلا حضور الغلام بإجابة الاستئذان، فحمدنا الله على كرمه وإحسانه في إنقاذنا من شقشقة لسانه، ثمّ اقتفينا الخادم إلى حجرة بادية الرواء، تتلألأ بأنوار الكهرباء، مفروشة بأثمن فراش، مشحونة بأبدع رياش، على اختلاف في الأجناس والأنواع، وتباين في الأشكال والأوضاع، فالتحفة الشرقية تقابلها طرفة غربية، وآنية الذهب تضارعها آنية الخشب، وقد قابلنا رب الدار باللطف والبشاشة، والتبسم والهشاشة، وأجلسنا مجلس الأخصاء، وحيانا تحية الخلصاء، وإذا المجلس قد جمع من أرباب الوظائف والرتب، بين ذوي الجاه والنسب، ولآخرين اتخذوا خدمة الحكومة لهم رزقا، فاتخذتهم لها رقا، وكان الحديث يدور بينهم في السياسة ويجول، وأحدهم يترنح ويقول:

٤،٢٤ أحدهم نعم، حبذا نصرة الجيش الفرنسوي على بقية الأحزاب فإنّ في ذلك لو تعلمون نيل بغيتنا وتحرير رقبتنا وانقضاء محنتنا.

آخر ما أبعد ما ترمي وما أسرع ما تحكم، فهلا نبأتنا لله أبوك كيف ترتيبك لهذه القضية واستقراؤك لهذه النتيجة، وما نحن وخذلان الأحزاب الفرنسوية ونصرة الجيش عليها.

and sparks of hatred. May God's curse be on them in both worlds! The terrible misfortunes I've suffered because of them and the dastardly actions they've perpetrated against me have almost made me succumb to a most undignified aversion. My brother sees all this happening and yet is prepared to overlook it. He tolerates the most unsavoury behaviour from them, while they in turn blame him and come out on top. When he tells them to do something out of respect for me, they refuse. God is my witness, every time I see my brother's money being frittered away in their hands and notice the ever-increasing confidence he has in them, my heart melts away and flows out through my eyes mixed with tear drops. Where the house steward is concerned—and 'Who's that?' you may ask. Well, «We count on God, and good is the trustee.»[190] He's a young man whose hypocrisy never errs; he never misses a trick inside the house. Cunning and treachery, stirring up resentments and disputes, these are all among his favourite pastimes. He will please an infant to enrage a grown man, and tempt girls with trifles, all so as to maintain his own luxurious lifestyle."

24.3 He kept up this diatribe for some time, muttering and grumbling. The only thing that rescued us from this deafening cacophony was the servant's return with permission for us to enter. Praising God for His generosity and kindness in ridding us of his babbling row, we now followed the servant to a pleasant room lit by electric lights and laid out with costly cushions and superb furniture of various shapes and sizes. Eastern ornaments were positioned opposite Western objets d'art and gold vessels were paralleled by others made of wood. The house's owner greeted us with a cordial smile, sat us in a place reserved for his close associates, and welcomed us as though we were genuine friends. This meeting, we discovered, was made up of high-ranking members of the government, people of prestige and illustrious ancestry, along with others who had entered government service as a means of earning a living and were now indebted to it. The discussion was focussed on politics. One of them was swaying from side to side as he spoke:

24.4 One of Them Yes, the right thing to do is to support the French army against the other parties in France. Did you but know it, therein lies our own liberation and the end of our sufferings.

Another I'm most impressed by your far-reaching aspirations and incisive judgment. Why don't you tell us—may your father belong to God!—how your research has led you to this conclusion? How can thwarting French parties and supporting the army against them affect us?

الأول أراك لست بعويص الرأي في السياسة ولا ببعيد الغور في استنباط الحوادث، ألا تعلم أرشدك الله إلى الصواب أنّ في انتصار الجيش قلباً لهذه الجمهورية، ورجوعاً بفرنسا إلى الملكية أو الإمبراطورية، فتأتينا بمثل أولئك الملوك والقواد الذين دوخوا الشرق والغرب، وقهروا الممالك وأذلوا الدول، وأصبحت كلمتهم هي العليا، فلا يقف أمام أغراضهم ممانع ولا يعارضهم معارض، وإني لأعلم علم اليقين ممّن عاشرت من الفرنسويين وصاحبت أنه لولا هذه الجمهورية لما وصلنا نحن إلى هذه الحال، وما نحتمله من الذل والصغار، واستئثار أولئك القابضين على زمام حكومتنا بالمناصب العالية والمرتبات العظيمة، ولما أغلقت أمامنا أبواب الترقي، وتقطعت بنا أسباب التقدم، فلو عادت فرنسا إلى مجدها القديم وسطوتها السالفة لزحزحتهم بإشارة، وأزاحتهم عنا بكلمة، ولأصبحنا نتصرف في حكومتنا بأيدينا.

ثالث دعنا بالله من هذا الخيال، واتركنا من هذا اللغو، ومثلك لا يحق له الشكوى من هذه الحال، فأنت متين العلاقة بالمستشار، قوي الرابطة مع الناظر، وما بينك وبين الوصول إلى المنصب الذي تتطلع إليه إلا قيد شبر، وأنت مع ذلك والحمد لله في غنى عن خدمة الحكومة بما لك من التالد والطارف، ولكن ماذا تقول في من هو في حاجة إلى البقاء في أسر الحكومة، وذل الخدمة مع سخط الرئيس، ونفور المستشار، وغضب الناظر، واستشعار المرؤوسين بذلك؟ فلا توقير ولا احترام ولا أدب ولا حياء، ويعلم الله أنه لولا الاحتياج إلى المرتب وقلة الحيلة في أنواع التكسب لقدمت استعفائي إلى الحكومة في الحال، ولما أقمت في خدمتها يوماً واحداً. ٥،٢٤

رابع وأنا والله لا أنتظر إلا أن يتمّ لي نصف معاش فأهجر خدمة الحكومة، وأخلص نفسي من هذه العبودية، ومن ذل النفاق، وقبح الرياء، وعنا المداراة، ثمّ أعوّل بعد ذلك على الاشتغال بالتجارة، فهي أهنأ عيشاً وأعظم ربحاً وأبعد بالنفس عن مواقف الهوان.

First I can see that, when it comes to analyzing events, you don't appreciate the intricacies of politics and fail to show the necessary insight. May God give you correct guidance! Don't you realize that, if the army party wins, the Republican system will be overthrown? Then the monarchy and empire will be restored. They'll bring us back kings and generals like the ones who conquered East and West, overwhelmed the Mamluks, and subdued entire empires. They had supremacy over all the peoples of the world. No obstacle could keep them from their goals, and nothing stood in the way of their aspirations. From my association with French officials, some of whom I've actually befriended, what I know for sure is that, were it not for this Republic, we wouldn't have reached the state we're in, nor would we be suffering the degradation involved in having to deal with the absolute monopoly possessed by the people who've grabbed hold of the reins of our government. They're occupying all the major positions and earning huge salaries. All gates to promotion are shut in our faces; the wherewithal of progress is cut off. If only France could regain her former power and prestige, she could remove these people with a mere gesture and drive them away from us with a word. Then we could begin to run our government with our own hands.[191]

24.5 Third For God's sake, put such fancies aside and stop talking nonsense! You've nothing to complain about in the present circumstances. You're on close terms with the Counselor[192] and have a direct link to the Minister himself. You're on the verge of getting the position which you've set your heart on. Not only that, but you're wealthy; you've enough funds, whether inherited or current, so that you don't need to be a government employee. But what about those of us who are still forced by need to be chained to the government and to be constantly humiliated—the boss gets annoyed, the Counselor is displeased, the Minister is furious, and it's the subordinates who feel it. There's no sense of respect or esteem, no manners or modesty. God knows that if I didn't have to earn a salary and get a living somehow, I'd resign immediately and wouldn't stay in government service for a single day.[193]

Fourth By God, I anticipate spending only half my life as a civil servant. Then I'll quit and save myself from this bondage, with all its humiliating hypocrisy, arrant deceit, and frenzied cover-ups. After that I intend to rely on commerce. It's a more pleasant way of earning a living, brings greater profit, and keeps one removed from degrading situations.

٦،٢٤ **خامس** ما أسخف الرأي وأحط الفكر، فلست تجهل أنّ خدمة الحكومة على أي حال أعلى قدراً وأرفع شأناً وأعز جاهاً، وجميع أسباب المعائش لا تخلو من الأكدار والمتاعب، وخدمة الحكومة أهون في هذا الباب حالا وأحسن مزية، ويكفيك أنك تستخدم التاجر وتسخره ما دام درهمك في جيبك والتاجر في حاجة أبداً إلى أصغر موظف وإن كان من أغنى الأغنياء وأكبر الموسورين، ولو تراهم إذ يفتخرون بينهم بزيارة الكاتب ومجالسة الملاحظ وتحية القاضي وإشارة المدير أسلمت أنّ خدمة الحكومة في أعينهم وأعين بقية الناس قد بلغت من الشرف والرفعة بحيث لو خيّرت أحدهم بين الخروج عن ملكه وعقاره وتجارته وأطيانه وبين التوظف في الحكومة لخرج منها خروج السهم من قوسه، ولانسلخ عنها انسلاخ الأرقم من جلده، ولأيقن أنّ السعادة كل السعادة في ما تحسبه أنت هواناً وذلاً وتعمده شقاء وويلاً.

٧،٢٤ **السادس** على رسلك! لا تعكس القضية، ولا تقلب الحقائق، ولا تحمل ما تراه من أخلاق أرباب الصناعة والتجارة والزراعة على أنه ناشئ من نفس تلك المهن من حيث ماهيتها، بل هو ناشئ عن الجهالة والوهم وضعف الفكر، فلو خلا أحدهم منها لعلم قدر نفسه، وعرف مكانته وأدرك نعمة حريته واستقلاله في عمله، وهو بلا شك أسعد من ذلك الذي يشقى بقيود الخدمة في الحكومة فيبيع لها حريته في مقابلة دنانير يعدّ لأجلها ساعات اليوم وأيام الشهر، يربحها الواحد من أولئك في يوم واحد وهو أمير نفسه وسيد دائرته ويا ليت آباءنا كانوا التفتوا إلى تعليمنا الصنعة وممارسة التجارة، ولكن بئس ما صنعوا وبئس ما خلفونا له، ولو كانوا أدركوا ما انتهت إليه حال الوظائف في الحكومة اليوم ولم يغتروا بما كان للحكام في الأزمان السالفة من الصول والطول والقوة والحول، واكتساب الجاه من المنصب والمال من الجاه، ولو علموا أنه يأتي زمان على تلك الحكومة التي أقاموا في يديها كالأيتام في يد الوصي يكون فيه الموظفون كالأطفال في حجر المرضع والعجزة في دار الإحسان، إن خرجوا عنها ماتوا

FIFTH What stupid, useless ideas! You can't deny that, whatever the case, government service is more prestigious and affords a higher status. No means of earning a living in this world is entirely devoid of aggravations, but government service provides the easiest conditions and causes the least hardship. For example, you can employ a merchant and laugh in his face so long as you have money at hand. But merchants always need the services of the most junior government employee, even if they're incredibly rich and well-off. If you only could see them boasting to each other about visiting the clerk, conversing with the adjutant, greeting the judge and addressing the governor, then you'd admit that government service holds a very prestigious place in the estimation of such people and of other classes as well. In much the same way, if you gave one of them the choice of either abandoning his wealth, property, trade, and lands, or joining the ranks of government employees, he would abandon everything like an arrow from a bow or a snake from its skin. What's abundantly clear is that the very pinnacle of happiness lies in what you regard as a terrible hardship and utter humiliation. 24.6

SIXTH Take it easy! Don't turn the issue upside down and alter the truth. Don't assume that the ethics you observe among practitioners of industry, commerce, and agriculture stem from the essence of those professions. To the contrary, it results from ignorance, illusion, and feeble thinking. If one of them were to abandon his profession, he'd appreciate his own worth; with an understanding of his own status in life, he'd acknowledge the boon of independent action and freedom of thought. He's undoubtedly happier than someone who has to suffer the trammels of government service, selling his very soul in return for a few paltry dinars, in returns for which he has to spend hours each day and days each month working. Anybody working in those other professions makes more profit in a single day than we do in our position; and they're their own masters and in control of their own environment. If only our fathers had given some thought to teaching us trades and giving us some experience in commerce! Instead, what they did do and what they did leave to us is completely useless. If only they'd realized the status of government service today, and had not been misled by the extensive authority and jurisdiction which people in authority had in days gone by, along with the power to acquire money by virtue of their high rank! If they'd realized that a time would come when high-ranking people in this government (in whose hands they were like orphans in the care of their guardian) would be like babies in the nursery or invalids in nursing 24.7

جوعًا، لعضوا الأنامل ندمًا وبكوا بدل الدموع دمًا على ما فرطوا في أمرنا.

الخامس إنك لتتكلم بكلام العجائز اللائي يقتنعن من دهرهن بالخسيس من المطعم والملبس، وأين أنت من طلب المعالي، وابتغاء المفاخر، واعتلاء المناصب، وخدمة الأوطان، والقدرة على النفع والضرر، وأين أنت من قول الشاعر: ٨،٢٤

ولو أنّ ما أسعى لأدنى معيشة
كفاني ولم أطلب قليل من المال
ولكنما أسعى لمجد مؤثل
وقد يدرك المجد المؤثل أمثالي؟

وإلى الله المشتكى من زمان صغرت فيه النفوس، وماتت الهموم، وخمدت الأفكار، وضعفت العزائم، ورضي الناس فيه بالخمول، والانكماش، والعيش والدون.

السادس إني لأعجب من أمرك أشد العجب أيها الفاضل، وكيف يغيب عنك الصواب فترى أنّ في خدمة الحكومة سؤددًا وعلاء ومجدًا وسناء، وما هي إلا النصب والشقاء والبلاء في أثر البلاء، وأنا أفصل لك الحال لتعلم أنّ بقاء أمثالك في الحكومة مع قدرتهم على التنحي عنها عجز وضعف وجهل براحة الحياة فأقول: ٩،٢٤

اعلم أنّ الرغبة في خدمة الحكومة تنقسم إلى أربعة أقسام، القسم الأوّل الرغبة فيها للمال، أعني لسد العوز وحاجة القوت وكفاف العيش، وصاحب هذا القسم في حال المضطر الذي حكم عليه الدهر باحتمال الهوان والأذى، ووضعته ضرورة طلب الرزق في رق العبد وذل الأجير، فليس له إلا تجرع غصص الصبر على هذا البلاء، حتى يجد له مخلصًا منه ومنصرفًا عنه، وهو مثلي يغبط كل صانع وتاجر ومزارع، ويتمنى لو أصبح داخلًا في زمرتهم، متمتعًا باستقلالهم وحريتهم.

والقسم الثاني الرغبة فيها للجاه، أعني علو الكلمة وقوة السطوة ومضاء الحكم وعزة المنصب، وهذا الميدان على ما ترى بعيد الشأو، واسع الأطراف، ليس لشوطه نهاية، ولا لدوره غاية، ولا بدّ فيه للجواد من كبوة، وللسيف من لبوة، وطالما كان ١٠،٢٤

homes—leave them and they'd die of hunger—then they'd have bitten their nails in anguish and shed blood instead of tears for the way they'd failed us.

FIFTH You are talking like a lot of old women, satisfied with a life that only provides threadbare clothes and poor food. What about our quest for the loftier ideals, bolstering our sense of pride and glory, rising to a high position and serving our country so we can do both good and harm? What of the poet's words: 24.8

Were I striving for a lowly livelihood,
a little money would suffice; I would not ask for more.
But yet I strive for a noble glory
and my peers achieve such a goal.[194]

We should complain to God about an age in which people's aspirations have dwindled, their resolves are dead, and all thought lies quiescent. People have lost all ambition; they are content to sit back in apathetic indifference and live a meagre life.

SIXTH Eminent Sir, I'm surprised that you can be so completely and utterly wrong. You seem to imagine it's a sign of authority and high rank, of honor and glory, to be a civil servant, whereas in fact it's simply humiliation and suffering, one trial after another. I'll explain things to you in detail. Then you'll realize that the reason why people like yourself remain in government service when you can in fact leave it, is that you're weak and incapable, totally unaware of the comforts of life. 24.9

I maintain that the desire to enter government service can be subdivided into four categories. The first is a need for money, by which I mean staving off poverty and earning enough to stay alive. Anyone into this category is in a state of compulsion whereby Fate has decreed that he should endure humiliation because of the need to earn a living as a matter of bondage and the contemptible status of hireling. All he can do is to swallow the bitter pill and endure such misery till he can find some way out. Like me, he envies the way of life of every craftsman, merchant, and farmer, and is forever longing to join their number, relishing their independence and freedom.

The second category involves a quest for prestige, by which I imply high status, important rank, wide authority, and executive power. As you can tell, this is a far-reaching and expansive field without any limits to its goals. Within it the rearing charger will inevitably stumble and the sword will miss its target. 24.10

اعتلاء المناصب وارتقاء المراتب داعية للرزايا والمصائب، ومجلبة للأحزان والأكدار:

والشر يجلبه العلاء وكم شكا
نبأ عليّ ما شكاه قنبر

ولو سلمنا أنّ صاحب المنصب نجا من المعاطب، وسلم من النوازل، وخلص من الخطوب، فهو لا يزال طول عمره في هم دائم وكمد مستمر، كلما ارتقى درجة في المنصب وجد فوقها درجة أخرى يحسد من يعتليها ويحقد على من يليها، مستعظماً لما فوقه، مستصغراً لما في يده، فيعيش ذاهلاً عن التمتع بلذة الجاه الذي يسعى طول حياته إليه غير راض عن نفسه ولا عن الناس، ولا الناس راضون عنه، وهذا هو منتهى الشقاء وملتقى الهموم والأحزان:

ذلك الخائب الشقي وإن كا
ن يرى أنه من السعداء
يحسب الحظ كله في يديه
وهو منه على مدى الجوزاء

وأخلق بمن كان دائم التطلع إلى غير ما في يده أن يكون أنحس البرية حالاً، ولذلك ١١،٢٤ زهد الراسخون في العلم من الفلاسفة والحكماء في المناصب، ورغبوا عن اغتراب غاربها وحذروا العقلاء من الاشتغال بها والسعي وراءها هذا كله إذا كان المنصب عظيم الجاه، نافذ الحكم، وكان الوصول إليه من طريق الفضيلة، والوسيلة نحوه وسيلة الشرف والعزة والشهامة والأباء والفضل والاستحقاق أمّا إذا كانت أسباب الوصول إلى المنصب كما تراها اليوم بيننا تقتصر على التوسل والتوسط والتصنع وإهراق ماء الحياء، لا يرتقي إليه إلا من بلغ أقصى الدرجات في علم النفاق والرياء، وفن المداهنة والموارأة، واستكمل آلاتهما من الذل والخضوع والاستكانة، والخشوع والصبر على احتمال الضيم والأذى كان المنصب على ما تعلم من حيث سقوط الكلمة، وضعة القدر، وحبس النفس، وتقييد اللسان، وفقد الحرية، وفظاعة المسؤولية، كان الفرار

Lofty position and high class have often been the cause of great calamities and disasters and the instigator of miseries and sorrows:

> High rank brings evil; how often did ʿAlī complain
> of news while Qanbar made no such complaint.[195]

Even if we concede that the person who holds an important position is free from harm and danger, he still spends the rest of his life continually straining and worrying. Every time he rises a rank in status, he discovers another one above it and envies the person who has been promoted to the post. He continually admires what is above him and strives to achieve it while belittling what he has. He lives his life, distracted from the enjoyment of the pleasures to be gained from the status that he spent his entire life attaining. He's satisfied neither with himself nor with other people, and they in turn are dissatisfied with him. This is the ultimate in suffering, and the very crossroads where distress and sorrow meet.

> That man is frustrated and distressed even though
> he may be reckoned among the fortunate.
> He considers all good fortune to be in his hands,
> whereas it is as distant as the Gemini.[196]

24.11 How appropriate it is that someone who continually aspires to gain something he doesn't have should be the most miserable person alive! That's why philosophers and wise men have always refused to accept important positions and disliked getting involved in them. Intelligent people have made sure they didn't chase after such posts and tie themselves down. All this was in the time when public office was still a great honor and commanded extensive authority. One could only achieve such distinction by proving one's excellence and nobility; the path to such positions involved honor, prestige, courage, fortitude, moral virtue, and merit. However, as we see it today, the road to high office consists solely in currying favor, acting as intermediary, and pouring one's lifeblood away. The only people rising to such levels are those who display the very highest level of hypocrisy and graft; they've mastered the crafts of sycophancy and concealment, both of which demand their share of humiliation, subjection, and passivity and a willingness to endure such injustice. As you know, public office now involves a loss of authority, a lack of status, an inability to express any opinion, a loss of freedom, and an

منه أجدر بذي الفضيلة وأحرى، والتنائي عنه أسلم له وأشفى، وكان السقوط منه والنزول عنه نعم المنصب العالي لذي الشهامة والمروءة والأباء والفتوة.

١٢،٢٤ والقسم الثالث الرغبة في خدمة الحكومة للعمل دون سواه تضييعاً للوقت، وتسلية للنفس، وصرفاً لأيام الحياة وقضاء لساعات العمر، ودفعاً للسأم والملل بالاشتغال بحاجات الناسولا يتألف هذا القسم إلا كل من كان فارغ النفس، خالي الصدر، خاوي القلب خلواً من كل فضل، لا تشتغل نفسه بغير الهواجس والوساوس والخيالات الفاسدة، ففؤاده هواء وأثقل شيء عليه خلوه من مشاغل متجددة تحول بينه وبين الخلو بنفسه التي صارت عنده إذا خلا بها كأنها خلية من خلايا الزنابير، أو وكر من وكور الأفاعي، وهيهات أن يبلغ المسكين غرضاً في هذا السبيل لأنّ من ضاقت عليه نفسه كان العالم عليه أضيق.

١٣،٢٤ والقسم الرابع الرغبة في خدمة الحكومة لمحبة الوطن وخدمته، وهذا بعيد المنال أيضاً، فإنه لا يتفق الجمع بين المحافظة على الوظيفة وبين الاستقلال في الرأي لمصلحة الوطن لما بينهما اليوم من الخلف والتناقض، ومن أراد أن يخدم وطنه فلا يقيّد نفسه بقيود الحكومة، بل يخدمه وهو خارج عنها مطلق اليدين كامل الحرية.

ثمّ أضف إلى ذلك كله مرارة العزل في بلد ينسبون فيه إلى صاحب المنصب كل فضيلة وينزعونها عنه عند سقوطه منه، فعندهم الرجال بالمناصب لا المناصب بالرجال على عكس ما قيل:

إنّ الأمـير هو الـذي
يضحى أميرًا يوم عـزلـه
إن زال سلطان الولا
ية لم يزل سلطان فضله

ولذلك رأينا الكثير ممّن كنّا نتخيلهم على السماع إبان المنصب علماء وأفاضل، أنهم إذا أصابهم العزل أقل الناس علما وفضلا.

atrocious level of responsibility. Any one person of moral integrity should turn the other way and avoid it; that would undoubtedly be better for them. People of steadfast courage and honor are achieving the highest possible status by renouncing it.

24.12 The third group involves government service as a means of wasting time and spending hours of one's life doing something or other. In that way, one can fend off boredom and waste hours fussing over other people's needs. The only people in that category are vacuous individuals who are totally lacking in any kind of virtue; their minds are only preoccupied by trifling concerns and futile fancies. Such people have no depth to them; the worst thing for them is to have no serious problems to solve that can distract them from the self-isolation they feel. If they're left to their own devices, it's like being in a hornet's nest or a viper's lair. The poor fools can never achieve their goals. Anyone who cannot tolerate himself will find the world yet more intolerable.

24.13 The fourth category joins the ranks of the civil service out of a desire to serve the country and help its people. This is also a futile objective because the attitude needed to remain in office and the independence of thought required to be of service to the country are mutually incompatible. Anyone desiring to serve his country should not tie himself down with government chains. In fact, he'll be serving it better by working elsewhere, a situation in which he will have a free hand. To all that you should add the bitter feeling of being sacked in a country where people attribute every kind of virtue to officeholders, only to strip them of such attributes when they fall from office. As far as they're concerned, people are known by their positions, not the opposite. That's the reverse of the old adage:

> The amir is one who becomes
>   an amir on the day of his deposition.
> Even if his authority ceases to exist,
>   his control of his own virtue continues.[197]

That's why we have seen many people, whose reputations while they were in office were such as to lead you to believe that they were scholars and men of merit, but who turn out to be the people least endowed with such traits once they were dismissed from their jobs.

فكيف يقبل عاقل الدخول في الحكومة وهو يجد عنها محيصاً وملجأ الأمن أضله الله على علم، ولذلك أخذت على نفسي أن أتخير لأولادي في تعلمهم العلوم صناعة يتعيشون معها أحراراً، وتكون معهم أينما حلوا وساروا، لا يسلبها منهم تقلب الحوادث وتغلب السياسة، وغضب زيد ورضى عمرو. ١٤،٢٤

سابع لا فض الله فاك، وأنا معك في هذا الرأي وهذا العزم.

الثاني اتركونا بالله من هذه الخطب المحزنة والأفكار المكدرة، وخذوا بنا في حديث غير هذا يفرّج عنا ما نلاقيه، ولا تجمعوا علينا بين ذل النهار وهم الليل، وهل لك يا فلان أن تقوم معي نرتاض ونتسابق بالبسكليت.

الأول أحسن من هذا أن تأتونا بالفنوغراف نشتف مسامعنا به.

ثامن أو قوموا بنا إلى عرس فلان، فقد بلغني أنّ فيه بوفيه لم يسمع بمثله.

الأول أنا معك.

الثامن لكن على شرط أن تقيم معي هناك حتى نستمع الغناء.

الأول لا لا، وإنما أحضر معك البوفيه ثمّ نذهب لسماع الموسيقى الانكليزية أو الأوبرا التليانية.

الرابع أنا لا أتوجه معكما لأني ذاهب إلى الكلوب.

السابع انتظروا بنا حتى نقرأ جرائد هذا المساء.

الخامس إن كان فيها جريدة فرنسوية عليَّ بها فهي أصحّ أخباراً وأغزر مادة.

الثالث اقرؤوا الجرائد العربية أولا واحدة بعد أخرى أو مع بعضها.

الثاني (يقرأ) «روسيا في الصين وأمريكا في الفلبين». ١٥،٢٤

الرابع ماذا جرى لعقلك يا مولانا، اقلب الصحيفة فمالنا ولهذه المقالات الافتتاحية فلنا فكر كما لكاتبها فكر.

القارئ (يقلب الصحيفة ويقرأ) «المراسلات» «الإسكندرية لمكاتبنا» «من اطلع على أخبار يوهانسبورج حكم بوقوع الحرب ولا شك أنّ العاقبة تكون

With all this in mind, why would any sensible person want to go into the civil service if he can find an alternative, unless, that is, God has led him astray? That is why I've vowed to choose another profession for my sons to practice, something they can use to earn a living as free men and that will be at their disposal wherever they decide to go and settle down. It will not be wrenched away by changed circumstances or political upheaval. They will be unaffected by either Zayd's anger or ʿAmr's pleasure.[198] 24.14

SEVENTH By God, that was a splendid and clear explanation! I thoroughly agree with your verdict.

SECOND By God, stop voicing such distressing ideas. Let's change the topic and talk instead about something that'll take our minds off our situation. Don't use daytime's humiliations and nighttime's anxieties for a combined attack on us. My dear A, can you join me in some exercise and bicycle racing?

FIRST A better idea would be to bring the phonograph for us to listen to.

EIGHTH Or else come to X's wedding with us. I've heard there's going to be a spectacular "buffet."

FIRST I'm with you.

EIGHTH But only if you'll stay with me and listen to the singing.

FIRST No, I'm not up for that. Let's go to the buffet, then move on to the Ezbekiyyah to listen to some English music or Italian opera.

FOURTH I'm not going to join you. I'm going to the "Club."

SEVENTH Wait a minute while we look at the evening papers.

FIFTH If there are any French ones, let me have them. Their news is always more reliable, and they have more in them.

THIRD Read the Arabic ones first, one after the other, or else a bit at a time from each.

SECOND (*reading*) "Russia in China and America in the Philippines." 24.15

FOURTH My dear fellow, what's gone wrong with your mind? Turn the page. What possible interest can we have in those editorials? Our ideas are just as good as theirs.

READER (*turning the page and reading*) "Cables. Alexandria to our offices. Anyone who has read the news from Johannesburg will have concluded that war has started. The outcome will undoubtedly favor the wronged party, namely Transvaal, against England, the wrongdoer. Should the latter be

للترنسفال المظلومة على انكلترا الظالمة، ولئن غلبت الثانية الأولى فتالحق منصور على أي حال على مدى الأزمان ولنا في الماضي عبرة. . .».

الرابع حسبك حسبك، أما قلنا لك لا تقرأ هذه المقالات الافتتاحية؟

القارئ قد تركتها وإنما أقرأ المراسلات.

السابع اترك الإسكندرية.

القارئ الزقازيق لمكاتبنا: «يثني العموم على حضرة ملاحظ البندر لاهتمامه بالكنس والرش».

الثامن أنعم به وأكثر الله من أمثاله في خدمة الوطن، عليك يا مولانا بالحوادث المحلية.

القارئ (يقرأ) «يسافر فلان إلى الإسكندرية على اكسبريس المساء، ويحضر فلان إلى مصر على اكسبريس الصباح».

الثامن اترك قراءة هذا المانيفستو أيضاً.

القارئ (يقرأ) «سبقنا فذكرنا أنّ مجلس النظار بحث في الجبانات والآن نذكر نص القرار وهو. . .».

الثامن جعل الله الجنة قراره، اقرأ غيره.

القارئ (يقرأ) «وصل سعادة السردار إلى أم درمان، وسيكون أهم ما يشتغل به السؤال كما حدث في السودان مدة غيابه».

الثامن سبحان الله، كنت أظن أنه سيسأل هناك عن قضية دريفوس أو سكة حديد سيبيريا.

القارئ (يقرأ) «يسم البوليس الكلاب الضالة».

الثامن نسأل الله الهداية والسلامة للجميع.

القارئ (يقرأ) «اكتشف فلان دواء للموت وكتب إلينا أنه من غرامه بصدق جريدتنا لا يفارقها حتى ولا في نومه على فراشه». ١٦،٢٤

الثامن سبحان الموفق.

victorious, then truth will win with the passage of time in any case. There are examples from past history"—

FOURTH Enough! Didn't we tell you not to read those editorials?

READER Fine, I'll stop reading them, and turn to the cables.

SEVENTH Forget about Alexandria!

READER "Zaqāzīq to our offices. The public are unanimous in their praise of the Municipal Superintendent for his attention to street cleaning."

EIGHTH May God bless him and provide us with more people like him to serve the country! Now, my friend, give us the local news.

READER "X traveled by express train to Alexandria this evening, and Y arrived in the capital on the morning express."

EIGHTH Stop reading this manifesto as well!

READER "We have mentioned previously that the Cabinet of Ministers has been looking into the question of cemeteries. We will now quote the full text of the report"—

EIGHTH May God afford it a resting place in Paradise! Now read us something else.

READER "The Commander-in-Chief has arrived at Omdurman. We learn from a reliable source that he is mainly concerned at this time with the question of conditions in the Sudan."

EIGHTH Good heavens! I thought he'd be concerned with the Dreyfus case or the Siberian railway!

READER "The police are poisoning dangerous dogs."

EIGHTH We ask God for guidance and safety for them all.

24.16 READER "Someone has discovered a cure for death. He writes to us to say that he is so fond of the genuine tone of our newspaper that he can't put it down, even in bed."

EIGHTH Praise to the Granter of success!

القارئ (يقرأ) «جاءنا تلغراف بأنه قد فجع الإسلام وانهدم ركن الدين وأظلم الكون، إذ قصفت المنون الشيخ فلان عن ست وتسعين سنة قضاها في البر والإحسان، فكان لنبأ موته رنة في قلوب أهل قريته خصوصاً وفي القطر المصري عموماً».

الثامن اسرع بالنظر في أخبار البورصة فلا بدّ أن تكون الأسعار هبطت لهذا الخبر هبوطاً فاحشاً.

القارئ (يقرأ) «نفيد حضرات القراء أنه لا يزال التحقيق جارياً في المسألة الفلانية، ولم يتم فيها شيء إلى الآن، ومتى تم نبادر إلى نشره إفادة لحضراتهم كما هي عادتنا في نشر الأخبار بأوقاتها».

الثامن أفادكم الله.

القارئ (يقرأ) «فاتنا أن نذكر أنّ فلاناً كان في مقدمة المشيعين لجنازة المرحوم فلان في الأسبوع الماضي، وكذلك فاتنا أن نهنئ حضرة مكاتبنا بالدير الطويل حيث رزقه الله بولادة مولود جديد فلا زال ممتعا بالرفاه والبنين».

الثامن جلّ من لا يغفل ولا ينسى.

القارئ (يقرأ) «لدغت عقرب ابنة في قسم الوايلي».

الثامن لا حول ولا قوة إلا بالله، هذا كله ناشئ من إهمال الحكومة في اتخاذ الاحتياطات الصحية ومن إهمال البوليس في ضبط مثل هذه الوقائع.

القارئ (للثامن) يكفيك يا حضرة القاضي من مثل هذه السخرية واسمعوا لي بالله هذا الخبر المهم. ١٧،٢٤

الثامن سمعاً وطاعة.

القارئ (يقرأ) «بلغنا اليوم أنّ الحكومة تبحث الآن في مشروع فتح شارع المرور، ونحن بلسان العموم وبالنيابة عن الأمّة المصرية الأسيفة نحذرها من عواقب هذا المشروع الوخيمة الذي يكون من ورائه رسوخ قدم الأجنبي في البلاد، وسنشرح لحضرات القراء مضار هذا المشروع وكل آت قريب».

Reader "We have received a telegram to the effect that Islam has been struck, the pillar of the religion has collapsed, and the world has been wronged. The fates have plucked away Shaykh B after a life of ninety-six years spent on pious and charitable deeds. At the announcement of his death, sorrow and sadness fill the hearts of the people of his town in particular and of the whole region of Egypt in general."

Eighth Take a quick look at stock prices. With this news, shares prices will inevitably go into a steep decline!

Reader "We would like to notify our esteemed readers that investigations are still proceeding in the such of such-and-such, but nothing has been concluded so far. As soon as it is concluded, we will publish it immediately in accordance with our practice of publishing news as it happens."

Eighth May God benefit you!

Reader "We have omitted to mention that C was at the head of the mourners at the funeral last week of the late lamented D. We also omitted to congratulate our esteemed correspondent in Dayr al-Ṭawīl whom God blessed with the birth of a child. May God continue to give him happiness from children!"

Eighth Excellent indeed is he who neither overlooks nor forgets.

Reader "A scorpion stung a girl in the al-Wāylī district."

Eighth God forbid! This all stems from the government's neglect of hygiene precautions and police negligence in stopping this kind of incident!

24.17 Reader (*to the Eighth speaker*) My dear judge, that's enough of your sarcasm and mockery! Listen now to this important announcement.

Eighth Hearing is obeying!

Reader "We have learned today that the government is at this moment considering a project to open traffic streets. In expressing the views of the people and deputizing for the people of Egypt who are distressed by the idea, we would warn the government of the consequences of this dangerous project which would lead to the penetration of foreigners into the country. We will be explaining to our esteemed readers the harm which such a plan would cause. As the saying puts it, the future is never far away. . . ."

الأول هذا الخبر لا يعلم به سواي، وقد أخبرتكم به فيما بيننا فقط فكيف وصل إلى الجرائد.

الثامن أبشر بقضية تلغرافات أخرى.

الخامس إني أنذركم أنه لا يبعد على هذه الحكومة إن دام إفشاء الأسرار للجرائد أن تستبدلنا باستخدام الحرس رجوعاً إلى القاعدة القديمة.

الرابع (للثاني) اقرأ بقية الأخبار.

الثاني لم يبق في الجرائد الثلاث إلا التلغرافات والإعلانات.

الأول عليّ بقراءة التلغرافات السياسية فهي أهم الأخبار.

قال عيسى بن هشام: وما قرأ التلغرافات حتى كثر اللغط في شرحها وتضاربت الظنون في تأويلها ١٨،٢٤

واشتدّ بينهم الجدال حتى كأنهم في امتحان يظهر كل منهم فيه براعة علمه وغزارة فضله، لا يتفق لهم رأي، ولا يجتمع لهم فكر ولما اشتعل بينهم الجدال اشتعالاً، خرجنا من بينهم انسلالاً، وتركناهم في مجاهل السياسة يهيمون تيهاً وضلالاً.

FIRST I'm the only one who knows about this project. I've shared it with you, but how did it get into the newspapers?

EIGHTH Give us some news from other cables.

FIFTH I'm warning you that, if secret information keeps being leaked like this, it's not out of the question that this government will start using guards instead of us; that would be a reversion to times past.

FOURTH (*to Second*) Read the rest of the local news.

SECOND All that's left in the three newspapers is cables and announcements.

FIRST Read the political cables. They have the most important news.

'Īsā ibn Hishām said: No sooner had the reader finished reading the political cables than everyone started arguing; opinions varied widely as they tried to interpret them. The argument became more and more heated; it was if they were all taking part in an exam where everyone had to prove the extent of his knowledge and virtue. No one agreed with anyone else, and there was a complete lack of unified opinion. As things heated up, we crept out, leaving them to meander through their politics and wander aimlessly in their delusion. **24.18**

مصباح الشرق ٧٤، ٢٨ سبتمبر ١٨٩٩

١،٢٥ قال عيسى بن هشام: وآن أن نزور المجلس الرابع من تلك المجالس والمجامع، مجلس الأمراء، ومحضر الكبراء، ذوي المجد والعلاء، والفخر والسناء، وأهل الوضاءة والوجاهة، والرفاغة والرفاهة، وأولي الرخاوة والرغادة، والسيادة والسعادة، فأممّنا مغانيهم قصراً فقصراً حتى كدنا نأتي عليها عدّاً وحصراً، فلم نجد بها غير الخدم في حمى الحرم، وكلما سألنا عن صدور مرابعها وبدور مطالعها، قيل لنا أنّ تلك الأهلة لا تنزل في الظلام منازلها، وهذه الثلة لا تأوي في الليل معاقلها، وعليكما بقصر الجزيرة أو ضفاف النيل عند دخول الشمس في الأصيل، إن كنتما تحاولان لهم ازديارا، وتبغيان اللقاء نهارا، وأمّا إن أردتما اللقاء في المساء، فعليكما بمحفل اجتماعهم، ومحل استمتاعهم، ومباءة الرائح منهم والغادي، وذلك هو «الكلوب» وهو النادي، فهم يسكنونه سكنى الأطيار في الأوكار، والآرام في الآجام، والكواعب في المضارب، وإذ هممنا أن نقصد قصده، ونرود وردة، تذكرت أنه لا يدخله من كان أجنبياً عنهم إلا إذا استصحب عضواً منهم.

٢،٢٥ فرأينا أن ننتظر من الغد أصيله لبلوغ هذه الوسيلة علنا أن نعثر فيه على من يصحبنا إلى ذلك المقام ممّن لهم فيه مكانة ومقام فلمّا حان الوقت المحدود، خرجنا للنزهة في مكانها المشهود، ومجالها المعهود، وقصدنا قصر الجزيرة المقصود، فإذا هو مجتلى المباهاة والمفاضلة، ومزدحم المباراة والمساجلة، ومضمار المقارنة والمشاكلة، ومعرض المغامزة والمغازلة، ومنزل من منازل التريض والارتياح، وبيت من بيوت الراح والأقداح.

فأعجب الباشا جمال المنظر والرواء من حسن الموقع وزخرف البناء، وسألني لمن هذا القصر من خلعاء الأغنياء، فقلت له وهذا أيضاً قصر من تلك القصور الشماء، كانت تفاخر به الأرض نجوم السماء، تصدر عنه البأساء والنعماء، وتندك له أركان القطر بالإشارة والإيماء، وتقذف سماؤه بشهب النقم، وتسيل جداوله بسيول النعم، وتكتنسه عقيلات الملك والشرف، فوق بساط النعيم والترف:

Miṣbāḥ al-sharq 74, September 28, 1899[199]

25.1 ʿĪsā ibn Hishām said: The time came for our fourth visit to these meetings, this one made up of amirs and important figures. Possessors of glory, prestige, honor, and majesty, they are people of purity and influence, of luxury and refinement, of ease and opulence, of power and felicity. We went to all their palaces one after another, till we had visited almost all of them. However, the only people we found living there were their eunuchs and servants. Every time we inquired as to their location, we were informed that the owners no longer lived in their own abodes; they did not shelter there at night. If you're trying to visit and see them by day, we were told, you need to go to the Gezira Palace or the Nile banks at sunset. In the evening, you need to go to their regular meeting place, the location they frequent in search of relaxation, namely the "Club." They treat it as birds do their nests, gazelles do thickets, and buxom maids do pavilions. However I now recalled that, if we were planning to go there, the only means of entry for someone who was not known to them was in the company of a member of their group.

25.2 So we decided to wait till the following afternoon before following our plan, in the hope of coming across a friend with the necessary status and prestige to take us. At the appointed time we took a walk in its illustrious location. We headed for the renowned Gezira Palace. It proved to be the very revelation of everything glorious and superb, the gathering point for contest and rivalry, the course for comparison and resemblance, the show ground for all kind of flirtation and dalliance, a haven fit for relaxation and enjoyment, a house for drinking wines and spirits. The Pāshā was duly amazed by the sheer beauty of the place and the decorations on the building. He asked me which wealthy profligate was the owner, and I replied that this was yet another splendid palace about which the earth used to boast to the stars in the sky. People both poor and prosperous emerged from it alike, and, at a mere gesture or signal, regional grandees would be subdued. Its firmament could hurl vengeful darts, while its rivulets could course with blessings. Its counterpane of refinement and luxury was covered in the acme of majesty and honor:

أيام كان بعز الملك متشحا
يختال في روضه الغر البهاليل
أيام كان له نهران فيضهما
للجود والري إسماعيل والنيل
والآن أصبح للآفاق مبتذلاً
كما ترى فهو بالسياح مأهول

فتألم الباشا وتوجع، وحوقل واسترجع، ثمّ تنفس الصعداء، وقال: لقد ضلّ من حسب نفسه من السعداء، فقلت له: لا تقرع سن الآسف النادم، فهذه سنّة في الدهر المتقادم، إذا تألق للمرء طالع سعده، فترقب له حلول الشقاء من بعده: ٣،٢٥

وكم نزل القيل عن منبر
فعاد إلى عنصر في الثرى
وأخرج عن ملكه عارياً
وخلف مملكة بالعرا

وخفض عليك فالدول دائلة، وسعادة الحياة خيالات باطلة.

وبينا نحن كذلك إذ مرّت بنا مركبة معلمة، تجرها الجياد المطهمة، فأشار راكبها بالسلام علينا، وأمر السائق أن يميل بها إلينا، وكانت لي به علاقة معرفة وصحبة، بل رابطة مودة ومحبة، وأعرف أنه صاحب مقام مفضل، في كل نديّ ومحفل، فصافح وسلّم، ثمّ شدّ على يدي وتبسّم، وقال: ما جاء بك إلى هذه المواطن، إلا التماس المغامز والمطاعن، فقلت له: لا، بل أنت الضالة التي كنت أنشدها، والسيارة التي جئت أرصدها، وأخبرته بالغرض المطلوب، من استصحابه لزيارة النادي أو «الكلوب»، لنقضي حاجة في نفس يعقوب، فقال قد أدركت رغبتك، وأجبت طلبتك، وسأكون لكما مساعداً ومرشداً في زيارتكما لذلك المنتدى، فهلما فاركبا معي نتنزه ونتجول، ريثما يتصرم النهار ويتحول، فبادرنا بالموافقة على هذه المرافقة. ٤،٢٥

Times there were when it was bedecked in royal pomp;
In its gardens strutted would-be clowns.
Days when its twin rivers bestowed both water and generosity:
Ismāʿīl and the Nile.
But now it is open for the world's masses,
As you see, it is populated by tourists.

25.3 The Pāshā groaned in despair, made his complaint to God, then gave a deep sigh. "Whoever reckons himself happy," he declared, "is mistaken." "Don't gnash your teeth in regret," I replied. "This is one of destiny's laws in its inexorable forward path. Mankind may well experience good fortune on occasion, but thereafter misery will be waiting:

How often has a prince descended from a rostrum
and once again become part of the earth.
Removed naked from his throne,
he has left behind a kingdom laid bare.[200]

"So calm down! Dynasties fade away, and all human happiness is mere futile fancy!"

25.4 While we were talking, a marked carriage passed by, pulled by a set of beautiful steeds. The owner waved at us and told his coachman to come over to us. It was someone whom I knew well, a good friend for whom I had great affection. I was aware that he was highly regarded and was a member of several clubs and gatherings. He greeted me and shook my hand. "What has brought you here?" he asked. "Are you looking for dubious haunts and dives?" "No," I replied, "not at all! You're actually the very person we need and the conveyance that I've come here to look for." I then told him about our quest for someone to accompany us on a visit to this "club" so we could fulfill our secret plan. "I understand your wishes," he replied, "and I'll be glad to do it. I'll serve as both helper and guide for this visit to the club. Come on up and sit with me; we'll go for a ride till the sun goes down." With that we hurried to respond to his invitation.

٥.٢٥ ولمّا توارت الشمس بالحجاب، واسود من الأفق الأهاب انبعثت بنا المركبة تتدفق في سيرها، وتسرع في مسابقة غيرها، فما هي إلا برهة حتى وصلنا ونزلنا، ودخل الصاحب أمامنا ودخلنا، وانتهينا من السلم إلى قاعة فسيحة الجوانب، مزدانة بمصابيح في تلألؤ الكواكب، تدخل منها إلى عدة غرف، مزخرفة بأنواع التحف والطرف، مزدحمة بجملة أناس مختلفي الأجناس، لا بشر عندهم ولا إيناس، وإن كانوا يبهرون الناظر بحسن الزينة واللباس، ويتألقون في حلى الياقوت والألماس، والكل في لغط وضوضاء، كأنهم في سوق بيع وشراء، وقد أخذ صاحبنا يرشدنا عن أجزاء المكان، وأسماء السكان، ويعرّفنا بفلان وفلان، ويقول أمّا هذه الغرفة الأولى فهي غرفة المنادمة والمعاقرة، والثانية غرفة المراهنة والمقامرة، والثالثة غرفة المحاضرة والمسامرة، فبدأنا بالدخول في هذه الغرفة الأخيرة، فوجدنا في وسطها منضدة كبيرة، عليها كتب منشرة، وجرائد مصورة، وحولها قوم من الأمراء تعبث بها أيديهم وأعينهم إلى المرآة، يشاهدون فيها جمال المنظر وحسن المرآة، وألسنتهم منطلقة بالأعجمية، دون اللغة العربية، في ميدان التناضل والتفاخر، والتفاضل والتناظر، فأخذنا مجلسنا منهم ناحية، وأعرنا حديثهم أذنًا واعية، وإذا أحدهم يقول والغضب يقطب في أسرته، لكبير من كبراء أسرته:

٦.٢٥ **الأول** أنا لا ينفع معي اللوم والتفنيد، ولا أقبل منك رأيًا ولا نصيحة، والله يعلم بما وراء ذلك ممّا تكنه الضمائر والسرائر، فإن كنت تريد بي خيرًا فاتركني وشأني، فأنا أدرى بالمصلحة لنفسي، ولا عليك من ذلك الدين الذي تعيرني به، فعندي من الملك والعقار ما يسدده ويوفيه، وكما أنني لا أتداخل في شؤونك، فليس لك أن تشاركني في أمري وتكدّر عليّ عيشي، والأولى أن تصرف جملة عنايتك بي إلى إدارة ثروتك فهي أحوج إليها مني قبل أن يأتي عليها أمناؤك ووكلاؤك وأنت في غفلة عنهم، وإني لأفضل إنفاق ثروتي في ما تشتهيه نفسي وتلذه عيني بدل أن أعيش محرومًا وغيري يختلس ثروتي ويكتنزها لأولاده من بعده.

As the sun went down and the horizon darkened, our carriage careened on its way, racing others in the process. In an instant we had arrived and were stepping down. My friend went on ahead of us, and we entered behind him. The stairway led to a spacious hall decorated with a constellation of lights. From there one entered a number of rooms adorned with the most magnificent furnishings and objets d'art. They were crowded with all sorts of people, unsmiling and unfriendly, all of them dressed in dazzlingly beautiful clothes with ruby and diamond ornaments. They kept shouting and yelling as though they were at a bring-and-buy sale. Our friend began to show us round the various parts of the place and telling us the names of people there. After introducing us to X and Y, he proceeded to inform us that the first room was intended for conversation and drinking, the second for betting and gambling, and the third for discussion and conversation. So we started by going into the last of these and noticed a large table in the middle upon which books were spread out. A group of amirs was thumbing through them, their eyes mostly focused on the mirror so that they could enjoy the reflected view. They were talking in a foreign language, not Arabic, all as a way of showing off and looking superior. We took our seats to one side of them and listened attentively. One of them was speaking to a senior member of his family; from the frown on his face, it was clear that he was furious: 25.5

First There's no point in blaming and reprimanding me. I refuse to accept your ideas or advice. God alone is aware of what secret schemes people harbor inside them. If you mean the best for me, then leave me alone! I know how to put things right for myself. That debt you're blaming me for is none of your business. I've enough possessions and property to honor it and pay it back. I don't interfere in your affairs, so why should you meddle in mine and spoil my life? The best thing you can do is to devote your entire attention to organizing your own wealth. Your need is greater than mine; you have to watch carefully in case your trustees and agents start pilfering it without you having the slightest idea. I much prefer to spend my money on things which give me pleasure and delight my eye rather than live in a state of deprivation while others filch and hoard it for their children to use later. 25.6

الثاني أنا لا ألتفت إلى هذا الكلام الفارغ، وإني أنذرك منذ اليوم أنك إذا لم ترجع عن ما أنت فيه وتسلّم إليّ إدارة ثروتك لتسديد ديونك وتصفية حسابك طلبت في الحال توقيع الحجر عليك.

الأول مثلي لا يؤثر عليه هذا التهديد والوعيد، ولست تجد في أعمالي ما تحتج به للحجر، أمّا الدين فهو أمر مستفيض بين الناس، لا يكاد يخلو منه ذو ثروة، والحكومة أول الناس وأكثرهم ديناً، ولئن لم تنتهوا عن السعي وراء الحجر عليّ فأنا أقسم لكم بكل شيء أحبه في العالم أني أتنازل حالاً عن جميع أموالي إلى أحد الأجانب يستثمرها لي ولا ينالكم منها شيء.

الثاني سترى من يكون الغالب منا والفائز فينا.

ثالث والله يا إخواني قدكرهت الغنى والثروة من فضول هؤلاء الأقارب، وقد آليت على نفسي أن لا أبقي منها درهماً واحداً لأحد من بعدي. ٧،٢٥

رابع الحمد لله على ضياع الثروة وانقضاء مشاغلها، وأنا اليوم أبيع ما بقي من الأطيان لأتمتع بثمنها في معرض باريس.

خامس وأنا أسأل الله أن يعجّل بربح القضية التي رفعتها على والدتي قبل حلول أيام المعرض لأكون معك.

الرابع وما يدريك أنها تستمر في المحاكم زمناً طويلاً؟

الخامس أنا لا بدّ أن أتوجه على أي حال إلى المعرض، فإن لم تتم القضية فعندي لأختي أوراق ومراسلات عثرت عليها في هذه الأيام، وقد قدّرت لها قيمة تكفي لسفري، وأخبرتها أنها إذا لم تسرع في نقدي هذا المبلغ طبعت تلك المراسلات ونشرتها، ولا شكّ أنّ طمعها في زوجها يدفعها إلى مداركة الأمر واشترائها مني.

سادس إني لأحسدك على هذه الفرصة النفيسة وأسأل الله أن يوفقني إلى مثلها مع عمّتي

سابع دعونا من هذه الوسائل الضعيفة وتعالوا بنا نجتهد لزيادة المرتبات. ٨،٢٥

SECOND I shall ignore all this inane talk. However, as from today I warn you that, if you don't mend your ways and hand over to me the responsibility for managing your wealth so that your debts can be settled and your affairs put in order, then I shall demand immediately that your legal competence be withdrawn.

FIRST People like myself aren't going to be influenced by such threats. There's nothing about my affairs to justify withdrawal of legal competence. Debt is a widespread phenomenon; hardly any wealthy person is free of it. The government itself is in more debt than most people. I swear to you by everything I love and value that if you don't stop your attempts to prohibit my legal competence I'm going to hand over all my money immediately to some foreigner to invest for me. Then you won't get any of it.

SECOND You'll soon see which of us is going to win.

25.7

THIRD By God, my brothers, the way relatives keep meddling has made me detest my wealth. I've promised myself to leave not a solitary dirham to anyone when I die.

FOURTH Thank God, my wealth's all gone. I don't have to deal with it any more. I'm selling the rest of my lands so that I can enjoy the proceeds at the Paris Exhibition.

FIFTH And I ask God to expedite a profitable verdict in the case I've brought against my mother before the exhibition finishes. Then I'll be able to come with you.

FOURTH Don't you realize that the case will be pending in the courts for ages?

FIFTH I'm going to visit the exhibition at any rate, even though the case may not be over. I have in my possession some letters and papers written by my sister. I've just stumbled across them. I've calculated that they're worth enough money to cover the cost of my journey. I've told her that, if she doesn't pay me that amount at once, I'm going to have these letters printed and published. Her devotion to her husband will undoubtedly force her to deal with the matter and buy them from me.

SIXTH I envy you such a precious opportunity and ask God to give me similar good fortune with my aunt.

25.8

SEVENTH Forget about such feeble expedients. Come on now! Let's try to get a raise in salaries.

السادس ماذا تفيد المرتبات وغاية ما يزيد مرتب الواحد منا خمسمائة أو ألف جنيه في السنة تكون من نصيب خياط أو عطار، ولكن علينا بالسعي في اصطياد ثروة تقوم لكل واحد بما يقضي به علو مقامه ورفعة قدره بين أقرانه.

الثاني لا تفسد فكرك بهذه الأوهام والأحلام فقد نضبت الموارد، وجفت الضروع، ومضت تلك الأوقات التي كانت تأتي لك بالثروة صفواً عفواً بلا تعب ولا نصب، وفاز بها الآباء والأجداد.

الأول لا تذكرنا ناشدتك الرحم بسيرة الآباء والأجداد ولا تقل أنهم فازوا بحيازة الأموال وبلوغ الغنى، فلقد قنعوا بالقليل، ورضوا بالدون، وظنوا أنهم جمعوا الكثير ونالوا العظيم، فما أقل فطنتهم وأصغر همتهم وأكبر غفلتهم، ويعلم الله أننا لو كنا مكانهم في زمنهم لأريناهم كيف تجمع الأموال وتقتنى الكنوز وماذا تقول في أحلام قوم كانت رقاب المصريين وأموالهم بين أيديهم طوع الشارة من إشاراتهم ولفتة من لفتاتهم، ثم هم يتركون لهم بعد ذلك هذه الملايين من الأفدنة يتمتعون بها اليوم دوننا، ومن كان يتصور منهم في أيامهم أنّ عمد الفلاحين الذين لا يعرفون ما الحياة الدنيا وما هو المال وما منفعته يصبحون أغنى من أبنائهم، أليس ذلك من تفريط السلف وبؤس الخلف ومن العار عليهم والخذلان لنا.

ثامن (وهو ينظر إلينا) إياك أن يجري لسانك بسوء في ذكر المصريين واحذر أن تعوده نفسك فإنه غير لائق بنا الآن.

الأول ولم ذلك حفظك الله، وماذا لقينا من المصريين من الجميل حتى نذكره لهم ويجري لساننا فيه من أجله بخير؟ ولكن لعلك تريد أنت أيضاً لأختك مصريا فلاحا يشرفك بالمصاهرة. ٩،٢٥

الثامن لا وإنما سمعت غير مرة من أكبرنا سناً حسن السياسة ووجه المصلحة لنا يلجئنا إلى التظاهر بالتودد للمصريين وإظهار الانعطاف نحوهم ليتعلقوا بأذيالنا وتنطلق ألسنتهم بشكرنا وحمدنا، فإذ تسامع الأجانب بذلك اضطروا إلى اعتبارنا واحترامنا،

Sixth What's the point of that? The biggest salary raise would only be five hundred or a thousand pounds a year. A mere tailor or carriage merchant makes that much profit. However, we have to do all we possibly can to grab enough wealth so that each of us can maintain himself in a style appropriate to his exalted status and his prestige among his peers.

Second Don't waste mental energy on such fanciful dreams. The wells have all seeped away and the udders are dry. Gone are the days when wealth would flow in without any effort or difficulty. Our ancestors and forefathers got hold of it for us.

First I beg you, for mercy's sake, don't bring up our forefathers' conduct or claim that they managed to amass money and riches. They were content with trifling, paltry sums. They thought they had collected a huge amount of money. But just consider how small their ambition was and how enormous their folly! God knows, if we'd been in their shoes in those days, we'd have shown them how money should be collected and treasures stored away. What can you say about the dreams of people who had the Egyptians and their money at their command, complying with any order or gesture they made, but then left millions of acres for the Egyptians to enjoy today to our detriment? Would any of our ancestors have imagined that peasant *'umdas*, people who in their days had no idea of what life in this world was about and what money was useful for, would now be even richer than their own children? That was gross negligence on our ancestors' part, condemning their descendants to a miserable existence. Their fault, our loss.

Eighth (*looking at us*) You should avoid malicious talk when talking about Egyptians. Don't make a habit of it. These days it isn't an appropriate thing for us to do.

25.9

First May God protect you, why should that be so? What good have Egyptians ever done for us that we need to mention them charitably? But then, maybe you too want an Egyptian peasant to marry your sister so that you can have the honor of being related to him.

Eighth No. But I've heard the eldest of our group say more than once that shrewd politics and our own interests dictate that we need to make a show of affection and sympathy toward Egyptians. They'll cling to our coattails and shower us with praise and gratitude. Then, if the foreigners get to hear about it, they'll be forced to respect our status. And you all know what such respect implies for us when it comes to finding ways to benefit from their lofty

وأنتم تعلمون ما وراء احترام الأجانب لنا من طرق الانتفاع بجاههم في هذه الأزمان التي لا تنبع فيها موارد الحكومة إلا من بين أيديهم.

الرابع أنا لا يتّسع عقلي لمثل هذه السياسة العميقة، ولا صدري لإظهار التودد والانعطاف كذبًا وزورًا للمصريين، وما أخالف طبعي في هذا الباب، بل أميل به نحو الأجانب فهم أحق بالتودد والمحبة، وأولى بالولاء والصداقة، وأجدر بالثناء والمديح، وجميع المصريين في عيني لا يساوون قلامة ظفر من أجنبي ولولا أبوك وأبوه لما قعدت بنا الحال ولما احتجنا للتنازل إلى هذه الدنايا فهما اللذان نهبا أموالنا وبدّدا ثروتنا.

الخامس أنا لا أحب أن يتشعب بنا الكلام إلى سيرة الآباء خشية تحريك ما في القلوب من الضغائن والأحقاد، وليس منا من يكاد يملك نفسه ولا يغيب عنكم ما عسى أن يجره اتساع الكلام من المكروه. ١٠،٢٥

أجنبي (داخل يقول للأوّل) لقد جئت لمولاي الأمير بأنفس اختراع في نهاية القرن، ودونك الصورة فانظرها وتأمّل في أجزائها تجدها تدهش الرائي إتقانًا وإبداعًا، وهذا شكلها وهي في الورق، فما بالك بحسن هيئتها وهي تجري في الطرق، وقد شهد لها كل من رآها بأنه لم يشاهد مركبة كهربائية مثلها إلى اليوم، وناهيك أنّ المعمل لم يصنع من هذا الطرز إلا اثنتين، واحدة أخذها البرنس هو هلوهنستين من أكبر أمراء ألمانيا، وهذه الثانية لك يا مولاي الأمير، وقد سعى أخوك ورائي سعيًا طويلًا ليلحظ الصورة بعينيه فضننت عليه بها لعلمي أنه يريد المبادرة إلى اقتنائها دونك ويفخر بها عليك فلم أبلغه أمنيته وفضلتك عليه تفضيلًا.

الأول أنا أعلم حسن عنايتك بي وأشكرك عليها، إنما أرجوك التعجيل بإحضار المركبة فقد أعجبتني جدًا وأخبرني في أيّ ميعاد يكون حضورها. ١١،٢٥

الأجنبي مسافة الطريق.

الأول أرجوك أيضًا أن تقصّر المسافة بإرسال تلغراف مكان الخطاب.

status, especially in these times when government revenues only come from their hands.

FOURTH My mind cannot cope with such subtle politics. I don't relish the thought of showing love and affection to these Egyptians, even for fraudulent purposes. In that regard I'm not going to go against my natural instincts. I'm more inclined toward the foreigners. They're much more deserving of our affection, loyalty, and friendship, and indeed of our praise and commendation as well. All Egyptians put together are not worth the nail-clippings of a single foreigner. If it weren't for your father and his, we wouldn't be in this state in the first place and wouldn't need to lower ourselves like this. They're the ones who stole our money and wasted our inheritance.

FIFTH I'd rather not start a quarrel by discussing our parents. I'm afraid it might arouse deep-seated resentments or malice. We can all barely control ourselves, and you know full well the harm which will be done if the conversation on this topic goes any further. 25.10

FOREIGNER (*entering and speaking to the first Amir*) I've brought your Highness the most precious invention of the end of this century. Take a good look at this picture and examine its different parts. For originality and sheer perfection it amazes the human eye. This is just a drawing; imagine how fantastic it looks going along the streets. Everyone who has looked at it agrees that to date they've never seen an electric carriage like it. Suffice it to say that the factory only produced two of this type; the German Prince of Hohelohenstein, a major prince in Germany, has taken one, and this second one is for you, Your Highness. His Highness your brother has been trying for ages behind my back to get a glimpse of this picture, but I've kept it from him as I know he wants to pre-empt you by buying it, and brag about it at your expense. I haven't granted him his wish, because I much prefer your Highness to him.

FIRST I'm well aware of the attention you've been paying to my affairs, and I thank you for it. My only request is that you hurry up and bring this carriage. I like the picture very much. Tell me, how soon can you get it? 25.11

FOREIGNER Only the time it takes to cover the street.

FIRST The best plan is for you to send a telegram rather than a letter.

الأجنبي سمعاً وطاعة، وهذه ورقة الثمن ألتمس منك تكليف الخاطر الشريف بإمضائها.

الأول ها هي الورقة ممضاة.

الأجنبي يتشكر وينحني راكعًا ثم يخرج بعد وضع الورقة في جيبه ويقول لنفسه، انتهينا من هذا فلنذهب لنبيع الثانية لأخيه.

الأول (مناديًا الأجنبي) عفواً وسماحًا يا عزيزي، قل لي بالله عن مقدار الثمن على التدقيق فقد نسيته.

الأجنبي العفو منك يا مولاي الأمير، المبلغ لا يبلغ إلا ستة آلاف فرنك وخمسمائة وستة وثلاثين فرنكا.

الأول أطلب منك خدمة لي، وهي أن تذهب إلى أخي وتخبره بأني اشتريتها بأربعة عشر ألف فرنك وأنه لا يوجد غيرها في معملها.

الأجنبي على العين والرأس وأنا دائماً في خدمة مولاي الأمير، ولقد كنت نازلًا على هذه النية قبل أن تكاشفني بغرضك، وإنما سأقول له أنك اشتريتها بثلاثة عشر ألف وسبعمائة واثنين وأربعين فرنكا ليكون ذلك على التحقيق.

الأول لك الله ما أدق فكرك وألطف حيلتك.

الأجنبي يسلم وينصرف.

الأول (لإخوانه) أنا على يقين من أنّ أخي يجنّ جنونه حين يبلغه هذا الخبر فيسعى في اقتراض مبلغ جديد لأجل أن يشتري مثل هذه المركبة، وهذه عادته تعلمونها، مازال يدأب في تقليدي في كل أمرحتى انتهى به الحال إلى بيع أملاكه جميعها. ١٢،٢٥

الثالث وماذا يعمل المسكين بعد ذلك؟

الرابع ما بقي له إلا أن يعيش من المرتب.

الثالث ألم أقل لكم إنه ليس لنا في آخر أمرنا إلا هذا المرتب، فهو وحده الكفيل بقوام حياتنا، ولا وجه لنا نقصده إلا بالسعي في زيادته فهلموا نعقد على ذلك اتفاقًا.

FOREIGNER Hearing is obeying. Here's the bill. Would you be so good as to bother yourself by signing it?

FIRST There's my signature.

(*The Foreigner thanks him and bows low. He then exits with the bill in his pocket. "That's it with this one," he tells himself, "now let's go and sell it to his brother."*)

FIRST (*yelling to the Foreigner*) I'm sorry, my dear Sir! Would you tell me the exact cost. I've forgotten.

FOREIGNER Excuse me, Your Highness! The cost is a mere six thousand five hundred and thirty-six francs.

FIRST I'd ask you to do me a service. Go to see my brother and tell him that I've bought it for fourteen thousand francs. Tell him too that there are no other models from this company.

FOREIGNER As you say, Sir! I'm always at your service, Your Highness. In fact I was already thinking along those lines before you informed me of your own intentions. I'll tell him that you've purchased it for thirteen thousand seven hundred and forty-two francs—to be precise.

FIRST What a clever idea! How subtle you are!

(*With that, the Foreigner says his farewells and leaves.*)

25.12 FIRST (*to his brothers*) I'm sure my brother will throw a fit when he hears this news. He'll try to borrow yet more money to buy a carriage like this one. As you all know of old, he usually copies me in every way he can. Things are now so bad that he has to sell all his possessions.

THIRD What'll the poor chap do then?

FOURTH He'll have to survive on his salary alone.

THIRD Didn't I just tell you that, when things get really bad, that salary is all we have left? It's all we have to live on. I can think of no better idea than trying to get it increased. Come on, let's agree on that amongst ourselves.

الخامس أما سمعت أنّ الارتكان على المرتبات من ضعف التدبير وقلة الحيلة.

الثالث أرشدنا هداك الله إلى طريق للثروة خلافه.

الأول أنا أرى طريقها في المضاربات.

الرابع وأنا أرى طريقها في تأجير أسمائنا للشركات.

الخامس وأنا أرى طريقها في خدمة السفارات.

السابع وأنا أرى طريقها في تزوج اليهوديات.

الثامن وأنا أرى طريقها في هذه الساعة أن نقوم إلى غرفة القمار.

الجميع أحسنت أحسنت فقوموا بنا إليها.

١٣،٢٥ قال عيسى بن هشام: فقاموا وقمنا على آثارهم نشاهد بقية أفعالهم، فدخلوا أوّلاً إلى غرفة المدام فتعاطوا منها ما شاؤوا، وانبرى أحدهم هناك لآخر يراهنه أيهما يشرب أكثر من صاحبه ووقف بجانبهما جماعة من الأجانب يحثونهما على المراهنة جهراً ويضحكون عليهما سراً، ورأينا اثنين يتباهيان ويتفاخران بقوة الجسم، فيقول أحدهما إني أحمل هذه المائدة بيد واحدة، ويقول الآخر وأنا أضغط بإصبعي على هذا الريال فأثنيه وأقاموا على هذا المنوال زمناً يتسابقون في النخخة والمبالغة، ثمّ ينتهي بينهم الأمر دائماً إلى الرهان حتى تخيلنا أنّ كلا منهم لا يأكل طعامه إلا مراهناً ثمّ انتهى بهم الحديث إلى وجوه متعددة، فمنهم من يقول إنه وثب مرة من فوق الناقة إلى الأرض فنزل على رجل واحدة، ومنهم من يقول إنه يكلم حصانه فيفهم عنه كلامه، وآخر يقول إنّ خليلته أقسمت له أنها لم تر في باريس راقصاً مثله، ثمّ دخلوا يتساندون إلى غرفة القمار، فما مضت عليهم برهة في لعبهم إلا وجرى بينهم ما يجري في مجلس القمار من فراغ الجيب واقتراض بعضهم من بعض، فإذا امتنع الرابح منهم على القرض تحوّل المفلس إلى خدم المكان يطلب منهم الإسعاف، ثمّ تولّد بعد ذلك الخصام واشتدّ النزاع حتى كاد يفضي بهم إلى ما لا تحمد عقباه.

FIFTH Haven't you heard that relying on one's salary suggests feeble intellect and little ingenuity?

THIRD Well then, God give you guidance, pray suggest some other way of acquiring wealth.

FIRST I see it in speculation.

FOURTH I see it in hiring out our names to companies.

FIFTH I see it in serving embassies.

SEVENTH My idea is marrying Jewesses.

EIGHTH I think our best plan at this point is to go to the gaming room.

EVERYONE What a great idea! Let's go!

ʿĪsā ibn Hishām said: They all got up, and we followed them to watch what they did next. They went into the wine room and had as many glasses of wine as they wanted. One of them started betting his friend that he could drink more than his colleague. A group of foreigners was standing next to them, encouraging them to take the bet and laughing at them behind their backs. We watched as two of them boasted about who was stronger: one claimed he could lift the table with one hand, while the other bragged that he could bend a riyal piece double between his fingers. They spent quite a while in this fashion, boasting and showing off. Whatever the case, things always finished up with bets being made; we imagined that none of them ever ate unless it was for a bet. Conversation now took a number of turns. One of them stated that he had leapt from the back of a camel and landed on one foot. Another insisted that he spoke to his stallion, and it understood him. Still another maintained that his girlfriend had sworn that she'd not seen anyone in Paris who danced as well as he did. Leaning heavily on each other, they now went into the gambling room. It was not long before pockets were emptied and money was borrowed. If the successful player refused to grant a loan, the bankrupt player would turn to the waiters and ask them for help. Soon afterwards they started arguing and quarreling among themselves in a way which we feared could only bring dire consequences. 25.13

فأسرعنا إلى طريق النجاة بالخروج، فخرج الباشا يضحك القهقهاء، فقلت له: أين ١٤،٢٥ سكب الدمع وتنفس الصعداء؟ فقال: جل الخطاب عن الحزن والبكاء، وهل نسيت ما رويته لي عن حكيم الشعراء؟:

هذي الحياة رواية لمشخص
فالليل ستر والنهار الملعب.

We hurried out in order to make a safe exit. The Pāshā followed me guffawing with laughter. "Where are your floods of tears and heavy sighs?" I asked him. "Fate has overruled grief or tears," he replied. "Have you forgotten the line of the wise poet that you've recited for me: 25.14

This life is an actor's drama;
night is a curtain, and day is a stage."

Notes

1 This article and the three that follow it (0.2–0.4) are narrated by ʿĪsā ibn Hishām, a name that Muḥammad al-Muwayliḥī revived from the famous collection of picaresque narratives—*maqāmāt*—composed in the tenth century by Badīʿ al-Zamān al-Hamadhānī (d. 398/1007). They were all published in the al-Muwayliḥī newspaper *Miṣbāḥ al-sharq* in the weeks immediately before their author began to publish the lengthy series of articles entitled *Fatrah min al-Zaman* that, in edited form, was later to become the book *Ḥadīth ʿĪsā ibn Hishām* (1907). In such a context, two things are significant: firstly, that these four articles would appear to constitute some kind of "dry run" for the series that is to follow; and secondly, that these initial articles address the extremely topical subject of the war in the Sudan in 1898, something however that Muḥammad al-Muwayliḥī completely excluded from the eventual text of *Ḥadīth ʿĪsā ibn Hishām.*

2 In these articles and all those to follow, Muḥammad al-Muwayliḥī replicates the prosimetric tradition of the pre-modern *maqāmah* genre by regularly inserting lines of poetry into his narrative. While he will often provide the name of the poet whom he is citing, sometimes he will not do so. For this edition, every effort has been made to identify the original authors of the poetry, but given the paucity of referential resources on the topic, that has sometimes proved impossible. The poet in this case is Muḥammad ibn Wuhayb (a Shiʿi poet from Basra, dates unknown); see Abū l-Faraj al-Iṣfahānī, *Kitāb al-Aghānī*, 75.

3 The title "Sirdar" was given to the commanding officer of the British armed forces in Egypt. In 1898 it was Lord Kitchener, and he was succeeded in 1898 by Sir Reginald Wingate.

4 Latin for "I came, I saw, I conquered."

5 The Arabic text here invokes the Abjad numerical system, whereby the symbols of the Arabic alphabet are assigned numerical value. By adding up the values of the symbols in this line of poetry, the number 1316 is reached.

6 This refers to Parliamentary Papers. See e.g., Marlowe, *Cromer in Egypt*, 322.

7 These lines by an unknown poet are quoted anonymously in, among other sources, *al-Maḥāsin wa-l-aḍdād* by (ps.-[?]al-Jāḥiẓ, 118) and in *ʿUyūn al-akhbār* (Ibn Qutaybah, 1:164).

8 The translation attempts to replicate the rhyming patterns of the original Arabic.

9 The minister's deficient knowledge of geography is illustrated here by his reference to the old Aswān Dam constructed in 1902. Fashoda, the site of a famous confrontation of British and French forces in 1898, is far to the South in Central Sudan.

10 In the Arabic text, al-Muwayliḥī inserts a parenthesis explaining that the surname of the French commander Jean-Baptiste Marchand means "merchant" in French.

11 Al-Muwayliḥī includes in the Arabic text a transliteration into Arabic of the French phrase, "marchand d'esclaves" (slave trader) before providing a translation.

12 Here again al-Muwayliḥī is playing on the minister's ignorance by punning on the surname of the French commander, Le Marquis Christian de Bonchamps—"bonchamps" meaning "good fields."

13 Yet again, al-Muwayliḥī is citing the basic meanings of these three proper names.

14 Since the Arabic word *fakhr* means "pride," there's a pun here.

15 This end structure mocks the Ottoman convention of bringing panegyrics to closure.

16 Abū Tammām, *Dīwān Abī Tammām*, 4:102.

17 Al-Muwayliḥī appears to have his particulars confused here. It is the Umayyad Caliph Yazīd who enters Damascus on a donkey. Furthermore, there is no caliph named "Abū Sufyān ibn Hishām." However, this might be a reference to the Umayyad Caliph Marwān II (r. 127–32/744–50) who was nicknamed *al-ḥimār* ("the donkey"), in which case his opponent in civil war was Sulaymān ibn Hishām.

18 From a line of poetry by Abū Nuwās. See *Dīwān*, ed. Ewald Wagner, 3:2–7.

19 Al-Maʿarrī, *Siqṭ al-zand* (1869), 1:209; (1948), 974.

20 Ibid. (1869), 2:8; (1948), 3:1021.

21 Al-Maʿarrī, *Al-Luzūmiyyāt*, 1:123.

22 The story is described in the Qur'an: Q Aʿrāf 7:138ff.

23 A well-known proverb. See Aḥmad Taymūr, *Al-Amthāl al-ʿāmmiyyah*, 320.

24 From Q Kahf 18:67–68, the passage in which Moses's encounter with al-Khiḍr is described.

25 This term originally meant "archer," but was also applied during the Ottoman period to military police and embassy guards.

26 Al-Maʿarrī; *Al-Luzūmiyyāt*, 1:416.

27 A line quoted anonymously in *al-Ḥujjāb*, which appears in al-Jāḥiẓ's *Rasā'il*, 2:50; attributed to an *aʿrābī* in Ibn Ḥamdūn, *Tadhkirah*, 8:204.

28 According to a tradition attributed to the Prophet, "a Qurayshī is worth two men of any other tribe." See W. Montgomery Watt, *Muhammad at Mecca* (London: Oxford University Press, 1953), 153.

29 Moses's words to Al-Khidr: Q Kahf 18:73.

30 The Pāshā's reaction is the result of a pun on the two possible meanings of the Arabic verb *S-B-Q*: "to precede" and "to race," from which come both translations: "precedents" and "racing steeds."

31 There is yet another pun here, this time on the verbal root *Sh-H-D*. The Pāshā interprets "shahādah" (the word ʿĪsā uses for "certificate") to mean "martyrdom." In pre-modern times, "shahādah" meant "martyrdom," but in modern times, as ʿĪsā later explains, it has also come to be used to mean "certificate" or "degree."

32 *ʿUmdah*: the provincial village headman, a figure who is later to become a major character in this sequence of episodes.

33 While the original episode continues without a break here, this point marks the beginning of a new chapter in the text of *Ḥadīth ʿĪsā ibn Hishām*. The title "Al-Muḥāmī al-ahlī" ("The People's Court Lawyer") was added to the third edition of the book (1923).

34 Al-Maʿarrī, *Al-Luzūmiyyāt*, 1:224.

35 Lines of poetry by al-Nābighah al-Dhubyānī, from his poem *A-min āli Mayyata rāʾiḥun aw mughtadī*. See e.g., Ahlwardt, *The Diwans of the Six Ancient Arabic Poets*, 10.

36 *Humāyūn*: the Persian word meaning "empire," and with the adjectival ending here, "imperial" (Ottoman).

37 A reference to the al-Muwayliḥī newspaper in which these episodes were being published.

38 Joseph's words in Q Yūsuf 12:33.

39 A line of poetry by Umayya ibn Abī l-Ṣalt. See Al-Jāḥiẓ, *Kitāb al-Ḥayawān*, 49.

40 Al-Maʿarrī; *Al-Luzūmiyyāt*, 2:403.

41 A line of poetry allegedly by a poet named ʿAbd Allāh ibn al-Mubārak ibn Wāḍiḥ (d. 181/797), a merchant, traveler, *mujāhid*, and *muḥaddith*, from Khurāsān.

42 Q Raʿd 13:17.

43 Q Ḥijr 15:74 and Hūd 11:82.

44 From the Q Zukhruf 43:32.

45 Al-Maʿarrī, *Siqṭ al-Zand* (1869), 203; (1948), 3:955.

46 Abū Tammām, *Dīwān Abī Tammām*, 1:161.

47 A line of poetry by al-Mutanabbī (*Dīwān*, 636); the standard version is *fa-mā l-ḥadāthatu min ḥilmin . . . qad yūjadu l-ḥilmu . . . .*

48 A line of poetry by al-Ḥuṭayʾah; cited in *Kitāb Sībawayh*, 1:443.

49 Al-Mutanabbī, *Dīwān* (Beirut: 1882), 245.

50 Al-Buḥturī, *Dīwān*, 3:1980. The *Dīwān* reads *muẓlimu* instead of *aqtamu*.

51 There is some disagreement over the authorship of these lines. They are attributed to the caliph al-Muʿtamid in al-Shābushtī, *Diyārāt*, ed. ʿAwwād (101); to "al-ʿAbbās" in al-Ḥuṣrī,

Zahr al-ādāb (repr. Beirut: 1972), 827, meaning Ibn al-Muʿtazz; the lines are in his *Dīwān*, ed. Muḥammad Badīʿ Sharīf, 2:375. But quoting the lines in his *Jamʿ al-jawāhir*, ed. al-Bijāwī (Beirut: 1987), 157, al-Ḥuṣrī says: *qad qāla al-Muʿtamid . . . aw qīla ʿalā lisāni-hi.*

52 No source for this line of poetry has been identified.

53 This point marks the beginning of a new chapter in *Ḥadīth ʿĪsā ibn Hishām*: "Maḥkamat al-Isti'nāf" ("The Court of Appeal").

54 This quarter is now downtown Cairo, with its broad streets and squares, as opposed to the older Fatimid city.

55 Al-Mutanabbī, *Dīwān* (1898), 281.

56 Ibid., 138.

57 A line of poetry by Abū Muḥammad al-Khāzin (poet of Isfahan and librarian to al-Ṣāḥib ibn ʿAbbād), in al-Thaʿālibī's *Yatīmah* (Cairo: 1947), 3:191.

58 In *Ḥadīth ʿĪsā ibn Hishām* this episode still forms part of the "Court of Appeal" chapter.

59 Al-Mutanabbī, *Dīwān* (1898), 381.

60 A reference to an injunction in the Q Tawbah 9:58ff.

61 These lines are attributed to "an Arab from the Asad tribe": see Al-Jāḥiẓ, *Kitāb al-Ḥayawān*, 3:86.

62 Line of poetry by Abū Firās al-Ḥamdānī, *Dīwān* (Leiden: 1895), 151.

63 This point marks the beginning of a new chapter in *Ḥadīth ʿĪsā ibn Hishām*: "Al-Waqf" ("The Endowment").

64 ʿAzzah's lover was the famous poet, Bashshār ibn Burd, while Nawār's lover (and husband) was the poet, al-Farazdaq. The line itself comes from *Dīwān Abī Tammām* (1905), 25; (1951–65), 164.

65 A line of poetry by Abū Tammām, *Dīwān Abī Tammām* (1905), 352; (1952–65), 4:42.

66 A famous line of poetry by al-Maʿarrī; see *Al-Luzūmiyyāt*, 63.

67 This point marks the beginning of a new chapter in *Ḥadīth ʿĪsā ibn Hishām*: "Abnā' al-kubarā'" ("Sons of Great Men").

68 These names all refer to consonants in the Arabic alphabet that are often mispronounced by non-native speakers.

69 *Bashibozuk* is a Turkish word used to describe an irregular soldier, a civilian serving in the military. In this context it obviously conveys pejorative significance.

70 This point marks the beginning of a new chapter in *Ḥadīth ʿĪsā ibn Hishām*: "Kubarā' min al-ʿAṣr al-māḍī" ("Great Men of the Past").

71 Al-Maʿarrī, *Al-Luzūmiyyāt*, 2:258.

72 On the night when the Prophet Muḥammad left Mecca in secret and traveled to Medina, his cousin ʿAlī stayed behind in Mecca and only traveled to Medina three days later.

73 This latter passage, describing Rāghib Pāshā's negative experiences with the Khedive Ismāʿīl, was omitted from the text of the fourth edition of *Ḥadīth ʿĪsā ibn Hishām*.

74 *Fulūs* means "cash," and *kurbāj* means "whip."

75 The entire section of this speech describing Muḥammad ʿAlī's conversations with the would-be governor of the Sudan and with the military reserve officers was omitted from the text of the fourth edition.

76 A line of poetry by Ibn Hāniʾ al-Andalusī, *Dīwān* (Dār Ṣādir), 131; in a *madīḥ* beginning *Taqūlu Banū l-ʿAbbāsi: hal futiḥat Miṣru? Fa-qul li-Banī l-ʿAbbāsi: qad quḍiya l-amrū.*

77 The function of the *muzawwir* was to show visitors round the tomb of the Prophet in Medina. Burckhardt, *Travels in Arabia*, 2:138; Burton, *Personal Narrative of a Pilgrimage*, 1:305.

78 The term *Ghawth*, meaning "aid," or "refuge," refers to the highest ranking saint (*walī*) in Islamic mysticism.

79 Q Zalzalah 99:7.

80 Al-Maʿarrī, *Al-Luzūmiyyāt*, 285.

81 "Abū Turāb" is ʿAlī ibn Abī Ṭālib's *kunyah*, or name theoretically referring to the bearer's firstborn. In this case, it is a name allegedly given to ʿAlī by the Prophet.

82 This point marks the beginning of a new chapter in *Ḥadīth ʿĪsā ibn Hishām*: "Al-Muḥāmī al-Sharʿī" ("The Shariah Court Lawyer").

83 In "Ḥadīth ʿĪsā ibn Hishām," 1018, Zakī Mubārak writes: "The division between wearers of the turban and tarboosh in al-Muwayliḥī's time was an object of seething dissension. The tarboosh wearers [those civil servants who had often received a modern and/or European education] considered themselves as the vanguard of the modern generation, while the turban wearers [the more traditionally minded shaykhs] regarded themselves as the guardians of the true religion."

84 Al-Maʿarrī, *Al-Luzūmiyyāt*, 81.

85 Al-Maʿarrī, *Al-Luzūmiyyāt*, 1:71.

86 Q Anʿām 6:53.

87 Lines attributed to Suwayd ibn al-Ṣāmit; see al-Maʿarrī, *The Epistle of Forgiveness* (New York: NYUP, 2013), 71.

88 The second hemistich is found in a line by Abū l-Walīd al-Ḥimyarī, see his *al-Badīʿ fī waṣf al-rabīʿ*, ed. Pérès, 109, beginning *talawwunan wa-manẓaran*. Perhaps a misquotation by al-Muwayliḥī, or a coincidence.

89 This point marks the beginning of a new chapter in *Ḥadīth ʿĪsā ibn Hishām*: "Al-Daftarkhānah al-Sharʿiyyah" ("The Records Office of the Shariah Court"). The office was situated below the main entrance to the Citadel. The approach to the building is described in detail in J. Deny's *Sommaire des archives turques du Caire*, 19.

90 Both al-Muwayliḥīs were apparently members of the Freemasons lodge run by Jamāl al-dīn al-Afghānī; Landau, *Parliaments and Parties in Egypt*, 96.

91 Al-Maʿarrī, *Siqṭ al-Zand* (1869), 61; (1948), 1:263.

92 Abū Tammām, *Dīwān Abī Tammām*, 4:311.

93 Lines of poetry by Ibn Hāni' al-Andalusī; see al-Rikābī, *Fī l-Adab al-Andalusī*, 152.

94 *Dhimmīs*: non-Muslim inhabitants of Islamic countries, so called because the Islamic community offered them a *dhimmah* (contract of hospitality and protection) provided that they acknowledged the dominance of Islam and paid the poll tax (*jizyah*).

95 The Clerk now proceeds to list all the locations in Cairo where these particular courts were to be found. Many of them still exist, but others have disappeared over time.

96 This point marks the beginning of a new chapter in *Ḥadīth ʿĪsā ibn Hishām*: "Al-Maḥkamah al-Sharʿiyyah" ("The Shariah Court"). This system of courts was the topic of a series of articles in *Miṣbāḥ al-sharq*, no. 27, October 20, 1898; and 81ff., November 16, 1899 et seq.

97 This line is often quoted anonymously, but is attributed to Majnūn Laylā by Abū l-Faraj al-Iṣfahānī in *Kitāb al-Aghānī*, 2:93.

98 The names of two palaces, often invoked in Arabic literature as symbols of former worldly glories and authority.

99 The first ʿUmar was the second caliph, succeeding Abū Bakr in 13/634; the second was one of the Umayyad caliphs (r. 98–101/717–20), renowned for his piety and frugality.

100 In Arabic the words representing these concepts have very similar consonantal patterns.

101 Al-Maʿarrī, *Siqṭ al-Zand*, (1869), 2: 223; (1948), 2066.

102 The author here is not only pointing out the inappropriateness of a Shariah Court official taking such inordinate interest in works of this category, but also parodying the flowery language which was used by Arab writers in order that their books should have titles, the two halves of which rhymed with each other.

103 No source for this line of poetry has been identified.

104 A line of poetry by Abū Tammām, *Dīwān Abī Tammām* (1905), 30; (1951), 186. I am grateful to Professor Geert Jan van Gelder for his assistance in interpreting this (one might say, typically) complex line by this poet.

105 A line of poetry by Ibn Abī ʿUyaynah; see Ibn ʿAbd Rabbihi, *Al-ʿIqd al-farīd*, 5:421.

106 Al-Buḥturī, *Dīwān*, 2:22.

107 Al-Buḥturī, *Dīwān*, 1:36.

108 Al-Maʿarrī, *Siqṭ al-Zand* (1869), 2:51; (1948), 3:1240.

109 A line of poetry attributed to Ḥamdah Bint Ziyād al-Muʾaddib, a Spanish poetess; see al-Rikābī, *Fī l-Adab al-Andalusī*, 99.

110 Literally: "I am a well-known person and a climber of tortuous ways." It is part of a line of poetry by Suhaym ibn Wahb al-Riyāḥī, see "Min Shawārid al-Shawāhid," *Al-Risālah* no. 749 (1947): 1263.

111 This entire article was completely rewritten by the author for publication in the book, *Ḥadīth ʿĪsā ibn Hishām*. In the book's third edition, the title "Al-Ṭibb wa-l-Aṭibbāʾ" ("Medicine and Doctors") is added.

112 While this original episode was published in 1898, Al-Muwayliḥī was to obtain direct information about this department when he became its director in 1910. There is presumably a direct reflection of his sentiments expressed here in the fact that he resigned his position in 1914.

113 Al-Mutanabbī, *Dīwān* (Beirut: 1882), 341. Most sources read *yakhtarimu* instead of *yakhtariqu*.

114 Apart from the first description in this article (until the end of 16.3), the remainder of the episode is totally omitted from the text of *Ḥadīth ʿĪsā ibn Hishām*. Once again, the similarity of its format and topic to those of the initial four articles in this series will be noted. The different chapter in *Ḥadīth ʿĪsā ibn Hishām* was entitled "Al-Ṭāʿūn" ("The Plague")—in the third edition and thereafter.

115 These lines of poetry seem to involve a range of possible sources. They are sometimes attributed to al-Sarī al-Raffāʾ; see Usāmah ibn Munqidh, *al-Badīʿ fī naqd al-shiʿr*, 37, etc. (with *-rabīʿi* instead of *-makāni*), but are apparently not found in the *Dīwān*. The second hemistich of the first line is taken from a line by al-Ḥusayn ibn Muṭayr and is often quoted (e.g., in Iṣfahānī, *al-Aghānī*). The second line is attributed to "al-Muʿarrij al-Nasafī" in al-Thaʿālibī, *Khāṣṣ al-khāṣṣ* (Beirut, n.d., 138) where the reading is *wa-wardun* instead of *wa-durrun*. In al-Thaʿālibī's *Man ghāba ʿanhu l-muṭrib* (ed. Shaʿlān, 30), this line is attributed to al-Muʿawwij al-Raqqī (Abū Bakr Muḥammad ibn al-Ḥasan—reading *wa-durrun*).

116 Lines of poetry by al-Maʿarrī, *al-Luzumiyyat* (a reprint of ed. Amin ʿAbd al-ʿAziz al-Khanji, Cairo: Maktabat al-Khanji, 1924, vol. I, p. 40).

117 This is a reference back to one of the four early articles above (0.2), published in *Miṣbāḥ al-sharq* (September 22, 1898), 23.

118 The term *qadhf* is used for a slanderous accusation of sexual misconduct against someone. Among the punishments for it is the withdrawal of eligibility to testify in court.

I am grateful to Professor Joseph Lowry for this information and for that on Ḥanafī texts on jurisprudence below.

119 Meaning *Al-Durr al-mukhtār*. (See the Glossary for further details.)

120 The Ḥanafī sources cited here are: *Al-Fatāwā al-bazzāziyyah* of Ibn Bazzāz (d. 817/1414) and *Al-Nahr al-fā'iq: sharḥ kanz al-daqā'iq* of ʿUmar Ibn Nujaym (tenth/sixteenth century).

121 The *Kanz* is another source on Ḥanafī jurisprudence by al-Nasafī (d. 710/1310). *Al-Nahr al-fā'iq* a commentary on it (see n. 120).

122 This line of poetry is quoted anonymously in Ibn ʿArabshāh, *ʿAjā'ib al-maqdūr*, where it reads: *yakrahu an yashraba min fiḍḍatin | wa-yasriqu al-fiḍḍata in nāla-hā*.

123 The clash between modernists and conservatives at this time was often expressed as being between the tarboosh-wearing class of Western-educated civil servants, and the turban-wearing class of shaykhs and others educated along traditional Islamic lines.

124 Q Muḥammad 47:7.

125 Al-Saʿd here refers to Saʿd al-Dīn al-Taftazānī (d. 791/1389), the author of a commentary on al-Qazwīnī's (d. 739/1338) *Talkhīṣ Miftāḥ al-ʿulūm*, itself an abridgement of the famous and much cited work on rhetoric by al-Sakkākī (d. 626/1229) entitled *Miftāḥ al-ʿulūm*. The work by al-Anbābī (d. 1896), twice rector of al-Azhar in the nineteenth century, is a further commentary on al-Qazwīnī's abridgement.

126 Q Baqarah 2:195.

127 Q Nisā' 4:59.

128 Q Kahf 18:29; Baqarah 2:256; Qaṣaṣ 28:56; Yūnus 10:108; Isrā' 17:84.

129 Q Yūsuf 12:68.

130 Q Āl ʿImrān 3:27.

131 Al-Mutanabbī, *Dīwān* (1898), 109.

132 Q Yūnus 10:12.

133 Al-Mutanabbī, *Dīwān* (1898), 366.

134 Al-Maʿarrī, *Siqṭ al-Zand* (1869), 1:197; (1948), 2:922.

135 A line of poetry attributed to "an Omani"; see al-Jāḥiẓ, *Kitāb al-Ḥayawān*, 6:219.

136 This description of the plague epidemic in 1791 (with a few minor omissions) is an extract from ʿAbd al-Raḥmān al-Jabartī's account in his *ʿAjā'ib al-āthār fī al-tarājim wa-al-akhbār* (1906), 203; (1965), 4:185.

137 A reference to the *mawāqif*, the places in which all of mankind will have to stand on the Day of Judgment before they are summoned to appear before God in order to hear His judgment on the basis of their deeds on earth.

138 For Muʿallim Ghālī, secretary of Muhammad ʿAlī, see *Mashāḥīr al-sharq* by Jurjī Zaydān [*Tarājim mashāhir al-sharq fī l-qarn al-tāsiʿ ʿashar* in the bibliography] (1910–11), 1:215ff.

139 Another quotation from ʿAbd al-Raḥmān al-Jabartī's account: *ʿAjāʾib al-āthār fī al-tarājim wa-al-akhbār* (1906), 4:187; (1965), 7:218ff.

140 A line of poetry by Abū Nuwās; see *Dīwān Abī Nuwās* (Cairo: 1898), 235.

141 Q Anfāl 8:60.

142 For a reference to this actual incident, see Muḥammad ʿUmar, *Ḥāḍir al-Miṣriyyīn aw sirr taʾakhkhurihim*, 174.

143 *Akalūnī al-barāghīth* ("fleas have eaten me") is cited in works of Arabic grammar as an example of mistaken usage.

144 The bulk of this episode of *Fatrah min al-Zaman* was not included in the text of *Ḥadīth ʿĪsā ibn Hishām*. The initial description was also used in a later chapter of the book, "Qaṣr al-Gīzah wa-al-matḥaf" ("The Giza Palace and the Museum").

145 This is one of several versions of a line by Abū Muḥammad ibn Ruzayq al-Kūfī (Iraq, fourth/tenth century), which in al-Thaʿālibī's *Yatīmah* (2:377), is quoted differently. In Ibn Khallikān's *Wafayāt* (ed. ʿAbbās, 4:46), the line is attributed to Asad ibn Ruzayq (with *raʾaytu al-ʿizza wa-nqaraḍā*). In al-Tanūkhī's *Nishwār* (2:221), the second hemistich is *hādhī al-wisādati kāna al-ʿizzu fa-nqaraḍā*. There are yet other variants. Note that *wa-raʾaytu* (as used here by al-Muwayliḥī) is unmetrical.

146 Al-Maʿarrī, *al-Luzūmiyyāt*, 1:50.

147 This is a reference to an actual incident in which the British sent troops to al-Azhar in order to force them to comply with quarantine regulations. The affair and its aftermath were described in detail in *Miṣbāḥ al-sharq*. See also the reference in n. 143 above.

148 Q Naḥl 16:112.

149 Q Naḥl 16:43.

150 A line of poetry attributed to ʿUlayyah bint al-Mahdī in al-Ḥuṣrī in *Zahr al-ādāb* (44), with different rhyme: *wa-lā yuraḍḍī l-qātilā*.

151 Q Ṣāffāt 37:61.

152 This episode of *Fatrah min al-Zaman* and the one that follows it was subsantially reworked for publication in *Ḥadīth ʿĪsā ibn Hishām* as the chapter "Al-ʿUrs" ("The Wedding"). Not only that, but the reworked chapter was placed later in the ordering of events in the narrative.

153 Al-Maʿarrī, *Al-Luzūmiyyāt*, 2:292.

154 Ibn Hāniʾ al-Andalusī, *Dīwān*, 344 (reading *amīlu*).

155 Q Anbiyāʾ 21:63.

156 Q Aḥzāb 33:53.

157 Unlike the previous episode of *Fatrah min al-Zaman* which was not used in the text of *Ḥadīth ʿĪsā ibn Hishām*, this lengthy discussion of the status of singing in Islam is included (albeit in heavily edited form). What is interesting however is that in the book version of the text, the explicator of the history of the topic is not ʿĪsā ibn Hishām, but rather a "Shaykh" whose views on the interpretation of Islamic texts are clearly more in line with the more liberal views of one of al-Muwayliḥī's colleagues and mentors, Muḥammad ʿAbduh.

158 Anṣār: the people who "helped" the Prophet in his community in al-Madinah (as opposed to the Muhājirūn, those who emigrated with him from Mecca).

159 Recited by the young women (*jawārī*) of Mecca upon the arrival of the Prophet; al-Jāhīẓ, *al-Bayān wa-al-tabyīn* (ed. Hārūn, 4:57). Other sources indicate they recited it on his arrival in Medina.

160 *Kāmil* and *wāfir* are the names of two of the meters noted down by al-Khalīl ibn Aḥmad (d. 175/791), the famous grammarian and prosodist of Basra, as part of his system of prosody. Saḥbān was a famous orator of the pre-Islamic period whose powers gave rise to the expression "more eloquent than Saḥbān." See al-Ziriklī, *Al-Aʿlām*, 3:123.

161 The speech that follows is intended as a parody of the verbiage employed on such occasions.

162 Without the insertion of the word "buffet," the lines of poetry are by Ibn Jad'ān; see Muḥammad ʿAbd al-Munʿim al-Khafājah, *Qiṣṣat al-adab fī l-Ḥijāz fī l-ʿaṣr al-jāhilī* (1958), 491.

163 A line of poetry by Laqīṭ ibn Zurārah (pre-Islamic), see al-Mubarrad, *Kāmil*, ed. Hindāwī, 1:180; also found in a poem by Muḥammad ibn al-Ashʿath, *Aghānī*, 15:60.

164 Al-Maʿarrī: *Siqṭ al-zand* (1869), 1:117; (1948), 2:559.

165 These lines are attributed to a member of the Banū Nashhāl. See Abū Tammām, *Al-Ḥamāsah* (Cairo: Būlāq, 1879), 1:50; airo, 1916, 24. In line 7 of this quotation, the reading *qawl* has been adopted.

166 Al-Maʿarrī, *Siqṭ al-zand* (1869), 40; (1948), 3:1174.

167 Lines by Qays ibn Khatīm; see Abū Tammām, *Al-Ḥamāsah* (Cairo: Būlāq, 1879), 95; (Cairo: 1916), 49.

168 A line of poetry by Ibn al-Rūmī, *Dīwān* 2:806 (where the reading *faqdā* is preferable to the unmetrical *fiqdān*).

169 A line of poetry by Sālim ibn Wābiṣah (d. 125/742); in Abū Tammām's *Ḥamāsah*, see al-Marzūqī, *Sharḥ Dīwān al-Ḥamāsah*, 1143.

170 Al-Mutanabbī, *Dīwān* (1882), 540; (1898), 375.

171 Al-Maʿarrī, *Al-Luzūmiyyāt*, 103.

172 Q Qamar 54:4–5.

173 Al-Maʿarrī, *Siqṭ al-zand* (1869), 1:144; (1948), 2:679ff.

174 This section (22.1–22.19) is one of the episodes/chapters that was omitted from the fourth edition of *Ḥadīth ʿĪsā ibn Hishām* (1927).

175 These initial two sections (22.1 and 22.2) are only to be found in the episodes of *Fatrah min al-Zaman.* The elaborate way in which each of the forthcoming sessions is described was obviously intended to form a vivid contrast with the actual situation that ʿĪsā and the Pāshā encounter in the episodes that now follow.

176 A quotation from a famous poem by Abū Nuwās; see *Dīwān*, ed. Ewald Wagner (1988), 3:2–7.

177 Q Kāfirūn 109:6.

178 A line of poetry quoted anonymously in several sources including al-Qalqashandī, *Ṣubḥ*; according to al-Damirī, *Ḥayāt al-ḥayawān al-kubrā* (Cairo: 1970, 2:90) in a chapter on *ʿanqāʾ mughrib*, often quoted by al-Qāḍī al-Fāḍil. In *Majānī al-adab* by Luwīs Shaykhū (Beirut: 1885, 6:311), attributed to al-Qāḍī al-Fāḍil himself, possibly incorrectly.

179 For a discussion of this story, see Fedwa Malti-Douglas, *Woman's Body, Woman's Word* (Princeton: Princeton University Press, 1991), 84–110.

180 A reference to a work by Aḥmad ibn ʿAbdallāh al-Bakrī al-Baṣrī (fl. ca. 694/1295).

181 Q Raʿd 13:33.

182 A line of poetry by Abū l-Aswad al-Duʾalī, according to ʿAbd al-Qādir al-Baghdādī, *Khizānat al-adab*, ed. Hārūn, 8:567. Anonymously in al-Jāḥiẓ, *Bayān* (4:63) and many other sources. All these sources read *fa-l-qawmu* instead of *fa-l-kullu.*

183 Line of poetry by al-Mutanabbī; see *The Poems of Al-Mutanabbī*, ed. A. J. Arberry (Cambridge: Cambridge University Press, 1967), 53.

184 My translation makes no effort to eradicate the complicated and verbose style of the original.

185 Al-Maʿarrī, *Al-Luzūmiyyāt*, 1:95.

186 Q Ḍuḥā 93:11.

187 Q Yūsuf 12:64.

188 This is a hadith of the Prophet Muḥammad. It is found in the two most famous collections, the *Ṣaḥīḥ* of al-Bukhari (d. 256/870) and Muslim ibn al-Ḥajjāj (d. 261/875).

189 Q Qaṣaṣ 28:56.

190 Q Āl ʿImrān 3:173.

191 The segment of this paragraph beginning with the words "nor would we be suffering"—with its reference to the British occupying forces (albeit without specifically mentioning them by name)—was omitted from the text of the fourth edition of *Ḥadīth ʿĪsā ibn Hishām.*

192 *Mustashār* refers to the British counselors who were attached to Egyptian ministries and whose function was to "advise" the minister on policy decisions.

193 Once again, the passage from "the boss gets annoyed" to the end of the paragraph was omitted from the text of the fourth edition.

194 Lines of poetry by Imruʾ al-Qays; see *Dīwān*, ed. Wilhelm Ahlwardt (London: Trubner, 1870), 154.

195 Al-Maʿarrī, *Al-Luzūmiyyāt*, 1:326. Qanbar is described in a footnote in this edition as ʿAlī's *mawlā*.

196 Lines 98 and 96 (in that order) of a long poem by Ibn al-Rūmī, *Dīwān*, i:70–71.

197 Lines of poetry by ʿUbayd Allāh ibn ʿAbd Allāh ibn Ṭāhir (d. 300/913); see Ibn Khallikān, *Wafayāt*, 3:121. Anonymously in al-Khālidiyyān, *al-Ashbāh wa-l-naẓāʾir* (Cairo, 1958–65), 1:101.

198 Zayd and ʿAmr are two names commonly used by Arab grammarians to illustrate syntactic usages in the language.

199 This entire chapter (25.1–25.14) was omitted from the fourth edition (1927).

200 Al-Maʿarrī, *Al-Luzūmiyyāt*, 1:65.

Index

About the NYU Abu Dhabi Institute

The Library of Arabic Literature is supported by a grant from the NYU Abu Dhabi Institute, a major hub of intellectual and creative activity and advanced research. The Institute hosts academic conferences, workshops, lectures, film series, performances, and other public programs directed both to audiences within the UAE and to the worldwide academic and research community. It is a center of the scholarly community for Abu Dhabi, bringing together faculty and researchers from institutions of higher learning throughout the region.

NYU Abu Dhabi, through the NYU Abu Dhabi Institute, is a world-class center of cutting-edge research, scholarship, and cultural activity. The Institute creates singular opportunities for leading researchers from across the arts, humanities, social sciences, sciences, engineering, and the professions to carry out creative scholarship and conduct research on issues of major disciplinary, multidisciplinary, and global significance.

About the Typefaces

The Arabic body text is set in DecoType Naskh, designed by Thomas Milo and Mirjam Somers, based on an analysis of five centuries of Ottoman manuscript practice. The exceptionally legible result is the first and only typeface in a style that fully implements the principles of script grammar (*qawāʿid al-khaṭṭ*).

The Arabic footnote text is set in DecoType Emiri, drawn by Mirjam Somers, based on the metal typeface in the naskh style that was cut for the 1924 Cairo edition of the Qur'an.

Both Arabic typefaces in this series are controlled by a dedicated font layout engine. ACE, the Arabic Calligraphic Engine, invented by Peter Somers, Thomas Milo, and Mirjam Somers of DecoType, first operational in 1985, pioneered the principle followed by later smart font layout technologies such as OpenType, which is used for all other typefaces in this series.

The Arabic text was set with WinSoft Tasmeem, a sophisticated user interface for DecoType ACE inside Adobe InDesign. Tasmeem was conceived and created by Thomas Milo (DecoType) and Pascal Rubini (WinSoft) in 2005.

The English text is set in Adobe Text, a new and versatile text typeface family designed by Robert Slimbach for Western (Latin, Greek, Cyrillic) typesetting. Its workhorse qualities make it perfect for a wide variety of applications, especially for longer passages of text where legibility and economy are important. Adobe Text bridges the gap between calligraphic Renaissance types of the 15th and 16th centuries and high-contrast Modern styles of the 18th century, taking many of its design cues from early post-Renaissance Baroque transitional types cut by designers such as Christoffel van Dijck, Nicolaus Kis, and William Caslon. While grounded in classical form, Adobe Text is also a statement of contemporary utilitarian design, well suited to a wide variety of print and on-screen applications.

Titles Published by the Library of Arabic Literature

Disagreements of the Jurists, by al-Qāḍī al-Nuʿmān
Edited and translated by Devin Stewart

Consorts of the Caliphs, by Ibn al-Sāʿī
Edited by Shawkat M. Toorawa and translated by the Editors of the Library of Arabic Literature

What ʿĪsā ibn Hishām Told Us, by Muḥammad al-Muwayliḥī
Edited and translated by Roger Allen

The Life and Times of Abū Tammām, by Abū Bakr Muḥammad ibn Yaḥyā al-Ṣūlī
Edited and translated by Beatrice Gruendler

About the Editor–Translator

Roger Allen retired in 2011 from his position as the Sascha Jane Patterson Harvie Professor at the University of Pennsylvania, where he served for forty-three years as Professor of Arabic and Comparative Literature. He is the author and translator of numerous publications on Arabic literature, modern fiction and drama, and language pedagogy. Among his studies devoted to the Arabic literary tradition are: *The Arabic Novel* (1995) and *The Arabic Literary Heritage* (1998; abridged version, *Introduction to Arabic Literature*, 2000).